Don't close your eyes. . .you may not wake up.

A year after Bradshaw's attempt to destroy her life, Marna Farlow joins Guardian in another paranormal adventure. Fred Keys' long time enemy, Pierre Lamontage, returns to possess Marna and he is not willing to let anybody stand in his way. It's a no holes barred game of cat and mouse that crosses from reality into the dream realm and if you die in one, you die in both.

Disclaimer:

The events, characters and places in this book are mostly fiction. Any resemblance to actual, physical people, places or events is purely coincidental.

Guardian WIT Book 2
Recover the Missing
Bonnita Pleisch

copyright 2013 by Bonnita L.Pleisch
ISBN 978-0615778549
0615778542
Cover Design and arrangement Bonnita L. Pleisch
Contributing artist
(Switzerland train/Castle) Bonnita L. Pleisch
(woman) Elena Sikorskaya / Shutterstock
(hostage)Lusiomages/Shutterstock
Author Photo) Crystal Grant

DEDICATION

(April 27, 1930 - May 30, 2012)

I dedicate this book to my Father whose time as a police officer inspired my desire to write characters that possess a passion for the innocent and a determination to pursue the guilty. I remember sitting up beyond bedtime and watching police shows on the television until I fell asleep on the couch or the floor. Rest In Peace, Dad.

Acknowledgements

It's always hard for me to write acknowledgements and dedications for a book because there are so many people that have influenced my writing over the years and at certain times in my life. A writer has to develop a system, or let the acknowledgement section take up half the book, and then nobody reads them because the names and places mean absolutely nothing to them, but to the writer sitting at the keyboard, they mean the world. These names are the people in our lives that have influenced our careers and the personalities of the characters created. They are people who have helped with information of a factual nature, alternatively, have helped with the accuracy of the text or have simply been there to listen to an idea and given me their thoughts on it.

Unfortunately, I can't get everyone down in one book, but remember to all of you who have mattered in my life or given me something to hold on to during the tough times, I love you all and I thank you with all that I have.

I'd like to mention two of those people today; my sisters who were there during my father's last days, by his side, when the rest of us could not be. I want to thank them. My sister, Nancy, whose gentle manner, sweet personality, and protectiveness of her family, helps me remember there is still good in this world. Nancy, you are one of the sweetest people I have ever had the pleasure of knowing. I'd like to mention my sister, Jamie, who no matter the cost to herself is willing to reach out and help someone else. You are a strong woman, Jamie, and one I am proud to call sister. I love you both, and thank you for being there when Dad needed you.

The third person I wish to mention is my brother, Steve, who in spite of obstacles thrown in his way, started on ventures no one else I know would have even tried. He worked hard to make them successful. You represent some of Guardian's insistence to go forth and solve issues despite the doors slamming shut before them. You are a strong and determined young man. I am proud of you.

I wish to say thank you to my husband's family in Switzerland. I had to capture your beautiful country in the pages of one of my books and decided to make it this one. Your hospitality and giving of love was refreshing and sweet. Thank you to those who welcomed us into your homes and answered my questions about your country and culture. We experienced some of the sweetest and unique cultural ways I had seen in a very long time. It was so nice to get to know you all.

Thank you to my own family who gives me the base for my characters. Some of the best qualities in my characters come from those around me.

As always, I'd like to thank those of you who help me polish my work and get it fit for viewing. Thank you all for whatever part you played in my life to get me to where I am today. Thank you to those of you who allow me to bounce my ideas off you and plot twists to see if it would make sense in the story line. Thank you to those of you who pre-read the manuscript and gave me your reaction to it. I value your responses.

Prologue

Demi Spencer's head shot up from her open Forensics 304 text: Blood Spatter and It's Tell Tale Patterns, where she had fallen asleep, startled awake by some sudden noise... Her emerald green eyes blinked as she tried to clear the fog from her sleep-garbled brain. The prison alarms! They were going off! She pulled her Fiery, red hair back behind her shoulders and grabbed her Guardian Personal Communicator (GPC) off the desk beside her as it vibrated a path to the edge. Strobes were flashing around her and she had to close her eyes to clear away the confusion. "Spencer." She said breathlessly. Her heart sank as she listened to the caller. "What? When? . . . Where? . . . But that's impossible . . . We just had Maximum serviced this morning . . . anywhere else. . . All right, send three teams to each of the other three blocks – a Blocker, a Telepath, and a Custodian. I want them on Lockdown and send six teams to Maximum. I'll grab Bryan and we'll meet you there !" Bryan? She called for him telepathically; trying to reach him by phone would be senseless with the confusion going on around them. She stood up and darted for her office door.

Outside your door! He answered her. She quickly unlocked her office door with her ID card and retinal scan, and then she joined him. The alarms blared mercilessly in their ears and the strobes nearly blinded her.

"What the hell happened?" He cried as she flew out of her office. This just didn't happen at Tarot Lockdown. He had been her partner for nearly eight years and not once had the alarms gone off at Tarot Lockdown, Guardian's psychic prison. They had both worked as Interrogators, usually double-teaming the more dangerous prisoners and a month ago, when Warden Green had retired, Demi had stepped into the position. He could think of no one who deserved it more, but he was pleasantly surprised when she asked him to take the position of Commander – her second in command – because she trusted nobody more. Their psychic connection had already developed during their long-term partnership, so using it now was a natural reaction to mayhem.

She ran to the door, leading to the cellblocks below, swiped her card and stood for her retina scan. After the machine buzzed her through, she held the door for Bryan and then followed him through. "Maximum's been breached !" She dashed for the stairs and headed down to the bowels of the building, Bryan, hot on her heals.

Bryan ran beside her as she half teetered, half stopped, to swipe her badge and gain access to the next staircase. "What? How did that happen?" He shoved his sandy blonde hair back with large fingers from one hand and held the door open for her to enter before him with the other, all the while not missing a step. He wore the typical uniform of the Guardian Security Team, a yellow polo shirt pulled taut over his muscled torso tucked neatly into the slim waistline of a pair of tan khaki pants. His tanned skin was a large contrast to Demi's Irish cream complexion.

"Martin doesn't know! He went to sign in for his shift and the door was open !" She stopped at the final door leading down to the Maximum Security unit, the unit specifically designed for the deadliest of the psychic criminals.

His arm shot out and his hand grabbed her bicep. "Demi, the staff?" They were breathless from their jaunt down the stairs. "Paula?"

She drew in a breath and her eyes became sad, full of regret. She worried her lower lip with her teeth. Paula was one of the newest additions to the Tarot team. She had been his replacement in the prison cellblock, a young woman with Telepathic and Feeler abilities, whom he had taken under his wing to train. This had been her first night out from the training program. She had been nineteen. "They're all gone, Bryan. All of them, Paula included."

His hands went to his hips and he spun on his feet, turning his back to her. With an anguished groan, he kicked the cement wall and slammed it several times with his closed fist. She went to him and put her hands on his back. Tears stung her eyes. "Bryan, I'm sorry. I know Paula was special to you, but we've a job to do now. Tell me now if you can't. I'll call somebody else." Her Irish lilt came out in her speech, but only for him.

He drew in a breath. "No. I have your back, Demi. It's just that she was so young, so promising. She reminded me of Kendra." Demi nodded in agreement. Kendra was Bryan's younger sister. She had disappeared during a family vacation in New York, ten years previous. She had been twelve. That was how Bryan had met Fred Keys, CEO of the Guardian Organization, and become part of the Guardian team. Kendra was actually the reason Bryan had accepted Keys' offer. It was why he was studying to advance to the World Investigation Team (WIT) division. Demi understood. She had lost someone she cared for too, a friend, and she also was working toward the WIT so she could return to California and pick up the trail that had picked up again and then ran cold just a few short years before. She understood disappointment.

"I know, but right now we've got to secure this level, assess the damage and call Keys. Can you do that?" She put authority into her voice to snap him back to the job at hand. "There are five other agents that fell beside her, Bryan; we have to do right by them, too." He looked at her and nodded. Then the two of them opened the door and crossed the threshold into chaos and carnage. Here it was, the spring of 2048, a month into her watch, and the unthinkable had happened. Somebody had breached the walls of Tarot Lockdown.

Chapter One

Frederick Keys Jeep sped into the parking area of Tarot Lockdown and kicked up stones on the cobblestone parking area as it came to a stop. He grabbed the roll bar above his head, and hoisted his lean frame over the side of the vehicle. The Psychic prison was one of the many smaller corporations under the Guardian umbrella. His thirty-five plus years as CEO at *Guardian Incorporation* had shown him that there was always a chance the impossible could and did happen, but a breach at Tarot Lockdown just didn't, not unless some unimaginable abilities were at work here.

Guardian Incorporation was a business title covering many branches centered on information and assistance to law enforcement. It was essentially above ground and withstood scrutiny, should prying eyes dig into the company or one of his agents' backgrounds. Guardian developed the company many years ago for use as cover for agents as much as a business hub for people looking for one of the many services Guardian offered to the public. Inclusion of these properties were*: Guardian Security Consultation and Protection Services, Guardian International Insurance Investigation Services, Guardian International Library Connect Services, Guardian Medical Connection Services, Guardian International Education Leadership* (comprised of teachers and professors ready to be loaned out to education facilities for short-term coverage) and *Guardian Security and Investigation Equipment*. The latter currently held the top selling position of machines and gadgets used by law enforcement and security companies worldwide. If anyone overheard the name Guardian, friend or foe alike, and wanted to check it out, they would find all the legitimate branches of Guardian except one - *Guardian World Investigation Team (WIT),* which was working under the (Black Ops) umbrella of the American government since the Bradshaw takedown a year previous.

Keys was fifty-eight years of age, but possessed the speed and agility of a man twenty years younger. He ran his hand through his salt and pepper hair as he jogged by three Guardian ME Vans and Two Guardian Forensic vehicles to the front entrance. Demi had said the aftermath of the attack had been devastating. His heart broke for the loss of life, especially his agents and their families. He pushed through the doors and stepped over the threshold, nodding at a couple of the agents as he made his way to the Front checkpoint; a wall that shared space with tempered glass enclosures and wide double doors equipped with retinal scanners.

As he made strides to the glass enclosed station in front of him, he pulled his badge out of his right breast pocket and handed it to the serious looking, dark skinned man within, "Frederick Keys." The attendant was approximately twenty-five, with flawless skin, whiskey colored eyes, and tightly curled hair that was black from the roots to the tips, which he had dyed a sandy brown. The young man studied him against his ID. He was a Feeler, a human lie detector. Keys could feel his probing and stood there to allow it.

"Okay, Dr. Keys, could you please step over to the Retinal Scanner?" Keys nodded, and then stepped up to a rectangular box on the wall, where twin red beams probed his eyes and then sent a picture to the computer within the station, verifying his identity. The young man buzzed him through the double doors and met him on the other side with his badge. The attendant reached for the in-house phone and hit two numbers, "Doctor Keys is here . . . Right, ma'am." He hung up the phone and lifted his eyes to the Keys who approved his directness. The boy would make a good agent one day. "Warden Spencer said she would be right up." Keys nodded and returned his badge to his jacket pocket, stepping over to an area that had a spread of chairs and stands, bolted to the floor as a precautionary measure. Bold colored magazine covers flashed at visitors from the stands, matching the brightly colored vinyl coverings on the chairs. He drew in a breath and blew it out through pursed lips as he looked around.

The facility was on high alert. Two guards stood on either side of locked cell block, steel doors that produced high electrical currents to interfere with resident's abilities and prevent contact with any partners on the outside. Unauthorized visitors, for personnel and prisoners alike, were turned away at the gates. In the Forty years Tarot Lockdown had been in existence, this was the first time it had to kick security up to its highest level. Only a very powerful adversary could have penetrated the defenses of this facility. Keys only knew of a few, none of which he wished to battle with.

"Dr. Keys." Demi said as she came up behind him. He turned and shook the hand she offered, and then fell into step beside her as she led the way to the stair exits. They had locked down elevators as well. "I'm sorry to drag you out of bed at this hour, but this couldn't wait until morning." She stopped slid her card through a magnetic key slot and stood for a retinal scan to allow her access into the cellblock area, repeating this process until she reached cellblock MS.

"No, I'm glad you did. What have you discovered?"

She stopped and turned toward him. The horror reflected in her eyes. "I'm not sure what I've seen, Sir. This is like nothing I have ever come across in all my years at Guardian or Tarot for that matter." She sighed, swallowed. "I can't explain it. The looks on their faces, where their bodies are located, I just can't explain it." She swallowed again, "You'll have to see for yourself." She turned and slid her key card, waited for another retinal scan, then opened the MS door, and let him enter before her. Bryan Rush came over to them.

"Dr. Keys," he offered his hand.

"Bryan." Keys shook his hand, and then started to wander the block. The MS section had about twenty-five rooms and could house as many as seventy-five high security prisoners at one time. The walls were solid steel, with small electrodes embedded within them to interfere with the residents' abilities, a precautionary measure to keep residents from harming the staff and calling for reinforcements. The floors were not equipped with any current, but Guardian blanketed the facility in electrical currents supplied by wind, static, sun, and storms. A team of highly trained scientists and environmentalists harnessed, controlled, and dispersed their supply, from a control hut, located elsewhere on the Island, by using special panels and various other collection devices, not too unlike a solar panel on a home, that absorbed the natural energy from these sources

This system usually worked without fail, but that system had failed them. Now, every room on the MS wing stood empty of living prisoners, housing only the dead. The agents' bodies were located at a center point in the cellblock and fanned out in a half circle. They were lying on their stomachs; arms stretched out above their heads. On their faces, an expression of frozen euphoria and acceptance, with a trace of shocked pain. He hadn't seen it since Callie had fallen eight stories to her death at the hands of Raquel Bradshaw and Pierre Lamontage last year. He continued walking, giving a passing glance to the bodies lying within the cells. The same expression was on all the victims' faces, until he came to the last two cells.

He sighed, here were the most heart breaking victims of all. The remainder of Bradshaw's young adult warriors, the ones too damaged to help. They were the ones responsible for the deaths of several Federal agents, from all government branches, during the siege a year previous. Loyal beyond a fault to their creator and would give that loyalty to no other. The reason, Keys suspected, they had died here tonight. Their expression was so peaceful, their dead eyes focused on something nobody else could see. Something suspended in a time only they knew. They lay on their sides or their backs where they had collapsed after the attack. Keys sniffed and turned as Demi and Bryan joined him. "Has the ME verified cause of death yet?"

"Preliminary findings on three adults were cardiac arrest," Bryan answered.

"How many lost?"

"Six agents, twenty Residents."

Keys swallowed, drew in a breath, and let it out through pursed lips. "How many missing?"

Demi drew in a breath, "Seven; Raquel Bradshaw and six of the Bradshaw experimental Teens from Generation L-2."

"Abilities?"

"I'm sorry?" She queried.

"Their abilities? What were their abilities?" He spoke in a controlled voice, vibrating with a fierceness she had never heard before.

"An Illusionist/Stager; a Blocker/Custodian; a Telepath; a budding Listener/Tracker; an Observer and a Locator," She sighed. "They were trainable and going to Guardian appointed foster homes next week."

Keys looked at the carnage around him, the bodies on the floor, the hopelessness of the victims and the stench of death all around him. He became dizzy with rage, started shaking inwardly. "Pierre," he breathed.

"Beg your pardon?" Bryan queried. Then he saw the look on Keys' face. "You know who did this?"

"I think so, yes."

"You mind sharing," Demi demanded, green eyes flashing. "Six of my people died here tonight. I've a right to know."

"I'll tell you this, Warden, the monster that did this, is the likes of which you've never seen before. He chose those children, with those abilities, for a reason and the fact that he teamed up with Raquel. Well then, that means one of two things. We've quite the job ahead of us because his plans involve her abilities or she'll be his next victim once her usefulness wears thin. He sighed, rubbed the back of his neck, drew in a breath, and let it out through pursed lips. "I'm sure they've been planning this a while. Could be they were working together during the Bradshaw investigation to undermine him. That would explain her presence in the hotel when he killed Callie. Has Raquel been getting extra privileges? Volunteering for extra duties? Anything like that?"

Demi's expression changed. "We've been letting her take the kids out in the exercise yard every day. She cooperated with us during the Bradshaw investigation. It was part of her modified program."

"One she counted on. They found a way to contact each other while she was with the children, she and Pierre. A weak point in the electronic bubble maybe. Was she partial to any particular area in the exercise yard?"

"I don't know, but I'll find out."

"Put someone on that. Has she had any visitors?"

"No, Sir."

"No," he said with conviction. "They wouldn't need outside help, not with the connection they share," he sighed. "He's Raquel's Lover," he said with conviction. "The one Rose Briar remembers seeing through her prison window, at night, during her captivity. The one Raquel was meeting while she was married to Bradshaw."

"Who's the lover?"

"One of the deadliest psychics we'll ever have to face." He pulled out his phone, dialed, and headed toward the door. Then he swung back, "Oh and, Demi?" She turned to look at him, "I want you and Bryan to pack your bags. He's not stopping with Raquel and the children. He's after another psychic, a much more powerful one. One he hopes to control. Find someone to cover for you and meet me at the airfield. We need your abilities for assistance with security." She nodded. Keys turned to the ME as he passed him. "Nathan."

"Sir?" a small man in green scrubs said as he looked up from one of the Guardian agent's bodies.

"I want all reports of your findings sent to me as soon as you're done." Nathan nodded. Keys walked up to the door, waited a beat while the guard let him out, and turned to jog up the stairs. "Come on, Tanner, pick up." He muttered as the phone insistently rang in his ear. Finally, when Tanner's voice did come over the airway, it was heavy with sleep.

"Williams," Tanner rubbed the back of his neck and glanced at the clock.

"Tanner, it's Keys."

"Keys?" Tanner said, quickly sitting up, and glancing at the clock again. It was 3:00 AM. "What's wrong?" He could hear the urgency in the older man's voice.

"Get Ventura and Heidi and meet them outside the Farlow house. I want the three of you to sit on Marna. Do not let her out of your sight !" Tanner slid his pants on and stood up.

"What's happening?"

"Nothing good." The line went dead. Tanner grabbed a T-shirt, pulled it on over his head and dialed Peter Ventura's number. "Yeah Pete, it's me . . . Keys just called and said we had to sit on Marna Farlow. . . . He didn't go into details, just said to do it. . . Okay, I'll meet you and Heidi by the Farlow home in fifteen." While passing the table by the apartment door, he grabbed his jacket, slid his phone inside the breast pocket, grabbed his security badge and slid that in a pocket on the opposite side. Then he grabbed his car keys, slipped on his shoes, and headed out his apartment door.

*****

By the time Tanner pulled his Retro Camaro onto Marna's block, he saw Ventura's Mustang already there. He passed it slowly, drove to the horseshoe turn at the end of the block, came back, and pulled in behind him. He grabbed the coffee tray off his passenger seat and brought it over to the Mustang.

Heidi rolled down her window, "Oh, man, Rookie, I think I'm in love. Will you marry me?" She teased as she took the coffee he offered her, and some sugar and cream. She fixed it the way she liked it, greedily took a drink and sat back in the seat, sighing. She was a handsome woman of thirty-five, with a straight sable mane pulled back away from her features in a single tail down to her hips. Her dark chocolate eyes weren't quite symmetrical, but they twinkled with mischief as she teased Tanner and winked at Peter. Her fine chiseled nose centered her face and led a direct path from her eyes to her slightly larger than normal mouth, and dimples formed on her round cheeky face when she smiled. Her body was lean enough to give any athlete a run for their money if they chose to challenge her physical abilities. Her psychic abilities were nothing spectacular; primary was Cloaker and secondary was Tracker, but her eye for detail when investigating a crime scene, made her one of the best and the toughest agents on the WIT.

Tanner grinned, "I somehow doubt coffee would sustain you for fifty years or so."

"You never know," she winked and took another sip of her coffee, while Ventura took his.

At thirty-eight, he was a new face to the WIT. He had transferred from the Security Consultation & Protection Team the previous fall, around the same time Tanner had joined the SC&P Team. His dark hair framed a milk chocolate, square-jawed face, highlighting eyes as dark and dangerous as a patch of unknown Forest, after sundown. His frame was 225 pounds of pure muscle and his mouth permanently formed a straight line unless he showed one of his rare smiles. He drew in a breath before he spoke, "Any idea what this is about?" He asked. He boasted abilities of the unusual variety. He was a Recognizer, Observer and a budding Tracker. The third was just beginning to show its presence. These gave him the ability to recognize latent psychics with the simple act of touching them or shaking their hand, see through complicated cloaks to warn others of coming enemies, and sense when and where someone was using a psychic ability within a 500-foot radius. Ventura informed Keys of Tanner's latent feeling ability months before. That insight changed Tanner's life forever.

"No. I was hoping you could tell me," Tanner shook his head for emphasis. His weight was considerably less than 225 lbs, maybe 195, but regular visits to the Guardian gym and battle ready stimulator rooms had chiseled out a muscled lean build on his 6'2" frame. His hair was a cross between mud brown and river black, but his eyes were a soft brown that held compassion and understanding for the people around him. Many teased him about his American pie looks, but underneath it all, he was pure business. His mother had been a Roma Gypsy, his father a Harrisville DA and the Guardian team gave him the best of both worlds. He could use all the talents he had acquired from both his parents' worlds. He was an accomplished officer, graduate of one of the top Criminal Justice programs in the country, and from his mother he had inherited the unique psychic abilities her bloodline offered.

He was an accomplished Feeler and a budding Custodian/Blocker. Meaning not only could he tell when people lied, making him an excellent interrogator, he could also extend his shield to protect another person from a negative energy attack or increase the strength of someone else's shield if they were in trouble or unable to use theirs. He could also block an enemy from using their ability or keep them from launching a negative energy attack. The latter only recently evolving. Keys told him it could happen. The more he used his abilities, the more they could evolve.

"Nope. Keys hasn't called to fill me in, yet," Ventura said. Almost as soon as the words were out of his mouth, his phone vibrated in his pocket. He pulled it out and looked at the screen, "Maybe we'll get some answers now." He raised the phone to his ear, "Ventura. . . Yeah we're outside the Farlow house now . . . Yep, we're all here . . . What? . . . When? . . . You really think he'll try tonight? . . . No, we'll stay on her . . . All right, we'll see you when you get back . . . We'll cover it . . . yep." He hung up the phone and ran a hand over his face."

Heidi looked at her partner, "that didn't sound so good."

"It's not," he sighed, "There was a breakout at Tarot tonight."

"What?" The other two queried in unison,

"Who, Pete?" Heidi queried not liking the feel of the situation.

"Raquel Bradshaw and six of Bradshaw's Teens. The ones that were going into foster care next week."

Tanner felt the urgency more than saw it or heard it "What else, Pete? Who broke them out?"

"Keys thinks it was Lamontage."

"The Seducer?" Tanner asked. Peter nodded. Tanner knew instantly why the orders for the protection detail. "Keys thinks he's coming for Marna," a cold, horrific feeling clutched his stomach.

"Yeah. Keys said we can count on it."

"My men described what he was doing to the other protesters during that riot on the road to the lodge, how Marna reacted to him. It was like something out of a horror flick. If he gets near her again. . ."

"Our job is to keep that from happening, Williams." Ventura got out of the car. "I'm going around back. I want you to stay here with Heidi," he took in a breath. "Heidi, call in Brandon and Misty. We need backup. If he does make an attempt tonight, we aren't going to be able to take him ourselves. He killed twenty-six people tonight and broke seven out of the high security wing of an impenetrable prison. We also suspect he's the one who killed Callie last fall. Three low level agents aren't going to stop him."

"Do you really think he'll try tonight?"

"Keys does." He pocketed his phone, checked his gun, and took a breath. "Check in every half hour. Open your channels and ready your distress signals," he said, just before he jogged across the street and disappeared into the night shadows surrounding the house. Tanner took a breath and let his eyes wander around the street. He couldn't help but wonder if Marna Farlow and her family would ever be able to live a normal life. Sighing, he made his way around to the passenger side of the car, while Heidi shifted to the driver's side. He slid into the passenger seat, closing the door and letting his eyes rise to the darkened upstairs windows of the house.

~~~~~

Marna moved restlessly in her sleep. First, she was hot, and then she was cold. She felt weighed down and then she felt as light as a feather. Then she was moving through space and time, landing in the middle of a grassy meadow with a barrier of forest on three sides.

The little cabin sat on a hill, surrounded by flowerbed and bursting with spring colors. Spring. She sighed. It was her favorite time of year. She loved how it filled the air with the freshness of new birth and fragrant perfumes from budding flowers. Marna looked up at the brilliant blue-sky and felt the warmth of the sun upon her face. Strands of her wavy dark hair broke free from the band holding it in place at the nape of her neck. The gentle breeze played it against her cheek. She tried to smooth it back into place and looked around. She was supposed to meet someone here, but she couldn't remember whom.

"There you are," she smiled as she recognized the baritone behind her.

"Jeff," she whispered his name, "I was wondering if you would ever come back." Birds burst out in song around her as she turned to look at him. Her breath caught in her throat. He was just as she remembered him when he walked the Earth beside her. His curly dark hair, lazy smile, and kind brown eyes accentuated his ruggedly handsome face. He stood before her, the sun shadowing his features. His button-up shirt unbuttoned at the collar and tucked neatly into the slim waistline of his jeans.

"I couldn't stay away." He raised a picnic basket with one hand and reached for her hand with another, "Come, we have lots to catch up on." She reached for his hand and allowed him to lead her back the way he had come.

The scene changed. It became dark and cold as she stood upon a stone terrace attached to a stone castle in some foreign land. Snow covered the hilltops around the castle. She was wearing a strapless blue dress with a matching shawl draped over her shoulders and a pair of white, elbow-length gloves. Her blue eyes, the shade of the ocean's depths, stood out against her pale complexion. Her jeweled shoes twinkled in the hazy moonlight as she spun around looking for Jeff. Her body convulsed with shivers from the wintery air. "Where are we Jeff? It's cold. I thought we were going on a picnic?" She turned around. Jeff was gone and in his place stood a man, she had only seen once. Fear shot warning bolts through her body. Her chest tightened. His dangerous good looks and black piercing eyes held her captive. "He is gone, Mon Cher, but I am here to bring you joy." He raised her fingers to his lips and kissed them. "Shall we dance?"

She wanted to say no, but he was quickly gaining control of her senses. No! She had to fight him, had to break away. "Jeff! Help Me."

"Fighting is useless. I always get what I want." He pulled her tightly against him and started dancing to the eerie waltz playing from within the castle ballroom.

"No!" she cried. "Somebody PLEASE !" She closed her eyes, dizzy with the sensations he was pouring over her. She tried to send out a psychic distress signal but couldn't tell if she actually got it out. He was slowly taking over her senses. Her distress signals to Rose were fad . . . Why was she fighting him. . . . She felt happy. The sadness of Jeff's loss was fading. Pierre spun her around the terrace, "Is this not better, Ma Cherie? Better then the emptiness you feel inside?"

Marna fought to gain control of her senses, but his hold was strong. "Jeff," she whispered.

The man before her changed form. "I can be he if you choose, my beautiful maiden, or I can make you forget him." He returned to his original form." and you can love me."

He spun her and crushed her to him again. "The world can be ours," he whispered seductively. She felt peace, joy, happiness. "You can feel the euphoria in my arms, my love or . . ." He raised her hand to his lips again, spun her around, and then let her go. She became dizzy and fell to her knees. "Not," he lifted his hand, closing his fist. The peaceful feeling left. In its place, a sorrow so deep Marna could not move. Tears flowed freely down her face.

"Jeff," she cried, "Where are you? Why are you not helping me?"

The man before her crouched and lifted her chin with a crooked finger. "He is gone, Ma Cherie, but I have the power to bring him back to you." The form changed. It was Jeff again.

"Come on, baby, we can be together again, just give in," Jeff said as the scene changed to the warmth of the earlier field.

"This isn't real," Marna whispered. She tried to get up but an unseen force held her down. Pain ripped through her body. She screamed.

"It is your choice, Ma Cherie, euphoria or pain," the stranger cried. "I have the power to take control, to make you do things . . . " POP- POP- POP . . . The form before her faded. The castle disappeared. A whirling black abyss threatened to suck her in. She screamed. It hurt to breathe. Suddenly she felt a warm blanket thrown around her; unseen arms surrounded her, pulling her back away from the whirling black Hole. The pain started to subside. She could breathe.

Put your shields up, Marna! I can help, but only for a short time! Tanner's voice came through the pain. She focused, but the effort to bring her shields up was so draining.

I don't think I c-can

Shields up, Marna! Rose's voice brought her back to reality as it shot through her head.

~~~~~

She bolted upright in her bed to the sounds of gunfire in her back yard.

Rose, what the?

I'll explain later. Tanner's got you covered now, but he's weakening. Put your shields up. I'll be there in ten minutes.

Marna drew all her strength and raised her shields, jumped out of bed, threw on her robe, and made quick steps to her bedroom window. She felt the unseen arms and warm blanket let go as she became more aware and her shields became stronger. She parted the blinds on her window and looked out in time to see Ventura and Tanner run toward the cemetery located on the hill behind her house, where Jeff and other Guardian agents' were buried. She panned the area and saw that they were chasing a retreating form in dark clothes towards the wood line. Seconds later, her doorbell rang and she cinched her robe at the waist, heading out her bedroom door to the front stairs, descending to the large living room below and to the front door. She looked out the window beside the door and saw Heidi Schaefer.

She opened the door, stepping aside. Heidi stepped over the threshold, gun ready, motioning Marna behind her and against the wall. The pale light of dawn was just starting to push the darkness of the night away. "Where are the children?"

"Sleeping."

"Good." Brandon and Misty came from the back and Heidi signaled them upstairs while she continued to check out the downstairs rooms. Moments later, the other two rejoined her in the living room and Rose came in, concern written all over her face. Heidi nodded. With relief, she went to Marna, pulled her into a hug and then set her back a few seconds later, searching her face with anxious eyes. "Are you okay?" Marna nodded. "The children?"

"Th-they're fine."

Rose drew a breath in relief. "I got your distress call and called Keys. He said Williams, Ventura and Schaefer were watching the house and that Tanner was covering your back with his Custodian abilities." She turned her attention back to Heidi but held her sister in a protective arm. Rose Briar was the sister Marna had never known she had. She had been born several years before Marna and her twin sister, Amanda. The doctors told their parents she had died shortly after her birth. During the course of Guardian's investigation into Amanda's death a year ago, the sisters were reunited. Rose had been living in Connecticut and working as a nurse. Now she lived on the Guardian compound two blocks away from Marna, and worked as a nurse at the compound clinic. Rose's abilities included cloaking, and Kything, which she used to assist Guardian when she could, but she had no desire to become a full-time agent. She had a family and enjoyed living a somewhat normal life. "What is going on?"

Heidi held up her hand as she watched Brandon Healy go to the patio doors, open them, and activate his tracking ability.

"Anything?" Misty Schofield asked her partner. She was a tall, forty-year old, wheat blonde with mixed Native American breeding in her pedigree, so her skin was more bronze than white and her eyes were the color of plumbs. She stayed focused on her partner letting nothing distract her from her job. Her average frame was dressed in flared jeans, boots and a button- down shirt left open just above her breasts. A jean jacket covered her weapon harness and completed her ensemble. She boasted a Listening ability as her Primary, a very rare gift that Kythers and Locators will earn as their abilities evolve. So rare that Bradshaw had tried to mimic it with his synthetic traits, resulting in devastating consequences to his subjects. However, hers was truly genetic and had developed so it had actually become stronger than the rest of them.

Brandon Healy was a great balance to his partner with a Telepathic ability as his Primary, and Tracking as his secondary. Now he tracked the surrounding grounds of the two-story home. He was a slender 6'4 " tall, weighing in at 185 pounds, with intense dark eyes and inky black hair framing a masculine jaw line and high cheekbones, exposing his Cherokee bloodline, "No. What about you?"

She tilted her head. Voices assaulted her. She started compartmentalizing them in her head. *"Hurry up, there's more than you who wants a shower, Dog Face...Can't you learn to put your dishes in the . . . Did you do the assignment last night . . . . Is your homework . . ."*

"We lost him..." Tanner said.

"Was it Lamontage?" Ventura queried.

"I don't know. He was too far ahead."

"Let's head back. I'll call Keys."

After she had pinpointed Tanner and Ventura, she tried to catch anything around them that might be their quarry, but she could hear nothing aside from some colorful language that Ventura was Spewing as he and Tanner made their way back to the house.

"No, nothing. Ventura and Williams lost him."

"You're a Listener?" Marna queried. She had been taking some classes at the Compound College and had just learned about the Listener in her Advanced Abilities class. Their ears were at a higher level of sensitivity and able to tune into higher frequencies connecting them to radio waves which would then transport a conversation from point A to point B, much like how a wireless network transmitted phone calls, smart phones, computers, etc. Their brain could then take all the sound information they gathered and within seconds, sift through the information, separate and hone in on a particular target or targets' conversation. However, the targets had to be within a certain radius and it went faster if the host knew the voices of their targets. It was a rare ability and very few people possessed it.

"Yes, I am," she said, offering her a hand. "Misty Schofield." She waved in Brandon's direction. "My partner, Brandon Healy." Marna shook both their hands in turn.

"Glad to meet you."

"Likewise. You and your family are quite popular among the ranks. The Bradshaw battle will go down in Guardian history." He sighed. "I'm sorry for the loss of your husband."

Marna cleared her throat. "Thank you." She drew in a breath. "I'll go make some coffee."

"Actually Ms. Farlow," Ventura said as he came in through the back door, "I'd like to speak to you for a few minutes."

"I'll get the coffee," Rose volunteered.

"Sure," Marna said as she stood where she was and glanced at the clock. "I hope this won't take too long. The children will be getting up for school soon. I also have classes today."

"We'll do our best to make sure you can move on with your day as quickly as possible. Please, sit down." Marna sat in one of the winged chairs centered in the living room and Ventura sat across from her on the couch.

"What's going on, Ventura?" Rose queried as she brought coffee in for everyone

"Keys got a call from Tarot Lockdown this morning."

"The Guardian prison?" She queried as she handed coffee cups to everyone and another pot spit and sputtered in the kitchen.

"Yeah," he accepted the cup she offered but held his hand up and shook his head when she offered him sugar and cream.

"What's happened?" Marna asked, placing her cup on the hardwood coffee table and folding her hands together in her lap.

"There's been a breakout."

Marna's hands stopped their nervous fidgeting. "Who?"

"Raquel Bradshaw and some of the genetically engineered teens."

She closed her eyes, got up to go to the patio doors, and looked across the backyard. "How did she break out?"

"She had outside help."

"The Seducer," she said with conviction. The dream, Jeff, was it all a cruel ploy to get her to let him take control?

"Keys thinks he'll come for you," Tanner put in. "He sent us here to watch your house."

She sniffed, "Anybody hurt?"

"He killed six agents, and twenty Tarot residents."

"Oh my . . ." Marna raised her hand to her mouth. "What makes Keys think he'll come for me?"

"Because he has already made an attempt once. He thirsts for power. The kind of power your magnifying ability can give him." Ventura studied her features. "I'm assuming it was him who induced the distress signal you sent out to your sister. Possibly he that Tanner and I just chased down."

"I-I don't know. It was a dream."

"Ms. Farlow, you should know by now, a dream that induces that kind of panic, with your genetic makeup, is no dream at all but a vision. Now answer me. Was Pierre Lamontage walking in your dreams just now?"

Tears tracked down her face. Rose moved to her side, and wrapped an arm around her. "Marna?" She turned to face Ventura.

She nodded. "Yes. At least I think it was him." She sniffed and Heidi pulled a couple of tissues from a box on the coffee table and handed them to her... "At first it was Jeff. He's visited me before and we've walked in this beautiful meadow."

"When?"

"At the funeral," She drew in a breath, "and a couple of other times over the last few months."

"You didn't think it important enough to mention?" Ventura pressed on. She raised her eyes to his, hers sparking in anger. "Can't I at least have my dreams?" She demanded.

"Ms. Farlow . . ." He trailed off with a sigh as his phone buzzed. He looked at the screen, then up at her. "It's Keys. If you'll excuse me," he got up and stepped outside, "yeah."

"Peter, is everyone okay?"

"Yeah. Whoever it was took off as soon as Tanner blanketed her."

"Has she been able to tell you the reason for the distress call?"

"She said she had some kind of dream. That she and her late husband were walking through a meadow," He sighed, "she said she's had these visitations before."

"She has. I remember one at the funeral, but it isn't Jeff. It's Lamontage taking on Jeff's form to trick her into letting her defenses down. Jeff had no abilities so he could not initiate a dream creating rendezvous."

"So what do we do?"

"We need to tell her the truth." Keys scratched the back of his head as he looked over the map before him. "I just took off from Tarot Airfield, so I'll be landing at the compound in . . ." He looked at his watch. ". . .about one and a half hours. Pull a Security and Protection team together and watch over the family until I get there. Have an investigative team start looking for a trail to the missing children. Kyle and Sasha are already in Zurich gathering Intel, have been for a year. "I think Lamontage is after the missing children as well. He feels he can take control of Marna, and form a collective of his own."

"I can't imagine their abilities are as powerful as the Farlow children?"

"No, they are more powerful. Arella is a Blocker and Dream Walker, I suspect she is a good candidate for Dream Weaving abilities as well, considering Heinderick has them. She also has a force field ability as Mary does, only more powerful. Heinderick is a Telepath, and possesses both Dream Walking and Dream Weaving abilities with signs of a budding Locater ability as well. Very important abilities for just about any plan Lamontage can come up with in psychic warfare." He sighed. "Those are just the abilities we know about."

"Well, if he's so powerful, why breakout Raquel Bradshaw? Her abilities are nothing to write home about. The teens he took with him, the two kids he's going after, and God forbid if he gets hold of Marna. Her magnifying power would make him almost undefeatable. Why bring a low-level psychic like Bradshaw with him? Far as I can see she'd be useless to him."

"She is. I'll see you soon." Keys hung up his phone and set it on the table before him, leaning back in the airplane seat to try to get a little nap before he had to hit the ground running.

Pete looked up as the gray of the morning sky started breaking up to show veins of blue through the clouds of the night before. The Farlow children would be getting up soon. He had to have a plan in place before they did. He slipped his phone in his pocket and went back inside.

"What did Keys want?" Heidi asked.

"Just giving me the battle plan."

"Which is?"

"We'll discuss that in a minute. Marna . . ." he gently urged her on, "I need you to tell me about your visitation last night."

Marna looked at the clock. "Can't this wait until after I get the kids off to school?"

"I'd like to say yes, Marna, but in order for us to be ahead of the game, I need to know what transpired in your dream vision last night, before the distress signal."

"Marna, you go ahead. I'll start breakfast."Rose offered.

"Rose, no, you've got your own family. . ."

"Kurt's got them covered. I have mid-shift at the hospital. Talk to Agent Ventura." Marna nodded as Rose took her cup and went into the kitchen. Marna looked at the clock, drew a cleansing breath, moved to the couch, sat back down, and started telling Ventura about her dream vision.

*****

Keys hit his breaks hard, spun his steering wheel around, kicking up dust as he jumped a puddle, and jerked to a stop behind a government issue SUV, before the sign Hillshire Family Park, which officials had closed down due to damage caused by recent flooding. He slipped his phone in his pocket and stepped out of his car advancing toward the crime scene tape stretched out between two trees. He showed the two uniforms his badge, then ducked under the tape, and almost ran into Devin Ruletto, the team leader of the dispatched Federal World Protection Agency team called on this case. He had served in the FWPA almost as long as Keys had been with Guardian. His hair was gray and balding, a shade darker than his eyes. His stocky build was encased in a black trench coat, thrown over a thousand dollar suit, and shining black shoes. He offered a hand to Keys.

"Morning, Devin." Keys shook his hand then fell into step beside him as they headed toward the public building that housed the showers. "Coroner says she's been there at least 6 hours." He led the way around a bend and onto a slate rock path.

"Who found her?"

"A couple of kids, camping over the rise, they came down here to take a shower and found her. Locals are interviewing them now." He sighed. "I recognized her from the Bradshaw case last year." He opened the door to the women's showers and let Keys go in ahead of him.

"Where is she?"

"Last stall on the left."

"Okay." Keys walked through the cement enclosure. The walls were dark gray and spotted with green moss. The stalls all had torn, slimy, plastic curtains covering the openings on the front. There were five showers on each side, perfectly symmetrical in every dimension. He gave the first nine barely a glance, but when he came to the tenth one, he stopped, slipped on a pair of latex gloves and pushed the curtain back.

There she was, laying on the cold cement floor, muddy puddles pooled around her, and cold water trickling from the shower head, her eyes unfocused and staring at the opposite wall. The expression on her face was shock? Pain? Dismay? Betrayal? He couldn't tell. She was naked, humiliated and all alone. "Guess he was through with you, Raquel, wasn't he?" There were no visible marks on her body, but then there wouldn't be, would there? "Pierre wouldn't leave any, would he?"

He crouched down to look over the body and the immediate area around it. "She yours?" Devin asked.

"Yeah." Keys sighed as he stood up. "Sh-ah, she escaped custody earlier today."

"From Tarot?" Keys nodded. "Who else?" Keys didn't answer. He moved aside to let the coroner in and then headed out the door. Devin fell into step beside him. "Come on, Keys, I have a right to know if we've got psychic sociopaths running around my jurisdiction."

"We're handling it, Devin."

"I bet you are," he looked at Keys, shook his head and sighed. "Let's hope you handle it before we have another Bradshaw situation break out."

"Psychic warfare isn't the object of this individual, Devin. You need not worry about that."

"I hope your right."

"I am. His desire is to control one person and take her as his own. That's what his immediate objective is."

Ruletto opened his mouth to speak, but an approaching tech stopped his flow of words. "Agent, Ruletto," Keys followed him over to the individual. They handed him a post card.

"We found this under her body." He handed him a post card in a plastic bag.

"Mean anything to you, Keys?" Devin handed him the picture. Keys looked it over. It was a picture of a snowy village built into a mountainside. The words written on it were German.

"Yes, as a matter of fact it does," he handed the picture back to Devin. "It means that I'm going to be taking a trip."

"What?"

"I'll explain it in a few minutes, Devin. Right now I need to make a call." He pulled out his phone and dialed a number. "Yeah, it's Keys. File a flight plan to Zurich. I think that's where Pierre is headed. . . Don't worry about Marna Farlow; I'll talk to her when I get back. . . Pierre and the Teens . . . Raquel is dead. He dumped the body in a campground shower stall . . . yeah I'll be there in a couple of hours." He took another look at the activity around the shower house and watched as they pulled the black body bag out of the building and into the coroner's van, and then he turned on his heal and headed back toward his vehicle. Marna Farlow's reprieve was over. It was time to defeat yet another monster. He slid behind the wheel of his truck and backed onto the road heading North on route 89.

Chapter Two

The professor shut down the LCD set up, "Dismissed," he said. Marna closed her textbook, slid it into her book bag and looked at her watch. It was 2:30 PM. She had just enough time to pick the cake up at the bakery, the movie at the video store and the various other party favors at the mall before the kids got home from school. She shut down her student computer tablet and slipped that into her bag as well. Standing up, she lifted up her book bag and grabbed her jacket, reaching behind her for her pen but brushed someone else's fingers instead. Startled, she turned on the balls of her feet, raising her bag as a means of defense and found herself looking into a pair of bright green eyes, with flecks of amber twinkling near the pupils, belonging to a man of 5'8", approximately thirty years old, auburn hair and a firm mouth. He sported a goatee, a little darker than the shade of his hair, and *a Kiss me I'm Irish*, green satin Jacket on a very lean and gangly physique. He was also standing in her personal space and did not attempt to move back. He handed her the pen smiling slightly with raised eyebrows.

"Thank you," she said, taking hold of the pen but he held onto it a moment longer than necessary before he let go and she could put it into her bag.

"No problem, Lass." His eyes held hers with a steady gaze. "The name's Martin -- Martin Freeman, and yea is?" Guess the jacket wasn't all for show she mused, his Irish accent was clear in his spoken word.

"Marna Farlow." Slipping by him, she stepped into the aisle and put some space between them. His closeness was sending her senses into high alert.

"Ah, aye. I was thinkin' yea looked famili'r. Yer face was on screens across the seas las' year, aye, even in Irel'nd. I was thinkin', even then, what a bonnie face it was." He smiled at her.

"You're a long way from home," she said as she started walking toward the back of the lecture hall. He stopped her with a hand on her shoulder and stepped in front of her.

"Aye, transferred last week. Dis' facility offers more than Dublin's community college." He smiled.

"Are you looking to join the WIT or one of the other Teams?"

"Waaat are yea studyin' for, Lass?" He grinned. "I may just soi'n up for the same."

"Marna," Tanner said as he started walking down the aisle toward them.

She waved and turned back to Martin. "Well, I hope your transfer gives you what you need." She smiled back. "It was nice meeting you, Martin, but I do need to be going." She started to walk away and he fell into step beside her.

"Tell me, Marna Farlow, are yea rushin' off to 'nother class roi'ht now or can I int'rest Yer in joinin' me for a cup av poor coffee in de student lounge."

Tanner met them and eyed the newcomer suspiciously. She smiled, and introduced the two men. "Tanner Williams; Martin Freeman; He's a transfer from . . . I'm sorry, Martin where did you say you were from?"

He grinned then turned to look Tanner in the eye. "Dublin county, Oirlan', Sir, been wi' Guardian for tree years nigh, workin' sec'rity on the Dublin base. Custodian, an' bloomin' Locator." He offered his hand and Tanner shook it warily, unaware that he had positioned himself between Marna and Martin. The next comment he aimed at Marna as he looked over Tanner's right shoulder. "I'm sorry, Lass, oi didn't nu yer be spoken for. Oi don't make a 'abit av movin' in on 'nother's territ'ry."

"Wh—Oh he's not," Marna shook her head. "We're —not – ah. . ." She cleared her throat, looking at Tanner and then at Martin again. "He's a friend."

Martin eyed the two of them. "Perhaps no. My mistake." He bowed. "Perhaps we can take a rain check on dat coffee than, Lass."

"Maybe. I'll see you Thursday, Martin."

"Thurs---?" He looked confused then grinned when Marna raised her brow. "Ah, in class." He winked. "Yea, we will, Marna Farlow." He nodded his head at Tanner. "An' yer, Mr. Williams, perhaps we'll meet ag'in."

"I'm sure our paths will cross again if you're staying on the compound."

"Aye, ya be shore ah dat. Good day, Sir." With another wink at Marna, he headed up the aisle.

"Oh, Martin." Tanner called after him.

"Aye."

"Where did you say you were staying?"

"I didn't," he grinned. "Investigashun 101. Treck subject into tinkin they've revealed somethin' they 'aven't," he chuckled. "A bit av a protective friend aren't yea, Tanner Williams?" Tanner didn't answer. "Well den, oi guess i'll tell yer, I've jist arrived on yer fair compoun' yest'rday, an' oi 'aven't a permanent livin' space yet, so i'm actoilly stayin' in wan av the spare dorms in the Barns buildin'." He grinned when Tanner just looked at him. "Wud yer loike the room number or is yer readin' sat'sfyin' yer c'rios'ty?" Tanner raised a brow. "Well, yer a Feeler ain't ya?"

"Yes, I am. And, yes, you pass the first level."

Martin grinned. "Well den, oi guess I'll be goin' afore oi lose points from me score. Agin. . ." He nodded his head. "Good day to ya." He turned and left. Tanner watched him until he walked out the double doors.

"What aren't you saying, Tanner?" She scanned his face with her eyes.

"Oh, so feeling is being added to your list of abilities is it?" His eyes twinkled with a teasing glint.

"No, a woman's intuition. I've relied on that a bit longer than I've relied on the psychic hotline," she tilted her head, "I've found it to be just as accurate, too." She leaned her hip against one of the seats, pushed her book bag further on her back, and raised her brow in expectation. "And it's screaming at me that you're hiding something."

He crossed his arms at his chest and glanced once more at the door, then brought his eyes back to hers. "I just find the timing of his transfer a little curious is all."

"Curious, how?" She queried. "People transfer in and out all the time. You know that."

"Did he initiate contact or did you?"

"What's that got to do with anything?"

"Could be a lot, could be nothing." He shrugged.

"He picked up my pen and handed it to me." She grinned. "Oh." She feigned a look of mock horror. "Maybe he filled it with poisoned ink, in the, oh, five seconds I had my back turned." She went to reach for it.

"Very funny," he said with a frustrated sigh. "I'm just saying it doesn't hurt to be a little careful in the wake of Lamontage's latest attempt, especially of new faces coming out of nowhere that try to get friendly."

"Tanner, look around you, we're on a college campus. There are tons of new faces. He's not the first guy that's asked me out for coffee at the lounge, or to study, or if they could copy my notes. He is, however, the first one that doesn't have a bad case of acne." She smiled and Tanner chuckled.

"All right, I get it. You don't want to sound the alarm every time someone talks to you but, Marna, throwing caution to the wind isn't the answer either."

"Is that what I'm doing because I talk to a fellow student on Guardian territory?" She drew in a breath, letting it out slowly, "Throwing caution to the wind?"

"You know what I mean."

"No, Tanner, I don't," she said firmly. "I can't--no---I won't live like a hermit because some psychic bad guy out there may or may not want a piece of me. I did that for almost a year when

Bradshaw was running the show. Back then, I had to because I didn't really know who I was or what I could do. I do now and if I hide every time a threat looms on the horizon, I'll be hiding most of my life. I can handle myself."

"He's a Dream Weaver, Marna, among other things," Tanner sighed, "and from what Keys says, he's more powerful than Bradshaw was."

"Bradshaw's play for power took pieces of my life I can't get back. He took pieces of the children's lives they can't get back. Lamontage won't have that chance. I know what to expect now. I know the world of the psychic mind, good and bad. I've dealt with both. Now you people have just got to trust me; trust my instincts." She turned and started walking up the aisle. "I'm stopping at the bakery and the **World Mart** before I go home. . ." She turned and looked at him as he stood there. "You are my escort, aren't you? I mean when was the last time you came looking for me between classes?"

"My class was next door. I just thought I'd walk you to your car."

"Of course you did. Mighty neighborly of you, Mr. Williams, but I do have to go. Isaiah's cake was ready an hour ago and the meat and veggie platters, for those of us that desire more sensible foods than chips and pizza, were ready for pick up a half an hour ago. After all, it's not every day you turn thirteen and his guests will be arriving by 6:30 for the rite of passage teen party." She grinned, "By the way, you may want to pick up something and change into jeans and a tee. He asked me to invite you if I saw you on campus today."

"Me? Why?"

Her look became serious, sorrowful. "He knows what you tried to do for Jeff, knows you tried to save him." She swallowed as the horrific scene at Bradshaw's desert palace came back to her. Jeff catching a bullet meant for Rose, Tanner's desperate attempt to staunch the blood flow, while they waited for rescue personnel, and the love of her life slipping away from her. "He looks up to you, Tanner. With Jeff and Pete gone, you and Keys are the closest things to a father figure he has. You go to his baseball games, basketball games, and you've helped him improve his football skills. Should it surprise you that he wants you there?"

"I-I guess I never really looked at it like that. I just felt a connection with him. . ." He trailed off.

"He feels it too. So are you coming or are you going to stand there with that goofy look of sheer surprise all over your face because I've got a schedule to keep."

He grinned and shook his head, jogged up the aisle and opened the swinging door, holding it for her to exit and then he followed her out. "I saw this great football at the **World Mart** store yesterday, pro-size; you think he'd like it?"

"I'm sure of it." They continued to chatter and exited the building, while a pair of unknown eyes watched them leave. He stood in the shadow of a nearby oak tree and pulled his personal video phone/computer (PVPC) out of his pocket as students filed out of various campus buildings, put it on private, and nodded to them. "Contact's been made . . . Ready to execute plan when you say . . . yes sir, I will hold my position." He ended the call and slipped it back into his pocket. He fell into a passing crowd of basketball players as they headed toward the college stadium for their afternoon practice.

*****

Marna pulled into a parking spot in front of **World Mart**, a large, mall-like department store nestled in the shopping center of the compound. She glanced at the bakery box in her passenger seat and smiled. She had asked the baker to do a sports theme and considering it was the tail end of football season, he had used the two teams that had been the Super Bowl rivals this year. He had even gone as far as using little football figurines at the centerfield yard line. Isaiah was going to love it. She was closing the driver's door just as Tanner's Camaro pulled in beside her. She used her key remote to lock her door and keyed in her alarm system, as he climbed out from behind the wheel of his vehicle.

"You're driving that thing and I still managed to stay ahead of you in my little hybrid," she teased, "and they sent you to protect me?" She clicked her tongue.

"You ran a red," he accused.

"Did not," she grinned, turning and heading toward the store entrance. "It was yellow."

"For about a half of a second."

"Still legal to go through."

"Says the woman with the special investigator badge."

"Yeah, I outrank you," she teased.

"In Civilian life, I would have outranked you and given you a ticket." He raised a brow.

"Well bully for me." Smiling, she led the way into the three-floor department store. "Sporting goods is on the second, party favors are on this floor down back. So I guess we part ways and I'll meet you at the register to check out."

"I can wait for you to get what you need. Then we can get the football."

She looked at her watch. "Tanner, it's going on three PM. The kids will be arriving home in half an hour. I don't believe in wasting time. Now go get your football and I'll get the favors." He nervously looked around. "Are you kidding me?" She looked around. "We are in the middle of a department store with a ton of witnesses. Nobody is going to try anything here. Come on, just go." She shooed him off with a wave of her hands.

"All right, but keep your phone on, a channel open to me, and your shields up." He ordered.

"Demanding sort, aren't you?"

"Marna," he warned.

"All right, all right. I'll do as you ask, oh great protector." She said and closed her eyes for a moment. She shut all other noises and sounds out and using her Kything ability, she opened a channel to Tanner. "*Testing one . . . two . . . three can you hear me? Oh will you look at that I made it rhyme.*"

Tanner grinned, shaking his head. "*Yes, I can hear you.*"

"*Good, then let's get this show on the road.*" I have a 13-year-old who's having his rite of passage party to Teensville tonight."

"*Yes, captain, I will.*" She opened her eyes. "Good, then let's get on with the shopping. I'll meet you by the register in 15 minutes."

"Fifteen minutes," Tanner repeated. "If you are not there, I will come looking for you with a club."

She raised a brow. "Clubs went out with the Neanderthals, Tanner, so did dragging women around by the hair. You approach the opposite sex with that attitude and you may be by yourself for a very long time."

"Funny." He stated as she grinned. "Just go do your thing and make sure you keep your intuition or senses, whatever it is you decide to use, tuned in to the atmosphere around you. I'd hate to have to tell Isaiah that you won't make it for his party."

She grew sober. "I'll be careful." She turned and walked toward the back of the store while he went toward the stairs, taking them two at a time, so that he could get the football and get back to her quickly.

She entered the stationary department, nodding at an associate as she passed him and started looking around the aisles for red, white and blue streamers, similar plates and napkins in honor of Isaiah's favorite football team. Once she had those in her shopping cart, she started toward the cards and gift-wrap section. She needed to get wrapping paper and a card so she could wrap up the Guardian Personal Computer/Communicator (GPC) she had picked up for him a week ago. It was the newest rage among communicating devices. Guardian designed it so they could sell it to civilian population. It worked like a hand held computer/cell phone, and had all the bells and whistles, including videophone, built in music player, a camera for video and stills, and an audio recorder. It was small enough to fit in one hand and store in a book bag or handbag. Tammy McGellen had one and Marna felt Isaiah was responsible enough to take care of it, so when she saw them on sale at the **Market World** mobile phone booth a week before, she signed up for a plan that included a phone for her and Isaiah. She had been using hers for just about everything, including recording her classes in video so she could listen during class and then transcribe notes later. She loved it. It was a useful tool for the organized person,

She saw the wrapping paper at the end of the aisle and steered toward it. It was then that she noticed the Piñatas hanging from the ceiling. Her eye caught one decorated as a football and thought what a blast it would be to fill it with football goodies, e.g., collectors' cards and statuettes for Isaiah's friends to take home. "Well, Tanner, I guess it'll be a little bit longer than originally planned," she whispered. A sign hung amongst them that said *ask for help*, so she started searching for the sales associate to help her get one down.

However, aisle after aisle, there was no one. Funny, he had been there a minute ago. He had been young, probably high school age. He was probably talking to his girlfriend on his own GPC, in some quiet corner somewhere, with the video on. "Hello !" She called and looked at her watch. She didn't have time for this. The manager would hear about her dissatisfaction of the young man's service. "Hope you aren't too fond of your job, kid," she breathed, and decided to go into the Lawn and Garden department next door to see if they could page the kid to give her assistance.

As she stepped over the invisible department line, she saw who she was looking for in a crumbled heap on the floor. He was out cold. Alarmed, she turned in time to see the shelf behind her move slightly seconds before she felt the crushing pressure of an arm go across her chest from behind and a needle prick her neck. A stinging sensation went through her vein as the attacker injected the drug into her body. *Oh God!* Someone was drugging her, a *Cloaker*! She could feel her cloaking ability trying to kick in. Her attacker was trying to tap into her magnifying ability and cloak them both. She fought against the pull of the power, but the drug was starting to take effect. She was getting dizzy, knew she was going to pass out. *Tanner . . . 911!*

Her attempt was weak. She didn't even know if she was getting through, but within seconds of sending out the distress signal, she felt something slam into them and break the hold of the attacker. She fell to the floor, hitting her head on the counter as she went down, the pain jarring her brain. Disoriented and confused, she grabbed the counter and pulled herself up, fighting the effect of the drug that was trying to pull her down into darkness. Her vision was blurred but she saw the two figures struggling just three feet away. Blood streamed from the wound above her eye. She wiped at it and looked around. She had to find a way to help Tanner. The attacker was bigger, stronger. She looked for something to throw and saw nothing, but her eyes did brush over the fire alarm on the wall. With no other option available to her, and Tanner in trouble, she reached for the fire alarm and set it off. The Cloaker gave Tanner a final push, knocking him off balance and causing him to fall into a shelf of potting soil. Then he threw up his cloak and took off.

Marna let herself slide to the floor and Tanner moved to her aid as the department filled with managers and associates. Tanner showed his security badge and told them to call compound security. He pulled a handkerchief out of his pocket and dabbed at the gaping wound above her eye, while she winced. "Clinic ambulance is on the way," another security agent said.

"No," Marna said, "I'm not going to the clinic. Isaiah's birthday."

"Marna, you need to be looked at." Tanner insisted.

She pushed at his hand as the room swam around her. "They can look at me here." Just then, the medics came in with a gurney. One went to check on the associate Marna had found, and the other went to tend to her. She heard Tanner tell them about the drug. They checked her eyes. The voices all meshed likened to Charlie Brown's teacher. Tanner crouched beside her, concern in his brown eyes. She stared into them. Someone somewhere said *Compliance* and *low dose*. She closed her eyes.

Someone was rubbing her head, brushing her hair away from her wound. She felt a prick in her arm. "Hey !" She cried and reached over with her hand to push the offending hand away.

Tanner took her hand in his. "It's okay, Marna, they're giving you something to offset the effects of the drug."

"Oh." She let them inject the stabilizing med. She closed her eyes. In a few minutes the noises around her stopped sounding so muddled, the underwater tunnel effect eased. She could feel the medic's finger poking around the wound above her eye. His voice sounded normal.

"We'll need to butterfly that. She can ride in the ambulance with the boy." The medic was in his thirties with strong, firm features, sandy colored hair and serious blue eyes.

"I'm not riding in any ambulance," she insisted. "Do what you have to do here. I've got an important meeting I can't miss."

"Ma'am, you could have a concussion. We also need to make sure there are no ill effects from the Compliance. We need you to at least go the ER to be checked out."

"Good luck with that." She started to get up but a wave of dizziness overtook her and Tanner caught her before she fell to the floor. He helped her into a nearby chair.

"Marna, you need to be looked at," he stated, the concern evident in both his voice and his eyes. He still held her hand.

"I'm not going to any clinic. Isaiah's party is tonight and I'm not messing that up."

The attendant drew in a frustrated breath and glanced at Tanner. "I can't treat her if she refuses."

"It's all right, I'll tend to her," Doctor Keys said as he made his way over to them. "You two tend to the boy."

"Are you sure, Sir? She could have a concussion."

"We'll keep a close eye on her." The attendant went over to help his partner. The teen had come out of the drugged stupor and was holding his head in his hands, answering the security team's questions as the emergency team examined him. "Let's see what we have here." Keys drew out a penlight to check Marna's eyes then he checked her vitals and doctored her cut with Steri strips and a butterfly bandage. "Looks like you were lucky this time, Marna." He turned his attention toward Tanner. "Why weren't you with her, Tanner? I told you to sit on her."

Tanner didn't say anything. He knew any dressing down Keys would give him was well deserved. No matter how much she protested, he should have stayed with Marna. It was a careless move on his part, a rookie mistake. "I'm sorry--."

"It wasn't his fault, Keys." Marna came to Tanner's defense. "I told him to go do what he had to do and I would be fine. I had some things to pick up for Isaiah's party and I didn't think anyone would be stupid enough to attack in such a public place, on a Guardian compound." She laid her head against the wall, closed her eyes, and swallowed back the nausea.

"I see," he sighed. "I admit I'm more than a little disturbed that someone could breach the security of the compound, but that was before Tarot." He drew in a breath. "Marna, he killed 26 people, 27 counting Raquel Bradshaw. Do you really think something like a Wrought Iron gate would keep him from what he wants? *That* being *you* at the moment?" His eyes scanned the destruction around the store before he brought them back to her. "Go home, have Isaiah's party. I'll stop by later, after we finish the clean up here." He turned toward Tanner, "Son, take her home, and this time stick with her. Do not leave her alone for even a few seconds. I'll have someone else bring her car home."

"Isaiah's cake. The rest of the things for the party," she objected. He waved his hand to one of the security crew. She was a tall red head, and she smiled as she came over to join them. Marna didn't recognize her. "Demi, could you get a list of things Marna needs for tonight's festivities, pick them up, then take her car and bring them to her house. She'll give you the address."

"Of course." He left Demi with them while she wrote down the items Marna needed and then headed off in a different direction. Marna and Tanner headed to the front of the store. She leaned heavily on him for support.

After he tucked Marna into the front passenger side of his car, Tanner looked around, making sure no one was watching then slid in behind the driver's wheel, backed slowly out of the parking space and steered toward the exit lane of the parking lot. Marna closed her eyes and laid her head back on the headrest of the seat. "I'm sorry."

"For what?" He queried as he smoothly turned into traffic, heading north on the two-lane road.

"For getting you in to hot water with Keys."

"It's not like I haven't been there before." He glanced in his rearview and took a left. "Besides, it was a rookie mistake, I should have known better." He turned onto a one-way road that led through the business center of the compound.

"What?" She glanced around. "You know a shortcut to my house, I don't?"

"We're being followed."

"What?" She started to turn around.

"No, don't look back." She quickly turned back around. "Check out the side-view." She did. "See the blue Grand Alliance, two cars behind us." She caught sight of the large Ford Sedan,exactly where he said it was. "He's careful. Stays two cars back. Only picks up enough speed to keep us in sight, but not enough to raise flags."

"He raised yours."

"I'm psychic, remember." His mouth quirked as he glanced at her then took another turn and glanced in the mirror again.

"Aren't you a funny one?" She teased.

He chuckled, "My senses are heightened due to the store. We can't go to your place with a tail. Let's see if we can get some backup." He reached toward his dashboard GPC and pushed a button. "Security and Protection," a voice came over the car speakers.

"This is Tanner Williams, badge number 31582. I'm driving a yellow 2025 Camaro, on Highland Avenue, Maine license plate Gary, Union, Adam, 569. I need an interference run for a suspected tail."

"Vehicle description?"

"Blue Grand Alliance, four-door, late model, two car lengths behind. Unable to report a license number at this time."

"Moving into position now," Ventura's voice came over the networked phone line then his Mustang pulled onto the road in front of Tanner.

"Position two is happening now," Heidi said just before she pulled out between the second car behind Tanner and the Grand Alliance in her hybrid Beetle. "He's moving up," she said as the Grand Alliance pulled out and moved ahead of her. "Guess he wants to play." She drew in a breath. "Maine Registration: Robert, Edward, November, 631"

"Don't tip your hand, Heidi. We don't want him freaking out," Ventura said. "Okay, Tom, you're up. Give us a chance to get through the intersection."

"You got it," Tom Fielding replied.

"Going into hover mode!" Tanner replied as he hit a button on his dash, turned to Marna, and said, "take a breath, Marna." The Camaro went straight up and pitched backward, as he slammed the pedal down. The intersection came at their windshield fast as the Camaro climbed in speed. Marna saw the truck out of the corner of her eye, gasped as Tanner expertly wove the hovering Camaro over car rooftops, and crossed through the intersection as the truck pulled into it and blocked the passage of any other car behind them. The intersection became a gnarled mess. The truck's trailer was above the legal hover level, therefore blocking the Alliance's efforts to follow them any further.

"Take the next left, Tanner, Hexon Hill," Ventura's voice came over the line, "travel a couple of miles and pull into an alley between Jenna's Tavern and Marty's Bowling Lanes. Spencer and Rush will be there in Marna's car. Switch vehicles and drive through the alley. You'll drive out into the business section in a few seconds. Take a right onto route 120 to the next intersection and get back onto Highland Ave, head south. Spencer and Rush will take your car back onto the main drag and head north toward the gates. Heidi, Keys and I will surround you the rest of the drive to Marna's place."

Ventura's instructions ended as Tanner saw the street sign for Hexon Hill, and turned onto the one-way road. He soon found the alley entrance, drove in between the buildings indicated, ending up in a circular back parking area between the two businesses. Each had their own dumpster. He released the car from hover mode, and let it slowly lower to the parking lot. Demi Spencer and Bryan Rush stepped out of Marna's car and exchanged keys.

"The rest of your party stuff is in the car."

"Thank you." Marna said, as she shook hands with the agents before she and Tanner climbed into her car and exited the alley, turning south on Route 120 into the business district, before turning onto Highland Avenue. Tanner reported their location and moved into traffic.

"We have eyes on the Alliance. Moving in," another voice Marna didn't recognize drifted over the airways, and then the radio went silent.

Marna laid her head back on the seat. "You okay?" Tanner asked.

"Yeah. Just a headache."

"The offset drug will sometimes give you that side effect. Have you got something for it?"

"I'll just close my eyes for a short time."

"You do that." He spared a look at her while she settled down and took a breath, letting it out slowly. The afternoon sun cut across her features in a slant and shadowed the nasty bruise that was forming on her head. He was glad he had asked her to keep her channel open. He didn't like the alternate ending if he hadn't. He looked in the rearview mirror. No hostile tail, but he did notice that Keys vehicle had appeared behind him. As he approached Kennicut Hill, he noticed Ventura's Mustang turn onto the roadway before him and Heidi's pulled in behind Keys. The convoy turned onto Camel Avenue. Sighing, he returned his eyes back to the road and shifted gears as he glanced at the clock. It was almost four PM. He would help Marna with the preparations for Isaiah's party. It was the least he could do.

Moments later, they pulled into Marna's Driveway in front of the home she acquired after Jeff had died and she had signed on as a special investigator with Guardian, which was a step between the Security & Protection team and the World Investigation Team. He knew by the few conversations he and Marna had engaged in, since their arrival months before, WIT was her ultimate goal. His too. They both wanted to become part of the team that brought people like Rick Bradshaw and Pierre Lamontage down, preferably in a fiery heap. After Jeff had died, he and Keys had become part of the Farlow family. They had remained a strong fatherly presence to the children and a constant support system for Marna. During the last few months, he and Marna had become friends, something he hadn't expected after his role in almost destroying her and her family during the Bradshaw investigation.

He glanced at the house. He had helped her find this two-story Chateau, one of the oldest homes on compound property. It had been the former home of Guardian founder, Sherman Worchester, newly renovated and placed on the market weeks before her move to Maine. It had five bedrooms and two bathrooms upstairs and the first floor had a kitchen, living room, dining room, laundry-room, pantry, and den. The previous owner had modified half the basement into a game room, complete with a modest pool table, which Keys, Ventura and Tanner had often used in pool tournaments with the family. Marna had soon learned to look forward to these gatherings and so had the children. The attached two-car, electric garage was new to the home and finished the modernization of it. Tanner reached up to push the button on her visor. The door noiselessly opened and he expertly pulled into it. The second space within was occupied by the family van. Marna had long ago sold the Hummer she and Jeff had owned as the family now needed a small bus to get around in.

The garage door closed behind them as Tanner grabbed his phone and climbed out from his side of the car. When Marna climbed out of hers, the room spun around her. She grabbed the open door for support. Tanner went to her aid. "Are you okay?"

"Yeah. Just give me a minute." She drew in a breath. "I'm just a little dizzy."

"You sure you want to go ahead with this party? You can always postpone it."

"No way," she said as the wave of nausea and the spinning room settled down. "Isaiah has been waiting for this far too long. He's been planning since January." She drew in a deep breath, closed her eyes, willed her body to comply with her mind, let the breath out between pursed lips, and pushed her door closed and then gathered her bearings. "I'm not going to let some psychic renegade ruin his party." She reached for the back door.

"I'll get the other stuff," he said as he placed his hand over hers to stop its movement toward the back door. She raised her eyes to his, an awkward moment passing between them, before he drew his hand away and smiled, "Let's get you inside first then I'll come back for it."

She cleared her throat, "Sure." He led her around the car and up some steps to a side door that opened into a mudroom between the kitchen and garage. They shed their shoes and could see the children had arrived home already because shoes lined up under their hanging backpacks. She looked into the kitchen through the single pane window on the door, catching the eye of her friend and neighbor, Arlene Fielding, who was assisting the twins, Elizabeth and Hannah, in making goodie bags for the party guests. Arlene's husband worked the WIT team and their four children hung out with Isaiah, Elizabeth and Hannah, who were close to their ages.

Arlene had agreed to watch the kids after school so Marna could do the last minute shopping for the party. She frowned as she caught sight of Marna's forehead through the glass and hurriedly opened the door. "Marna, my goodness, what on earth happened?"

"Got in a fight with a counter and lost." She smiled. Arlene put and arm around her and walked her to the table.

"I'll go out and get the rest of the birthday stuff." Tanner volunteered.

"Thanks, Tanner, I'll make some tea." After Arlene seated Marna at the table, she grabbed the teakettle, filled it up and put it back, turning on the flame underneath it. Then she grabbed three cups from the cupboard and arranged them on saucers, popping some herbal tea bags into them. Seating herself at the table with Marna, she asked, "Now how about telling me what really happened."

"I told you."

"Marna. Feeler. Remember?"

"Can't get away with nothing around here can I?" She chuckled.

"Not with those that care about you. No." She sighed, "Does this have anything to do with the other night?"

"Probably, some Cloaker took a shot at me, tried to grab me out of World Mart."

"Oh my . . . did they catch him?"

Marna shook her head. "No. He managed to slip through security." The teakettle whistled. Arlene got up, made the tea, returned to the table, placing Marna's before her, and setting an extra cup at the empty spot across from her. "Guess it's a good thing Tanner was with you."

"Yeah. Guess so." Seconds later, he came through the door laden with bags of the party favors, just as Keys, Ventura, and Heidi came in through the front door.

Heidi walked over and took a couple of bags from Tanner's arms. "Okay, Marna, where do you want us to start?"

"Wha. . .?" She shook her head. "No. I can't ask you. . ." as she stood up, the room swam before her, nausea overwhelmed her. She faltered. Keys went to her side and helped her back into the chair. He pulled out a penlight, and rechecked her eyes.

"You really should have spent the night in the hospital."

"No. Besides I have my own Concierge doctor right here," she smiled at him. "Isaiah's party will happen tonight, just as he planned."

"On one condition," Keys insisted.

"And that is?" She challenged.

"You go upstairs and lay down for a little while. We'll take care of things down here."

"I can't. There is so much to do. I can't leave that up to you."

"Compromise?" Arlene asked, recognizing Marna's tone. "How about you rest on the couch and stupidvise?" She twisted at the waist to bring her eyes to Keys'. "Is that acceptable, Boss?"

"I guess it'll have to be." He chuckled and stepped over to assist Marna into the living room and onto the sofa. Hannah appeared beside him with a thin blanket and covered her up with it. Hannah wore her dark hair in a single tail reaching to her waist. Her blue eyes clouded with concern.

"I'm okay, sweetie, really, just a little bump on the head."

Mary appeared beside her sister. "Aunt Marna, did you fall down?" She looked up at her aunt's head.

"You could say that." Mary was such a beautiful child, her dark ringlets, tied back in two neat tails, reaching her shoulder blades and her eyes huge and blue were full of compassion for her aunt. Mary was an Empath; she could feel the pain of others. She was six. She and her twin brother, Jacob, were the youngest of the eight children. She reached for Marna's head wound but Marna reached up quickly to take her hand.

"It's okay, I can make it better." Mary's Empathy had morphed into a healing ability when she combined her ability with Marna's magnification ability to save Hannah from certain death. All work stopped and everyone looked toward the couch. The memory of Mary slipping into a coma the last time she used her healing ability was still fresh in their minds as well as the terrifying weeks after when all involved wondered if she would ever return to them.

"I know you can, Baby, but I think we'll just let it get better on its own." She took Mary's hand, kissed it and smiled. "Why don't you go with Beth and Hannah and help with the goody bags?"

"Can I?"

"You sure can."

"Come on, Mary," Hannah said, reaching out her hand. Mary took it and followed Hannah out to the kitchen.

"Sooner or later you're going to have to let her use the ability," Keys said as he sat on the coffee table in front of her, "so she learns to control it."

"Every time she wants to use it, I have horrific flashbacks of the cave. We almost lost her because of that ability."

"Because it caught us by surprise, Marna. She's been training with me now for several months. A lot of agents, good agents fell, as well as many civilians, including Jeff, during the Bradshaw investigation, but thank goodness Mary wasn't one of them."

"That ability takes so much from her."

"Not as much as the Bubble Shield did during the siege, and she managed to come out of that okay. She never even needed extra rest to recuperate."

"But to take on somebody's pain, just to relieve them of the injury."

"The sensation only lasts for a few seconds and then she's left with hardly any effects. She's ready to use it, Marna. It seems to me that a controlled environment would be the best place for her to start improving it."

"Not tonight." She looked beyond him, toward the kitchen door. "Isaiah. Hi."

He walked slowly into the room and looked at her, then at Keys. "What happened?" His speech harbored the squeaks of a voice starting to change.

"It's nothing, just a little bump. I'll be fine."

"It's nothing?" He scoffs. "That's what Mom said."

"Isaiah !" Marna said

"We're going to have to run again. Aren't we?"

"No, Son, you aren't," Keys assured him.

"Hey, buddy, come on," Tanner said. "Let's go set up things down stairs."

"Sure." He followed Tanner toward the basement door. Marna dropped her head back on a couch cushion.

"He'll be okay."

"Will he, Keys?" She brought her head back up and caught his eyes with her own. Keys was not only a doctor to her, he was a friend. "Seriously, will he?" She sighed. "We start to have some semblance of a normal life and then something like this happens and they're reminded of the night that threw them into some horror flick that keeps trying to rewind." A tear slipped down her face. "I'm not sure how to talk to him. At least with Jeff around I thought we had a chance, but with him gone. . ."

"I'll talk to him," he said while patting her hands. "You get some rest right now, before the guests get here. Do you need something for the headache?"

"Arlene has gone to get me something. I don't want anything too strong. The dizziness is easing up. . ."

"Marna?" Rose came into the room. "My gosh, are you all right? I just heard about it from Serena." Serena Blackwater was a friend of Rose's they went to the same aerobics class together.

"I'm fine, Rose, really. But if you could just go supervise the decorations for the party, I'd appreciate it."

"Do you need some tea or something? Water maybe?"

"I'm fine. Arlene is getting me a pain reliever and I believe they are starting to clear the dining room for dancing."

"All right, I'll go help out. You give me a holler if you need anything."

"I will."

Keys got up. "I'm going to go down and give Tanner and Isaiah a hand downstairs. You rest, Marna. It looks like everything is under control."

"I will." She watched him go and then lay back on the cushions, closing her eyes to wish away the throbbing in her head. The house hummed with activity around her and it felt comforting. She shifted her position and could feel herself drift until she dozed off.

~~~~

Like movies on a screen, she saw time pass before her on the walls around her, her life as a child, as a teen, her life with Jeff. The loss of her sister, Amanda and Jeff. The joy and sorrow of it all ripped through her.

She saw her parents as they kissed her and Amanda goodbye that final time, her grandparents when they came and told them of the fatal accident and again when they put the house up for sale. The girls had to move out of state with them to finish their last two years of high school elsewhere.

"She saw the party she and her high school sweetheart Jeremy had attended. They had both taken a taste of the candy bowl and the fountain of forbidden drinks. They had both been unfit to drive, but she didn't stop him from getting behind the wheel. She didn't care enough to and because of her selfishness, she had lost him that night and she had received a serious injury that almost cost her the ability to walk.

She collapsed on the rocky surfaced floor of the canyon she stood in as the pain and shame of guilt weighed on her. "Stop it! Please make it Stop !" She cried.

"Your sins will follow you no matter where you go, Ma Cherie. But I can make you forget." A hand touched her head. All the pain faded. The reels of memories stopped flashing on the walls. He lifted her to her feet and the scene changed. They were alone by a flowing brook. "See, my love, look around you. I can give you this." He waved his hand around. Marna looked around. It was peaceful and pain free. All she felt was love and joy. This is what she wanted, no fear, no pain of loss, just peace, love, and joy.

"Step away from her, Pierre." Marna turned toward the newcomer.

"Amanda?" There she stood, her flowing white gown blowing about her in the gentle breeze. Her long dark strands of hair, lifted away from the features that mirrored Marna's. Her large blue eyes, so full of rage, they flashed.

"Amanda, my love, why don't you join us?"

"No, Pierre. I will not and I am telling you one last time, step away from my sister."

"I will destroy you."

She chuckled. "You can't harm me here, Pierre. Your Dream weaving power only haunts the living. But my sister will not become one of your victims." She briefly looked at Marna and Marna saw her falter a bit, " Marna, raise your shields." In a flash Marna saw Amanda fly through the air and slam against the rock wall across the stream.

"Manda !" Marna cried. Pierre grabbed her arm.

"Forget her !" Pierre commanded and grabbed her to him. "You will be mine."

"No." Marna fought to raise her shields and instantaneously she felt his hold on her weaken. Her shields went up. She pulled back and looked at him. She could see him fight for control.

"Marna, they need you to help them !" Amanda cried. Marna looked toward Amanda. She saw Jacob and Mary join hands, concentrating on Pierre. His power over her faltered and he weakened. Then she saw him raise his hand and push them back. They went to their knees. "Quick, Marna, help them !" Marna ran to their aid and as soon as she joined hands with them, she felt the power surge through her and extend to the children. The children stood up. Mary raised her hand and lifted Pierre off the ground slamming him into the rock wall opposite the one Amanda had slammed into moments before.

He turned vicious eyes back on the trio and raised his hand, making a fist. Marna could not breathe. In seconds, a force field bubble went up around them. Marna's breath returned. Pierre's attack eased as Marna felt another layer of protection cover her, the security blanket! Tanner! Mary raised her hand and waved it sideways. Her action threw Pierre further upstream, into a deeper level. The children laughed. Pierre stood up angrily. "You will feel my wrath !" He cried and faded into the background.

The force field dropped and Marna felt a tugging. She fought against it. "Great job you two, but we have to go." She reached for their hands, but they ignored them. They looked at her hands and backed away. "Mary, Jacob, what's the matter? Don't you want to go to Isaiah's party?" The children looked at each other, confused. Then they spoke in a language Marna recognized as German. "When did you two learn to speak German? Is that another gift?"

Marna felt herself forced back away from them. "No !" She pulled forward.

"It's not them, Marna . . ." Amanda said. "It's not Mary and Jacob."

"Have you lost it here in dream land, Amanda? Look at them. It's definitely Mary and Jacob."

Amanda shook her head. "No, see for yourself." Amanda gestured toward the rock wall before her; another reel of memories started playing before her, only this time, they were Amanda's Memories. She saw her go into labor, her delivering quadruplets. Her being told that only two survive while Bradshaw was handing the other two to a nurse and giving them to some stranger who walked *away with them. Rose in Bradshaw's office, looking at files. Marna's reaction to learning of two other children that Amanda never knew.*

"You've got to find them, Marna. He wants to destroy them. They are very powerful."

"What are their names, Amanda? Where are they?" Marna felt herself yanked away. "NO !" She fought the pull. "Amanda, tell me!"

"Go, Marny, find them." Amanda and the children faded. Marna felt herself pulled back through space. The weighed down feeling returned. She could hear voices.

~~~~~

"Marna, Wake up !" She was shook violently once. Her eyes opened. Keys, Tanner, Ventura, Rose and Heidi were above her. All with concern etched into their features.

"Oh my . . ." Marna flipped the blanket off her, swung her legs around and sat up, resting her head in her hands.

"Marna, tell me what's happening," Keys demanded.

"My head, it feels like it's going to explode," she said as she started rocking on the couch.

"Mary, no !" Arlene said. Through the pain and confusion, Marna heard running feet from somewhere behind her and instantly she felt Mary's hands on both sides of her head. The onlookers watched as a halo of light encircled the two of them. Almost instantly, Marna felt the pain ease and Mary's little body quivered in concentration. Within seconds, the halo of light dissipated and the pain left Marna's head. Little Mary's legs buckled. Tanner caught her when she started to fall and brought her around to the front of the couch, sitting her beside her aunt. Her big blue eyes looked up at Marna.

"Is your head all better?" She asked as Keys ordered someone to get his bag and he started examining Mary.

Marna rubbed her little head, "Yes it is thank you." Tears slipped out of her eyes as she worried her bottom lip that something unthinkable was about to happen to Mary like it had the last time.

"Good." She raised her little finger up to Marna's bandage. "It's all better," she whispered

Marna looked at Keys for verification. He reached for the bandage and gently pulled it away. He saw the wound had closed and was well on its way to healing.

"She's right." He accepted his bag and pulled out his stethoscope to listen to Mary's heart, check her vitals and finish examining both of them to make sure there were no ill effects. Mary was pale and fatigued, but her breathing was steady and her vitals were strong. He asked someone to get both of them a drink of water. Rose went and returned with two tall glasses of water.

"Is she all right?" Marna asked, concerned.

"Aside from a little fatigued, as I would expect from the use of such a powerful ability, she's good to go. What about you?"

"I feel good." Marna said, and realized she was telling him the truth. Aside from a little fatigue herself, she did feel good.

"Then I'd say Mary did very well with her healing ability, wouldn't you?"

Marna looked at the child beside her, "Yes, she did." She kissed the top of her head.

"And if I'm not mistaken. . ." He looked at his watch. "Isn't there a very special party starting here in, oh fifteen minutes?"

Mary brightened, "Isaiah's Birthday !" She jumped up and ran back toward the kitchen.

"Yes there is," Marna stood up, faltered a little, accepted Keys help until she felt steady enough, and then thanked him and caught his eyes. "We need to talk before you leave tonight."

"I'm not leaving," he said. "I'm bunking in the den for tonight just to keep an eye on you and Mary, so we'll have plenty of time to review exactly where you went just now."

"Good." As their conversation ended, the doorbell rang and the first guests arrived, putting off any conversations between Keys and Marna about the strange encounter she had just had.

Chapter Three

Marna stood at the railing of her back porch watching Kurt, Tanner and the boys read the instructions to set up the six-man tent she had specifically picked up for Isaiah's after party, slumber party. He had permission to invite three of his guests to stay on for the overnight festivities of ghost stories, stargazing and nighttime, glow-in-the-dark, flag football. After the third try ended in collapse, Kurt grinned and joked around with the boys. "Who needs a tent anyway? We can always just sleep under the stars, isn't that right, Ray, Ray?" He patted his son on the back.

Ray had his father's bushy brown hair and freckled skin, but his eyes were the clear blue of his mother's, not the Hazel gray of his father's. At the age of thirteen, he learned quickly that in order for peers to accept you, you had to believe that parents had one purpose in life, to embarrass and humiliate you. "Yeah, Dad," he said dismissively and went to the back of the tent to pull up an aluminum pole to reset it into the ground and secure the hook to pull it taut. Marna grinned.

"Kurt loves camping," Rose said, handing Marna a cup of tea after stepping onto the porch.

"I see that." She took a swallow, turned around, and leaned her hips on the railing. "Does your family do a lot of it?"

"Two to three weeks during the summer and some long weekends throughout the camping season," she sighed, "At least we did before last year changed our lives. I guess we may have to rearrange that until we build up our vacation time again." She smiled, "We actually have a private camp site up near the Canadian border, on the coast. It was nice to get away from the city occasionally. Maybe you and the kids can join us this year?"

"I think I'd like that," she said wistfully.

"Like what?" Keys stepped onto the porch, drinking a cup of coffee, himself.

"A family camping trip," Marna said smiling.

"I think that would be a wonderful idea." He returned her smile, walked over and watched the teamwork below, not saying anything for a few seconds. "There is nothing more bonding than a good weekend of fighting off mosquitoes and other unmentionable critters."

"Always got to be one cynic in the crowd," Rose said, shaking her head.

"Am I being a cynic? My apologies." He winked and looked toward Marna. "How are you feeling, Marna?"

"Better. No dizziness. A nagging headache is about all I have left."

"Glad to hear it," he gestured to the patio set. "Join me?" She nodded and followed him over, sitting across from him. He took another drink from his coffee cup and sighed. Rose, sensing their need for privacy, skipped down the steps and went to help with the tent.

"How's Mary?" Marna asked, concern lacing through her words.

"Oh, she'll sleep real well for you tonight, but other than that, she's bounced back quickly. She and Rose's Desiree are watching a Disney flick."

"A princess flick no doubt."

"I think so, or Alice in Wonderland. One of those far out fairy tales, yes."

"Nothing wrong with believing in happily ever after," she said.

"Not at all." He chuckled, drew in a breath and let it out between pursed lips. "Speaking of happily ever after. . . Marna, you fought against us hard to stay in your dream vision. I need to know why?"

"I know. I'm sorry. I felt everyone pulling me back, but you're right, there was something happening that made me want to stay."

"You were in distress, Marna. You can be killed in a dream vision if an attacker chooses to end your life." He stared into his coffee then lifted his eyes back to hers. "What was so important that you risked death?"

"Amanda was there."

"Not an unusual event, she often communicates with you in that way."

"So were the two children Bradshaw took from her. Arella and Heinderick."

"Aha. That changes things a little." He sighed, sat back, and crossed his arms frowning. "Maybe you should tell me the whole story from the beginning." Marna told him the entire vision. He listened intently, was thoughtful in some places, asked for clarification in others.

"Amanda actually said Pierre wanted to destroy them?" She nodded. "I see."

"I don't think I'm his only target, Keys." Keys sighed wearily. "We haven't been able to confirm nor eliminate that probability." He leaned back in his chair. "I am curious, however, why they made themselves visible to you. According to my sources they don't even know of you or the family's existence."

"Dream Walkers?"

"Yes they are, but still, they would have to be able to open a channel to you and target your dream to walk within it."

"Amanda?"

"That's a possibility. She died over a year ago. She's had plenty of time to search the Dream Realm, discover the children, and bring them to you."

"When we discovered them last year, you said you had agents searching for them. What have you discovered?"

"My Intel runs dry in Switzerland. That's where Bradshaw gave the children to an agent for placement. They separated them there. They sent one to handlers in Geneva, the other to Zurich. However, all we have are the family surnames to go on. Both names are very popular names in that part of the world. No first names or addresses to follow." He drew in a breath. "However, agents on the ground there have sent some good Intel on sightings and observations over the last year but whether their covers were blown or some other reason spooked them, they've gone underground. No new Intel for several months now.

"But they were together in my dream. They both spoke German."

"Not unusual for Dream Walkers or Dream Weavers, for that matter, to find each other in the realm of psychic dreams . . ."

"Dream Weavers? Wait a minute, Keys. What is a Dream Weaver?"

"Dream Weaving is an ability that branches from an illusionist or staging ability as the host matures. Though there are reported cases of it coming to light on its own. without the prerequisite ability, it is very rare. A psychic with this ability can take hypnotic control of a target's subconscious while they sleep, and bring them into a dream environment/story of his choosing. He can control what his target sees, or does, and how they see and do it. He can make the dream environment comfortable or uncomfortable for his target."

"He can also control how the dream ends if a Dream Walker is not there to counteract that ending. A good example of that is the never-ending dream of falling off a cliff or a building and waking up before you hit the bottom of the canyon or the pavement below. Someone shooting at you and you wake before you feel the bullets pierce your body or the dream hyper jumps to another scene. If the Dream Weaver wants his target to meet their demise, he keeps his target in that hypnotic state until they hit the canyon floor and/or the pavement or until the bullets pierce their flesh. This causes their target to die of a cardiac arrest. Autopsies usually show no injuries consistent with such a fall, though it has happened on rare occasions – a mystery of dream study – the brain will send signals to the rest of the body that the victim has suffered this type of injury or injuries. In the real world, the patient was literally scared to death. These people have no history of heart trouble at all. As I said, to the real world, it's a medical mystery. To those of us in the psychic world, the sad reality is well known."

Marna paled, felt sick to her stomach. "And the only one who can counter act this effect is a Dream Walker?"

"The Dream Walker can introduce alternate endings to a target, like Jacob did for you in the hallway of doors when he led you to Bertha." Marna nodded, she remembered the incident well. "I suspect that your vision earlier started as a Dream Weaving event induced by Lamontage."

"What? Are you saying that Lamontage is a Dream Weaver?"

"I suspect that is true, yes. He is an accomplished Seducer, Illusionist and possibly a Stager. Dream Weaving isn't that far-fetched."

"But why me? Why am I a target for him? I have no abilities that threaten him."

"I suspect killing you isn't his goal." He sighed and put his elbows on the table, leaning forward. "Pierre Lamontage is a very powerful psychic. I have come up against him once already. A battle, until your encounter with him last year, I thought I had won. A battle in which I lost someone I cared for deeply." He swallowed.

Marna put her hands over his, "I'm so sorry, Keys."

He blinked several times, smiled through watery eyes, and patted her hand. Then he cleared his throat, "Lamontage was powerful even then. I was on a Guardian task force developed to go after Lamontage and the the newly forming Liberatores terrorist groups. We suspected he was the one calling the shots, but so far none of his men were willing to turn on him."

"I lived in Paris at the time, with my wife Elizabeth." He smiled as his mind took him back. "Lizzy is what I called her. We'd been married a couple of years and she was my world. I still felt like a newlywed in her arms and like I could do anything, be anything I wanted to do or be. I was indestructible as long as she was by my side. We were both on the task force. One night I was called to a sighting of him and left her with a promise to be back before daybreak."

~~~~~

"You bring my man safely home to me, Mr. Keys", Lizzy teased.

He brought his hand to her cheek and caressed it with his thumb. "I will. It's probably just a false alarm. Lamontage doesn't usually travel alone and rarely does he allow anyone to see him, until after the deed."

"Still, don't let your guard down, Fred. He may be your brother, but he couldn't be any more different. He's a vicious man who only believes in power and causing pain."

"I'll be careful." He caught her chin between his thumb and forefinger and gently lowered his lips to hers. When he pulled away, he could see the fear in her eyes. "Don't, Lizzy, don't think the worst. You know that's not good for you."

"I just wish I could be there with you?'

"Not an option," he said softly, and brought her in for another kiss, deeper than the first. "You just get that paperwork done and I'll see you when I get home. We'll watch our favorite movie again."

She smiled. "Alright." She stood on her tiptoes and kissed him again then watched him catch the elevator and closed the door.

"Where did you go?" Marna asked as Keys got lost in the memory of seeing Lizzy's face that last night as the elevator door slid closed. A tear slipped from his eye and tracked down his face.

"The task force was called to a government building. I was the first to arrive." He drew in a breath as he returned to his memories. "Lamontage had the same choices I did on how to use his abilities. He chose to use his for death and destruction. I chose to join Guardian and take down men like him. His dominant ability, even then, was his Illusionist ability. It's a form of hypnosis. It works

*like that of a mirage in the desert. The brain makes you see water when it isn't there. He makes you see
things that aren't there, but that night he chose to make me see reality in the cruelest way possible."*

~~~~~

"What reality, Keys?" Marna gently prodded. She wanted to be patient because it was obvious
that the memories Keys was sharing with her were very painful for him.

He ran a hand over his face. "The death of our parents."

Marna fell back in her chair. "Lamontage is your brother?"

Keys sniffed. "Technically speaking, yes. We were both products of Bradshaw's lab as was
Elise Riley."

"The children's pediatrician? The one that Bradshaw had killed last year?"

"Yes, and we all came from the joining of two donors. A college couple who needed money
for tuition. One was pre-med and the other was pre-law. We were pegged A-1." He drew in a breath.
"He paid good money to those kids for their contributions. In the earlier part of his experimentations,
he used surrogates, and then he got bolder and started using couples such as Amanda and Peter."

"Pierre and I grew up together, in Bradshaw's laboratory, available for his experiments and
training with various trusted individuals he brought on board. As much as Pierre never yearned for the
love of parents, I did and I searched for them, hoping that when I found them, they would care enough
to help me escape Bradshaw. I couldn't find them but Lamontage did. They were both successful in
their chosen professions. She was a highly respected Washington D.A. and the other a top name in his
chosen profession of Oncology. He had found them and on that night, they became his chosen victims
to show me how powerful he was becoming."

~~~~~

*When I arrived at the government building, he had them on the balcony in some kind of
hypnotic trance. They showed no fear, only a peace that I could not describe. Still can't to this day, but
I know it well. I've seen it several times during my time with Guardian. I begged him to let them go. He
only laughed at me. He was terribly cruel even then. Causing pain to others made him feel powerful.
He loved that control. With a movement of his hand, he held me back with some kind of psychic energy,
with his other hand he ordered them to leap to their death. I remember screaming. He then turned his
attention to me, closed his fist and twisted it. I could never remember feeling that kind of pain, before
or since, that he induced on me that night. I thought he was going to kill me. I collapsed, could barely
move, and when he finally let his control go, I knew I had a couple of broken ribs and God knew what
else. He crouched before me.*

"Why don't you kill me, Pierre?" I asked him with the little breath I had left.

"You, Brother, are worth more to me alive than dead." His black eyes bore into mine.

"What does that mean?"

*"That means that I will take whatever is important to you until you are begging me to take you
into my world. I will start tonight with your lovely bride."*

*"No! Don't hurt Lizzy! I will do whatever you want, Pierre, but please leave her alone." He
induced more pain on me until I collapsed to the floor, then I heard him leave."*

*"I was paralyzed, couldn't move, it hurt too much. Precious time passed, I don't know exactly
how much, but when the spasms finally did stop, I reached for my communicator to call for back up. At
that moment, I heard agents from Paris law enforcement moving into the building. I knew if they found
me there, I would have to explain why I was at the scene where two people had fallen to their deaths
and it would take precious time away from my getting to Lizzy, so I moved out as fast as I could with
two fractured ribs and possibly other internal injuries. I took the stairs, went to my car, and managed
to get around the security bubble.*

*When I arrived at my building I ran, half hunched over, to the front door with my gun and
banged on the glass. The doorman opened the door and looked at me in shock.*

"Dr. Keys, are you okay."

I slammed a card in front of him with the Guardian dispatch number on it. "Call this number and tell them I need back up now!"

"Yes, sir." He turned to his phone and dialed the number while I ran toward the elevator and practically pushed an awaiting person aside, showed them my badge, told them it was an emergency and took their car to my apartment. When the car opened at my door, I saw my apartment door open and I heard Lizzy screaming.

The emotions that engulfed me were like nothing I had ever experienced before, nor have I experienced them since. The fear, the anguish, the hate, and the anger, it overwhelmed me. It took control of me. I moved into the apartment, gun ready. I knew other Guardian agents were coming, but I also knew that Lizzy was in major trouble now. I didn't have time to wait for them. She screamed again, and then there was nothing but silence. It was a silence so loud my ears could hear my own heartbeat. I ran down the hall to our room and barged in. She was on the floor, her eyes full of desperation, drool leaking from her mouth. There were several candles lit all around the room and he was there. . .

"No !"

"You are too late, Brother." He laughed. "She will die at my hand." A tear slipped from her eye and tracked down her face, but I wasn't going to allow him another attack. Lizzy was fading fast and I had to get her away from him. I felt such rage at that moment. Rage I had never felt before. He laughed. "That is it. Feel the rage. Feel the anger. Feel the power of hate, anger and darkness." He came up to me and whispered in my ear. "Come serve me, Brother, and together we can conquer the world!"

I barely remember what happened next. I twisted, raised my gun and fired twice into his torso. He fell backwards, knocked some candles down. The flames caught the window drapes and engulfed them quickly. Fire was all around us. He lifted his hands and tried to take control of me again, but my emotions had channeled into some kind of telepathic power. It had made my shields strong enough to deflect his attack and hold him off. It wasn't long before he passed out. At that moment, I was stronger than he was. I ran to Lizzy, picked her up, and barely escaped the flames myself. I somehow got her out of the building and to the front yard, just as more Guardians and emergency personnel arrived. The last thing I remember is looking back at the house and seeing him standing by a window as the flames engulfed him."

"Lizzy didn't make it?" Marna asked.

He shook his head and sniffed, "She was on life support for a few days, everything modern day medicine and Guardian had available to them and we couldn't save her. The internal damage was too much. I knew she would not want to go on like that so I had them disconnect life support. It didn't take long for her to fade away from me.

~~~~~

"I'm so sorry, Keys." Marna took his hands, and Keys sniffed. She knew how horrible it was to see the one you love slip away from you. She could understand and feel his pain. "So why do you think he's back and why has he locked onto me?"

He stood up and walked to the railing, noticing briefly that the tent project was almost completed. He turned around and leaned against the railing. "After your sighting of him last year, I had some of my best agents reassigned to Switzerland to start a methodical search for similar deaths to Cassie's, those of my parents and Lizzy's.

"And?"

"We found that there is a chapter of the Liberatores running in Switzerland, Zurich, to be exact. They are parallel to Guardian in every way but what they stand for and what they do. Where we provide protection and justice. Their biggest service is Assassins for Hire. Questionable clients hire them through underground channels to assassinate high-ranking, government officials, though they will do just about anything for a price. Raquel Bradshaw, I'm assuming, planned to take a position as co-pilot, beside Lamontage but he got what he wanted from her and disposed of her. "

"The remaining Bradshaw Children." Marna filled in the blanks.

He nodded. "I'm afraid he's recruiting them for his organization and according to the Tarot report, they were the ones with the most powerful abilities, which explains why he chose them."

"Again I say, why me? Why is he coming after me?"

Keys returned to his seat. "Isn't it obvious, Marna? He wants control of your Magnifying ability, and your ability to form a collective when joined with other psychics." He sighed "and the only way to get that is to get control of you."

"But his control can only last so long. Eventually I would fight his control and break away. He must realize this."

"I suspect by then, he has gained his control by using his love, fear or lust, whatever he wants to use, you will not leave him. What he has given you so far is so endearing and soothing to your soul . . ."

She nodded. "The virtual visions of Jeff, my chance to be with him again," she said quietly.

"Yes. He'll give it to you in daily doses and eventually it will be like a drug. It will be like an addiction. He will have complete and utter control over you and your emotions. It will get to a point that if he threatens to take your time with Jeff away."

She nodded. "The need for it will override my need to have free will."

"Exactly, and his brainwashing will be complete. Most likely Stockholm Syndrome would be in play." Keys knew of a more vicious control that was out there, but he prayed Pierre had not picked up that ability in the years he had been underground. It was more likely to evolve in the abilities of a Seducer than it was in any other psychic. They called it Possession and the results of that kind of control were devastating to a psychic that went through the cycle. The best scenario was becoming a servant to the Possessor, totally losing your free will and the worst scenario was madness or death. He felt a chill go through him but it wasn't because of the coolness of the evening.

She cleared her throat. "Wow. Guess I never thought myself that vulnerable." She lowered her eyes to her cup.

"Pierre's specialty is finding people's vulnerability and using it to control them. He has already proven that you can't fight one of his Dream Weaving attacks, Marna, without the help of a Dream Walker. He's taken free will from you, more than once. He has also tried his Seducing powers on you, again showing your vulnerability to him. Every time he launches an attack on you, there is one common denominator."

"My inability to let go of Jeff." Tears pricked her eyes.

"Your need to have back what you lost," he said gently.

Angrily she stood up and walked to the railing. "Why can't I have my dreams? Dark forces have already taken the rest of my world from me. Why can't I at least have that one little thing?" Angry tears rolled down her cheeks.

"I understand your pain, Marna, but Pierre is a powerful adversary. Make no mistake about that. You are not a Dream Walker and you cannot fight him alone. Unfortunately, he has set his sights on you, for whatever reason. When you sleep at night, your guard is down. It may be a good idea to have a Blocker come in to protect you at night, just for added security."

"No."

"But Marna."

"No, Keys." She turned to face him. "I want to play the offensive with this one. I don't want to hide from him. I spent almost a year running from Bradshaw. I won't run from Pierre."

"Marna, you're still learning the scope of your abilities."

"And so were you, when you first encountered him."

"And he almost killed me!" He took her shoulders and made her look at him. "Marna, please, for God's sake, be reasonable!"

She stared him in the eyes, determination settling in the blue depths of hers. When she spoke, her voice was steady and controlled. "I will not be like a spooked pup, Keys. If you want me on the WIT team, then I will no longer play the victim. I want in on the chase of Pierre Lamontage. I want to be there when we take him down, and I want to be there when we destroy him. This man will not take the things that matter from me. I will be the one doing the taking this time. I will be the one who walks away the victor."

"Marna, I admire your courage, but what about the children?"

"Do we need them?"

"I don't know what we'll encounter when we finally catch up to Pierre."

"You said it yourself. I have the ability to form collectives. If need be, a collective will bring him down." She drew in a breath and let it out. "Can my shields be made stronger? Can I become resistant to his control?"

"I suppose if you know what to look for, what to be aware of, and then you may have a chance to keep him out."

She crossed her arms. "Do you know where he is now?"

"No. Chances are he goes back to Switzerland."

"Find him. Spring break starts a week from Monday, and I've always wanted to go to Switzerland. Our cover story will be a skiing vacation. While we're there, we look for him. I'll have Rose and Kurt come with us. Rose is just discovering Blocking abilities, so she and someone else, maybe Schafer or Tanner, can keep the children safe while we look for Pierre and get ready to put an to end him and his organization for good."

"I admire your spirit, Marna, but taking down an organization the size of Liberatores is dangerous at best."

"A snake dies if you cut off its head."

"That may be true in the Animal Kingdom. But in the world of Organized Crime, there's always another ready to step into the lead position."

"Worse case, we cripple it and it takes a while to rebuild and come back. By then Guardian gathers more Intel. Right now we concentrate on taking down Lamontage."

Keys sighed, drew in a breath, gathered his thoughts, blew it out again, and spoke pointedly. "Marna, don't get me wrong. I admire the way you are ready to move forward on this. It's the go get 'em attitude I look for in all my agents, but I'm concerned about your reasons why. You may be too close to this. You have investigative experience. I don't challenge that. You and Jeff were the best at what you did, but I need to know you are moving forward with a level head and not one filled with revenge."

Marna put her palms on the table and leaned in until she was within inches of Keys face. "Keys, I will not let another person take over my life again. My head has never been clearer, my path never more direct. You want to bring Lamontage down, so do I. I have a better understanding of psychic investigation now than I did last year. It's a learning process, and I'm a quick study, so stop trying to shrink me, and let's get on with it."

"All right, I'll get in touch with my agents in Zurich and see what new Intel they have. See if there is any word on Lamontage. Then we'll start making plans, but if you have any more dreams about Jeff, do not take them at face value. Remember, Lamontage is a Dream Weaver and once he has you, he will not let you go."

"Got it."

*****

After she said goodbye to the last guest, Marna wandered around the house tidying things up. The boys were out in the tent, you could see the flashlights from the French doors, leading to the back porch. The other children had long since gone to bed. She wandered about her home and allowed herself to reminisce some. When they had permanently moved to Maine, shortly after the Bradshaw investigation had officially closed, they had stayed in one of the apartments while waiting for a unit big enough for their populous, to open up for them. The garage was a nice extra.

She looked around the interior of that home now. The front door opened to a small hallway between the den and kitchen. Her kitchen was the largest she had ever had. Marble counter tops circled the entire room, minus the space where the mudroom door led to the garage, with complimenting maple wood cupboards, complete with built in refrigerator, stove and dishwasher. The stove had a Microwave unit attached above it and included a bread oven as well as a conventional. A breakfast bar occupied one section of the wall, facing the living room, complete with four stools. Saloon style doors, attached by a lattice trim separator, extended from the opposite wall to the breakfast bar.

Beyond them was a spacious dining area with a table big enough to seat ten to twelve diners. A hutch was snug against a wall, displaying Amanda's old China. They had found it in a storage facility in time for Christmas dinner.

A lattice wall separated the dining room from the living room, which had laminated flooring, complimenting western, stucco walls, cherry furniture, including a coffee table, two wing chairs, a love seat and an L-shaped sofa with a lounge seat attached. A large 46-inch plasma TV hung on a wall above a surround sound, home theater and media system.

On the corner of the living room and hallway, rising to the second floor was a flight of wrought iron stairs, which led to the second floor, containing five bedrooms and two bathrooms. Four rooms occupied one end of the hallway where the children slept, and the master suite with an attached bath, was on the end above the living room. The concept was open; almost loft style, there were no walls that blocked the second floor from one's vision, with the exception of the wrought iron railings, and silk plants that lined the landing.

It was a comfortable home and it sat on one of the largest lots in the Guardian compound. Three acres of grass surrounded her home and a patch of wooded land stretched between the back of her property and the little cemetery on the hill that Jeff laid in. It was those same woods that Ventura and Tanner had lost track of the Peeping Tom the other day.

She sighed, dried her hands as she finished washing the last party dish in the double stainless steel sink, placed them in the strainer and made her way into the living room, pausing to straighten out some magazines and coloring books on the coffee table, before reaching for the remote and turning on the television.

The local news channel had preempted the drama she liked to watch to talk about the suicide of some foreign, government official, in downtown Washington. "Keys!" she called. Keys quickly came in through the patio door. She pointed to the screen, too shocked to say anything.

Prince Akeem Basheed died at the scene this afternoon after he walked into the path of a fast moving bus. Witnesses say he was holding his head and crying out in pain, which could account for his apparent confusion about where he was and explain why he stepped directly into the path of an oncoming bus. Police are investigating the accident, but believe it could be an apparent suicide and are looking to see if he had a medical history of tumors, or some kind of psychological disorder, that could have caused the man to take his own life.

Basheed was attending the Senate hearings about the unbiased terrorist attack on a subway in his country three months ago that killed 150 Macerians and 15 United States service men on their way to a U.S. base that had been active in his country since the oil conflicts. He and his father, King Rakeem Basheed, had been allies with our country since 2025 when his small country, Maceria, won its separation wars from Arabia and became an independent state. Since then they have been a target for several terrorist groups operating in the area. We will keep you updated as the story unfolds. Now for the weather . . .

She turned to look at him. He watched the TV for a few more minutes then turned his head to meet her eyes with his own. "His target?"

"Could be. We'll check with the ME and then we'll see if he is seeking to leave the country."

"When will we know?"

"I'll have agents tag the bus stations, train stations and airports."

"Do you really think he'll let himself be caught that way?"

"I don't know. But it's worth a try. We play on his ego. He believes he's above average in intelligence and that we are not able to catch him. So let's work on proving him wrong." He took her shoulders and leaned in to give her a fatherly kiss on her forehead. "You get some rest, Marna. I'll see if we can trace him." She nodded and then watched him as he grabbed his jacket, heading toward the door.

"How soon will you know?"

He turned toward her. "Marna, just go to bed. I'll leave Tanner and Martin to work security around the house so you can get some rest."

"Keys, we discussed this . . ."

"No, Marna, you discussed, I listened, but in my expert opinion at this time, you are not ready to try and fight Lamontage on your own. Just accept the added security and get a little peace of mind. We'll start testing the strength of your shields tomorrow. Goodnight, Marna." He opened the front door and disappeared into the darkness of the night. Letting out a frustrated growl, she threw herself on the couch, grabbed a pillow, and pulled it close to her chest.

Tanner stepped through the door and stood watching her. He wondered if he should step out and leave her to her thoughts. Instead, he cleared his throat. She started and turned around. "Oh, Tanner, I didn't hear you come in."

"Sorry. Keys said I should ask you where you thought I should set up for the added security."

"I guess you and Martin can set up in the den." She got up off the couch and led him into the den. It was a room with paneled walls and laminated flooring. The tempered glass, trim line, desk was against the wall opposite the door, with a modern, fast-paced computer set up on it. Beside the desk was a standard sized window with insulated curtains and white blinds. Against another wall to the right of the desk, was a daybed made up in muted tones, so guests could be comfortable when she converted the room to a guest room. A built in closet approx four feet long and three feet deep at the foot of the bed, and shelves on one side of the closet allowed plenty of space for folded garments. The other half had an aluminum bar for hanging garments.

The main key pad for her current alarm system was on the wall next to the closet, and that key pad emitted wireless information to the house windows and tied in the code to the keypads that were on the walls next to all entrance doors within the house. "Will this work for you?"

"It'll be fine." He smiled and went about connecting wires to various USB plugs on the computer while she watched.

"What's all that for."

"It's a bypass system, that will allow us to interconnect your current security to a video surveillance set up, which we'll set up so we can watch all angles of your property for intruders." He turned to her and smiled. "Martin is out setting up the wireless camera's now." Marna stepped forward with interest as the monitor split into four sections and displayed separate areas of her property, the video changing every few seconds...

"Wow, fast work."

"Yeah, Martin's a wiz with electronics." He turned toward her, noticed the strain and weariness on her face, laced with concern. "We've got your back, Marna. You've got nothing to worry about."

"That obvious, huh?"

"Not really. Feeler, remember."

"Oh – ah – yeah. Would you guys like some coffee? I was going to make some tea. I can start a pot of coffee as well." She smiled. "There is some leftover cake if you like too."

"That would be great. Sure." He pulled his phone out of his pocket. "I'm going to give Martin a call so we can run checks on the camera locations."

"Sure." She smiled, but stayed a moment looking at him. He raised a quizzical brow. "Something else?"

She cleared her throat. "No, if you'll excuse me." She turned and left the room. Tanner watched her go then lifted his phone looking at the screen. "Yeah, Martin, station one-clear, station-two clear . . ." His voice faded as Marna entered into the kitchen. She set the teapot on the stove and reached in the cupboard for cups, teabags and coffee. Then she went to the bar, and pulled the cover off the glass, cake display case and cut three slices, setting them on paper plates.

She sat on a stool and leaned on the bar as she waited for the tea water to boil. Then she glanced at the television. They were still showing clips of witness testimony from the Prince's supposed suicide. Her thoughts drifted back to Amanda. Oh how she wished she could talk to her. Rose was a nice comfort but she and Amanda had shared a history. She closed her eyes and let the memories wash over her. It sometimes brought Amanda closer to her . . .

~~~~~

When she opened them, her eyes caught something in the hallway she turned quickly. It was Amanda. Her dark hair cascaded beyond her shoulders to the center of her back, in soft gentle curls, and she wore a white robe-like garment. A soft light haloed around her. She blinked and looked again. "Amanda?"

"About time," Amanda chided "I've been trying to reach you since our encounter earlier." Amanda's eyes, so like her own, scanned her face. "I see Mary's healing power has advanced nicely."

Marna raised her hand to her head. "Yeah. It did. No coma this time."

"Good. How was my boy's party?" She said. "I want details."

"It was lovely, Amanda." I tried to make it everything he wanted it to be."

Amanda studied her a moment and swallowed. "Of course you did. You were a wonderful choice to look after my babies. I'm glad you agreed to do it."

"So am I." Marna sat up and swiveled herself toward the apparition of her sister. "What are you doing here, Amanda?"

"You called me."

"Wha—No. . .I . . ." She stopped and smiled. "The Psychic Hotline." She pointed to her head.

"Yes, Darling, the Psychic Hotline. You should be used to it by now."

"I don't know if I'll ever get used to it."

"You were burning up the lines with your stress signals. Tell me, Lil' sister, what is it that has you all tied up in knots?"

"Lil' sister? You were only born three minutes before me."

"Still makes me older," Amanda said quickly and walked around the bar, stepping through the saloon doors. Marna shook her head. The who's older arguments used to be a way they would amuse themselves on family outings. "But that's not why you wanted me here, now is it? You're scared and irritated and you want to talk to someone about it. Someone who will listen and not dictate. Who better than a ghost? Especially if it's your sister. It's not like you have to worry about her gossiping or

anything." Amanda spread her arms out and let them drop to her side. "Another downfall to being dead, ugh."

Marna laughed. "I do miss you, Manda."

"Of course you do. Now spill it. I only have so long before the cosmic whosit; whatsit calls me back to the great beyond."

"Another one has come out, Manda."

"Another what? Can you be a bit more specific? It's been a while since I've decoded your cryptic sentences."

Marna sighed, got up, and walked to the counter. "Another enemy has crashed into our lives, Manda, someone who wants to hurt us, no, me, wants to own me, another psychic criminal, homicidal maniac, all of the above." She turned around and leaned her hip against the counter top.

"You mean Pierre?" Marna nodded. Amanda sighed. "I was afraid his Dream Weaving the other night wasn't just for theatrical reasons." Amanda turned her eyes toward Marna. "It's not the first time is it, Marna?"

"No. He's done it before." She drew in a deep breath and blew it out. "His full name is Pierre Lamontage, and he is much more powerful than Bradshaw. He runs an assassin for hire organization and . . ."

"He wants your magnifying ability."

"Yeah, and according to Keys, his abilities are rare and powerful."

"Seducer, Illusionist, Stager, Dream Weaver?" Marna nodded. "I've heard of him from other spirits. He's considered deadly. But Marna, you are more powerful than he."

"Am I really? I'm not so sure."

"Marna, look at what you have already. Cloaker, Medium, Dreamer, Magnifier, Kything, Locator . . ."

"Loca . . .? Manda, I don't have a Locating ability."

Amanda looked around the room, and pointed toward a book that Isaiah got for his Birthday. "Pick that up." Marna raised her brow. "Just do it." Marna shrugged, and reached for the book. "Now just hold it, close your eyes and focus on Isaiah."

Marna did what Amanda asked. Like a movie playing in her head, Isaiah came into focus, and she saw that he was listening to one of his friends tell a story. It was just flashes but she recognized her house and the back yard. She saw the tent and the time of day. She dropped the book, drew in a breath and stumbled backward. "When . . .?" She looked at Amanda for an explanation.

"It's been coming for a while, Marna, but your discomfort with your abilities always pushed it back, but now you need it, and it is affirming itself within your psychic makeup."

"Why now?" She demanded, "Why not before?"

"Be honest with yourself, Marna, you already know the answer to that."

Marna thought of the two children in her dream. "The children, Arella and Heinderick. Your children . . ."

Amanda nodded, and Marna swore she saw a tear sparkle on her cheek. "Bring them home, Marna, please. You're the only one that can."

~~~~~

A loud whistle caused Marna to bring her head up sharply. She must have fallen asleep. The teakettle was whistling. She looked around the room. Amanda was gone. Her sister had visited her in her dreams. She quickly got up and turned the kettle off as Tanner came quickly from the den.

"Everything okay?" he queried.

"Yeah, I dozed off on the bar." She smiled as Martin came through the French doors. "You know what, I think I'm going to forego the tea and just go to bed. I'm suddenly feeling very tired. Coffee is done and the cake is on the counter." She smiled at both of them, came through the saloon doors and headed toward the stairs. Before she started her ascent, she turned to them. "If you need extra blankets there's some in the linen closet by the laundry room and I'll wish you both a good night." She smiled and headed upstairs.

As she made her way through the upstairs hall, she went right instead of left so she could check on the children. Joseph and Jacob shared the first room she entered. She went in, and pulled the blanket up over Jacob's shoulders because he had kicked them off. She kissed both boys and moved on. The next room belonged to the three girls. They all wanted to share the room, even though they could have arranged for two to a room, but their reply was, 'us gals need to stay together.' She smiled at the memory.

She quietly walked in and turned off the electronic bedtime aides. Then she checked the nightlight and kissed each of them in turn. Then she moved on to the next room, which David and Moses had claimed and turned into a dinosaur lair. She stood in the doorway and grinned. She had gotten so she could tell when Moses was using his Astro ability, and she kneeled behind his lower bunk and whispered, "Time to come in, Moses, and leave the older boys alone." Within minutes his physical body took a deep breath and grinned then he looked up at her.

"Sorry, Aunt Marna," he whispered. "I just wanted to hear some of their stories."

She moved some of his hair back from his forehead, speaking softly, "Enough for tonight. Stay in your body and go to sleep."

"Yes, Ma'am," he smiled and she bent to kiss him goodnight. Standing, she checked on David and pulled the blanket up around his neck. Kissing the flats of her fingers, she gently laid them on one his cheeks. "Good night, sweet boy." She turned toward the hall and stepped out of the room, closing the door behind her. She didn't go into the next room as it was Isaiah's and she knew where he was. She ventured to the end of the hall and entered her own room, closed the door, and took off her clothes, slipping into a pair of lounge pants and a tee. She glanced at the portrait of Jeff that sat on her bedside table. He was standing by their Humvee, in his customary khaki summer trousers and short sleeve cobalt blue polo. She gently caressed it with her fingers.

"I miss you so much," she breathed, before she went into the bathroom to do her nightly ritual, and then returned, grabbed her book from the desk and crawled in between the sheets.

When she opened the book, a picture of her and Amanda fluttered out from between the pages. She lifted it and looked it over then sighed as she thought about the children asleep down the hall, and the two children taken from the family at birth, not allowed to know their family. She returned her eyes to Amanda's and sighed. "I will bring them home, Amanda, I promise you. She replaced the marker in the book and concentrated on putting her shields up, and then laid her head on the pillow. She felt that familiar, cozy blanket circle her mind. *Goodnight, Tanner,* She contacted him through a channel she opened to him, *No investigating behind any closed doors up there while I'm helpless to fight you off,* she smiled and reached up to turn out her light.

Downstairs, as he looked out over the backyard, Tanner grinned when he saw the light patch, representing her room, on the grass go black and he craned his neck to look at her window. *I somehow don't see you as helpless.* He chuckled. *But you have my word, no investigating behind any doors you don't invite me through. Good night, Marna.* Shaking his head, he turned and headed back in to the command post.

Chapter Four

"Isaiah, don't forget to pack your research notes!" Marna called up the stairs as she checked items off her list. After she was back in the kitchen, someone knocked on her front door. She poked her head around the lattice trim and waved Tanner in. He entered the hallway with a suitcase and a carry-on bag. Marna smiled. "Looks like you're ready to go. What time's the flight leave?"

"Keys said around two p.m."

She glanced at her watch. "Good, gives us a couple of hours." She smiled. "I could get used to having private jets at my disposal."

Tanner grinned. "It does make things a little easier."

"No long road trips to the airport and no changing planes with eight kids in tow. That's like opening the big gift under the Christmas tree."

Tanner laughed. "I'm not sure I would liken it to that, but it is convenient. Have you ever been to Switzerland?"

Marna immediately became wistful, her expression sorrowful. "No. Jeff and I talked about it as a second honeymoon sometime, maybe our tenth anniversary. Guess that isn't happening."

"I'm sorry." Tanner looked awkwardly at his wristwatch.

"No, I am." She swallowed. "I shouldn't have unloaded on you. I just hate how unfair this is, me living a dream without him. Just doesn't seem right." She sniffed, turned her back on Tanner and busied herself with checking things off her list.

She felt his hands on her shoulders. "Hey, don't be so hard on yourself, Marna. Putting your life back together after such a loss isn't always easy for those left behind. It takes time."

"I feel like a puzzle missing pieces," she said stepping away from his hands.

He moved his hands to his pockets as she turned toward him. "You'll find them soon enough," he encouraged, "and they'll be stronger for the healing. You'll be stronger."

"I have to be; for them." She nodded toward a wall portrait of the children.

"And you will be." Running feet on the stairs brought their attention toward them.

"Aunt Marna, is there room on the plane for Frizzy Bear?" Mary queried as she jumped off the bottom stair. Frizzy Bear was Mary's only possession she had taken with her when they ran from her home. He was a 12-inch bear with a plush outer layer, purple and white in color, and a button sewn on to replace the blue eye that went missing that same day.

"Of course there's room for Frizzy on the plane." She played with a misplaced curl atop the child's head. "I wouldn't have it any other way." She smiled at Mary and crouched down to give her a hug. When she pulled away, Mary put her little palm on Marna's cheek.

"Why are you sad, Aunt Marna?" The child's face showed signs of sadness now too, as her empathy kicked in.

She used her fingers to arrange a few more unruly curls, and sniffed. It was too late now to redirect Mary's concerns. She sniffed. "Nothing, Baby, I'm just missing Uncle Jeff is all."

Mary sighed and wiped a tear off Marna's cheek. "I miss him, too."

"I know you do." She smiled. "But we're going to be okay." She kissed Mary's forehead. "I promise." She drew in a breath, and let it out, trying to neutralize her emotions. "Now, that's enough sadness for the day. We're going on a vacation to Switzerland; all expenses paid. It's a place where few people get a chance to go during their lifetime." Emotions in check, she smiled at the child. "Are you all packed?"

"Yep. I wanted to find out 'bout Frizzy Bear is all."

"Well you found out, now scoot upstairs and make sure the others are on track."

"Ooh, I get to check on everybody else?" She smiled, her blue eyes round and intense with excitement.

Marna grinned. "Yes you do."

"Okay !" She stood up, quickly turned around and accepted the tissue Tanner offered her. .

"Thanks," she cleaned off her face then blew her nose, "for the words of wisdom, the tissue, and for listening."

"What are friends for?"

She stared at him for a moment, remembering the road they had traveled, and thought how ironic that statement was, given their past. "Are we, Tanner?" He looked confused. "Friends? Have we been able to get to that level?" Her eyes were intense, thoughtful.

"It would be easier for partners to at least cross that threshhold," Keys said. They both looked his way when he appeared, as if by magic, on the opposite side of the bar, placing a brief case atop of it. "I'm sorry, the door was open. I figured it was all right to just come in."

"Of course you did," Marna said, stepping further away from Tanner and raising a brow at Keys. "However, do tell. What do you mean, partners?"

"I put a rush on your semester grades."

"Why?"

"I need the two of you, in a professional manner, on this case assignment."

"I don't know if I'm ready for that," Marna objected.

"Trust me, based on your grades and experience, you're more than ready; you can step in to a Level One WIT position without hesitation. However, like any other law enforcement agency, maybe even more so in our establishment, you need a partner. I won't let you do field work without one."

"What is that? Level One?" Marna asked.

"Guardian Security levels determine what cases you can be assigned to,, and whether or not you need a senior agent to cover your back."

"I see."

"It's based on your experience in law enforcement before you come to us, and whether or not you've completed the class study required in Psychic Investigation to be given the reins on an investigation." He captured her eyes with his. "In the psychic world, our world, there are many level perpetrators we go after, and you have to be strong enough to face them. That also plays a part in what your level is."

"I get it. It's like rookie level in the psychic world."

He grinned, "Something like that. Tanner will be entering at the same level. He doesn't have a partner yet either. You two are familiar with each other, and from what I've seen over the last year, you seem to get along okay, so I'm asking if you would try it on for size, if it doesn't work then we can change it later." They both nodded. " You'll need to have each other's back. You do not go through a door; you do not investigate anything without being in the company of the other. Do I make myself clear?" Again, they nodded. "If I hear that either of you have ventured off on your own without consulting me, or the senior agents on this or any case, then I will take you off the team. Understand?" They nodded.

"Good." He opened up his brief case and handed each of them a gun and a WIT badge. "Tanner, I'll need your security badge back."

"Yes, sir." He reached for his belt, pulled off the badge, and handed it over to him.

"You'll be working the missing person angle of the case to find Arella and Heinderick, and hopefully bring them home. Then you will be backing up Kyle, Sasha, Peter and Heidi, when the time comes, to go after Lamontage."

"Kyle and Sasha?" Marna queried.

"The agents assigned to this case for the last year. They have plenty of Intel to share with us when we arrive, but for now, here is what you need to know before we set down in Switzerland." He tossed a file to each of them. "It will give you a general idea of what we're up against. We'll have a briefing at the Zurich Compound before we join forces with Sasha and Kyle to complete the assignment."

"Okay." Marna opened the file and started skimming through it. Her breath caught when she saw the photos of Arella, it was one of the two children that had dream-walked into her life that first night. "How did you get these?"

Keys didn't have to see what she was looking at to know what she meant. "She was spotted in a park in Zurich, feeding some swans." He drew in a breath.

"Where is she?"

"We don't know her exact address. She was in the company of a couple named Sweizner. They are either her adoptive parents or her handlers. We aren't sure. We found them with facial recognition software through DMV; records list them as German Swiss, but their address was bogus. We don't even know if they're still in Switzerland. They went under a few months ago. Kyle and Sasha wrote all the information down in their journals. Read it and know most of the info before the briefing in Switzerland."

"Do you think they spotted your man?" Tanner asked.

Keys shrugged. "Possible but many people take pictures every day in that area. It's a tourist attraction. He blended in. He followed them to a German restaurant, waited outside, but they never came out. He went in two hours later and they had disappeared. The wait staff he talked to claims they had eaten and left through the front door, but he never saw them come out."

"You think they helped them disappear?"

"Or they never left the building. All he saw was a fine foods restaurant with two floors of dining area. We have a background check in the works on the owner of the restaurant. It has several layers of bogus shell companies attached to it, so it's taking some time. We've gotten as far as a property owner in France. Could be an apartment in the restaurant somewhere but without a legal warrant, we aren't finding out."

"To do that we'll need the cooperation from the locals and the FCP, one of Switzerland's levels of Federal police. After we're settled, I'll give a couple of my contacts a call and see if we can't get things moving."

"How are we going to find them?" Marna asked. "We don't even know where to start."

"We'll worry about that when we get there. For now, just study the file and get some of the information down. I also want to give you your cover IDs." He handed them packets with IDs, passports, and other official papers they would need for their aliases. "Look them over and memorize them. We've done deep backstopping, going back five years and surface backstopping for beyond that, so if someone does any research, it will ring true and hopefully keep your covers intact."

"Wait a minute, I'm the nanny?" Tanner asked, looking horrified.

"Yeah." Marna busied herself looking over the paperwork to hide the grin on her face.

Keys grinned at Tanner's exasperation. "Most of the nannies in the park will be women, and what better way to draw them into a conversation than a strapping young man. After last year's Bradshaw incident, Marna's face is better known in national circles and it will be easier to keep things under control if we keep the object of Lamontage's desire under wraps."

"Marna, as you can see, your identity is a bit more elegant. You are the wife of an elite businessman whose fingers are in many pies, some hovering in a gray area. You are on vacation while he is there making business contacts, so you are left alone often and looking for ways to amuse yourself."

"Okay, so who is this absentee husband?"

Keys pulled out another envelope. "That would be me." Tanner chuckled and Marna's face filled with dismay.

"That's just wrong, Keys," she said, shaking her head. "The children don't even look like you and I don't have daddy issues." She looked at him, trying not to laugh, but Tanner couldn't keep the laughter from bubbling over. Keys' face filled with mock shock but his lips twitched.

"I'm sure you don't, but we'll make it work. I, however, am the perfect age for the trophy wife syndrome and you, my dear, fit the bill nicely." He lifted her hand and kissed the back. Now Marna did laugh, tears streamed down her face. Tanner couldn't help but join in and Keys just stood there, eyes twinkling.

"Touché'." She said, drawing in deep gulps of air. "Okay, Darling, how is this set up going to allow me the freedom to investigate?" She challenged him with a lift of her chin.

"It gives you and Tanner the chance to test the waters. I'll be in the pool to pull you out, if you find you've gone too deep. Just think of me as another layer of protection. You also need someone who speaks the language and I happen to be fluent in it."

"Of course you are," she said, closing her file and looking at him.

Next, he pulled out two small boxes and handed one to each of them. "These are your ear buds. Make sure you wear them whenever we are in the field."

"What? No psychic hotline on this one?" Marna challenged.

"Minimal use of psychic channels is recommended when going up against an enemy like Lamontage. It's safer that way. There are times that we won't have the surveillance opportunity as we had with Bradshaw, and we may have to rely on mere mortal police work. If that is the case, you will have these communication devices. They are two-way communicators complete with GPS chips. Not only will we be able to communicate with you and listen in on conversations, we will be able to locate you if you fall off the grid for some reason, during the operation. It's a safety feature in case we cannot communicate with you through the, as you so elegantly put it, Marna, psychic hotline."

"Comforting," she said, looking at the device. It was very small and the color of natural skin, so it would easily blend in, once in place.

"Marna, as investigators, no matter the field, we have to be prepared for everything. However, to communicate with each other in a crowded room and avoid any possible Listeners, Trackers or even Readers in our midst, I want us to use the ear buds. This will avoid any issue we may have with our shields when it comes to combating these synthetic abilities.

All agents have them. It is an added safety feature to help protect your psyche from Lamontage. He is not your typical psychic adversary; he is much more powerful than Bradshaw ever thought of being. Therefore, until we bring him down, we will be mixing traditional techniques with Guardian techniques. Understood?" Both of them nodded. "Good. Is everyone packed? I'll check with the pilot, if you want to start loading your luggage into the van." Marna nodded, excused herself and headed up the stairs, while Tanner headed out the door with his two bags.

"Yeah, Marty," Keys said into this phone. "Are we on schedule?" Upstairs he could hear the excited talking of last minute arrangements and he could see out the window that Tanner was talking to Rose and Kurt, as they waited patiently for the rest of their party to head to the airfield for the long international flight.

*****

Marna leaned back against the reclined seat and closed her eyes for a moment. She could smell the food the staff had served for dinner: meatloaf, potatoes and corn. It mixed with the fresh coffee that someone had started brewing. They had been in the air now for five-and-a-half hours and coming upon a refueling stop at a compound in Ireland in about 45 minutes. Switzerland was six hours ahead, making it 8:00 PM there when they left, so it was 2:00 a.m. there now. The brief stop would take twenty minutes and then it would take another hour and forty minutes from Ireland to the compound in Zurich, where they would get some sleep, have a briefing, and then start their investigation.

Marna had spent the last several years of her life working with Jeff in the private investigation and security business. Their clients knew **Farlow and Farlow** for their high success rate, 98 % of their cases closed satisfactorily. She was in familiar territory in the investigative setting. However, fitting in the psychic angle was a little different and a bit frightening. Secretly, she was grateful Keys was using traditional methods as well as psychic methods her first time out. It would give her a chance to find a healthy balance.

Marna stood up, stretched, and stepped around Mary's little legs as the child slumbered in the seat beside hers. She bent to pull the covers up to the child's chin and move an unruly curl from her forehead. She could smell coffee coming from the kitchenette and despereately needed a cup. On her way there, she stopped and checked on all the children. Isaiah was the only one awake. She smiled at him, went to get her coffee, and returned, sliding into the seat across from him. "Couldn't sleep?"

He smiled sheepishly. "I kinda promised Tammy I'd write down a description of the trip."

Marna grinned. Tammy McGellan was a young girl that Isaiah went to school with and the family had lived next door to them briefly the year before. She was a good friend and Marna suspected his current crush. "The plane ride is kind of boring, don't you think?" She studied him. Every day that went by, she could see his father in his features and his manner. Peter Nymphis had been the love of Amanda's life and he had died trying to protect her. Isaiah had his dark hair, serious brown eyes, and though he was entering the awkward stage of adolescence, he had his father's determination to be his own man and not conform to the demand of others.

"Yeah, I guess." He shrugged, but Marna saw something pass through his eyes that concerned her.

"What's wrong, Isaiah?"

He sighed. "I've been having dreams again." Marna sat back, not showing her alarm. She swallowed a mouthful of coffee. Isaiah's premonitions came in spurts. He had foretold of Mary's coma and Jeff's death, though at the time they didn't know it but in hindsight, it was clear. His premonitions caused him massive anxiety because he couldn't understand the symbols within them. They were mere flashes of incoherent pictures skittering across his mind with no apparent solution. Marna understood, because for years she suffered in silence over the hallway of doors.

"Do you want to talk about them?" she encouraged, taking another sip of coffee and scanning the plane for Keys. She caught Tanner's eyes instead. He made a show of excusing himself from a conversation with Demi Spencer, and got up. She shook her head slightly as he passed by their table heading toward the back of the plane.

"It was very strange. I was in some building." He closed his eyes, and focused. "A museum I think."

"What kind of museum, Isaiah? Can you look around and see what kind of museum you're in?"

"An air museum I think. . ." Keys joined them at the table. "Jacob and Mary are there. We must have gone there together."

"Is it Jacob and Mary, Isaiah? Look closer . . ." Keys took the boy's hand, closed his eyes and focused.

*****

"Hey, you weren't here before," Isaiah said as Keys materialized beside him.

"You're right, I wasn't. I've come in to see if I can help make sense of what you are seeing. Now where are Jacob and Mary?"

"I think they're playing in the virtual cockpit over there." He pointed across the room.

"Well, let's go." The two of them walked across the room. Around them were fighter planes and jets from every era of wars. When they reached the virtual cockpit, Isaiah reached out and touched his sister's shoulder. She spun around. Isaiah stepped back. The child looked similar to Mary, very similar to Mary, but there was a subtle difference in the set of her eyes and the shape of her mouth. The boy poked his head out of the cockpit. Where Jacob's hair was curly and unruly, this boy's was straight and neat. He jumped out and stood in front of the girl.

"Wer sind Sie?"

Isaiah stepped back. "What?"

"Er fragte Sie, wer Sie waren Junge, jetzt ihm antworten?" she stated.

"Doctor Keys, what's going on?" Isaiah said looking at the two of them. "Why are they talking like that? What's it all mean?"

"They want to know who you are and what you want."

"But they know who I am. What's this all mean?" Isaiah's voice was tense from frustration.

"Take a breath, Isaiah." He put an arm around Isaiah's shoulder to offer comfort and to keep him from closing down the vision. "Just stay with me. I'll explain it all momentarily." He turned to the children. "Was sind eure Namen, und wo kommst du her?" He made his tone non- threatening to keep them from running away.

"Arella." look alike Mary said, pointing to herself.

"Heinderick." She said pointing to look alike Jacob.

"Weißt du nahe bei einander leben?" He continued.

They looked at each other and laughed. "Nein," Arella said laughing. Then she pointed at him again. "Er lebt in Deutschland, ich lebe in Schweiz."

"Sehen Sie sich oft?" he pressed.

Heinderick shook his head sadly. " Nein. Nur in unseren Träumen. Sie sehen uns nur in Ihren Träumen. Aber wir sind verbunden." With a wave of their hands, they took off around a corner, and when Keys and Isaiah followed they were gone. The vision faded and both of them returned to the present.

*****

"What did they say?" Isaiah asked

"The boy lives in Berlin and the girl in Zurich. They said that they only see each other in their dreams and that we only see them in our dreams."

"What's it all mean? And why do they look so much like Jacob and Mary?"

Keys looked at Marna and she drew in a breath, letting it out slowly. She sat her coffee down and took his hand. "Isaiah, they are one of the reasons we are going to Switzerland."

"What?" He pulled his hand away and sat back. "Who are they?"

Marna took her coffee cup in both her hands, studying it for answers. How could she explain this complicated mess to a thirteen-year-old? She drew in another breath, tipped the cup toward her, studied it some more, then let it back on its bottom and raised her eyes to his. "Isaiah, last year when your Aunt Rose went into Bradshaw's files, she discovered that Mary and Jacob were not twins. They were actually two babies in a set of quadruplets."

"Yeah, mom said the other two died. We often lit a candle for them when we celebrated Mary and Jacob's birthday."

"They didn't die, Son," Keys said. "They were actually taken from your mother at birth and given put in to a sort of foster care."

"Wha-?" Isaiah brought his head forward and ran his hand through his untidy curls. "Why?"

Marna drew in a breath and released it. "Because Bradshaw was an evil, vicious man, he knew no boundaries when it came to his desires, no matter who it hurt."

"He ---That was them in my vision?"

"Yes, they've appeared in my dreams, too. They are trying to contact us, or your mother is trying to give us a message concerning them. I haven't figured it out yet. Was she in yours?"

"Not that I remember," Isaiah said. "What does she want?"

"She wants me to bring them home, Isaiah. She wants me to find them and bring them home. Reunite them with you guys."

"What if they don't want to come? What if they're happy where they are?"

"I guess we deal with that when we get there."

"Why can't we just leave them where they are? It's been six years. They don't even know who we are." His voice was starting to rise.

"Isaiah, lower your voice. I haven't told the others yet." She looked around at the other children. They all slept on. Isaiah brooded and crossed his arms. Marna put her hand on his forearm but he pulled away. "Isaiah, please don't do that. Don't pull away from me." He turned his back, causing her to pull her lower lip between her teeth and chew it. "Isaiah?"

"I'm tired." He laid his head on the seat pillow and closed his eyes. She went to reach out to him, but Keys shook his head and gestured to the kitchenette with his chin.

Marna followed his direction, and crossed an arm over her midsection, resting the elbow of the other on the hand of the first. She brought her forehead down into the palm of the second hand. Rubbed vigorously, then dropped both arms and paced, stopping to look up at Keys. "That wasn't exactly the reaction I was expecting," she hissed.

"Give him time. He'll calm down."

"He's never turned away from me before."

"Marna, he's not turning away from you. He's turning away from a nightmare that doesn't seem to want to end. Even dead, Bradshaw continues to disrupt his life."

"I probably shouldn't have told him."

"He would have figured it out. He knows Jacob is a dream-walker. He would eventually confront the boy and confuse him. You did the right thing."

"What if the others react the same way?"

"We cross that bridge when we get to it. Right now let's just take it one day at a time, shall we?" She nodded.

The PA system cracked to life. "Dr Keys, we are starting our descent onto Guardian Compound 2014 in Meath, Ireland, for refueling. Please turn off electronics, all loose items secured, and fasten your seatbelts. "

Keys pulled the microphone attached to his headset down to his mouth. "Okay, Marty, what's the ETA?"

"Fifteen, sir."

"Good." He drew in a breath and turned his attention back to Marna. "Best to make sure the kids are all fastened in. We'll deal with Isaiah's open dissatisfaction after we land in Zurich, Okay?" She nodded and headed back to her seat, checking the kids as she passed them. Keys nodded to Tanner. He slid into the seat across from Isaiah, and belted in, starting a conversation with him. Marna was relieved to see Isaiah respond. Sighing, she slipped back into her seat and belted in just as they hit turbulence. She grabbed her seat armrest, closed her eyes and took a few deep breaths to get through it.

*****

The flight from Ireland to Zurich was uneventful, for which Marna was thankful. Isaiah seemed to have come out of his brooding mood, and he hadn't mentioned Arella or Heinderick. She was grateful for that. She wanted to have them all together in one room to tell them that herself.

She watched the runway pass by as the plane taxied to a stop on the Guardian airfield in Zurich. It was thirty miles from the outskirts of Zurich on property adjacent to the Zurich airport.

Guardian had bought it from a developer several years before during the Oil conflicts to offer their agents a safe haven.

Another developer was in the bidding for the property, but Guardian had not only won the auction, but the approval of the people for their Private Security and Protection Branch over another shopping center.

Many of the employees that worked within the walls were Swiss, a condition for a foreign buyer. Few foreign workers drew a paycheck from the compound, unless they were working on a current case that included the land within the boundaries of Switzerland or surrounding countries, excluding France and Italy. Guardian had to notify the local law enforcement, as well as the Federal police, about all activity involved in any investigation they conducted, and apprehension of any suspect, especially if it was a Swiss citizen. The burden of proof rested on the shoulders of the visiting law division or they left the country empty handed.

The living quarters were not as numerous as those in Maine were, but they were sufficient. They all had an air of efficiency, which was common within the country. Most had shower stalls and no bathtubs to conserve water. Apartments and homes had many windows that brought in the natural light to conserve electricity. It was common to see more people walk, bicycle or use public transportation to get where they were going, rather than use a car. The Swiss food was rich, but the physical activities the natives engaged in daily, e.g., mountain climbing, skiing, or simply walking several miles for the sheer enjoyment of the beauty around them, counteracted that.

The compound wasn't as expansive as the Maine compound, but it was no less impressive, more compact, as was much of the property in Europe. Instead of houses, such as the ones in Maine, there were half a dozen motels, hotels and rooming houses spread throughout the property, with a few apartment buildings to accommodate long-term residents or large families like the Farlows. They all had the charming exterior of the traditional Swiss Chalet. Marna knew their long-term stay was in an apartment building called Starlit Wonder, just added the year before when Guardian was able to add a few more acres to their property.

It mainly housed suites for larger families of the agents on short-term assignments or visits. It was one of the quirks of being an agent employed with the company; you never had to worry about a place to stay when you traveled abroad if you stayed on one of the worldwide, Guardian compounds. Starlit received its name because of the domed, tempered glass ceilings in the living spaces that could allow for stargazing on those nights when a family just wanted to hang out and look at the wonders of their universe instead of the whodunit on the local network.

The morning was still dark as she ushered the children into the lobby of the main building and checked through Security, accepting keys for one of the second floor apartment suites. After what seemed like hours, she was closing the last bedroom door on the last slumbering child.

Next on her to do list was to make coffee and study the file until she could sleep a few hours. She found a station on the radio that was actually broadcasting in English and turned it up a little. Then she sat down on the leather couch, opened the file on Arella to read the Intel Kyle Rigby had discovered and written in his notes.

It looked like Arella had been his target while Heinderick had been the responsibility of his partner. The first dated entry was a year previous.

*****

Subject: Arella Elizabeth Sweizner
Age: 5
Recorded abilities: Dream Walker; Blocker

April 20, 2047

Arella seems to be a well-adjusted five-year-old, though her caretakers seem to be constantly looking around in a defensive manner. They remind me of hunted animals. The only steady thing I can see, with this family, is they faithfully take Arella out walking around Zurich at least once a day. Always in the early morning, when leisurely foot traffic is low but business traffic is at a pace where it would be easy to blend if need be.

April 21, 2047
Arella's favorite thing on these walks seems to be feeding the swans. She comes armed with a bag of breadcrumbs or her caregivers buy her a small handful of feed.

April 22 . . .23 . . .30 . . . 2047
There is something off about Arella today. She is almost fearful of her caregivers. They aren't letting her walk too far away from them, and they seem harsh. I think I'm going to do a little research on them. The reports are wrong. They are of Middle Eastern descent, maybe they are actually Bradshaw's buyers and not her Caregivers. Maybe the child heard or saw something that is making her fearful of this couple or is there something else . . .?

May 1 . . . June 15, 2047
I made contact with Arella. I felt it was time. I started feeding the swans and ducks and they came. I made sure I was near where they usually were so I could hear what they said. They spoke Arabian but I did pick up a few words. They were talking about publicity getting to critical levels and that if the media didn't let up on the story, they would have to go into hiding until things died down. The man said that they could dress in traditional Muslim wear to protect their identity if need be. Arella seemed nervous, anxious, and even fearful.

June 16 . . .The visits are coming less frequently.

June 17 . . .June 18 . . .June 19 . . . I've made contact again. Arella has talked to me. She is a sweet child. Knows every swan and has named every single one. She knows which one belongs to which mother, and how long it was before they took their first dive. She's really a delightful child. I have to be careful, if I get too obvious they will spook. They think I am a music teacher for the local school and have actually talked to me about how much Arella likes music. They seem relaxed with me. I'm being careful not to infiltrate too quickly so as not to raise suspicion.
June 20...
Sometimes I hate this job. I wish I could just take her and run. She is such a wonderful child, and so bright, so sweet and giving. Why does it seem all the good ones are the ones to get hurt?

June 21. . . 22 . . . 23 . . . 24 . . . August 1 . . .
Marna skimmed over a few more pages, it was more of the same. She sighed. Surveillance. It was such a status quo, tedious job. True, you have to know your subject pretty well; the restaurants they frequented, the route they chose to travel most, their address, what they like to do for leisure time, and in Arella's case, that she was home schooled. The daily walks with her Parents/Handlers was a way of giving her the daily dose of fresh air a child required, or to prevent the child from going stir crazy. She yawned, rubbed her eyes, got up to refill her coffee cup and returned to look at the next entry.

August 15, 2047 . . .   Her breath caught in her throat. The cave day. The day she and Jeff's little world started to crumble around them. They could no longer hide from the world or

Bradshaw. A couple of Bradshaw's men, gone rogue, had kidnapped Hannah. Guardian was working on a plan to get her back unharmed. Then Tanner appeared on the scene, Hannah's injury, Mary's surprise healing power, her coma. She thought she would have to trade one child's life for the other. The next two weeks had been a horrendous nightmare for her. A media frenzy, whose aftershocks were felt as far as Switzerland, obviously. She stared at the entry written two weeks later.

August 29…
     The handlers are scared. I noticed they would hardly let Arella two feet from their presence. The parental male figure has been on his phone several times arguing with someone that the press is too much, that they needed to go under, especially with the child's picture being splashed all over the front page of the tabloids. He said people were looking at Arella curiously, even suspiciously. He's demanding transportation out of the country. It doesn't look like he's getting his way.
August 30. . .No sign . . . August 31. . . No sign of . . . Sept 1. . . No sign of Arella . . .
Sept 5…
     It's been several days since I've seen Arella and her handlers, and I do believe that is what they are. After observing them for this long, I am almost sure of it. The trail is cold. Farlow's arrest is all over the tabloids and news channels. I'm worried. . .
*****

     Marna closed her eyes and swallowed back the fear, drawing in a deep breath and laying her head back on the cool leather cushions. Another day she'd never forget. The day Tanner came to her in Mary's hospital room and arrested her for several murders, her sister's and brother-in-law's included. She relived the nightmare in her head and everything that followed the arrest. She remembered the humiliation of the media branding her a witch, and the attacks in jail. The whole process that Bradshaw had put her through while he was setting up his plot to get control of the children, and the final leg of the plan that set her world on a downhill spiral that led to the ultimate end of her life as she knew it.
     She couldn't breathe. She tossed the journal on the coffee table and pushed herself off the couch to walk to the opposite wall and look out the window that claimed most of the space. There were bars on the outside of the window. Just like in her cell. The Stager's black mist, in her cell, cutting off her ability to breathe. She drew in some more deep breaths and drank in the view of the mountains. The bars should actually make her feel more secure, but instead she felt trapped. Trapped in the nightmarish memory she could not forget. She focused on the mountains in the distance instead. The rising sun gave them a high definition quality, colored in the customary blue with the romantic cap of white. She drew in a breath and blew it out. She repeated this several times. Her heart slowed. The pounding headache eased. Her breathing became easier. She raised her shields in case the feelings she had were more than just anxiety and lack of sleep. She closed her eyes. Remembered the last few months she had with the children. The bond they were developing. She became more relaxed.
<div align="center">~~~~~</div>

     "Too much coffee always makes you edgy, Marny, you know that."
     Marna smiled. "You do have a way of appearing at the most private of moments, Amanda." *She turned around to look. Amanda's apparition leaned against the partial petition separating the kitchenette and the living room.*
     "It's this ghost thing. It's like having GPS chips in every family member and monitoring them all from one huge room filled with screens. I come to you all, but sadly, the only ones who see me are you and Hannah. You oughta try---" She chuckled at Marna's raised brow. "Shutting up now."
     Marna laughed. "Good idea." She slowly walked over and slid onto the stool by the ghostly body of her twin sister. "So, what brings you to my presence tonight, Manda? Did I think too loudly? Did my moment of remembrance send aftershocks into the afterlife?"

Amanda's eyes swept over Marna's features. "Hmm." She said. "You need to stop dwelling in the past, Marny." She sighed. "Or how are you ever going to look to the future?"

"Maybe I don't want to," Marna said, gazing into the nothingness before her. "Maybe I like my life the way it is."

"For a while maybe, Marna, but not forever. What happened didn't happen so that you would go this life alone. You were never meant to do it alone."

"I'm not alone, Manda. Somebody very dear to me gave me eight beautiful gifts to fill my life with." She smiled as she turned her head toward her sister. "And if this investigation goes as planned, there will be two more that will need me to help them adjust."

"True, they are the most wonderful of all gifts, but this investigation ..." Amanda got up and floated across the room. "Is your first with Guardian, as an agent. You need to be able to focus on it. If you don't let go of the pain of the past, you will never be able to deal with what the future may hold."

"I won't be too distracted I can't get the job done, Manda. I know the dangers of a distraction. I've done enough investigating to know that.

Amanda studied her again. "Hmmm. How does it feel to be in the saddle again?"

"I have to admit, I don't dislike it. I kind of missed it." She drew in a breath. "That was one thing Jeff and I did well together." She smiled. "Would I be too presumptuous to say we were the best?" She looked into her coffee and swirled the brown liquid in her cup. "I just don't know if I can do it myself. There is so much that I depended on him for."

"You can do it without him. I believe in you and so would he. You just have to believe in yourself."

Marna pushed herself away from the counter, and walked back to the window. "The problem is, Manda, I don't know if I can. When Jeff died, a part of me died with him."

"So bring it back to life, Marna. Don't let it roll into the abyss."

"I'm trying, Manda, but I think I'm losing that battle," she whispered.

"Then fight harder."

"I don't think I can."

"Of course you can, you're a Greenwood girl."

"Doesn't make me invincible, Amanda. That was you." Marna drew in a breath and exhaled loudly. "You always were able to pick up the pieces faster than me."

"Really?" She sighed. "I've tried to tell the powers that be that they had the wrong twin, but they wouldn't believe me." Marna laughed. Amanda smiled. "There she is. I knew she wasn't gone forever." Marna shook her head. "What was it that put you in such a desperate mood anyway?" She moved to the coffee table and looked down. "Surveillance? Yeah that would make me cry, too."

Marna cleared her throat, went to the table and pulled out pictures of Arella, and laid them on the table. "One of the Guardian agents had her under surveillance last year while everything was going on in the states. That's his journal. Seems that the media frenzy in the states, because of her resemblance to Mary, spooked her handlers and they went underground. They haven't had another sighting of her since September."

"Heinderick?" Amanda asked.

"I-I don't know, Manda, Tanner's in charge of his file. We're meeting for a briefing later. Kyle's partner was responsible for him."

"You'll find them, Marna, I know you will. You have to." Amanda started to fade away.

"Amanda, please don't go."

"I have to, Marna, You get some rest now. I'll be back." The apparition faded.

~~~~~

Marna breathed in deep and sprung forward on the couch. She had dozed off again. She should realize these things because she only converses with Amanda in her dreams. The journal lay before her on her lap. It was still quiet in the apartment. She was tired. Bone tired, and she knew that if she didn't get some rest she would absorb nothing at the briefing. Pushing herself up off the sofa, she went to the panel on the wall, engaged the privacy screens on the windows, turned out the lights, lay down, pulled an afghan over her and slipped into a dreamless sleep.

Amanda faded back in with another apparition. "Why didn't you let me talk to her?" Jeff demanded.

"When the time is right, Darling. She's not ready yet." Amanda put a ghostly hand on his bicep as he moved forward.

"She's got to be ready to deal with what's to come, to be ready to handle it and to make that connection for her own safety and the safety of the two children."

"You can't rush these things. I'll bring you to her when it will give her closure, not pain. Come on, she needs to rest. The weeks ahead aren't going to be easy." The apparitions faded as Marna turned in her sleep.

*****

The smell of fresh coffee drifted through the fog of Marna's sleeping brain. She opened her eyes. Elizabeth stood before her with a fresh cup in her hand. Her wavy dark hair pulled back in a single braid reaching the center of her back, and her crystal blue eyes sparkled with warmth and excitement. She heard more commotion as she came fully awake. "Guten Morgen, Tante Marna."

"Huh?" She said.

"That's good morning, Aunt Marna, in German. Hanna and I have been studying while Isaiah and the boys made breakfast."

"Breakfast?" Marna swung her legs quickly and looked toward the kitchen. Isaiah and Hannah were loading dishes into the dishwasher, while David, Moses and Joseph poured drinks into the glasses that Mary and Jacob had sat on the table with the other dishes. "Wow." She accepted the coffee.

" Danke schön." She smiled at the girl's frown and whispered, "That's thank you very much."

"Ohhh." Elizabeth said, just before she headed back to the kitchen to help finish the arrangements.

As soon as she took her first drink of coffee, she remembered the photos and journal she had left out, and her eyes quickly looked toward the coffee table. The closed file was under the securely closed notebook.

"I took the liberty of reorganizing your file for the briefing." Tanner said from somewhere to her left. Her head turned in that direction. He was in a crewneck sweater, over a grey-collared shirt, and light blue Khakis. Her hand quickly went up to her hair to smooth it out some. "Sorry, I didn't see you there."

"The kids invited me over in exchange for a recipe for pancakes."

"A recipe for . . ." She grinned, not finishing her thought, and raised her coffee cup to her lips. "Not sure how I feel about the idea of my partner being in my house when I wake up in the morning. It's – ah awkward."

"I promise it won't be a habit." He raised his free hand, palm out and drank some of his own coffee.

"Okay. As long as we're clear on that. Girl's got to have her space before she starts making public appearances." Her blue eyes danced. He studied her for a moment and opened his mouth to say something, but Jacob's voice rang out from the kitchen.

"And don't forget the park later, Tanner." Jacob said from his concentration of folding napkins. "You promised."

"Already in the day planner, Son," He grinned at the boy, making his brown eyes dance a little.

"Park? But the case?"

"I'm the Nanny, remember? I figured it would give them a chance to release some that pent up energy from the long flight, and maybe make a few Nanny Connections."

"Ah, good idea." She said. She noticed his eyes also showed some fatigue. "You looked over the file?"

He reached out and put his coffee on the table, pulling his file back with him. "Yeah, you weren't the only one burning the midnight oil. Seems Agent Rhinestone took a few trips to Germany to search birth certificates, adoption certificates and foster homes. Flashed Heinderick's pictures around a few parks, and finally hit pay dirt sometime in June. She found him in a middle class neighborhood outside a military base. A couple by the name of Vonbracht legally adopted him back in 2042 from an adoption agent representing an orphanage from the states."

"Legal adoption?"

"Yes. By all appearances it was on the up and up." He sighed.

"All appearances?"

He pulled out a document. "The birth certificate was forged." He handed it to her. She looked it over. "The child is listed as born to a single mother, age sixteen, father unknown. Our agent looked the mother up and found her in a New York law office." Marna looked at him for clarification. "She's actually forty-five and an attorney. Her identity was stolen six years ago, by an organization she went to for information on Invitro Fertilization . . ." He waited for her response.

"Heaven's Gate."

"Give the lady a prize. Yes, Heaven's Gate."

"There's the connection."

He nodded. "She said that they turned her down, saying something about not wanting to have children in single parent homes. She went to talk to a lawyer, but he said that because it was a private establishment . . ."

"They had the right to turn down who they wanted."

"Yes." He sat back. "Truth be told, she had no history of psychic abilities in her blood line."

Marna nodded knowingly. "Probably the real reason she was turned down." She sighed. "She doesn't realize how lucky she was. Marna looked over the forged birth certificate.

"Well, she does now." Tanner said sitting back in his chair. "She moved on, went to another clinic, was able to successfully be impregnated, gave birth to a healthy baby boy, and never gave the clinic another thought, until . . ."

"Last year, when the official story hit the airways making the connection between Bradshaw and terrorism, she saw exactly how lucky she was."

"Yes," he smiled. "You're finishing my thoughts, Farlow, get out of my head."

"Turnabout's fairplay, Williams," she raised her brow, "God knows you've been in mine enough."

"Touche', Farlow," he held her gaze a moment before he raised his hands in mock surrender, "I concede."

"As you should," she returned her attention to the file, to hide her own smile, "did Sasha find him?"

He cleared his throat, and mowed through the disconcerting turmoil in his brain. He gave it up to the fogginess due to lack of sleep."Yes, she went to the address, pretended to be an adoption official on a follow-up visit."

"What happened?

"They let her in, spoke to her, and she asked all right questions, but when she asked to speak to the child, they became defensive and closed mouth—said he was at his grandparents for a few weeks and that they would call her when he returned. They became rude and practically pushed her out the door."

"Surveillance?"

"She watched the place for a few weeks, caught sight of him once or twice, with a few other boys his age, but he was never outside the house without the presence of the father or mother. Then one day she went to continue surveillance and the house was empty, abandoned. With the change of the wind, a For Sale sign was on the front lawn, and there was no trace of the owners. She gained entrance and saw that they had left in a hurry. Only thing left behind was some trash and a few toys. When she did a thorough search, they found this. He handed her the Tabloid page. It was a picture of Tanner leading her out of the hospital in handcuffs, and an inset of a comatose Mary in the hospital bed.

"The arrest."

"Yeah. Looks like my carelessness hurt more than you and your family," he sighed.

She looked at him. "Tanner, you were under Bradshaw's influence. Don't forget that same vigilance is what got those charges dropped. Once Keys was able to let you know what was really happening to you; you did a good investigation, getting solid evidence that proved my innocence and I was released."

"The charges never should have been filed in the first place," his eyes strayed to her neck and she knew what he was remembering.

She raised her hand to her throat. "Let's put it away, Tanner, it's what we do in the next few weeks that will matter now. We need to focus our energies on that."

"Don't be sad." Mary came over to the couch. Marna quickly folded the Tabloid page and handed it back to Tanner, quickly guiding her shields to protect Mary's empathy from her emotions.

"We're not, Sweetheart, sometimes adults talk about things that make them feel a little down, but we're better now." She looked at Tanner for affirmation and he nodded.

She smiled, "Good, because breakfast is ready."

"Great. We'll be right out."

"Okay." She ran back into the kitchen.

"You good?" She asked, looking back toward him.

"Yeah. You?"

"Yeah. Let's go see what they've done to kill the pancakes." She grinned. He chuckled and waved her forward. He took one more look at the file on the coffee table, felt the twinge of regret for a few more seconds before he put it away and went to enjoy the breakfast the kids had worked so hard to produce.

After the last pancake was gone, Marna and Tanner finished the dishes and washed up the kitchen. Rose came over, kissed Marna on the cheek and told her Keys had sent her over to be with the children while she and Tanner went to the briefing.

Marna left instructions for the children to clean up the apartment, unpack their things, make up their beds and take showers so that when she and Tanner came back, the children could go to the park with Tanner as promised earlier. With a few groans and minimal protests, they all agreed. Desiree and Ray had agreed to help the kids pick up, so they could watch some television and try to figure out what the TV people were saying. For each correct word, they would give themselves three points. Marna left the apartment laughing at their imagination, and in a much lighter mood than she was before. She looked at her watch as she and Tanner started walking to the main hall of the compound.

When they arrived, they fell into step with the others that were arriving. Six total agents, Peter and Heidi among them. "Hey, congratulations you two, I hear you made it to the first wrung of the WIT ladder," Peter said.

"Yes we did," Tanner shook hands with him.

"Well, we're going to be working the Lamontage angle. I guess you're going to be teamed up with Kyle and Sasha."

"Yeah, we read through their files. What can you tell me about them?"Tanner pressed.

"Kyle's a bit of a cowboy at times but he's good. He gets what he goes for, though he needs bailing out of sticky situations sometimes. I suppose that's why they teamed him up with Sasha. She runs a little closer to the line." He waved to a couple of agents as they went into the building. "He's the one that broke into Bradshaw's office last year and found the files that told us about the clones and Arella and Heinderick. His assignment wasn't to find that information, but he went for it anyway. Almost died getting it. Tate had to go in after him. That's when Keys sent him over here to do the surveillance. I suppose it was to keep him out of trouble as much as it was for his blood hound tendencies."

"What are his abilities?"

"Kyther and Blocker."

"And hers?" Marna asked.

"Tracker and Locater."

"I'll introduce you inside," He looked up and saw Keys appear at the door and wave them in. "And the games begin. Shall we?"He waved them ahead of him. Marna and Tanner walked toward the building, with Peter and Heidi following them in.

When they entered the building, they followed Heidi and Peter down the tiled hall to a door that said Conference Room 5. A sign hung on the door Reserved for Investigation L456 briefing 10:00. Behind them several FCP entered after them, Switzerland's equivalent to FBI and Homeland Security in the USA. Marna watched them walk to the front of the room, and join Keys at a large board where there were several pictures, a timeline, and some comments.

Ventura put his hand on her elbow and steered her clear of the foot traffic, to the table laden with coffee, cocoa, cheese, various kinds of bread, small, thin slices of meat, yogurt, granola and a thermal milk dispenser. He stopped before the coffee Carafes and poured her a black coffee in an espresso cup then nodded toward the spread on the table. "You might want to grab a little something to eat. This is going to be a long morning."

"No thanks. The kids made breakfast before we left. The coffee is well needed though," she saluted him with her cup, before she took a swallow, and then looked the room over. "What is all of this?"

"This is a briefing for an international task force, Guardian slash Keys' style."

"International . . .?" She drew in a breath. "Does the investigation really require all of this?"

"Switzerland, Germany, France, Italy, United Kingdom, United States, even Ireland have all been effected by the Liberatores in one way or another. They all want a piece of Lamontage when we bring him down. Over the last thirty years, he and his organization are suspected in at least 1,000 attacks worldwide and a hands breadth away from conviction in at least 50 world leaders' assassinations, but nobody could ever pin anything on him because of his method."

"The psychic angle."

"Yeah, hard to get a conviction, when the murder weapon is mind over matter and not tied to ballistic lab rats."

"But what does this have to do with the attack on Tarot and the kidnapping of Amanda's Children?"

He studied the board, looked at the photos of the children, their caretakers, and the lines that were drawn to the center circle housing the name of the organization. "I think we're about to find out. He guided her toward the table where Tanner, Heidi and two other agents sat amongst four empty chairs. He nodded at the two newcomers as he sat down, and proceeded with introductions. "Marna Farlow, Tanner Williams, this is Kyle Rigby and his partner Sasha Rinestone. They'll be assisting you with the search for Arella and Heinderick. They've been on the case for the last year, so feel free to pick their brains."

Rigby reached over and shook both their hands. "Marna Farlow: you're a bit of a celebrity in the ranks of Guardian. It's a pleasure to meet you."

She smiled. "I hear it was you who got the files we needed to bring Bradshaw down, along with a few other records that helped us find out just how far his tentacles reached. Then you started searching for my sister's children. Thank you."

His face flushed red," just doing my job." .

"Don't forget the unnecessary risks," Ventura said under his breath. Heidi to smile and Sasha cleared her throat.

"Depends on who you ask," Kyle said defiantly. The comment went unanswered as two agents came by and handed them all folders with the same case number that was on the door sign. Keys stepped away from the other officials and up to the podium.

"Good morning." Beside him, a young woman in a navy blue, skirt suit translated what he said into German. "I'm having our security personnel give you all a folder of information about the case we are about to discuss and in turn I will have agents come up and explain their parts in the investigation thus far."

"For now take a few minutes, have some coffee and breakfast, and get familiar with the file before you. Briefing will start at 10:00 sharp." He turned to the table behind him, grabbed a red case, turned back and made eye contact with Marna, motioning her toward the coffee table. She excused herself. Kyle watched her go. "She's his next star."

"Jealous, Rigby?" Ventura challenged.

"Not t'all. If I have to lose the crown, I'd rather it be to her than the likes of you. She's at least better looking." He raised his brow and looked sideways at Peter. They all chuckled and their eyes followed Marna as she went to meet Keys.

Keys poured himself a coffee and offered her a refill. "You look tired, Marna. Did you sleep at all?"

"Not much." She took the coffee, fixed it and let her eyes take in the room. "Amanda visited me."

He took a sip of coffee and sighed. "I see. What was it she wanted?"

"She gave me a pep talk about not living in the past because it blocked what was waiting for me in the future."

"Maybe you should listen to her."

She looked at him and raised a brow. "You two holding out on me?"

He sipped at his coffee. "Just concerned about you, Marna." He looked at his watch and handed her the case he had in his hand. "You'll need this. It's a Guardian PC Tablet, standard equipment for all of our agents."

"I have a Tablet already."

"While that may be okay for your personal use, Guardian records and software are a little sensitive to be keeping in files next to your class notes. This also has a compatible screen dock for your phone, so you can exchange information with the two.." He tapped a screen app with his finger and a two dimensional version of her GPC 2000 came up, "Just set it on there, and hit the synchronize icon here," he pointed to a small rectangular task bar, "and the process start immediately, finishing in seconds. They are meant to work as a team."

"The wonders of modern technology.." She smiled, took the machine and headed back toward the table as he went back toward the front of the room, glancing at his watch.

"Again, good morning, Agents, and welcome. I trust those of you that traveled yesterday have no ill effects." People chuckled as they looked around the room. He waited a beat for the translator to finish her sentence then he smiled. "Today we come together in a joint effort with Guardian WIT, FCP,

Interpol, and several other members of intelligence and Federal forces from Germany, Ireland, and Italy."

"We're all here to work together toward one goal; to bring down the Liberatores Organization and its founder Pierre Lamontage. He and his and his organization are responsible for the deaths of several diplomatic leaders and many terrorist attacks throughout the European territories and the United States over the last several decades. He is also the main suspect in the more recent deaths of the Arabian Prince in Washington, DC and the massacre at Tarot Lockdown a week and a half ago, that claimed the lives of six Guardian agents and several Tarot residents. Raquel Bradshaw, another resident, was murdered after the escape from the prison,"

He used a laser pointer to point out the picture of Prince Basheed, and each of the agents and residents in turn on the board. He went into the details of the attacks. Marna flipped through the pages of the file as he spoke. She saw the crime scene photos of the Tarot attack. Her heart went to her feet as she saw the children. She gasped and brought a hand to her mouth. The other agents looked toward her. Her hand trembled as she shifted through pictures. "Hey, are you okay?" She felt Tanner's hand on her bicep.

She looked up from a photo. "They were just children, Tanner." Her eyes welled with tears. The others looked back toward Keys, deciding to leave the comforting to Tanner. "I thought Bradshaw was a cold Bastard, but there are just no words to describe him." She looked down at the picture opposite the crime scene photos. Lamontage stared back at her with soulless eyes.

Tanner instinctively put his hand over hers. It was cold. "We're going to get him and put a stop to him, Marna. We are. That's one of the reasons we're here."

"Of course." She swallowed and glanced down at his hand. It wasn't unpleasant to feel that type of comforting touch again, but she pulled hers free as Jeff's face flashed before her and she busied herself with moving the Tarot crime scene photos over, face down, on the opposite side of the folder. In the next photo, Arella's face looked up at her. Keys called Sasha and Kyle up to take over their part of the briefing. The agents excused themselves and headed up to the front of the room.

"Gutan Morgan." Kyle said into the mike and was welcomed with several echoes of the same greeting. "My name is Kyle Rigby and this is my partner Sasha Rinestone. We are Guardian WIT and our assignment for the last year has been to locate and gather Intel on these two children. He used a laser pointer to point out Arella and Heinderick. They were actually two of a set of quadruplets born to this couple." Sasha put up pictures of Amanda and Peter and sent a sympathetic look in Marna's direction. Marna lowered her eyes, feeling the loss of her sister deeply in that moment.

Tanner looked her way, "Are you okay?" She nodded.

The briefing continued. "Amanda and Peter Nymphis. They were one of the many victims of Heaven's Gate's Invitro Clinic. The children are believed to be the victims of a kidnapping orchestrated by this man." He waited, while Sasha put up Richard Bradshaw's picture on the board next to Lamontage's.

Marna's breath caught in her throat. Tanner reached over and squeezed her hand. He knew the memories assaulting her right now. He wanted to offer her his support and encouragement. Ventura caught sight of the automatic gesture and made a mental note of it, exchanging looks with Schafer.

"As you all know, he was killed during the siege of his compound last year, orchestrated as a joint, effort between Guardian and several other U.S. government agencies. However, we have discovered that placement of these children was done in 2042 in the homes of the handlers for psychic combat training." He raked the laser pointer over the Vonbacht couple and the Sweinzer couple. "We have further discovered that these particular handlers were under Bradshaw's directive and not found through any agency. That was the cover story to make the placements appear to be legal adoptions."

"We set up surveillance of each child. Copies of the journals are in your files, so you should be aware that when the General Media went after Marna Farlow last year, in the States, and she and the

Nymphis children were all over the front pages of the tabloids and internet newspapers, our handlers went underground. We lost track of both of them." He drew in a deep breath.

"However, during the process of trying to recapture their trail, we discovered some rather disturbing Intel." He dragged his pointer down the line to the center circle. "Both couples have known ties – be it well buried underneath some deep cover stories – to the organization Liberatores, an organization run by this man." Sasha did an imaginary circle around Lamontage,"Pierre Lamontage. Information on him is also in your packet and Dr. Keys did a good description earlier, so we won't go in to his details. He is dangerous and he is deadly, remember that. Do not attempt to bring him down by yourself or by one agency. We are all going to have to work together and combine our resources to chop the head off of this viper." A few nods and murmurs of approval went around the room.

Sasha took over the briefing as Kyle stepped back and took a bottle of water from a waiting assistant. "These couples are actually high ranking officials in the cloth that makes Liberatores and they set up Bradshaw to claim these two children. She pulled her laser pointer out and briefly raked the beam over the children's displayed photo. They identified themselves to him as Middle Eastern Generals in the organization known as National Iranians for Allah. A terrorist organization that believes the Iranian philosophy that fast pacing the end of the world will gain favor with Allah."

Marna's hand went to her mouth. Her eyes filled with the horrifying knowledge that she had been a pawn right along with Bradshaw and Amanda in Lamontage's end game. "Questions?"

A hand went up in the front row. It was a woman that Marna recognized from the plane. "Yes Demi?"

"Do we know if these children are even in the country still?"

"We have heard nothing to the contrary from our Intel." She turned to her partner for confirmation. He shook his head,"or any chatter that they have made it over the border."

"What are the security measures we're taking to keep him in the country?" Another agent asked.

"We are working with Swiss officials to heighten security on all bus stations, train stations and airports. The Swiss have also increased their security along their borders and have saturated the entire country with Lamontage's picture, the picture of these two couples and the children so that any attempt by Lamontage to get them out of the country will be next to impossible without being recognized." Sasha drew in a breath. "Any other questions?"

"What is the battle plan once we get this sucker in sight?"

Sasha smiled and said. "I'll hand the reins back to Doctor Keys to explain that strategy." Keys came over to her, shook her hand, and patted her back. He shook Kyle's hand and waited while they left the small platform, giving him a chance to gather his thoughts.

"Martin, to get to your question, the strategy to capture Lamontage is to proceed with much caution. Make sure your Shields are the best they can be. He is a very dangerous man with synthetic abilities, and his method of killing is as unconventional as you can get. As you saw in the Tarot photos, he does not harm with physical wounds. His attacks are all psychic. We have brought in several Blockers and Custodians for this assignment to offer extra layers of protection for our agents."

"Where does that leave our mere mortal brothers?" someone asked with a heavy English lilt. Snickers went around the room. The government officials looked uncomfortable and a little miffed. Keys knew he meant the regular law enforcement brothers.

"We will be forming teams of six to eight. They will be a mixture of Guardian agents and, as you so eloquently put it, our mere mortal brothers. I expect Guardian agents to cooperate fully with the locals both at the County and Federal level. Their number far outweighs us greatly. One thing Guardian will not do is step onto territory we are not welcome. They are our hosts and we will give them respect and honor their positions. We will also protect them from the damage that psychics like Lamontage and his soldiers and the weapons they have at their disposal can cause. If you feel you are too great to work in conjunction with our local officials, then Guardian is no place for you. Do I make myself clear?" Murmurs of agreement went around the room. "Very well then, I am going to hand over the next phase of this briefing to my friend Norman Schizner from Fedpol. He is going to tell you what measures they have put in place."

A man of about fifty, and in great athletic shape, stepped up and exchanged air kisses with Keys. Keys stepped back and let him take over the mike. Another young woman, this time English speaking, stepped up to interpret what he was saying about security being heightened and the history of terror the Liberatores had unleashed in Europe over the last thirty years. The lights went dim, and all around the room panels of the wall slid into themselves, revealing large LCD screens. Constable Schizner readied a laptop and a program for a power point presentation.

"The Liberatores' main objective, from the day they appeared in the ranks of organized crime, was to strike fear into the hearts of Europeans and other enemies. This they have done quite well. This organization was founded in 2014 by Pierre Lamontage." A younger version of Pierre appeared on the screen. "To build his organization, he specifically recruited soldiers with and without psychic abilities, and those not afraid to use them for less than wholesome goals. Another requirement to get into his organization, you had to be willing to die for the cause. His cause. A one world order, a world by which he reigned as King." A screen appeared with the world webbed together and connected to Pierre.

He is the suspect in several bombings over the last thirty years. These include several embassies, an international train carrying government dignitaries after a top secret summit in Kuwait in 2021, and an attack on a U.S. base in Iraq in 2030 that killed 150 coalition troops sent on a mission to Iran to reclaim an American Drone stolen by Iranian Terrorists." He drew in a breath to give himself a chance for a drink of water, allowing the agents to study the images and absorb the information.

"Pierre's main goal is power, and he doesn't care how he acquires it. If you get in his way, you die for your trouble." He showed several pictures, including one of Keys' wife Elizabeth. "Elizabeth Keys was one of Guardian's top agents. She met and married Frederick in 2013. In Spring of 2015, they were on a task force to infiltrate and bring down the Liberatores. If they could, they were to bring in Pierre. We had no idea at that point how powerful this man was."

Marna had heard the story from Keys so as the speaker retold it, in painful detail, she studied the woman's face. She had been beautiful. Her hair, midnight black, fell below her shoulders in rich, dark waves, held in place with a Robin's egg blue headband. High cheekbones, prominent underneath a cross between a deep copper and deep brass skin tone, hinted at a Native American bloodline. Her eyes were a penetrating whiskey color with flakes of gold near the pupils, and her mouth, chiseled between a slender nose and an oval edged chin, upturned in an easy and warm smile with lips the color of a mid-summer sunset. Marna tried to imagine what she would look like today if Lamontage had not claimed her as one of his many victims.

Her eyes slid to Keys, who was busily playing with some imaginary thread on his pants. Kyle, too, was watching him closely. Maybe he was worried the man would break down. It was still too painful even for him to look at her picture. She felt a kinship with him. She understood his pain after her loss of Jeff. *She was beautiful, Keys.* She wasn't sure if her message would get through to him or if he had his psychic veil down, but he looked up at her and nodded once. Kyle glanced her way and she passed him a quick smile. He quickly turned his attention away from her and back to the speaker, but not before, she saw something pass through his eyes. She just wasn't sure what. Brushing it aside, she turned her attention back to the speaker as well.

"Five Guardian agents died in that task force, during that pursuit through Europe in 2014-2015 and Guardian was forced to pull back. Pierre was presumed dead after his attack on Keys and his wife, though his body was never found. We followed the chatter through the next several years, even dispatched forces to try to pick up his trail, but he did not surface again. The Liberatores, however, were in full tilt, especially during the great oil conflicts of 2020 - 2035, when the oil-rich countries in the Middle East pulled together and enforced sanctions on the U.S. and some of her allies. Europe stood side by side with the USA, Ireland, Switzerland, Italy, France, Israel and Afghanistan and came to our aid with airstrikes against Saudi Arabia, Iran, Russia and China.

Liberatores was a silent partner to the terrorist countries during that conflict, and frequently did their bidding. Many other bombings plagued our united countries. We attributed them to his organization. At the same time there was a revolution of sorts, later dubbed the American Freedom Conflicts, going on in America between government forces, under the direction of their president, Fatih Arjmand Winters, a ruthless dictator, and a well-known militia group called Friends of Freedom or FOF. The president had ties to Iranian terrorists and the Liberatores. Whether he crossed paths with Lamontage or not, there is no documentation verifying that so we don't know for sure, but authorities did verify his ties to Iran and the Liberatores at the end of the Conflicts in 2035." Marna vaguely remembered that troubled time as she grew up during it, but she learned the political instances in college in 2038 when and the first American history books, containing the whole horrific story came out in time for her American History class as told by those exiled and survivors of horrendous imprisonments under the NDAA umbrella, by the government, and suspected government assassinations. It had been a dark time for her country, and, she prayed, a lesson learned by those so willing to let a master manipulator in the highest-ranking office. A descendant of the FOF organization now held office, and they were a constant reminder of what the country had gone through and how it had been rebuilt from the ashes of a destructive war.

"There are many murders and unexplained deaths during the period of 2020-2035 that shared the traits of Pierre Lamontage's style, but . . ." he reached into his file and pulled out a photo, hanging it among the victims. It was a picture of Cassie Martin. "Last year, during the Bradshaw investigation in America , Guardian agent Cassie Carter was murdered at a luxury hotel. The hotel was located on the outskirts of Harrisville NH. The murder had Lamontage's signature. Lamontage also attacked Marna Farlow with his seducing abilities, bringing her to the brink of collapse before he released his control over her. He has been making attempts on her for several months. Pierre Lamontage is back in the game and so are we." He nodded his head and left the podium. Keys came to it, glancing once at his wife's picture, sniffing, clearing his throat and continuing. Kyle looked down at his pants and brushed something off his lap. Marna frowned, curious about his behavior. Was he that indifferent to Keys? That rebellious to authority?

"Before you came to this briefing, it was set up so that you were placed at certain tables. If you look around those tables now, there are certain faces there. Those faces are your team." He cleared his throat again and two FSS agents came over to Marna's table, claiming the empty seats. The one remaining, Marna knew, belonged to Keys. "Get to know your team, exchange information and study the files. They are your backup. Dismissed."

With an explosion of applause, Keys left the podium and made his way to the table. "Marna, Tanner, Kyle, Sasha, Peter and Heidi, I'd like you to say hello to Agents Klein and Stocker with the Swiss FSS, and the two others heading this way are Agents Weiner and Ricker of Interpol. They will be joining our team. After exchanging pleasantries and basic information, they agreed to meet later that day at Keys' office for their strategy then said their goodbyes.

Marna was thoughtful on the walk home. "Are you okay?" Tanner queried. "I know that briefing must have opened up some old wounds."

"Yeah it did, for more than just me. I'm sure Keys had his own demons he was fighting."

"Yeah." They turned toward the Starlit. "Do you want to go to the park with me and the kids?"

"No, I think I'll pass. I'm kind of looking forward to a nap."

"Okay, but, Marna?" She looked at him as he opened the door for her. "You need to keep your shields up tight. Don't leave him a way to get in."

"I won't." She smiled at his concerned frown. "I'll ask Rose to stay with me. Maybe Kurt would like to take Ray and Desiree to the park with you and the kids."

He nodded with his lips firmly together. "Okay, I can live with that." He followed her into the lobby, and then they separated. His apartment was down the hall a couple of doors from hers. She could hear the buzzing of excited voices and glanced at her watch. It was almost lunchtime. She unlocked the door and stepped in. The kitchen was abuzz with activity. The girls were preparing lunch and when the kids saw her walk in, they all yelled a greeting. Rose got up from the floor where she and the triplets were playing a game of Monopoly, and walked over to give Marna a hug. "Hey, how'd it go?"

"Informative." She sighed as she put her jacket and purse on the chair and dropped her folder onto the coffee table. "Seems Pierre Lamontage has been around for a lot longer than I thought, and he's been a very active, naughty boy during several upstarts against us and Europe."

"Well he is a Psychic Terrorist."

"Did you find that in a book somewhere? Because that is a description I don't believe I've heard before." She smiled as she watched the kids do an assembly line for cold cut sandwiches.

"It's a new world out there, Marna. During the Conflicts, people exiled to America and other safe countries, bringing with them their secrets, strengths, abilities and cultures. Gypsies, tribes, Natives of Voodoo and Witchcraft, all trying to find a safe place to just live and raise their families in peace. We were young, but I saw a lot of scary crap on the street. You might have been a bit sheltered with our parents and then our grandparents. But believe me they're all out there, and their descendants that were born in whatever camp, village or community their people set up. They came by sea, by plane, by car and foot and wagon need be, some traveled for many months to reach their destination. Immigration laws were totally ignored during the battles so we just don't know the scope of power and natural abilities there is out there, to say nothing of what Bradshaw was doing in his lab during that time; creating those like me, Keys, Lamontage, Elise and their descendants that are just waiting for the right time to come forward and use what he gave them to reek destruction and mayheim."

"Yeah, that's the scary part, Rose, what happens if one of those hidden do come out and Guardian can't beat them? What if I can't beat them? what if Lamontage is that one?",

"A little cynical aren't we?" Rose crossed her arms, and raised a brow.

"I'm sorry." She smiled. "I'm just tired, I guess. I need a nap. Too much sorrow and too many images of death in my brain, I guess."

"Then take one. Wake up refreshed and with a new perspective."

"Yeah." She smiled slowly then drew in a breath, "on that note Tanner would like to take the kids to the park but he feels a little uneasy about me being here by myself without the extra protection Keys ordered, so I thought maybe Kurt and the two kids could join him while you stayed here and practiced your Custodian abilities?"

"I think that's a lovely idea. I'll call him." She picked up her cell and ventured into the living room. Marna yawned and went into the kitchen. "Looks great, ladies."

"Thanks, Aunt Marna." Hannah said. "I made the sandwiches and Beth made the veggie soup. It's homemade."

"Mmm, sounds delicious." She grabbed a piece of bread while all the others took their seats and Rose quickly stepped into the kitchen, hanging up her phone.

"Wow, does it smell great in here," she said snatching a piece of bread. "You girls did a great job."

"Thank you, Aunt Rose."

"So did Kurt say he'd do it?" Marna queried as she took the large soup bowl from Beth and sat it down, serving it to the children.

"He thought it was a great idea," she said.

"What's that?" Mary asked.

"Uncle Kurt is going to go to the park with you and Tanner this afternoon. He's going to bring Desiree and Ray."

"Yes!" Isaiah cheered from the end of the table.

"I take it you like that idea?" Marna queried, raising her brow.

"I'll have somebody to hang with, somebody who understands me."

Marna tried to hide her grin behind a bite of bread. "Just make sure you hang where Kurt and Tanner can see you."

"Aunt Marna." He objected.

"Don't argue, Isaiah, please. You're not familiar with the area, and I want you to be safe. It's not like you've got to hold their hands or anything." The rest of the kids snickered. Marna gave them all her well-rehearsed mother stare and they started shoveling soup into their mouths. "I just want you where they can see you. Okay?"

"Fine." Brooding, he turned his attention back to his soup and didn't look up the rest of the meal. When Tanner came to pick them up, he met up with Ray out in front and the boys trailed by a few feet. Marna shook her head.

"Isn't there an owner's manual or something I can add to my library?"

Rose grinned and gave her a side hug. "You're doing fine. He's just testing his boundaries."

"Seems that's all we do is disagree these days." She sighed as she put the last of the dishes into the dishwasher and turned it on. "I just don't know." She turned around and leaned her hips against the counter. "I don't know if I can do this alone."

"You'll do fine, Marna. Come on, you're tired and you've heard a lot of info that you have to absorb. Go lie down and get some rest. Things will look better when you wake.

She smiled. "You're probably right." She gave her a hug and went to lie down. Sleep overcame her almost the instant her head hit the pillow and Rose added an extra layer of protection. However, twenty minutes into her slumber, voices started invading her mind.

"Arella, come back here."

"When can we go to the park, Momma?"

"It is not safe there anymore."

"But I want to go!"

"No, you must stay with us."

"Why won't somebody help me?"

"Guardian's in Zurich, Sir."

"Let the games begin." An evil laugh filled her sense.

She woke up and cried out. Her head throbbed. Rose ran into her room. "Marna what is it? Did Lamontage attack?"

She drew in a breath. "No, no." She grabbed her head. "I'm not sure. Voices. My head. It hurts."

"Was it a dream?"

"No, it wasn't a dream."

"Maybe I should call Keys."

"Yeah, maybe you should." Marna fell back onto the pillows, breathing deeply. She was sweating profusely and she tried to control the violent trembling overtaking her body. She had no idea what had just happened but one of the sinister voices she had heard before. It was Lamontage and the whispered cry for help was Arella. She knew it. She felt it. She didn't know how she did, she just did.

Chapter Five

"Coming !" Rose set the teacup on the table before Marna, and went to answer the door, returning moments later with Keys.

He sat in a chair across from Marna and caught her eyes with his own. "Tell me about the experience, Marna. Everything. Don't leave anything out." Marna broke eye contact, carefully sat her teacup on its saucer, and got up to walk toward the window overlooking the distant mountains, giving herself a moment to gather her thoughts. Keys watched her movements. She was tense. Frightened. "Take your time."He coaxed.

Drawing in a breath and letting it out slowly, she started to tell him. "I had gone in to take a little nap while Tanner had the kids at the park. I didn't sleep much last night and the meeting being so long this morning, it was a lot of information to take in, my mind needed time to process."

"Understandable," he said, leaning back in his chair and watching her retrace her steps, until she sat back down. "Then what happened?"

"I'm not sure how long I was out, but these uh..." She looked his way, his expression was blank, no sign that he thought she was losing it. ". . . Voices, I started hearing voices."

"I see." He leaned forward. "Any you recognize?"

She nodded. "Lamontage." His eyes betrayed his concern. "But it was only for a moment, and it wasn't a vision or a dream. He didn't know I was there." She sighed. "At first I heard others, a woman talking to Arella, then a man and then like a radio station it flipped to some guy warning Lamontage that we were here." She lifted her eyes from the nervous movement of her hands to his face. "That Guardian was here."

He drew in a breath, leaned forward to rest his elbows on his knees, dropping his eyes to his hands as his fingers formed a steeple, then he too returned his gaze to hers. "You said you heard some woman talk to Arella. Was it our Arella ?"

Marna was sure of her next response. "Yes, it was."

Keys got up, put his hands in his pockets, and went to the windows to study the mountains. After some long agonizing moments, he turned toward her once again, ran his hand over his mouth, and sighed. "Marna, I need you to do something for me." She nodded. "I need you to close your eyes and focus on one of your children, let's say Isaiah and Ray. Focus on their voices, on how they talk, on what they might be talking about."

"Keys, I highly doubt that will . . ."

"Just trust me." He said.

"All right." She closed her eyes and did as Keys instructed.

"Now clear your mind of all other clutter. Chase any other thought from your mind," he said softly. Voices filled her mind, mostly snippets of conversation, nothing that made any sense. It was as if a radio was flipping stations in her head. Her brow furrowed. Her head started to pound. "Easy, Marna, don't break your thought process. I know it's uncomfortable. It usually is the first time out, but just stay with me. Relax, ignore the pounding, and ignore the discomfort in your brain." Moments later the creases in her brow eased up. She started hearing things more clearly.

"*Will you relax; he can't get in any trouble there,*" a man's voice.

"*The bars are so high,*" a woman's voice.

"*You can't protect him forever,*" a man.

"*Mary, stay within my sight,*" Tanner's voice soothed her nerves. "Hannah, could you?"

"Sure *thing Nanny Tanner.*" She teased. "*Come on Beth.*"

"*Hi. You're new here,*" a strange woman's voice said.

"Stay focused on Isaiah," Keys said as he noticed her concentration ease.

"I'm thirteen, a teenager. I don't need a babysitter. Tammy doesn't. She just doesn't trust me." She finally settled on her quarry.

"Hey look at this !" Ray said.

"Cool, that's tonight." Isaiah said.

"Want to go?"

"Are you kidding, she won't let me out for that. It's beyond that ridiculous bedtime she's set for me."

"She might if Dad takes us."

"Maybe."

"It is your vacation after all. Dad is someone she trusts, right?"

"Yeah, it is my vacation." Isaiah said stubbornly.

"Come on, let's go find him."

She opened her eyes and recounted what she had heard as Keys listened intently then smiled. "What just happened?"

He took his glasses off and made a point of cleaning the lenses. "Marna, have you experienced any new abilities you haven't shared with me?"

She looked at him and was about to say no then remembered the night in the kitchen with Amanda. "Locator," she told him about her late night talk with Amanda on Isaiah's birthday.

"I see. That clarifies why this ability has surfaced."

"What ability?"

"Listening."

Marna was shocked. "B-but I thought that was a synthetic ability? One designed in labs like Bradshaw's"

"Psychics are finding new and amazing things in their realms every day. Listening is an ability that doesn't manifest by itself, most of the time the implantation of synthetic genes is suspect if it is not predetermined by Locating or Medium abilities. Your magnifying ability probably turbo boosted it along from your Locating ability, because most of the time the predetermined ability is bypassed by the strength of listening as it moved to the surface."

"So I'm a psychic eavesdropper. Great. I'm already slipping all over the place on banana peels where Isaiah is concerned." She shook her head and picked up her teacup to go and make another. It wasn't so much that she felt she needed it, but she needed something to do.

"Isaiah is thirteen, the time when one is trying to experience and define their independence. It's perfectly natural."

"And every authority figure in his life grows fangs and claws." She passed him a sideways glance.

"I've never heard it explained so poetically before, but yes, I suppose that's true. Rose, you have a boy of the same age, what is your input?"

"Depends on who you're talking about; I have a forty-year-old who thinks he's thirteen, or could you mean the adolescent child in my care?" She grinned, Keys chuckled and Marna just smiled and shook her head.

"Well I just heard our adolescent boys making plans to double team your forty – who thinks he's a thirteen-year-old – into taking them somewhere tonight."

"Ooh, intriguing," she grinned, "any idea where?"

"No, they both sounded very excited."

"Whatever it is, you can bet it will be very loud and very active," Keys chuckled.

"Most likely," Rose agreed. She popped open her PC tablet and started an internet search. Marna finished making her tea and offered one to Keys, which he accepted gracefully.

"Let's talk about this Locating ability, shall we?" He interjected, joining her in the kitchen.

"Rose, you want tea?"

"Yes, please, I would love some. That apple and cinnamon one would be great." Marna smiled and pulled a box of herbal tea out of the cupboard. "There isn't much to tell really, Amanda told me I had the ability and she told me how to test it."

"And did you. . . test it . . . I mean?"

"Yeah, with a book Isaiah got for his birthday . . ." She put Rose's tea on the table. "Amanda asked me to pick it up and focus on Isaiah. Tea's done, Rose."

"Be there in a minute. I'm searching the area to see what dreadfully awful band or fight is on tour here."

Marna laughed and turned her attention back to Keys. "I saw him and his friends in the tent telling stories. It was uncanny." She sat down.

"Got it !" Rose called from the other room. She got up, secured her PC tablet against her body and joined them in the kitchen, opening it and showing them the picture of the latest rage in music bands.

"Raging Vampires?" Marna asked, her brow furrowing at the promotional photo of the four-man band dressed in full costume, each holding a female victim in their arms. "Oh my." She lifted her fingertips to her lips, "You have no problem with this group?"

"At first I did, but then I researched them." Rose took a sip of her tea after she handed the tablet to Marna. "They're this generations' equivalent to Kiss or Queen or any number of hard rock bands from past generations or The Underworld Rock band from ours. They just took what was out there in the media to pull in the Macy and Trey fans from The End of World Trilogy. There's no profanity, no demeaning language toward women, or half-naked dancing on the stage. Just a lot of hoopla, flash, noise and a good ballad thrown in here and there for good measure. Besides Kurt will be with them. They'll be fine."

"So you've decided he can go, if this is what it is?"

"If they can get tickets, sure." She reached for her phone on her belt, looked at the screen and smiled. "Oh, Kurt's texting." She nodded and looked up from the screen. "Am I good or what? He wants to know if you have a problem with the hard rock to the heavy metal band category. He would like Isaiah to accompany him and Ray to a Raging Vampires concert tonight at the Opernhaus here in Zurich. He promises not to fill them with too much junk food and not to let them wander off. He called the hall and they have a few tickets left. He reserved three. They're holding them until four this afternoon. He just wants to know so they can go and get them after they're done in the park."

"Now what would he have done if I had said no?"

"Probably scalped them or begged me to go with?" She winked.

"You're sure this band isn't going to warp him into some creature of the night?"

Keys chuckled and when she looked his way, he quickly raised his tea to his lips with one hand and waggled his fingers with the opposite. "I'll leave this decision to my trophy wife."

"Oh you're good," Rose said.

"Nope. Just a business man who knows when not to offer his opinion."

"Good call," Marna said, her lips twitching. "A sign that I've trained him well." They all laughed and Marna relaxed. "If you guys have no problem with the band than I guess Isaiah can go."

"I'll let them know," she texted back, "You'll be his hero."

"Yeah for about five minutes." Marna mumbled.

"Ah, the trials of raising teens," Keys stated quietly as Rose put her phone down. "It works out well, though. Tonight, we have been invited to a Masquerade party, Marna, as Mr. and Mrs. Francois Kestin."

"Wow, that was fast," Marna stated.

"Well, we can't let any grass grow under our feet in our pursuit of Lamontage." He placed his teacup on the table. "It's being put on by a Fortune 500 business man with suspected ties to the Liberatores. He has a seasonal castle on the outskirts of Zurich. He throws this big kick-off party every year. His name is Zorich, Benjamin Zorich. His business is high-tech spy aides, listening devices, phones, spyware, etc. He has buyers all over the world. Some of his product is the advanced facial recognition used by the CIA, FBI and Homeland Security. All those higher end security branches. Perfect way to launder the money taken in to support the cause." He sat back in his chair. "His holdings average billions of dollars. The flags went up when Interpol investigated one of his companies for supporting a Mosque with known terrorist connections about six months ago."

"Why didn't they bring him in?"

"They did. They couldn't get anything to stick. His lawyer used the religious angle. Religious beliefs are the hardest thing to prove or disprove when it comes to money laundering. He simply said that he chose it as a charity. That his companies are run through his business manager and he just signed the checks."

"What about the manager? Couldn't they get him to flip on this man?"

"He was dead within seventy-two hours of Zorich's questioning. Skiing accident. A cable car came loose."

"Well that's not suspicious," Rose interjected.

"Tough to prove. Eight other people injured, and one other person dead. The resort got sued and he was just given up as collateral damage to the resort's poor maintenance of their equipment."

"Of course he was," Marna said, shifting herself in her chair. "So, what are we supposed to be doing tonight?"

"Something that'll become a lot easier with that new ability of yours." He took a final drink of his tea and stood up. "Listen," he winked. "The theme is Grimm's Fairy Tales. He likes to remind people that the fairy tales originated in Europe."

"Let me guess, you want to go as Cinderella and Prince Charming?" Marna queried.

"Actually, no, we're going as The Frog Prince and Tiana." They laughed. He shrugged. "It's all the costume store had left, and I found a Rapunzel for Rose." Rose's brow went up. "I need you there for extra protection for Marna in case Lamontage happens to be amongst us, especially if she's taking her new ability for a test drive. Not to mention, it was either that or a dwarf."

"Rapunzel is just fine." Rose nodded. "Do I get a spinning wheel too?"

"Gracious, let's hope not! Those things were a challenge to carry around." He grinned. The women chuckled.

"This just might be the highlight of the trip." Rose leaned her hip on the bar. "Do we get to take pictures?"

"They've hired a professional for that." He turned and walked toward the door. "Keep in mind ladies that we are on the clock tonight."

"Of course." They nodded, trying to keep a straight face. "Will you be sending a car, Dear?" Marna called in a sweet voice.

"Yes." He grinned. "The costumes should be arriving around three, the party starts at eight. Make sure you wear the mask, Marna, and do something different with your hair. We want to minimize the chance of guests recognizing you. We'll leave before the unmasking at midnight. Good afternoon, ladies." He turned to go.

"Just one more thing," Marna called after him. Keys turned around expectantly. "Will you be bringing your own lily pad or will they be supplying one?" Rose laughed. Marna's lips twitched.

"I've got one reserved in the Champagne pool already, but thank you for caring." He winked again and left. Marna turned to Rose. "Champagne pool? Not only do I have my father for a husband on this assignment, he's an alcoholic. Geesh."

"Yeah, too bad you couldn't get Tanner to play sidekick on this one."

"What?"

"Got to admit, he'd be a better choice for a husband on a Switzerland vacation, and besides, I think he's sweet on you."

Marna looked horrified. "What?" Her face turned ten shades of red. "Sweet? Are you on drugs or something? He's a friend. He feels responsible for us because he tried to save Jeff and he couldn't." She drew in a breath and let it out slowly. "Besides, there's never going to be another Jeff for me."

"Probably not, but you're still young enough to have a full life in every sense of the word. I didn't know Jeff that long, but I doubt he'd want you to be wasting away behind closed doors."

Marna scoffed. "Amanda said pretty much the same thing." Rose's brow went up. Marna smiled. "In one of her dream visits, she told me pretty much the same thing."

"That's creepy."

"Not really, sometimes it's a comfort." She sighed. "You never know how much you value their advice until they're gone. Amanda would be quick to give it, not so quick to take it." She started tidying up the kitchen.

"No, that's not what I meant. I mean it puts me a little off balance that I had a sister who thinks like me, gives advice like me, and I've heard resembles me some, but I've never met her."

Marna chuckled. "You would have liked her. It's true there are similarities between you two, however, you are a bit more mature than she was."

"Thank you for that." She frowned. "I think."

"It was meant to be a compliment." Marna smiled. "Amanda was the type to throw caution and restraint to the wind. During her teen years, we all wondered what kind of drama we were going to be privy to on a given day. . . That is, until she found Pete." She glanced at Rose. "He was a calming influence on her wild years, and the best thing that ever happened to her." She sniffed.

"The happily ever after we all search for."

"Yeah." There was a knock on the door. Marna smiled. "Sounds like our costumes may be here."

Rose looked at her watch. "Maybe." Marna went to the door and looked through the peephole. A deliveryman stood on the other side holding two large boxes. She looked over her shoulder at Rose, grinned and nodded. Then she opened the door, signed for the packages and after giving the young man a fair tip, closed it. She handed the correct one to Rose and grinned. "Shall we go try them on?"

Rose thought for a moment. "You bet." Like two girls who could not wait to try on their prom dresses and show them off to their best friend, they ran toward the two closest bedrooms and disappeared within them.

*****

Elizabeth, Hannah and Mary assisted Marna, as she dressed for the party. Mary watched in wonder as the two older girls turned her simple aunt into a beautiful princess before her very eyes. "You look like a fairy princess, Aunt Marna," she said.

"Why thank you, Mary." She reached out and ran a finger down Mary's cheek. "Hearing that from you, I know we've done it right because you know what princesses are supposed to look like."

"Yes I do," Mary stood tall and proud.

"We're done." Elizabeth said proudly, pulling a hand mirror from the top drawer of the dresser and handing it to Marna. She was impressed. The girls had worked together, Elizabeth on makeup and Hannah on costume and hair. The finished product was amazing. They had pulled Marna's dark hair into a fountain bun with some curls cascading down gently around her face, The Tiara' rhinestones winked in the room's low light from its perch on top of her head and Mary's chosen heart pendant glittered against her skin from the square cut bodice.

"Wow, you girls are my Fairy God Mothers tonight. What a great job!"

Mary's gentle laughter rang out in the room. "Silly Aunt Marna! Cinderella was the one with the Fairy God Mother, not Tiana."

The other three laughed.

"You're right, Mary. I'm sorry. Where would I be if you didn't keep me straight?" She bent down, kissed Mary's forehead, and stood up. Glancing at her watch, she asked, "Where's my mask?" Mary ran over to the bed and ran back to give it to her. It was a soft blue to match her dress with imbedded glitter in the painted surface. She slipped it on and caught her reflection in the full-length mirror across the room. Even those who knew her would not recognize her. For the night, she had placed colored contacts in her eyes, turning them a soft brown with golden flecks of Amber winking in the low lighting. The mask hid most of the top half of her features and she had been learning how to speak with less of a New Jersey accent and more grammatical pronunciation. Her hair was still a rich midnight color, but with the style the girls had done, including the glittering hair net and straightening tool she had brought from home, with the exception of the appointed curls around her face, her natural curls were all but gone. The dress was a style that included a hooped skirt and fitted bodice that masked the size of her body from the sight of curious eyes. "You did well ladies. I look good."

"You don't need us for that, Aunt Marna," Hannah put in. "You're beautiful anyway."

"Ahh, thank you, Hannah." She turned and gathered the young girl in a hug and held her close. How close they had come to losing her just a year before. She set her a short distance away from her. "And so are you." Hannah smiled a smile that went right to her eyes. Clearing her throat, she straightened up. "I guess we should go out to the other room and await my date for the night."

"Yeah, I can't wait to see Dr. Keys in his frog costume," Elizabeth said and they all laughed.

"Neither can I," Marna echoed and put her arm around the two older girls. Hannah grabbed Mary's hand as they headed toward the bedroom door.

"Whoa, Aunt Marna, you look bee--u--ti--ful," said Jacob when she entered. Tanner and the other three boys looked their way.

Marna smiled at the boy and tipped her head. "Well thank you, Jacob." She turned her head toward Tanner while she spoke the next few words. "Has Kurt picked up . . ." she trailed off when her gaze collided with Tanner's eyes. The look he gave her was one she hadn't seen in a long time. It was tender and caring. The emotion was raw and real. His guard was obviously down.

Within seconds, Tanner blinked and his guard went back up. Whatever she thought she had seen was gone. "Uh . . . Yeah." He cleared his throat. "They left about forty minutes ago." He tried to make his smile casual. "You look nice."

"Thank you, kind sir." She grinned. "Guess I'll keep up the appearance of the mysterious trophy wife pretty good in this get up, eh?" She playfully twirled before him. They all laughed. A knock on the door brought their attention away from Marna's playful dress-up game.

"I'll get it !" Elizabeth said and ran toward the kitchen. "Wow, Aunt Rose, you look almost as good as Aunt Marna."

"Almost, my fair niece?" Rose said as she stepped over the threshold and Desiree ran further into the apartment calling Mary's name. "I'll have you know, Rapunzel kicks butt !" She grinned. "Haven't you seen Tangled?" Elizabeth laughed, Mary and Desiree giggled. Rose walked over to Marna and drew her into a hug. Marna appraised her sister's outfit. The dress had a lavender bodice glittering with sequins, a sheer orchid over layer covering a lavender hooped skirt and sleeves that puffed at the shoulder and narrowed at her elbow where the same sheer material hugged her lower arm, coming to a point at her middle finger, with sequins winking as she moved, around the hem. She wore a similar mask to Marna's only colored purple, and a golden blonde wig styled in folded braids that reached to her knees and looped back up to the base of her skull.

"You look lovely, Rose."

"But I do concede, Marna. You will definitely be the belle of the ball. Cinderella, look out !" Everyone in the room laughed.

"Stop it," Marna said as her face turned several shades of red.

"Oh, and isn't that sweet. She blushes," Rose teased. Marna was about to respond when the intercom buzzed.

"You are so saved by the bell, big sister," she said as she moved over to the wall, smiling. She pushed the button. "Yes?"

"Your driver is here, Mrs. Kestin."

"Thank you, we'll be down in a moment." She lifted her finger off the button and turned toward the kids. "Must be Keys is going to meet us there. Looks like you'll miss seeing him as a frog." A chorus of disappointed "ahs" went around the room. "I'm sorry, but I'll make sure I get plenty of pictures." She went to give them each a kiss. "Now you all know the rules. Don't give Tanner a hard time and Moses, no astral projection tonight."

"All right, Aunt Marna." The other children looked at him with a smile. They all knew how he liked to practice his ability at night, taking unsupervised walks around the area while everyone slept.

Mary's little brow was bunched up in confusion and Marna was sure she saw concern. She crouched as low as her dress would allow her. "Mary, what's wrong?

"Who's Mrs. Kestin?"

"Ah." She looked up at Tanner, who smiled. "That's a make believe name I'm using right now. We're play acting, kind of like you do when you play dress up."

"Oh, okay." She smiled. "But shouldn't we be Kestin, too?"

"I think that's what Tanner uses for your name when he speaks to others." She looked at him for verification. He nodded. "But you only have to use your first name when you talk to people. That way you don't have to use the make believe last name."

"Oh, okay, but what about when we go back home?"

"Then you can use your own name, but while we're here in Switzerland, we will be under the play name. Okay?"

"Okay." She nodded, "As long as I don't have to change my name again. It gets terrible confusing to keep doing that."

Recognition donned on Marna's brain. That's why the child was concerned. She was thinking of the year before. "No, baby, not this time. You are Mary Ellen Nymphis Farlow today and for every day that you want to be that. This is just like playing hide and seek. We are hiding under a different name for the week we are here. Think of it as play acting in a school play."

"Oh, like Santa's elves at Christmas time."

"Exactly, Darling, just like that." She kissed her forehead. "Now we've got to go, but you be good for Tanner. Rose and I are going to go now. I'll see you in the morning."

"Okay." She kissed Marna on the cheek then whispered in her ear. "You do look pretty."

"And so do you." She touched the child's nose with her forefinger, and then stood up giving Tanner final instructions on evening chores, meals, as well as emergency numbers. Then she waved goodbye and headed out the door to go to work.

*****

Staying within the boundaries of their cover identities, they used their cover names when addressing each other in the conversation. They kept their masks in place to make sure their very curious driver would not recognize them as he kept using his rearview for checking them out as much as for checking out the traffic behind them. Marna was simply the wife of a very shrewd French businessman, whose second language was English, which she spoke almost as good as the French she threw about in the back seat. Rose complied, because she, too, was very fluent in French as well. One of the classes Marna had recently taken in Guardian Tech taught you how to adopt a cover ID as your own and learning several foreign languages was at the top of the list. Luckily, French was a class she had already aced and German was one she had just come through. Next on her list was Russian.

However, all chatter and cover identity slipped from her mind when the wrought-iron gates before them separated and they began their drive up a mountain road. In the distance, a well-lit castle glowed against the night sky. The gleam became more detailed and more defined as they got closer. Shortly thereafter, their limo pulled up in front of a medieval styled castle. The rook towers finished off the many stone sides of the generously spread building and they were capped off with cone shaped roofs, decorated with many white lights winking in the night. Marna knew it had to be thousands. The front door was an arch with a wooden walk bridge leading up to it. The walk bridge crossed over a moat that was actually a lined marine life trench with several species swimming about in it, including native lizards. The massive building was centered on a stretch of land that went as far as the eye could see, marred only by the smaller buildings spread about. One side of the castle was a view of snow-capped mountains and the other a view of Zurich with its lights twinkling like the stars above.

Their driver stopped behind a line of other limos, horse and buggies and, yes, even a few carriages styled like Cinderella's pumpkin. "Hey, Maryse," Rose said, using Marna's cover name. "I don't think we're in Kansas anymore." She watched in awe as men in white pantaloons and blue double-breasted jackets assisted each guest from their means of travel. Then they directed drivers uniformly onto a small cobblestone road that led to a distant building and parking area. The building, Marna assumed, was most likely a stable that took care to have men available to feed and groom the horses while their owners enjoyed a night of fantasy. The music drifting from within the stone building was a mixture of classical and polka, orchestra style.

The driver grinned as he inched his car forward when another vehicle left the line. "It is like this every year," he said with a heavy German accent. "Herrn Zorich's annual Masquerade Ball is the social event of the season. It is a time to escape the real life and live what you call it, hmm, the fantasy life?"

The two women laughed. "I think so, yes," Marna said, keeping her ID intact. The car inched forward some more as another Cinderella stepped out of a framed pumpkin structure surrounded in lights. "This place is amazing," she said. Within minutes, it was their turn as their driver pulled up to the footmen. The back door opened and a white gloved hand reached for them, assisting them out of the car and over to the footbridge. His partner closed the door and signaled the driver to move on.

Marna and Rose revered all that was around them. "Marna, pinch me. I think I'm in one of your dreams. I expect Amanda to pop out at any moment."

"You and me both." Marna smiled.

The ear-bud in Marna's ear crackled. "Don't let the outer shell fool you. The blood money that built this place is all over Lamontage's hand."

"There you are, darling," Marna smiled. "I was wondering when you were going to start whispering sweet nothings in my ear." Rose covered her mouth as she laughed. Marna grinned at her. Keyes chuckled. "However, it would have been nice if you would have let me imagine myself a princess for just a tiny bit longer, you old spoil sport."

"Later. Right now, don't stand out there and look like you've never been to a scene like this. Remember your cover and keep it real. You are used to this type of lifestyle."

"Hmm.... I thought I was the ignored wife."

"But I do like to show you off."

"All right, all right. We're on our way." She sighed and opened her purse to pull out her GPC. Looking at the screen, she pulled up the GPS tracking program APP that tracked their ear - buds. Guardian had installed it before she left for the trip. She saw three blue dots representing her, Rose and Keyes floating amongst the other neutral gray ones representing the unknown guests. Once the operation moved forward, they would send a sequence of numbers to other phones belonging to people of interest, and they would become red dots. She hit Blueprint and in a few seconds, the phone pulled up a miniature 3-D blue print of the castle before them. Keys' dot showed him next to several gray dots and one red dot. "Who is with you, Keys? I see red."

"Herrn Zorich, if you will excuse me, I have just gotten word that my beautiful wife has arrived."

"Gotcha." She typed in Zorich's name. She heard Keys excuse himself again and turned toward Rose. "Let the games begin." She put her phone back into her clutch and then the two women crossed the footbridge to meet Keys on the other side and ease into the enemy's camp.

*****

Hours later, Marna leaned against one of the arched doorways of the ballroom. The marble floor glistened in the low lighting of the grand room, echoing years gone by. There was laughter and muffled talking as many couples danced across the floor, the clicks of heals and boots bouncing back at them from the castle walls. She tried not to laugh as Keys made his way toward her in his frog suit. His jeweled brass crown winked at her. He grabbed two drinks from a passing tray and handed one to her. "Anything to report?"

"Not yet," she said taking a sip of champagne. "Just party conversation. You know the kind. Does Suzy want to spend $100 on a pair of shoes at the local shoe store? . . . Whether they should fire their Irish nanny and hire a more respectable English one? Should they sell their ten-bedroom house in the mountains for the fifteen-bedroom house by the lake?" She grinned and he chuckled, "just normal everyday water cooler talk."

"You seem to be enjoying this." He chuckled and looked around. "No signs of anyone trying to intrude?"

"Nada. Just a peaceful, enjoyable evening though I have been asked to dance by a couple of English gentlemen."

"And you didn't accept?"

"Uh, uh. I told them my heart was lost to a frog and they moved on to the next princess. I think they're looking to raise their status."

This time Keys burst out into rolling laughter. "It's refreshing to see you relax a little, Marna," he said.

"It's the costume," she said and smiled as Rose came back from the refreshment table with two small plates of sweets. "Thank goodness there is no diet patrol here as I'd be so busted," she said, handing the second plate to Marna.

"Me, too." She lifted a cream-filled pastry to her mouth and took a bite, closing her eyes in ecstasy. "M-m-m-m. Got to say this about the Germans, they know how to make a woman smile." Rose grinned.

"Are you enjoying yourself, Rose?" Keys asked.

"Immensely. However, if I have to laugh at one more handsome prince asking me to let down my hair, I just might ban Desiree from ever reading a fairy tale again."

Keys chuckled and looked at his watch. "It's 9:30 now. I'll make our excuses to our host at 11:30 so we can depart before the unmasking. We don't want to chance blowing our covers."

"Kill joy," the women said. They synchronized their watches with his. "Very well then. Keep listening and if you hear something suspicious, let me know."

"Yes, Prince Frog, I promise not to go get myself killed without first notifying you," Marna teased. Rose grinned. Keys' eyes narrowed from behind the eye slits in the frog head. Marna grinned, "You do know it is really hard to take you seriously in that get up."

"Look beyond it and remember I am a Remote Influencer." With that, he turned and left.

"That sounded like a threat," Marna called after him, but all he did was raise his hand and wave as he walked away. Marna turned toward Rose. "Didn't that sound like a threat?"

"Unh, unh, I think it was more of a promise," Rose stated watching him walk away.

"Yeah, I think so, too." She was about to go after him when something stopped her. It was something she had heard. She held up a hand to wave off Rose's concern.

"Have you seen that costume?" Marna shifted to the next snippet.

"She is one hot Rapunzel." Marna moved her eyes and caught a couple of young men checking out Rose. Blocked it out, grinned, and moved on.

"It's cooling down outside."

"Well it is only the end of March . It's always cool." She shifted to the next, surprised at how easy it was for her to adapt to her new ability.

"We need passage out of Switzerland tonight." Marna paused and blocked out all other conversation. The voice she had picked up was a man with a German accent.

"You know that won't be happening." The second voice was male as well, but his nationality sounded French. *"The plan is not in place yet."*

"She is only a child. She does not understand."

"Make her understand. You are her father."

"In name only. They never meant for her to be ours. You tell him that we need passage to Paris and we need it tonight or we will find our own and he will not find Arella, ever!"

"You stupid vile, little man, do you think you're strong enough to go up against him? Do you?" She heard air escaping lungs and a grunt. More sounds of someone taking a beating.

"Please stop."

Marna focused on surrounding sounds, trying to identify where the conversation was. There were no echoes, so it wasn't another room within the stoned building. She heard a soft whispering sound, a rustling of leaves, whistling as if through a wind tunnel. They were outside! She focused again as more sounds of fighting drifted to her ears, music in the background. Not just any music, it was the same music was playing in the ballroom right now! She looked across the room. Five French, doors stood open. A stone terrace was visible as the curtains blew in the breeze. She grabbed Rose's hand and led her into the empty hall. "Arella's handler is on the terrace and he's in trouble. We need to help him."

"What about Keys?"

"No time! Cloak up !" She grabbed Rose's hand and they joined their cloaking ability to form an impenetrable cloak. A heavy, thick mist surrounded them. They made their way down the empty hall through a distant entrance into the ballroom that came out by the terrace doors and slipped onto it undetected. When they were safely away from the doors, they heard tortured moaning.

They followed the sound around some tall shrubs, moving slowly so no one could detect their movement. On the terrace floor, Bernard Sweinzer had curled up in a ball to defend his body from the insulting blows of his attackers, but now the man above him bald and white was fixing a silencer onto a forty-five. He bent down and drew Sweinzer to his knees. He remained on his knees but bent at the waist, holding his ribs. "You know how disappointed he gets when his people do not obey his orders. I knew you couldn't be trusted. You have lived in limbo too long, Bernard, adapted to the Western ways too easily. I knew you would eventually crack and want to run. Too much trust in everything the infidels have brainwashed you with for years."

"You call me a radical? Look at what you people do in the name of all that is holy. You kill and maim. You commit genocide. But I am the radical?" Bernard challenged.

Marna opened her channel to Rose. *Rose, go get Keys.*

I'm not going to leave you here.

We don't have a choice, if we both go; he's as good as dead. Just go, I'm going to try to distract him. Keep your channel open.

He also said little, if no Psychic contact. Too easy for Lamontage to trace.

This is why I am physically sending you. No time to argue. Go!

Staying cloaked, they separated. Rose went toward the doors and slipped in unnoticed while Marna inched toward the assailant, picking up a vase on her way. As she drew closer, she raised the vase in the air and swung as hard as she could on the back of the bald man's skull. The vase broke and her quarry crumbled to a heap on the floor. She dropped her cloak and knelt beside Sweizner. "Are you okay?"

"I will be." His accent was German with a Middle East undertone. He was obviously the product of mixed heritage. He allowed her to help him over to a stone bench to sit down. Then she knelt before him and pulled a handkerchief from her purse. He pushed her hand aside. "I do not want your help. I will be fine."

"Sure you will." She gave him the handkerchief. "If you don't bleed to death internally. That was quite a beating you took."

"I am a man of honor. I can take whatever is given to me, including beatings." He pushed himself up. She heard a pop just before shock filled his features and he pitched forward, clawing for her, blood spattered her dress and her face. Shocked, she took a step back, raising her hand to her mouth. Then she saw him, a dark silhouette by the house.

"Wh-who's there?"

The silhouette came closer. "I'm hurt, my love. I'd thought by now that you would know me." He was backlit by the moon and his face was in shadow, but Marna knew who he was. She remembered every inch of that body. Every pitch in that voice.

"No. You're not real." She stepped back. "This is a joke. A cruel, cruel joke." She drew in a breath as his hand reached out to her. "Come, darling, walk with me." His voice was soothing, easing her into trusting what she was seeing. She felt her defenses start to tumble. She could not raise her shields as his green eyes bore into hers. "I can be who you want me to be, who you desire me to be."

"No," she whispered, but she was losing the battle. He drew her into his web.

"You're beginning to feel it, aren't you? The pain is lifting. I can see it in your eyes. Don't be afraid to grab it. Darling, come with me. We can leave all the pain behind. Be together forever."

She wanted it to be true, badly. "Jeff," she breathed, and reached out for him, but stopped herself. "No, this is an illusion." Even as she walked toward him with an outstretched hand, she knew she should be walking, no, running away. Her head started to pound. She could feel both Rose and Keys trying to shield her, but the hold he had on her was too strong. They couldn't penetrate the wall he was trying to build around her psyche and when she tried to let them in, her head pounded more. She winced.

Sensing interference and knowing his time was short; he took her hand and drew her to him. "Does my touch feel like an illusion, Darling?" He ran his hand up her arm and to her face. Then he lowered his lips to hers and drew her in with a kiss. She responded. Knowing he had to act quickly because she had reinforcements on the way, with his other hand, he pulled a syringe out of his pocket, and drew it up and flipped the cap off. He aimed for her neck.

"NO! !" Rose cried and the syringe went flying. The illusion faded and Marna stepped back. The person before her was not Jeff, but one of the young men who had escaped Tarot Lockdown. He went to grab for Marna with both hands, to drag her with him, but Rose lifted her hands like she was accustomed to the new power flowing through her and the boy went flying, landing a few feet away. Keys ran forward and grabbed Marna as she started to crumble to the floor. The boy's eyes narrowed as he looked at Rose, then he jumped to his feet and ran. Rose started after him.

"Let him go !" Keys ordered. "We'll have another chance !" He cradled Marna in his arms as Zorich ran out.

"What happened?" Zorich demanded.

"She was attacked after she witnessed the murder of the man over there." He waved to Sweinzer lying prone on the terrace floor. "Please call for my car. I need to get her medical care." He responded in German. Zorich nodded, ordered some of his men to call the police and then called for the Keys car. Bryan and Demi jumped out and assisted them into the car and then they sped off the castle property and headed for the compound.

"What happened?" Bryan demanded as he threw his red bubble on the roof and blew through traffic lights, pushing the speed limit to get back to the compound medical facility.

"Marna was attacked by a Stager. Took on Jeff's identity." He did a preliminary exam of her eyes and heart.

"Wait wasn't there one among the escapees?"

"Yes, looks like Lamontage is helping them develop their abilities."

"Well at least now we know what his plan is." Bryan yanked the wheel to turn onto the highway.

"No comfort in that. He's not looking to create a mirror version of the Farlow collective. He wants a team of his own Psychic assassins, and Marna is the key to his whole damn thing. He gets control of her, he'll be unstoppable." As soon as the compound came into view, he yanked the car right then left and pulled into the emergency parking lot. Four medical attendees pushed a gurney to the car and then headed back for the building after they laid a motionless Marna upon it.

"Pulse is eighty and holding. Pupils are reactive to light. Breath sounds in both lungs normal. Respirations, thirty-two. They continuously called out her Vitals as they disappeared behind the double doors of the ER leaving him and Rose to await news of her condition. They sent Bryan and Demi to do security at the apartment in case the escaped stager planned another attack. Keys did not believe it likely because what Lamontage wanted was laying here in the ER.

*****

Rose sat in the waiting room twisting her wedding band on her ring finger. Keys sat down beside her. "How are you, Rose?"

"I'm not the one in the Emergency Room."

"No, but you are the one whose new ability probably saved her from Lamontage's latest attack."

"Does that happen often in this Psychic world of puzzles? You get over excited and Bam! -- a new ability hits you between the eyes without warning?"

He leaned forward, elbows on his knees, and placed his fingers together then used them to arch his hands apart. "No, not always, but I'm not surprised it happened. You are a Custodian, Blocker and a Cloaker thrown in for good measure. All mostly passive abilities, but when you weren't able to protect Marna with a mental shield, your body took that energy and morphed it into an active ability; Telekinesis, so you could protect her from a distance."

"Is that, like, you know a one-time thing or is it something that is now part of my genetic make-up."

"Oh, Rose, it probably always was a part of your genetic make-up. It just took a stressor to activate it. Someone you love was in trouble and needed your help."

"Is it always that simple? The Cloaking took hours to learn."

"As you mature in your psychic skin, you may develop more abilities that will build on what you already have. Now, it's just a practice of pulling it up when you need it and controlling it, forming it to fit your style. You may even be able to get some tips from Beth as she's lived with this ability all of her life."

Rose chuckled. "That she has." The clinic doors swung open and Tanner strode through. He moved quickly to their seats.

"What happened? Is she okay?"

"I think she'll be fine. Somehow, either Lamontage knew we were going to be at that party or he had some of his people there for unrelated issues they tracked when the girls started using their Psychic channel."

"Do you think we're Compromised?"

"Let's hope not. We're going to need our cover long enough to find his wife." Keys pulled out Sweinzer's ID. It had his address and car tag number on it. "If we don't, she could take Arella and dig deeper into the woodwork."

"When did you lift that?" Rose queried.

"About the same time you sent our Stager through the air." He smiled, and then averted his attention to the nurse making her way toward them."Molly, How is she?"

"She's got a bit of a headache, but I doubt we'll keep her here. She'll probably do better to recover at home. She just needs some solid sleep and to be surrounded by her family. Her shields will probably be weak for a few hours, so it might be safe to have a Custodian or Blocker with her while she sleeps. You can go in and see her now if you like."

"Thank you." Keys got up and motioned Tanner and Rose ahead of him. "I'll be right along. I'm just going to call Bryan so he can let the kids know she's fine." They both nodded and went in.

Molly watched them go, but made no attempt to return to her duties. Keys looked at her. "Is there more, Molly?"

Molly drew in a breath, let it out, and collected her thoughts before she raised her eyes to meet Keys. "Keys, Marna Farlow is one of the most powerful psychics I've come across, how can this man and his coherts get beyond her defenses?"

Keys sighed and looked down the hall toward the closed door, leading to the examining room. "Because she wears her weakness on her sleeve, Molly. She has to let go of the past to enable her to fully defend herself against an enemy like Lamontage. As long as she holds on to Jeff, he'll keep using him as a weapon against her."

"Too many more attacks like tonight, and she won't have the strength to fight him, Keys. Her defenses are weakening."

"I know, and so does Lamontage." Nodding his head once, he excused himself and pulled out his cellphone. Molly glanced once more in the general direction of the examining room and moved on with her duties.

*****

They brought the Stager in, hands tied before him, to the presence of their master, circled by many others, and forced him to his knees. His head hung in shame. He had seen others go through the punishment. He knew what was coming. That alone was enough to turn his insides to mush. "Look at me boy," The Master ordered. He raised his green eyes to the merciless expression of his Master. "Where is your quarry?"

"She got away." He spoke softly.

"Louder, boy, I didn't hear you."

"She got away, Master." He drew in a breath.

"Did I give you an assignment too difficult for you to handle, boy?"

"No, Master, others came to help her."

"What others?"

"A man and a woman. The woman had telekinetic powers. Master, she caught me off guard."

"Did I not teach you to be ready for anything?" The boy was silent. "Did I not teach you that butting heads with Guardian officials would be difficult and unpredictable?"

"Yes, sir." His voice grew soft again as tears welled in his eyes.

"Stop mumbling, boy, I can't hear you."

"Yes, Master, you did." He spoke loudly.

"Hmmm. I am disappointed in the results of your assignment, Bradley, and I can't ignore that. What kind of Custodial leader would I be if I did not discipline you when you did something that displeased me as quickly as I reward you when you do well?" Lamontage turned and walked a few paces away. "I need to make an example of you so others will know not to repeat your mistakes." On the last word he turned around, his medieval clergy robe swooshed around his ankles making an ominous sound, his hand stretched out, palm facing the boy. "This will hurt me more than it does you." He closed his fist, and twisted it. The Stager's body convulsed with pain.

" AAAAAAAAAAAHHHHHHHHHHHHHHHHHHHHHHHHHHHHHHH !" The Watchers stood rigid. They knew if they so much as turned away and the Master saw them, they would be on the platform of pain next. In seconds, though it seemed hours to the Stager, Lamontage unclenched his fist and the boy's body stopped convulsing. Drool came from his mouth. His eyes were open and aware. His body ravaged still with the memory of the pain.

Lamontage approached and nodded to his men. They pulled him up to his knees, holding him as his head lolled to the side. "Let that be a reminder to never fail me again. I can inflict so much more than that." He nodded. "Take him to his quarters and send the Healer to him." The men nodded, and then one tossed the half-conscious boy over his shoulder and removed him from the room. "Now", he turned around and looked over the young women within the room, "Who will share my meal with me tonight?" They all smiled with anticipation, each wanting to be the one he chose, because they knew that to share a meal with Lamontage was a step up in status among the other young women in the organization. His eyes combed the onlookers and settled upon a dark haired, blue-eyed beauty in the back row. "Iris, approach." Smiling, she made her way down to him from the coliseum benches and stood before him.

She stood about five foot eight inches with fair skin, and her belly was swollen with his child. He placed a hand on her face, then he let it drop to her belly and let it rest. "My son is active today."

"Yes, Master, he is." He smiled at her, his face filling with pride. A dozen subjects carried his children, but Iris still held favor in his eyes. She was well behaved and willing to listen to directions. Yes, she would do nicely. He snapped his fingers at the women in servants clothing standing by the open doors of the theater. "Make her presentable. Wave her hair, and pretty her face up a bit. You know what I like. Then choose a purple robe for her tonight." He looked at her smiling face. "Tonight you will tell me all about my son." He returned his gaze to the servants. "Bring her to my quarters when she's ready." He dismissed the others and then left the theater for his two-story castle that marked the center of their camp.

Yes, tonight he would have a substitute for his beloved Marna, for she managed to get away from him once again. He would have the young woman fulfill his Marna fantasy as he had others do before her. As he had Raquel do before she stepped over the line and tried to make him forget his Marna by trying to become her. Nobody could do that, absolutely nobody. Nobody had the power to share with him that Marna did.

Chapter Six

Marna set her teacup down on the coffee table. The children had long since gone to bed after several hours of awaiting word that she was okay. Elizabeth had been the last one to retire because she had talked at length with Rose about telekinesis. Beth was excited that she could share her knowledge and experience, little that it was, with someone else.

Despite the pounding headache plaguing her, Marna smiled. She could foresee Elizabeth having a future in Guardian. The child had often told Marna that she was already looking into using her abilities to help others. She would fit right in. She sighed and stared at her reflection in the darkened windows of the terrace door. She hadn't even looked that far down the road yet. Now she allowed herself a few minutes to ponder it, the kids growing up, seeking out an education, looking toward their future. What dreams would the children chase when they reached that point in their lives? Would they continue in Guardian or would they venture off and make their own path? She closed her eyes and tried to imagine where they would be, where she would be ten, fifteen, even twenty years down the road.

~~~~~

"Tough to think of that isn't it?" Amanda said from behind her. Marna started and spun around, her hand over her heart.

"Amanda, you really have to stop sneaking up on me like that." Amanda was sitting on the afghan she had left crumpled on the couch moments before.

"Oh come now, don't take all my fun away," she said, appearing at the opposite casing in the blink of an eye. *"It's bad enough I have to be dead isn't it?"* She pouted prettily and looked at the couch. *"And may I ask why, after what you've been through tonight, are you sleeping there instead of on that nice comfy bed in your room?"*

"I guess I have a thing for leather couches." She grinned and brought her eyes back to Amanda. *"What is it you want, or should I ask what are you up to?"* She raised her brow.

Amanda grinned and reached out to her. *"Take my hand, Marna, someone wishes to speak with you."*

Marna raised her brow. *"If I refuse?"*

Amanda shrugged. *"Then I guess I disturb your dreams all night and you wake up looking like the lead in a bad horror flick."* She grinned, and Marna chuckled, but she was intrigued. Bertha? Elise? Who in Amanda's realm of existence would want so desperately to talk to her that they would send Amanda to her at this time of night? *"Come, Little Sister. You need to take this journey with me tonight, and no, I'm not telling you anymore, because it would spoil the surprise."*

"Well, we wouldn't want that, now, would we?" Marna smiled and grasped her sister's offered hand. Almost immediately, she felt herself pulled through the familiar misty tunnel that delivered her to the sandy beach , she had come to accept as Amanda's temporary home, her vacation spot, a place of rest between stops until her work was done; whatever or whenever that would be.

Marna secretly hoped it wouldn't be soon, but she also knew that would be unfair to Amanda because she must long for that time to come when she could join her husband, Peter, and their parents. The place where eternal peace, love, and rest awaited her. She felt her feet sink into warm sand and opened her eyes. The sun was shining and the sky was a glorious blue. As if it would ever be any different here. The surf was soothing her soul as it gently lapped the beach, and the breeze had the sweet earthy smell of mid-Spring, Amanda's favorite time of year. She closed her eyes as the rays from the sun bathed her in their warmth. "Why would you even want to leave this place, Amanda? It's so peaceful."

"I still have work to do," she glanced at her sister's face turned up to the warmth of the sun. "Right now, that involves guiding you down a path you probably won't take on your own, Marny." Marna opened her eyes and brought them to Amanda's face.

"Come on," Amanda said, leading the way. Marna started following Amanda, her bare feet making indents in the sand as she moved. She looked up and stopped. She hadn't noticed it before, but there was someone sitting on a bench at the center of the beach. Marna gasped. Amanda turned toward her and studied her features. "Marna, what is it? That wasn't exactly the reaction I was expecting."

"No, this isn't real, this is a trick. You – you're not real." She started backing away. "How did you know about this place? Amanda's place?"

"Now, you start questioning what you see." Amanda raised her hands palms out toward her sister. She saw fear and puzzlement fill Marna's eyes. "Marna, sweetie, it's okay. This isn't a trick. This is real. I'm real." She pointed to the bench. "He's real." Marna shook her head, tears welled in her eyes and she backed away.

"No," she looked at the sky. "Keys, for God's sake, where are you?" She asked. "Tanner? Rose?" No soft voice answered her pleas. No psychic hotline opened in her mind. She looked at Amanda again, a tear rolling down her cheek.

The newcomer got up from the bench and started moving toward them. She recognized the stride. The way he held his body, the way he pushed his hands into his pockets as he moved toward them. The crooked smile that had won her heart when he had stood beside her in the rain, and that unruly dark hair her fingers had run through so many times during their years together. Love radiated from his eyes when he stopped before her. "Jeff," she managed to whisper though she fought to breathe.

"Hey." He just looked at her, didn't reach for her or grab at her. He wanted to give her the time to absorb it. The silence boomed around them like thunder.

"No. This can't be real." She stepped back wiping away her tears. Her body was as tense as a coiled snake ready to strike. He stopped his strides. "This is another trick by Lamontage," she accused. "This isn't real."

"Columbus day. Parks Terrace. 2044." Marna raised her hand to her mouth, the day he asked her to marry him. "You ordered the Rainy Day, Pork." More tears glistened in her eyes. Because it had been raining the day they had met, pouring for that matter, their meal choices of that night had always been a private joke. Lamontage would not have known that, it had been their secret. A detail she, herself, had forgotten until now. There was no way Lamontage could use that against her. The apparition that stood before her had to be Jeff. "And I ordered."

"Rain-boiled chicken," she whispered, as more tears came. "It really is you."

"Yes, Baby, it is." His smile lit up her entire world as it always had. He took her hand and kissed her fingers. "Walk with me?" She nodded and allowed him to lead her down the beach. Amanda slipped away.

When they had walked in silence for a while, glorious moments of serenity to Marna, if only she could stop time or remain here with him at her side; she stopped and stared out at the rolling waves, the soft breeze playing with the loose strands of her hair. She knew why he had come. "You've come to say goodbye," she simply said and searched his face with knowing eyes. It glowed with the peace she had only read about in Sunday school. A peace she still didn't quite understand, but saw in both his and Amanda's face. Both of them torn from their lives too soon, yet both trusting the unknown enough to move on, and trusting her enough to go forward, to let those left behind remember how much they had loved them.

He reached for her left hand and played with the stone of her engagement ring. "It's time, Baby, time for me to move on, and time for you to let go. You're making yourself vulnerable by holding on to us, to me."

She nodded., "I know." The words came out in a sob. " It's just so hard. They took so much from us. So much we were meant to do."

He shook his head. "We've done what we were meant to do, Marna. What you do from here is what you were meant to do without me." He moved some of her hair behind her shoulder. "What you and others were meant to do. Don't think of what you experience from here on as what was taken from us, but what is given to you and whoever will be beside you." She shook her head. "Shh." He placed his finger over her lips. She closed her eyes, relishing his touch. "Yes, Marna, you will find love again, and what you do together will be beyond what we could have even hoped for, but you have to let me go. Let us go -- to be able to get there." He caught a loose strand of her hair and brushed it behind her ear.

"Jeff, it's time," Amanda said. He nodded.

"No." Marna said, reaching for his hand and looking deep into his eyes, but she knew Amanda spoke the truth. It was time, time for him to move on and time to let go. "There's so much I want to say. So much, I want to ask you. Isaiah's having such a tough time right now, and I don't . . ." Jeff placed a finger over her lips again, and she closed her eyes not wanting to see him disappear from whatever they had right now.

"Look for the answers within yourself, Marna. They're there. You just have to be willing to listen."

"Jeff." Amanda said. He nodded again. Then he lowered his lips to Marna's and she felt his kiss to the depths of her soul. When the kiss stopped he pulled her close whispering in her ear, "One day we will be united again, my love, until then believe in yourself. Never forget that I love you." His whispered words echoed in the rolling sea. When Marna opened her eyes again, he was gone, and all she saw was a bright light fade out above the water.

"He's gone." Amanda said.

She nodded. "I know." She turned to look at her sister, wiping at the tears on her face. "I know." She let her eyes stray to the sea again.

"He wanted to give you closure. That's why he tapped into my energy. He had no abilities so he could only get to you through another psychic in this realm." She smiled. "He wanted to make sure you had the kind of closure the things of the world couldn't give you."

"I guess I should say thank you."

"You should, yes." Amanda didn't move toward her, sensing she needed the time. "But I won't require it."

"You never do."

"He's right you know. You will find love again. Another who is meant to do wondrous things with you."

"So you both say." Marna turned to look at her. "I suppose one day, I may even agree with you."

"When you're ready, Marna. Not until." Amanda approached her, and reached for her hand. "It's time to go back now."

Marna nodded, and took her sister's hand, then paused. "How do you handle it Amanda?"

"Handle what?"

"The separation from Pete? The loneliness?"

Amanda took a breath. "I just take it one assignment at a time, Marna. I know I still have things to do before I can rest, but I know he waits for me. Now he and Jeff can fish all they want while they wait for us." They chuckled. "The point is, Marna, you aren't alone in this. I'm meant to be with you until you don't need me anymore and I'm not pushing to finish my guardianship." Amanda smiled. "And when the time comes for me to move on, I'll know that you and my children will be well looked after by the right person,"

"You're that confident?"

"I have no reason not to be." Smiling, Amanda raised closed eyes to the blue, blue sky and they were pulled into the mist.

~~~~~

The next thing Marna knew, she woke up on her couch, in the living room of the apartment. She felt no pain of loss. No regret of what could have been. Just peace, balance and a closure she hadn't felt since that horrible night on the floor of Bradshaw's kitchen when her whole world just slipped from her grasp.

"Until we meet again, Jeff. I love you," and for the first time in months, Marna slipped into a sleep so restful that she had no dreams or disturbances, and she didn't even feel the blanket of security that Tanner wrapped around her. He smiled as he felt the peace radiate around her. A peace so strong, so total that even from his apartment two doors down, he sensed it

*****

Marna gazed at the Alps through her bedroom window. Her mind tumbled through her late night visit with Jeff and Amanda repeatedly. She tried to dismiss it as a dream, but she knew it was real. Jeff had said goodbye and oddly enough, she didn't feel the crippling pain she thought she would when she had stood by the rolling sea as the last of his essence had faded away. She had finally let him go. She glanced down at her ring finger at Jeff's modest teardrop diamond, and the matching embedded wedding band winked back at her. She had not taken it off since he had placed them there four years before, but now, as her eyes lifted to the black box sitting beside her prop set, she slipped them off and placed them in the velvet bed, lifting them to look at them. One day she would pass them on to one of the girls. Until then, she would keep them safe.

Sighing, she placed them in a hidden compartment in her suitcase, then slipped the Cubic Zirconium set on her finger and watched as they glittered in the sunrays that streamed through her window. If people didn't look too closely, they would buy the realism. She shrugged and turned toward the mirror, did her hair in a French twist, and appraised her outfit. For today's lunch excursion, she had chosen a spandex/cotton mix, Robin's egg blue, dress with spaghetti straps coming just above her knees with an off white, three-quarter sleeve, jacket. It hugged her curves, and screamed designer threads. Her matching Stiletto-heeled sandals gave her about four inches in height and highlighted her muscled calves. She took a complete turn to make sure she looked the part of a much younger, much richer, business tycoon's wife and reached for her matching clutch on the bed.

Today, she and Rose were going to lunch at the restaurant Kyle had mentioned in his journal. Tanner was taking the children to a matinee at the neighborhood theater and then to the park to meet the neighborhood Nannies. Keys was going to be at an upscale commercial building to put the final touches on their cover. He was going to rent an office for their new Swiss headquarters for an online social networking site.

Isaiah and the twins were going to help him with that part of the family's cover. They were going to be the first profiles on the site's network and try to use it to make a connection to Arella and Heinderick. Demi and Bryan would be the first adults to try and reach out to the handlers. Keys had people working on a deep cover for them already. Specialists from the task force would monitor and research all parties that signed up. They would also be watching for members with suspected or known Liberatores connections. Taking a final look in the mirror, she left the room and headed toward the kitchen to wait for Rose.

Keys was pouring a coffee for himself when she stepped into the living room and looked toward the kitchen. "Make yourself right at home, Boss."

"Thank you, I did." He raised his cup in salute to her. "Would you like one?"

"Sounds lovely." She reached out and squeezed Hannah's shoulder as she passed her, sitting in the overstuffed chair. Hannah looked up from her English book and grinned, then returned to her painstaking steps of putting together a five-paragraph essay.

"Where are the others?" she asked Elizabeth, who used her telekinesis to lift the other living room chair and used the Swiffer sweeper to clean underneath it.

"Getting ready to go to the park with Nanny Tanner."

Marna chuckled. "Don't call him that."

"Well that is who he is on this trip?" She grinned.

Marna smiled. "Yes, but you still need to respect him."

Elizabeth rolled her eyes, but nodded. "You're taking all their fun away, Dear." Keys said in a soothing fake husband kind of way, while he sipped coffee by the counter.

"Or teaching them to respect their elders," she caught his eyes as she entered the kitchen and accepted the coffee he offered her. "Depends on how you look at it or who is making the request."

"Got me there," he lifted his cup in surrender and took another sip. "You look lovely by the way."

"Just trying to stay in character." His eyes caught sight of the dummy wedding set on her left hand as she placed her clutch purse on the table, and reached into the fridge for some leftover breakfast cheese to offer him. Then she sat at the table. "How am I doing?"

"Very well," He sat across from her, "Herrn Zorich called this morning, wanted to know how you were.

Marna sat the cup down and smiled sadly. "I see," she rounded her cup with both her hands. "I take it we didn't raise any suspicions."

He shook his head. "No, just the opposite, Herrn Zorich and his wife have invited us to their home for a dinner party next week to make up for the way things turned out."

"What did you tell them?"

"The truth, that we would be leaving to go back home by the weekend, and would have to respectfully decline their generous offer."

"And?"

"They thought maybe a trip to the theater later this week. They have a box and thought you might be interested in an opera."

"Persistent," Marna took up a slice of cheese and chased it down with another swallow of coffee. "How are we going to dodge the bullet without raising suspicions?"

"I'll think of something," he said, looking at her. "We have to keep your identity under wraps."

"Well, I've been meaning to color my hair. Maybe now would be the perfect opportunity," she grinned and looked sideways at him. "What's your feeling about blondes, Dear?"

He choked on his coffee. Marna leaned back looking at him, patiently waiting. When he could breathe again, she raised her brow in expectation. "Let's not do anything drastic, Marna," he said drawing in deep breaths. "Guardian has many ways of changing looks without going to extremes." He grinned. "Besides, I prefer redheads." Before she could reply, her doorbell rang. "Hmmm, saved by the bell," he said, taking a cleansing breath.

She smiled, got up, and went to answer the door. Tanner took a step back when the door swung open. She raised a quizzical brow. "Hello, Tanner. You just saved Keys from having to talk about his favorite attributes in a mate."

Tanner cleared his throat and stepped into the room, skirting Marna. "I'm sure you temporarily fit every one of them," he said, blinking back the burning desire in his eyes. Marna looked different this morning, and it wasn't just the way her outfit hugged her body enough to make a man want to explore every curve underneath it. It was her composure, the lightness in her speech. He couldn't read auras like Little Mary, but he bet Marna's would dictate relaxation and peace. That's what it was. She seemed at peace with life, herself, and the shadow that had lingered around her since Jeff's death.

"Thank you." She closed the door and turned her attention to Keys. "See, Keys, now there's a man who knows how to compliment a lady." She winked at Tanner. "Maybe you should take some lessons from him."

"I'll schedule that as soon as we return stateside." Keys stood up chuckling, and glanced at his watch. "As of right now, My Dear, I have to take the next step in our facade. You enjoy your lunch and try to keep your admiring groupies at the restaurant. Wouldn't want any strays following you home."

"What's that supposed to mean?" She queried.

"Well, my dear, you do look lovely in that dress." He turned and winked at Tanner. "Doesn't she, Son?" Tanner cleared his throat and nodded, not sure how to answer. Keys had seen the effect Marna had on him. It had been a brief response, but it was there. Tanner looked toward the floor. Keys patted his bicep before he left. "I'll stop by tonight." He said to Marna before he left.

"Hmmm. . . Guess the old goat does still have it in him." She grinned.

"Guess so." He caught her gaze with his own. For the first time, she seemed to notice how bright his eyes actually were and how they foretold the emotions within the person, Gateway to the Soul she thought and smiled.

"Hmmm . . ." She felt shaky and unsure of herself so she turned away to look around the kitchen. "I'll go let the kids know you're here." He nodded. She left him in the kitchen while he took a cleansing breath to regain his composure. She returned to tidy up the kitchen and place the cups in the dishwasher. He stepped aside as she started the machine. Her perfume filled his senses. "What are your plans today?" She asked as she leaned a hip against the machine, feeling in control once again.

"Infiltrate the Nanny defense at the front line." He grinned as he moved the subject to a much lighter topic. She chuckled, shaking her head.

"Good luck with that," she smiled, and turned her attention to the children as they all gathered in the kitchen, Isaiah trailing behind. She sighed and slid her gaze toward Tanner. He shook his head and silently told her not to worry about the boy's brooding. She nodded, kissed Mary, Jacob and the triplets on the forehead before they all trooped out of the apartment. "Good luck with that too," she whispered before closing the door and then finished tidying up the kitchen.

*****

Marna smiled at the waiter, while he seated she and Rose at a table by the window, overlooking the busy epic center of Zurich and handed them their menus. "Would you Ladies care for a drink?" The waiter asked with a heavy German accent.

"Renee?" Marna asked, using Rose's cover name. Her sister looked lovely in the salmon colored skirt set and matching pumps, she had chosen for their lunch date. It came to her knees, and complimented her athletic build. She slipped off her waist jacket, showing the definition in her muscled biceps, when she placed her forearms on the table. She had chosen to wear her hair in a French Braid and she carried a matching clutch. She finished the look with diamond stud earrings, similar in style to what Marna's were. The only difference was Marna chose to wear a string of pearls, while Rose chose a simple silver chain.

"I think I'd like some Chardonnay, white, please." Rose answered.

"I'll have the same." Marna stated, and then opened up her menu, looking for the English section of the laminated folder.

"Place looks pricey." Rose stated, glancing around rather cautiously.

"That's what expense accounts are for, Sis." She grinned, catching Rose's eye.

"Expense account?"

"Yep." Marna pulled a credit card from the front pocket of her clutch. "Guardian card."

"huh. The only expense account I've had was for nursing conferences and to us, **Croydens Family Dining** was splurging. This," she held her hands, palms up to indicate the dining room, "is totally foreign to me."

"Welcome to the good things in life." Marna grinned

Rose chuckled, and then opened her own menu, looking over the lunch specials. "Hear anything?"

"Haven't started eavesdropping yet," she kept her eyes on the menu as the waiter brought their drinks and placed them before them.

"Are you ready to order yet?"

"Could you give us a few more minutes, please?" Marna requested.

"Certainly," the waiter left, but stayed within their line of sight so they could flag him over when they were ready.

"Great, a babysitter." Rose said.

"Pardon," Marna looked at her and smiled like they were having a conversation about the menu.

"Waiter. Hovering."

Marna casually scanned the room and caught sight of him. "Yep," she returned her attention to the menu. "Alpine Macaroni. Now that looks delicious." She folded her menu before her and took a sip of her drink. "What about you?" Their hopeful waiter stood ready to move as soon as Rose put her menu down.

"I think I'm going to go with the Grison beef stew and some bread." She grinned. "That way I can pretend that I'm not spending as much on lunch as it costs to reserve a plate in a presidential fund raiser."

They chuckled. "Don't worry about it. Look at it as sort of a stake out if it makes you feel any better. We are working after all," Marna said, flagging the waiter.

With hardly any effort at all, his fluid movements brought him gracefully to their sides. He took their orders, and then glided out of sight. "Now that's just creepy," she said as she watched him disappear through the swinging kitchen doors.

Rose chuckled. "Get anything?"

"Not yet." She tilted her head and focused. Snippets of conversation drifted in and out of her range of hearing.

"I hear they're separating."

"Really?"

"I don't know what to do Momma. All he does is get into trouble."

"What's the teacher say?"

"Adolescent hormones." Marna almost laughed, glad to know she wasn't the only one dealing with a strung out teen.

"Who's the new meat in town?"

"I don't know, but I sure would like to . . ." Marna felt herself blush at the various ways the young man would like to get to know the new mail clerk at his office. Rose raised a brow. Marna waved her off and quickly moved on.

"They killed Abbud, Mother. . . What am I going to do? . . . They will be coming for me next . . . How am I supposed to protect her?" Marna stopped and looked around. She hoped to see the woman she had just heard. Rose recognized the look threading through her features and raised a quizzical brow.

"What is it?" she whispered.

"Not sure yet." Marna whispered, careful to look around the room and make sure there wasn't another person in the room, who seemed to be listening too. "I need to make a phone call." She pulled her GPC out of her clutch. "Watch and make sure no one follows me." She smiled. "If they do, spill the Chardonnay on them."

"Oh, Marna, not the Chardonnay." Rose looked pained.

Marna left the table and looked at her phone, as if she was trying to get a signal. After looking back at Rose, who discreetly shook her head, she sidestepped into what looked like a cloakroom where, consequently, she could see the whole dining room without someone seeing her. She continued her search. She saw several people on their phones, video phones and GPCs, but a woman at the bar drew her attention. She was hunched over a cup of tea sitting before her, holding a phone tightly to her ear, wearing a uniform similar to other restaurant staff. She was slight of build, with a long dark braid that brushed her hips. The hand that held the phone was closest to Marna and it was dark-skinned with red polished nails. She focused trying to pick up the conversation again.

*****

"*No, Mother, I have to leave here. They will be coming for me. I'm risking a lot calling you. . . When can you wire it? Enough to get train tickets for Arella and me . . . We will be wearing Abaya with veil. . . Yes Momma, we will stay in the apartment. . . See you soon . . .*" The conversation stopped. Marna watched the woman slip her phone into her back pocket and push herself away from the bar.

The woman was thirtyish, Arabic, and making her way toward the back of the restaurant where it divided into two hallways. She turned her face toward the entrance of the restaurant. Marna raised her phone and took her picture. She scrutinized the photo. She couldn't be sure, the face was thinner and more drawn than the pictures at the briefing but she suspected it to be Arella's handler. She dialed Keys' number. He picked it up on the third ring. She heard laughter in the background.

"Yes, Darling." He said, playing the role. She heard his muffled, "Excuse me," and then she heard the background voices become more distant. "What is it, Marna?"

"Keys, I'm sending you a picture. I think it's Arella's Handler, but I won't swear to it. Can you run facial recognition on your tablet? I heard her making plans with her mother to take the train with Arella. She told her mother she would recognize them because they would be dressed in Abaya with a veil."

"That's a type of Islamic clothing for women and it sounds like she's planning on adding a face veil so nobody can recognize them. She's going to run."

"It sounds like she's trying to protect Arella."

"Yes, it does, but I'm afraid she may put herself and the child in more danger. In a disguise like that, she may stand out more than blend."

"What do you want me to do?"

"Stay on her. I'll wrap things up here and offer you and Rose backup. I'll send Ventura the picture for definite identification and then send him, Heidi, Demi and Bryan over to give you some more back up."

Just then, the restaurant door swung open and four men in fatigues came in. Marna sensed their energy instantly. She knew Lamontage had sent them. She threw up her cloak. "You better hurry, Keys. I have a feeling things here are going to deteriorate fast. We just got company." She hung up on his orders for her and Rose to stand down until backup arrived, and sent out a message to her sister. Raquel was her clone, if they saw her, their cover was blown and her sister could be in serious trouble. *Rose, get away from the table! Cloak up and stay out of sight, now!*

Rose grabbed her bag, opened it to start searching for something, got up from her seat, and moved toward the back of the restaurant. She slipped into the restroom, thankful it wasn't coin oriented like the ones at the bus and train stops, and raised her cloak. *Marna, what's going on?*

Lamontage just sent lunch guests.

What?

Keys is on his way, and he's sending a team, but until then you and I are the only ones to build a wall of defense.

What? Rose looked around the bathroom.

Arella and her handler are here somewhere, she's trying to escape. Lamontage somehow found out about her desperate attempt to get out of Dodge. He sent his men to collect Arella, and my guess is to kill her handler. Where are you?

Restroom.

Meet me in the hallway outside the door. I'm on my way. She closed her channel and weaved around the tables. She saw the four men sitting at a table in tight conversation, eyeing the back hallway. Great they knew where to look. "Come on Keys," she whispered as she eyed the couple sitting at the table next to theirs holding hands. "How sweet," she said under her breath. A waiter was coming the other way with an order of pasta and two full glasses of red wine. "Perfect, though I am sorry to spoil the mood." Under the cover of her cloak, she quickly put her foot into the path of the waiter and tripped him. The pasta and wine dumped onto the table and into the laps of the young couple. The couple jumped up and started yelling at the waiter, delivering a long string of words that Marna would recognize in any language. The four men looked their way and laughed. It had worked. They were amused and kept watch for the outcome.

She slipped into the hallway undetected and dropped her cloak. Rose dropped hers and went to join her. "What are we going to do?"

"Find the apartment that Kyle couldn't." We need to get the Handler and Arella to safety and under Guardian protection. Come on." Joining hands to strengthen their abilities and mold them together, they made their way down the hall and up some stairs to a closed, private dining area.

*****

Tanner made his way to the benches where the other nannies sat, and claimed one that was empty. "I was wondering if you would be coming back with your brood." A young woman, dressed modestly in a black skirt and gray sweater, approached him. He recognized her as one he had spoken to the last time they had come.

He smiled and folded his paper, placing it in his lap. Then he stretched his arm out on the back of the bench and let his eyes wander to Mary and Jacob on the swings. "They've got to get out or they start bouncing off the walls."

"I hear you there." The other nannies grinned and whispered to each other. He let his eyes stray their way then brought them back to the girl before him. He guessed her to be 23, with red ringlets brought up in a tasteful bun, Irish blue eyes and pale skin with a smattering of freckles flecked across her cheeks and the bridge of her nose. "May I sit?" She queried.

"Please." He made room for her on the bench. He had dressed modestly in a pair of gray khakis and a white dress shirt. "Name's Tanner and yours?"

"Polly." He chuckled. "I know, what else, huh?" She shrugged and chuckled herself. "My mother loved the Pollyanna book as a child, so she named me after the heroine. I shortened it to Polly, as I got older. You'd be amazed at what they come up with in school when you've been named after a book." He could hear the Irish lilt in her voice and occasionally a word would slip out that betrayed her Irish heritage.

"Kids can be cruel."

"Ye bet your hide they can be which is why I became a nanny. Guess I wanted to protect kids from the viciousness of others." She smiled, squinted against the sun, and brought them back to his. "What's your reasoning? It hasn't historically been a man's career choice, now has it?"

"It's 2048 and we still quibble over what a man's job is vs. what a woman's job is?" He raised a brow then did another head check on the kids. He saw Isaiah by himself, brooding once again. "Got a cure for that?" He nodded his head toward Isaiah.

"Git him a girlfriend," she said with a grin.

He couldn't help but grin back. "That's your best answer." He brought his eyes back to hers. "Really?"

She chuckled. "Come on, his parents have even denied him the right to have the traditional crush on his teacher or nanny phase by hiring you. The lad's dying over there." Tanner couldn't help but laugh.

"You have an unusual outlook on things, Miss Polly." He shook his head and brought his eyes back to hers, which sparkled with an innocent youthfulness he found very appealing.

"So I've been told." She held his gaze. "You haven't answered my question, Mr. Tanner."

"Hmm, and what is that?"

"Why a nanny?"

"I like kids," he stated flatly, looking at her. "And where else would I be able to meet one as charming as you?"

"Oh my." She waved her hand in front of her face, and the other nannies giggled. "You're just raisin' me body temp' thar', Nanny Tanner." She grinned. "Maybe we should go out for drinks later to see if we can cool it down."

He grinned as his eyes sought out Mary, whom he had lost sight of for a moment. He got up and frantically scanned the grounds for her. "Mary!"

"Right here!" she yelled as she popped her head through the tunnel at the top of the jungle gym slide.

"She's a cute lil' bugger." Polly said. "Reminds me of another little one who used to come here, but her hair wasn't so dark and didn't have the curls."

"Really?" Tanner turned toward her, hiding the anticipation well.

"Yeah. What was her name? Abella, Amelia, Arella! That's it. She was adorable, but her parents were the hovering kind, Middle Eastern I think. I remember her because she was American, most likely adopted. Her parents didn't like her talking to strangers much."

"Well some parents are a little more anxious then others."

"Yeah, I guess. Oh well, it's been a while, going on a few months now since I've seen them here, but if it weren't for the hair, they could be sisters."

"They say everyone has a double."

"I guess they do." She smiled at his profile as he watched Mary use the slide. "So how about it?"

"Hmm, what's that?"

"Drinks after you get off duty."

He ran a hand over the back of his neck as if he was thinking it over then shrugged. Maybe he could get some more information from her. "I think that is probably the best invitation I've gotten in a long time." Polly smiled. "Sure. Give me your number and I'll call you."

"Give me your hand." He obliged and she pulled a pen out of a pocket in her skirt, touched the tip with her tongue and wrote her phone number on his palm. "I git off at seven," she said.

"I'll keep that in mind." He felt his phone vibrate in his pocket, and lifted it to look at the screen. It was Keys. "If you'll excuse me, I have to take this. It's the boss."

"Sure thing, Nanny Tanner." She put her hands behind her back and rejoined the other girls. They slapped high fives. He brought the phone to his ear.

"Yeah."

"Tanner, how's it going?"

He turned to look toward the women. Polly winked at him. He grinned and turned back. "Not bad. I've made a connection or two. How's Marna doing on her end?"

"She's at the restaurant believed to be the last residence of Arella and her Handlers, but Liberatores knows of it too. Four of them just showed up. Rose and she are trying to keep a low profile, but they need backup. Can you get the kids back to the apartment and join us? I can't seem to contact Demi and Bryan. They left on assignment to try and find leads to Heinderick."

"On my way." Quickly he hung up the phone to round up the kids and head back toward the apartment. As he climbed behind the steering wheel of the van, he dialed Kurt and asked him to be at the apartment so he could take over with the children, then he shifted the van into drive and turned into traffic. trying hard to hide his anxiety from the kids.

*****

Rose moved around the kitchen quietly so as not to alarm anyone responsible for the space. She opened doors to rooms and investigated their darkened depths. She hoped to find a door within them. One that was using the pantries or pots and pan closets as a cover, but she found none. Drawing in a breath and letting it out in one long, quiet sigh, she gave up and stepped out of the last accessible one, silently hoping Marna was having better luck. *Marna, no luck in here, what about your end?* There was no reply and when she tried to make a connection, all she got was silence. Something was wrong.

She retraced her steps and looked through the porthole style window in the swinging door. Her breath caught in her throat. Marna was on her knees, back against the wall. A man was standing above her, taser in hand imprisoning her sister in some kind of electronic force field created by the purple stream coming from it. They must have modified it to imprison not only Marna, but her abilities as well. Rose moved further back into the kitchen to avoid detection. Thoughts started going through her mind. She tried to think of a way to distract them, if only long enough for their backup to arrive. Backup! She had to let them know of this new development. However, opening a channel could mean them discovering her, if there was a Tracker amongst the soldiers in the other room. She reached for her phone and slipped noiselessly into one of the pantries, closing the door quietly. She hit speed dial. Keys picked up. "Rose. Development?"

"Keys, what's your ETA?" The tone in her voice alone was enough to alarm him. Reception was poor, and there was no background noise one would typically get in a restaurant, but the main thing that made his stomach clench was that it was Rose on the phone, not Marna.

"What's happened, Rose?" His foot pressed down on the gas and he swung out and around the slower Fiat in front of him. Tanner was in the car behind him, and he followed his action. Something was wrong.

"The men, they have Marna in some kind of purple force field. They've blocked her abilities."

He jerked the wheel left to exit off the highway. "Dammit! I thought I told you two to lay low!" He swerved\to avoid a collision with another car in the opposite lane as he skirted around a southbound car turning off the main road. "Where are you?"

"I'm in a pantry, in a commercial kitchen."

"Tell me what you saw, exactly." He pressed the pedal to beat a light and get through an intersection. The convoy behind him did as well. Rose started to explain things to him.

In the car behind Keys, Tanner felt his heart plummet. His anxiety turned to a cold ball of fear in the pit of his stomach. The girls were in trouble. Keys had started driving as if it was a life or death situation. He debated with himself about whether he should try to open a communication channel to Marna, find out if she was okay. His concern for her well-being won over his common sense as a Guardian agent. He strengthened his shield and readied himself to send out an extra layer of protection to Marna if he was able. *Marna? What's going on?* She didn't answer. It was as if he had connected to a dark abyss. *Marna? For God's sake, answer me.* He focused hard, hoping to get something back.

C-can't mo-ove.

What's going on?

El. . .tic . bar . . . . r . . . bl . . . . k . . .ng . . . .bil . . . .ties. The connection ended before he could get a lock on her to shield her. His phone vibrated in his console.

He reached out and hit the car connection button. "Yeah, Keys." He said breathlessly.

"Tanner, the girls are in trouble."

"I know. I just contacted Marna. She sounded like she was in pain. I got that she couldn't move, and I think something about a barrier. What the hell is going on?" he demanded as he jerked left to follow Keys.

"Liberatores attacked at the restaurant," he said, honking at a couple of kids who jumped back up on a sidewalk as he raced by them over a crosswalk. "I've contacted the authorities in the area. They're already at the restaurant trying to clear out the lower level dining room without warning the men. I've talked to Rose. She said the men have some kind of altered taser beam on Marna that has her encircled in a type of electric field. It's rendering her helpless. Rose is hiding in some kind of closet. She's watching things from a safe distance. I told her to observe until we get there. We don't want them getting control of them both. There are too many of them."

"Dammit !" Tanner hit his steering wheel in unbridled furry. "How did they get the drop on her? Wasn't she using her cloak?"

"She had dropped it to search for the door to the apartment." He sighed. "We're almost there, Son, keep your head about you. If you go in there guns blazing, you could be signing her death warrant."

"Don't worry about me, Keys. I'll keep myself straight. Worry about a way to get to them before they see us coming and hurt Marna." They ended the conversation as the restaurant loomed before them. Unmarked vehicles were scattered about the parking lot, men he recognized from the briefing escorted patrons and employees quietly out of the building. The Guardian team pulled their vehicles into the parking lot and checked in with the Fedpol officer in charge.

Keys shook hands with him and introduced the team. "Did you bring the blue prints?"

"Yes," He brought them to his car and pointed out an area circled in red. "We believe they are here. This is a private banquet room upstairs reserved for weddings and special occasions." He drew in a breath, glancing sideways at the older man. "These women trapped with the Liberatores, they are good agents, no?"

"Two of my best."

"Then they will know how to handle themselves in a crisis, yes?"

"Yeah."

"That is good, because Liberatores, they are not known for taking much pity on enemies."

"I'm aware of that, Kent." Keys bent over the blueprints. He pointed to the area circled in red. "That's the banquet room and kitchen?" Kent nodded. He noticed certain things that spoke how experienced the Fedpol were at dealing with the Liberatores. There were four sets of windows on the east side of the room, and Fedpol had parked all the cars strategically on the west side to hide their presence. Kent had discretely positioned officers at key points, but blended them well with the surroundings so the men upstairs would not know what was going on if they happened to look out the window. He was pleased with their strategy. His finger traced an invisible line to some extended rooms that had one entrance door and one window on the east side and a fire escape. He grinned. "What's this right here?"

"Storage rooms, maybe."

"Maybe," but Keys knew differently. That was the apartment. Rose must have missed it. He nodded and walked a few paces away before taking out his phone. Tanner's eyes looked toward the upper level, trying to scrutinize their point of entrance to rescue the sisters. "Well at least they won't know we're here," Ventura said, looking around. "Looks like the Fedpol are well rehearsed in this type of situation.

"As long as they stay engrossed in what they're doing up there and don't retreat." He knew that eventually they would have to come back down and his heart sank. He knew they did not intend to leave Marna behind. Her only hope was that Rose could keep things under control until they could get up there and offer their support.

Keys typed quickly on his GPC keyboard. *Apartment off kitchen--north-northwest--Search, breach and offer security, but do not attempt escape. Guardian back up is assessing the situation for extraction.*

*****

Rose moved out of the pantry and quietly made her way back to the door, peeking through to check out the situation. Marna had her eyes closed, and concentration etched into her features. She saw the force field dim slightly, a smile barely audible on her sister's face, but it all left as quickly as it came. Marna discreetly looked toward the kitchen. She was trying to let Rose know something. Rose felt her phone vibrate. She moved back against the wall and looked at her screen. Sighing, she moved away from the door and fell back against the wall. The Calvary was here. She opened her phone and printed one simple word. *Hurry.*

She looked out the window, closed her eyes, and focused. She prayed no Tracker was among the soldiers. When she attempted to connect with Marna, she confronted the dark abyss as well, but she could see the electronic field dim. *I know where the apartment is. Guardian backup outside.* Marna looked at her captor, saw he was busy looking toward the other three as they continued their search, and then she moved her head toward Rose.

She felt Marna's transmission grow stronger. *Get Arella. . .n. . . get out!*

Her captor looked toward her and saw the dimness of the field. "There is someone else here !" Involuntarily Marna looked toward the kitchen. "In there!" he ordered. "You two, go get them!"

Rose opened a connection to Keys. *They made me!* She tucked her phone into her pocket and shut down all transmissions. She pulled her Glock 19 from her clutch, and then she waited until the approaching men were close enough to the door then kicked it into them, and watched as they stumbled backwards. Raising her gun she fired a few shots to cover herself, and waved her hand toward the Taser. It flew from the captor's hand.

The force field broken, Marna took a deep breath and quickly rolled away from the men and under a nearby table. She was too weak to help Rose, so the best thing for her to do was try to stay out of sight and reach of the enemy so she did not compromise her. She closed her eyes and laid her head against the wall, breathing deeply. Her pulse was irregular and dizziness accompanied the tingling in her body, and then the nausea set in. She swallowed hard, closed her eyes and willed her body to return to regular functions.

Rose raised her hand again and pulled the taser toward her as the soldier tried to retrieve it. Then she fired a few more shots, forcing the men to take cover before she vaulted over a nearby table and reloaded. She listened intently for approaching footfalls. The next thing she knew, she was lifted by her arm and swung in a half circle, before her attacker let go and she flew into a nearby wall. Her head hit plaster and her gun flew out of her hand, and skittered under a nearby table.

Shaking her head to clear it, she saw him coming at her again. She grabbed the legs of a nearby stool and slammed it into the head of the attacker closer to her. He fell to the floor. Then she rolled over and pushed herself to her feet, swinging around and kick-boxing the second one toward the stairs, watching as he tripped over his fallen commrade and tumble down them. The first one, recovering from the stool attack dived for the Taser and aimed it at her, she dived for her own gun as the beam hit the wall. Then she rolled over shooting the the man with the Taser as ge aimed for another shot. He fell foward. Rose again waved the Taser toward her and picked it up, this time, tucking it into her waist band. *Marna, where are you?* She opened the connection as she heard more shots from below. She raised her hand to the back of her head and winced as she felt the stickiness of her own blood on her hand. Great, she was going to need stitches, she was sure of that.

Rose, get Arella and get out! Rose peaked around the table. The leader half dragged, half-walked Marna backwards with a Magnum 45 barrel to her head. "You leave or I kill her."

Running feet on the steps caused Rose to blow out a breath in relief. The Calvary had arrived. Keys was the first one on the landing. He ducked below the protective wall, holding up a hand for the others to check their approach, catching sight of the man on the floor. His eyes saw the blood on the wall and frantically searched for Rose, he caught sight of her behind a wet bar. He raised a brow and she nodded her head. Then he spoke to their adversary. "There is no way out. Fedpol has surrounded the building and two of your men are already dead. Let her go and you live." Holding his gun before him, Keys stepped into the banquet room and kept the soldier in his sight, saying. "You hurt her and you die."

"I do not fear you." The soldier said. Rose came from behind the bar gun in hand, aimed at the soldier. Tanner, Schafer and Ventura came from behind Keys and fanned out on either side of the soldier. Shafer looked at Roses head.

"You good?" she asked.

"I'm fine," She assured her, never taking her aim off the soldier.

Keys picked up his conversation with the soldier again, after a wary glance at Rose. "You don't have to, but there are countless agents and locals out there who want a piece of Liberatores and they don't care which piece they get, because in their eyes, every one of you are responsible for the number of good men and women they've had to bury over the course of three decades now. So you can take your chances and go through that window behind you, or you can take your chances with me." Several red beams showed up on the boy's shirt and forehead.

"Will you look at that? You're lit up like a Christmas tree, Son, Make one wrong move and you'll have enough holes in you to classify as Swiss cheese." The man moved his eyes around nervously. "And let's say you do make an escape. You've failed your mission. You'll have to face Lamontage." The boy's posture changed. "Oh yeah, we know about him. He and I go way back. I know what he can do to a person, how he can turn your insides to mush and make a man cry out in so much pain, he'd rather die than continue to feel it."

"But Pierre doesn't allow that, does he? No. He'll bring you to the brink and make you wish for it, and then he'll stop. He'll do it several times before he mercifully gets tired of the game and finish the job." Sweat started beading on his forehead. "Because I can tell you right now, boy, you will fail. There is no way I'm letting you walk out of here with her." He raised his gun. "I'll kill you myself first." All the guns in the room took aim. Marna closed her eyes. The soldier's hold faltered.

Marna had a split second to act and she did. She stomped on his foot, elbowed him in the stomach, and twisted away from him to give enough space between them for Keys to seize the opportunity and put a bullet in his hand. The gun flew from his grasp as he cried out in pain. Rose took him down with a shot to his knee. He crumbled like a broken doll, dragging Marna down with him and valiantly reached for his weapon. "I don't think so!" Rose cried, waving the gun toward Ventura. Tanner grabbed Marna's hand, pulling her to her feet and holding her against him with one arm circled protectively around her shoulders, as she leaned into him for the support as much as comfort. He kept his weapon on the soldier with the other. Rose faltered and Keys moved in to assist her into a chair as Ventura grabbed the gun, put it in his waist band and Heidi covered him while he cuffed the man.

Keys lifted his radio to his lips. "Building secure. We need medics in the banquet room, now." He grabbed a towel, and looked over Rose's head wound, then he gently pressed the cloth to it. When the medic came upstairs, he gave him his orders then asked Heidi to sit with her. He made his way to Marna whoTanner had assisted onto a nearby chair. "Are you all right?"

Marna nodded. "Yeah, I'm just a little wiped is all." She looked toward her sister. "What about Rose?"

"No stitches. The medic is gluing the wound up now, but I'll send her home with orders to rest for the night. Kurt will take good care of her." Marna nodded and watched as Rose got up and moved toward them. Other than the slight falter earlier, she had bounced back. For someone who didn't want a full time agent's position, Rose was made for it.

"Did you get them all?"

"one dead downstairs, one dead up here and one in custody."

"Wait a minute." Rose interrupted, "that's only three." Keys nodded. "There's one missing. There were four. He must have slipped by when I was pinned behind the buffet table." A shot rang out from the direction of the kitchen.

"Arella !" Marna cried, stood up, but her legs wouldn't hold her, she stumbled. Tanner caught her, and sat her back down.

"Stay with her." Keys said to Tanner as reinforcements from the other task force teams came up the stairs. "The rest of you with me." Marna watched anxiously as Ventura, Heidi, Rose and Keys pushed their way into the kitchen.

"God, please don't let them be too late." Tanner put his arm around her and she laid her head on his shoulder. He pulled her close, dropped a kiss on the top of her head, and waited for the emergency personnel to come and check her out.

Chapter Seven

When the Guardian team slammed through the kitchen door, a quick glance around showed them what Rose had missed. On the wall that was facing east, there was a door between two baker's racks. A security door, with ,a digital keypad lock, was in place . Rose had thought it to be a vault of some kind so she had passed it by. "Of course," she said. Now the door stood partially open because, making a big gaping whole in the wall and the keyboard hung by a couple of wires.

"Guess they forgot their key," Ventura said as he pulled his gun, and the others did the same.

Keys motioned Ventura and Heidi to one side of the door, Heidi low, Ventura high, and then he signaled Rose to be low on his side. Ventura rose three fingers, counting down. When he folded the last finger down, he spun on his left foot, lifted his right, and hit the door hard, leading the charge and ducked into the shadow of a small entry hall, just before the fourth Liberatores soldier took the first shot. The other three-team members moved in as Ventura pinned him down with three shots to give the others time to get into position.

"Guardian WIT!" Keys yelled, "Give it up or go down like the others !" The man returned fire. They took cover on either side of the open doorway, leading into the small kitchen. Their quarry started running for the bedroom. The one room in the four-room-apartment, with the only window. It was large enough for a person to get through but small enough for the oak wardrobe, standing beside it, to successfully block. The window had no bars, as was customary for other buildings in the country, and someone had opened the shutters, leaving the curtains blowing in the breeze. Ventura assessed the situation with a quick eye scan.

"Rose! Window! Heidi! Cover !" Ventura yelled as they moved in. Ventura ran forward as Heidi forced the soldier to duck for cover behind the bedroom door by riddling the walls around it with bullets. Ventura reached the kitchen table, tipping it over then covered Heidi as she ran to join him. Rose focused on the wardrobe and it quickly slid in front of the window. Ventura emptied his Magazine as Keys and Rose moved behind a counter to the left of the table and slightly ahead of them. "Reload !" He called out as he switched places with Heidi, and she took over his point position.

The soldier yelled out a string of curses, fired more shots at them and rolled over the bed, placed horizontal to their position, falling into the space on the other side. "I will die before I betray the Master!" he yelled.

"Son, you have nowhere to go. The only way out is by us. The window is closed off."

"Then I will die where I stand!"

"Be reasonable, Son. Pierre doesn't deserve your loyalty. Do you really think he will welcome you back after this? You failed your mission, failed to bring him what he asked" The soldier did not answer. "You know you have a better chance with Guardian than you do with Lamontage."

"The Master loves me. He loves us all. He only punishes us to make us better men so we may be honorable servants to him and his cause. We are not afraid to die in service to a man as great as he." Alarm flitted across Keys' features. If circumstances did not change, this would not end well. The only difference between Pierre's followers and past terrorists he had dealt with was that they worshiped a live man who made them believe he was God and the only reward they had coming was the absence of punishment.

He pointed to Ventura and Heidi and looped the air with his finger, communicating that he wanted them to circle the apartment and see if they could come in behind the boy. They had to diffuse the situation quickly.

While they slinked off, Rose crab-walked to take their holding spot, her head was beginning to throb, but she ignored the pain, keeping her gun aimed at the open doorway. They could hear praying but the boy made no attempt to rise above his cover to shoot. "Son, Pierre's version of love is power. You serve him without failure you give him power. He rewards you by letting you live. If you fail him, you suffer for your failure in the most excruciating, painful way he can make you suffer." The boy didn't answer. "You know I speak the truth, Son, You've seen it. He makes sure you do . . ." The boy answered his plea by spraying more bullets across the kitchen, forcing him and Rose to shrink even further back behind their cover.

While Keys tried to reason with the young man, Peter and Heidi cautiously made their way through a small dining room decorated in colorful rugs, wall hangings and modest furniture, to a closed door. Peter motioned Heidi to the side of the door while he pushed his back against the wall and reached for the knob. He turned it cautiously before he opened it as noiselessly as possible, peaking around the casing. It was the bathroom. Across the room was another door that stood half-open. They moved cautiously across the tiles of the bathroom floor, and heard quiet sobbing. That was never a good sign. A sense of urgency filled the empty space between them. Heidi activated her cloak so it covered them both and they made their way into the room as cautiously and as slowly as they dared as precious moments ticked away. They pressed themselves against small wall that worked as a privacy screen for the toilet area. Ventura reached for the door. They heard more shots. Peter pulled the door open and ejected himself in a dive and roll, Heidi covered from the door casing, From within the room, the soldier cried out something in German and Keys answered him using the same language. A final shot rang out, followed by a thud.

Heidi dropped the cloak and Ventura stood up,and swung the gun around 180 degrees, then looked toward the bed and sighed, he kicked the boys gun away from his hand and holstered his own weapon as did Heidi. The soldier was face first on the faded wood floor in a pool of his own blood, a bullet hole in his temple. "Clear !" Ventura called out. Keys and Rose came in from the kitchen. Keys let out a tortured sigh. "We can't save them all, Keys," Peter stated, "He was dead the minute we cornered him. If not by our hand, then by Pierre's, so he chose to end it by his own."

Keys ran a hand over his face, "I know." he blew out a breath. "Clear the rest of the apartment and then help forensics go through this place." He looked toward the window. "I'm guessing Aaminah took Arella and escaped through that window, long before we breached. I'll call Kyle, Sasha, Demi, and Bryan to help with the canvas."

"Rose, come with me. I want to know what you and Marna saw before it all went south." Rose nodded, holstered her weapon and then handed the collected taser to Keys. "This is the weapon they were holding Marna captive with. I don't know if maybe our people can go through it. There might be something in the makeup to help us nail down Lamontage."

He took it and looked it over. "Good work, Rose." he studied her features after handing the weapon off to one of the forensics personnel with strict orders to notify him of the makeup as soon as they knew it. "When we're through here, I want you to go home, get some rest. Let Kurt and the kids take care of you for a change. You took quite a rap on the head." She nodded.

"Okay," she said. Keys nodded, and he and Rose left the apartment.

When they found Marna, she was drinking a glass of water and Tanner was hovering with his hand on the butt of his holstered gun. Keys smiled, and spoke to Tanner, "We'll take it from here. I want her statement. Tanner, I want you to go in and help Peter and Heidi with evidence collection." Tanner nodded, caught Marna's gaze, smiled and squeezed her shoulder, then headed toward the kitchen.

"Arella?" She asked. Keys put his finger up, shook his head stepped away and pulled out his vibrating phone.

Rose sat down beside her. "Looks like she and her Handler were gone by the time we breached."

Marna shook her head and closed her eyes. "So close."

"I know." She put her arm around Marna and let her eyes slide to Keys.

Keys sighed as he listened to Demi give him an update on the search for Heinderick. "I'm calling you off that trail right now, Demi . . . I want you and Bryan here to canvas the area for the girl and her Handler . . . Marna heard the woman making plans to bolt. We need to stop her. If she gets that girl out of the country, there's no telling when, if ever, we will get her back. Fedpol is locking down all the stations but I have an uneasy feeling about this. I fear that if we don't get to her first, chances are Lamontage will. We can pick up Heinderick's trail later. What's your ETA? All right, I'll see you then." Keys hung up and paused as the coroner made his way through the banquet room and into the rooms beyond. He returned to Marna, pulled a chair out, and sat across from her, "How do you feel?"

"I'm okay. Just a little shaky," she paused. "Arella?"

He took a penlight out, checked her eyes then her reflexes, and then her pulse. "We think they used the window and fire escape before we got here. We have people canvassing now." He drew in a cleansing breath, satisfied she had no ill effects from the taser attack. "Tell me what happened, from the beginning."

Marna started with the lunch and her eavesdropping on fellow patrons, the entrance of the four men and their retreat. Then their moving to the second floor and her search of the main banquet room while Rose searched the kitchen." He was thoughtful for a moment. "Then what? How did they know where you were? Were they following you?"

Marna shook her head saying, "No, we were careful. We didn't tag any followers on our way. They came in several minutes after we had already been here. I don't believe they knew we were here or even who we were. They didn't act like they were even looking for anybody in particular." She shook her head and continued. "My view was obstructed for a spell. I was in the coat room talking to you." She flicked her eyes at Keys then brought them to back to Rose. "Did you notice anything?"

Rose shook her head and picked up the story. "No. As soon as you told me to cloak and disappear, I did. What little I did see was them getting a corner seat next to the wall with a vantage point of the whole dining area."

"Watching and waiting," Keys voiced his opinion," for whom and why, your guess is as good as mine, but I'd be willing to bet, taking into consideration what you heard, Marna, it was probably Arella and her Handler." He cleared his throat and took down a few notes. "What about here? What happened up here?" He encouraged her with a smile. "How long after their arrival on scene before the situation escalated?"

Marna furrowed her brow. A headache was viciously trying to take hold behind her eyes. She drew in a deep breath before she spoke. "Twenty minutes maybe. When we met in the hallway, we found the stairway and came up. I was looking for hidden seams in the wall that might give way to a hidden door and Rose was covering me." She shrugged. "I just didn't think they'd come upstairs so I de-cloaked. I figured the search would go faster if I could put my full concentration on finding the entrance to the apartment."

"How long before Rose's position was compromised?" Keys pressed on.

"I don't know exactly. Ten or fifteen minutes maybe." She closed her eyes, fighting off the headache while trying to remember details. "I sent Rose into the kitchen. I figured we could get things done quicker that way, find Arella and her Handler, and be on our way before anyone was the wiser."

"So what stopped you?"

"It wasn't long before I sensed someone behind me and I spun using some defense moves. I cut the guy's lower legs out from under him. He went down. Before I could react to the next guy in line and throw up my cloak, he blasted me with the taser. I couldn't move and I couldn't use my abilities to try and get word out to Rose that we'd been discovered."

"What did they say?"

"I-I don't know. I'm a little foggy on the details." Her eyes strayed over his shoulder as the coroner rolled the body of the young soldier by them.

"Marna, look at me." She obeyed. "I'm going to take you back there, we'll have to connect, and then we'll go back there together. Do you understand?" She nodded. "Good. Now close your eyes and open up our channel." He paused a moment to be sure she was relaxed. "That's it, let everything else drift away. Good . . . We're coming up the stairs. The four men are sitting at a table downstairs. You and Rose are just coming off the top stair. . ."

*****

"It's a private banquet room." Rose said.

"Yeah, the perfect cover for a hidden apartment. Let's see if we can find a hidden door."

"Are you serious, Marna? This isn't Anne Frank," Rose protested.

"This building is very old and refugees hid in many countries, some for years, in hidden apartments or rooms."

"Switzerland was always neutral. They never joined the war. Some have even accused her of letting the Germans move Holocaust victims through the country by train on the railroad system." Rose said.

"True for World War II, but the Conflicts were different. Switzerland wasn't able to stay neutral and many refugees hid from government tyranny in many different countries." Rose looked unsure. "Come on, Rose, we don't have time to argue this point right now. Humor me. "

"All right."

Keys and Marna were walking through the memory as ghosts through Scrooge's dreams. "How are you doing this?" She looked at him for an answer.

"It's called Space Continuum, a facet of my Remote influencing, one of Bradshaw's tweaks to my development. It's a collective ability, it enables us to walk through memories in 3-D with great attention to detail. Now, what happened next?"

Memory Marna turned from her search of the wall. "Rose, go into the kitchen and look there. We'll get done faster if we both take a room."

"What about cover?"

"I think we're safe. If they were going to trust their luck, they would have come up here by now. I'll keep an eye out. Just keep psychic contact to a minimum in case one of them is a Tracker. We'll use one of modern day's wonders," she held up her GPC, "Texting."

Rose looked at the stairs, unsure about what to do next. "I don't know."

Marna took hold of her shoulders and squared her so they were mirrored images. "The longer we take doing this, the better the chance is that we blow our cover. Now go into the kitchen and check the area out. If what I heard is correct, then we haven't much time. Now go." Rose nodded, holstered her gun, and went into the kitchen.

"So you thought you were safe?" Marna nodded as she watched herself search for seams and push on panels.

"I was so focused on finding that hidden doorway that I totally dismissed the possibility that they would come looking as well," she sighed. "Rule number one of Investigation Theory: Always be aware of your surroundings."

"And not long after Rose went into the kitchen you felt the intrusion behind you?" She nodded.

I had time to finish checking the panels on the north wall before the hairs on the back of my neck stood up. They watched as Keys' abilities showed the men coming up the stairs and fanning out around Marna who had her back to them.

Not long after their arrival on the scene, she turned and went in to self-defense mode as she had described earlier. She became aware of the intrusion and then stood up, spun on one foot, while simultaneously lifting her leg and knocking the first man off his feet. She managed a few more self-defense moves and sidekicks before the second man pulled out the taser and zapped her with it.

"I fell completely under their control. I couldn't sound the alarm and I couldn't call up my Magnifying ability to help me strengthen my shield. Nothing. All I felt was this energy around me. All I saw was this purple mist."

"Did they speak, Marna? Say anything that might lead us to Lamontage or the Liberators?"

The apparition Marna thought very hard. "They spoke some but it was German. I made out some of what they were saying."

"Tell me," Keys encouraged. Marna closed her eyes and put herself inside her head during the moment of the attack.

"Crush her. She has seen us."

"Nein. I think she is the one the Master wants."

"What?" The leader pulled out a flyer Lamontage had handed out to all the soldiers before he sent on them on their missions. He laughed and patted the younger man on his back. *"You are right Adolf. She is a great prize indeed, a nice bonus after the girl and Ahminah. Keep her under until we finish the search and then we will take her with us to present her to the Master."*

"How will we get her there, Herr Meichster?"

"I have Compliance. It will put her out for long enough. She will not be able to fight us." The men all laughed. Marna started to tremble.

*****

"Okay, Marna, we're closing the door now. You did well." Marna nodded. She opened her eyes and Keys turned to Rose. "Is that when you came into the picture?"

"Yes. Things got quiet and I went to check on her. That's when I saw what they did – ah," She cleared her throat. "What they had done to her."

Marna picked it up. "It was my fault she was discovered. She contacted me and I gave her away by looking toward the kitchen." Keys nodded.

"But none of you noticed if they were using any psychic abilities?"

They both shook their heads. "No, I don't think so," Marna said. "They would have discovered Rose long before that if that was the case. They only knew she was there after I looked toward the kitchen."

"Okay, so chances are, Arella and her Handler are still somewhat safe. They weren't able to notify Lamontage they had slipped away." The women shook their heads. "Good, we have some time advantage here. However, Their access to Compliance causes me great concern. That is the one drug that can wreak havoc to psychic abilities. Pierre has taught them well."

"With Pierre's abilities, it would seem odd that he would need any kind of synthetic drug to help him keep things under control."

"He is powerful, but he is not taking chances with someone such as Marna. Especially if he sends out his lower level to no ability personnel to retrieve her. They have to know Guardian is involved by now. Liberatores is not just made up entirely of psychics like Bradshaw's was," Rose said. "I don't think the men that were here today were psychics."

"Why do you say that?"

"They showed no use of any abilities. I think they are what they portrayed. Foot soldiers sent out on a mission to locate and retrieve."

Keys nodded. "He doesn't know the scope of Arella's abilities so send the expendable people first. The Guinea pigs." He was thoughtful a moment and rubbed his chin. "You're probably right, Rose," he nodded. "Good observation. They were armed with Compliance and the altered taser, so they were ready for both kinds of trouble." He got up from his chair and motioned to one of the other agents. "Marna, are you feeling up to helping with the search of the apartment?" She nodded. "Good. Let's get to work."

Marna set the water down on a nearby table and followed Keys into the apartment. The first thing she noticed was how tidy the living space was. Whoever was raising Arella had been meticulous about the home. The kitchen was what Marna had come to realize as the norm for Switzerland homes. In their desire to use space efficiently, Swiss designers had built appliances, cupboards and shelves in to the walls. Marna walked through the kitchen, opening cupboards, and looking at Disney Princess dishes, glasses, and silverware. She saw floral patterned plates, coffee cups and sterling silver utensils. A teakettle rested on the narrow four-burner stovetop and beside it, a teacup filled with water and a tea bag emerged in it. "She was interrupted," Keys said. "Fits in with our theory that she must have heard the commotion in the banquet room, either when you were confronted or when Rose came on the scene."

Marna nodded. "Makes sense." Marna reached out and touched the cup. "It's still warm."

"Means they aren't that far ahead." He lifted his radio but kept from saying anything because Marna had taken hold of the cup with both hands and closed her eyes.

*****

The woman was terrified. She looked at the glass walls encasing the train schedule, her reflection stared back at her. She was wearing a black Abbaiya with a face veil. Her eyes searched out the departure of the next train to Stuttgart. Marna zoomed in on the schedule, but the woman looked to the floor as two men passed behind her before Marna could get a read on the schedule. When the men have passed, she discreetly turned in the opposite direction and hurried toward the escalators. There was no child with her but she hurried down some stairs. Trains are stopping below. She looked behind her. Marna felt the woman's fear and the urgency in her heart as well as the tears on her face.

She stumbled, almost fell, quickly regained her balance and turned to the right. She went through yet another door. More tracks. More train sounds. She stumbled and fell to her knees, words of prayer flowing from her mouth. She looked behind her and continued to run. Soon she was out of the station and on the platform. Many other passengers were awaiting their train. She continued to run, Someone stepped into her path. She backed up and turned but she stopped, horror showing on her face, more words in Arabic. She backed up coming to the end of the platform. She cried out. Turned and jumped. A train is coming. . .

*****

Marna gasped, "Oh my gosh!"

"What is it, Marna?" Keys queried.

"The Handler. She's at the Zurich train station. They've found her. I couldn't see them clearly, but I know they are from Liberatores. They were wearing the same clothing as the men here. She's terrified. The last thing I saw was her jumping off the platform and onto the tracks. There was a train coming. Everything ended. It felt like she was lost in a dark tunnel."

Keys grabbed his GPC and hit a button on the mini-keyboard. "Sasha, you and Kyle head to the Zurich train station. The Handler may be there and look for the child, too, but don't look for them together. The Handler may have left the child hidden and tried to lead the pursuers away from her. Call me when you've done your search and you know the answers."

"Can you get anything else?"

Marna tried again then shook her head. "No, it's gone or she is. . ." She swallowed. "I don't know which."

"We'll know soon enough. Come on. The others are searching the rest of the house. They think they've found Arella's room." Marna nodded and allowed him to lead her into the dining room and across a soft brown carpet to two small rooms side by side. The first one was the master bedroom. She entered it first. Aside from the blood pool on the floor, very little was disturbed. She noticed the wardrobe blocking the window and put the pieces together herself.

The furnishings were, like the rest of the apartment, modest but comfortable and durable. The vanity dresser was the only thing she could see that the female Handler had either splurged on or her husband genuinely loved her and he bought it as a token of that love. Marna touched it and closed her eyes, trying to call up more loving images of the young woman that had been Arella's mother.

She saw flashes of a smiling face, olive in skin color, eyes a compassionate brown, hair pulled back in a modest braid. She saw flashes of her carrying a birthday cake, a casserole. More images of her crawling through a dining chair tent, teaching lessons at the dining room table. The images presenting themselves to her were that of a loving woman, someone who deeply cared for the child entrusted to her, not the domineering psychopath suggested at the briefing. She didn't feel the woman was that wrapped up in the Liberatores organization. She felt she was trying to run from it. She lifted her hand off the dresser and drew in a breath letting it out in a soft sigh. "Keys, I'm not seeing the evil woman that FEDPOL painted. This woman genuinely loved Arella. I think they both did. I think they wanted to run from Liberatores not toward it."

"Which would make them public enemy number one in Lamontage's eyes."

"Which is why they killed Abbud and why they came after Aaminah."

"This puts her in very real danger, Arella, too." Marna's voice became urgent. "Keys, we need to find them and soon."

"We're doing everything we can, Marna. Come on, maybe you can get something off Arella's belongings. Let's go." Marna followed him through the adjoining door into a small bedroom. There was a small built in closet. Against the far wall was a castle-framed bed, complete with royal red satin sheets and twin rooks forming both sides of the headboard. Across from the bed, against the eastern wall, was a small single mold desk and chair, on top of it, a worksheet with today's lesson word spelled out in German, with crayons beside it. Some of Arella's homework no doubt.

A small vanity table with a princess grooming set upon it, the brush missing, took up space beside the desk. Marna could see Aminah brushing Arella's hair while the child sat on the small throne chair pushed up to it, the seat cushion also done in royal red. Next to that, a built in dresser stood, with drawers left open and clothing strewed around it. They had packed in a hurry. Aminah was spooked.

Marna reached out for the small hand mirror and closed her eyes. Immediately she saw flashes of Aminah hurriedly throwing the child's cloths into a small overnight case. A little girl with straight dark hair and Mary's features, dressed in a dark blue cloak, stood nearby, clinging to a princess doll and the missing brush. They spoke in German as Aminah hurried about the room.

~~~~~

"Momma, what's wrong?" she asked

"We need to go, Arella, now."

"Go where, Momma? Are we taking a trip?"

Aminah, also in a dark cloak, knelt down before the child. "We are going to go see Gross mutter Adala for a few days in Stuttengart, and then we are going on a long trip."

"Where to, Momma?"

"Someplace safe, my darling girl, some place safe."

~~~~~

The images changed and Arella was alone in a room. Marna could hear muffled sounds. She listened intently. A PA system! She focused harder. Arella was among some large dark objects. Marna concentrated on details. Arella curled up against shadowed forms of all shapes and sizes. There was something familiar about them. Paper dangled from the forms around the child. Tags! Marna opened her eyes and drew in a sharp breath. "Marna, what is it?" Keys asked.

"Luggage. Arella is among luggage bags. Aminah was running at the train station, away from a threat. What if she was also running away from Arella to keep her safe? Is there an unclaimed baggage room or storage room at the train station? Could a child as small as Arella be artfully hidden among the bags?" She looked earnestly at him. "Keys, take my hand."

"What?" He was confused.

"Allow me to magnify your Remote Viewing and influencing. Maybe the two of us can pin point her location."

He nodded, wondering why he hadn't thought of that to begin with. "It's worth a try." He reached for her hand. Marna still clung to the little mirror with her other one and they both closed their eyes. Soon images started flashing before them. Voices murmured in their ears. Bodies rushed by. Sounds of trains coming and going echoed in the recesses of their minds. The PA system called out track number, departures and arrivals.

Keys, see if you can find Arella.

Keys' trained mind quickly shuffled through all the distractions and soon they were looking at the world through Arella's eyes. Marna was seeing things as if she was looking at a split screen. She saw Arella huddled among some bags and then she saw the door to a darkened space through Arella's eyes. Slits of light were streaming through. *I see her.*

So do I.

Arella looked around her space. "Wh-who's there?" she whispered in German, her voice trembling.

Friends. Keys said. *Have you learned to talk in your head, child?*

Arella closed her eyes and nodded. *Yes, but momma and poppa don't like me to. Especially to people I don't know.*

We've met, Arella, in a dream. You helped me get away from a bad man. Do you remember? Marna assured her.

The pretty lady with the white dress, my dream mommy?

Marna smiled. *Close, but no, that was my sister. Do you remember? I look like her.*

Oh, yes. You're pretty too. You made the bubble bigger.

Marna grinned. *Yes I did. Arella, my friend and I want to help you again. But I want to do it here, not in a dream. I need to know where you are. Can you help me with that?*

I don't know. Momma brought me here. She told me to stay until she came. Bad men were after us.

Do you know how long you've been there?

For the first time, Arella's communication expressed dismay. *It's been a long time and I'm scared she's hurt.*

Don't *you worry, Arella, more of my friends are trying to help your momma too.* Marna interjected

Okay.

My friend is going to help me find you. Can you help him?

Okay.

Keys took over the communication. Okay*, Arella, we're going to look around.* Within moments, Marna was seeing what Keys was seeing and vice versa, They were a combined power, seeing through Arella's eyes, they were in a large closet like space on a lower shelf. Arella was against a wall with several luggage bags surrounding her. Slits of horizontal light were reflecting in her eyes and on a nearby bag. *Arella, can you get up on your knees and look at one of those white tags on the bag in front of you?*

Arella did as he requested. **Claim number 2263 LAX to ZURICH November 2047**. *Good, Arella, now very carefully move the bag aside and look around the room.* Again, the child did as they said and looked around the room. Keys and Marna saw a large room, with a concrete floor and bricked walls. Metal shelves were standing throughout the room, evenly spaced. On each of those shelves were many luggage bags. Through Arella's eyes, Marna could see a light brown door with a vented window built into the center of it,it was across from her hiding place. Eureka! They knew where she was. Arella's mother had hidden her in the storage room for the station's lost and unclaimed luggage. *Arella*, Keys stated. *I want you to stay where you are. I have people nearby who can help you.*

When will they come?

Soon, child, soon. But I don't want you going with anyone unless they tell you that Marna and Fred sent them. Do you understand?

What about, Momma?

If Momma comes back, tell her to wait with you. We are coming to help. Okay?

Okay. They drew in a breath and broke the connection. Keys heard track five called in the background, during their connection with Arella. He would tell his people to start there. He dialed Kyle on his GPC.

They picked up immediately. "Kyle, take Sasha and go to track five. Meet with your FEDPOL partners and get to the unclaimed baggage storage room by track five. Arella is hiding in there. Marna and I will meet you there. Get inside and call for Arella. Tell her that Marna and Fred sent you. Go now. Lamontage's men may already be in the area." He disengaged his GPC and looked at Marna. "You ready?" She nodded. "Let's go." He turned to Ventura. "Ventura, you and Shaefer oversee the search here. Rose and Tanner will escort the evidence back to the compound. We'll meet the four of you there," he took in Tanner, Rose, Heidi and Peter with a glance. "Rose, you go home and get some rest." Ventura agreed to the orders and watched their backs as they, and then he walked by Tanner and clapped his shoulder as he noticed Tanner's eyes on them as well. He was unhappy they were leaving him behind. Marna was his partner. He felt responsible for her safety.

*****

Bystanders had seated themselves on their luggage, some had leaned against the wall and some had sat on the offered benches, but all watched in horror as various civil servants jumped down on the stalled track six of the Zurich station. Most of the onlookers had seen the woman jump onto the tracks and the conductor desperately trying to stop its approach by hitting its emergency brakes as well as it traditional. They heard the engine squeal its defiance and saw the bright sparks fly from metal grinding on metal. Now they all sat or stood in shocked silence. Nobody had actually seen her get hit but the conjecture was there. Demi Spencer and her partner Bryan stepped into the track area searching the sea of heads for Andreas Schultz and Avril VonCutz of Fedpol. When she finally made eye contact, they waved and she nodded, making a path through officers interviewing countless nervous passengers, straight to them. "What have we got?" She asked Andreas.

He shuffled through his notes. "Depends on who you talk to," he said. "I've talked to at least twenty eye witnesses and the only thing they all agree on is that a woman in Muslim dress, seemingly being pursued by four men in street fatigues, jumped onto track six as the 2:20 was coming in to the station. From there it goes in many different directions. Some say the train hit her, some say she made it across and onto platform seven, and some say she disappeared in a puff of smoke. Then they again agree that three of the four men pursuing her stopped short of jumping on the track after her and took off. The fourth one jumped down after her. Some even say they heard a gunshot at the end."

"So they agree on the beginning event and the end event, but the middle is what gets all muddled up?" Schultz nodded. "Thanks Andreas. If we'll agree that the first and last thing witnesses saw actually happened and what happened in between is unclear. We'll extract that for our reports." He nodded again. "Keep us posted." Demi bobbed her head once and headed toward the track.

"What are you thinking?" Bryan asked.

"That a woman protecting her child would not have committed suicide unless she knew said child was safe or that she could get a message to someone to ensure said child's safety. She would do what she could to lead the threat in a totally different direction and return to the child later, even if it meant making it look like she died."

"You think she's still alive?"

"Unless the investigators find proof she died there, then yes I do." They reached the end of the platform. Demi shoved her red ponytail behind her shoulder, crouched, and jumped to the tracks below. She walked over to the crime scene units. "What have you found?"

"Lots of blood and tissue on the tracks," one of the investigators said, "but we can't determine if they belong to one person or two. We did find the Abbaiya worn by the woman, and a face veil.

"Is this it?" She queried accepting the brown paper evidence bag, the woman offered her.

"Well there was more, but some body parts were left intact, so they've body bagged them and shipped them to the Coroner's. She did say she could conclusively say that body was a male." She pointed toward a space in front of him. "The place of impact would have occurred here, but the train would not have finished braking until a good 150 yards that way." He pointed toward an area down the tracks where a solid bold black seven was marked on a metal sign nailed to a wooden post. "This was a train due to stop on track ten,so their braking was premature and it took time to stop." He looked at her. "Lots of tissue, brain matter, blood, and body parts to work with on this jigsaw puzzle, especially if the body got caught under the train, and then there is the matter of matching parts to victim."

Demi sighed. "Okay, when you fill out your reports, make sure Fredrick Keys from Guardian gets a copy, too."

"Will do," he stepped away as she folded her arms and studied the tracks before her. So much blood and tissue everywhere you looked. She crouched down and got as low and as close as she could to study the stains and debris without contaminating the scene.

"Anything?" Bryan queried, crouching down beside her.

"Not sure. Something doesn't feel right."

"Coming from a Feeler, I'd say that statement alone would make me raise an eyebrow."

"I know there is a lot of blood and debris but is it enough for two bodies?"

"Demi, I usually don't question your instincts but with human remains, the debris field can get pretty wide, especially in this kind of an impact. They're going to need to try and get DNA to positively identify if that woman died with the pursuer, and even with today's advances in DNA technology that could be inconclusive."

She straightened her back but remained crouched, "A few of the witnesses reported a gun shot at the end. Why would they fire on her if the train had done their job for them?" She glanced over her shoulder at him.

He shrugged. "Maybe they wanted to make sure she couldn't get away."

"Or slow her down." Her eyes caught sight of something. "There," she pointed and got up, taking purposeful steps toward track seven. She stopped and pointed down. "Spent casings." She crouched down, pulled a glove out of her pocket, slipped it on, and picked up a casing to look it over," a Glock 45, That's a big boy's gun. Hmmm. Lamontage is brave letting his kids play with such a dangerous weapon. You got an evidence bag on you?"

"Yeah. I grabbed a couple from the crime scene people. Here." He put on gloves and held it open while she slipped the casing into it. Then he sealed it, wrote the information on it and turned it over to a nearby CSU Tech, "hey, can you label this and file it please?" The Tech nodded and took possession of the bag.

"Now, if he was here on track six when he fired then to hit his target with a train coming in about to block his view, his target would have to be . . .," She calculated three things in her mind; the speed the train was coming in at, how long it would take, at that speed, to come to a complete stop using emergency means., and the time the shooter had to fire before the engine blocked its view based on the position of the spent casings. She used her fingers as a gun, took the position she thought the killer could take with limited time and swung slowly to her left, stopping just behind the engine. "There. Come on." She stepped over the tracks and under the police tape, briefly examined the engine for bullet holes, and then walked around the front of it.

When they reached the other side, she studied the tracks under the engine and the ones close by. "Hello there." She put on another glove and crouched down. Bryan looked over her shoulder. She carefully moved aside some small pieces of driftwood to reveal what she had zeroed in on.

"Gravitational blood droppings." The drops formed a perfect red teardrop shape, the thinner, upper point leading the experienced hunter in the direction the wounded subject had gone.

"Has anyone reported finding a gun?" She queried, lifting her chin toward the cluster of CSU techs.

"Let me call Schultz and see." He stepped a pace away while she searched for more drops. When he returned, he stated what she feared most. "He said thus far, no discovery of a firearm has been reported.

"So we have a terrified woman, wounded, hunted, trying to protect her daughter and a missing gun. Great ingredients for catastrophic pie." She narrowed her eyes and looked in the direction she thought the blood drops were leading. "Looks like she went toward platform seven. Let's follow the bread crumbs, see where they lead, and hope we get to her first. I'll call Keys and update him." She pulled out her GPC, while the lab techs extended the area for evidence collection per Bryan's instructions. Then, she and Bryan headed toward platform seven, eyes glued to the ground. Every few feet they found another blood drop showing them the direction of their quarry. Demi responded to Keys when he answered the phone. "Keys, we may have a problem," she said, her Irish lilt coming out in her speech. That was when Bryan realized how worried she really was.

*****

Aminah slipped coins into, yet another rest room coin dispenser, and with a shaking hand, opened the door and pushed her way beyond it while the automatic lights came on before the door closed securely behind her. She had to keep moving. She couldn't stay in one place for long. She couldn't let them find her or her efforts to save Arella would be lost. She sighed as the noisy hustle of the station faded away and she leaned against the wall, wincing. She took the shirt she had been using to splotch the bleeding in her shoulder and buried it deep in the trash bin, throwing still more paper towels on top of it. In the commotion of the terrified onlookers , she had seized the opportunity to hide between stopped trains, and torn off the Abbaiya and face mask and toss it into the debris on the tracks as she was running from her pursuers. Unfortunately it didn't stop them from shooting her. Their aim was true, and the bullet seared a path deep into her fleshy shoulder as she ran away.and lost herself in the confusion of the accident aftermath. "Aah," she lifted her arm to the sink, tore some more paper towels from the dispenser, and soaped them up trying to cleanse her wound the best she could. Then she reached into the large shoulder bag she carried and pulled out another of her husband's t-shirts.

She was grateful for the years in her homeland. War was ever-present at every border, and around every bend. If you were traveling, they taught you to be prepared. It was second nature for her to pack items to use as bandages, and wound packing – survival skills, her parents had called it – she called it necessary.

When she had washed away all the excess blood, she examined the wound using the rest room mirror. She took the scissors from her bag, cut the first slice in the new shirt, and cut strips. She gritted her teeth as pain ripped through her arm with each rip of the material. When she had produced all the strips she needed, she started taking the thinner strips and packing the wound, then with the larger strips, she wrapped the shoulder, using duct tape as the outer layer to keep the blood from seeping through the bandages and exposing her to prying eyes. Her brother-in-law was a doctor and when she and Arella got safely to her husband's family in Stuttengart, Germany, they would be able to rest and be protected until they could board the plane to America where her family hid, under false names, in a small town not even listed on road maps.

It was a refuge where she and Arella would be safe from Lamontage and his evilness. She leaned against the wall, and slid to the floor as dizziness engulfed her. She closed her eyes awaiting it to pass. When she opened them again, shadows moved about outside the door. "This restroom is occupied," she stated in German, while she pulled the gun and pointed it at the door. The knob turned, but the lock did not give. The shadows paused. They were speaking English. "I said this restroom is occupied. Please go away and find the next one." Tears formed in her eyes. She had never had to kill anyone before, but she would not make it easy for her enemies to kill her and take both Arella's parents from her. She loaded a round into the chamber as again the knob turned and the occupied light flickered.

*****

Bryan and Demi followed the gravitational drops across the rails, onto platform seven and into the station. They were fearful that the amount of people moving about the station would degrade the trail. Traces of bloodied footprints caused them some aggravation. "She's wounded," Demi said, "so she's going to try and stay away from people. Come on let's check closer to the walls." They veered right and went toward the walls. Demi pointed at some drops on the floor and followed them. "Look at the wall," she said pointing out some rusty red smears on the white bricked walls and glass partitions.

"She's getting weak," Bryan verified, recognizing the smears as places where she may have leaned against the wall to catch her breath.

"Blood loss," Demi stated.

"No doubt. She needs medical attention but she's a fighter." He pulled out his phone. "I'll give Schultz a call and tell him to send some more man-power to canvas. She couldn't have gotten far." Demi nodded as she searched the floor for more drops. She found what she needed and signaled Bryan. He said goodbye to Schultz and then rejoined his partner. "Let's go." They followed the drops down a hallway to a rest room. Demi tried the door. It was locked. She looked around the area and noticed a security person a few hundred feet to their left. She motioned Bryan to stay and went to speak to the guard.

Before she spoke, she pulled out her ID, "Demi Spencer, Guardian WIT. Have you got a pass key to the rest rooms?" The man nodded. "Give it to me, and then you and your team clear the immediate area. We have reason to believe there is an armed fugitive hiding in your rest room over there." He nodded, handed her the key, pulled his radio to his lips and started immediately clearing the area of bystanders. Demi rejoined Bryan, pulled her weapon, fit the key in the security strip slide and opened the door with a jerk. It was empty but they were sure their girl had recently occupied it. There were bloodied strips of cloth under a layer of paper towels in the garbage dispenser, some of which were exposed over the edge. Demi was about to replace her gun when a shot rang out in the station and a woman screamed. They quickly left the rest room and a woman dressed in a housekeeping uniform ran toward them.

"She's nuts, I tell you! She just tried to kill me! There was blood everywhere. She must have killed someone !" The woman was shaking and crying.

"Where?" Demi demanded.

"Restroom 10. . . by the food Kiosk." She pointed toward the north end of the station. "I went in to clean it and if I hadn't seen her . . . Oh my . . . I'd be . . ."

Demi waved four security personnel over that were running toward the commotion. One of them was the one she had spoken to before. "Post someone by this door. Someone stay with her and get her statement." After she handed the woman safely over, she pointed to the remaining two. "You two with us !" The four of them ran for the restroom, while Demi lifted her phone to her ear, calling

Schultz of Fedpol while Bryan called for backup from Guardian. "She has a gun, Schultz. Glock - 45, the one that the witnesses said they heard.".

"She's on the run, Keys," Bryan stated. "My guess, she's looping back to get Arella. She has a gun. Glock - 45 and she's wounded, she's running for her life and I don't think she's going to leave without the girl !" He confirmed their location; cut transmission then slipped his GPC into his pocket.

They reached the bathroom in question, opened it with the pass key and Demi's heart sank when she saw all the blood smears and pools about the rest room. She ordered the security team to secure the area until the tech team got there and then she called Keys.

"What's your ETA?"

"Ten minutes."

"Better make it five. Ahminah is looking for an escape for her and Arella. She just took a blind shot at a housekeeper. If she doesn't die first, she'll get the child and leave the country by any means necessary. Bryan and I will do what we can to head her off but you better hurry and convince her we aren't the enemy." After ending her call, she and Bryan left on a run toward the tracks to try to cut Ahminah off before she got to track five and retrieved the child.

Chapter Eight

Keys and Marna pulled out their badges as they jumped from the car and jogged to the front entrance of the station. After showing them to security, they pushed through the barricades immediately. Kyle and Sasha met them on the inside. Sasha spoke as they all fell into step together. "We've locked down all the exits and security is evacuating as quickly and as orderly as they can while still checking IDs. FEDPOL is assisting them."

"Has anyone verified if the three assailants are still on the property?" Keys queried. They all stepped onto the escalator leading to the lower tracks.

"If they're still on the premises, they're hiding or have changed appearances, Sir. The descriptions given to FEDPOL have not led to any arrests," Kyle verified.

"What about the Handler?"

"No one has reported seeing an injured woman yet. She's spent many years blending in with the people in this country. She's a well-rehearsed Liberatores member. She could be half way to Germany by now."

"No," Marna said, shaking her head. "She wouldn't leave without the child."

"What makes you so sure?" Kyle demanded.

"Because when you become a mother, your entire focus changes." She glanced Keys way. She knew what she was talking about as she had experienced those very feelings last year.

"She is not a mother. She was the appointed Handler of Arella until such a time when they told her to hand her over to Lamontage and the Liberatores for further training. You'd do well to remember that, Agent Farlow."

Marna stopped in her tracks, turned and stared him in the eyes. "Ahminah is not that person anymore, Agent Rigby. She hid that child in a baggage room to protect her and then got shot trying to lead the Liberatores away from her."

"She just shot at an innocent maid, Farlow! Does that sound like the nurturing mother to you?" Kyle's gray eyes flashed.

"She'd just been shot, Rigby! They're hunting her! How'd you expect her to react?" The two agents faced off in silent glares. Blue eyes clashing against gray, experience against intuition, neither willing to give in first.

"Enough !" Keys' voice raised a notch. "Whatever Ahminah's motives are, we have a young girl in need of our help and protection. Put your focus on Arella and put your opinions aside. Let's do what Guardian does best. Protect the innocent." He focused first on Rigby who sliced his hand through the air and turned away, and then Keys brought his eyes to Marna who nodded, "can you hear anything, Marna?"

Marna tilted her head slightly down and to the right and started shifting through the miscellaneous talk about the station. She pushed voice after voice aside as she searched for those that would give her the clues she needed. "*They're evacuating.... I don't know...Wow, this is cool...Mommy what's going on.... It's a safety drill sweetheart... Ich werde mein Zug wegen dieser Scheiße verpassen .... Zug Absage für morgen verschieben ... Ich weiß nicht, irgendeine Art von Task-Force suchen, vielleicht ein verlorenes kind... Rufen Sie mich zurück mit der neuen Zeit ...*"

"*Have you found her yet?*" Marna's head shot up.

"*Nein, but I found her bloodied clothes in a restroom on the bottom floor by a storage area. She must have the child there.*"

"*Let's go...*"

"*What we do when we find her?*"

"*She has betrayed the Master. We kill her and take the child.*"

"Keys, she's near the storage area. They're headed here now." Marna's eyes reflected her horror. "They're going to kill Ahminah and take Arella."

Sasha looked around the lower level. Her eyes briefly caught sight of a door silently closing behind a woman as she passed through it. "There !" She pointed over the hundreds of evacuating heads.

"Sasha is there any psychic activity going on?" She tilted her head and tracked. After a few minutes, she shook her head, and then stopped. "Wait a minute." She focused more. "Yeah, I'm getting something."

"Marna," Keys looked at her. Without having it spelled out for her, she knew what he wanted.

"Give me your hand, Sasha." Sasha looked at Keys, he nodded and she reached out. Together they closed their eyes. Marna focused and soon she and Sasha's powers were working together. Sasha was tracking, but her tracking was different. Her mind was drawing out a map to where the signal was coming from. Then she heard a young girl's trembling voice call out to Marna.

Marna, where are you? There is someone in here but it isn't Momma.

Who is it, Arella? Is it a worker?

No. They're knocking bags off shelves but not putting them back and they're angry. Should I run?

No. Don't move, Arella.

I'm so scared, and Momma's not here. After a moment of no communication, Marna felt an overwhelming fear coming from the child.

Arella, what's happening?

They shot him, Marna. He asked them if he could help them find something and they shot him. There was a long pause and more fear. Someone is outside the door, looking in. It's Momma. She's opening the door.

Gasping, Marna broke contact. "Did you get it?" she asked Sasha. Sasha nodded, still amazed at what Marna's magnifying ability did for her.

"I know exactly where she is." She started on a run toward the back of the station where, only moments before, they had seen the door quietly close and wordlessly the others followed.

*****

Ahminah pushed the door slowly, but it would not swing open. Something was obstructing it. She looked down and raised her hand to her mouth stifling the scream. A booted foot blocked the door. She gagged as the coppery scent of blood drifted to her nose. She heard commotion from the inside, men speaking in German and Arabic. Her heart went cold. Arella! They were looking for her and Arella. She pushed with all her strength, trying to get an opening large enough for her to slip through but small enough for it to go undetected. After pushing for a few more seconds, the body moved slightly and gave her enough space to move inside the room.

She closed the door silently, and slipped into the shadows of the aisle on her right and stood for a terrifying moment. Had they heard her? Had they seen the light from the hall? She listened. Her eyes scanned the room until they rested on a shelf in the middle of the room where Arella's eyes stared back at her from a tiny space above a bag. She quickly lifted a finger to her mouth and shook her head once.

She listened to more of the conversation between the men. Instantly, she knew what her fate would be and knew that she could not and would not escape from it. She was weakened from blood loss and fading fast. She had to do something to lead them away from Arella. She had to find a way to save her daughter.

She had seen Guardian Agents in the station. She knew they were looking for her and Arella. She had recognized the woman from the media reports the year before. Marna Farlow. The woman the Master so desperately wanted to own; Arella's true blood, her biological aunt, the Magnifier that would make him the most powerful psychic of all. The one no one could stop. She also knew that Guardian had a better chance of keeping Arella safe than she did. She looked around. Another exit door stood behind the men at the end of the aisle they were inspecting.

She needed a diversion. She saw the bags and the glass vases on the shelf beside her. They would do nicely. She pushed them off, moving quickly down the aisle and hiding behind the end-cap of the shelf. The clatter echoed against the cement walls. She heard running feet coming closer to her hiding place. They inspected the aisle the bags had fallen into, the one next to hers. A little closer, she just needed them to get a little closer. When she heard them move into the aisle, she slipped into the one beside them. While they inspected the mess, she pushed with all the strength her injured arm would allow and heavy bags fell on top of them, slowing them down. She ran for Arella, shooting blindly behind her. When she reached Arella, she pushed the bags that concealed her to the floor then took her hand and pulled her into the safety of another baggage aisle, slipping into the shadows.

"Ahminah, you have no escape," the leader said. "You come to us willingly and the Master may show you a merciful end."

"Momma?" Arella whispered in a shaky voice. Aaminah pushed her behind her as they slipped into another aisle trying to make it to the exit door.

"The Magnifier is here with other Guardian Agents. She will not let you get away with the child! Arella is her blood. She will not let you take her."

"We take you both back. The Master will be very pleased." He silently signaled his men to fan out so he could narrow down her escape options.

Aaminah backed toward the end of the aisle. "I heard you talking. I know you will not bring me back alive, but I will not let you have Arella. I will kill you first."

"Is that any way to talk to your brother, Aaminah?" He moved into another aisle as he and his men pinpointed her location.

"You are not my brother, Aadil, not anymore."

"You dishonor me, Aaminah."

"Not dishonor, Aadil. I see you for who you are. A man who has a thirst for power ..." At that moment, a servant ripped Arella from her grasp, and she screamed. Aaminah turned to shoot, but they grabbed her, and slammed her into the metal shelf, her arm wrenched behind her, causing a resounding crack to echo eerily in the room and the gun fell from her hand. She cried out in pain.

"Momma !" Arella cried as the men dragged her from the baggage aisle and before Aadil. Aaminah cradled her arm as they forced her to her knees.

"Silence, girl." Aadil ordered. Arella closed her mouth and struggled against the man holding her, but her mind was desperately reaching out for Marna. "Any last words, sister?" Aaminah stayed on her knees in proud silence. The man behind her raised his gun.

They're going to hurt her.

We're coming.

At that moment, Keys and his team met Demi, Bryan and the security forces outside the door. Aaminah saw the commotion and thought delivery from her fate was there, but it was not to be. Aadil fired the fatal shot just as Keys and his team pushed through the door.

"MOMMA !" Arella's agonized voice bounced back at them from the walls around them. "NOOO !" The Guardian team moved in and Kyle took out the man standing behind the sprawled form of Aaminah.

"Get the girl!" Aadil ordered and headed toward the door, but Demi and Sasha moved in, rapidly firing their guns and emptying their clips, forcing him back into the shadows of the room.

"Get to the other door !" Keys ordered Bryan and Kyle as he covered Marna who ran down the aisle a man was using to escap with Arella. Gunfire exploded from the aisle when Marna disappeared from sight.

Marna! He opened his channel to her.

I'm all right. She moved silently down the center aisle as she listened intently for the slightest of sound. *Aaminah?*

Keys reached for Aaminah's neck to check for a pulse. Gunfire littered the floor around him. He returned fire and dived behind another shelf. *She's gone. Arella?*

Haven't found her yet. Marna advanced further down her aisle keeping close to the shelf. When she peaked around the end-cap, she recognized material from Arella's robe sprawled into the aisle. She moved quickly toward the robe, praying the child was all right. When she had almost reached it, someone jumped her from behind. She hit the floor face first, her gun sliding out of her hand. Arella screamed. Marna rolled over and tried to get her bearings. She could feel blood streaming down her face. She saw her assailant reach for something in his waistband. Fear gripped her heart in its icy fingers. He was pulling out a taser similar to the one at the restaurant. She rolled out of the way, as the beam hit the floor. "Not this time, sucker !" She dove behind some large boxes as she shook her head to clear the cobwebs. Glancing around, she saw her gun against a book case four aisles down from where she was.

Marna! Keys voice called through their channel.

I could use a little back up, Keys, she relayed back to him as she dove behind a pile of boxes seconds before the taser beam hit the top box.

"You have nowhere to run, Magnifier. I will bring you to the Master and reap the reward!" her attacker advanced toward her.

"You and who's army, sucker?" She tucked and rolled behind another pile of boxes as the beam burned into the end-cap of a nearby shelf, narrowly missing her.

Marna, what's going on?

Love to chat, Keys, but I'm a little busy right now. Guy has another taser. Where's the backup? She scanned the floor for her gun. Two more shelves and she would be within reach of it.

Kyle's on the way.

Great, but I had a little more maturity in mind. She tucked and rolled into yet another pile of boxes as the taser beam followed her trail. Gunshots littered the floor. Her attacker dove for a pile of boxes. She dove for the next row of shelves.

Gee, Farlow, you could have waited to start the fireworks until I got here.

Sorry, the other guest was a little yancy. She pulled back as the attacker lifted his gun and sent a spray of bullets her way. "Hey errand boy !" Kyle yelled The man turned, Arella freaked and started running toward Kyle. The attacker turned on her.

"No !" Marna dove for her gun, lifted it, aimed at the man's gun hand and shot the weapon clear out of his hold. Arella crouched where she was. The attacker turned on Marna and aimed the taser. Kyle ran toward Arella, shooting the man in the ankle, bringing him down and then he placed himself between the man and the child. The taser flew out of the attacker's hand and when he rolled over to scramble after it, Kyle appeared above him cocking his gun, aiming the barrel at the attacker's head.

The man froze and looked from the taser to Kyle. Kyle raised a brow, speaking in Arabic. "Are you really that stupid?" The man thought it best to retreat his hand and remained prone on his stomach on the floor. "Guess not." Marna got to her feet and ran toward Arella, picking her up in her arms and hugging her. Bryan appeared, and covered the prisoner, while Kyle pulled a zip tie from his pocket, and secured the captive's hands. The man yelled out. "I'm sorry, did that hurt?" Kyle queried, and then glanced toward Marna, who nodded at the questioning look in his eyes.

Report! Keys demanded through their psychic connection.

Situation is under control. Kyle communicated. *What about Aadil?*

He slipped out. I found an open duct in the back. Arella?

We got her. He glanced toward Marna. The child had buried her face in Marna's neck and he knew by the shakes claiming the little body, she was sobbing. *She's safe.*

Bring her in. Keys closed communication and Kyle glanced at Marna. "Aadil got away." His eyes moved to the cut on her head. "You okay?"

She wiped the blood from her face. "I will be." She kissed the sobbing child's forehead, sniffing. "Let's go." Kyle nodded, grabbed the taser and sliding it into his waistband pulling the assailant to his feet forcing him to walk.

"Time to face a real hard-nosed judge." He pushed him forward and the man limped on. Bryan took a last look around and followed the others.

*****

Keys tapped the back of the Guardian coroner van and returned to the Guardian ambulance where a medic was stitching Marna's head wound and another was checking Arella out, "How is she?" He asked the young man in charge of Marna as he was putting the bandage over the wound.

"She should go to the hospital for a cat scan," the attendant said.

"Perhaps, but I'll look after her."

"All right, Dr. Keys. You know the drill."

"I do indeed," he smiled. "Thank you Stan."

"Yes, sir."

"Marna, if you aren't going to follow medical advice, perhaps you shouldn't get injured." He winked at her.

"Tell that to the bad guys," she pulled her hair back. "How's Arella?"

"The attendants gave her a mild sedative. Sasha and Kyle are with her now, trying to get a witness account from her."

"Can't that wait?"

He shook his head. "The best thing with children is to get them talking right away. There's no doubt this will affect her. She saw the woman, she perceived as her mother all these years, gunned down in front of her. She's going to need time to heal." Marna nodded. Kyle stepped into her line of sight.

"Kyle."

"Keys." Marna studied the two. Something in Keys demeanor changed when Kyle was around. She couldn't quite put a finger on it.

"Job well done, Son,"

"Thank you, Sir." He nodded and Marna could swear she saw pleasure in his features, but it was more than just the reaction to a job evaluation. However, she didn't have time to reflect too much on her thoughts because Kyle turned his gray eyes on her. "I-I'm sorry for earlier, Farlow. I've been told I can jump to conclusions before all the facts are in." Marna chuckled and looked toward the ground as he continued. "You were right. The girl says her mother was trying to get her to you. Guess she had changed her way of thinking."

Marna shrugged. "It happens." She tilted her head so their eyes met. "How's the prisoner?"

"He is on his way to the compound with Demi and Bryan for interrogation. This is actually a historic event. First time since the Liberatores started pinging on the radar, that one of them has actually been taken alive."

"Congratulations."

"Right back at ya, Farlow." He sighed. "We worked well together, seemed to be in sync."

"Yeah, we did."

"Hope we can do it again sometime."

"I'm sure we will."

"Yeah." He reached out, patted her arm and smiled. "I'm going to go back and see if they're ready to release Arella. Sasha and I can bring you back to the compound." Then he was gone. She watched him leave, wondering why she was looking for a reason to call him back.

*****

Bryan and Demi entered the interrogation room together as they had always done. Demi sat down across from the suspect and Bryan stood behind him. The man played with the bandage on his hand. A pair of crutches leaned against the wall, by the door, leading to the holding facility on the compound. Demi slapped the folder on the table causing the man to jump. "What's your name, sir?" He looked at her but didn't answer. "According to your prints, it's Khabar Ashimar Kassab." He still did not answer. "I also ran your prints through a few data bases and you are a very mobile man. A bombing in Israel, an assassination in Lebanon, a kidnapping in the states and a terror attack in London. Wow, I must tell you, Mr. Kassab, it doesn't look good. Now you're down for kidnapping, ending with the execution of Aaminah Akil and the attempted murder of two American Federal agents. Not good, Khabar, not good at all."

"I do what needs to be done to serve the Master. Aaminah had betrayed him. The child is his."

"Oh." She pulled out some papers and slid them over to him. "You know what you're looking at, Khabar?" She waited a beat. "It's a DNA test. Arella's. She is in no way shape or form the property of your Master. Her parents were Amanda and Peter Nymphis. She has two remaining blood relatives. Two aunts that can take legal custody of her, Marna Farlow and Rose Briar. Your Master, or whatever it is you call him, didn't make the short list."

"He will get what he wants."

"Not this time, friend. Pierre Lamontage has no idea what he is facing. There is no way he will get his hands on Arella, Marna or the children. It's a fantasy. A sick fantasy woven by a sick man who believes he is God."

"He is God. He will kill you with his hand. I've seen him do it and he has others that he is training. His children."

"He's a very powerful psychic called an illusionist, who can take control of your mind through hypnosis and make you believe he is hurting you. Nothing more, nothing less. Just a glorified magician."

"Do not speak ill of the Master," his eyes warily looked around. "There are others that do his bidding. Others that can call upon the very spirits and kill."

"Wow! Talk about a snow job." She put the photos back into her file. "He really has you believing that he can." She shook her head and got up. "Hang tight, I've got to confer with my partner." She got up and went over to Bryan. "Let's leave this Bozo alone for a few minutes, let him stew." Bryan nodded and they left the room.

In the observation room, they went to the coffee pot and grabbed a cup of coffee. "You want a shot at him, Bry? Given his culture, maybe he'll have more respect for a man."

"I could try." They turned toward the two-way window.

"What the . . .?" Demi's words trailed off as they watched the observation monitor in horror, a black mist surrounded their prisoner's throat and he started clawing at it. Bryan and Demi slapped their coffee cups on the counter, and took off for the interrogation room.

When they reached the door, it would not budge. It was as if someone or something was holding it closed. "Look out !" Bryan yelled. Demi stepped back as he pulled his gun and shot out the lock. Still the door would not move. They both pushed against it. Finally, he and Demi raised their weapons and shot at the door. They heard a thud. Instantly Bryan pushed it open. A body lay before the door filled with holes matching the gun shot pattern on the door, and across the room, the other door clicked shut.

"Go !" Demi yelled as she moved to their prisoner, but before she even felt for a pulse, she knew he was gone. She turned to the man by the door. He was alive but barely. He was trying to say something. She moved closer to him. "You cannot protect her…," he said as his final breath left his body and life left his eyes.

Bryan rushed back in the room. He looked at the prisoner and then at her. She shook her head. Then she returned his quizzical gaze and he shook his head. She looked back at the young man on the floor. He wasn't very old, maybe twenty. Most likely, a Cloaker sent to cover for the Stager who had committed the actual killing of the witness. The attack had been swift and deadly. Drawing in a breath, she stood up and pulled out her GPC.

*****

Marna stepped out of Kyle and Sasha's car. Dusk was just darkening the skies of Zurich. She had spent the afternoon in a conference room introducing Arella to her new family, through pictures, including the still absent Heinderick. The child's reaction had been much as she expected.

"I don't understand?" She had been very puzzled, *"what do you mean my dream Mommy is my real Mommy?"*

"You were taken from your real Mommy when you were born, Arella. You and Heinderick both."

"Why?"

"You and Heinderick are part of a very special family. You can do very special things and men who wanted to control those special things wanted to control you and your brother."

"But my Momma?"

"She ended up loving you very much and she was trying to hide you from them. That's why she wanted to get you to me this afternoon. Your real Mommy is my sister, Amanda."

"I have brothers and sisters?"

"Yes." Marna chuckled. *"Several as a matter of fact. There are eight of them, nine counting Heinderick."*

"Will they like me?"

"Of course they will." She had gotten up to hug the child. *"How could they not?"*

Now she stood in the parking lot of the hotel heading toward the decisive moment. She had called Rose requesting she and Kurt deliver the news so that when she arrived, they would be ready to meet their sister. Arella's little hand slipped into Marna's as Kyle grabbed the two suitcases and the one small chest that carried all of Arella's belongings from the trunk of the car. Sasha took the bags so he could carry the chest. Taking a breath, Marna started the entourage toward the hotel lobby.

She buzzed ahead so when she reached the apartment door, Rose was waiting. "Hey."

"Hey." She hugged her. Rose crouched down to eye level with Arella. "Hi, Arella. My name is Rose. I'm very happy to meet you."

"Thank you," Arella whispered. She clung tighter to Marna's hand.

Rose looked at Marna. "They're all in the living room."

"Thanks Rose." She glanced at Marna's forehead and shook her head. "Can't stay out of trouble, can you?"

"You should see the other guy," Marna quipped. The rest of them chuckled. Marna squeezed Arella's hand. "Well, kiddo, let's say we do this?" Arella nodded and with a smile and a quiet thank you to Kyle and Sasha, the sisters headed into the living room, with Arella between them.

What Marna saw brought tears to her eyes. There was a banner covering one wall of the room. It was the children's version of a family symbol: a scallop shell split into ten sections, with Marna's name at the bottom center and a section devoted to each child's name. She recalled the symbolism the scallop shell held from her college class days, but the ones she remembered most were love and pilgrimage. Her family was both, whether it was here on earth or watching from beyond the boundaries of this earth. Every family member was taking a pilgrimage and spreading their love to each other. She swallowed the lump in her throat. The children could not have picked a better symbol to represent them.

        Hannah approached it. "You like it?"

        "It's beautiful, Hannah."

        "Momma thought it suited us."

        Marna turned her head to look down at the child. "Momma?" She looked around the room. "Your mother gave you that idea?"

        Hannah nodded. "She visited me this morning. She said we were going to meet our sister and we needed to make her feel welcome."

        Marna swallowed. "You did well." She hugged Hannah and then called everybody over. "Everyone, I'd like you to meet Arella." A murmur of hellos went around as Arella clung tighter to Marna's hand. She smiled down at the child. "Arella, this is Isaiah, Elizabeth, Hannah, Joseph, David, Moses, Jacob, and Mary." Marna pointed out each of the children as she said their name, and when she came to Mary, Arella stared at her in amazement. Her curious eyes turned to Jacob. "We have met before, in dreams, yes?"

        Marna crouched down. "No Arella, it wasn't Jacob you met, it was Heinderick --- another brother who looks like Jacob. One we are trying to find, like we found you."

        Arella turned sad eyes to Marna. "Are bad men after him, too?"

        "Yeah, sweetie, they are." She smiled and pushed some hair from her face. "We're going to look for him and try to help him get away before the bad men find him, okay?" Arella nodded.

        Rose cleared her throat. "I think Tanner is picking up pizza for dinner on his way here. Why don't you girls take Arella and get her settled, show her around a bit."

        "Okay." They nodded and Mary reached out her hand to Arella. Arella hesitated. "It's okay, Arella, you're my sister. You can hold my hand. I won't hurt you. You don't have to be scared anymore. We take care of each other in this family." Marna covered her mouth, drawing in a breath. Mary had repeated a phrase she had heard her older siblings and the adults around her say many times. Arella slowly let go of Marna's hand and took Mary's offered one. A sign of trust? Maybe, but it was definitely a move in the right direction. The girls went off as the rest of the family crowded around Marna and asked about her adventure.

*****

        Marna smiled as the Girls went for another round of Sorry. It had been a common gift under the Christmas tree, year after year, as she and Amanda had consistently worn out the favorite board game. She had seen it on the shelf of the World Mart store and couldn't help but buy it for her family. It was nice to see that through decades of changes some things could remain the same. She brought a plate of chocolate chip cookies over to the table with four glasses of milk and set them down, glanced at the clock and smiled. "Half an hour before bedtime, girls."

        A collective groan went around the table and then Elizabeth said, "Can't we stay up a little while longer, Aunt Marna?"

        Marna grinned. "Nice try, ladies, but I've already broken bedtime by an hour-and-a-half in honor of Arella's arrival. Now you all need to finish your game and hit the sheets. I think Tanner has a full day planned for you tomorrow as far as activities go for your live lesson learning."

        "That I do, starting with museums and a few galleries," Tanner said as he stepped over the threshold and into the kitchen. "Listen to your mother, ah, I mean your aunt. I might even let you stop at a few of the street vendors during our travels."

        "Yay !" The girls said in unison,

"I want a hat," Elizabeth said.

"I want one of those neat hair clips with my name in German," Elizabeth chimed in. "What about you, Mary?"

"A new toy," Mary said. Marna smiled. "Arella, what are you going to get?"

"I already have what I want," she said. Marna smiled at the child's simple answer.

"Walk me out?" Tanner requested.

"Sure," she said. "Half an hour, girls." She walked with him to the door and stepped into the hall with him. "Thank you for the pizza," she said.

"My pleasure." He searched her face with his eyes. "How are you feeling? Kyle told me about the fight."

"I'm fine," she assured him. "It was just a little bump. That's all."

He caught her chin with his hand and looked it over. "I should have been there."

"Tanner . . ." She gently stepped away from his touch. "You were where Keys told you to be. Kyle and I handled it. He's a bit immature and lacking in the common sense department sometimes and I've heard the stories about his trying to hold the ball instead of playing with the team, but when push came to shove and when it mattered, he had my back."

He drew in a breath and not knowing what else to do, put his hands in his pockets. "I just feel a little protective over my partners. Something I need to work on I guess."

"Tanner, I understand your sense of responsibility toward me and the kids. I really do. You were there during the most horrible night of my life and you tried to save him, I know you did, and you've been there every day since, but you can't be there all the time. Sometimes you just have to trust me to do it on my own." She smiled. "You're a good friend and there isn't anybody else I'd rather have covering my back, but there will be times when somebody else will have to. He nodded, afraid to speak for fear she might sense the turmoil going on within him. She reached out and touched his arm. "We good?" He nodded again. "Great, I'll see you in the morning. Keys thinks we should get an early start to try and pick up the trail."

"I'll bring the coffee," he said with a sideways smile.

"Good." She stepped up on tiptoes and kissed his cheek. "Night, Tanner, sweet dreams." With those innocent words, she stepped back into the apartment. He stood a few more minutes staring at the closed door, fighting the urge to open it and reenter her presence if only for a few more precious minutes.

"Man, you are so losing it, Williams," he said to himself and turned to retreat to his apartment next door. A young woman stepped out of the shadows of the hallway, her October blue eyes flashing, the only betrayal of her mixed heritage, as Tanner's door closed behind him. She stood in the low lighting of the hall as the glitter on her bronze skin twinkled. Her black lace scarf covered her ebony hair, pulled into a braided bun. Her bare feet peaked out from her dress that fell to her ankles in a flare of multi-colored layered skirting, and the bodice was a dark, black lace pulled taut over her ample breasts enclosed in blue satin and the straps crossing over her shoulders embroidered with blue satin roses.

She pulled out her phone, dialed and spoke to the other party in Romanian. "You were right. They're here. . . I can't do it here . . . I'll be at my parent's farm at Christmas time. . . You take her or I kill her . . . He will honor our families' commitment or suffer the consequences . . ." She hung up the phone.

Tanner's door opened. She quickly stepped back into the shadows and waved her hand. Her cloak went up. Tanner locked his door and started down the hall. She smiled. Perhaps Christmas would come early this year. She closed her eyes and focused. Tanner felt a pain go through his head, quickly his hand went up to his temple, another door opened. "Hey, Tanner?" Ventura said as he stepped out of his apartment. She released her hold and peaked around the corner.

"Hey, Pete," Tanner said as he rubbed his temple.

"Headache?" Ventura queried, falling into step beside him.

"Yeah, it's been a long day," Tanner verified as he reached for the elevator. "I was restless and thought I'd go down to the cafe for some tea, listen to their guest singer. I might as well stop at the gift shop and pick up some aspirin, too."

"Here," Ventura said, tossing him a bottle. "Try these. They work better."

Tanner looked at the bottle, shrugged, and stepped into the car when the doors slid open. "Mind if I join you?" Pete asked. "I don't drink tea, but a cup of espresso will do me just fine." Tanner waved him into the car just before the doors slid closed.

The woman stepped back into the shadows of the hallway. A sign from the Gods no doubt. She turned on her heal, opened the exit door, lifted her skirt, and hurried down the stairs.

The first thing Tanner noticed when they got to the cafe was the amount of people. He glanced at his watch. "They must have some mighty fine coffee here," Ventura stated.

"Adalia is playing tonight." The approaching host was a blonde-haired woman with gray eyes. We were all thrilled when we found out she was on the tour list." She smiled. "She's on break right now. Just two in your party?"

"Yeah," Tanner stated as they followed her to a quiet table among three others, on a riser section of the room, surrounded by railings and petitioned off from the balcony by windows now open to let in the spring air. Couples occupied the other tables.

"Who's Adalia?"

"Only the most sought after vocalist this side of Romania. She's one of the hottest artists on today's pop culture."

"Am I going to need earplugs for this presentation?" Ventura teased.

She giggled. "Gosh no. She sings more folk-type music and haunting melodies. Her voice is so beautiful. Critics have said that it's the best one to come around the pop culture in decades."

"Really?" Ventura clicked his tongue. "Well this I got to hear. When will she return?"

The girl looked at her watch. "Due to return in five." She handed them menus. "Enjoy the show." Smiling, she wandered to the other tables to pick up dishes, chat and take orders.

Ventura let his eyes scrape over Tanner's features. "How's the head?"

"The edge is gone, but it clings. Funny, I never suffered too many headaches ..." He turned his attention to the menu.

"Until Bradshaw's attack," Ventura finished. "Have you talked to Keys? Maybe something was left behind by Bradshaw's intrusions, some ghost tracking maybe."

"No. They don't happen all that often. I think it's more the use and evolving of my abilities than anything else."

"Maybe . . ." The PA announcement cut Ventura off.

"Ladies and gentlemen, please welcome back ADALIA !" The crowd burst into applause and hoots of encouragement as the dark-haired beauty came onto the stage. She wore a tightly fit, off –the-shoulder bra top, and a long slim A-line skirt in peacock blue and pink with a slit clear up to her hips on both sides where fine toned, bronze-skinned legs, covered in skin - glitter. twinkled in the low lighting of the cafe. Her gold, studded medallion belt boasted embedded emeralds that matched the emerald studded collar around her neck and the dangling emerald earrings peeking out from her hip-length, coal black hair as she swung it behind her bare shoulder and broke into a peppy song about having a party with friends in a rock house cafe, swinging her hips belly dance style. She sung the lyrics in Romanian first then in English as the enthusiastic crowd clapped with her and some of the young girls, dressed in brightly colored clothing, got up and mimicked her dance moves. Adalia smiled, and encouraged her fans with a point and clapped to the beat as she danced on the platform in the middle of the room.

"Now that is easy on the eyes," Ventura stated softly as the Server delivered their orders.

"Isn't she wonderful?" The young girl asked.

"She is at that," Peter said. He winked at the girl. "I think she's got my buddy bewitched with her beauty." The girl laughed and left the table, as the music changed and Adalia moved into a soft, caressing ballad. Peter glanced at Tanner, chuckled, and shook his head. "Keep that up, Williams, you're going to have to marry her." When Tanner didn't answer, Ventura slapped his arm.

"Huh, wha . . ."

"Where are you?"

"Sorry?"

"She's probably married with six kids back home on the farm," Ventura teased.

Tanner grinned. "Sorry, lost in thought I guess." He sipped his tea.

"Well if ain't her then it's got to be another member of the female gender. Only a woman would get a man that far away from reality." He took a sip of his espresso. "Wanna talk about it?"

"Naa. It's just something I've got to work out on my own."

"I see." The music changed again. Adalia's voice became mournful. "Give her time, Tanner."

Tanner's head lifted from his tea. "I'm sorry."

"The woman that has you all tied in knots. Give her time. She may have a lot she's dealing with, too."

"I know." He smiled at his friend. "Patience has never been a virtue of mine."

"This one may be worth the wait, my friend."

"Yeah, she may be at that." He smiled at Ventura, reached for his teacup and raised it toward his friend. "Thank you."

"Anytime." Ventura took another drink of his Espresso. "As for me, I'd like to get a piece of that. But those baby-blues keep scanning right over me." Tanner grinned and turned his attention back to Adalia as she swooped into another heartstring folk song. The more she sang, the more he seemed to drift away on her lyrics. Eventually he fancied he understood them.

"Let me in your life
Let me relieve your pain
I can lead the way
make you forget the strife
She will only increase the hurt
not give you what you deserve
She just wants to flirt
It's love for you I will serve."

The chorus of the song seemed to whisper in his head repeatedly in her haunting voice. The headache slipped away as the melody comforted him and he relaxed. The rest of the room seemed to slip away, leaving only him and Adalia. Her blue eyes raised and sought him out and she whispered softly, alluring. "Let me in, Tanner." He shook his head and drew in a quick breath, looking around.

Ventura quickly put his hand on Tanner's arm. "Easy there, cowboy," he said as Tanner looked his way. "What was that?"

"I-I don't know, I must have dozed off. I had some weird dream."

He thought quietly for a moment and then thought better of sharing his experience with Ventura. "You know what, I can't recall it. I think I'm just going to head back to my room." He stood up and dropped a twenty on the table. "I'll see you tomorrow."

"Yeah, sure." Ventura watched him go and then brought his eyes back to the performer. Her blue eyes scanned the room, coming to rest on Tanner's back in a look that almost seemed too intimate.

She must have sensed his eyes because she returned her gaze to his, lingered, and moved on. Ventura dropped another bill on the table and headed out of the cafe, and as he passed the poster hanging on the window of the cafe, announcing the Adalia performance. He quickly looked around, ripped it from the tack, folded it up, and slipped it into his jacket pocket, moving to the elevator.

*****

"Okay, Isaiah, time to say goodnight to Tammy," Marna said as she walked to Isaiah's bedroom door and saw him in a private chat room with TamSam101 on HomeSpot.com, the social network that Keys had started.

"I'm helping her with her Social Studies paper. She's doing it on the witch trials. I thought we would be a great resource for her considering our roots go back that far."

An involuntary chill claimed Marna's spine as she remembered the horrifying story her Aunt had relayed to her in the dream realm. "I see. Well, how much farther have you got to go?"

He typed a message to Tammy and she immediately responded. Isaiah read the words on the screen and then he looked at Marna. "She says fifteen minutes tops."

"All right then lights out, Isaiah, I mean it. Tanner has quite the itinerary planned for you guys tomorrow and I suspect you're going to need your sleep."

"Fine." He rolled his eyes in answer to her orders.

"Perhaps you'd like to say goodbye now. Hmm?" She crossed her arms, and rose her brow.

"All right, fifteen minutes." With no further protest, he turned his attention back to the screen and returned her post. With a sigh, Marna moved on to the next room. The boys were already in bed. Jacob was sleeping, and the other three were chatting about their day tomorrow, planning their moves.

She grinned, "I think you should just let Tanner tell you what's going on." A collective groan filled the room. He is the adult in charge of you, so you do what he says, just like you would with me, okay?"

"Okay, Aunt Marna."

"Good." She kissed each of their foreheads and smiled. "No strolls tonight, Moses." He giggled as she left the room and moved on to the girls' room. "How are we doing in here?" Marna said as she entered the room.

"Shhh," the older girls whispered and pointed to Mary's bunk. Arella and Mary had fallen asleep side by side. Mary with a protective arm around Arella, and Arella with an arm around her doll.

Marna felt a tug in her heart. She smiled, kissed both girls on the forehead and hugged the others, leaving the room and closing the door behind her. A warm feeling filled her soul. The children had immediately taken to Arella, and she knew that Amanda had to be smiling down from her beach knowing that her child was safe in the arms of family. "One down, one to go. Manda, I promise you I will get him back."

"*I know...* "came the whispered reply. A gentle caress of a breeze surrounded her and was gone as quickly as it had surfaced. She looked around the room, glanced once more at Isaiah's door to make sure it was dark under it, and she proceeded to clean up the dishes and the pizza boxes before she headed to her own room to get some sleep.

<p style="text-align:center">~~~~~</p>

Isaiah walked on the dark street. In the fog, he saw signs in German but couldn't read them. He heard something behind him, causing him to spin around. A figure emerged from the shadow. "Jacob, what are you doing out here?"

The boy stared at him, wide-eyed and frightened. "Have you come to help me?" the boy whispered.

"Help you? Help you do what?" Isaiah reached out with his hand. "Come on, we've got to get back before Marna realizes we're gone."

"He's going to hurt her."

"Hurt who? Jacob, you're not making any sense."

"He's a bad man."

Isaiah narrowed his eye, and realized his mistake. "You're not Jacob, are you? You're Heinderick." He looked around. "Have you come to tell me where you are? We've found Arella. She is with us. We'll come for you, but you have to tell us where to look."

"It's dark and it's cold. My parents brought me here. They told me it was a school, but bad things happen here."

"Bad things?" Fear gripped Isaiah's heart. "What kind of bad things? Heinderick where is here? Who's with you?"

"I do not know, but the Master kills with his hands. I am frightened, Isaiah. I was happy with my family. Why did they give me away?" His lips puckered and he sniffed. "What have I done wrong?"

"Heinderick, can you tell me anything that might help us find you?"

"They are coming. I have to --- No! I am sorry --- I will not do it again----a-h-h-h ...," The screams echoed in the air until complete silence replaced them. Through the fog, Isaiah saw a shadowed, cloaked figure emerging. He dived into a nearby brush, and closed his eyes.

"I know you are here, boy," an angry voice boomed across the night. Isaiah curled up, willing himself to wake up. "You cannot, boy. I have control of your dream now. It will end on my terms as will your waking cycle." The heavy footsteps grew closer. Isaiah swallowed and looked for an escape. Suddenly a road appeared beside his clump of bushes and an arrow pointing left and before him stood his mother. "Come, Isaiah, run and don't look back !" Amanda helped him up, urged him ahead of her. . .

*****

Marna awoke to Hannah viciously shaking her. "Aunt Marna, Isaiah's in trouble we have to help him."

"What?" Marna looked at her clock. It was 2:00 a.m. "Hannah, what are you talking about? He's sleeping."

"Momma came to me! She says he's in trouble in his dream and he needs our help!"

Marna sat up, and grabbed her arms. "What kind of trouble."

"She said someone named Pierre was chasing him."

She jumped up. "Have you tried waking him up?"

"Yes, but he's sweating, and crying and won't wake up."

Marna took Hannah's hand, grabbed her GPC and summoned Keys. "Marna, what is it?"

"Pierre's launching a dream attack on Isaiah. Amanda contacted Hannah and said we needed to help him."

"I'll be right there !" He ended communication and grabbed some sweats throwing them on as he sent out distress calls to the team.

Isaiah breathed heavily as he continued to run. His side hurt and his head was starting to pound. He didn't see a rock in the path and tripped, twisting his ankle, but limped on. "Fight him, Isaiah," Amanda ordered.

"I'm trying, but I'm so tired, and my ankle hurts."

"Come on." She took his hand, and pulled him in to some brush, leaning him against the tree. "Breathe deep, Son, rest for a moment." She looked over his ankle. It was swollen and bruised. "Stay put, Isaiah, it's time to call in the Calvary." She focused on Hannah and Marna both. One of them had to see her.

"Momma !" Hannah cried. The others in the room looked at the corner Hannah focused on. Hannah listened for a moment and Marna saw her features contort with fear. Isaiah's face was so white it was almost translucent, his breathing labored. Hannah looked at them. "She said Isaiah's tired and he can't run anymore because he hurt his ankle." Marna pulled back the covers, and sure enough, Isaiah's ankle was swollen and turning purple and blue with bruising. She raised a hand to her mouth. Hannah continued to relay Amanda's message. "Pierre is not far behind them and if he catches up with them she can only help Isaiah for a short time. She said only the Collective can fight him off."

"The Collective? How?" Marna asked.

"You join him in the Dream Realm," Keys said as he walked into the room, "and you fight Lamontage."

"I-I've never done that," Marna whispered. "I-I don't know how."

"It's not something you can do by yourself, Marna. Arella and Jacob will have to help you." The children looked at Keys. "Your magnification, the Collective and their Dream Walking abilities will all be needed, but you can only do it for a short time. The more Dream Walkers you have, the longer you can stay. Three is usually a good number, but two will do for a short time." He turned his attention to the children. "Are you two willing to help your brother?" They nodded. "Okay, Arella and Jacob's abilities can get you there, but you'll all have to do your part to ward off the attack once there. You don't have enough time nor power to beat him in the Dream Realm. He is too powerful, but you can weaken him enough to retrieve Isaiah safely. I'll be here monitoring. If I'm needed, I'll join you." They all nodded, as did Keys. The family joined hands gathering around their brother and with a final look at Keys, Marna reached out and took Isaiah's hand. Immediately she felt the pull as did the rest of them, and they landed on a country road hazed over in fog.

~~~~~~

"Stay close," Marna cautioned the family. She squinted to see through the mist. "Isaiah?" she whispered.

"Over here." Amanda's voice came from the brush beside them. The family ran into the brush. Isaiah was leaning against a tree. "He's very weak, Marny. He needs to get out of this realm."

"Working on it, Manda." She turned to Isaiah. "How did he get him here in first place?" she demanded.

"H-Hein-ick," Isaiah said between gulps of air. "He's in trouble. C-contacted me through dream. Th-they caught him. P-Pierre st-stole the dream." Isaiah closed his eyes. "He's close -- I can track him."

"Alright, let's change this dream." As she took their hands, Amanda started to get up. "No, Amanda, stay with him."

"But you may need my help."

"Isaiah needs someone with him, Manda. He's injured. Stay with him, and don't let him use his abilities at all. Shield him. I have a feeling Lamontage has tracking abilities. That's how he knew Heinderick had connected to Isaiah, and he continued to use them to track down your distress call to Hannah."

"Oh my, I never gave it a thought."

"It's not your fault, Manda, just stay with Isaiah." Amanda nodded and watched them go. "She's getting stronger isn't she?" She said to the apparition that shimmered to life behind her.

"Yes, she is. You should be proud." Keys said. "It won't be long before you can join Peter and rest, Amanda."

"Watch over her Keys. Don't let Bradshaw's psychic nasties get their claws into her."

"I won't." He sighed. "But it's going to be a tough battle to get them all. He had years to create them. Lamontage is only the beginning."

"I know, and the Conflicts brought others that can be just as dangerous if not more so, but she's become a force to be reckoned with. This realm is rocking with news of her and the rest of the prophecy."

"Unfortunately, the good people are not the only ones who are hearing of her reputation."

"I know, but you and Guardian will be her sanctuary."

"We will try, Amanda, we will try." He smiled and turned his attention to the family moving down the country road. This was only the beginning for Marna and the whole Guardian collective. With a heavy sigh, he shimmered out.

Marna and the children ran down the road to an open field. "Arella and Jacob, do you think you can create a barn in this area?" They nodded. "Then let's do it." In seconds, a barn appeared with a fenced-in pasture and several horses running around in it. The two children looked at each other and giggled. Marna nodded. "Nice." She grinned. "Now for the inside." She led the children inside. "A few lit lanterns." They appeared. "Hay spread on the floor down here, and stacked in the loft. Hay clogged the loft. "Okay, let's not get too carried away." Several bails disappeared and a pitchfork appeared. "Cute," she shook her head as they giggled again. "Let the games begin. Children link." They all grabbed hands and a surge of electricity went through them all. Their thoughts became one; their abilities became one. They could read each other's thoughts, see what each other saw and do what each other could do. They were one. They were a Collective. Arella held tight to Marna's hand on one side and Elizabeth's on the other. She was frightened, yet oddly comforted. She fit and she knew she belonged. "Moses bi-locate and show our guest how to get here."

An essence of Moses body appeared before them and ran out of the barn. His feet carried him to the road. "Clear skies everyone." The fog cleared and the stars came out. Pierre caught sight of Moses. "Return, Moses !" Moses' form evaporated, but the bait was set and seconds later, they heard his approach.

"You cannot hide from me !" He bellowed as he approached the barn. "I have waited too long for this!"

"Do not break contact." Their communication came through psychic thoughts only. They didn't need words between them to communicate and they understood this.

He burst through the doors and laughed as he faced them. "I knew you would come if I trapped the boy."

"Careful what you wish for," Marna hissed. He raised his hand. "Force field !" Marna ordered. Mary and Arella joined their forcefield abilities. A bright purple and white mist surrounded them. His attack sparked off it and bounced back at him knocking him back.

"The children cannot hold for long," he hissed approaching them.

"Long enough !" She smiled. Elizabeth focused and all the lanterns fell to the floor shattering and catching the surrounding hay on fire. They trapped Pierre by circling him with four walls of fire. "Doors !" The front barn doors closed and latched from the outside. "NOW !" Marna ordered as the flames engulfed the beams on either side of Pierre. Tongues of flame trailed up to the loft. The girls dropped the Force field and Marna picked her up while Elizabeth picked up Arella and they ran from the building to the safety of the surrounding grounds.

"I'll be back !" Lamontage bellowed from the burning building.

"I bet you will," she whispered as the dream realm evaporated and the family was once again standing above Isaiah in his bedroom.

~~~~~

Isaiah bolted upright in bed and Marna sat down beside him, pulling him into her arms rocking him. "Shhh… It's alright. It's over now." Isaiah clung to Marna as she rubbed his hair, kissed the top of his head and held him until his trembling subsided. When he became calm, Keys stepped forward.

"Marna, would you mind if I talked to Isaiah for a few minutes?"

She looked like she was going to object, but she knew that the information Keys needed to get was important if they were to help Heinderick and defeat Lamontage for good. "Of course," she nodded and turned to the others. "Come on children, let's go back to bed."

"Will Isaiah be okay?" Mary asked feeling the fear and the pain cascading off him through her empathy.

"Of course he will be, sweetie." She crouched down to meet her glance. "I'll bet if you go give him one of your Mary hugs, he'll feel even better." Mary smiled, nodded and ran to the bed, climbed up and wrapped her arms tightly around his neck. He sniffed and hugged her back.

"G'night, Isaiah. Only good dreams the rest of the night."

"Night, squirt." He smiled through fresh tears and tousled her head. She giggled and jumped down to join the others as they headed out the door.

Marna turned toward Keys. "Keep it short," she said and smiled at Isaiah before she stepped out and closed the door.

Keys cleared his throat as he walked around and pulled the desk chair to Isaiah's bedside. "How do you feel, Son?" Isaiah shrugged. "It's a harrowing experience, I know. A Dream Weaving attack is far from pleasant, but you made it out alive, some can't say that." Isaiah nodded, sniffing, and rubbing his hand under his nose. Keys handed him a handkerchief. Isaiah took it and blew. "You said it started as a visitation from Heinderick?" Isaiah nodded. "Isaiah, I know this is painful and hard to relive, but I need to know everything that transpired before Lamontage attacked. Can you do that for me, Son?" Isaiah nodded. "Please take your time, pull it together, and then start when you're ready."

Isaiah drew in a few breaths and then closed his eyes as he tried to recall everything that Heinderick said to him, what he said to Heinderick and how he tried to help him recall certain things that might help them rescue him. "When they found him, he begged them not to hurt him, said that he was sorry, and it wouldn't happen again." Isaiah raised his eyes to Keys. "He's scared Keys, real scared. We have to help him."

"We will, Son, we will." He reached down and patted the boys back. "You did well tonight, Isaiah, now how about we take a look at that ankle." Keys gently moved the foot around, checked Isaiah's pulse, and felt around the anklebone then smiled. "I'm going to set up some X-rays at the clinic tomorrow, first thing, just to make sure nothing is broken. Until then, I'm going to wrap it up and leave these with your aunt." He pulled a bottle of pain pills from his pocket. "It'll help you sleep and ease the pain a little." Isaiah nodded. Keys handed him the water bottle and two painkillers, wrapped his ankle and placed it on an extra pillow. He then helped the boy settle in for the night, and, left the room, meeting Marna in the hall. He glanced at his watch. It was 4:00 a.m.

"How is he?"

"I gave him a couple of these." He handed the bottle to her. "They've got a mild sedative in the mix so it will help him rest. It'll be a couple of days before he feels it's safe to sleep again. I'm also going to set up X-rays at the clinic for him just to be sure he didn't break anything." Marna nodded. "Where's Kyle?"

"In the kitchen with the others having coffee. The only one missing is Tanner. Ventura said he was sick earlier so he let him rest, didn't call him in."

"Hmm." Keys said wiping his mouth. "I'll check on him later. For now, I'm going to brief everybody on what Isaiah told me, leave Kyle here to block him, then everyone is to take the morning off and get some rest, including you, Marna. I'll send a well rested agent up from Fedpol for security so you can rest." Marna nodded and followed Keys into the kitchen. All talking stopped when he entered. He poured himself a cup of coffee and started filling them in on what Isaiah had told him.

"Kyle, I want you to stay with the family on extra security detail. If Heinderick has made contact once, he may do it again and open up the possibility of another attack by Lamontage. He now knows what the family is capable of, so his strategy will change. Bet on it." Kyle nodded. "Sasha, I'm going to team you up with Rose. You two will be on training detail with Arella. She's got a good handle on her abilities already, but I just want to make sure we know the full scope of them." Sasha nodded. "Demi, you and Bryan team up with Ventura and Heidi and surf HomeSpot.com. See if we can lure anybody out of the cover of the Liberatores compound. Some of our Fedpol counterparts have started scratching the surface but with these new developments, I think the quicker we find a way to breach, the better for Heinderick because they're either going to move him or turn him if we don't. At least that would be my next move if I were Lamontage." A chorus of agreement went around the table. "Marna, you and I are going to recapture our cover IDs and take our son to the hospital tomorrow. Start pushing some buttons to see what lights up."

"Okay."

"For now everyone go to your quarters and get some sleep. Report back here at 1200 hours to start your assignments." After a chorus of good nights, everyone left but Ventura, Rigby and Keys. When Kyle went to Isaiah's bedroom to start his blocking vigil, Ventura turned toward Keys.

"Is there something you need, Peter?"

"Could I have a word with you?" he queried. "Something about the investigation?"

"Sure." He turned to Marna. "Go to bed, Marna. Kyle's with Isaiah and I'll be camping out on your couch. You get some rest."

"Okay." She wished them goodnight and went to her room. Ventura led Keys into the den, closing the door behind him, and pulling out the poster of Adalia.

"What has you in such a state, Peter?" Keys asked.

"This." He handed him the poster.

Keys looked at the poster. "What about her?"

"Tanner and I went to the Cafe earlier. She was singing there."

"I hear she has a lovely voice."

"Something weird went on with Tanner while she sang. It was like he was in a trance or something."

Keys looked at the picture again and then up at Ventura. "What was she singing?"

"I don't know. Some haunting love song in Romanian," he waved it off, "but that's neither here nor there. The point is that Williams looked like he did when Bradshaw had a hold of him. He was complaining of a headache and feeling restless. Do you think Lamontage could be influencing him?"

"I doubt it. He's built strong shields over the last year, but I'll look into the possibility. I'd be more than willing to bet there was something else at play here." He glanced at the picture and up at Ventura.

"Her? But all she did was sing."

"She could be a Maestro Songbird."

"A Love Witch?" Ventura chuckled, shaking his head. "I thought that was just a legend."

"There is no such thing as just a legend in the psychic world, Peter. A Maestro Songbird is rare and unique to the gypsy line, but the ability is real. How many fans fancy themselves so in love with musicians that they stalk the object of their obsession or scream themselves into oblivion at rock concerts? How many couples choose a signature song because they give it credit for the moment they fell in love? Cultural music sooths the soul and the artist reaps the benefit. The difference between that and the psychic phenomenon of the Maestro Songbird is that they seek out their targets, make eye contact and drop subtle hints to the recipient's brain through hypnosis that they're interested. Then she invades the part of their brain that caters to a man's desires and she draws them to her with her haunting melodies. She becomes their heart's desire. She becomes their obsession. They fall completely under her control until she decides to release them. That is usually after they are stupidly and hopelessly in love with her and all they want to do is give her happiness."

"What happens if she releases him and he realizes she's not what he thought she was?"

"There are written cases of the man's heart exploding in his chest if he betrays her or resists her."

Peter's brow furrowed, "that's just damn scary, Keys."

"Most psychic enemies are, Peter." He looked at the paper. "She has all the signature marks of a Maestro Songbird, but I think I'll have Sarah Justice and Misty Schofield research her and see what they find."

"Why do you think she's targeted Tanner?"

"Hmmm." He looked at the picture again. "His mother was a Gypsy from the South Carolina Clan. I'll have the girls start there and see if the lines cross anywhere. We might get an answer. For now, just keep Tanner away from the Cafe."

"Can't we counteract this someway?"

"We can try to block her but if she has already initiated contact, we may need to find someone for him to fall in love with and fast. According to the legend, that is the only way to counteract a love witch's attack. Know of any willing Maidens?"

"Keys, you are a sick man." Ventura said, raising his eyes to Keys.

Keys chuckled. "When the girls research, I'll see what type of blocking is successful against this type of attack. For now, just keep him away from her."

"Easy job... Right. In case you haven't noticed, she's beautiful and he's single and good looking."

"Well it says here tonight is her final showing, so we'll do something to keep him busy on this case until we get more information on her. Then we'll initiate a counter attack on her."

"Alright."

"Go get some rest Peter. She's not going to go after him tonight. A Love Witch is like any other woman. She needs her beauty rest."

Ventura chuckled. "Aren't you the wise one tonight?"

"Comes from little sleep. Go get some rest. Tanner will be okay for tonight."

"Okay." Keys walked him out, then picked up his GPC and dialed the Maine compound. He could joke about this latest threat, but Ventura was right to worry. A Maestro Songbird was easy to fight if all she possessed was her primary ability, but more deadly abilities usually accompanied it, especially if the object of her desire had enough will power to resist her. Tanner was one that would put up a fight because the object of his desire didn't even know he waited for her.

Chapter Nine

"Beep, Beep !" Marna opened her eyes to the obnoxious sound of her alarm, the scent of freshly brewing coffee, and frying bacon. She rolled over to glance at her clock. Large red numbers flashed 10:00 a.m. "Oh my. Half the day is already gone." She threw back her covers and swung her legs over the edge of the bed, sliding her feet into her slippers. She reached for her cotton robe and slipped it on, "who on earth is cooking?" She feared the children had gotten up ahead of her and imagined a mess that would take hours to clean up, but when she opened her door, she didn't hear voices or noisy clatter, just the someone moving pans around quietly in the cupboards. She made her way to the kitchen. Keys had coffee brewing, a large pan of scrambled eggs cooking on one burner, and bacon spitting noisily on another. She leaned against the mold casing of the bar, "Keep this up and I may really have to marry you."

Keys chuckle and glanced her way. "Good morning to you, too. How are you feeling?"

"Like I overslept and missed the school bus."

He shook his head, "You are not late for anything. You have your own driver today," he motioned to himself. "I will be taking care of all of your travel arrangements." He smiled and waved at the table. "Have a seat and I'll get you some coffee."

She looked around. "Where are the children?"

"Tanner is with them in the den going over the itinerary for the day, via the internet, and Isaiah is still sleeping"

"Did you brief Tanner?"

"Yes. He was somewhat disappointed that we didn't include him last night, but I told him the situation was under control, and considering he wasn't feeling well, he was more help listening to his body and resting. The headache was probably a sign of over extending himself because of the constant use of his Blocking ability." He placed coffee before her then went to the stove to flip the bacon.

"He's feeling better?"

"Yes. I believe so." Keys didn't go in to the Maestro suspicions, but knew he had to offer her some explanation due to the fiasco of the year before. Despite what the boy had done to redeem himself since then, the memory would always be on the edge of her mind and ready to feed her doubts. He placed a basket of hot biscuits on the table in front of her and sat across from her. She took one and started to butter it. "Tanner's abilities are evolving quickly and fierce headaches are sometimes a part of that, but he's not and will never again be a threat to you or your family, Marna." She stopped buttering her biscuit and brought her eyes to his, placing the biscuit and the knife on her plate.

"Logically I know this, Keys. Most days, I even believe it . . ."

"But the uncertainty is there when a situation or an action takes you back."

She nodded, "Does that make me a horrible person?"

He smiled and shook his head. "No, just human."

"There is a 'but' in there somewhere isn't there?"

He cleared his throat and folded his hands before him. "Having a partner means trusting them, Marna. It's imperative to have that in place in all situations. In light of how your acquaintance with Tanner began, I can understand your hesitation, but in his defense, he has gone beyond what is required to prove he can be trusted, especially to you. He's a damn fine agent."

"I know. Like I said, most of the time I don't think twice about it, but then someone mentions he has a headache or he forgets something or he's not well and I ask myself 'Is it happening again? Has somebody gotten in?' The walls go up, and the process starts all over."

"The walls will come down and stay down eventually, Marna. He knows you can't help but have doubts at times. He even has doubts himself, though he wouldn't admit it, but sometimes you have to stamp those down and go with pure instinct. That's what is going to get you through those rough moments and solidify your partnership."

She lifted her eyes to him. "Maybe a partnership between us isn't such a good idea, Keys. Maybe it would be fairer to him, to me, to clients and to other agents if we weren't partners."

Keys sighed. Her concerns were well founded, but in the 30 plus years he had run Guardian, he had yet to find a new team that didn't have some type of growing pains. "If I thought that, you wouldn't be partners. You two fit, Marna. Building a relationship of trust comes from working together and getting to know each other well. All of which will happen, you just have to allow it to."

"I'm sorry." She sighed, playing with her napkin. "I don't even know why I just said what I did." She raised her eyes to his.

He placed a fatherly hand over hers, stilling her fidgeting with the napkin. "Moving on is more than just letting go, Marna, you have to make changes too. I'm pretty sure working with Tanner will help you get there."

"You're probably right."

"I am. There will come a day when you believe it too. Remember that." She bobbed her head once.

The den door opened and the children joined them at the table wishing them a good morning. Keys placed a large bowl of eggs and a platter of bacon on the table, and they dropped the conversation.

An hour and a half later, Marna was at the door, telling them to have fun on their ventures. She smiled at the short argument over the elevator buttons and glanced up at Tanner as he paused by the door. "Can you call me with an update on Isaiah later?"

"Of course. How are you feeling?"

He grinned. "Better. Thank you for asking. Keys said it was probably the over extension of the new Blocking abilities ." He smiled. "How about you? Any ill effects from the fight yesterday or the dream encounter last night?" His eyes shifted to her head wound before returning to hers.

She shook her head. "Head's fine and I think Isaiah got the worst of Lamontage's attack."

"Poor kid." He glanced in the general direction of Isaiah's door. "I hope it didn't freak him out too much."

"Lamontage is a scary enough Dream Demon or Boogey Man, whatever you want to call him. I'm just glad we were able to break the dream-event."

Tanner crossed his arms. "Speaking of which, whatever made you think of a barn fire to fight him off?"

"Something Keys told me a while back. I think fire is a good way to thwart, if not destroy this man. He tends to veer away from it."

"You could be right, Agent Farlow."

"Let's hope it's a good enough assumption to bare some fruit. Guardian is investigating the possibility, and developing defense weapons accordingly." For a moment, there was a roaring silence between them. Marna felt foolish for doubting him even a small amount.

"Uncle Tanner ..." Mary called. "Come on! I want to go to the museem."

Tanner grinned and turned his attention to Mary. "It's museum and yes, we'll go." He went over and started filing the kids into the elevator, but before the doors closed, he popped his head out. "Hey, Marna, we're going to have a picnic lunch in the park at around 2:00, if you'd like to join us. The Cafe kitchen has put together enough food to feed an army."

She nodded. "If we get things done, I think I will."

"Fair enough," he nodded and ducked into the elevator. Marna was about to step back into the apartment when the second elevator opened and Demi and Bryan stepped out.

"Keys in there?" Their faces showed their concern and disgust.

"Yeah, what's wrong?" Demi handed her a HomeSpot.com profile of a young girl with dark hair and blue eyes, she was in her mid- teens, wearing a white linen cloak, and she was in the late stages of pregnancy. Marna knew the face, well, a much older version of the face. She turned around and stepped in to the apartment. Keys was looking over a copy of the print out.

"Another Rose clone?" Marna asked.

Demi looked at Keys and he nodded. "Yeah, she was among the pictures and information we confiscated from Bradshaw's safe. We managed to find the others and place them in suitable homes but we couldn't find her. Her name is Iris VanGardt."

"Where is she?"

"Lamontage's compound," Demi sighed. "She contacted my alias on HomeSpot. She's scared. Her due date is coming up fast and she's alone, no family. She preaches how wonderful the compound is and how the Master has so much love to share. Practically begged me to come and visit her to see for myself." She sighed. "However, she also told me of other young women, especially a young girl she befriended, a Melissa Gait, that disappeared after they delivered. I think among all the valor she presents, she's nothing but a scared young girl."

"What were the common traits of the others?" Keys queried.

"They all had high functioning, rare abilities, such as Iris. Her abilities are Hyper-memorization, Telepathy, and Telekinesis. Those are just the ones she was open about."

"How did she know to contact you?"

"She didn't. My profile cover is an Irish immigrant on the run from an abusive husband."

"How was she even able to get to a computer? Nevermind paying the homespot membership fee?" Marna furrowed her brow. "I'm sure Pierre isn't letting his people get too close to the outside world."

"One of the Liberatores is sweet on her. He loans her his GPC, I'm assuming he paid the fee too. She's only been there a year. Like Heinderick, she was placed there by her Handlers."

"Pierre is gathering what's left of Bradshaw's kids," Keys mused. "The ones we don't get to first." Keys brought his eyes back to Demi. "Has she told you of any others, like she and Heinderick, who have been brought in to the compound over the last year?"

"Yeah, about six, all female, all in their mid to late teens, all impregnated within the last year." Demi sighed. "Three have been reported to have left the compound after giving birth, leaving the child behind. No contact after leaving. They just disappeared."

Marna fell into the chair behind her. "He's using them as his own breeding stock with him being the sire."

"That's my take."

"But Heinderick is so young, and he's not female."

Keys cleared his throat. "That's his way to you, Marna. You are the ultimate prize. That's what the dream event was all about last night. He was baiting you. " Keys said with a knowing sigh."If he fathered children with you, he could create the ultimate psychic family. A powerhouse not easily brought down. That's why he is using seducing tactics with you. He doesn't want to kill you. He wants you in his bed and under his control."

"Dream on Tarzan," she put the picture down, stood up to face him. "Let's give him what he wants and I'll destroy him from the inside."

"I've already made contact. I've established my cover, and the backstopping is finished," Demi stated, "I'm going in."

"What? Keys you can't let her do this." Marna insisted.

"It's the only thing that makes sense Marna. We can't chance you going in. We don't know how much damage he may have already done to your resistance." He sighed, " Demi will lay the groundwork. We need to get a read on his security, his personal habits and his schedules. "You'd be his prisoner from day one, You'd have no freedom. Demi would be just another lost soul. She goes in under the name of Meagan Cartwright, a vulnerable young woman in need of salvation from an abusive man. She's the perfect target for Lamontage's seducing ability, and possibly, because she's older, she may become one of his favorites. He begins to trust her. The more trust she builds, the more freedom he gives her, and with more freedom comes the ability to breach the compound. Once she's in, she'll look for Heinderick, find him and secure his safety. That's when you and Tanner make your move with the extraction team, Marna. Then we take him down."

As much as she hated to admit it, he was right. The plan was solid. "When do you meet her?" Marna queried of Demi.

"Eight tonight at Zurich station."

"Be careful," Keys said as he moved to his brief case and pulled a small packet, handing it to her. "It's all here. The Guardian camera watch, and the listening device in the binder of Mark Twain's Huck Finn. To the untrained eye, it will look like nothing more than an old hardback book, but in the fine threads of the binding is your antenna wire and device. He opened the book to show her the microphone and antennae. The device looked like a glue drop. Use this only if you have to. An old radio sequence can pick you up, but you have a higher risk of a tracker honing in on your psychic channels if you use those. When you feel you are in the clear use this. He handed her a very small ear-bud. That will keep us connected, and it is under a special Guardian code not used by any other law enforcement agency. Lamontage is suspicious by nature, and you will be under scrutiny when you first get there," Demi nodded, "You're flying solo in there, Demi, no back up but what devices we can send in with you could be your life line. You're GPC will most likely be the first thing confiscated, so hide yours, and in the envelope is your cover ID GPC. Once he takes that, it may be enough to satisfy him. Take your personal one, and find somewhere safe to hide it in your quarters."

"Will do."

"Your first target will be Heinderick, locate him and notify us for extraction."

"Okay," She opened the enveloped and looked over its contents. As far as she could see, she had everything she needed and said so.

"Good. Go home, find the appropriate attire to fit your cover, and then keep your head down for the day, we don't want to chance anyone from the compound seeing you and blowing your cover before you've had a chance to get through the gates."

"Yes sir." Isaiah came hobbling out of his room on crutches Keys had securedfor him, and joined them by the kitchen table.

"I'm ready."

"Then I think we should go, don't you?" The three of them left the apartment, caught the elevator to the lobby, and went over to leave the Key. "Patty, we'll be at the hospital the rest of the morning having Isaiah's ankle tended to. Any calls come in forward them to my alias cell."

"Sure thing, Mr. Keys." The pretty receptionist said.

"Thank you." He waved Isaiah and Marna ahead of him, and then opened the door for them to exit first."

*****

Tanner, Kyle and Sasha herded the kids out of the museum and headed for the park three blocks away. Tanner glanced at his watch, and then at his GPC for the sixth time in the last forty minutes. "Got a hot lunch date, bro?" Kyle asked.

"Yeah with two Guardian cover agents, nine kids and their aunt if she gets a moment," he scoffed, "so hot it's sizzling."

"hmm." Kyle said putting his hands in his pockets as he kept pace with Tanner. Sasha hovered around Mary and Arella a few paces ahead. "Well, Marna is kinda sizzling."

Tanner slowed, and glanced sideways at Kyle. The disapproval threaded into his words. "Kyle, really? She's still mourning her husband.?"

"Whoa, Tiger, I said she was hot, I didn't say I wanted to feed her a love potion. Besides she's a bit territorial for me."

Tanner chuckled. "I heard she kind of let you have it at the station."

"That's putting it mildly. With all the flaming arrows searing into my flesh, from that lady's blue peepers, I'm surprised I didn't burn.."

Tanner laughed, "Marna will let you know if she isn't happy with you."

"Yeah, I kind of got that." He chuckled. I did do a little research on her though." He slid his gaze toward Tanner again. "You two have a colorful past."

"I wouldn't call it a past, Kyle, we met under some unfortunate circumstances, and I wasn't myself. Somebody else controlled my actions because I was ignorant. I didn't know enough about psychic abilities to recognize the signs. My actions caused her a great deal of pain," he sighed, "I'm grateful she's willing to work with me despite it all."

"So why did Keys make you partners? Considering everything, I would think a bit of space between you two would be a better move."

Tanner shrugged. "You'll have to ask him that. - - - Hey David, don't do that." Tanner moved forward a few paces, and stepped between David and Joseph as the former started squirting water at his brother with a water gun he had picked up at one of the street vendors and Joseph was starting to get irritated. Their conversation about Marna unfinished, Kyle watched as Tanner made his way through the children and smiled. Hmmm, very tight lipped about Miss Marna, wasn't he? Made him wonder if there was more interest there than he let on.

"I do love a challenge, Williams," Kyle muttered.

Tanner confiscated the water weapon, and slid it into his jacket pocket, then slid his hands into his pants pocket, slowing his pace a little to stay steady with the boys. Why had Keys kept him and Marna partners, knowing their past? He furrowed his brow, thinking of the conversation he had with Marna the night before. Snatches of it came back to him. . . *I understand your sense of responsibility toward the kids and me* . . . was that what he was feeling? A sense of responsibility? . . . *but you can't be there all the time. . . . You just have to trust me to do it on my own* . . . was she telling him she needed space? Telling him that she really didn't want him hovering around her? . . . *You're a good friend* . . . was that all he was, all he would ever be? . . .*'Tanner, let me in'* . . .There was that voice again. Soft, sensual, alluring . . .calling to him, wanting him to come, wanting him to be a part of . . .

"Tanner !" Kyle yelled. Tanner snapped back to the present, Arella and Mary giggled. The kids, Sasha and Kyle stood at the entrance to the park, and Tanner was about three feet beyond it, oblivious to the fact that they had stopped. He looked around and grinned.

"Guess I was on automatic pilot."

"You were on automatic something," Kyle said, "switch back to manual. I don't know about everybody else but I'm starving," He took all the kids in with a glance. "How about we snatch up a piece of grass and eat that fantastic lunch that was packed for us."

"Yeah !" The children's voices blended in one big roar. Sasha led them in to the park.

Tanner started following them, but Kyle stopped him with a hand on his shoulder, "You sure you're okay?"

"Of course. I was just a little distracted."

"Distracted is missing a bird that flies by, you were out in left field, man. The kids all called your name, and you didn't hear them."

"They did?" Kyle nodded. "Sorry, guess I just spaced."

"Sorry does no good over a dead or wounded agent, Pal. Pull it together and file whatever it is that is driving you to distraction, because if it happens again, I go to Keys. We can't risk that kind of error in the field, Williams, especially not with a nemesis like Lamontage."

"It won't happen again."

"See that it doesn't." He held Tanner's gaze for a few seconds before he said, "Come on, let's go eat," Tanner nodded then followed Kyle into the park.

"What do you think that was all about?" Ventura asked Heidi as they stood by their car across the road. Keys had sent out a picture of Iris over the airways, and they had just finished questioning a clerk at the hotel across from the park. They witnessed the situation with Tanner, though they couldn't hear the exchange between the two men, they could see the tension in their forms. "I don't know." She glanced his way. "You think something is going on?"

"I'm a little concerned about Williams. He's been distracted the last couple of days."

"Leave the rookie alone. He's in love," she chuckled.

Ventura scoffed, "Yeah and we both know with whom, but I don't think that's the main cause of his distraction," he shook his head, "I think it's something paranormal. Could be a new ability breaking through, but I'm going to keep a close eye on him. We can't afford any missteps on this assignment."

"You're not going to go tattling to Keys on the rookie are you?"

"Not yet, but if he doesn't pull it together, I may have to. For his safety and anyone who may be working with him. He may need to go to the facility in Maine to make sure there is no weakness or ghost tracking in that channel Bradshaw breached."

"Oh, Ventura, you are a kill joy."

"Yeah, but at least I'm a safe one." He started the car and pulled into traffic heading south toward the train station.

Tanner was leaning back on his hands, when he heard her voice. "Are we terribly late?" He turned around and smiled. Keys and Marna were making their way toward the picnic sight. He waved.

"There might be a few scraps left if you chase the ants away." He teased.

"And here I thought they packed enough for an army."

"They did." He nodded toward the activity area where the kids were playing. "And they enjoyed it very much." He grinned. Marna smiled down at him.

"Well if that's the case then I guess it's okay." She set her purse in front of them. "How was the sight-seeing?"

"Informative. Zurich is rich in its history and beauty." His eyes scanned the park to do a mental head count. They sat in comfortable silence for a few moments as Keys went to confer with the other agents, and then he brought his eyes back to her. She had chosen to wear her hair loose today in rolling waves down her back and pinned back away from her face with shell clips. Her sunglasses were large and metal rimmed, protecting her eyes from the afternoon sun that bathed her in a golden light. She was wearing a light beige sundress with an elasticized bodice that fit snug around her breasts, and gathered in an empire waistline than allowed the skirt to flare out to just above her knees. Her brown, wedge heeled sandals were a good match in color to her attire. A matching Bola jacket lay softly on the blanket beside her. She looked distinguished enough to actually be the trophy wife she was pretending to be. "How's Isaiah doing?"

Marna drew in a breath. "He has a hairline fracture in his ankle."

"Sorry to hear that," he sighed, "sucks to have to spend vacation that way." He flipped to his side, and pushed himself up on his elbow. "How'd your day as Mrs. Kestin go?"

She brushed a loose hair off her cheek, and caught it behind her ear. "Uneventful. We went and checked out the branch offices of HomeSpot, spoke to a few of its business contacts, and had a meeting about expanding with a few of the board members."

"What's the verdict?"

"I think he just might keep it going after the mission for – ah," she rubbed her calf then looked at him. "Charlie horse, I probably ought to ditch the heels and walk it off." Tanner stood up and reached for her hand to help her up. She stood, and held his hand for balance while she slipped her sandals off, and when she was done, she raised her eyes to his. "Thanks . . ." She trailed off when their eyes met. His had darkened with such intensity it made her heart stop. "Tanner?"

"Huh?"

"Walk?"

He called out to the others that they were taking a short walk then he waved her ahead with his free hand, as she limped forward and let it slide out of his grasp as she became more sure footed. The wind gently played with strands of her dark hair and she carelessly swung the hand holding her sandals at her side, and pushed forward. He fell into pace beside her, pausing to pick up the soccer ball, that had rolled away from the triplets, and toss it back to them. David jumped up, hitt it back into play with his head, and waved at Tanner. The sounds of the city moved around them, but the noise wasn't intrusive, just there. "It's a lovely day," Marna said as they stopped at the rail fence and looked down at the swans swimming gracefully in the water below them.

"It is at that," Tanner said as he leaned forearms on the fence and moments later pointed out the young ones trailing behind the swan that was the purest white of the flock. "Beautiful sight isn't she?"

"Yes," she smiled, glancing his way, "she is indeed," smiling, she reached up to her mouth and rubbed the corner, "you've got a little something right there." He reached up to rub at it, but missed. "No, it's right . . ." She took her thumb and gently rubbed at the item, while her fingers rested on his cheek, it was a piece of watermelon. "There," She grinned, looking up at him as she wiped it away, "got it." Her hand remained on his cheek. The moment seemed natural between them, almost intimate. He reached up and gently took her hand in his. He saw intensity in her eyes, but he also saw confusion. There was a battle going on within her, he could feel it. His eyes moved to her pink tinted lips. He could imagine taking them with his own, tasting them, just a quick taste, a moment of stolen pleasure. His eyes moved back to hers. He could smell the delicate lilac of her shampoo. Feel the warmth of her breath, his pulse thundered in his ears. Every ounce of his being wanted to reach out and take her in his arms, show her what he felt . . . But he could feel her conflict . . . The truth sliced through him like a double-edged sword. She wasn't strong enough to make the decision to step back, but he was.

He drew in a breath and stepped back, still holding her hand. "I must have been saving it for later," his voice sounded harsh even to him. He searched her eyes. Something had passed between them just then and he knew if he had taken what she was offering, they would both regret it. Jeff was still there, she was still feeling the pain of his loss. Tanner could not bring himself to take advantage of her with that wound still seeping in her heart. Starting a relationship with her now could only lead to heartache for both of them. He cleared his throat, "we should – ah – we should probably get back."

She glanced at her watch. "Yeah, I guess we should. It's later than I thought."

"How's the Charlie horse?"

"Much better, thanks for asking," Marna said. Tanner pushed away from the railing and stepped aside, offering his hand to assist her off the riser they had stepped on to look at the swans, and then they headed back toward the picnic area. Both lost in their own thoughts. The silence between them was louder than the surrounding traffic.

*****

Demi paced. She was at the appointed meeting space, on the platform by track six. She glanced at her watch, it was eight-thirty, and *she's late. That can't be good.* Demi sent the message through her psychic channel to Keys.

Give it fifteen more minutes, Keys sent back to her, *before we consider the mission blown,* Demi nodded. Keys, Bryan, Kyle and Sasha were monitoring machines in the device van while Tanner, Rose, and Marna were across the road from her and Ventura and Heidi were in the station watching for the welcoming committee. Keys had positioned them for back up if Demi needed it and equipped them with camera sunglasses and ear-buds for communication and surveillance. The team in the van watched them all on various monitors. The plan was for the party in question to meet with Demi, and then they were to fall into formation and take turns following them to the Liberatores compound.

Keys was Reclined in a chair, wearing the helmet attached to the GRV2000 surveillance machine. The others in the van watched what was unfolding at the Metro station on the monitor of the GRV2000. *And, Demi, I want communication kept to a minimal. They could be watching you from somewhere nearby to see if you're law enforcement undercover and let's not forget, the Liberatores may not be built of pure psychics, but Lamontage would not be in an organization without having several in the ranks, and Iris is a Rose clone.*

Sorry.

Don't be. Just be careful, Keys interjected. The 8:00 p.m metro train pulled in to the platform twenty minutes late and temporarily blocked their view. Like a light bulb going on, Bryan put it together. "The train! That's it! Ventura, Schaefer move in, their taking her by train! Get on that train !" Ventura and Heidi ran up to the security gate, flashed their badges to the guard, and he waved them through. As they were running down the escalator, the GRV2000 went blank and all the monitors filled with electrical interference lines, Keys sat up alarmed. The train started pulling away from the platform.

"Ventura, Schaefer, report! I'm blind here!"

After a few seconds of endless silence, and the train was on its way, the interference faded away, but the GRV2000 stayed silent. "Keys," Ventura's breathless voice came over the ear-buds, "we didn't make it, they've got her," they all glanced over the monitors until they came to the ones monitoring Schaefer and Heidi. They saw them standing on the platform Demi had been standing on moments before, Heidi leaning on her knees breathing heavily and Peter pacing like a trapped animal. "And, Keys, she was incapacitated. Two Liberatores, Middle Eastern descent, held her between them as they boarded, and then moved quickly to seats in the back.."

Total silence filled the empty space between the mission team. Did they know who she was? Did they all just watch the beginning of an execution of one of their own? "What about the girl?"

"She was with them, but it looked like she was calling the shots."

"Dammit, Keys! You never should have let her go in there alone !" Bryan accused.

"Then we'd be down two agents right now !" Keys turned his back and paced away, while Bryan seethed.

"Keys." Sasha called. "I'm getting something over the audio."

"They must have turned off whatever they were using to jam signals." Keys went over to the main listening board, and pulled out the headphone plug. The train sounded in the background.

"*What will he do to her?*" A female voice said.

"*It is good thing he just wanted her incapacitated, Iris, you are favored. With others he had us kill them.*" A calm male voice said.

"*I was lonely nobody would talk to me because the Master favored me.*"

"*So you bring outsider in*?" A third, more angry voice came over the airways. "You do not know she is who she says she is."

"*You saw the bruises on her face! She can't be lying about that !*" The girl defended her choice to invite Demi in. There was shuffling. Iris cried out.

"Akim, stop, you bruise her, you make Master very angry." The calm voice filled with a warning tone

"The Master should show young girls how respect men. They should not speak those tones to us. There are some in Liberatores who are very offended, and some are angry with him. There is talk of revolt against him."

"That be very dangerous."

"Then he should respect us !" They heard a clattering then the audio went silent.

Sasha played with buttons and looked up at Keys, shaking her head, "It's gone. Either the bud was discovered or the motion of the train finally dislodged and fell to the floor.*"*

"Sasha, rewind the audio," Keys ordered, he had heard something near the end. She rewound the tape, and replayed the last part of it. All eyes were on Keys as he tilted his head. "There, did you hear that? It's the PA announcing the rail stops and exchanges, they aren't going to want to change trains in the middle with too many people aboard, too many chances for discovery, they'll wait until the last stop and get off there. That's where they'll continue their journey and if they want to keep her under, which is what I suspect, until they reach the compound, they'll have some kind of faux medical transport waiting for them. If we can get that information, we'll know where to start looking."

"Of course the train will have to lay over there, refuel and clean up before they start on a return journey," Ventura said.

"Giving us time to get there and talk to the train personnel," Kyle said.

"Exactly," said Keys, "Looks like we're back in business."

"I'll start working on the clean up immediately, Sir."

"Great Sasha," he smiled at her and turned to Rose, "Rose, you and Tanner will remain with the children. I think we may need Marna's expertise on this mission. and I need Blockers on them. I'll have Fedpol send over a couple of teams to help with security."

"The rest of you go home and pack one backpack of clothing and essentials. Be prepared for some rough travel and some possible camping out. We may be gone for a couple of days so make sure you have enough ammunition and use your shoulder holsters for your weapon transport. Make sure you carry an extra or backup also snug to your body. The closer we get to Liberatores territory, the more you are going to need to be on your guard at all times. Any questions?"

"Keys, I got it," Sasha said from her seat by the soundboard. They all gathered around the board and listened carefully. Soon they heard the comments first in German, and then in English. The announcer went down the list of stops, and the final one was Spiez, from there people change trains to Visp, Lenk or Sion.

Keys looked at his watch, "by rail the trip is approximately an hour and a half, we'll hop the jet to Bern, and from there we'll drive to Spiez, and find out what we can. By the time we board the jet they'll have at least a forty-minute head start. Get yourselves moving and meet me at the compound Airfield as soon as possible." They all synchronized their watches to Keys', and quickly headed for their cars. When they were gone, Keys looked at the still blank GRV2000, "hang on, Demi, just for a while longer." Then he moved to the front of the van and headed to his temporary living space as well, glancing at the mountains in the distance. He could think of better ways to enjoy the Alps and the glaciers, but life deals the hands it deals and tonight he had an agent in trouble.

*****

Demi woke with a start, drawing in a deep breath. The air was damp and musty. She coughed. She could feel the cold impersonal surroundings grabbing at her. The unexpected shiver convulsed her whole body. She reached for her ear-bud to turn it on. It was gone. Oh no. What had happened? She tried to think, but a dense fog short-circuited her senses. My Gosh had the mission failed, was she dead? Was she a prisoner? She moved her hands and feet, though they felt somewhat disconnected, they were still functional and not tied down. She breathed a sigh of relief, and felt around for her book, it wasn't there. Where were her belongings? She swung herself into a sitting position. Dizziness engulfed her. She shook her head to try and clear it then lifted her hand to her forehead as the pounding started again. Her feet recoiled as they touched cold, hard cement. She looked down--cement floor-- then she lifted her head so she could scan the room with her eyes, the pounding persisted in her brain.

She was in a small 8 X 10 foot room. It was cold. She was sitting on the edge of a hard cot-- one of the few pieces of furniture in the room. Her feet were bare. The walls around her were bricked cement, painted white. Another shiver convulsed her body. Her mouth felt like cotton. Her head continued to pound. She tried to focus and it started coming back to her. The train had pulled in to the station in front of her. Iris had stepped out with two men flanking her then she took Demi's hand, while the two men moved to flank Demi. She remembered the prick in her shoulder, the sensation of her surroundings swimming around her. She drew in a breath. They had drugged her with a powerful control drug. She remained conscious, but not able to control her body with her mind, she wasn't able to let anyone know what was happening. She was aware of her surroundings, but could not respond to them. That's why her head pounded so.

Where was she? She looked around for a window to see what was outside the walls. The room was windowless. The air went colder if that was possible. It went through her fall sweater and broomstick skirt to prick at her skin. Goose bumps formed on her arms. She felt panic rise in her throat. Had backup been able to follow her? It had all happened so fast. Did they know where she was or was she on her own? Against the opposite wall was a dresser and a bedside stand was directly to her right. A vanity table, oddly out of place, was to her left. She stood up, lifted her skirt and moved to the door. Then she reached for the knob, turned it but nothing happened, they had locked her in. " 'ey let me oyt av 'ere!" She remained inside her Meagan skin, but banged on the door. A small window slid opened and Blue eyes stared back at her.

"Shhhh," Iris hissed. "You looking to get punished before the Master even purifies you." Demi stumbled backwards, hitting the dresser when the door opened. She grabbed at the top of it to get her bearings. She was still very unsteady. Purify? What did she mean by purify? Iris stepped in.

"Iris, waaat is goin' on, an' waaat yer meanin' purifies? Why am oi locked up loik an animal. Oi tho't dis place wus aboyt love an' acceptance. That's waaat yer towl me." Demi was using her Irish accent, keeping it heavy, as she moved against a wall, putting as much space between her and Iris as possible. The only light in the room was a kerosene lamp, setting on a corner table. Demi almost knocked it over as she moved to her right. She leaned into the wall giving the outer appearance of being terrified.

"You're always locked away from the others until after the Master has invited you to his quarters for inspection and purification, but not to worry, I think you will be one of his favorites like me. We are an elite group we are." She walked over and ran her hands through Demi's hair. "Your hair is such an unusual color, the red with the golden highlights, is that natural?"

"Ya it is." Demi said slapping at Iris' hand, "what is purificashun, oi don't want ter endure naw freak tests or anythin' liken ter dat. me auld man 'as put enoof bruises on me body. an' Ah've 'ad more broke bones in de tree years we've been mates than anyone else 'as 'ad in a lifetime."

She let go of Demi's hair, "Master only hurts those that betray him or our people. If your motives are true, Meagan, you have nothing to fear," she walked across the room and started pulling beauty supplies out of a vanity. "Your motives are true, Megan, aren't they?" She tilted her head in Demi's direction. Demi smiled, but the girl was making her nervous. It was a good thing she had opted for a good old fashion hand to hand with another agent in a monitored gym match earlier to get bruises, instead of makeup, because they would have blown her cover by now. "T'be sure they are. Waaat a ter'bl' tin' ter ask. Da me injuries luk fake ter yer?"

"Of course not," Iris shook her head, "come over and sit at the vanity, I have to prepare you for your first meeting with the Master." Demi moved toward the vanity, with the slightest of hesitations, to stay in character. As she sat in the chair, Iris started playing with her hair. Within seconds, there was a knock on the door. "Robe up and enter." There was some shuffling outside the door, then a body, completely robed from head to foot in a white robe, with a white mesh veil covering her face, floated toward them. Demi shivered as she likened her to a ghost. The woman started when she saw Demi. "Beautiful isn't she, Sashika?" Iris asked, "The Master will be very pleased with his offering." The woman nodded. She had in her arms, a tray laden with fresh fruit sparkling water, cheese, and soft bread. "Put it on the bedside stand, Sashika?" Again, the woman nodded. Demi watched her movements. They were very fluid and somewhat familiar but she brushed the familiarity aside, thinking the drugs were clouding her judgement. How could she possibly know this woman? "Thank you, Sashika. Please draw Meagan a Lavender bath. I will be bringing her in soon. The woman nodded, glanced again at Demi and moved quickly out the door.

"What's wi' da coverin'?" Demi asked.

"No one can come near you until after your purification unless they are covered to protect their souls from the sins of the world that you possess." She proceeded to pin Demi's hair up.

"Now wait a minute ---" Demi's voice rose.

"Sshhh. . ." She ran to the door and listened as footsteps came up the hall, stopped and moved on. She returned to Demi. "The men here are not like the men in our world. You are an outsider, and in their eyes and the Master's you are bringing the dirt from the world into our community. Master will purify you and cast the evil within you away before he can let anyone near you. Please don't be difficult, Megan, it is as I told you. I do not have many friends here as I am an outsider, but I did as the Master said, and I am now in top favor with the Master. We are to have a child. Please just do as you're told and we can be good friends for a long time. The unusual color of your hair will bring you favor with the Master, I'm sure, but if you become disruptive and disobedient they will hurt you or worse and me too for bringing you here . . . " She bit her lip to try to control the tears that welled in her eyes. "Please, Meagan, don't be difficult. I beg of you."

"I'm sorry," Demi did her best to be contrite. "I da not wish yer any trouble. Oi wanted ter come 'ere ter 'av waaat yer 'av, an' if yer say dis purificashun stuff is gran', den i'll believe yer. Oi jist don't want ter be 'urt by a man again."

Iris smiled, "It doesn't hurt, Meagan, it is the most wonderful feeling in the world. The Master takes you to a world of complete and absolute peace after he cleanses you of all the pain you've suffered. He offers you happiness and satisfaction, but you have to let go of the old you, and embrace the new person you will become. You have to become submissive to him. He will then take you in his arms and love you like he loves the rest of us. He will protect us if we are true to him and if we are not we are punished." She shivered and smiled, "but let's not think about that. Come, I need to finish your hair so you can undress and step into the Lavender bath Sashika has drawn for you, then you must eat your fruit to ready yourself for the Master. Demi sat down again, raising her shields. Of all the times she had needed them, she had a feeling she needed them now more than she had ever needed them before. She had to figure out where she was, and then find her book to notify Keys and the rest of them. Her eyes scanned the room. Under the small cot was a small plastic storage container and in it she saw her personal effects, minus her clothing. Now if she could just get the time to use it. She wished she knew when the ear-bud had fallen out, so she would know for sure her cover wasn't blown. She could only hope that she had lost it before anyone in Lamontage's army had found it.

*****

Demi stood before a full-length mirror as Iris flittered around her with a curling iron, doing the finishing touches to her hair. "There, Meagan," she said as she curled the last end around her finger, and finished, "you look beautiful."

"I fale loike a street walker, waaat is it wi' al' dis paint on me face?" She screwed her nose in distaste, and then looked down at her attire. She was wearing a simple white cotton gown, the hemline brushing the floor as the very softness caressed her feet. There was no embroidery or decor of any kind just a simple, sleeveless gown with Velcro enclosing the back center seam. "An' waaat is it wi' dis dress, oi fale loike a virgin bein' offered up for sacrifice ter da gods."

"Of course not, Silly, but you are starting a new life." Iris went across the room and poured them both some fruit juice that had been brought in.

"Then why am oi feelin' so terrified roi nigh?" Demi looked at the mirror again. "Waaat if oi don't want ter do dis? waaat if oi ask ter be broot back ter Zurich or ter be put back on de train? Oi promise i'd walk away an' never luk back." She turned toward Iris, whose back was facing her."

Iris turned and smiled at her, walking over and handing her a glass of juice. "It's okay to be nervous, we all are the first time we meet the Master, but it will be fine, I promise," she spoke in a soft easy voice and took a drink of juice, "trust me, you'll feel so fresh, so pure when he is done with you," her smile widened. "It's like becoming a new person,"

"Who wouldn't want dat?" Demi said, taking a swallow of juice.

"I can't think of anyone, can you?" Iris' eyes hardened, "Agent Spencer." Demi swallowed her mouth full of juice before she choked.

"Who's Agent Spencer?" Demi looked at her with eyes as innocent as she could make them look.

"Don't lie to me, Demi Spencer. Sashika recognized you." The woman from earlier who had brought the fruit in. How did she know Demi? She tried to think of something that would key her in to the woman's identity but all she had was that vague sense of familiarity she felt about the woman, nothing came to her. Right now, she had to think survival. Had this woman already blown her cover? She had two choices, lie and possibly anger the girl more or try to make an ally out of her. She chose the latter. "Look, Iris, I can explain," Demi said as she went to put her glass on the bedside stand. Instead, she stumbled when the room suddenly started swimming and spinning around her, she reached for the wall to keep her from falling. "What have you done?" Iris grabbed her glass from her hand and set it on the stand.

"It's just a little something to make you relax, Demi, that's all. The street name for it is Compliance. It's a mixture of Haldol and Jet" She assisted her into a chair as she started to falter. "In our circles it's called the psychic date rape drug, because it interferes with the brain waves, and eventually your shields.

"How . . .?" Demi shook her head; she was starting to feel confused, and foggy. Sensations started flooding her body. She continued to fight them. Her arms and legs began to feel heavy. She was becoming less able to control her actions or her shields.

"How did I find out?" She shrugged, reaching into her pocket and pulling out the ear-bud. "This fell out of your ear on the train. When it hit the floor, I discreetly pushed it under our seats. When the opportunity presented itself, I picked it up and when we stopped, while the guards struggled with you, I slipped the little prize in my pocket," she shrugged. "Who knows, I may need it sometime." Approaching footsteps echoed in the hallway, Iris quickly slipped it back into her pocket. She leaned real close to her ear. "Are you ready for your debut, Demi, because your chariot is here," a knock resounded on the door. Iris quickly left her side and went to the door, unlocking it and swinging it inward. "Take her to the training room."

The men approached, and slipped their arms under her armpits, lifting her and practically dragged her out of the room, while she struggled to walk. Iris closed the door, pulled the ear-bud out and looked it over again. She could sense him before he stepped over the threshold. She fisted her hand to hide the ear bud, and slid it into her pocket as she turned to face him. "Master," she said as he walked into the room, and kneeled before him, her head bowed. "I ask for your forgiveness."

Pierre looked at the young woman before him. His brown eyes narrow slits, his salt and pepper, hair pulled back in a tail trailing down his back. His lean body encased in casual jeans and a t-shirt. He placed his finger under her chin, and lifted her face so he could look into her eyes. "You disappoint me, child, I had such high hopes for you."

"Had?" A single tear slid down her cheek. She trembled as she sensed his anger with her.

She pleaded with him, "but, Master, I did as you asked, I- I gave her the drugs, I had them bring her to the training room. She's awaiting her fate now."

"But it is you who brought the woman upon us, Iris, you broke the rules, you must pay the consequences."

"Consequences? b-but master what about my baby, our baby?" she sniffed.

"Not to worry, Iris, the child will be fine." He raised his eyes to the men that entered the room from behind her. "Take her to the extraction room, and have the team start the process."

"The extr. . ." Iris' heart went to her throat. She was seven and a half months pregnant, they were going to take the baby and put it in the Gestation machine, to finish his term, and then take it from the machine on his due date. The process had been around for just over thirty years and recently introduced to Pierre by Raquel Bradshaw when she had stolen the blue prints for the machine from her husband, and given them to Pierre during their torrent affair. She had died when her usefulness had run out as well.

He had tested the process on other fetuses from other girls who had betrayed him and tried to run away near the end of their pregnancies. Both the children had been born healthy, but had later developed lung related issues, and had died before the age of two. It turned out that the machine was leaving scar tissue on the lungs, leaving them vulnerable for collapse and respiratory infections, so he had brought in scientists who had reworked the machine, and now her baby would be the first to need it. The baby would no longer need Iris. "NO !" She struggled against the men as they held her arms. She was only seventeen. She wasn't ready for her life to end.

"Not to worry, Iris, until this little mishap, you have been a loyal subject in your service to me. I will dispose of you in a very humane way."

Tears were freely falling down her cheeks now. She started begging him, "Please, Master, let me make it up to you. I will kill the intruder myself to prove to you I can be loyal, just please let me raise my baby, he needs his mother."

"Oh, a mother he will have, Iris, it just won't be you. He stared her in the eyes. Sashika will take over that role as soon as the child is able to be removed from the Gestation machine." He nodded to the men and they led her out of the room as she struggled to break their hold. She was only seventeen and her life was over. She would never see her baby or watch it grow. What had she done?" Suddenly, she remembered the ear-bud. All electronic devices had honing devices built into their make-up nowadays, didn't they? She had one shot at this even if she didn't survive maybe her baby could, if Demi would be willing to help her.

She saw the bend in the hallway coming up fast. The stairwell to the training room was a few feet down and on the right. She was not only running for her life, but the life of her child. She let her knees crumble beneath her, taking the men totally by surprise. With the extra weight of her pregnancy, she had the advantage. She slipped from their hands. They cursed. Their weapons slipped from their hands and hit the floor, making them reach for them first. She took the moment to scramble to her feet and run. They cursed again.

There was a linen carrier two doors down the hall on the left. Iris pushed the girl aside, and pushed the cart into her pursuer's path. She heard them run into the cart and stumble as she turned around the next bend. The training door was within her grasp. Her private room was further down the hall, as was the entrance to the beautiful English garden where she had snuck out and taken many quiet strolls with the young Liberatores soldier who had allowed her to use his GPC. They would think she was running there to escape to the forest beyond.

She heard boot against metal. One of them had kicked the linen carrier. She grabbed the doorknob and quickly plugged in the code. The door buzzed and she swung it open. She smiled as she realized her many nights with the Master weren't wasted. He had taken her around the compound, and she had memorized all the codes. All she had to do was see them used once. A talent she hadn't shared with him, and one she had managed to hide for the whole year she had been here. Even in his bed, during their most intimate times when shields were down and connections were at their strongest, she had kept that secret for herself. She pushed the door closed, and slipped into the shadow of the stairwell, standing perfectly still, holding her breath. She listened as running footsteps came to the door and paused. She shrunk even further back. Praying they wouldn't see her. Seconds later, she heard yelling from the other end of the hall and the footsteps moved forward.

Cautiously she stepped into the pool of light made by the stairwell unit, and then picked up speed and moved down the stairs quickly. She reached the bottom floor and cautiously opened the door, slipping through as soon there was an opening big enough for her to enter, and then she let it close silently behind her. She stayed close to the wall as she moved forward, and passed cautiously by all the lower level classrooms checking for the soldiers and the students. Today was Saturday. School was not in session, so nobody would see her but she kept her eyes moving just the same. Sometimes students had makeup tests, or papers to write.

When she reached the corner of the hallway, she looked around the edge of the wall. One guard and it was a lower level soldier. She sighed in relief, just a small obstacle. His phone rang; he answered it and started speaking in German. Iris heard her name. She quickly looked around for a place to hide. Across the hall from her was the sports supply closet for the school buildings. She quickly crossed the floor, stepped in and closed it quietly just as the guard passed by in the hallway looking around. Slowly she breathed out in a long sigh.

The baby kicked at her swollen belly, protesting how tense his mother was no doubt. She rubbed where he had kicked, and drew in a few deep breaths to relax, then Seconds later she heard the stairwell door open and close then others followed. He was searching all the lower rooms. She looked around the closet, looking for something. She was too close to let him win now. Her eyes continued to scan the room, and then she saw it. A wooden bat lay atop some boxes opposite her in the closet. She snatched it up into her hands, stepped back into the shadows, gripped it and listened, her senses on high alert. He was very close. She started counting down the doors as she heard them open . . . four . . . three . . . two . . . one. Adrenaline pumped, the baby kicked, she held her breath, watched as the doorknob turned, and she raised the bat. She had won the softball championship for her high school with her homerun swing. She prayed it wouldn't fail her now. Not until you see the whites of their eyes . . . She remembered that phrase from History class but couldn't remember who had said it. The door swung open slowly she saw him step in. He raised his flashlight, and started circling the deep closet, but before it could fully illuminate her, she swung out quickly and felt sick when she heard the cracking skull, felt his head cave to the bat.

Blood spattered back at her, covering her dress. She smelled the copper of it, felt its warmth on her face, and gagged. Then she watched the soldier fall backward, landing half in and half out of the closet room. She stood in frozen silence, as she stared at him sprawled out on the floor. Like some horrible horror flick, the incident repeated itself, in her mind's eye repeatedly. When he didn't move, she tossed the bat aside and swiped at the blood on her face, then wiped her hands on her chest, smearing blood all over her white linen dress and stared at the soldier. His eyes saw no more. Her stupor lasted a few seconds more until the radio cracked to life. "Chicken's not in the garden." She recognized the voice as belonging to one of the men who were pursuing her.

"Floors five and four have been cleared too," another voice confirmed.

She sniffed and swiped at the tears on her face. She drew in a breath, stooped down to grab his radio, stepped over the guard's body and ran down the hall toward the training room. There wasn't much time before they realized the guard from the bottom floor hadn't checked in yet and they would call to find out his progress. When he didn't answer, they would abandon their systematic search of the upper floors and head down there. She had to get to Demi, and then get the two of them out of the training room and out of the building. It wouldn't be easy, because the drugs she had given the woman were still at the height of their power. However, there was only a brief window of time where it would be possible to escape, and that was closing fast as she ran toward the last door on the right of the hallway.

When she reached it, she quickly punched in the code and pushed the door inward. The training room was the room the Master used his dark abilities to beat people into submission in. He would gain control of their mind by inducing unbearable pain and sadness before he would reward them by tricking their mind into thinking they got their heart's desires. Most were easy to bring around, as they'd rather have the peace and tranquility he offered verses the pain the session started with, but then there had been others that were so strong willed that she had literally seen them take the pain until they died. That is what Demi's fate would be. He would keep her alive, until he grew bored with the game. She was special, she belonged to an old enemy he had said. He would bring her to the brink then pull her back several times before he would destroy her. Iris had seen that as well. It was horrible to watch a person go through that day after day, but Demi would, unless Iris could help her, and then maybe Demi's people could help them both and save her baby.

She slipped her hand in her pocket to double check and make sure the ear-bud was still there as she slipped into the room and closed the door, disarming the alarm. This would be the last room they checked because of the alarm. They thought it the most secure in the building but that would only buy them a short time while they searched the rest of the house. Just a couple more steps and then she and Demi could escape out the exit that led to the lower gardens. They could go into the thick forestry and make their way to the lake, and await Demi's people there. She was so close to freedom, she could taste it. She heard the radio crackle to life. "Manson, check in with status of bottom floor, over . . ." Her breaths quickened. Time was about to run out and there was Demi slumped in a chair in the center of the room, awaiting her first training session, illuminated by a single frosty blue lantern. Iris moved toward her quickly.

Chapter Ten

The Guardian jet landed at the Bern airport precisely forty-five minutes after they took off. The agents went from the jet to the convoy of vans waiting outside the hangar as a distracted Keys gave them their orders. He, Marna, Kyle and Sasha were in the lead van followed by Ventura, Schaefer, and four of their Fedpol counterparts in the second, and Bryan headed up the team in the surveillance van, which trailed the other two. With him were a team of surveillance specialist from the Zurich office and Barry McGellen from the states. Marna studied Keys profile from the passenger seat as he drove off the airfield. "This isn't your fault, Keys."

"I cleared the assignment," he said, his voice gruff. "I don't know maybe I just wanted it too much, maybe what happened to Lizzy clouds my judgment, whatever it was that influenced my decision, consciously or subconsciously, this is on me. Demi's fate is on me, whatever that may be."

"She wanted this assignment, Keys." Marna stated, "She knew the risks going in."

"For the most part, her powers are passive, Marna, I should not have let her go in alone. I should have arranged for active backup."

"You did, none of us considered that the situation would deteriorate that way."

"I should have. . ." He sighed. "I should have explored all the angles, made a plan for all of them. I failed her, I alone have to live with that."

"Keys," the radio cracked to life as Bryan's voice came over the airway.

Keys snatched the mike from the console, bringing it to his mouth. "Yes, Bryan?"

"Earpiece honing just came back online; it's showing us a location in Lenk. I looked it up. Before the Oil conflicts it was a cooperative farming village of about 2000 people, circled by forestry and glaciers. During the conflicts, they couldn't do a lot with their farming as the government had taken control over the import/export businesses, and needed resources weren't reaching them. People were dying from exposure and illness. There really isn't anything there anymore but a few tourist hotels and some company called **Subgonomic INC**. The employees operate the farms now. The only rail service going in and out of that town now, verses twenty years ago, is freight."

"Of course. I remember now, Subgonomic bought the village in 2035. It was nothing short of a ghost town by then. They wanted to start a line of groundbreaking vegetable and fruit products that supposedly could grow in any climate. The media reported the CEO as saying, "seeing the cooperative farms were already in place, it would make it economical to start the company there." He won a relatively new reward equivalent to the Nobel in 2037 after he marketed his line of peaches under the brand line of **Swiss Perfection**. He now has a complete line of canned vegetables and fruits grown year round. He promises a fresh line within the next five years. Hmmm. Bryan run a check on him and let me know what you find."

"Already in progress Keys."

"Good." He released the mike, put it back on its mount, and flipped on his earpiece. "Ventura, pull to the left lane with me and let Bryan take the lead, he's got a possible location on Demi. The signal in her earpiece just came back online."

"Moving over," Ventura stated. Keys eased up on the accelerator, turned his signal light on, and eased into the right lane. Ventura followed suit and Bryan eased by them then slowed to a steady fifty as the other two vehicles took up position behind him. He turned toward Marna, "Marna can you contact her?"

"I'll try," Marna closed her eyes and tried to communicate with Demi. *Demi —, Demi, can you hear me? It's Marna.* Marna felt confusion, disconnection, and fear. Then out of the confusion, one word came through that struck fear into her heart and it would in every heart on the team *Blown*. Marna's eyes flew open, and her head swung around. "Keys, her cover's been blown."

"Pierre, knows who she is." His facial muscles bunched and released. The airways fell silent. A blanket of fear covered the convoy liken to that of the darkness in a mid-December night.

"Did you hear anything else?" Bryan's urgent voice came over her earpiece.

"No, Bryan, I'm sorry. But I've felt that fog and confusion before," she looked Keys way, "the party Amanda went to when we were teens.'

"They've drugged her," Keys slammed the heel of his hand into his steering wheel. Marna started at the force of the blow. "All right, team, game plan changes. Demi is in trouble, I've seen Pierre's work. If we don't get to her soon . . ." Their ear-buds cracked to life.

"Hello is anybody out there?" A child like voice whispered in their ears. Everybody dropped their conversation and turned their eyes toward the lead in each vehicle. Nobody spoke, just waited until Keys gave orders on how to proceed.

"State your name and your business on this line," Keys answered.

"M-my name is Iris and we need help."

"We?"

"M-me and Meg--I mean Demi. The Master is going to hurt us. I got away, but they'll find me soon," Keys heard her sniff, "They were going to take my baby and k-kill me . . . He's going to hurt Demi bad and then kill her too, I can't stop him, he's too powerful. Please help us."

"Iris, this is Dr Keys with Guardian WIT. Can you tell me where you are?"

"Lenk, Switzerland. We're in the main building of the cooperative farm community, near the glaciers at the end of town. We're in the training room. He does bad things in here. We're safe until they can't find me and they find the dead man in the hall." She sniffed, "I had to do it he was going to hurt me." Keys could hear her quiet weeping.

"We're on our way, is the room upstairs or downstairs?"

"Bottom floor, the room on the end. . ."

"They're coming downstairs. They're going to find him. . ." Keys heard the panic in her voice.

"Iris, listen to me. Find somewhere to put the ear-bud, and leave it turned on. There is a tracking device in there, and then I want you to find someplace to hide." He heard a sharp intake of breath, a hissing of a radio in the background.

"Iris, what's happening?" Keys demanded.

"Here they come," she whispered, "I'm going to hide, Demi, they're coming to help us. . . Hurry before it's too late. . ." Keys heard some slight commotion then the line went silent.

"Radio commission shut down. Psychic communication only."

"What about Pierre, he can track us," Marna stated.

"We'll just keep communication to a minimum. If he finds that ear-bud and transmissions are going, he'll know we're coming and we may be too late for Demi and Iris." Marna nodded, "Radios power down . . ." silence filled the vans. All ear buds and communication devices shut down. *Ventura! ETA*

'Bout twenty minutes, Keys.

Make it fifteen! The rest of you suit up and ready yourselves for a frontal assault! He stepped on the accelerator as he passed a road sign that stated Lenk, **Home of Subgonomic INC 25 miles.**

*****

Iris listened from behind a wall in the training room, a hidden crawl space. She had found it totally by accident one day while cleaning the room.

~~~~~

There had been a heavy rain the night before and she had found a puddle by this one section of wall. She had looked the ceiling over and it bore no signs of leaking water, so she had gotten down on her hands and knees and looked closer at the lower baseboard. It was then that Iris had noticed a hidden switch. She had fussed with it, but it wouldn't budge. It had been jammed up by paint and soon the Master had come back to let her out. She memorized the pass-key and had returned later that night, after an evening with the Master.

After entering the room, she went directly to the wall, and pressed the trigger lever and it still wouldn't give. She looked around the room for something thin and strong enough to slip behind the lever to give her the leverage she needed to pop the lever. She found a screwdriver. She thought about chipping away at the paint around that, but something like that would leave traces behind, so she placed the screwdriver into the indent behind the lever and tried to pop it open but still it stayed frozen within the white paint.

She had sat back on her haunches and closed her eyes trying to visualize ways to open the door. Within seconds, she felt something bump her knees. When she opened her eyes, the wall section had opened to reveal a large crawl space, and a tunnel leading away from the training room. She scooted back, frightened, and looked around. Had the master seen what she was doing? Was he playing games with her mind to punish her for her disloyalty? However, there was no one else in the room. How had the secret door opened? She looked under the door at the trigger lever; it was still in its closed position. She had tried to recall what she was doing, the moments before the door had opened. In her mind, she had practically begged the door respond to her efforts and it had. Realization hit her, she could move things with her mind. She was Telekinetic. To test her theory, she looked at the door again and ordered it to close, it did. Excited, she used her ability a few more times to turn things on, move things around, and then returned her attention to the door, opening it again. Then she crawled into it and ordered it closed. She had followed the tunnels throughout the old home to several rooms on the main floor and the back exit, facing the glaciers. Despite her exciting discovery, she had kept it a secret, even from her Liberatores Lover. Tonight, this very moment in time, she was glad she had.

~~~~

Subgonomic had built the home during the time of Conflicts and she was sure forces that had joined the worldwide rebel resistances had occupied it to flee capture sometime during that time. Until that time, Switzerland had remained neutral in any historical conflict, but if they wanted to continue to remain a free country, they had to resist the attempts of the UN forces to take them over and they did. It had been a bloody time in history and a time where you never knew who your enemies were or who your friends were. Even families turned on each other, some wanted worldwide socialism, others wanted worldwide democracy. Either you took a side or you died in the crossfire. There was no neutral territory at that time.

Pierre's organization was the only one she knew of that had managed to stay a free agent and it was only because he was not discriminatory of who he destroyed or erased to remain that way. He had assassinated many officials on both sides, earned his money, and built Subgonomic to cover his real reason for existence, to cause irreconcilable pain and destruction. Guardian WIT was the only organization holding him at bay, because they were the only ones strong enough to fight him at his level. She knew Pierre added several of the community homes to Lenk after the Conflicts, because what the enemy hadn't destroyed, Pierre had when he took over the commonwealth of Lenk to build Subgonomic INC and the surrounding village. She had learned it in her history classes over the years, and again here in the community as part of her home school requirements. The difference? In the books on the compound, he was represented as a god, savior of the world. The knowledge was designed to inspire loyalty and worship. It had to moist, including her, until tonight.

The main building had been a carry over, and one Pierre had lovingly restored because it was located at the entrance gates to Lenk, a physical statement of his control. The small, modernized farm buildings created a Semi circle at the front of the building, the glaciers behind them and the farming property was in a cluster to the right of all the buildings. There were no modernized vehicles in the community as most walked to their destination and others used horse and buggies. Hardly any currency

exchanged hands within the walls of the community except at the import and export hub and all the proceeds went into the hands of the village officials, appointed by Pierre. It was their responsibility to take care of financial needs of the village. The community members never noticed the absence of currency because village dealings were cash free.
.   The Blackstones would ask Molly Maefield, the elderly tailor, to make clothing for their children. In return, Ms. Maefield would receive freshly canned fruits and vegetables from the family's garden. Weincher's Tree Nursery would tend to the forestry land, separating them from other towns. They'd plant trees and prune the forest. The wood from the fallen trees would then be traded with other merchants for the basic needs of their family. Then there was the church, standing proudly, dead center of town, where everyone would go for Pierre's teaching services. Their leader, their father, their master. Pierre used this public building to reinforce his power and control by having the public chastisements or executions of disloyal subjects and servants who had failed in their missions or obligations to him. Through these, he would make it clear, especially to the young and impressionable attendees, that failure was not an option and conformation and obedience was required for personal safety and satisfaction. The ones who accomplished their missions would be publicly rewarded.
         To the outsider's eye, it would look like a beautiful life to adapt to – minus the executions and chastisements that were never spoken about outside the community – simplicity, no currency so no greed. Women walked around in ankle length garments, working with other women to make flour and butter, feed the farm animals, and supply for their family through trading, baking, and going back to basics.
          The older woman, few that there were, were busy knitting blankets, and tending to the shops in the small business community that housed trading hubs. Everyone pitched in and everyone contributed. What a grand life! But the untrained eye was just that; untrained. The experienced knew the dark side. They knew that the town's population tilted toward young girls, pregnant or raising children and they had no husband unless the master saw fit to share her with a loyal soldier or subject. They knew that once within the gated community, there was no way out and they knew that the search that was going on right now would end in the death of a disloyal subject and one that wasn't the mother would raise another baby. Yes to the experienced eye, the community would not look so much the fairy tale.
         Iris was experienced. She knew she had to find a way to escape the walls of this place but she also had to help Demi. Why had she been so selfish? How could she have been so blind that she lured another innocent into this hell on earth and why, when Sashika had come forth with her report about recognizing Demi from childhood, had she done what the Master had ordered instead of helping the woman escape? She knew of these tunnels, knew there was a way Demi could have escaped unharmed. Instead she had drugged her, and now they both would die if Guardian didn't get there in time.
         Her breath caught when she heard the alert go over the airway about the body on the bottom floor. She felt the pounding of footsteps on the floor above, and the stairway leading down. She turned the radio off and moved deeper into the tunnel, but stayed within earshot of the training room. She heard the lock buzz, and the entrance of three, maybe four guards and then she heard Pierre's voice, "search the rest of the floor and the gardens." She silently hissed out a breath.
         "But, Master, you shouldn't be left alone. Numann picked up foreign activity on the airway. If the activity continues, we need to be ready to leave."
         "I have sent word out to my driver. He has the vans ready. If we need to run, we'll be ready," he paused and looked toward Demi. "I want a few minutes alone with this woman."
         "Yes, Master." Iris heard them retreat, just before she heard the door close and the security lock buzz into active status. She heard the Master move toward Demi
         When the steady footdrops stopped, Iris heard him sigh."Who are you, Demi Spencer?"

Iris heard him draw in a breath, and she closed her eyes. She knew what was coming next. *No,no,no,no.* Her head started shaking.

 Iris, what's wrong?

 Who's there?

 My name is Marna, I'm a friend of Demi's, and I sense your distress, what's wrong? Tell me what's happening.

 He's going to hurt her . . .

 "Guardian !" Pierre bellowed in other room and the screams . . .

     *****

Marna grabbed her head and started screaming. Kyle grabbed her and shook her. "Disengage, Farlow! Disengage!" Keys pulled over, the other vans followed his lead, knowing there had to be something bad going down. Marna continued to scream, holding her head. Her body started rocking in the van seat.

 "Block her, Kyle, now!" Keys ordered.

 Kyle closed his eyes, raised his shields, and opened a channel to Marna. He focused his energy on blocking the pain receptors in Marna's head. He could feel the pain, the distress. It was all he could do to keep focused, but he had the experience, he had the strength. *Marna disengage!* He ordered, and worked at mixing his energies with hers, essentially short circuiting the negative energy attacking her. He was building a virtual wall to deflect the negative energy causing her the pain. Eventually, the pain eased, her screams leveled off to whimpers, and her eyes began to focus.

 Shields up, Farlow! Marna stopped rocking her body. An action she wasn't aware she was doing. She felt tears slide down her face. Kyle looked into her eyes and spoke in a more soothing, more comforting voice. "Are you with me, Farlow?" She sniffed, but nodded. He disconnected from her when he was sure she was on solid ground. "That was quite an episode. What was going on?"

 New tears poured down her face. "It's Demi, I was talking to Iris and then I got a distress signal from Demi." She covered her mouth and looked out the window. "I tried to strengthen her, tried to find out her location, but the pain, oh my god, Kyle, he's doing awful things to her, he's causing her so much pain and sorrow," she sniffed again, "I tried to talk to her . . . to assure her we were on our way, and then the pain . . . I felt it. . .it was excruciating. I don't know how one body can handle it, I was getting it second hand and I thought my brain would explode." She choked back a sob. "I felt her despair, Kyle," She shook her head sadly, "then nothing, just a void where our connection had been."

 "The Bastard killed her." No one had seen Bryan come into the van. All eyes turned in his direction. "Is that what happened, Farlow?" Marna stared at the man, felt his heartache. He was in love with his partner, she wondered if Demi returned those feelings.

 "I-I don't know, Bryan," she sighed, "I lost contact with her."

 "Can't you get it back? You're trying to tell me the all-powerful Marna Farlow can't pick up a transmission from another psychic. Maybe all the stories were nothing but fables after all?" He glared at her. Marna's lips moved, but no words came out.

 Kyle stood up, stepping between Bryan and Marna. "Stand down, Rush, you're out of line !" He said.

 "Enough!" Keys ordered as the men faced off. He ignored their angry silence and turned concerned eyes toward Marna. "Marna, are you okay?" She nodded. He crouched down to look her in the eye. "Do you think you could try to make contact again?"

 "Keys, you can't be serious!" Kyle's voice raised a notch. Keys put his finger up to silence his protest, while he continued to look at Marna. "Bryan and Kyle are both blockers, and Bryan is a Custodian as well. They can protect you from negative energy attacks by putting walls up that deflect them and reinforce your shields. I will be there with you as well, you won't be alone, I promise." She nodded. He stood, went to the radio and ordered someone else to drive Bryan's van and he called Sasha to his van to drive. Then the four of them sat in the back of the van and joined hands.

Marna took a breath as she felt their abilities join forces. They were a unified strength. They were of one mind. She opened her channel cautiously as the van pulled back into traffic. *Demi? Demi, it's Marna can you hear me?* She waited patiently for an answer. Only silence answered her query. *Demi, please tell me you're okay. We're very close to Lenk now. Tell us we made it in time.*

Not there. The reply was barely audible, but it was a reply. A collective relief washed over their little circle.

Marna focused hard to get a sense of where the signal was coming from. *Demi, what do you mean?*

Help Iris. . .

Bryan sent his own message, *Demi, it's Bryan, we need to know where to find you, please help us.*

Can't.

Marna focused not on Demi but on what was going on around her. She sensed movement, darkness, flashing lights, no, passing lights. She closed the channel and backed away. She looked at the others to confirm her suspicions. They all drew in a breath and breathed it out in a hard sigh. "He's moving her." Keys said.

"Do you think he knows we're coming," she asked.

"I'd bet money on," He ran a hand over his mouth. "The question is what did he leave behind for us?" He sighed heavily, "and how long before she is no longer of any value to him and she becomes disposable like Raquel?" Marna's eyes strayed toward the window as an old castle property came into her field of vision. A tour bus was driving up the private drive, and as they drove on, she could imagine the clanging of the ten foot, iron gates as they closed it to secure the property. For some reason it made her shiver.

*****

Demi's body jerked as whatever vehicle transferring her, came to an abrupt stopped. Pierre had blindfolded her, so all she had to rely on were her sense of smell and hearing. She was on her side on a carpeted surface that smelled of cedar and grease Her hands were bound tightly before her, and her feet were bound tightly at the ankles. Her body was folded into the fetal position because when she tried to straighten out, her feet hit something hard and sharp. A chain saw? She concluded that the vehicle had to be some kind of forestry service vehicle, maybe a tree farming business? She had not felt the sun on her face, so it was obviously dark where she was. However, there had been flashes of light, and a steady stream of air coming from somewhere. She was either in the trunk of a car, a storage container on the back of a pickup or a van with a very silent driver. She was so cramped, she could barely feel the lower extremities of her body. Why was she still alive? Pierre had found out who she was. Here cover was blown. Compliance had weakened her resistance, and he had gotten in. Why did he let her live?

<p style="text-align:center">~~~~~</p>

After he had discovered she was Guardian, he had sent sensations through her body with just the wave of his hands; fire seared through her, it was so hot she thought she would spontaneous combust. Then she had felt the cold, her body trembled from it, her teeth chattered. Then came the fear and the overwhelming sorrow. He made her watch as she and her childhood friend, Suzannah, had played and then she disappeared. He had gotten into her head and taken her back to Tarot Lockdown, made her watch as he executed her colleagues. He had dialed her emotions like telephone numbers, and played them out on the screens around the training room. She had heard her heart thunder in her ears, had felt the pains in her chest as her heart started protesting. Her breath had become hard to take. Then he had stopped it all. She had gasped for air, her heart had calmed, sweat had poured down her face and she had been able to get a message to Marna about being discovered. Someone else had come in to the room, whispered in his ear.

He had turned toward her, grabbed a handful of her hair, and pulled so hard her head jerked back and she was looking directly at him. The evil flashed in his dark eyes. "We will finish this later." He let her go and her head had fallen forward again. Her body had ached from his psychic torture. Tears streamed down her face. He had turned to the man beside him. "Get the buses. Load the nobles. Destroy the rest. Leave Guardian a very clear message. Take the buses to RUHE, get the nobles settled. My brother needs to see what happens when he intrudes into my world. He wants war, he's got it."

The newcomer's head had swung toward her. "What about her?"

She had heard his chuckle, evil dripped from it like blood. "Oh, I am not done with her." He lifted her chin so she looked directly at him. "I have great plans for this lovely creature. She will be mine. I will possess her. Fred must understand the consequences of his actions." He let her head drop again. "When I'm done with this one, Fred will not even recognize her, she will be so devoted to me and my cause, and it will be like seeing a new person,"

"Master, she's Guardian." The man protested.

Pierre turned on him. "You dare to argue with me?"

The man had trembled and stepped back. "No master," he bowed his head and rose his hands in defense. The boy was young. Curly blonde hair, blue eyes, fair skin and still in need of much guidance at his tender age. The only reason Pierre didn't strike him down that moment was that he had seen a desire for more and a deep sense of loyalty in him when he had taken him from that godforsaken farm in Ireland three years before. He took the boy's hands in one of his and touched his head with the other. "Dear, Quenton, you have nothing to fear, I would never harm you unless you betrayed me. The boy nodded not looking up. He kissed the boy's head. "Find Sashika and then take our guest to my transportation and load her in the unit, then step into the driver's seat. You will drive me." The boy's head snapped up, his eyes shined with joy and honor.

"Really, Master?"

"I wouldn't ask if I didn't mean it. I'll give the orders to James for the rest of it. Our guest is now the responsibility of you and Sashika, take care of her, she will be your kin soon, and her one desire will be to serve me. I'll see you by the escape gate in fifteen minutes."

"Yes, sir." Quenton watched him go. He then turned to Demi, "you should feel honored, you are now among the chosen – the nobles – this a great day for you indeed." He swung his gun onto his back, shifted his radio onto his belt, and went to work on Demi's restraints. He sensed, rather than saw her in the room. He looked up and Iris stood there heavy with the Master's child.

"Quenton." She whispered. He reached for his belt. "Please don't, Quenton. You know he'll kill me, and take my child. I'm running." Tears were streaming down her face. "But I can't go without her. I need your help."

"You deserve what you get. You betrayed him." He reached for his belt again.

"Quenton, please !" She cried. "I'm begging you. I don't want to die. You heard him, he's killing us all."

"Only the underlings."

"Is that what people have become to you, Quenton. Underlings and nobles? Can you so easily discard them? Was my judgment of you so wrong? Was my love for you so off?"

"Don't speak of that," he ordered stepping toward her. "Nobody must know of that. Ever."

She studied his face, her eyes moving quickly over his features. "My God, Quenton, have his warped words turned you so viciously?" Tears fell down her face. "Do I mean nothing to you?"

"You confuse me, you wretched woman." He turned and walked away, then pulled his gun and quickly turned back toward her. "You will come with me, and I will turn you over to him."

"You will have to kill me first." She glanced Demi's way. She had to get away. It was clear to Iris, she would have to leave Demi behind because if she forced his hand, Demi could end up dead and Iris would end up back in Lamontage's hands, her child stolen from her, and her body thrown on the street with the rest of the ones he would discard. She swallowed, backed up. "Then where would your standing be. If I meant so little to you then pull that trigger and kill me now !" She turned, jumped back into the passage, and closed the wall behind her. Quenton stood, gun held at the now empty space before him. He could not do it. He stood there a few seconds, the silence echoing around him, her final words booming in his ears. He could not put her down, he had loved her and loved her deeply, but the master could never find out about their relationship. Lamontage would kill him if he found out Quenton had fallen in love with one of the chosen. However, loving her made him owe her this chance.

"Good luck, Iris." He whispered, holstered his gun and undid the tape restraining Demi's arms to the chair. He caught her as she sloped forward, grabbed the duct tape from a nearby table, and taped her hands and feet. Then he threw her over his shoulder, and retreated from the room, locking the door behind him, buying Iris a precious few minutes.

~~~~~~

"Take her inside and secure her." Pierre's voice brought Demi back to the present.

"Yes, Master." She heard Quenton's voice just before she heard something click, and then felt the warmth of the sunshine on her face. Quenton lifted her and tossed her over his shoulder. She feigned unconsciousness because she knew that if she didn't, her training sessions with Pierre would begin sooner rather than later and she would have no time to get her bearings; get some idea of where she was. Her senses told her the trip had been mostly uphill. The air was different, thinner. They were at a higher elevation. The temperature had been warm, then cool. Her ears had popped several times during the trip. They had definitely climbed to a higher altitude. As they neared their destination, she had heard helicopters, and even some air traffic. They were obviously at a place where escape by air was not going to be difficult if Pierre felt the need. Quenton carried her into a dank, damp place. Footsteps echoed against walls of stone or cement. Maybe a castle? Quenton continued up several more steps, unlocked a door, dropped her onto a bed, and chained her hands and feet, spread eagle, to the frame. The final touch was the duck tape on her mouth.

"Don't bother," a woman's voice said. "Ain't nobody going to hear her up here 'cept the rocks and the trees, and maybe a few forest animals." Mocking chuckles filled the room. Footsteps retreated across the floor, the door shut, and a heavy lock moved into place with a resounding click. Demi remained quiet. She listened for the slightest hint of noise, a shuffle of feet, a cough, the rustle of clothing, a sneeze, anything, but only silence thundered around her. She opened her eyes to look at her surroundings.

She was in some kind of rock walled, circular room with barred windows. Beyond them, she saw the tops of trees and the afternoon slant of the sun. The only furnishings were the bed she was on, a crude table and chair, a water basin and pitcher, and a single wardrobe. Her heart sank. Great. Rapunzel let down your hair. Her thoughts wandered back to her least favorite childhood fairy tale. She swung her head so she could see the restraints around her wrists. They were metal cuff bands of solid steel attached to chains that lead to another steel cuff closed around a metal framed, headboard. She yanked a couple of times on them, but they were solid. She shifted and looked at her feet. The same restraints held them in place. She was in a hopeless situation. Her only hope was to try to give Marna an idea as to her whereabouts. She shifted her head some, closed her eyes and concentrated. *Marna?* Nothing was getting out; her words came back at her. Something was blocking her transmission. A Blocker! Of course, he wasn't about to leave her alone and unguarded. Reality hit her and hard. Unless Guardian found her, and soon, the situation would become desperate. Pierre Lamontage had full, unbridled control of her. That thought and many others, each more horrific than the last went through her mind, but they all came to a stop, when the door opened and he came through it. His menacing presence made her cower on the bed.

"Ahh, Miss. Spencer . . ." he grinned evilly, "let's get acquainted, shall we?" She yanked on her restraints as he approached her. He looked toward the right. "You may leave now, Sashika." Demi looked in the same general direction as he. A woman came from the shadowy depths of the room.

"She tried to contact them." She hissed.

"Of course she did." He nodded toward the door, "dismissed," Sashika nodded, and floated away. He returned his attention to her." It's rude to wish to be elsewhere when your host is trying so hard to make you comfortable." He was wearing a white cloak and a cross suspended around his neck on a silver chain."

"Hosts don't chain their guests." Her Irish lilt was apparent in her speech.

"Oh, but you are special." He reached out and traced a finger down the side of her face to her lips, lingered, then continued the caress to the plunging V of her neckline. "My brother surrounds himself with beautiful women."

"He's a good man." Demi instantly regretted her words, because his face darkened in anger, and his eyes captured hers. She knew what was coming. "No, please," she begged, just before she felt the confusion as he took over her mind. He closed his fist over her chest; her breathing became tight, labored. Perspiration beaded on her brow. She was suffocating.

"Frederick Keys is a coward, and you will soon learn that." He raised both hands to the ceiling, fisted them, pulled them down to just above her chest, the pain seared through her. She screamed arching her body, trying to make it stop. Tears filled her eyes. He opened his hands and she collapsed onto the bed. He released his hold on her lungs. She gasped for air. The tears now streamed down her face. "You will be loyal to me and no other." She had barely caught her breath when she felt the heat build in her core. She thrashed. Fire burst out all around her body. She yanked and pulled, trying to get away from it. The heat seared through her, she felt herself burning up. She screamed. Then the flames died down and the fire within retracted. Her wrists and ankles felt slick, from the blood trailing down her arm. Her struggling had chafed both wrists and ankles raw. Her head had rolled to the side.

He gently turned it back toward him. She was too weak to fight him. "I can continue to bring you pain, Demi, or I can bring you Euphoria." He brought his hands over her body again, she closed her eyes and braced herself for more of the same, but instead of pain, her body was weightless, her emotions filled with gentle joy. She saw herself running on a beach. A young man chased her. When he caught up to her, he embraced her so gently, and his hands caressed her so lovingly, she felt safe, secure. The gentle laughter echoed in the room around her. She closed her eyes as he kissed her. Felt his lips on hers. She felt elated. Euphoria. "It is up to you what you get." Her eyes opened, and the face above hers, was Pierre, not the young man on the beach. "I can give you either." His hand moved down her side. She pushed her head back into the pillow, moved to avoid his touch. He let out a cruel laugh. "You make the choice." He got up and walked toward the door. "Sashika." He said when he opened it. "Tend to her wounds, and give her a low dose of Compliance. I will be back later."

"Yes, Master," Sashika shuffled in as the slamming door echoed in the room around her. Demi felt felt the prick of the needle, the burning of the liquid as it seeped into her veins, tears leaked onto her cheeks. The room swam around her, confusion and then mercifully the darkness came.

*****

"Dear God." Keys breathed as he slowed his vehicle, staring straight ahead. Marna lifted her head from the crook of her arm and looked through the windshield. Smoke billowed in the distance. Emergency lights reflected off a large steal sign engraved with Lenk Community,home to Subgonomic INC. Police vehicles barred entrance onto the private road that lead to the largely private Community. Keys put the van in park.

"What do you want to do, Keys?" Ventura queried.

"Stay put. Marna and I will go talk to the locals." He glanced at Marna. "Ready?" She inclined her head once, and followed him out of the van. Then they walked up to the officer he thought to be in charge, and Keys showed him his badge. "This is my associate, Marna Farlow." The man shook both their hands. "What can you tell me?" Keys and the man spoke for a bit in German, while Keys translated for Marna. "He said they got a distress call about an hour ago from an unknown female who said there was about to be a mass murder in the Lenk community, and that many innocent people would die. She said Lamontage and the Liberatores were responsible."

"Demi?"

"No. He said the caller was young." He sighed, looking out over the horizon. "My guess would be Iris."

"Survivors?"

Keys shook his head. "He said they are still hoping, but the reports he's been getting back have been very bleak."

"Can we go in?"

"He's radioing ahead to get us a pass." Just as he spoke, the man walked up to them and spoke some more in German. Keys nodded and said, "Dunken," he then turned toward Marna, took her elbow and steered her back to the van as he flipped on his earpiece. "We're going in." He and Marna separated at the van and climbed in, and as soon as the cars moved away, they moved onto the road and headed toward the compound.

*****

Sashika stared at the woman on the bed. She had grown more beautiful with age. Demi had not recognized Sashika, but then it had been many, many years. Sashika had known from the moment she had seen her in the preparation room. Demi Spencer, child from a prominent family, Brentwood High golden girl, gifted, bright, lovely. She could go on with all the adjectives about dear Demi but the fact remained, the star of their small California town had left them if favor of joining Guardian to help find Suzannah Peraz. It had been the talk of the town. She had gotten her Diploma while away and even taken some college courses, she was quickly becoming a rising star in the Guardian organization, but Suzannah Peraz was still among the missing, and she would remain so.

The moonlight speared through the bars on the window, and sliced across Demi's features. Sashika had reported her discovery to Iris, but Iris had wanted to keep it a secret. Humph, poor little Iris, always ignored, shunned and brushed away like an annoying gnat. She was needy and nobody wanted to be bothered with the spoiled princess, but since the day the dark haired, blue-eyed beauty had walked through the doors she had monopolized the master's attention. It was sickening really to see how much he doted on the little twit while Sashika had practically begged for a smile or even a caress that meant more than hello. She had always wanted to be a noble in the community, a chosen one. One the master could never get enough of, but the scar across her face had always repulsed Pierre. She knew it. She had even asked him to approve surgical removal but he had said no, that the scar was what made her distinguished. She turned toward the mirror. The veil hid her face. She removed it. The scar went from above her left eye in a diagonal slant across the brow, the bridge of her nose, and continuing across her cheek down to her jaw.

Sashika ran her fingers over the jagged white line and bolt, scar. She had been sixteen, kidnapped, dragged into a car, driven to another county, dragged into a cabin in the redwood forests of California, tortured and raped repeatedly for three years to fill her captor's sick fantasies. She had screamed, she had cried, she had begged, but the vile man had ignored her pleas. She had prayed someone would find her, believed that if no one else could, Brentwood's golden girl would. Demi would not give up until she did, but that day had never come and Sashika, had become nothing but a shell of her former self, a far away memory of a young blonde haired, hazel-eyed child laughing and hanging out with her best buds. When she realized nobody was coming for her, she had ignored the pain, ignored the horrible things she suffered and prayed for death.

Three years later, suffering from Stockholm's syndrome, he took her hiking, tethered to his waist like a dog. At least it was better than being locked away like a prisoner in the windowless little cabin they lived in. They were going camping. She cooked their meals and kept the camp tidy while he did his hunting. He told her that if she tried to run, he would hunt her down like an animal and skin her alive. She had been a victim of his cruelty for three years. She knew he would do as he threatened so she obeyed his wishes without question.

However, one night the beans had burned because she was getting water from a nearby creek. He was furious. He tied her wrists to an overhanging tree branch, as if she was some animal he had brought back, and whipped her with a rope that had several little knots tied in it to increase the damage it caused and his pleasure. Though she tried, she could not protect her face and the knots that slashed across it, causing the injury. Her tears and blood mixed together and she had tasted both as they poured down her face. She prayed he would kill her prayed her body would just quit and she'd be free from his maniacal control, because she just couldn't take it anymore. However, something else that had changed the circumstances of her life.

During the vicious attack, his body froze, and lifted into the air. Suspended by invisible strings and thrown into some rocks before it fell lifeless to the ground. Pierre had walked into her life. She had fallen in love instantly. He had been so gentle, so caring. He told one of his servants to tend to her wounds, and gave her a veil to cover her bandaged face as the wounds healed. She had been his faithful servant ever since. However, no matter how faithful she had been, she had never gotten the one thing she wanted. To be his Lover. He had placed her on his servant staff, where she had remained in the years since, not once invited to share his bed. Even after the wounds had healed, she left the veil in place to hide the grotesque disfigurement that had marred her once beautiful features. However, this did not bring her to the master's side for more than service. He kept her on as a personal servant to his chosen ones, but he continued to ignore her existence and take people like Iris to his quarters. She did not understand it. She was ever faithful, and the ones he chose never were, so when Demi came into the community, she thought she had seen her chance to win his favor. She went to him to report Iris' betrayal to prove to him that she was the loyal one.

His decision to destroy Iris had secretly pleased her. He had even offered her the privilege to raise the child, yet, he still had not invited her to his bed. However, he had rewarded her by making her supervisor among the servants. It not only bumped her into his inner circle, but now she watched over his next conquest. What he didn't know was that Demi was a powerful adversary and she wasn't going to be easy to control.

Demi mumbled in her sleep. Sashika spun toward her wanting to listen, possibly bring more information to the master, but she heard him approach. She quickly lifted the veil back in place, and turned to face Pierre. He was dressed in silk lounge pants and a robe. With every movement his body, the silk moved softly against his muscled torso.. "Master?"

"Give me the key to her restraints, and leave us, Sashika. I want to begin her turning."

"Yes, master." She quickly handed him the key, crossed the floor, and left the room. Anger seethed within her. Once again he would pass her over for another as long as the target's mind and spirit could handle his toying.

Pierre removed his robe, and draped it over the chair by the bed. He took in Demi's sleeping form with his eyes. She mumbled softly. Sashika had bandaged her wrists and ankles, and then taken the time to dress her in a soft white, gown with a dipping neckline and wide straps. It molded her curves, and increased his desire to own her. "Well done, Sashika, well done," he whispered. What a beautiful specimen she was and she was Guardian. The satisfaction of turning her, possessing her, was just too exciting to explain. He could imagine the feel of his hands moving down that body, turning it, possessing it. He drew in a breath as visions of Lizzy passed through his mind. He hadn't wanted to kill her, but she had not been willing to go to him. "You will be my next act of revenge, Demi Spencer. Fred will feel the heart wrenching emptiness of loss, I will finish what I started with Lizzy, and you will be next on the menu." He took the key and unlocked the restraints.

Demi was under the influence of Compliance; she would not, could not, resist him. He brought her arms across her chest, and placed her hands on top of each other then he moved his hands down her legs, and undid the restraints around her ankles, laying her feet gently on the bed. He straightened to look down at her with a sick smile forming on his face. The joining promised to be explosive. The energy she expelled was among the highest he had experienced thus far.

He positioned his hands above her body about six inches, and moved them in an upward slide, starting at her feet and stopping above her torso. Then he closed his eyes, drew in a deep breath, and commanded the energy of the natural surroundings to enter his body. He felt the flow take hold, smiled as he strengthened, and then clenched his fists above her torso. She gasped, and her body arched. Her eyes flew open, and settled on his face. His eyes took hold of her gaze and she couldn't look away; they prodded, they intruded. "Feel the euphoria, Mon Cher, let go and feel the joy of no pain, no sorrow. Just a deep warmth and euphoric pleasure." He did it again, held her longer, she moaned as sensations she had never experienced took over her body, he felt her energy heed to his command. Demi could not resist whatever he did to her. The Compliance made her submissive to his wishes and his desires. He held her until he saw her body twitch, trying to get away from the energy waves traveling through it. He could sense, as well as feel her weaken. He released her again and her body fell to the mattress, listless, her breaths coming in deep, labored gasps. Sweat beaded her brow.

He smiled, "tonight, Mon Cher, we begin a journey you will not soon forget. Tonight, you start to become mine. You cannot fight it, so do not try. Soon you will only wish to serve me. My touch will be the only one that can satiate your desires. Your emotions will be wrapped up in pleasing me." He cupped her cheek with his hand and whispered, "oh don't look so sad, Mon Cher, I promise you, to be possessed by a man such as I will give you so much satisfaction and joy. The life you had before that will pale by comparison." He drew in a breath and kissed her lips. She wanted to turn away, but he held her fast. "Please do not resist, the more you fight the joining of our minds and souls, the more painful it will become and your mind will die," he ran a finger from her cheek to her hair and then ran his fingers through it," you will die. Please Mon Cher, because I prefer to give life not death, do not put me in that position. Death is a necessity of life and if it is required it will be."

He lay down beside her. His fingers caressing her arm, tracing the outline of her body, she felt fire burn from within wherever he touched. It was like thousands of hot needles penetrating her, prodding, and scorching her from within. A tear slipped out of the corner of her eye. She couldn't speak, she couldn't fight him, She could only obey. "Do not fear the joy I'm about to give you, my love. Euphoria is a gift." He moved her hair aside. His lips grazed her neck then grabbed her ear. His breath was hot on her lobe. "You are about to enter into a world like no other. I will leave you wanting more, and you will not want to disappoint me. Ever." He pulled her into his arms, pushed the straps of the gown off her shoulders, rubbing them, claiming her lips with his own, bruising them, biting them, and owning them. His breaths became quick and fierce as his psychic paths forced their way into her brain to connect.

Demi felt his probing and searching. His forceful desire became unquenchable as his psychic tentacles attached to every connection and control she had in her brain. He heated her senses until she thought her head would explode. The pain was excruciating, she cried out, but could not disengage, he alone had the power to do that. She felt the darkness in his soul invade hers but could not resist him, and shivered. He pulled away, looked down at her and chuckled. His hands were rough, his intentions viciously evil. She felt her head throb as his connections became sure and steady. His will pushed hers away, he explored, invaded. He took control of her thoughts and processes. She resisted at first but the pain it caused was more then she could bear. She screamed, he laughed. He held her fast against him as she tried to pull away. Soon she no longer fought him because she had no energy to do so; he was sucking it from her.

When her resistance faded, she felt the rising of an unquenchable desire to get what he offered. She was climbing to something unknown, something frightening, but she couldn't break away. She felt him lead her to the edge of some dark abyss and seconds later allowed him to pull her into it. Her mind burst with a high she had never felt before. It was something sinful, something--addictive. Fear and pain started to fade away as she felt something of herself fracture under his control. She heard someone scream in the distance. A voice cried out NO! It was familiar yet she couldn't identify it and before long, she forgot her interest in it. Her only desire was to please him. White-hot flames were devouring her. Her heart pounded in her ears.

He completely took her over, blocked any outside channels leaving only the one connecting her to him, and claimed her in a twisted mass of evil desire, temptation and longing that only he could satiate. She heard his maniacal laugh in the distance. At first, it was low, then it became louder until it bounced off the walls around her and assaulted her ears. Demi closed her eyes against the pain of electrical currents travelling throughout her body, she screamed. She tried to move away, but he had imprisoned her wrists with his hand, pinned her body with his own. "Do not fight it let it flow. The first time is always the hardest," his voice whispered breathlessly into her ear," but she wasn't listening anymore. Her mind had taken her away from the pain, away from the raping of her body, mind and soul. She shut out the horrors, lifted herself, her mind, above it all to a serene, relaxing place.

She was singing by a river as ducks passed by and she remained motionless, her connections locked out. Across the river, the castle where Pierre held her prisoner, surrounded by unforgiving terrain and cold stonewalls. She felt happy, euphoric. He sensed the change in her, her body stilled beneath him. She no longer fought his mind control. He smiled in the darkness and allowed himself to complete the cycle, and then he disengaged from the psychic as well as the physical joining. "You did well, Mon Cher, you rest now. Tomorrow will be soon enough to continue your journey." He kissed her forehead, grabbed his clothes, slipped them on, and left the room without noticing the small smile that appeared on Demi's face through her tears.

*****

"Dear God," Marna whispered as they drove through the gates and checked with the law enforcement within the compound. It was a blood bath. Bodies strewn everywhere, including whatever children, Pierre had deemed unworthy. It had grown dark and the moon light hardened the reality even more. It looked as if people were going about their business when the Liberatores soldiers gunned them down where they stood. Signs of struggles and people running were everywhere. Her eyes wandered over the buildings. They all burned, with the exception of the church in the center of the village. Marna stared at the cross still hanging strong on the little steeple. How ironic that people serving such an evil master, could put the symbol of love and forgiveness in the center of the very carnage he created. Local firefighters were combating blazes all around the community with streams of water from heavy hoses and choppers flew over dropping water loads from skies. "He had them all killed." She wiped at her face. An officer ran across the compound, speaking excitedly in German.

"Marna, will you excuse me," Keys said. She absently waved him off.

"Do you think . . ." Bryan's voice was breathless beside her.

"No, Bryan, no. I sensed them moving her. He didn't kill her."

Keys rejoined them. "They found fresh tracks at the back gate. He must have taken some of the villagers with him, the tires suggested large buses were used recently to leave the compound via the back way They're dispatching units now to try to pick up their trail. Do you sense anything, Peter?"

Ventura looked at Marna and held out his hand. "May I." She nodded and placed her hand in his. Her magnifying ability increased the strength of Peter's tracking ability, much as Sasha had experienced at the train station, he was in awe by what he saw. What Marna's magnifying did for his tracking ability. Their eyes flew open together. "There, in the church," Ventura said. A scream went across the village. "We got this." Peter said and was the first one to run toward the little white church, with gun drawn, while the others followed suit.

They landed their backs against the wall, guns aimed up, fanning themselves out on opposite sides of the door, and waited until agents covered both entrances before they synchronized their breech. When Keys said three, they kicked open the doors and moved in. Lying on the floor, in a pool of blood, highlighted by the altar light, was Iris. She was crying uncontrollably.

Keys holstered his gun and the others covered him as he approached her. "Iris." He said softly. She spun around and raised a knife. They readied their guns. "Stand down !" He ordered, fearful they might shoot. Keys saw the blood originated not from her, but from a small child sprawled on the floor underneath her. The gaping wound in her back, suggested a soldier had shot her while she ran for safety, possibly after another had gunned down someone she loved first. She had bled out on the floor of the church. He slowly reached down and closed the child's eyes."

Marna holstered her gun, and crouched down before Iris. "Iris, I'm Marna, Demi's friend. She reached her hand out. "Give me the knife. I know what happened here was horrible, incomprehensible, and I know you don't understand why or how people can do this to others, but we're not here to hurt you, I promise. We're here to help."

The girl looked at her and Marna caught her breath. She had known Iris was a Rose clone, but seeing it close up shocked her. She was seventeen, pregnant, alone, and terrified. She let herself conjecture that she was probably looking at the same face of her older sister, as she had looked, when she had escaped Bradshaw so many years ago. Her heart twisted in her chest. Iris was confused, hurt, betrayed and trusted no one. Too many had betrayed her in the worst of ways. "Please, Iris, this is not doing you, or your baby any good. You may not care what happens to you, and in the wake of what you just witnessed, I can even understand that feeling. But what about him? Does he have a right to live? These agents are trained professionals and they will kill you if you threaten them or another team member so please, Iris, don't force their hand."

Iris raised her other hand to her swollen belly and looked at Marna. A tear slipped from her beautiful blue eyes and tracked down her cheek. She looked at the knife in her hand as if she didn't know what it was doing there and let it slip from her grasp. Marna dropped to her knees and pulled the teen into her arms, letting her cry. Kyle retrieved the knife. Keys knelt down and assisted Marna in sitting Iris on a pew, and then began a quick examination. She pulled away. "It's okay, Iris." Marna crooned. "He's a doctor." Iris relaxed. Keys checked her over.

"I can't tell for sure until we get her to the clinic, but it looks like she's okay. No visible trauma. Bryan, call the medics." Bryan stepped away and dialed his phone. Keys looked at the girl. "Iris, how did you escape?"

She picked at her simple white dress. "A tunnel. . . In the wall."

Keys looked around. He saw no opened panels. "Not here . . . the main building." I hid here when I saw," she sniffed, "when I heard the gunfire go off. She glanced at the child, now covered by Ventura's jacket. "Sally came in here for help. She ran from the guns – she came in here and fell down. I tried to stop the bleeding . . ."

"It's okay." Marna said. The front doors flew open and the paramedics came in. Keys motioned to Iris to get on the gurney. "Help her out, gentlemen." They did. "Do you have a baby viewer on board?"

"A small one, sir."

"Hook it up." They did and Keys took control of it. He covered Iris' legs to her abdomen then lifted her dress. She reached for Marna, who grabbed her hand. Keys hooked the machine up, gelled up the contact head of the wand, and started running it over her abdomen, watching the computer screen.

In seconds, a 3D image of the infant took form on the screen. Keys let out a sigh of relief when he saw the sepia toned form sucking its thumb and the bleeping of its heartbeat and respirations in the sidebar. Both were within the right levels. Seconds later, it kicked out at its mother's stomach and she laughed. "Looks like he's no worse for the wear."

"It's definitely a he?" Iris asked.

"I'd start looking under boys names." He smiled and disengaged the machine, cleaned her up, pulled her dress down, covered her up and strapped her in. He turned toward the paramedics. "I want her brought to the clinic on the Guardian compound in Zurich. My name is Dr. Frederick Keys. I am now her attending. I'll radio ahead." They nodded. "Before you go, Iris, do you have any idea where he took Demi?"

A fresh tear strayed down her cheek. "I heard him say the Ruhe."

"Tranquility?" He thought for a moment. "Must be the name of some place he owns here in Switzerland. Anything else?" He queried. She sniffed.

"He has no intention of returning her to you, no matter what he says, he wants to possess her." Keys face grew dark. Marna watched the others' expressions become anxious. Bryan became enraged.

"Okay. Thank you, Iris." He patted her shoulder gently then turned toward the medics and nodded. They left the building.

Marna turned toward him. "What does she mean, he wants to possess her?"

"He wants to break her." Bryan said, and then slammed his fist into a nearby pew. Marna jumped.

"What?" She turned toward Keys. "B-break her, what's that mean exactly?"

"He wants to create a psychic bondage or tie down by intruding into her mind and inducing a euphoria so powerful she won't want to leave. She will become his servant."

"Dear God, Keys, please tell me that isn't as bad as it sounds."

"I'm afraid I can't, Marna, it's a horrific and painful experience for a psychic to go through. It usually happens over several severe sexual encounters and mind intrusions, which happen simultaneously that only a Seducer has the power to inflict. He starts by feeding a pleasant sensation through a body, equivalent to ecstasy, and then he gets access to the mind through eye contact and psychic hypnosis. The target is even more powerless if the Seducer is using a drug such as *Compliance*.."

""And he is," Marna said and Keys nodded.

"The drug *Compliance* works like a date rape drug, but it is even more dangerous for the psychic. It breaks down all the defense mechanisms they possess, and it makes them powerless against intrusions of any form. His invasion takes control of all the channels, shutting them down, leaving only one open between the he and the target. The more advanced the Seducer is the more controlled and intrusive his invasion can be. Near the end of the encounter, the Seducer releases an energy current through his target that comes from combining their psychic energies. This phase of the process can be very painful to the target, and the target may buck and try to disconnect from the Seducer physically, to break away from the pain but it will be to no avail. A less experienced Seducer can lose control at this point, cause death to the target. However, a Seducer with more experience will have a means of keeping their target tied down such as restraints or in most cases, the physical body already engaged in sexual activity with the target, which makes the surge more physically pleasing to the Seducer. The two energies fuse together and bonds start to form between the target and the Seducer. The process breaks her spirit and it will leave her totally adherent to him." He sighed.

"He's raping her?" Marna's voice held horrible conviction.

Keys nodded. "In more ways than one."

"How many sessions of this process will happen?"

"At least six," he said with a sigh, "but not sequential, that kind of abuse to a target's mind will most definitely cause a break if it doesn't kill them. My experience with Pierre tells me that Possessing Demi would be a way to strike out at Guardian and at me. He's not going to kill her. He's going to take control of her."

"You can't trust that, Keys," she interjected.

"Yes I can, and I can do it with conviction. After each session, Demi will retreat into what experts call a happy place, a place that has no pain, no sorrow, no regrets, a euphoric place, and if he completes his conversion, she will stay there and only trust him to protect her and make her happy. This is what possession is all about. He wants her to respond to him and him only."

"How long between sessions?"

"The interim between sessions could be a day or two, more if he spaces the sessions out, and they will go until the process is complete, but if he plans on starting the conversion immediately. Demi's time is already running out."

"If he succeeds in taking control of her?" She pushed, not sure, she wanted to know the answer.

"It's curable with treatment through meds and psychiatric rebuilding, but if he goes too far he will cause a psychotic break or a psychosis episode she may not return from."

Marna ran a hand through her hair. "Then we need to find her now and stop him." She said.

Keys sighed heavily. He looked years older. Lizzy's death still haunted him and now Pierre was working on taking another family member from him. She wondered how often this case brought him back to that apartment in Paris. "Well we can't do anything from here. We'll go back to the hotel, get some sleep, regroup, and try a new plan of action in the morning." The others agreed, and in a brooding silence, they left the building.

*****

Heinderick tossed and turned, he tried to sleep but the eerie silence of the new room echoed around him. He turned onto his back and thought about his dream sister. He hadn't seen her in a while. Maybe he should go to the realm and try to contact her. He heard the doorknob on his door turn, and quickly closed his eyes. The hallway light sliced into the room. Only about thirty people had come with them to this place. Pierre had left the rest behind. He was one of the ten children who had left with the master. He heard shuffling feet, and then felt gentle hands pull the blanket up over his shoulders. He rolled to his side, not opening his eyes. He recognized her smell. Sashika. She was in charge of him now. Master left Rosina behind. He had cried when he found out. Rosina was kind and loving. Sashika was cold and very devout to the Master. Seconds later, he heard her shuffle away and the door closed out the light.

Instantly, he heard muffled voices outside his door. He climbed out of bed, and tiptoed to the door, peaking through the keyhole. "I thought you were watching our guest, Sashika?" Malina queried, she had been with the servants' team for 20 years. Her dislike of Sashika's brooding around all the time was apparent to everyone. Heinderick had listened to her tell some of the stories of her early years in service to the Liberatores and Pierre. He shivered.

"The Master is with her."

"Already?"

"I guess he figures he must move fast with this one. She is Guardian."

Guardian? The word rolled over in his six-year old mind. What was Guardian?

"I highly doubt he has training in mind, Sashika, because of who she is. He's going to possess her," Malina continued. "The Master has had problems with Guardian in the past, particularly the leader."

"If that is his wish," Sashika said.

"Hmm, you're too young to remember." The older woman wasn't being harsh, just truthful.

"Remember what?"

"There was only one other woman the Master wished to possess, but her heart belonged to another."

"Who was that?"

"Her name was Elizabeth, I think. The Master was obsessed with her."

"Why is he not with her now?"

"She was married to his brother, who also happens to be the Guardian Leader."

"So what happened?" That would explain a lot of the master's behavior about Demi.

He tried to possess her, but his powers were not as strong, nor did he know how to control abilities as well. She fought him, and he killed her. Almost killed his brother too, but the apartment they were in caught fire."

"I am surprised that stopped him, considering his abilities."

"Fire suppresses his abilities; it sucks all the energy from the natural power around him which is what he draws the energy from. The energy that powers his abilities."

"You should not talk of the Master's weaknesses, Malina. That is private. You could end up like the others."

"Only if he finds out I did, and the only one around to hear is you, but I would think twice before you betray me as you did Iris. We do not take betrayal lightly in our ranks. None of us wishes to feel his wrath so we watch out for each other. Many of us have served the Master from the beginning, and an upstart like you could be lost very easily. So I would watch your step."

"Is that a threat, Malina?"

"Take it as you wish, but you need to decide if you are a mindless robot or one of team." The woman raised a brow when Sashika looked to the floor. "He has a type, Sashika, and you are not it, be grateful for that. You have minimal psychic energy. He wishes to only join with those that are strong in spirit and psychic mind. They are who make him most powerful. Their energy fuels his power. I've seen him drain the life out of those that are weak and discard them like trash." She paused to study the younger woman. "Choose your way carefully, Sashika, because if you choose wrong, it is you who will end up like the others, not I." Giving the girl a final appraising look, she turned and went up the stairs.

Sashika drew in a breath, looked around to make sure no one had heard the conversation, and sunk to the steps, burying her head in her hands. She knew Malina was right. Knew that the screams coming from the Master's chambers at night weren't all in pleasure and she had known of others to disappear after a night with him, but it did not quench her desire to be with him.

"Sashika." Pierre came down the stairs. "I was looking for you."

Sashika jumped up, and bowed. "Yes, Sir?"

"I am done my session with our guest. You may return to your post and make her comfortable. He started to walk away, but turned. "Oh, and leave the restraints off, I don't think she'll need them, she's actually quite compliant now."

"Yes, Sir." She watched him go and felt a chill go down her spine. His eyes were so cold, so unfeeling. Why would she notice it now? Hadn't she seen him many times after his 'Sessions' with others, why would she just notice now how his eyes gleamed with a twisted pleasure? She shook it off. Her talk with Malina was overshadowing her common sense she could not let it. She shook her head, and headed up the stairs toward the tower room. Heinderick backed away from the door as quietly as he could and returned to his bed where, despite the icy fear that filled his soul, he soon fell into a restless sleep.

~~~~~

The forested area was familiar. The trees were tall, and the grass as bright and green as it was after a springtime rain. Heinderick whistled as he ventured down the little dirt path. Flowers bloomed all around him, and birds sang from the trees. He put his arm out as a beautiful little blue bird flew down and landed on it. "Good evening to you bluebell." The bird whistled a string of notes to him. "I'm sorry. I'll try not to be gone so long next time. Is there anything I should worry about?" The bird chirped and flapped his wings. "Good then, fly on home to your family." The bird lifted off and flew into a tall fir tree.

"Don't you wish you could do that in the real world?" Arella asked, coming from behind a tree.

"Then it wouldn't be much fun," he grinned. "Where have you been Arella? I've walked here many nights and you have not been here," he stated sadly, "I thought you had left me".

"It hasn't been safe, Heinderick. That man came last time, we had to fight him." Arella stepped into the path beside him and kept pace.

"It is tonight," he said and sat on a rock, inviting her to join him. They spoke in German, their native tongue.

"Why do you say that?"

"Look around you?" He invited. "All the paths are closed." He was right. All the paths had gates across them. His face saddened. "It was not his path I followed, it was hers."

"Whose?"

"He has another one. I heard her screaming."

"Did you shut her out like I taught you?"

He nodded. "Why does he hurt them like that?"

"Because he's mean, Heinderick, he tried to hurt our family. But Aunt Marna, she is very strong, and she hurt him."

"When is she coming for me? I don't want to do what he says anymore. He makes me hurt people. They're make believe, he says it's only practice but what happens when he wants me to hurt real people, Arella, I don't want to do that. What am I going to do? He'll hurt me if I don't obey him."

She took his hand. "Aunt Marna is coming for you. They left this morning."

He sighed sadly. "If they've gone to the other place, they won't find me."

"Why?"

"He moved us," he sighed, "he left a lot of people at the old place I think he hurt them. Sashika, the person who takes care of me now, says that if we don't behave and do as Master says, the same thing will happen to us."

"Well what happened?"

"I don't know but I heard big guns. I think he killed them." His eyes widened in fear.

"Aunt Marna better hurry up and find you."

"Yeah . . . Did you hear that?"

"Hear what?"

"Shhhh . . . listen," he whispered then cocked his head. "It's over there," he pointed toward the bank hidden by thick brush and tall trees. "Someone is singing." He took her hand, "come on," together they followed the melodious voice to some berry bushes, crouched, and peeked through. They saw the backside of a woman with red hair. Her hair fell in rich waves to the center of her back. She was sitting on the riverbank, staring at the ducks in the river, just singing an old children's song. She had a crown of flowers on top of her head and she barely moved. The two children approached then fanned out so they flanked her on each side, and moved in. "Who is she" Heinderick asked, "and why does she look so sad?" He reached out and touched her cheek, she didn't move.

"I know her," Arella said in a frightened whisper. "She left with Aunt Marna to come get you."

"Wha ---"

"Her name is Demi," Amanda said coming toward them, "and she needs your help," she walked up and accepted a hug from Arella, and played with Heinderick's hair. "This is her dream, Heinderick. She summoned you though she isn't aware of it. She's scared. You sensed her need and you *came to her," She took them both in with her eyes, "You both did. That's what dream walking is all about. Pierre is hurting her, and she needs you two to get word to your Aunt Marna." She looked around. "He's closed all of her paths to connect to her friends, so you have to help her find them and tell them where she is."*

"B-but I don't know, Momma, I don't know where we are. I was in a van with no windows."

"It's over there." Amanda pointed to the old stone castle across the river," Demi stared at the building while she sang, "It's his Castle and it's somewhere here in Switzerland, but we need to be able to find it when we search." Her eyes strayed toward it then she brought them back to Heinderick. "Guardian just needs a clue . . ."

"Guardian?" Heinderick puzzled over the word.

"Have you heard that before, Son?" Amanda asked.

"The woman that cares for me spoke of it earlier. She is taking care of someone for the Master. She said she belonged to Guardian so he was moving faster with this one." He looked toward Demi. "Her?" Amanda nodded. "She lied to the Master about who she was. The Master was very angery. He will not spare her any pain. He does not like to be lied too. Sashika is the one that told him of her lie."

"Who is Sashika?

"She works for the Master. She takes care of me, and her," he pointed to Demi. "She is the one who knows where he keeps her."

"Then she is the one we must focus on."

"Run, he's coming," Demi's head turned toward them quickly and her eyes were wide and clear. "Get away !" Her body went stiff and rigid just before she let out an agonizing scream and her body arched before it collapsed on the riverbank. Her eyes focused on something that wasn't there, and then clouded over. Amanda ushered the children into some nearby bushes and back down the path they had been on before they had walked to the river bank.

~~~~~

Heinderick bolted up in bed, heard Demi's screams, and rolled over on his side, covering his head with the pillow, trying to drown it out. Miles away, in the little bedroom she shared with her new sister, Arella cried out and sat up in bed. Rose and Tanner ran into the room, guns drawn. The little girl let Rose grab her into her arms and take her into the living room with a bewildered Mary watching. When she had stopped sobbing, she told them of her dream walk. Tanner immediately dialed Keys at the hotel.

Keys rolled over, grabbed his cell off his bedside stand, glanced at the LCD screen, and brought it to his ear. "Keys."

"Keys, Demi made contact with Arella and Heinderick through a dream walk and Amanda was there. He's got them stashed in the mountains in a castle. It's by a body of water, a lake, maybe and Sir, near the end of the dream it appears he may have caught Demi trying to make contact, she warned them away just before she collapsed."

"Dammit !" Keys sat up on the edge of his bed, and drew on his robe. Keep her blocked, use an extra layer if need be, if I know Pierre he's going to do some prodding to try and find out exactly who Demi contacted, then he'll be after them and I don't need to tell you if he can find Arella . . ."

"He'll find Marna."

"Yes. I'm afraid Demi is only a stepping stone and once he possesses her, he's going to use her to find the real prize . . ."

" Marna." Tanner's heart sank to his stomach.

"So I don't need to tell you how important it is to keep those children safe. They are the one thing that he can manipulate Marna with."

"Not to worry, Sir, I'll tighten the activities to the compound area."

"I'm going to call in some more security for the children. No matter how dictatorial you have to become, Tanner, do not let any of her family out without supervision. Is that clear?"

"Yes, Sir, Very."

"Good, I knew I could count on you. If Arella is up to it, I want to talk to her and get information on the dream."

"Sure." There was some shuffling on the other end then Arella came on the line and the two spoke while Keys took notes.

Chapter Eleven

Keys waited at at the entrance to the cafe of the Cambrian, a hotel nestled in the mountain village of Adelboden, with a spectacular view of the Swiss Alps. The establishment was equipped with accommodations from single rooms to Presidential suites. It also included extras such as a spa, a bar and a restaurant, It was a big draw for skiers, tourists and business personnel, which is why he thought it the perfect place for them to blend in while they figured out their next move. He had told them to dress in business attire for this morning's meeting, and when they were out and about, because they were there under the pretense of expanding the HomeSpot networking site.

HomeSpot was a great way to help Guardian set up long-term cover IDs for their agents. It would be easier to backstop them from the beginning of their career with cast iron covers, and if they needed to change them, it would be easier to get the information out there. The site had started out as part of their cover for this mission, but the more Keys thought on it, the more he liked the idea. Guardian had many uses for a social networking site where they could freely monitor, control and secure information to protect their agents. Members would pay an annual fee to have their domain, a safety feature for his agents and those that became a part of it. Members could set up virtual 3D chat rooms for private and professional use, so they could keep their identities secret and safe. Each room would have secure passwords, which the administrators of the pages would have to choose and notify their guests what they were to enter the room. Video conferences would be an option if they owned a GPC or a GPC app on their computer. High security checks would be mandatory for anyone opening an account and that would be appealing to most people who did not want strangers to have the easy access other networks e.g. Facebook, twitter and MySpace had allowed in the past.

People would use credit cards and online accounts to pay their fees, allowing the Guardian security team to keep a database of the members. A database that was accessible by law enforcement agencies across the globe, via a Guardian Gateway. They would attach red flags, to anyone who registers, if they have a questionable profile or neighbors. They would also add a safety feature that would alarm the webmaster team if anyone gets on the site that might have characteristics to put them on the terrorist watch list. Eventually he would put a student team in charge of checking backgrounds. They could set it up as a work scholarship program for the Compound University.

The whole set up would be safer for his agents if the enemy put them under scrutiny, or if they needed immediate exposure to be launched into an investigation. It was a wise addition to the Guardian team and he was surprised they hadn't done it sooner. Each agent would have a profile and be listed as employed by one of the business corporations under the Guardian umbrella. They would have job histories and a realistic pasts. These practices were very similar to those of the old time CIA, before the Conflicts, and they had worked it for decades with satisfactory results. Some of the lower level CIA agents still practiced this strategy today. It would improve Guardian's ability to run more efficiently and securely. He sighed and stilled the thoughts in his mind to focus on why they were there, and what was on the agenda for today.

Keys had booked the presidential suite and two junior suites, using cover IDs. Technical agents had been working around the clock to set up their profiles on Homespot.com for the last few days to establish the desired history they needed to satisfy curious outsiders. The suites gave them enough space to spread out, but they were close enough to connect immediately if needed. He had also arranged a business meeting with the hotel manager to present HomeSpot to him as a cover story. No cover ID worked well unless there was some ring of truth in it. This is why the CIA had made a history of linking their operatives with a legitimate company and why Keys chose to do the same.

He spoke a few words in German to their server, gave her the total number of people in his party, and followed her to two large tables in the back, which they pulled together, before she went off to get the breakfast menus. He took a few minutes and spread out the map of the surrounding mountains and a copy of the property registry in those mountains. It was a lot of ground to cover in a short amount of time, but they had no choice. Demi's and Heindrick's lives hung in the balance and they depended on the team to get them away from Pierre Lamontage.

The last thing he brought out was the ear bud he had retrieved from the emergency personnel at the Subgonomics Community. That could be the most important key of all. He wanted to combine Marna's budding Locating ability, Sasha's Tracking, Kyle's Blocking and his own Kything ability to try to get the same results they had gotten at the train station. However, this time he was going to sketch the path on a large transparency sheet, placed over the map before him. He hoped the two together would lead them right to Lamontage's doorstep. If his plan worked, they could possibly have Demi back before nightfall. If it didn't and they somehow tipped Pierre off that they were closing in then he would rabbit again and possibly figure Demi wasn't worth the trouble and pull Heinderick even further away from Marna and his family.

He sighed at their dwindling options and waved as Marna and Kyle arrived at the entrance to the restaurant. His brow furrowed when he saw how easily Marna accepted Kyle's guiding hand, at the small of her back, as they weaved through the tables and how the smiles they exchanged were spontaneous and warm. "Hmmm," he breathed but now was not the time to analyze whatever was happening between them. He buried the questions in the back of his mind as the young people reached the table and Kyle pulled a chair out for Marna. She smiled and thanked him then studied Keys' features as Kyle moved on to take the seat across from her.

"Keys, you look like hell. Didn't you sleep at all last night?" Marna queried.

"A little. I got a call from Tanner."

Alarm crossed her features "Tanner? What's wrong? Are the kids okay?"

He held up his hand to stop her onslaught. "Arella had a dream walking experience with Heinderick and Amanda. A dream, which I believe, Demi called them into."

"What? Demi?" Anger replaced her alarm, "why didn't he call me? They're my kids!"

"He was going to, but I told him not to."

"That wasn't your call, Keys." She hissed,

"Marna ---." Kyle said reaching over and placing a hand over hers as it fidgeted angrily with one of the table napkins, her hand stilled under his.

Keys looked from one to the other, and cleared his throat. "I'm sorry if I've overstepped my boundaries, Marna, but it seemed the right thing to do at the time. Rose and Tanner had the situation under control, and I saw no reason for both of us to spend the night in sleeplessness. The contact was initiated by Demi, and she gave them some hints as to where she was, but unfortunately we think Pierre interrupted the contact. . ." He raised his hand again to stop another protest, "he didn't enter the dream, and Amanda removed the children quickly before he found out who she had contacted."

"But?"

He looked at her and scrubbed his face with his hands. "But," he sighed heavily, "he will not stop until he finds out who Demi contacted, and the more he goes ahead with the process of possession . . ."

"The weaker she gets," Kyle finished the sentence for him.

"Yes, Kyle," his eyes grazed over the boy's features and came to rest on Marna's, "I'm afraid he'll use her to find you through the children."

"Through the children?"

"To him, they are only tools, Marna, tools that will eventually help him get to you. You're the main attraction. He wants to possess you and your magnifying ability. Demi was his first step. You're the reason she's still alive. When he gets what he wants . . ."

"He'll kill her too." Marna stated flatly and pulled her hand from Kyle's grasp. "I'm the reason he is doing all of this? Demi?" She swallowed and regained her composure before she lost complete control. "I'm the reason he attacked Demi?"

"No, Marna, his selfish desires are the reason he does what he does, but in his eyes, you are his prize." He sighed, "But you're not alone. He has an old score to settle with me too. Getting Demi, getting to you," he paused, "it'll all bear fruit for him if he breaks down my defenses and the Guardian organization."

"Well then you better have a damn good plan as to how we are going to stop him in his tracks." Her blue eyes flashed. Kyle watched from the sidelines. He admired Marna's inner strength. Most people would have pulled their tail between their legs and run in the opposite direction after everything she'd been through since her association with Guardian, or they would have simply fallen apart in the wake of such realizations but no, she wanted to meet it head on. He looked down at the hand that had just held hers and smiled slightly. He could still feel the warmth of it, the strength in her grip on the napkin. When this mess was over, if she was willing, he was definitely going to make it a goal to get to know Marna Farlow a lot better. She was a complex, intriguing woman, with too much sorrow in her recent past, he wanted to remedy that problem.

"What plan is that?" Her voice brought him out of his private thoughts. Keys had just said something and she wanted to know more.

"I think I'll wait until the others get here to share that with you."

Kyle cleared his throat. "They should be joining us soon. Ventura called as we were heading out the door. He said they were running a few minutes late but his team should be down soon, and Bryan was in the shower when we left the suite." No sooner had he said the words, than Keys saw the others come into the restaurant, so he flagged them over. The dining area was still empty, so they made their way over quickly. The Server delivered menus instantaneously to their arrival.

It took a few minutes for them to order and for their coffee to arrive along with a basket of bread, spreads and various cheeses, for them to enjoy. "So what's the plan, Keys?" Ventura asked before taking a bite of toast, loaded with Nutella, then chasing it down with a swallow of Espresso. "Which do we do first? Pound down the doors of the locals, so we can extract info from the wary or go ripping up the records buildings? I haven't had a good sparring match since we left the states. I'm up for either." The team chuckled and Keys smiled, shaking his head.

"Nothing quite so dramatic, Pete, as satisfying as that may be, I have something a little more subtle in mind."

"Well share it with us," Bryan stated, "because right now, Pete's plan sounds pretty damn good to me." They all paused and waited while their Server delivered their breakfast entrees and walked away.

"We'll need the cooperation of Marna, Kyle, and Sasha but I think it might prove faster and far more efficient."

"Anything, Keys, Demi is one of my closest friends," interjected Sasha.

"Of course, Keys," Marna agreed with Sasha, "just tell me what needs to be done."

He placed Demi's ear-bud on the table before Marna. "I want you, myself and Sasha to join abilities. We're going to draw a road map right to Lamontage's doorstep."

"What?" Marna looked confused. "Keys, even if that ear-bud reveals Demi's surroundings to us, neither one of us has the ability to draw a map of her whereabouts. You know that."

"And the only way I can track someone is if their abilities are actively being used, not to mention radius. They could be way out of range for us to plug into them," Sasha stated.

"Under normal circumstances, Sasha, yes, you'd both be right, but Marna's magnifying ability changes the rules." He turned toward Marna. "Marna, I want you to take Demi's ear-bud and concentrate," She reached for the bud, but he put his hand up, "after you have established an open connection with Sasha." Marna nodded. She reached her hand toward Sasha. He turned toward Kyle who awaited word on his role in the drama unfolding. "Kyle, I want you to offer extra blocking. We don't need Pierre realizing he's being breached, that wouldn't be safe for anyone, but most of all Demi." Kyle nodded, and clasped Sasha's hand. If the breakfast crowd thought the goings on amongst the Americans, at the corner tables strange, they kept it to themselves, because not a one spared them more than just a passing glance.

The three participating became one, each of them feeling stronger for the joining. A channel opened, connecting all three. The joining launched them into a foggy mist and placed them in another psychic realm equivalent to the dream realm. A forest of trees filled the white space in their mind's eye, and then a country road led them to a four-way crossroad.

*****

Okay this is weird. Kyle voiced the words in his mind.

Somewhere Keys' voice drifted to their subconscious. *Kyle, block them.*

Okay, he shrugged and raised his virtual hands as more trees filled the area. *Way cool.* Both the women heard his telepathic messages. He glanced Marna's way and winked, *I could get used to this.*

It is amazing, isn't it? Keys appeared beside him.

Where'd you come from?

Really, Kyle? After everything we've seen on this mission, you had to ask that? Sasha stated.

Yeah, right. He glanced over at Marna and smiled again. She was amazing. *This magnifying thing is something special isn't it.*

Yes and every known Psychic in our realm wants to own it, but let's not wonder in the magic of it all right now. There will be time for that later. Marna will tire quickly supporting three additional Psychic minds. Here's what I want you to do. Kyle keep blocking, while Marna reaches out to Demi, and Sasha, when Demi responds you get a lock on her location. We'll keep her talking as long as possible. He paused a moment while they all got on the same page. *While you do that, I'm going to sketch the path you draw in our minds on to the transparency and it should give us a road map of sorts to where he is keeping Demi.*

Of course, Marna interjected, Keys nodded. *That's brilliant, Keys,* Marna stated.

Sometimes it pays off to mix a little of the old investigation tools in with the new. Let's get started, shall we? They all agreed and focused.

Marna focused on Demi. At the physical table, she took hold of the ear-bud with her free hand, while the others secured their hands and focused with her. *Demi, can you hear me?* Marna asked. She felt fog, confusion, fear and darkness. A darkness so cold, so empty it made her tremble. They all felt it, but still kept the chain connected.

Miles away, sedated on the tiny cot, Demi fought to come out of a *Compliance* controlled sleep. In her mind, she wandered aimlessly in Pierre's dark abyss. She was Cold, lonely, scared and . saddened. She had displeased him by reaching out to the children. He had done another training session with her almost immediately, but this one was more violent. She could still feel the pain and the rage he had for her. The hate he reflected on her because of what she belonged to, whom she worked for. He had been very angry with her and he had hurt her, violated her in many different ways. Her head had felt like it was going to explode and she felt she would die, but then he took it all away. He gave her the bliss of euphoria. He promised her she would continue to get it if she would behave.

Now the pain and anger was back because someone was talking to her, someone besides him was trying to contact her. She curled up in that dark place, and covered her ears. She wanted them to go away, leave her be. Why wouldn't they let her be happy? Why did they want her to be in pain? Maybe they would go away if she didn't answer them.

Her physical body, lying on the cot, moaned softly in her sleep. By pure luck or simply fate, Sashika had stepped out to get the master's companion, for the night, ready for him. At least it wasn't she. No training tonight. Tears streamed down her face. She didn't know what was worse, the training or the deep loneliness of being left in this hole, this abyss, where it was so cold, so evil, you could feel it closing in on you. *Demi, can you hear me?* The voice returned.

Please go away or he'll hurt me again. She begged.

At the table, Marna felt Keys gentle pressure on her hand. He wanted to talk to Demi. *Demi, this is Dr Keys. Please. We've come to help you. We want to make sure he never hurts you again.*

She shook her head to the abyss and choked on a sob. *Can't. Too powerful. Go away, please.*

Marna joined the conversation. *Demi, it's Marna.*

Marna? Demi looked around. Marna was important, Marna was powerful but the Master was more powerful.

Yes. I'm with Dr. Keys and some others from Guardian we're going to help you, but we need to know where you are? Can you tell us anything?

No no no no no, go away, Marna, even you can't fight him.

I can and I will. What about Heinderick? Is it fair to leave him under the control of Pierre? You know what he'll do to him. Come on, Demi, he's a child, does he deserve this?

She raised her hands to her ears. *No, I don't want to hear. I don't want to be hurt again. So much pain. I can't, please don't ask me to, please don't ask me to."* Her voice had become child-like and had drifted off to nothing. A soft humming filled the darkness. Keys decided to approach it a different way. It was obvious Pierre had already done some damage to Demi's mind.

Demi, remember Suzannah? Do you remember why you joined Guardian to begin with? You promised her parents you would find her and bring her back to them. Have you forgotten that promise?

Suzannah is dead. Master showed me.

He's not your master, Demi. Only if you let him get total control of your mind will he become that. He is only showing you what he wants you to believe. He wants you to give up your reasons for fighting.

No, no no no no. I don't want to fight. I want him to make me happy. He will, he promised if I be good, he would make me happy, I-I'd never have to hurt again. She covered her ears and started humming again.

Keys! Kyle's voice hissed through their thoughts in alarm and the connection was broken. Marna was slumped over the table and Kyle crouched beside her, pushing her hair away from her face. The other patrons around the room had started to jump up from their seats or turned curious eyes toward their table.

"Get her upstairs, Kyle." He ordered and pulled her chair back while Kyle cradled Marna in his arms and he made his way through the crowded restaurant.

"Herr, Kestin, brauchen Sie mich, um einen Arzt zu holen?" The stunned Server appeared beside him asking about medical treatment.

"Nein, I'm her doktor uh Arzt." He slapped some bills in her hand and hurried after the others, who were already heading up the stairs to their suites.

*****

Kyle sat by Marna's bedside. Keys had asked him to block her while she slept and he and the others had set up camp in the Suite's sitting room. Many thoughts sped through his mind. Keys had said if they had stayed in the enhanced state too long, Marna would tire, but her collapse seemed due to something else entirely. He closed his eyes and tried to remember anything that had seemed out of the ordinary during the excursion into the psychic realm, something that could have caused her to collapse or short circuit. Other agents knew him, would call on him for his analytical and observation skills, but they failed him now. There was something there but he had been so in awe of Marna's ability that he had not paid as close attention to his surroundings as he should have. He cursed under his breath, and pushed himself up from the chair to walk to the window and look out at the mountains. Demi's voice haunted him. She sounded so lost, so pained, so childlike. He had come across some real winners during his eight years with Guardian, but nothing like the Nemesis they were facing now. How could one man break down the most powerful among them?

"How is she?" Keys voice came from the door.

Kyle turned around, resting his haunches on the window seat, "still out of it," he swallowed, "She hasn't made a peep since this morning." He glanced her way, rubbed his face, and accepted the mug of coffee Keys offered him. "How's it going out there?"

"We're making progress," Keys took a sip and studied the boy's features. "What's on your mind, Son?" Concern etched his features, and Keys read it as more than what one would feel for a fellow agent. There was something else there too; anger, regret, frustration and they were all tumbled together in the tempest forming in the boy's eyes.

Kyle scoffed as he slid his eyes sideways to look at Keys. "You haven't addressed me like that in a while. Guess I'm out of the dog house." He said haughtily and took a sip of his coffee.

"You seem distraught. Agent Rigby seems a bit cold, and Kyle seems distant."

Kyle chuckled wryly, "never stopped you before."

Keys drew in a breath and let it out in a rush between pursed lips. "We can't have this discussion now, Kyle."

"I Know, we're on assignment, too many ears, yada yada, I've heard it all before."

"And you'll hear it all again. It's a decision we both agreed on. Now, we can exchange verbal blows or you can tell me why you've been so jumpy since Marna's collapse."

"Focus on work, keep your eye on the ball. Keys rule number 497 or something."

"Or something," Keys nodded. "Kyle, I'm afraid the conversation you want to have is not proper here and now. We have an agent whose life depends on us finding her, a young boy who has no idea why a homicidal maniac wants to hurt him, and another agent who seemed to have short circuited for no apparent reason, I need answers, Kyle, not reconciliations," Keys voice became hard, insistent. "If you have answers for me, let's have them, otherwise take up your post and put the rest away until it's a more appropriate time."

"All right." Kyle hissed and put his cup down on a nearby dresser. "I get it." He pushed himself away from the window seat and stepped a few paces away, drew in a breath and let it out through pursed lips. "I'm sorry. I'm just a little tense,"

"We all are," Keys said calmly and waited. He sensed Kyle had more to say.

"Something happened, I saw, no I felt something pushing the boundaries of our connection. I sensed it coming out of left field. I turned to look . . ."

"And?"

"That's just it . . . I can't remember what I saw, only what I felt. All I know is we were not alone in that realm. There was something evil, something wanting to get at Marna. I went to increase the blocking and . . ."

"She collapsed." He nodded. Keys pushed away from the window seat to walk up to Kyle. "Was it energy? Another psychic intruding?"

"I don't know, dammit !" Kyle ran a hand through his hair, retreated back the way he had come, passing Keys. "I can't put my finger on it. All I know is whoever or whatever was there, I felt an abundance of negative, dark energy.

"And it was directed at Marna?"

"Yes, but it was different than what we felt surrounding Demi; more disjointed than that. Almost like a funnel cloud trying to come together and spin out of control, but for some reason it just couldn't cement itself into a whole."

Keys became thoughtful. "It sounds like an immature psychic trying to launch a negative energy attack, but lacked the power they needed to penetrate your block. Pierre has his share of incompetence in his employees, but I somehow doubt it was one of his or he would have been on the heels of that attack. "

"But why Marna, and why now if they had no connection to Pierre?"

Keys shrugged. "We've been preoccupied with this investigation. They may have thought it a good time to breach our defenses." He sighed and glanced Marna's way, "we'll find out more when she wakes. Why don't you take a break, I can send Bryan in for a spell."

"No, I'd rather stay, if that's okay?"

Keys sighed, "Of course, but keep in mind you are no good to us if you burn out as well."

He nodded, "I will. If I think I need a break, I'll get Bryan myself."

"Okay," Keys watched him as he returned to his vigil in the chair, by Marna's bedside, and sighed quietly. Then without another word, he stepped out of the room, closing the door quietly. Someone had delivered two large pizzas while he was talking with Kyle. They lay open and steaming on the table. He went over, grabbed a paper plate, grabbed a cheesy slice, and joined the team as they studied the map. Several property listings, in Peter's bold hand, were in a column on the board, beside the map, and they had eliminated many of them with a red line through blue letters. "How are we doing?"

"We've narrowed it down to a couple of old castles in Thun and Tarasp." Peter slid some notes over to him and pointed out the areas circled with red ink on the map tacked up on a second board by the first. "Right here on the lake is the Thun castle. The owners have modernized and remodeled in the years since the conflicts. A man by the name of Pete Willow bought the place as a summer get away, in 2035. The second place is almost on the border of Austria in Tarasp. It's in the Swiss Canton of Graubunden. It stands on a rise of rocks. Before the conflicts, it was a popular medieval museum. The castle itself has a history dating back to the 1200s. Austria owned it, and though enemies attempted many sieges, it never left their hands until 1900, when some major inventor of mouthwash, Karl August, bought it while it was in a state of decay and restored it. That restoration took sixteen years. Three years later, it was opened to the public as a tourist attraction, until 2023, when the municipality of Tarasp – population 250 – was taken over and controlled by a chapter of the German Republic of *incarnated Third Reicht* from Austria. These groups joined forces with the, *European Brotherhood of Allah*, and many other terrorist organizations, during the Conflicts, who wanted to control Europe and its choke-holds to control the world through the dispersion of oil." He drew in a breath.

"After the Conflicts, the occupiers retreated from the castle and the town, because of Switzerland's rising cooperation with America to go after war criminals, and slunk back into Germany and the castle stood empty once again. Of course, the members couldn't leave without their greed taking hold so what they couldn't carry of the treasures and what they hadn't already sold they destroyed. The town stood empty for many years; a ghost town, until a Middle Eastern Prince bought the place in 2032 and rebuilt the town and the castle. Now it's population is close to 350, close to what it was in the early 2000s,ranging from small children to retirement age. It's now pretty much the international web based business hub of the world from *World Clothing inc.* to *Handmade Trinkets and Toys* and they are all booming thanks to the tourist populations from Austria, Germany, Italy and America. It is known for its mixed population of Muslims and Christians living and working together in their community. It is peaceful and self-reliant. A large Mosque and a Chapel both claim space in the center of the town and the two religions worship without conflict. It was one of the top ten amazing places in *Tour Me* Magazine last December for skiing, shopping, and Holiday getaways. It's got accommodations from High end inns to small overnight no tell motels, for people looking for the occasional over nighter or the perfect vacation get away spot," he cleared his throat, "and other, under the radar, entertainment."

"What is the Prince's name?" Keys queried. Ventura shuffled through his papers, but Keys felt the certainty go through him, before Ventura even said the name, "Akeem Basheed of . . ."

"Maceria."

"Wasn't he the one killed in Washington last month?" Sasha asked, understanding dawning on her.

"Under mysterious circumstances."

"I thought they said it was suicide."

"They did, I don't agree. His actions had Pierre's assassination style written all over them."

"Why would they want to kill him?"Ventura queried.

"I expect Pierre knew we'd figure out the connection sooner or later and Basheed could and would most likely cooperate with us if we asked him too.

"Well then, I guess we have our link," Ventura stated.

"Maybe, but my guess is the property reverted to his family when he died. We need to get solid evidence before we approach one of the most prominent members of the Noble community in the Middle East to search one of his properties for the leader of Liberatores." Keys sighed. In his gut he knew, as Ventura did, that they were right on track. "Don't forget we are but a small team here. We aren't even written on the book as government special ops, so they need to trust us and we need assistance from FEDPOL and local," he nodded toward Ventura's notes, "What else have you been able to find out about the ownership of the castle?"

"During the off season, Basheed rents it out to keep it functional and well cared for year round, to corporation meetings and retreats, some weddings, religious retreats and business conferences."

Keys walked toward the board, and studied the circled castle. "Bryan, see if we can get those records. Cover the last three years. See if any corporation uses the castle regularly, especially Subgonomic or another corporation under that umbrella. It may take some digging, but find it. Then call King Basheed and present him with what you found. See if we can't get his written permission to search the castle and its grounds. It'll be quicker than a warrant."

"On it." Bryan said. He took out his cell and headed toward one of the presently unoccupied bedrooms, off the sitting room.

"We've got him, Keys." Ventura said.

"We've got a lock on a possible location. Don't ever underestimate Lamontage, Pete, those that do wind up dead." Keys drew in a breath and ran his eyes over the roads that led up to the castle. There was only one that directly led to the castle, but if he were Lamontage he would make damn sure there was an escape route, most likely by air, and that is what Guardian had to make sure, this time, did not happen or they could lose him, Demi and Heinderick forever. They would not get another chance, because catching a flight to Russia, after gaining entrance to Germany would not be difficult and he knew that people from the former KGB of the Soviet Union were once again trying to rebuild the communist country. They would welcome him and his dark ways.

If that happened, they would join ranks with China and North Korea and Pierre could be lost to them forever with Demi and Heinderick as his prizes for this round. "Damn, Pierre, what are you up to?" He breathed. He glanced toward Marna's closed door. They were all due back in the states in three days, but they were no closer to their goal than they had been when they boarded the jet a few days before. Sure, many Liberatores, from the Switzerland chapter were in body bags, but not the best of the best. Pierre had taken them with him, Keys was sure of that. It was a double-edged sword really. He knew, in his heart, that Marna was Pierre's ultimate target, but Keys strategy to defeat him would have to include her, because there was none more powerful than she was. He needed her. They all did. The Collective of combined powers was the only thing that could beat Pierre. Bradshaw was a mewing kitten compared to the roar in a lion like Lamontage.

"Keys." Bryan interrupted his thoughts.

He turned to look at the young man. "Yes, Bryan."

"Here is the list you asked for." Keys took it from him and looked it over. "Subgonomic isn't on it, but a sister company is," Bryan pointed to a name halfway down the list.

"Swiss Advantage Produce," Keys said the words quietly.

"It's the company label for the fresh produce due out later this year." Ventura patted Bryan on the shoulder. Sasha came over to join them

Keys smiled at the young agents standing before him. "Pete, call King Basheed and using as much diplomacy as possible, tell him who we are and refer him to Fedpol's Cyde Bauer to verify our mission and identities. Then call Federal World Protection Agency and tell them we believe Pierre Lamontage is using Basheed's property to hide a kidnapped Gardian WIT Agent, and need the cooperation of the locals in Tarasp Switzerland, and the Canton of Graubunden. We'll need back up from FEDPOL as well. Then let's all get some sleep so we can hit the road early in the morning."

"What about, Marna and Kyle?" Sasha asked.

"I'll brief Kyle and he can brief her."

They all nodded and went to their own accomodations as Keys stared at the map. After mulling the new information over some more, he sighed and headed toward Marna's room.

*****

Marna drew in a deep breath and opened her eyes, at first she forgot where she was then she recognized her room in Keys suite. She looked around the darkness, trying to orient herself. She knew it was late because darkness pressed in on her, the kind that brings with it a heavy silence. Kyle was slouched in sleep, in a chair beside her bed, his breathing slow and steady; his forehead was resting on his palm as if he was trying to nurse a headache, while his elbow rested on one of the floral arms of a winged chair. She smiled, drew in another breath, and shifted upwards in her bed. What had happened? Had she fallen? Had she knocked herself out? She tried to remember.

Then it all came rushing back. They had joined their abilities to find Lamontage's safe house. Like a bleep on radar, they honed in on Demi, she was talking to her, and Keys was talking to her. Sasha's magnified tracking worked like they hoped. Keys was trying to remotely view the path, but then something interrupted the joining, something interfered with their connection. What was it? She closed her eyes trying to focus on those last few moments before everything went black. Something harsh and evil invaded her space, She felt cold, icy arms surround her. She sat up and drew her knees to her chest, resting her chin on them. Kyle had noticed it too, he had turned to look at her, worry filled his eyes, but then, and then...."ugh, it's gone." She whispered. She shifted her head so her forehead rested on her knees. Evil tried to intrude their safe little bubble, no, not the bubble, her, something or someone tried to invade her channels, her mind, but it wasn't Lamontage, it was someone else, a different feeling altogether. Untrained, Unmastered. Bradshaw's consistent intrusions had made her an expert in how that felt. "An intrusion by whom?" She muttered.

Kyle stirred. She turned toward him, rested her cheek on her knees. "Hey," she whispered as he scrubbed his face with his hands, smiled, and leaned forward. His elbows rested on his knees and his hands clasped between them.

"Hey, yourself," he whispered, "welcome back." He reached up and pushed her hair behind her shoulder.

"How long have I been out?" She looked around the room for a clock.

He glanced at his watch. It was eleven PM. "Twelve hours." His eyes moved over her features. "How are you feeling?"

"I've got a pounding headache." She said rubbing her temple. "Feels like I tied one over and missed the fun that goes with it. Are you sure they didn't lace the coffee with Vodka?"

He chuckled, "If they did, they didn't share it with the rest of us." He took a breath, smiled, and spoke softly. He enjoyed this moment between them. Quiet. Relaxed. Intimate. "I think I saw some aspirin or some such thing in the bathroom. I'll be right back." He gently squeezed her hand, and pushed out of the chair to move to the bathroom. She watched him go.

"Have you been here all day?" she queried.

"Yeah," he returned, handed her two pills and some water. "Keys thought you could use some extra blocking."

"I'm sorry."

"Don't be." He shook his head, "I volunteered. He was set to ask Bryan to relieve me."

"I guess I should be saying thank you."

"No need. You'd do the same for me."

"I don't block." She grinned at him, threw back the pills, chased them with water, and threw the covers off. Then she swung her legs around and pushed herself off the bed, teetered, and fell into his arms as dizziness engulfed her. She could hear the pounding of his heart as her head rested on his chest. His arms tightened around her to keep her knees from buckling under her. She could feel the warmth of his breath on her temple, smell the faint scent of coffee. She stayed in the comfort of those arms until the spell passed and balance returned then she gently pushed away. "I – I'm sorry." She said and looked up. A storm surge brewed in his gray eyes. She couldn't look away. She felt the heat, feared the wave may carry her away. She chuckled to cover the thumping of her own heart. "I'm sorry, I don't usually fall for men I barely know," she said softly.

He studied her, thoughtful and uncertain, "I don't mind, if you don't." His voice thickened. His eyes raked over her features, the intensity in them deepened as they settled on hers, drawing her into the tempest blowing out of control within them. "Marna, I . . ." He breathed. His hand slid upwards from her waist, over her back, his touch leaving trails of heat in its wake. He brought his hand to her cheek. She couldn't look away. His thumb gently caressed her lips. Her protest to his taking of liberties died in her throat when he leaned down and captured her lips with his own. They were warm, firm. The kiss was hot, passionate, awakening something she thought long gone. A small cry escaped her as he pulled her tightly against him and swung her around, backed her into the wall, and pinned her wrists against it. The kiss deepened, it became more passionate, more demanding. His hands slid down her arms molded against her sides as they traced her body outline, awakened her desires.

Marna put her hands against his chest, but she could not muster up the strength to push him away, though her head was telling her she should. The attraction was there, "Kyle." His name came out in a whispered plea, as his kisses trailed across her cheek, as his hands clasped hers, and then reclaimed her lips again. He groaned. Their connections opened and he was feeling energized. Marna too felt this strange new energy. She had never felt it before with anyone. She felt him enter her mind and explore, learning things about her, feeling things. A closeness, a joining. She let go of her reserve and connected to him, exploring, and learning. "What's happening?" She breathed, when they came up for air, her voice trembling, but not wanting it to stop.

He pulled away slightly, looking into her eyes, seeing the passion, seeing the confusion. Knowing the pleasure they could give each other. It would be explosive. "I-I'm not sure, but I like it." He kissed her again. This time with more tenderness, and palmed her cheek. Their chests heaved with the intensity of all they were discovering but had never before experienced. It was like a rush of adrenaline, a high that was above anything a synthetic drug could give you.

He had heard of this kind of connection happening when Psychic partners became intimate. Read about it in textbooks but had never before experienced it. Their energies mixed and left them raw and open to their partner, they could learn everything, every thought, sadness, every intimate detail about the one they were coupling with. They literally became of one mind, body and spirit, a biblical aspect of it all, but very true. Marna's magnifying power enhanced it, intensified it. It was a double-edged sword in the field. It could tear you apart or hold you together. A partner could instantly feel when their partner was in trouble, hurt, scared or even dead. Why so many psychics sought companionship outside the psychic circle for a temporary companion to sow their wild oats. Why those that didn't, fell so deeply in love that some died within days of each other because they literally could not live without the other, losing their lifetime mate felt like losing a part of himself or herself. He had seen what it did to another. Those that did survive, found it very hard to break away from that bond and move on to another. It was a lonely existance.

The carefree, dangerous part of him wanted to throw caution to the wind and do what both their bodies were screaming for, but the part of him that wanted more than just a conquest was telling him to put on the brakes. This wasn't how he wanted it to be, especially not with her, not with this woman who came out of nowhere and demanded his attention. Taking a deep cleansing breath and pulling her hands to his lips, he kissed her fingers, he stepped back, but kept the distance between them short. Marna looked at him in confusion. He closed his connections, shielding her from his thoughts. She frowned. "I'm sorry, Marna. That was a mistake. I had no intention of – well – of that." He let go of her hands, put his up, palms out, turned his back to her, and took a breath, running his fingers through his hair. Every nerve ending in his body sparked with energy.

"I didn't push you away," she said, drawing in a breath, "I'm sorry, I've just never felt anything like that." She was glad the wall was there to hold her up or she would have collapsed from the let down.

He turned toward her. A tear streaked down her face. He approached her, wiped it away with his thumb, but pulled his hand back quickly. He sought out her eyes with his own. "I won't lie to you, as my reputation will tell you, if it had been anyone else, we'd be tearing up the sheets right now, but this is not what I want with you, Marna." She looked confused. "What I want with you is a chance to get to know you, develop something deeper, meaningful, but I won't start it like this." He waved a hand around the room. "A hotel suite in some far away land." He caught her biceps in his hands. "When we connect, if we connect in that way, I want it to be on American soil after we've gotten to know each other a lot better. I won't ravage you like some street walker." He sighed, took a stray piece of hair, and pushed it behind her ear. "You demand respect, Agent Farlow,." He chuckled, "and I'm letting my intentions known." His eyes warmed, "When we get home, when this thing is over. I want a chance with you." He grinned. "A chance to develop something meaningful because I care." He grinned, "I think I've cared, ever since you went superior on me at the train station." She let out a tearful chuckle as he reached out and caressed her cheek with his knuckles.

"Kyle." She said softly.

"No. Don't say no, just say you'll give it some thought, Marna, that's all I'm asking."

Marna stayed quiet a moment before she spoke. Then she sighed. "All right, I'll think about it, but that's all I can give you right now."

He looked down at her so sweetly and caressed her cheek so intimately with his finger. She almost recinded on her decision. "Just call when you're ready, Agent Farlow, I'll be by the phone," he whispered. With that, he kissed her lips once more and groaned softly as he rested his forehead on hers, took a deep breath, and smiled. "I'll be waiting," his voice was as soft as a caress.

A knock on the door caused him to let her go. He winked, straightened his hair, and pivoted on his feet to go and open it while she turned to wipe the tear tracks off her face. At the door, he took a deep breath, got control of his emotions and reached for the knob. When the door swung open, Keys was on the other side.

"Is she awake?" He asked softly.

"Yeah, she just woke up." Kyle's voice was controlled, husky, but if Keys noticed, he didn't say a thing.

"Good. I've just gotten some information I need to share with the both of you." Kyle stepped back to let him in and the moment for he and Marna slipped away as Keys sat them down to talk about the trip to Tarasp.

*****

Marna stood by her window overlooking the Alps as the moon rose high above them. Images of her and Kyle's encounter flashed through her mind like a medley of movie clips. He was reckless, carefree and adventuress. He energized her, made her feel alive again. Then there was Tanner, their moment in the park not far from her muddled thoughts, would they feel the same thing she and Kyle did if they ever connected in the same way? Tanner was responsible, reliable, caring and always put others before himself. He was the ideal man to take home to meet the parents. He made her feel safe when she was with him. Was safe enough? She felt the weight of the object in her hand. The metal was cold. She hadn't worn it since they'd said goodbye, but the connection still held her. She uncurled her fingers that fisted her right hand and looked down. The moonlight twinkled off the diamonds, embedded in the gold. Her wedding band, the only thing left of her and Jeff's life together.

<p style="text-align:center">~~~~~</p>

"Open the windows. It's still pretty steamy in here."

Marna grinned and turned around. "Amanda." She leaned against the casing of the window seat. "How'd you know?"

"Know what?" Amanda said as her apparition floated across the room and stood opposite her twin. "That you needed me?" Marna nodded. "Do I really have to explain this to you again?" Marna chuckled as Amanda did a nasally impression of their third grade English teacher, "Come on, Greenwood, study your notes, even Hannah gets this Medium thing better than you."

Marna sniffed and grinned. "Ms. Bloomberg."

"The old bat." Amanda studied her sister. "You were rocking the boat again, and I don't mean maybe." She fanned her face. It was getting hot enough to boil the ocean on the other side." Marna's mouth dropped and then closed and then her face turned crimson, "Don't worry, Darling, it's rather lonely over their right now. I'm the only one who saw you getting all hot and bothered. It was almost like watching a movie scene," she performed an exaggerated sigh, "A love story, one of those hot and steamy scenes, just before the hero and heroine – ahhh the memories – you know the ones." Marna looked horrified. "Don't worry, I would have turned off the lights if it had gotten more involved, but don't deny me a little fun." Amanda raised an eyebrow. "I was actually tempted to dump a bucket of cold water on the two of you just to keep from you two starting a fire.."

"Oh my . . ." Marna walked around her sister, her shoulder grazing Amanda's, a coldness brushing over her. "Couldn't you have, oh I don't know, turned around or something?"

"Hmm, I did think about stepping in, just to remember what it felt like – " Marna turned to look at her sister horrified. "I said I thought about it, I didn't say I would have done it." She smiled wickedly at her sister. "Besides why all the drama? You have two hunk-a-stud muffins dying to make you part of their lives and all you have to do is say the word." She played with her nails. "If I were you, I'd take them both for a test run; see what connection blew me away."

"Amanda !" Marna hissed.

Amanda shrugged and turned to sit on the window seat. From the waist down the apparition disappeared. Marna grinned, shaking her head before she looked down, through watery eyes, at the ring she held in the palm of her hand. Then she walked back to the window seat , sat beside her sister, and let the ring fall from her grasp to the cushions. "I see, I thought that was settled."

"I can't help it, Manda, he's always there." She sniffed. Amanda reached out and let her hand hover above Marna's.. She could almost feel the enveloping warmth of the grasp.

"Look, Marna, I know it's hard to let go, but he made it a point to give you closure, he gave you his blessing to move on with your life. Why aren't you doing it?"

"I'm scared, Manda." she whispered.

"Of what, Marny?"

"Of letting them get too close. Of opening my heart for that kind of pain again, of . . . I don't know." She got up and stepped away from the window seat.

"Losing them like you lost Mom and Dad, like you lost Joe in that car crash, like you lost me," Amanda stated, "like you lost Jeff." Marna looked away, swallowing. "You don't have to say it, it's written in the way you throw that wall up every time someone gets close."

"There are so many holes in my life, Amanda. I don't know how many more can pierce my heart, my soul, before it just implodes."

"You're young and vibrant, Marny, you were not meant to walk this earth alone."

"I'm not alone, Manda, I have your children."

"Who fill a void, no doubt, but they don't fill that part of you that cries for a pair of strong arms to hold you when a the storm rages outside at night. For that, you need more and you've got two pairs of those arms ready and willing to take on that challenge." Amanda smiled, her eyes understanding. "Marny, there is so much you have yet to experience," she floated up beside her and drew circles in the air with her finger, " right there, waiting for you to grab it,,"she grinned wickedly, waved her hand and two scenes unfolded in the space before Marna, the one with Tanner in the park and the one with Kyle in her room hours before. "Most women pray for one but you, my dear, have two hunka-hunka burning loves just waiting for you to give them the go ahead." She whistled and waved her free hand before her face. "Is it possible for a ghost to get flushed, because I'm telling you, I'm feeling the heat just thinking about it."

Marna chuckled shook her head, and turned around. "You always made life so simple, Amanda."

"Because it is, lil sister, you just have to look at it with less abstract thinking and lower expectations." The apparition faded some as it smiled. "Oh bother, gotta go, energy's low."

"Manda?"

"Hmmm." She turned while her form twinkled in and out.

"Thanks."

In answer, Amanda's form held up the sign language symbol for 'I love you' and she faded away.

~~~~~

Marna opened her eyes, drawing in a breath. She was sitting on the window seat in her darkened room. The moon, now on the descending side of its cycle, glowed through the trees. She hugged herself. "I love you too, Manda."

"*I know*," Whispered the darkness. Marna smiled and glanced at her bedside clock. The Red letters read 5:00 a.m. she pondered the thought of getting another hour or so of sleep but voted to get the kinks out with a hot bath instead. Then she would pack and go down to the cafe to have a quiet cup of coffee, before calling Tanner to check on the children and see how Isaiah's ankle was doing. The day to return to the states was fast approaching and even though she would miss the beauty of Switzerland, she instinctively knew that the children needed normalcy—well their type of normalcy – and routine in their lives, especially Isaiah. She knew he enjoyed the freedom of homeschooling and physically discovering the history around him, but he missed the comradeship of his basketball teammates and a special young lady with Red braids. She grinned and retreated to the bathroom, turned on the water as hot as she could stand it, searched the cupboards for some bubble bath, found it under the sink and poured a generous amount in. While the tub filled, she moved into her room to pull some comfortable traveling clothing out of her suitcase, and then returned to the bathroom, closing and locking the door. When the tub filled, she tied up her hair and sunk into the water, sighing. For a few minutes, she would just be a woman, in a luxurious bubble bath and shut the world out.

While Marna enjoyed her bath, Bryan was pacing the sitting room, in the junior suite, across the hall. He had also risen early and started the coffee. He had not slept much the night before. He tossed and turned all night, his mind and body never relaxing enough at the same time for him to fall into anything but a sleep that was haunted with images of Demi and what Pierre Lamontage was doing to her. His heart ached. He pushed himself away from the window, and tried to busy himself with packing the few belongings he had brought with him on this trip. Then he carried the hiker's backpack to the door and placed it on the floor. He looked around the room to make sure there was nothing left behind. He then lay on the bed, and closed his eyes for a second, trying to open a connection to Demi as he had last night, and many times before that. When he reached nothing but the confusion and fear that Marna had run into before, he opened his eyes and realized he wasn't alone. He lifted himself up on his elbows and looked around. It was then that he saw it, just a shimmer at first, but it eventually took on the form of a young boy who looked just like Jacob Nymphis Farlow. He was too startled to do much but stare.

You are Bryan, no? The boy connected to him telepathically.

I am.

She has spoken your name in the dark. I have heard her.

Wh-who has? He looked around the room. It was just he and this apparition, if that is what it was.

The one in the tower. The one who screams.

Bryan closed his eyes. "Demi." He spoke the word aloud but it was no more than a whisper.

You are coming to get her, no?

Yes, Son, yes we are. You're Heinderick, am I right?

It is my name, yes

Then we're coming to get you too. We're leaving soon.

You will hurry, no?

We are trying, why?

I heard talk among others that are here. The Master is preparing to leave soon, but your friend, Heinderick sighed, *He does not think her strong enough.*

Strong enough? Brian tried to make sense out of his cryptic message. *Strong enough for what?*

To become one of his. The apparition started to fade. *I must go, they will be coming for me.*

Coming for you? Wait. What do you mean?

He will take me with him.

No. Can you find a place to hide? For you? For Demi?

I will try. The apparition faded, Bryan opened his eyes, gasped and bolted up in bed. He had fallen asleep but the encounter with Heinderick was more than a dream. He believed the boy had actually reached out to him. He was a Dream Walker wasn't he? Bryan swung his long legs off the bed, and scrubbed his face with his hands. What was the boy saying again? He tried to clear the fog of sleep from his mind, and thought back to the conversation. His head came up quickly. Lamontage was leaving! Things weren't working out with Demi, and he had plans for her, not good ones. He pushed himself off the bed and began to pace. He had to try to contact Demi for her sake and the sake of the child.

He closed his eyes and focused on their connection. There it was the fog, the fear, the helplessness. He swallowed the painful emotion building in his throat. He had to get through that barrier. *Demi? Demi?* Nothing came through. Their connection wasn't strong enough. Not without help. Then it came to him. Marna! Her magnifying ability. She could strengthen him, strengthen his connection to Demi! He hoped it would be enough. He looked at the clock. 6:15 a.m. "Wake up call, Farlow, I need you." He hit the screen on his GPC and hit Marna's speed number.

"Bryan?" Marna's voice filtered over the audio, but she had blocked the video. "What is it? Is everything okay?"

"Marna, I'm sorry to bother you so early, but I just got a dream visit from Heinderick."

"Heinderick?" he heard the concern in her voice. "What's going on? Is he okay?"

"I need you to help me get in touch with Demi, if we can't get through to her, we may lose them both."

"Oh my. . . Does Keys know?"

"I haven't called him yet. I figured we'd try this on our own first, if we got results, then we could call him." He drew in a breath and let out a sigh. "Can I come over?"

"Sure, I'll unlock the door."

"Good, thanks." He signed off and headed for his suite door, careful not to wake anyone else before he left. When he stepped into the hall, Marna was waiting for him, by the door of the Keys' suite. Her hair fell, in dark waves down her back and black leggings encased her form, complimented with a long, thigh length sweater. She waved him in and closed the door quietly behind her. Keys moved about the kitchenette, setting the coffee to brewing. He looked at Marna. She shrugged and raised her eyebrows, nodded her head and led him to the sofa in the sitting room. Keys had already been awake when he had called so she had to tell him what was going on.

"Morning, Bryan." Keys said.

"Sir." Bryan said, bobbing his head once.

"Fill me in while the coffee brews."

"Didn't Marna?" She shook her head.

"No. I want to hear it from you, Bryan." Keys said with a smile. "If I've learned anything in this business at all; it's that to get a clear picture, it's best to hear it from the person who experienced it." Bryan nodded and launched into the whole dream visit while Keys and Marna listened intently, nodding and asking questions to clarify anything they didn't follow. When the coffee finished brewing, Keys got up and returned with three cups on a tray and choices of cream and sugar. "What makes you think you can break through, Bryan? Marna has made several attempts and has failed." Keys queried.

"I'm a telepath. My ability to connect with targets, outside the psychic realm, is more accurate than those that use other methods. Demi and I have a connection. We've been partners for years. We've watched each other's backs. Our relationship is deeper than hers and Marna's," He turned toward Marna. "No offense."

"None taken." She watched Bryan's body language, his facial expressions, and she believed he was being very honest with Keys, with the exception of one minor detail. "Bryan, how long have you been in love with Demi?"

His head swung in her direction, his blue eyes flashed. "What's that got to do with anything?" His tone had become angry, wary.

"A lot if it's true," Keys said, "answer her." He raised a quizzical brow.

Bryan looked from one to the other then sunk into the chair behind him, drew in a breath, and let it out in a forced sigh. "Ah – " His eyes watered. "We've been involved for five years now."

"Since the Pueblo case?" Keys queried, with a tone of understanding, Bryan nodded.

"Pueblo Case?" Marna asked.

Keys cleared his throat. "One of the longest running cases Guardian has ever been involved with."

"What?" Marna was confused. Demi was legendary, among the students at the compound University, for being the youngest agent ever to join Guardian. She was barely eighteen when she became a full time agent and sixteen when she worked her first case with them in 2037. Someone took her friend, a young girl, on her way home from school, just two minutes after she and Demi had parted ways at some old park. Demi had always had special talents and at that time, she was a budding Locator as well as an accomplished Custodian and Feeler. They had never found the girl, Suzannah was her name, but Demi never gave up.

"I thought Suzannah's disappearance happened when she was sixteen?"

"It did." Keys sighed. "The human remains of Luciana Pueblo, a fifteen-year old girl, was found in 2043, in a waterpark, during some remodeling. She was listed on the national missing persons data base back in 2031. Information states she was from Brentwood, California. Demi knew the family.. It was the same MO, same victimology, as Suzannah Peraz. Both mixed heritage, both between the ages of 15-18. We believe the same Unsub was involved in both cases."

"But there was six years between abductions. That's a long time for any kind of serial to go before taking another victim."

"Demi thought so too, so we started checking out other small towns in the northern part of California. Because of the Freedom Conflicts, it was harder to find information. Cyber attacks destroyed many computer files, so it involved a lot of leg- work. We had to find detectives that were still around, track down family members of suspected victims and paw through old records, notes, and police reports dating back to election night 2020, before all hell broke loose. We found Lu Yang, who we believed to be one of his first. She was a young woman of 18, Chinese American, lived in a small mountain town called Willow Creek California, and had just come back home from visiting L.A.U. She and a few of her friends had gone to Raging Creek Pub that night, a local bar, to have a meal and a couple of drinks. She wanted to tell them about her visit to the University. The time-line indicates that they were there from 6:30 PM - 8:30, and then they left. The last time they saw her was when they said goodnight out in front of the bar. Polls were still open so parking was minimal and she had parked a couple of streets up, she never made it home."

"Did they ever find her?"

He nodded. "But not right away. At first, they thought she was lost in the riots. A lot of people went missing that night, some as yet to be found, so not much advancing was made on her case until three years later when she was discovered in the Redwood National forest. A couple of hikers found her; she was on a public path, bludgeoned to death, and then dumped for the animals to finish the job."

"My god, that poor girl," Marna said, swallowing back the bile in her throat, "but how's this tie in to you and Demi?"

"The same day the body was found, within hours of the believed time of death, another young woman disappeared, from Orick California this time. May 21, 2020." He drew in a breath, "mixed race — Native American and White – this time and . . ."

"Three years later the same thing," Marna finished for him.

"Yes, like clockwork. Three years every May and July, in the small towns clustered around the Redwood forest. They'd find another body and another girl would disappear, except for the Suzannah and Luciana cases. He broke pattern. There were six years between them. They were both from the same town. However, they never recovered Suzannah's body or that of Luciana's until they found her in that park. We had one other girl we could loosely tie to the case. Marianna Cassidy, she was an Irish American, her family immigrated here during the conflicts and she disappeared in 2040, her body is also yet to be found. After 2040 it all stopped."

"Twenty years is a long time for a serial to operate."

"We figure the confusion of the Conflicts helped him out," He sighed.

Marna nodded, "Which ended in 2035, and by 2037 Computers were up and running again, so it was harder to go unnotice. Almost all informational Data bases, salvaged from the conflicts, reloaded."

"Yeah, and then in 2040 Cassidy disappears."

"And he's back in business. Probably in his forties or fifties, assuming the old time serial profile holds for beginning." Keys and Bryan agreed with her analogy.

"Like you, Marna," Keys interjected, "I call Bryan and Demi in on occasion to consult, where I think their skills would be helpful." Keys sighed, "Demi wanted in on the investigation. The girl was someone from her hometown, and there were similarities to Suzannah's case.."

"Being back in Brentwood, working on a case similar to Suzannah's, well, it got to her. We'd get a lead, follow it, and then it would fizzle out. The only thing we were able to verify was that the 2020 case was the beginning run of a serial leading up to and ending with the Cassidy Case.." He drew in a breath and let it out in a long drawn out exhale. "Best we could put together, with the records and ME notes from all the remains of the victims, was the guy was consistent with his weapon of choice for the beatings. All of them had scars consistent with a nylon rope with evenly spaced knots. There were also signs of remodeling of radial breaks and spiral fractures, on all the victims Their captor fed them well, but their hands showed signs of manual labor, gardening etc . . . They were in good health. Two of them did show signs of recent childbirth, however. Pueblo and Yang. "

"Stockholm's," Marna stated.

"Yes that was the general consensus," Bryan verified, "Reading the findings, knowing that Suzannah could have been taken by this monster, it broke Demi's heart and one night we went out for drinks to just forget it all, all the ugliness, all the despair of those left behind. Just for a while. We had a few, she cried, I comforted and . . ."

"One thing led to another," Marna finished his statement and he nodded, "and you two have been together ever since?"

"Yes." He pushed himself off the chair, looking down at Keys. "I know, Sir, there are no rules on the books about personal involvement, but there are about carrying on a personal relationship if you are partners. That's why we've kept it under wraps, but it's that very relationship that has made us better partners and it's that relationship that makes me believe I can connect with her now, even if Lamontage has screwed with her mind."

"Have you tried to connect to her by yourself?" Keys queried.

"Yes, and I get to the very edge before I run into a fog of confusion, pain, and fear," he sighed. "She's scared and she needs a safety net, I think I can give it to her, but I need Marna's magnifying ability to reach her."

"Why now, Bryan?" Keys queried, "Why come forward now and not before?"

He cleared his throat and looked Marna's way then back at Keys. "Heinderick came to me in a dream," he swallowed, "He said she calls my name in the dark, and that we didn't have much time because there was talk among others that Lamontage was leaving and that he was abandoning Demi because she wasn't strong enough – ah—strong enough to become one of his."

Alarm immediately spread across Keys features, "he said that?"

Marna swung her head toward Keys. "Keys, what's that mean?"

"Nothing good, Marna," Keys said, "nothing good at all."

"Please, Keys, let me try to contact her?" Bryan pleaded, "If that Bastard hasn't taken complete control of her mind, I can get through, I know I can. I have to let her know we are coming so she has something to hold onto. Some thread of hope to keep her grounded, to keep him from convincing her that we've given up on her."

Keys was thoughtful. Bryan was right. His unique relationship with Demi, and Marna's magnification ability combined could be the break they needed to get through to Demi, but it could also prove to be the opportunity that Pierre needed to get hold of Marna. It was a catch twenty-two, but was it worth the risk? He stayed silent a moment longer then looked from one to the other. "If I give the go ahead for this, you have to keep your shields intertwined, and you have to constantly be aware of what is going on around you. We're still not sure what the attempted intrusion on Marna was yesterday or who initiated it. We can't give them a second chance. They nodded, and then Marna glanced Bryan's way, and reached for his hand. "Just one more thing," he said. They raised their eyes to his. "You said Heinderick was able to contact you?" Bryan nodded. "Contact him, tell him to get as close to Demi as he can. It'll be easier to extract them both if they're in close proximity." They agreed and as Keys sat back, Marna and Bryan closed their eyes, and then opened channels to connect and merge abilities and strength.

~~~~

Instantly they felt it, the surge of energy, the combining of abilities, and the becoming of one entity to help their downed comrade. *You with me, Bryan?*

Yes

Okay, you take the lead this is your show.

Nodding, Bryan concentrated on Demi. He and Marna appeared on a darkened path with a veil of dense fog hovering around thick forest, and heavy underbrush. Flies and mosquitoes buzzed around them, but never landed. He turned his head toward Marna. *This stuff is so thick we'll need a machete to cut through it.* Instantly, he felt the weight of a handle in the hand that extended before him. The conjured machete had a pearl handle and the blade formed from surrounding energy, represented by multiple colors. Startled by its unexpected appearance, he almost dropped it. He quickly glanced at Marna. *Did you?* She shook her head.

Not knowingly, She communicated with a shrug, *this whole magnifier thing surprises me every day. Maybe it took your thought process and created the holographic representation of the object you needed. Keys would explain it as a typical process that goes on while you're dreaming – I mean this is a dream realm.* He nodded. She continued. *Your mind tends to give you the things your dream actions demand, in the story unfolding, and you move about from one place to another without the sequential process that plagues us in reality.*

Yeah. He agreed, turning the weapon around in his hand. *I don't recall ever having a weapon appear out of nowhere in any of my dreams. At least not in 3D.*

Maybe the Magnifying ability advances the common to the impossible if given the right circumstances. She too stared at the weapon. *I don't know this is all still new to me.*

He nodded, waving the weapon skillfully in the air before them. *No wonder so many enemies want to claim you. Your abilities could inflict some real damage if controlled by the wrong person.*

Marna swallowed. *Thanks for reminding me . . . Shh* She said as she heard something come out of the veiled darkness. She tuned in her Listening ability.

I can't find the boy, Master

Form a search party. I want every inch of this place searched before the plane arrives. What should we do with her?

I have plans for her . . . Now go, we haven't much time.

Yes, Master.

The first voice had been female, the second male. Suddenly she felt a familiar probing. She winced, her knees buckled, causing her to fall into Bryan who quickly offered his support. *Marna, what is it?*

He knows we're coming! He's trying to breach! She raised her free hand to her head, clinging desperately to Bryan's with her other, knowing that if she broke contact, they would both become vulnerable.

Hang on! Bryan increased his blocking, Marna felt relief start to circle her psyche, enabling her to increase the thickness of her own shields.

Cloak Marna! Keys ordered from somewhere beyond the parameters of their psychic realm. *What?*

Just do it! Immediately, Marna raised her cloak. It surprised her by how it responded to her beckoning. It formed a half-sphere around her and Bryan, glowing and twinkling like the stars on a clear night, as it rose and encircled them. She hadn't seen a shell like this since the siege at Bradshaw's compound a year before. At that time, Mary's emphatic ability produced it when it plugged into Marna's magnifying ability. Bryan's abilities were Custodian and Blocker. Could her magnifying ability be combining with his to make an ultimate block? Maybe it was the unusual energy in this realm that made all abilities stronger and more dream-like. She looked at it in wonder. Multiple colors faded in and out, and periodically the shell would zap when a negative charge hit it.

Marna felt her strength return. *Keys, did you know about this?*

Not really, no, but I thought it was worth a try. On the same token, I highly doubt it will work in the real world, but you can use it as added protection in the dream realm. Are you okay?

Just peachy. She looked around once more. *I'm beginning to think this character is the spawn of Satan himself.*

You're not alone in that thought, Marna. Lamontage leaves that impression on many. How close are you to making contact, Bryan?

Hard to tell. The electrical charge weaved into this Fog is interfering with my telepathic communication.

Do your best, our time is limited.

So is Demi's, Marna stated, *Lamontage is making plans to leave the castle and take Heinderick with him, but Demi has become disposable.*

He's changed his plans for her. He's going to leave her as a calling card to Guardian, most likely incapacitated or dead. Either way would be too late for her. You need to find her and/or Heinderick, deliver your message, and come back so we can get on the road.

Got it. She turned her attention to Bryan. *Let's go.* Bryan still looked stunned. He brought his eyes to Marna's face. *Bryan, we need to move.*

Yeah. He looked at her, not moving an inch. She raised her brow causing him to snap out of his stupor and resume the position of moving forward through the fog. Another negative attack bore down on them, the shields electrical deflection made them both jump. *He's working overtime.* He gave the shield a sweeping glance as another negative charge sparked loudly. He grinned and shook his head. *Have I told you recently that I am glad you're one of us?*

No, She grinned, *but nothing I can do or we can do together will make a bit of difference if we can't get to Demi.*

Right. Machete in hand, he tightened his grip on her hand before they advanced through the fog as it closed in behind them. Bryan started reaching out to Demi. *Demi, I need to know you're okay. Please answer me.* They moved forward.

Chapter Twelve

Demi moaned in her sleep and rolled over on the cot. In the shadows of the tower room, Sashika sat in her usual chair, reading The Dark Side of the Psychic Realm, a textbook from one of the master's classes. She placed the book on the seat cushion and went to Demi's side. Sweat beaded Demi's face, her complexion was gray and when Sashika reached out to roll her over, she could feel the heat radiating through the thin cotton material of the nightdress. "Girl, you're burning up." She whispered. She grabbed the basin off the bedside stand, filled it with cool water, and then brought it back, tossed some washcloths into it, and placed one on Demi's forehead.

"You're rejecting his control, you are." She whispered to Demi. "Don't get your Irish temper up, Demi. Serving the master is a privilege. You'll only get worse if you continue to resist." She exchanged cloths. Demi mumbled something Sashika didn't understand at first, so she bent in closer.

"Bryan." Demi whispered. "Bryan."

Sashika straightened, a knowing gleam in her eyes. "Hmmm. Who's Bryan?" Demi called out his name again. "Whoever he is, he's obviously important to you. Maybe that's why you're so resistant." She changed the cloths again. "Do you have a lover, Demi Spencer? Is his hold on you so strong, you've built a barrier the master can't break through?" She sighed, "He doesn't give up easily, girl. If he desires you, he will win but you may not live to reap the rewards." She swapped the cloths again. "What a shame," she stood up clicking her tongue, "I need to go tell the master of this development." She leaned in, "sweet dreams, Demi Spencer, we'll see what gets you first. Will it be Infection eating away at your brain cells, or the master's anger?" Smiling, she pushed away from the bed, sauntered across the floor and out the tower door, leaving it unlocked. Their guest was going nowhere. She wasn't strong enough. She left the bindings undone and closed the door silently behind her.

~~~~~

Trapped in her mind the walls of her prison cave were icing over. Demi was feeling cold one moment then hot the next. *What's happening to me? I can't think . . .He hurts me so much. . .I'm so cold . . .so alone . . .I'm scared. . . I think I'm dying. . ."* She hugged herself and moved about the dirt floor, pacing. Her feet were so cold. She shivered.

Demi, it's Bryan, Sweetheart, please let me know if you can hear me. Please tell me, you aren't lost to me forever. Demi gasped and listened again. *Demi.*

Whose there? The voice was familiar, yet unfamiliar, distant, yet closes by. *Where are you?* Suddenly the fog thinned, and two backlit silhouettes appeared at the edge of her prison, she backed away from them. *Who are you, what do you want?*

Demi, it's us, Bryan and Marna, we're here to deliver a message to you.

Bryan? I don't know a Bryan or a-a-Marna. Her teeth clattered. *The ice on the walls thickened.*

Yes, Honey, you do. Fight his control. Reach beyond the barrier he's put around your mind.

Confusion and fear contorted her features. She shook her head and backed away. *No, he'll hurt me. No if I be good, he'll make me happy.*

No, Demi. All he has for you is more pain. Think, Demi, think. Think about California. The Pueblo case. The ice on the walls thinned, Demi stopped her back-pedaling. The darkness dimmed. He was reaching her! She tilted her head studying the silhouettes. Bryan swallowed back the lump forming in his throat. Marna reached out and touched his bicep, nodding to encourage him to continue. *Demi, we know where you are, we're coming, but you need to hide, you need to keep away from him, he plans to kill you. He knows you're rejecting him.*

She backed away from him. *He'll find me. He knows things.* She searched the room with wide eyes.

Bryan noticed the ice on the walls grew thicker... He was losing her again. *Demi, remember Lucia Pueblo, remember it was our first time. It was the first time we shared our love, the first time we admitted how we felt. Remember I told you I would help you solve that case if it was the last thing we did together. Well it hasn't been solved yet. Marianna, your friend Suzannah, they depend on you to find out what happened to them and bring them back home. Remember the attack on Tarot, remember Paula? You were there for me let me be there for you. Let me hold you up now.*

Tears streaked down Demi's cheeks, but her eyes were clearing, she was focusing. The ice was thinning once again. Somewhere within her, a thread of reality reached out and attached itself to Bryan, and gave her a lifeline. How long it would stay attached, with Pierre's constant attacks, Marna didn't know but she prayed it would be long enough for them to reach her. For this moment in time, they had her; she was lucid. *Bryan, Marna? What's going on? Where am I?* She looked around.

You're locked in a prison of your own mind, created by Lamontage. He's been trying to possess you for days. A flicker of fear passed through her eyes. *No, no, no* Marna cried silently to herself. They had to be very careful with the conversation. Lamontage's name brought fear to her, a warning that his control was still very much present.

How'd you find me?

*That doesn't matter we can't stay long. I'm here to tell you we know where he's keeping you and Heinderick, and we are coming for you. You just need to hang on a little longer. Can you do tha*t? Her head jerked as she nodded. Bryan was going to give her something to think about besides what Lamontage could do. Someone else to protect. Good. Maybe that would keep that thread connected. *Find Heinderick and keep him safe until we arrive. We're going to extract you both.*

I take it this is Bryan. A female voice, laced with the sound of Ireland, said from the shadows. Marna's alarms went off. A jet stream of current came from the shadows, trapping Demi in the bluish shield, Marna remembered well from the restaurant.

Bryan's heart tumbled in his chest. Instinctively, he tried to go toward her, but the negative energy threw him backward, causing Marna to fall too, the machete hit the ground, the darkness lifted and Sashika stood in the middle of the abyss, holding the taser that kept Demi prisoner.

Bryan . . . Get out! Demi cried telepathically. Bryan pulled himself to a sitting position and caught a glimpse of Sashika flipping a switch on the taser. The Laser's beam became more intense and a deeper blue. The beam slammed Demi into the wall. She gasped, grabbing her neck, she couldn't breath. Sashika was trying to kill her! He froze, if she died in this realm, would she die in both? He didn't know-- this psychic facet was new to him--dreams mixing with reality. He didn't know how to fight that kind of power, but he did know he could not gamble with Demi's life. He looked around desperately for a weapon, saw the machete lying on the ground a few feet away and scurried over to it. He wasn't sure it would work but he simultaneously grabbed Marna's hand and thought about a hunting knife, instantly the weapon changed its form.

Marna, shield! He ordered. Understanding what he was doing, Marna quickly dropped the shield and prayed his aim was true. Sashika turned to look toward them when she heard him yell and he let the knife fly, sinking it deep into her chest. Her knees buckled and she collapsed to the floor. Her form and that of the taser faded, freeing Demi from its death grip. Demi gasped, and pushed herself to a standing position and looked around the abyss. The walls were shaking, akin to that of a high magnitude earthquake. *Bryan go. git out ah here.* Her Irish lilt came through as she watched the walls crumble around her.

We're coming for you, Demi! You and Heinderick must find a way to hide from Pierre.

I know, now go! I Love you Bry, with ahl my hart! Marna led the way as they ran blindly through the foggy brush until they reached their destination, returning to the real world. Taking deep breaths, they opened their eyes and found themselves in the suite sitting room where they had started. Bryan looked at his watch two hours had passed. Keys face revealed nothing, his look was somber.

"Keys?" Marna asked.

"We're ready to roll. You two get your bags and load them into the van. Demi may have had some fluent moments with you, but unless we get there soon, the advances you just made will be for nothing.

"Let's roll then." Bryan said and he and Marna left the sitting room to go to their prospective rooms, and get their luggage.

*****

Demi's eyes shot open and she gasped, her heart was pounding and her head was screaming out in pain. It was all she could do not to scream verbally herself. She reached up and pulled the washcloth from her forehead, swung her legs off the side of the bed, and pushed herself into a sitting position. She grabbed her head and rocked. Good God what had just happened? She looked around the room and when she turned her head to the right, he was there. Heinderick. His eyes were wide, and his stance was unsure. "Heinderick?" He nodded. "Good, My . . ." She trailed off as a drum solo played out in her brain. "My name is . . ."

"I know who you are."

She raised a quizzical brow. "Really?"

"You're Demi and your friend's name is Bryan. You both know my family." His delivery, though heavy with a German accent, sounded so grown up, she almost forgot she was dealing with a six-year old.

"Well, good now that we've cleared that up, we need to get out of here." She looked around. "Wait a minute, how did you get in here? They lock the doors."

"She left them unlocked."

"Who?"

He turned around and pointed to a spot under the window. Demi tried to turn her head, but the drums got harsher and more intrusive so she moved a bit slower and turned at the waist. Sashika lay crumpled on the floor. She pushed the child behind her, walked over, and knelt down to check the woman's pulse. There was none. The body was warm she hadn't been dead long. It all came back to her. The realm, Bryan, Marna, how many days had she been under Pierre's control? Based on her Olympic sized headache, it had been days, maybe even weeks. The last thing she remembered was Lamontage attacking her the first night she was there. Her eyes grazed over the woman's body and she saw the taser in her hand. Whatever game Lamontage was up to, no one was safe from his deadly blows in either the dream/psychic realm or the real world, but neither was he safe from your weapons, the worlds intersected somehow, so when you died in one, you died in both; there was no waking up. "Glad to know that." She mumbled.

"Huh?"

"Nothing." She knelt down, grabbed the taser from Sashika's limp hand, and searched her body, finding a small backup weapon in an ankle sheath. She took it, looked it over, set it on kill, and handed it to the boy."Hold this. If we get separated, you use it if you have to, do not let them take you away from here." He looked frightened, but clasped the weapon tightly. Then she stood and reached for his hand. "Come on, we need to get out of here and find a place to hide until my friends get here." They started toward the only door in the room but stopped when there was commotion outside it.

"Master?" A male voice said. More commotion.

"Is Sashika done?" Lamontage queried.

"I haven't heard a peep."

"Well let's have a look." She heard the doorknob turn and the door opened slightly. She shoved Heinderick behind her, and moved them both against the wall by the arched doorway of the sleeping quarters. She checked the taser, made sure it was on kill mode, and got ready. She may die in a stand against them, but she would take as many of them as she could with her. She turned toward Heinderick.

"If things start happening, Heinderick, you run, and you keep running until you are safely away from this place, and then you hide until my friends arrive. Do you understand what I'm saying?" He nodded. "Good." She said, shoving him further behind her.

"Master, I have some questions about the flight. Boston has cancelled all private flights, in or out of the airport, some kind of terrorist threat. Do you want to try Kennedy or Newark?" Demi heard a third voice come toward the door and they muttered something intangible. The door closed and they moved away from it. She drew in a breath and let out in a heavy sigh, then pushed Heinderick in the opposite direction. They moved to the back of the room, and like an answered prayer, she saw a partially opened window. She moved toward it and pushed it open the rest of the way. Outside, built into the castle wall, she saw cement steps, probably put in when the building was renovated, leading to the lookout tower above her room.

She grabbed his shoulders and looked him in the eye. "Heinderick, you go into that lookout tower and you stay there no matter what you hear in here."

" Vat about you, mein Fräulein? "His German accent was heavy, but she was able to understand what he said.

"I may have to stay on this rollercoaster a bit longer."

He shook his head. "Nein, Fraulein, he vill kill sie."

"I'll be okay as long as he thinks he owns me." She looked around the room, saw paper and pencil, on the stand by her bed, rushed forward and grabbed it, scrawled some words on it then she gave it to him. "You give this note to Bryan, Marna or Dr. Keys. I'm trusting you to have my back, Son,"

"Okay." He whispered, and then he reached around her neck, and hugged her tightly. She heard more commotion by the door she had to move quickly, if her plan had any hope at all of working. She turned to Heinderick, picked him up, and placed him on the steps urging him upward then secured the window. Then she tore her bed apart, ripped both sleeves of her dress, tipped over the bedside stand, and chair – making as little noise as possible – threw the basin of water all over her, moved to Sashika's side, zapped the woman with the kill stream, above her heart, screamed, and collapsed, still holding the taser. The door swung open and they all ran in. She sensed him before she heard him. The Guards cursed in French as they dispersed about the room.

" Ce qui s'est passé?" Pierre cried and moved to Sashika, lying two fingers over her Carotid artery.

Demi feigned Catatonia. She stared down at the body, with no show of emotion. "Répondez-moi! Qu'avez vous fait ?" more French. Demi rocked her body, tears forming in her eyes and spilling over onto her face as if his harsh words had triggered them. Her drama teacher would be pleased. Lamontage reached out, dragged her to her feet, and shook her roughly. Still she gave no response. It wasn't until he grabbed her face and made her look into his eyes that she felt him prodding. She fought him, looked away, raised her shields, and emptied her mind of any other thoughts or connections besides the ones he had created. Her eyes moved to Sashika. She shivered. Okay, Demi, this is your Oscar nomination performance. You win, he trusts you, you lose and he buries you beside Sashika. Two could play at his mind games or so she hoped.

She brought her eyes back to his, felt more prodding, then she looked away slowly, her eyes again settling on Sashika's body, as if it was the first time the scene was registering in her mind and then at the taser in her hand and she started screaming. She pulled away from Pierre, slapped violently at his hands, and back-pedaled herself toward a corner opposite the body, screaming some more. When her back hit the cold wall of castle, she threw the taser to the ground, put her hands up in a defensive pose, and turned to run. Pierre caught her around the waist and pulled her tightly to his chest. He spoke to her in English this time, "Moa, Cher, Shh, it is okay. Tell me what happened. It will be better for you." He shook his head, when another person approached with a vial of Compliance. His surface probe had found no indications that Demi had fallen out of his control.

Demi pulled away and looked up at him. "Shh-she was going to kill me. She said you told her to." He didn't answer. She pushed away. "I-I fought with her, I-I only wanted to get the taser from her. She came at me. I-I had no other choice." She looked down at her wet dress, shook her head then raised troubled eyes toward him. "Master, you said I was one of yours, you said I was a good girl." She swallowed, choked back a sob. "Why would you want her to kill me?" She cried. "I don't understand !" Many emotions passed through Pierre's eyes; confusion, anger, disbelief and finally triumph. Got him. She nearly jumped out of her skin she was so excited, but instead she fell to her knees and doubled herself at her waist, retching, and then looking up at Pierre. "Please, Master, whatever I've done to displease you, I'm sorry. I'll make it better. Just don't kill me !" She cried, and bowed her head.

Pierre looked down at Demi, then toward Sashika, his thoughts racing with the possibilities now before him. He had done it. He had done the unthinkable; he had turned a Guardian. Pride swelled in his chest. He raised his eyes at one of the men who came in behind him.

"We leave within the hour. Have the plane ready."

"Yes, Master." He left the room, and Pierre reached down for Demi's chin, lifting it with his finger. "Stand, child." Demi did what he asked and re-bowed her head when he pulled his finger away; he smiled at the meekness of her actions. After a moment, he spoke, "seems your actions have left me a job opening. Know of anyone who would care to step into Sashika's shoes?"

"I can find someone, Master," she stated, adding just the correct amount of tremble to her voice to make her fear believable.

He chuckled. "You are refreshing." He pulled the pin that held her hair up. "Keep your hair down, I like the way it frames your face." She nodded. "Manson," He called toward another guard.

"Yes, Master."

"Take Demi to Malina have her run a bubble bath for her, and make sure she has a nutritious meal. Tell her to have her sized for a purple – no – green robe," he lifted her chin again and looked into her eyes, "It'll bring out your eyes," then he directed his next comment to Mason, "Then bring her to my quarters on the plane. She'll be accompanying me on the flight."

"Yes, Master." He walked up and took Demi's arm, then looked toward Sashika. "What about her?"

"Leave her. The rodents will enjoy the feast." Demi tried to keep her face neutral as she swallowed back the bile gathering in her throat. She had been successful in convincing him, but how long could she keep it up? How long before she would end up like Sashika? A feast for rats? She looked once at Sashika's body as they escorted her from Pierre's presence, then she heard the heavy door shut, and prayed it would not be long before Keys and the team would get to Heinderick and pick up Pierre's trail. She could only hope it would be before Pierre noticed him missing or before he saw beyond her facade.

Three hours later, Keys pulled the Guardian van up behind three Cantonal Police cruisers, two medic trucks, and four Fedpol vehicles in Tarasp. He told Sasha to stay with the surveillance crew to watch the grounds and warn of any movements that may indicate escape, and then he climbed out of the vehicle to approach Herr Schultz, the officer in charge of the operation. Shultz was approximately fifty years of age, and Keys had consulted with him on several cases over the thirty plus years he had been a part of Guardian. He offered his hand. "Herr Schultz."

The older man smiled Shook Keys hand and spoke with a moderate, German Accent, "It is good to see you, Herr Keys. I heard you were in Schweiz."

"Likewise, mien Freund, Wie ist die Familie?"

"They sind gut, und you? Have you found a frau to take care of you yet?"

Keys chuckled, shaking his head. "Nein, Nein, mein freund, there will never be another Lizzy." He grew somber.

"That saddens me, Freund, it has been too many years," he patted Keys bicep with one hand, and still held his hand with the other. His eyes held the compassion of one that loved his wife deeply, laced with concern that his friend continued to hold on to a love that was long gone. "You think za mann das Schloss Tarasp is za same that killed your Lizzy?" Keys nodded, "the mann that leads the Liberatores, und is verantwortlich for many Terror attacks und government Morde here und in Europa?"

Keys nodded somberly. "I do, ja, Kristof, further investigation has also suggested that Pierre Lamontage is responsible for Prince Basheed's assassination in the states last month."

"That is what ihre mann say when he called, ja." His eyes were serious, when he caught Keys' gaze. "You haben Genehmigung from the King to enter the schloss, ja?" he sighed, "we do not vant to make Feinden of alliierte."

"Keys handed him the email he was holding in his hand." Kristof read it through.

"Then we go. We get this mann verantwortlich for your sadness and many others."

"Yes we do." Keys nodded at his friend, and then he returned to the van.

He placed his ear-bud in and flipped it on. "It's a go." Kristof waved his men to their vehicles, grabbed a gun from one of his soldiers, and hopped onto the back of the last vehicle, waving the convoy, of law enforcement vehicles, forward. They moved away from the town of Tarasp and headed North on Fontana, which turned onto Sparsals. A few miles out, they saw the lake on the right, and the castle loomed on the hillside on the left. Eventually they came to a road that took them off Sparsals and headed up to the castle. The convoy pulled into an old public parking lot, left over from the castle's museum days.

"How do you vant to fortfahren?" Kristof asked over the Radio. This is one road to Schloss?"

"I think we go by foot from here?" Keys replied. He wanted the advantage of the element of surprise. "Any level of surprise in our column is a plus."

"As you wish." He signed off and a few more feet up the road, they pulled the vehicles off the road and into a thicket of trees. The team armed themselves with Tasers, rifles, and various other standard issue weapons, and then waited within the vehicles for briefing. Each team leader briefed their members.

Keys turned to Sasha, "activate CC12048-EX." Sasha hit a few keys on the computer. It hummed as it fed a few lines of data over the screen. The Guardian development team had been working on the program since they took possession of all of the equipment and computers from Bradshaw's compound. They liked the camouflage program for his compound, but they wanted it further developed to use on a larger scale and made more portable. The prototype was on the Guardian surveillance van they brought with them today. It targeted the optical nerve and used electrical energy to form a cloak, of sort, over a team in the field that blended in with its surroundings. It wasn't dissimilar to the process used by a Cloaker

The teams heard a crackle of electricity as the cloak went up and their mouths dropped as they stopped and stared at the multicolored mist that enclosed them in a half spherical shaped cover. Schultz smiled, and looked toward Keys. "You always surprise me with your gadgets, my Freund," he chuckled. You spoil my mannschaften, they vill vant to go to America with you, ja?"

Keys chuckled. "This is a combat shield, designed to hide soldiers' field location from approaching enemies. We're hoping to put it on the market, after we patent it and allied governments approve it. This is the prototype for us to test drive." He winked. "You'll be the first one on my list when it does become available."

"I am happy you bring it with you." He patted Keys on the back and grinned. Then he shook his head as he ordered his men to gear up. They slipped knives into sleeves strapped around ankles and under shirts. Leaders dispersed bulletproof vests and other weapons. He turned toward his van and opened it up to disperse his teams' weapons and gear. When both groups were ready, they met around the cantonal equipment truck. A satellite map of the grounds and the castle hung on the side of the truck. The team listened as Keys and Schultz joined forces with the Fedpol leader and showed them how they were going to go in from all sides. They spoke in German, and Kyle interpreted for his team. "The walls were reinforced when the prince bought the property, but if we successfully hit the four entrances," Keys was pointing them out on the map, "simultaneously with synchronized movements there will be no forewarning to those inside, and we will gain access. I want teams A and D on east and north entrances," he pointed them out, "and I want B and C on the west and south entrances," he pointed those out as well. "We get into position, we wait for all to get into place, and we attack. Synchronize your watches before you begin your approach."

Schultz looked at Keys. "Keys, you und ihre team, with me." Keys nodded and he took them all in, slipping into German once again. "Let's go get us a terrorist." They all nodded, and Keys started back toward his team to make sure they understood the plan.

Marna and Kyle were standing in front of the vans, helping each other fasten their vests in place. When he heard Keys words, Kyle said, "music to my ears."

"Kyle, this is no time to be a hero," Keys said, stopping his trek toward the van and facing the younger man. "Lamontage is beyond dangerous and I can't tell you how much he would enjoy taking down as many Guardian agents with him as he could. Don't give him advantage over our people by being cocky." Anger flashed in Kyle's eyes. Marna averted hers, as the two men faced off.

"Yes, Sir." Kyle's tone was bitter as he pushed by him and joined the others.

Marna paused. "You were a little hard on him, don't you think?"

Keys let his eyes follow Kyle's progress to the others before he brought them back to hers. "Kyle has a history of throwing caution to the wind. I thought it necessary to remind him to keep his feet firmly on the ground."

"He's a good agent and a strong fighter, Keys. I've seen him in action I don't think you have to worry about that."

"As have I, Marna, and I'd like to see him live to reach his full potential," he smiled, "a cautionary word here and there does the boy no harm." He waved her ahead of him. "Why don't you join the others?"

Figuring more words in Kyle's defense would be of no use right now and possibly reveal certain things she was feeling, she herself didn't understand yet, she turned and led the way toward her team. She, however, made a note to herself to find out why there was so much tension between Keys and Agent Rigby. She came up beside Kyle and smiled. The one he gave her was a bit too cocky and bold. Maybe Keys was right, maybe a word of caution now and then didn't hurt. She moved forward as the teams dispersed into the forested hillside, the castle crowned. Keys watched her go then went to the van, checked in on the surveillance crew, and Sasha on the computer. Then drawing in a breath and letting it out between pursed lips, he grabbed a rifle, knife, and his Glock, following Marna to where the others waited.

As soon as they were all within sight of the gates, but far enough back to keep themselves hidden, they hunkered down to await further instructions. Marna made her way to Kyle's side. He was counting when she approached. "You okay?"

He looked at her and smiled. "Never better." Then he returned his eyes to the gate and started counting again. Before she could ask more, Bryan moved over to them. Marna glanced his way. He looked scared.

"Bryan, what's wrong?"

"I can't get through to Demi. She's not answering my telepathic communications."

"Maybe she's got her shields up so Lamontage don't know we're coming." She tried to reassure him, but she too had tried to contact Demi and had only gotten as far as opening a connection before some force slammed it shut. However, she hadn't sensed Lamontage's evil in the block. "Have you tried Heinderick?"

He nodded. "He's not answering either."

She was about to answer, but their ear-buds came to life. "Team A in position." She lifted her hand to her ear to turn up the volume, and block outside interference.

"Team B in position."

"Team C in position."

"Team D In position; waiting on your word, Commander."

"Show time, boys and girls," Kyle said, and tensed.

Bryan put a hand on Kyle's shoulder. "Wait for Keys to give us the word, Kyle."

"We can't," he had discovered something that Schultz had missed, and other than the teams at the gates, radio contact had been shut down. "I'll explain later." Kyle moved forward.

"Kyle !" Bryan hissed. Marna's hand went to her mouth as Kyle belly crawled to the edge of their wooded area refuge. Bryan undid his holster strap holding his gun in place, pulled the Glock out, loaded the chamber, and moved three trees forward covering Kyle.

"Keys, what the hell are your men doing?" Schultz's voice whispered over the ear-bud. Keys moved quickly forward, followed by Ventura.

"Dammit, Keys, Kyle's at it again." Ventura hissed as he came up behind Keys and Marna.

"Kyle, hold your position, do you hear me?" Keys ordered.

"Keys listen to me . . .," Kyle demanded.

"Leave it to Schultz's men! We have a plan already in progress. Lamontage gets wind that any Guardian is here, Demi becomes a casualty and so do you. You will hold your position." Kyle bounced his forehead off his arm several times, giving Bryan a chance to catch up to him.

"Are you out of your mind, Rigby, you want to be reckless, do it when Demi's life doesn't hang in the balance." Before Kyle could explain what was causing his disregard of orders, Team A brought down the gate guards with their Tasers. The two-foot soldiers crumpled to the ground, the grip on their guns going limp. Team-A took their quarries weapons, and dragged them away from the gate, around the corner of the wall out of sight. Kyle got to a crouched position and moved toward the gate. He ignored Keys' voice bellowing in his ear. Instead, he told him what they had all missed.

"Keys in exactly six seconds two more men are going to come to the front gate on the inside, they'll notice their buddies aren't there. Team-A isn't going to make it back in time. If we don't take them out, they'll sound the alarm, and we'll have a bloodbath here. Then we're all dead. Would you rather have that?" He shut off his ear-bud, and he waved Bryan forward. They quickly took position pressing their backs against the castle wall on either side of the gate.

"Are you sure about this?" Bryan asked.

"Yeah. I was counting from the wood-line. Something our Cantonal police and Fedpol friends missed. Lamontage must have upgraded security. He was expecting us." He raised his finger to his mouth as rhythmic footsteps approached the gate from both sides and opened a psychic connection to Bryan, starting a two-way communication. *They're going to come through with rifles, Rush, be ready.* Bryan nodded and flattened himself tighter against the wall. Team-A reappeared around the corners of the wall and headed toward the gate again, the footsteps stopped and changed direction. The nozzles of the rifles came out first, just as Kyle had predicted. *Three, two, one!* With gloved hands, Bryan and he grabbed the muzzles and swung the guards 180 degrees, slamming their quarry against the castle wall, the cantonal team stunned them with their Tasers from six feet away. Kyle was right, if he and Bryan hadn't have acted, their presence would have been exposed, and the cantonal team downed.

"Nice work, you two." Keys said as Kyle switched his ear-bud back on. Marna let out a breath she didn't know she was holding. She looked toward Keys. He nodded and moved away.

"We're going in now." Bryan said, but Kyle stayed silent. Marna didn't miss that or the pained look that passed through Keys eyes before he turned away. Other teams around the castle walls confirmed their entrance as well but Keys was no longer listening. He and Marna watched from the cover of the forest boundary line, as a team of six--Kyle, Bryan, two Cantonal and two Fedpol officers--entered the front gates. Officers from Fedpol moved forward and retrieved the four guards, handing them off to the medics.

Keys body was tense. Marna sensed every muscle in his body was bunched and ready to pounce if his agents ran into trouble. The only sound that came over the airwaves was the heavy breathing of the agents. It dragged on for what seemed like hours to Marna but it was only moments before Bryan came back on. "Keys, Courtyard's clear, unnaturally so." Marna tensed, Keys glanced her way then caught Ventura's eyes. "There is nobody in it. No guards but what we just took down. I'm having déjà-vu." Keys caught Schultz's eyes, and they all gave the signal for the rest of the team to move forward. With weapons ready for any unexpected occupants, they approached the castle wall, and entered through the gates. Bryan was right. Marna could feel it. It was déjà-vu.

"Spread out, check the buildings." Schultz ordered and stepped to Keys side. "Why don't you and your people check the tower?" Keys nodded.

He flipped on his ear-bud. "Marna, Bryan, Kyle and Pete, meet me at the tower entrance." He pulled his gun and moved toward the south side of the castle.

Moments later, they were all waiting for Keys to open the door so they could start their ascension on the tower steps. Keys grabbed the knob, nodded at Ventura, on the opposite side of the door and flattened his form against the wall. Marna pulled her weapon, slanting her position to see what would be in the immediate line of vision, and Kyle took up her mirrored position beside Keys. All four of them loaded their chambers, and aimed. Keys ticked down with his fingers, starting at three. When the last finger went down, they kicked the door open. Marna immediately went into a defensive crouch, letting out a breath when no gunfire met their entrance. She moved in swinging her upper body to cover the right of the lower chamber room while Kyle crossed her path and did the same for the left. Ventura and Keys took up the rear as the door silently closed behind them.

The lower chamber was quiet too quiet. Keys signaled Marna and Kyle to the rooms on the right. He and Ventura took the ones on the left. They would clearl them and meet in the end kitchen before they continued upstairs. She and Kyle were the first ones in the kitchen. It was modernized, with commercial sized appliances, and a wood stove for heating in the center of the room. This was the center of the activity, the hub of the room. A teakettle keeping warm on the wood stove.. Marna looked toward Kyle, who nodded, and turned his back toward her, while keeping a constant sweep of the room with his gun, ready for intruders. Marna lowered her gun, and placed a hand on the teakettle. Kyle looked toward her, she nodded, "still warm," she whispered. He nodded toward the pantry tucked into an inlet of the room. The door was closed. She nodded back.

Resuming her position, her gun hand leading her steps, she moved to one side of the inlet, her gun aimed at the pantry door, while Kyle approached, holding his gun up with on hand. He grabbed the doorknob with the other, glanced Marna's way, and waited for her to nod to verify they were on the same page. With one quick movement, he swung the door outward, but neither of them was ready for what happened next. The immediate exposure of the room showed nobody within it and as he turned to clear it, Marna saw a form drop from somewhere within, knocking Kyle to the ground. His gun slid across the room, and the assailant immediately plunged a knife downward narrowly missing his throat because Kyle maneuvered the hand holding it to the right, the blade sliced his cheek, while he averted it. The two men rolled about on the floor. She aimed her gun, following the struggling men about the floor, praying for an opening. "Come on, Kyle," she breathed, "give me an opening." She tensed, waiting for her chance.

Kyle rolled the man below him, and slammed his fist into the man's face, opening a cut on his cheek, holding the wrist, of the hand, with the knife off. The attacker managed to break his legs loose, bring them up and kick out, Throwing Kyle over the stove, slamming his rib cage on the edge, and his head on the corner of the bricked wall. Kyle was stunned, and tried to push himself up with one hand, using the wall for support, while holding his other arm across his midsection. He looked toward the assailant who sprung himself to his feet, yelled and ran after him, ready to plunge the knife deep into his flesh.

Marna fired four bullets into his chest. The attacker crumpled to the floor, and the life force left his eyes seconds later. ,The knife fell from his hand, and Kyle eased himself to the floor, his back sliding down the wall. Marna swept the room with her gun, then she crouched to check the downed man's pulse after she kicked the knife away from his hand. She didn't expect any, but she wanted no more surprises. Satisfied, she went to assist Kyle. With him leaning on her for support, she walked him over to the table, in the center of the room, and helped him lower his lean frame into a chair. "You okay?" She queried. He nodded, and then reached for the back of his head with his hand. There was blood on it when he brought it back. Marna grabbed a towel from a nearby counter, and bunched it up on the wound. The rest of her team ran into the room, guns ready.

"It's okay," Marna said, "we got surprised by a servant hiding in a ceiling tile or something in the pantry." They all looked at the man on the floor. Keys holstered his gun and moved to Kyle's side, crouching down to look him over.

"Marna, go with Bryan and Pete to clear the second level. I doubt there is anyone here or they would have come running, after the shots."

"What about Kyle?"

"I'll stay with him." She nodded, and Kyle took over holding the towel in place while she gave him a final smile and followed the other two out the door. After they had left, Keys turned back toward Kyle. "You okay, Son?"

"Yeah, thanks to Marna." He winced when he tried to sit up. "She took him out." His eyes moved toward the downed man.

"She's a crack shot." He agreed, looking over the wound on Kyle's head then his cheek, then checking Kyle's ribs. Kyle drew in a sharp breath when Keys examined his ribs. "Looks like you may have cracked a rib or two, we need to bind them, steri-strip the cut on your cheek, and you're going to need stitches in head wound. Did you come across any medical supplies while you were clearing the room?."

"Yeah, in the pantry." Keys unbuttoned his holster, pulled his gun, and moved into the pantry, pointing it upward then toward the back and around the small 6 X 6 space. He saw where the assailant had hidden. There was a ceiling tile missing where the heat ducts met, it offered just enough space for a small man to perch himself and lie in wait for an attack. He wasn't surprised they had missed him. Satisfied there were no other concealed enemies in the little room, he holstered his gun, and looked around the shelves. The medical supplies were in the back of the room all together in a plastic tub. He pulled out what he needed, and flipped on his ear-bud.

"This is Keys. I have an 11-99. I need a medic in the lower level, tower kitchen and call for an ambulance. My team is clearing the top level now."

"How bad?"

"Agent injured and one of Lamontage's men is down."

"Medic on the way."

"Thanks." As he stepped out of the pantry, he caught sight of the assailant's knife half under the open door, where it had stopped when Marna had kicked it away. He saw the blood on it and quickly glanced Kyle's way. The boy could have ended up dead instead of injured. A chill went up his spine. If it weren't for Marna, they could be calling for a coroner instead of an ambulance. He swallowed down the gripping fear that rose in his throat, and returned to Kyle to do what he could with his injuries.

*****

Marna, centered between the two men, moved cautiously up the stairwell to the upper level of the tower, guns trained in angles to protect each other, and their eyes constantly moving about, looking for shadows and suspicious movement of any kind. They moved sideways up the stairs one at a time. They didn't want another incident such as in the kitchen. Ventura reached the top level first. He gave them the all clear sign for the immediate area, and motioned to the one closed door at the end of a narrow four-foot hall. He moved down first. Marna, gun trained ahead of her, moved down second, and Bryan with his back to Marna moved backwards down the hall, gun trained behind them The Tower door had a modern dead bolt. Ventura grabbed the doorknob, and nodded to Marna. She tilted her head to listen for any conversation or voices of any kind, she shook her head. He turned it. It was unlocked. Marna nodded and Ventura swung it open. She entered first, sweeping the room with her gun leading the way. Nobody was an immediate threat. Bryan moved in behind Marna and Ventura took up the rear, securely closing the door behind them.

Marna Swept around the corner of a double arch doorway and saw the body on the floor, she signaled for Ventura while she went and felt for a pulse. She shook her head, Ventura holstered his weapon. "Clear" Bryan called from deeper within the room, and then returned to join them. The bedroom chamber was split into three rooms in an open concept theme; An entry section between the outer hall and the sleeping chambers separated by the double arch doorway, and then a smaller dressing area in the back, also separated by the sleeping chambers by an arch doorway, only smaller. Marna holstered her gun and rolled the body over. Her breath caught in her throat as she scrambled backward. "Dear, God !" She breathed.

"What is it?" Ventura queried.

Bryan drew in a breath and let it out in a sigh. "Marna and I saw her this morning in our communication with Demi." He ran a hand through his hair. "I killed her with a knife in the dream realm."

"And she died here?" Ventura took a step backwards. Marna looked up at Bryan.

"She was going to kill Demi, Bryan, you had no choice."

He put his hands on his hips, and caught Marna's eyes with his own. "I know, but I'm not used to my dreams becoming reality when I wake up."

"You don't know that to be true." Marna said. "Look." She pointed out a jagged burned on her chest.

Ventura crouched down. He looked over the injury. "Looks like a Taser kill to me."

"Lamontage?" Marna queried.

"Could be . . . Maybe he wasn't happy with her nightly jaunt into the dream realm without him."

Marna's head shot up. "Did you hear that?"

"What?"

"Shh." They all listened and it came again. A tapping sound, quiet but steady.

"Sounds like it's coming from the back of the room," whispered Ventura.

Leaving the body, they all pulled their guns and headed back to the dressing area. The tapping got louder. Ventura saw the shadow on the window first. The outline of a weapon in their hand. He put his arm up and swung it back telling everybody to move back. Someone was on the other side of the window trying to open it. He Nodded Marna over to cover him, then ducked below vision level, scooted until he was directly under the window. Marna loaded a round in the chamber and aimed. He reached up from the floor, using the middle casing of the window for coverage, and carefully pushed up on the latch. The window swung inward, and a small body fell through, yelling and landing in a heap on the floor by Ventura. He lifted his head and looked up the barrels of all three guns. " Nicht schießen !" Heinderick cried, throwing his weapon down. Don't shoot! and he pulled his knees up to his chest trying to protect his small body.

"Heinderick?" Marna said softly, lowering her gun quickly.

He slowly lifted his head up when he heard his name, and stared at Marna. " Du bist die Frau aus dem Traumreichs, meine Tante." Marna had picked up enough German to figure out what he was saying--You are the woman from my dreams, my aunt.

She looked at Ventura, but Bryan started talking to Heinderick in fluent German. "Wo ist die Frau, die in diesem Raum Demi war?"

" Sie ging mit dem Meister, um mich zu retten,"Heinderick said, hanging his head, "erzählte sie mir in der Suche Zimmer zu verstecken und nicht herunterkommenegal was ich gehört habe."

"Dammit !" Bryan said and fell into a chair.

"Bryan, what is it?" Marna asked.

"Lamontage is gone, and he took Demi with him."

"What?"

Heinderick walked over and pulled a paper out of his pants pocket, giving it to him. Bryan took the paper, unfolded and read the note.

Bryan, Marna and Keys
This may be crazy, but I think I can stay undercover with Lamontage as long as he thinks he has me under his control. The situation with Sashika would have made him suspicious, so I had to act fast to save Heinderick. If you are reading this, we are already on our way back to the states. His private jet is landing in New York or Newark depending on where it will be easiest for him to get in undetected. You've tracked me down once, I have faith you can do it again. Don't worry I'm fine. I know what to expect now and I think I know how to fight him and keep him, and his control at a distance. As soon as I get some privileges, I will find a way to contact you. We can't let him get away, we are too close and I am the only one with an inside track.
** I'll see you soon.**
Demi.

He handed the note to Marna and rubbed his face with his hands, while she read it through. Her eyes met his, "I'll get this down to Keys, you guys search around up here, we'll call a coroner and Keys can check Heinderick over. Uncover everything, maybe there is a clue here somewhere." She smiled and reached out for Heinderick's hand. He slipped his into hers shyly and she returned her eyes to Bryan's. "We'll get her back, Bryan. You have to keep believing that." He nodded and started searching the dressing area without saying another word.

An hour later, agents were combing the tower room and the kitchen for clues and evidence, and Keys was nodding at the medics as they loaded Heinderick and Kyle into a helicopter. He gave them orders to take them directly to the clinic in St Moritz, and he would join them there. Marna waved as Heinderick looked out the window. Kyle reached over and squeezed the boy's shoulder, and then the helicopter lifted out of the courtyard, and headed toward St Moritz.

Keys rejoined Pete, Bryan, and Marna as they looked over the bagged evidence. They had placed all the evidence they thought had pertained to Demi in a separate box from the rest, hoping something could lead them to where Lamontage was going next. **Bag one**: clothes from the plastic tub, under the cot that Demi had been wearing the night they kidnapped her. Bryan looked over each evidence bag that held all the missing blanks of Demi's captivity in 3D. A white cotton gown that had a couple of strands of Demi's hair, perspiration, blood and some tear tracks on it, restraints that were tied on the bed, in the tower, same story. Bryan tried not to visualize the unthinkable things Lamontage had done to her during her captivity. He looked at the bag that held the strands of her hair again and drew in a breath. "Bryan, somebody else can box this stuff up to go to the lab, you don't have to do it," Marna said stepping up beside him.

He dropped the bag into the box. "You think she can do it?" he asked turning his head in her direction, his arms resting on the edge of the box, his eyes tortured with uncertainty. "You think she can keep him in the dark long enough for us to find her."

Marna thought about her next words carefully before she spoke them. "I think Demi is a smart woman, and an even smarter agent. I think whatever she puts her mind to, she'll do."

He sighed, "I hope you're right."

Keys walked up to them. "The jet is meeting us in St Moritz, in two hours, to fly us to Zurich. We'll get a good night's sleep there, and then we take off in the morning for the states." Marna nodded. Secretly she was glad they could arrange to get back to Zurich tonight. She wanted to see the children, hold them in her arms, and bring home their brother so they could meet him. She remembered what Amanda had said--- gosh was it really only a month ago---they needed to find out the what and the how it would all fit in to the scheme of things and how they would keep Demi from becoming one of the casualties in Lamontage's war.

St Moritz was a beautiful city, and Marna couldn't help but be amazed at the beauty of the Alps surrounding it. The cobblestone streets, the high-end stores and the restaurants, it was a city built around tourism, but caught in the breathtaking beauty of its surroundings. A fresh layer of snow blanketed the landscape, from the valleys below her to the tips of the slopes in the distance, and wondered about the longevity of the Switzerland winter in this city. Large churches marked the landscape with old architecture. Their steeples reaching to the clouds above and footpaths carved their way through the mountainous Terrain around her. One of these days, she would come back and sample the beauty of this land without marring her experience by chasing a homicidal maniac through it. The driver pulled into the airfield, and they went through their private security check in, before boarding the Guardian jet fueled and ready to go. Within minutes, they were in the air and on their way to Zurich. .

When the seat belt sign went off, she ventured from her seat to the seat beside Kyle, a couple of sections down, and then she dropped report forms and a pen on the table before him. Kyle was reclined back, both eyes closed. His features were strong, with a straight nose and firm lips set in a square jaw and perfectly distanced eyes. The only thing keeping him from perfection was the ugly gash the knife fight had left on his cheek; they had used the medi-glue to close up it up and six stitches to close up the gash on the back of his head. Evidence of the rib wrap, the doctors had put around his midsection, was clearly defined through his loose fitting tee. A bottle of subscribed pain pills rested on the table before him. She reached for it, and looked at the label. "I can't pronounce it so they've got to be good, but they aren't going to do you any good if you don't take them." She folded her legs up underneath her, still holding the pill bottle and the fingers of her other hand lightly brushed his shoulder.

He sighed, and his good eye squinted open, "I don't like pain pills, they make you act like an idiot, say things you wouldn't normally say, and they cause drowsiness. All things I could do without right now."

She shook her head. "Afraid you might miss something?"

He grinned, reaching for the pills, taking hold of the bottle, intentionally letting his fingers rest over hers for a moment, before taking them. "Somethin' like that." He opened the compartment by his seat and dropped them in it, wincing as he pushed himself up. She had him lean forward as she readjusted cushions behind his back. "What's all of that?" he asked, finger combing his hair, and indicating the pile of paper work. A piece of his hair caught on the glue line, in his cheek and she instinctively reached for it to remove it gently. Her fingers felt the uneven line of the cut. The scene from earlier replayed in her mind, how close that knife had come to his throat. She paused, her eyes moving to his. His hand reached up and enclosed hers. "It's fine, I'm fine." He brought her hand to his lap, "thanks to you."

She cleared her throat and looked down at their hands, not in any particular hurry to pull hers free then she brought her eyes back up to his. "You would have done the same for me," she smiled, "actually did if you recall the train station."

"I have a feeling you would have been okay." He smiled and shifted himself so he could look at her, without twisting at the waist. He glanced sideways at the clipboard she had dropped on the table. "You give me the impression, Farlow, that you could be pretty self reliant if you needed to be," her cheeks colored, he grinned and looked at the clipboard. "Now what is all of that?"

"Report forms for today's incident. I figured we could fill them out together," she caught his eyes with hers, "less stress for both of us."

"I agree." He reached for another pen that was on the table, but drew back with a grunt and grabbed his ribs. He changed position and tried again but Marna put her hand over his.

"Let me," she said, lifting her hand and reaching for the pen, bringing it back to him. He rapped his fingers around it, enveloping her hand as well, and keeping his face inches from hers.

"Thanks." He said as she inched her hand from his grasp. He took the clipboard and looked the papers over. Marna had filled most of it out and explained it well. He added a few things here and there for clarification, but he was done within minutes. He put the clipboard down, and turned his attention back to Marna. "Done."

"Thanks." She detached the papers from the clipboard, slipped them in an awaiting folder, and pulled them toward her. He put his hand on the folder as she readied to leave. She looked up at him, an unspoken question in her eyes.

"You think you could find some coffee in the kitchen? I would love a cup but getting around right now isn't all that easy." His voice was soft, alluring.

"It would be," she said, her voice matching his, as she reached across his body to retrieve the pills, "if you take your medicine." He watched her through lowered lids. Felt her closeness a little too much. He leaned back to give her more room, as her body curled backwards to return to a sitting position beside him. She held the bottle up for him. He reached up and took the hand the bottle was in, pulling her toward him.

"If I promise to be a good boy and take my meds, Dr. Farlow, can I get you to join me for a cup of bad coffee from the kitchen?" She couldn't breathe. His nearness was confusing her thoughts, her resolve. What was it about this man that his mere presence could throw her in to such a tailspin? She traced the lines of his face down to his lips with her eyes where she hesitated; he curled them upwards in a lazy smile. Flashes of the night in the hotel room whipped through her head. She felt her cheeks flush, and then she drew in a breath and pulled away, he loosened his grip on her hand so she could retrieve it.

"I-I don't know, I probably should spend some time with Heinderick."

Kyle moved his eyes around the plane. Keys was conversing with Heinderick fluently in German. "I think Keys has him pretty well occupied right now." She looked around the plane, fearful that all eyes were on them, but her fears were unfounded. Bryan and Ventura were sleeping with their backs toward them, and her glance in Keys direction verified Kyle's observations. Nobody was even looking their way; much less caring about their high intensity exchange. Marna drew in a breath, regrouping and letting go of her own anxiety.

She smiled "Sure, I'll go get it now." She pushed herself up from the seat, and away from his section. Kyle watched her go and admired the grace by which her body moved. He couldn't help but fantasize about holding her in his arms one day. However, he didn't want it to be just another one-night stand with Marna. He felt something for her, and he wanted a chance to see what that was, or where it might lead.

He dropped his head back on the seat, closed his eyes, took a cleansing breath, swallowed, and looked again at the pill bottle. Every nerve ending in his body screamed in pain, but dare he be that off guard with Marna so close? "It's not unmanly to take a pill, Rigby."

Kyle raised his eyes from the bottle label. Ventura peered down at him. Rigby tightened his arm around his midsection, and let the hand grasping the pills collapse into his lap. "Funny man."

"I try." He glanced Marna's way. "She's a fine woman." He brought his eyes back to Kyle. "One of the sweetest I've ever had the pleasure of working with. Not to mention, smart, damn good with a gun, and not afraid to face the enemy head on. You should have seen her and the kids go up against Bradshaw last year."

"I've heard. She's a legend among the ranks."

"So you've said, but what do you really think about her, Rigby?"

"What's that supposed to mean?"

"Come on, Rigby, I've been around the block a few times, I know when there is an attraction building. You damn near burned a hole in the seat just now and the smoke almost set off the alarm."

"So, I'm attracted to her. You said it yourself, she's fine woman I'd be blind if I wasn't."

Ventura chuckled, "yeah you would, wouldn't you?"

Kyle heard the edge in Ventura's voice. "I'm sorry am I trampling on your stomping grounds? Cause if I am, I'll back off. Funny thing though, Marna doesn't talk about you like there's anything romantic between you."

When he spoke, Ventura's voice was hard as steel, but he kept it low so as not to attract attention to them, "you listen, you immature moron! Jeff Farlow was a good man. I wouldn't chase after his wife and dishonor his memory that way." Ventura glanced toward the kitchen, then brought his eyes back to Kyle's, lowering his voice to a menacing whisper. "Tread lightly, Rigby, because if you cause her any pain, I'll kick your ass myself. She's been through enough, more than any one person should endure and she doesn't need some teenager with his hormones out of wack counting her as a notch in his conquest belt." Ventura pushed up from the table as Marna arrived with the coffee.

"Pete, you want to join us for coffee, I'll go get you some."

"No, thanks, Marna." He smiled at her. "I've got some more evidence logging to do."

"How's Bryan holding up?"

"He's doing okay considering." He glanced back at Bryan reclined, sleeping in his seat. "He's just holding onto the belief that Demi will be okay until we get there."

"Demi's strong. She'll probably get through this better than the rest of us."

"You're probably right, Marna. Excuse me." He glanced at Kyle. "Kyle."

"Pete.." Ventura walked away. Marna handed Kyle his coffee. "Thanks."

"What were you guys discussing? It seemed pretty serious."

"Oh you know, guy things," he shrugged, "comparing battle scars and stories."

"Oh." She smiled. "I'll bet Pete has some good ones, he was special ops during the Freedom Conflicts." She grew solemn." Men like Pet is why Jeff became an MP. We used to light a fire in the brick fire pit in our back yard, and we would sit on a blanket, and he would share his stories with me."

"I'd like to hear some of those if you're willing to share. From what I hear, he was a good man, an honorable man."

"He was." She smiled sadly. "He was, ah," she cleared her throat, "we discussed him becoming part of the PS&S Team when the Bradshaw investigation was over . . . I never suspected, a year ago, I'd be doing this without him." She sniffed, "I'm sorry," she wiped at a tear tracking down her face and dropped her hand by the table. "It gets to me every once in a while."

"No need to apologize," he took her hand in his, "what you had with him was very special and it always will be."

"Talking about him helps."

"Then tell me those stories," he pulled his hand away, and circled it around his coffee cup, "I'd love to hear them."

She smiled. "Maybe just a couple," she whispered and grinned, "But only if you take your medicine."

"You are ruthless," he grinned.

"I can be." He swallowed down the pill and laid his head on the back of the seat while she launched in to one of the stories Jeff had shared with her. Funny, it seemed like a lifetime ago.

Through lowered lids, he watched her face tint with many emotions as she talked about her husband, happiness, sadness, loneliness and love. He found himself wishing he could have met the man, but he also felt like he was in competition with a bigger-than-life memory; and how does one compete with that? Maybe Ventura was right. Pursuing her right now could be a mistake. He sighed sadly, as she laughed and sighed and had long moments of silence where she had to gain control of her emotions. He was careful to be attentive and not show that her attachment to her Jeff made him melancholy, and eventually, mercifully, the meds took hold and he fell asleep. He didn't even notice when Marna pulled a blanket from the storage bin above his head, and covered him up with it and walked away with a smile on her face, joining Keys and Heinderick for some Chocolate ice-cream.

Chapter Thirteen

The time following their arrival in Zurich was a whirlwind of debriefings, and hospital waits, while doctors tended to Kyle and Heinderick and then released them. Then there was more debriefings as the International Internal Investigation Team (IIIT) grilled Marna and Kyle about the incident. Crime Scene techs then verified their account with forensic and ballistic evidence... More waiting, while they tested her Glock and confirmed that she fired no more shots than were necessary, to bring the attacker down to save her partner.

Six hours later, they were heading home in the back of the car Keys had sent for her. He had taken Kyle home and arranged for Sasha and Bryan, as well as himself, to stay at Kyle's place for added protection, while he slept and recuperated.

Marna was exhausted. She laid her head back on the seat. Flashes of her trek across Switzerland passed before her eyes. A small throbbing had started behind her eyes. The car slowed, and then stopped at the gates of the Zurich compound and the driver commenced in a conversation, with the guards at the check-in housing. She heard the hum of the window rolling down, and felt the night air kiss her face. She opened her eyes, and glanced toward her window. A young man's head and shoulders filled the open space. He was young, maybe nineteen. He had slicked his blonde hair back with some kind of hair product smelling of a manly musk, making his features sharply defined in the low light of the night. His eyes were Hazel, with flecks of blue and green flashing as he smiled at her, "ID please, ma'am." He was clean cut, but she felt uncomfortable with the way his eyes probed and intruded into the depth of hers. She felt even more violated when he moved them from her face and combed down the length of her body, taking his time before he returned his gaze to her face. She raised her brow, "Seen enough, sailor?" The driver coughed to cover his snicker, but the teen's gaze did not falter, his lips upturned lazily.

"Yes, ma'am." he challenged.

"Glad to hear it," She pulled her hand out of her purse, mustered up a weary smile and handed him her leather ID case. He took a long moment to study her face again, and then turned toward the enclosed housing. She saw movement behind the tinted glass.

"They're clear," the kid said, and turned back toward her, gave her the ID back, and then smiled again. "Have a good evening Ms. Farlow. Welcome back." Then he backed away and the driver rolled her window up. She shivered as the last of the evening draft fought to stay in the car, and then exchanged a chuckle with the driver before she brushed her discomfort aside and glanced down at Heinderick who was studying her closely.

"What?" She queried.

"Du nicht like him?" His words came out in a mixture of German and English.

"What makes you think I didn't like him?" She smiled at him.

"Dein Lächeln war gefälscht." your smile was fake.

"Very observant of you, Heinderick." She grinned at him. "You're half right, he was obnoxious and rude."

"Why?"

"Why what?" She said as the car slowed to a stop in front of their building, and she reached for the door handle."

"Why du nicht like him?"

"Woman's intuition." She grinned at his puzzled look and leaned in closer to him, speaking conspiratorily in his ear. "I'll explain it to you In about ten years." She pulled away. "Come on let's go meet the rest of the family." He nodded and opened his door.

Moments later, they were outside her apartment. She knelt down before Heinderick. "Are you ready?" He nodded, glancing at the digital photo she had given him on the plane. Tanner was thoughtful enough to get all the children together, take them to the park to take a snapshot, and then he picture expressed it to Marna on her GPC so she could print it out, and give it to Heinderick to study on the trip home. He had even added a caption with all their names, in order, left to right, so he could get to know them by sight before they got home. She had been touched beyond words that he had thought to do such a thing. He didn't have to, it wasn't required, but he did it because he cared.

The adjustment was going to be tough enough on the boy without the added stress of putting names to faces amongst the routine of first introductions. "Okay then, Peter James Nymphis Farlow, it's time to meet the rest of your family." He smiled. Marna had already called their Guardian lawyer to start adoption proceedings, and changed his name to Peter James (PJ) for short, after her brother in law. Peter Nymphis had never been big on a junior in the family, but somehow she didn't think he'd mind this once. She did the same thing with Arella; she changed her name to Amanda Sue, after her mother. When they got back to the states, they would do it legally in honor of their rebirth and new life. When she sent an email asking Tanner to broach the subject with rest of the family, he did and the vote had been unanimously in favor of the choice. That way they would always have a part of their parents with them.

Brushing some fingers through his hair to straighten it, she put her key in the lock, but before she could turn it, the door swung open, and Tanner stood before her. He was dressed in a red polo that fit tightly over his muscled torso and tucked into the slim waist of his black Khakis. He had feathered his dark hair back from countless sweeps with his fingers and his eyes were warm and welcoming, like he was genuinely pleased to see her. His exuberance was contagious as was the smile that went straight to his eyes. "Welcome home," he said in a soothing voice.

"Thanks." The emotions that engulfed her when she saw him, took her by surprise. Instinctively, she went into his arms and he wrapped her in their warmth. She wanted to relish in their strength and unload all of the trials of the last few days. He held her tightly not sure what to make of her actions, but wanting the have the moment. His cheek rested on her head

Her feelings for Tanner were so different from what she felt for Kyle. With him, they were gentle, caring, sensual and deep, with Kyle it was electrifying heat when they touched, it was so intense, and the shock waves alone could take out an entire room. How was she supposed to acknowledge one set of emotions, without understanding the others? Was it just a physical attraction with Kyle? Forbidden fruit? Her head throbbed. She raised her fingers to her temple.

Tanner reached for her elbow she looked up at him. His eyes were alert as they studied her features. "Are you okay?"

"Yeah." She smiled. "No intrusion, just a migraine. It's been a long few days."
She ran her hand through her hair, and then looked toward PJ. "This is Tanner, a friend of ours."

Tanner blinked, but brought his attention to the boy and offered him a hand. "Hello, PJ. It's nice to meet you." The boy shook his hand, but never spoke.

"Where are the others?"

"In the living room, anxiously waiting to meet their brother."

"Then let's go." She brushed everything aside, and urged Heinderick/PJ ahead of her.

"Go ahead. I'll make some tea," he said, "Some tension tamer may help with that headache."

Their eyes locked for the briefest of moments before she said, "Thanks," and headed into the other room. He watched her go, he could not outwardly explain the relief and thrill of having her back home; near enough to see, to touch, to talk to . . . he didn't finish his thought *'knock it off, Williams, your time will come, when she's ready to hear it.'*

When they had gone through the doorway and deeper into the living room, the conversation started. Arella was the first to speak. "Heinderick, you're okay." Tanner smiled as he poured water into the kettle, and placed it on the stove, turning it on. His GPC vibrated on the table. He stepped over, and hit a button to allow video. Keys swam into focus on the screen.

"How are things going?"

"They're in the other room chatting."

"But . . ."

Tanner glanced toward the doorway then back at the screen. "I don't know, Keys, Marna came home with a furious headache. She says it's just a migraine, and she's probably right, but past experience makes me a little wary."

"It has been a rough few days, Son, she could be suffering from just that."

"True, but I'm still a bit concerned."

Keys looked thoughtful. Tanner was a Feeler, he knew better than to question his concern. "Hmmm, why don't you just plan on sticking close by? We don't know what Lamontage's next step is. I still find this whole retreat out of character for him, and why did he leave the boy behind?' He looked thoughtful then shook his head. "Lamontage wants a confrontation with Guardian. I just wish I knew when and where.." He glanced toward the left of the room then back at the screen. "He's gone somewhere to regroup and take his plan to the next level. I just wish we were a little more informed of the rules. ."

Tanner sighed. "Any update on his whereabouts?"

"They traced the flight from St. Moritz to Geneva to France to, JFK. He's doing much to confuse the radar, but he knows Guardian can track him. A driving service at JFK took him to Boston to meet with his own private Caravan of – well for lack of a better word – and I mean no offense to your mother, Son, Gypsies and I guess they took them the rest of the way."

"None taken, Sir. Were they able to trace the caravan any further?"

"We have a description and plate on the vehicle that Demi and Lamontage were in, but the plate came up empty, probably bogus. The satellite search turned up empty as well. They must have separated to be as inconspicuous as possible."

"So he's vanished. What about Demi?"

"The driving service remembered her. They said she appeared unharmed and not in distress. He thought they were married. She wore a ring of some type on her finger, and she was dressed in street clothes."

"They were wearing disguises, so they could get through any road block and customs."

"That would be my guess," Keys verified.

"So where do we go from here?"

"We go home and we regroup. Demi trusts us to pick up her trail and we will. The questions more pressing to me are why was the boy left behind? Why the states? and why now?"

Tanner shrugged. "He's not exactly anonymous in Europe anymore. They've linked him to the Liberatores, and he's a person of interest in several assassinations and terrorist attacks, since this dance through Switzerland. Maybe he's looking to set up shop elsewhere. He killed most of his followers when he fled the Subgonomic village in Lenk."

"Could be," Keys agreed, "but I guarantee he has not given up his desire to possess Marna, and that's what scares me."

"You and me both," Tanner stated. His heart beat a little faster in his chest. Keys had no idea how much that thought scared him.

"Stay close, Tanner, but get some sleep. We depart at seven AM. We'll try to piece it together when we get home. I think it is safe to say this battle with Lamontage may be over with the safe return of the children, but I think the war is just warming up."

"Will do, Sir," he signed off the conversation.

"Something important?" Marna queried, as she came through the doorway, and the teakettle started whistling."

He turned toward her, smiled, placed his GPC in his pocket, and moved to turn the water off. "Keys was checking in," he poured boiling water into two cups, glancing her way. She looked pale, drawn, and just plain worn down. Every impulse in him wanted to take her in his arms and hold her until it all went away, "how's the head?"

"Still there," she said taking the cup he offered her, "I think I've got a million little construction workers pounding the corner poles for a foundation up there." She leaned against the stove. "How was your audition as Mr. Mom?" she queried, wanting to change the subject.

He looked at her, grinned, and took a drink of tea, leaning his hips against the counter and sliding his eyes in her direction. "Should we start with the bickering over who the best looking band member of Mammas Boys is; Tory or Dylan? Or should we go to which Disney princess is the real thing and which one is just a clone. Or maybe we should veer toward why, at thirteen, we should not be thinking about the setting of a ring we would like to give a certain redhead back home. . ."

"Oh, tough one," Marna winced and took another drink of tea.

"Yeah, young love," he winked, "or we could possibly jump right to the why and why not of astral projecting into our sisters' room, in the middle of the night, and scaring them senseless by pulling the blankets off of them." He raised his brow, took another sip of tea, and smiled mischievously, his eyes twinkling.

"He didn't."

"He did."

"I sense a grounding coming on," she said tapping her cup with her fingernails.

"Not necessary. We took care of every grievance." He grinned.

She winced. "Dare I ask how?"

He chuckled, and stared at the liquid in the cup for a few seconds, before returning his eyes to her. "Diplomatically."

She stopped herself mid-sip and looked at him. "Why do I get the feeling you're enjoying this little game of 'I got a secret.' "

"Because I am," he grinned, "very much so." He took another sip.

"You are a strange man, Tanner Williams."

"So, I've been told." He held her gaze for a moment then sighed dramatically, "all right, I cannot continue to look into your eyes, when they reflect so much pain, and withhold information, it's just not right." He reached out and pushed a stray hair behind her ear. For a moment, they just stared at each other, and then he cleared his throat, drew in a deep breath, letting it out slowly. "The boy band discussion ended on an agreement about a third member being the best looking, the other two forgotten and peace restored. Cinderella won the princess crown, because she is what most girls wish to become. The ring was advised to be put on a back burner until Mom got home; a discussion I gladly hand off to you and Patty McGellan," he waved his hand in her direction.

"You're all heart, Tanner."

"Why thank you . . . and the astral projecting was counter attacked by a little telekinetic joke of a sheet flying into the boys' room on a basket ball and a certain little guy being scared straight . . ."

Marna nearly spit out her tea. . . "You didn't," she brought her eyes to his, trying not to laugh as she pictured Moses reaction to the sheet shrouded basketball.

"I'm wounded, you would even suspect such a thing, I don't even have the ability," he shrugged, and pushed away from the counter. "I just happened to be looking the other way when Elizabeth did," he winked, "turnabout being fair play and all that." He grinned and she shook her head, wondering if she was would have to include a psychologist's phone number on her rolodex. "Where are they now?" he asked.

"Isaiah is setting up a cot in his room for PJ," Tanner looked puzzled then he remembered.

"Oh, that's right, my bad, you're going to change their names."

"I don't want them having anything that connects them to the last six years of their life. I want them to have a fresh start."

Tanner studied her features for a moment. "Anyone ever tell you, you are a special lady, Marna Farlow?"

"Not recently, no," She smiled, and raised fingers to her temple, trying to massage the pain away.

"Well they should. Amongst all the chaos and the danger from entities unknown, you think of some tiny little detail that will make a major difference in someone's life." He took her teacup from her hand, placed it on the table, and then he took her hand and led her to a chair, had her sit, and started to knead her shoulders, then her neck. Marna felt the tension slip from her muscles. Then he moved to her head, and started working the base of her skull and moved his fingers upwards. She let out a sigh. "That's it, just let it out."

"You have magic fingers, Tanner Williams."

"So they say.,"

"They being?"

"Ah, Mrs K. Nanny's do have some privacy rights don't we?" He smiled as he felt the knots in her muscles just slip loose under his fingers and she relaxed. He worked steadily for twenty minutes. "How's the head?"

"Mmm, much better," she reached for her tea and took a sip, screwing up her nose "but my tea is cold."

"I'll make fresh while you go get the kids settled for the night. They've already had dinner.. Hein – I mean PJ – is probably exhausted, and Isaiah is on his chat date with Tammy." He glanced at the clock on the stove.

"Sounds like you've got their schedule all figured out,"

"Of course I do, I'm a Nanny. Remember?"

"What time do we leave in the morning?" She stood, casting a glance over her shoulder.

"Seven."

"Maybe you should think about going getting some rest too. I know how exhausting this brood can be. So I hereby release you from Nanny duties and you can leave."

"Oh, didn't I tell you," he walked to the sink and refilled the teakettle, putting it on the stove. I'm staying here tonight."

"Excuse me?"

"Keys and I thought it a good idea to keep you and the children under watch until we leave Switzerland, and we are safely out of Liberatores territory. You took down one of their soldiers, and have their leader on the run. You're probably on their wanted, dead or alive, list right now. Keys is staying with Kyle tonight, so I told him I would stay here."

"But . . ."

He rose a brow, "Really, Marna? You're not going to fight me on security now?" He crossed his arms and stood there, an immovable rock.

"Arrgh! When will you people realize I can take care of myself!" She demanded.

His lips quirked. "We all can, but I am your partner and you're exhausted. You've the added stress of a migraine so iust consider me a shot of sleep aide. You can go down for a solid eight and wake up refreshed, headache free."

She eyed him, and knew she would not win the argument. "Fine," she hissed and left to check the children. Tanner watched her go. She was right, she could take care of herself, but it made him feel better if he was there to offer her backup. He flipped the burner on, grabbed his laptop and set it up on the coffee table in the living room. He had gotten a strange email from his parents' old lawyer and he wanted to find out what it was about, considering he hadn't heard from him since his parents had passed sixteen years previous.

He smiled when he heard all the children say goodnight then Marna's soft voice returning the sentiment. She really was incredible. Her head was causing her much discomfort and yet, she still put everyone else before herself. She was a wonderful woman and an even better parent. He sat back on the couch and just listened as she stopped to read a story to the young ones, and then took the time to listen to all of their adventures while she was gone before she said good night. Then she made steps to her bathroom and turned on the shower.

It all seemed so natural, him sitting in her living room, opening and checking his email, while a 24-hour television news station played on in the background. He grinned and opened the email from the lawyer. He narrowed his eyes and frowned. Then after looking over the information twice, he called the number on the email, left his name and number, and disconnected. He would try again later. He brought his hand to his mouth and kept turning the information over in his head, until the teakettle whistled and he pushed off the couch

He moved about, pulling down the needed ingredients, using fresh leaves instead of the prepackaged teabags. The herb he had chosen was supposed to encourage relaxation and well-being. It might help Marna with her headache. His muscled arms rippled as he moved about preparing the cups.

Shortly, he felt her there. When he turned around, she was leaning against the door casing, just watching him. Her hair was damp and wavy, loose down to the center of her back. She was wearing a sweatshirt and lounge pants with a pair of boot slippers. She wore no makeup or enhancements on her face, but he thought she was the sexiest woman alive. He drew in a breath, and the smell of strawberries filled his senses. Letting it out in a slow sigh, he carried her tea over to her. She thanked him, before she took a sip. "I'm sorry," she said, wrapping her hands around the cup, enjoying the warmth.

"For what?" He raised a quizzical brow and braced himself on the casing above her, with the palm of his hand. Then he took a sip of his own tea.

His closeness brought with him the scent of spring rain. "I shouldn't have jumped on you like that, Tanner. I know you and Keys are only doing this because you care. I know Lamontage is a formidable enemy, and we all have reason to worry."

"Yeah, we do," he said, bringing his eyes to the brown liquid in his cup. His mother used to read tealeaves. He secretly wondered what she would tell him right now about this woman before him. How she fill his thoughts every waking moment of every day. Why was he here again? Her closeness confused his thoughts. He brought his eyes back up to hers. The blue depths pulled him in, feelings started to surface. He was losing the battle of keeping them at bay. He remembered the satisfaction of holding her earlier.

"It's just that sometimes I wonder if it will ever end. Will I ever have a normal life?"

His sideways smile was lazy, seductive. "Normal's overrated," he said softly.

"Funny," she said softly, feeling his presence way too much. Her heart beat increasing with every word. Her thoughts became jumbled. "Jeff used to say that."

"Jeff was a wise man," His voice was husky, emotions too strong to ignore overcame him, he put his tea down on the table then reached for hers and placed it beside his. She seemed as captivated by the moment as he did. He raised his hand and palmed her cheek, caressing it with his thumb. She leaned her face into his palm. Words he wanted to say caught in his throat. He tilted her head, his breath warm on her face. Then he brought his other arm down and snaked it around her waist, while he tunneled his first hand through her hair. He lowered his head purposely and captured her lips with his in a gentle, sweet kiss. It was caring and soft, not demanding, not bruising, just lips slipping in unison, with hers. The strength in her legs gave way. She leaned in to him to keep from slipping to the floor.

Her arms went around his waist, her hands exploring his back through the material of his shirt, her heart hammered against her rib cage.

When he came up for air, his eyes were darker in their intensity and he searched her face, speaking in a whisper, "Frumoasa mea Iubirii," My beautiful love. He spoke the words in Romanian, his mother's native tongue. A language she had taken with her and held close to her heart when her family had joined a great exodus to America, during the conflicts, to seek a better life.

Marna didn't know what it meant, but she loved the way he said it. It was so musical, so mystical. He brought his fingers to her face, caressed her cheek with the back of his hand, his eyes searching every line as if memorizing it, then he again cupped her face, his thumb feather light on her lips. "Marna, I . . ." her name came out in a whispered declaration, almost a desperate plea. He lowered his lips to hers again; she melted into him, returning his kiss with matching intensity.

He brought his hands down her spine to the small of her back, ran them up her body outline and pulled her tighter against him. She felt doors open between them, connections made, shields dropped, leaving them vulnerable to each other. Their kiss became deeper, bonding. His heart--his entire soul--was open to her, she could feel what he felt, the depth of his feelings for her, the desperate need he had to hold her in his arms, the love that had grown and bloomed so quietly, so sweetly, so steadily, for months, until it completely took over his soul. All of it was there for her to see, and to feel. He drew her into it and tears filled her eyes. She had never seen or felt anything so beautiful. Her heart ached. She pulled away as a lone tear tracked down her face, "why didn't you tell me?" she whispered.

"It never seemed the right moment," he whispered back. He brought his hand up to her face, palmed her cheek, his thumb tracing her lips, his breath warm on her face, smelling of peppermint tea, his eyes inches from her own, fire burning in the depths of them. He sensed a hesitance in her, and he felt a pain slice through his heart. Did he reveal his feelings too soon? Should he have opened the doors and let her in? His eyes raked over her features. "Maybe now isn't either." He started to pull away.

She didn't stop his retreat, more tears tracked down her face. What she had felt, what they had just experienced together, the feelings, the depth of them, they were so tender, so complete, that when he pulled away she had felt the emptiness heavy on her heart. Her fingers gently touched his face, traced it with a feather light touch. "God, Tanner, I'm so confused. I don't know what's happening here. I don't know what this thing is that is developing between us. I need time to figure it out. I need time to figure me out, my feelings. I don't want to start something, I might not be able to finish. Her eyes moved over his face, "Can you understand that?"

He looked at her, gently wiped away the tears tracking down her cheeks. "Marna, I'm not asking you to go forward with something you aren't ready for. I'm just telling you it's there. What I feel for you is real, but I can wait. We can wait. Do you understand what I'm saying?" She leaned into his hand.. "All I'm asking is that you'll at least allow the possibility. Don't shut me out."

"Tanner, I. . ." She sighed, worrying her lower lip with her teeth. A storm of emotions passed through his eyes; pain, love, hopelessness. She couldn't give him the assurance he desired. Could she even give him hope? He stepped back and turned away from her. She touched his shoulder and he shrugged it off, putting more distance between them, before he turned to look at her. She dropped her hand, and lowered her eyes. What he offered scared her. To commit to something that deep scared her. Two men had approached her in as many days, and all they wanted was a chance. Could she get beyond her fear of moving on to give them that. "Maybe when things settle down and we're home and I can think things through better, or maybe I'll be stuck in this rut forever. I just don't know."

Tanner reigned in his emotions, his desires, his needs, all of them; got control of them and replaced his shields. He had laid it all out to her and it was up to her now. He ran his hands through his hair before turning back to her. The muscles in his face bunched then relaxed. He swallowed. The silence thundered between them as he thought about his next words very carefully. He didn't want to be harsh, or his words to cause her anymore pain, but he wanted her to understand where he was coming from. "There is always going to be another investigation, Marna, always going to be another obstacle in the way. It's called life. It may always be complicated, but you have to rise above it. He's not coming back, Iubirea mea, and I know how deep your love for him ran, but you can't go through life loving a ghost. I don't think he would have wanted that."

"Tanner, I . . ."

"Don't," He raised his hands, palms out and brought his eyes to hers. They weren't full of betrayal or anger. They were full of love and understanding. "I'm a patient man, and what I feel for you is real, So. Very. Real.," his voice was husky, "it's not just a roll in the hay, I'm looking for here. I love you, Marna, and when you've finally realized how much I do and you want to stop drifting, I'll be there to give you a hand up, but I can't forget what just happened nor can I make it less than what it was, so don't expect me to." He sighed and swallowed. "I'll talk to Keys as soon as we get back to the states, because to be perfectly honest with you, I don't know if I can handle 'just partners' after holding you like that," he reached for his GPC and looked at the caller ID, then before he left the kitchen, he kissed her gently on the forehead. Marna crossed her arms, watched him go, and drew in a deep breath, trying to regain control of her emotions, feeling the cold after absorbing the warmth of his arms, his touch, his love. However, she didn't go after him, she didn't stop him. She heard him speak into his phone.

"Yes this is Tanner Williams," he cleared his throat, "You're office sent me an email . . ." He moved out of hearing range to finish his call. She looked at the tea on the table and decided she didn't want it after all. She doubted he'd want his either. She dumped them both down the sink and headed to bed. As she passed through the living room, she stopped a moment and watched his back. Could she be letting go of something very special? She hadn't felt emotions that intense in a long time. Though she enjoyed Kyle's company, what she felt that moment with Tanner was so much deeper, she could have gotten lost in it, in him.

She took a step toward him. He stopped his typing and raised his head, but didn't try to look in her direction. Without another word, she turned on her heal and went to bed. Tanner turned to watch her go, fighting the urge to follow. When he heard the click of her door close, he got up and moved to the window to look out over the dark night. Tomorrow they would return home, get back into their regular routine. He didn't really want to lose her as a partner, but to have her that close every day. He sighed.,. Maybe they could get beyond this, set it aside, and when she was ready, they could discuss it further, but for now, he had to let it go. Lamontage was still out there, still a threat to her, still a threat to her family and he would not let him get to them. That's what he had to focus on now.

Marna stood in her room leaning against the door, the thoughts going through her mind mirrored Tanner's. Could she continue to work with him, knowing how he felt? Could she let go of the past and move toward him, as he wanted? Could she have that all consuming love with Tanner? What about her feelings for Kyle? Were they purely physical? A lustful attraction? She was dangerously attracted to him, but she didn't know if what had started in that hotel room could turn into something lasting and meaningful. She didn't have the same reaction to him that she had had toward Tanner. She knew nothing about Kyle, he was a mystery, but Tanner she knew him; he was honorable, responsible, sturdy, and caring. He would give everything in him to a relationship to make it work. What would Kyle give away from the bedroom? She had seen him take chances, seen him risk a mission to be a hero. Could she have that kind of recklessness in her life? Could the children? Her head throbbed again. She closed her eyes.

Moving on with her life was proving to be so hard. "God, Jeff, I miss you so much. I miss what we had together." A tear slid down her face as she walked over to her bed, "Why couldn't I just go to sleep and find out the last year was just a horrible, horrible nightmare or someone's cruel idea of a joke? I could wake up to your crooked smile and have you tell me that it was just a dream? Reassure me it was all going to be all right." She flipped off the light and slipped between the sheets, pulling the extra pillow close to her chest, maybe she could imagine she held him in her arms and it would all go away. Maybe going back home was a good idea, maybe she could get back to her regular routine, she could have a normal life or as close to normal as these twisted gifts would allow her. She fell asleep remembering two kisses from two very different men.

~~~~~

Marna tossed and turned, and around two AM, she finally fell into a restless sleep disturbed with images she didn't understand.

A symbol filled her field of vision. She was wandering through the forest, on an overgrown path, alone. She was wearing a pair of fatigues, but camouflaged for the jungle. Foreign symbols she had never seen before were carved into trees around her. She stopped to study another one as she walked along. It has two capital A's side by side with an arrow slicing through them. she unsnapped the holster strap on her hip, resting her hand on the but of the gun, before she pushed away from the tree and continued down the path. There was a rustling in the bushes to her right. Startled, Marna pulled her gun and pivoted on the balls of her feet, pointing it, ready to fire. She let out a heavy sigh when she saw who stood before her.. "Why are you here?"

"Sasha." She brought her hand back to her side, looking around. "Guess I could ask you the same thing." Sasha looked at the symbols as well. A thought occurred to Marna and fear clawed at her throat. "Sasha, do you have dream weaving abilities?" Sasha shook her head. "Dream walking?" Again, the young woman shook her head. "Ahh, hell." Marna walked up, grabbed Sasha's arm, put her behind her and backed her further into the brush.

"What?" Sasha queried.

"Lamontage." Marna searched the horizon. "I think we're about to become the stars in his latest nightmare movie script.

"Double hell." Sasha echoed Marna's earlier sentiment, looking around, "What do you think he's up to?"

The scene changed, they were deep in the forest. The clearings and the paths were gone. Sunlight barely made it between the canopies of leaves. Monkeys sounded off and swung from tree limb to tree limb, a big cat cried from somewhere off to their right. A wolf cried from somewhere deeper in the foliage. A Coyote's triumphant bark sounded off to the left, Marna brought her gun up, the barrel parallel to her nose, facing upward. She nodded to Sasha who pulled out her gun, and did the same. The look on Sasha's face exposed the fear she felt within. Marna looked her in the eye. "Sasha, listen to me," she hissed, "the only way we're going to survive this, is together. There has to be a reason he pulled us into this vortex, I'm not sure what his sick game is, but I'm not about to let him win. Do you understand?" Sasha nodded. She thought about their combined abilities. Sasha was a tracker/ locator. Lamontage wanted them to find something. Something he wanted them to go after, otherwise it would be no challenge to him. Demi! "Sasha, can you get a lock on Demi."

"I-I don't know, I don't have anything of hers to use as a guide."

Marna's eyes were constantly moving, forever searching. Then she remembered the appearance of the Machete when she and Bryan pinpointed the castle. "You, don't need it here, Sasha." Sasha looked at her. "I don't have time to explain, now, but just close your eyes and combine your locating and tracking ability."

"Okay." Sasha closed her eyes as she focused her energies on finding Demi, Marna kept a close eye on their surroundings. Finally, Sasha opened them and turned her head toward Marna. "A house, north of here."

"Did she know you were there?"

Sasha shook her head. "No. She was sleeping on some kind of canopy bed."

"Drugged?"

Sasha shook her head. "I couldn't tell."

"All right, we'll go with what we have. Lead the way."

Sasha went in front of Marna and they started making their way through thickets and heavy brush toward Demi's location. . . ever wary of their surroundings.

~~~~

Demi awoke with a start. She was not sure what had awakened her, but she was sensing trouble. She pulled the coverings off her, swung her legs over the side of the bed, and slipped her feet into the slippers left for her, pushing herself to standing. She grabbed the robe at the foot of her bed, and walked over to the window to look out over the forested terrain. She knew there was a country road, beyond the stockade fence, cutting through the New Hampshire Mountains, but rows of trees obscured it from the house. A private road led from the town road to the house through a canopy of Oak and Maple trees. It was dark when they arrived the night before, but Demi had seen the beautiful Villa from the many lights spaced around the horse shoe driveway. A Dark eyed beauty, with wavy dark hair had met them at the door.

~~~~

She stood about 5'2" tall and weighed in at about 145 pounds of pure muscle. She camouflaged her height some with three-inch heels to compliment the ankle length, white linen skirt, and a peacock blue, peasant blouse. She chose to decorate her home in a Western tone with buffalo statues and paintings in the hallway. She hugged Pierre like a long lost lover, and raked her eyes over Demi with obvious disapproval. "An Irish girl, Pare? I never took you for a green lover." Demi had to tamp down her biting retort, in order to keep up appearances, she had to make him and those around him believe she was under his control.

"She is a means to an end Jezzy, When is Morgan due our way again?"

"Whatever have you got up your sleeve, Darling," She eyed him suspiciously.

"I thought an exchange, but new information has come my way that makes someone else much more valuable to me. A change in plans is called for and killing her seems such a waist, when Morgan can make it a bit more rewarding for me."

"What's in it for me?" She queried inspecting Demi closer.

He placed a finger under her chin, and lifted her face so their eyes met. "You get to live."

Anger flashed in her eyes and she pulled free of his hand. Her guards, guns aimed right at Pierre and Demi, instantly surrounded them. Instantly a Taser went off, trapping him and Demi in a bluish shield of electrical current. Jezebel Amanar stood before him, staring him directly in the eye, "You'd be best, Pare," she hissed at him, "to remember I am not one of your mindless robots." She waved a hand quickly, her bangle bracelets clattering on her arm. The intensity of the beam increased. Demi groaned and fell to her knees, sweat appeared on Pierre's brow. "I will not hesitate to destroy you or your green trash." She waved her hand again, more clattering. The bluish beam let up and Pierre drew in a deep breath, Demi collapsed, two guards grabbed her and held her between them. "Next time you even think of laying a hand on me, I will kill you," she said. Pierre grabbed her wrist, his breathing labored. Her guard readied the taser again, but she held him off raising her other hand. She turned and stared Pierre directly in his eyes. "Right now, your abilities are not reliable Pare. Your brain feels like mush. You try you burn. I am stronger and more capable then you and you know it. Any attempt to launch an attack at me, will most certainly result in your imminent death and you know it."

"Gypsy Witch." He spoke between clenched teeth and labored breaths, but let go of her hand.

"Morgan will be here in a month. She may bring me 500K, you will get 150K, and I will keep the rest to compensate for keeping her on ice for you." She waved her hand again, more clattering of her bangles. She turned toward her men, as they came toward her, flanking Pierre. they grabbed him by his biceps. Then she turned to a young servant awaiting orders in the background. "Sallvi, take his Irish trash upstairs to the Princess room."

"Yes, Ms. Jezebel." She moved forward and she traded places with one of the soldiers as they stepped back. Demi leaned heavily on her.

Jezebel then turned back toward Pierre. "You're lucky, Pare, she fits many descriptions on my waiting list, or we'd have nothing to discuss and you would both die." She nodded to the soldiers and watched as they practically dragged Pierre out of the house. Then she turned toward Demi. "You will be closely watched, but treated well, don't try anything stupid, because whatever Pare did to you, think tenfold, and that's what I can do to you." Demi downcast her eyes, feigning meekness, "You behave, we'll get along just fine and your stay here will be comfortable, " You become difficult," she drew in a breath and let it out, "let's just say your stay, what you just experienced, is just the beginning." She gestured up the stairs with her head then she moved into the drawing room.

~~~~~

Demi's eyes took in the room she was standing in. She did not turn on the lights, because she did not want to alert anyone of her wakefulness. The house was silent. They had locked the bedroom door; she had tried it earlier. She had simply traded one prison for another one, but at least this one, she had a better chance of survival, or so she hoped. She puffed out a breath and looked around the rest of the room. It was done in pastel colors and Romanian rugs. A canopy bed stood in the center, draped in a satin comforter the color of a midsummer sunset, and trimmed with white lace; the same white lace that draped the windows.

She looked around, the bedposts, head and footboard, were all painted a princess white with etchings of flowers and delicate designs carefully crafted into the surface. She reached out and felt them with her fingertips. As prisons go, she could think of worse ones. She drew in a breath and let it out slowly. This was the end of the line for her unless she found a way to escape and soon. Pierre said he had found a better bargaining chip and that she had become useless to him. Who? He was looking for an exchange, she knew for whom, and she could not let that happen. She could not let Marna fall into Pierre's hands. She brought her fist to her lips and swallowed back the bile as she thought about what he planned for Marna. She knew what she had suffered, she could only imagine the horrors he had planned for Marna. She pulled the silk robe about herself and wrapped her arms around her mid-section.

Her mind raced. She brought her eyes back to the window. Was there a town nearby? If she made a break for it, would she get to safety before they caught up to her? Would she find help? Could she have time to warn Marna and Keys about the upcoming threat? She started to formulate a plan. She had to gain the trust of Jezzy. Pierre had called her that. She had to gain her trust, so she could gain a little freedom. Did the woman know who she was? Did she know of Guardian? Was she aware what Lamontage was involving her in? Of course she was, hadn't she taken control of Lamontage? Didn't she threaten him? Demi had actually sensed his fear and anxiety. This woman scared him. What had he called her? A Gypsy witch? Was that truly what she was? Had Demi fallen into the hands of the lost tribe of the Ambrosian Gypsies? The legend the college had an entire class about? She shivered. If she had, then she needed to get away, and she needed to get away fast, because they had mixed their psychic abilities with the art of black magic and had become the most powerful people in the Dark Realm, especially during the Conflicts. They valued no one. They were on the side of neither the government forces nor the FOF. Demi turned as she heard movement by the door. She froze when she saw the silhouette in the half-opened doorway.

"Couldn't sleep?" Demi bowed her head, and raised her hands in a defensive motion, but didn't utter a word. The figure approached her, slowly. "Put your hands down, I'm not going to hurt you." Demi slowly, carefully lowered her hands, and backed up as the newcomer moved forward, until her knees hit the window seat and she sat down hard on the cushions, again she put her hands up. A gentle hand took them and lowered them. "You poor thing. I can only imagine the horrors you went through at his hand. He is an evil man."

Demi looked at her again, and then looked away. She was a much younger version of Jezebel with a few exceptions; she had the wavy dark hair, but green eyes instead of the dark. Her skin was bronze in tone, and flawless. She wore a spaghetti strapped nightgown, floor length, with a sheer robe pulled over it. Her eyes continued to study her quarry. "Look at me." Demi cautiously looked her way, but not before she put her shields in place. "That's better, now we can talk like women. She reached for the chair by the dressing table and dropped her slender form into it. "What's your name?" Demi looked confused. "Come now, he didn't do that much damage," she studied Demi's face, "or did he?" Her eyes never faltered. Something flashed in them. "Is he that much of a heathen that he stole your identity?"

"Demi." Demi mumbled.

"Say again?" Esmeralda Amanor tilted her head to listen more closely.

"Demi – he calls me Demi.."

"Ah, now we're getting somewhere. Demi what?"

Demi shook her head.

"No worries, we'll figure it out later." She waved her hand, dismissing the issue. She leaned back in the chair. "Do you know how long you've been with him?" Demi shook her head.

Esmeralda studied her. "Interesting. Do you have a logodnic?"

Demi raised her eyes to Esmeralda's. "What?"

"A fiance, a betrothed," she leaned forward and whispered conspiritorily, "a Lover?"

Demi shook her head, she could not let the woman find out about Bryan. "I belong to the Master." Demi whispered, again lowering her eyes.

She scoffed. "He's about as desirable as a skunk, come on, femeie, you must have felt that forbidden desire for someone in your life other than Pare?" Demi shook her head. "Then you have been deprived. He has stolen so much from you."

"He is good to me," her voice trembled.

"Is that why you look like you are about to jump out of your skin?" She got up, touched Demi's hair. In character, Demi cringed. Esmerelda pulled her hand back. "Such beautiful hair, like fire at it's brightest. Tomorrow I start giving you back what he has taken. You are my charge, Demi, whoever you are, and I will give you your life back." She put the chair back by the vanity. "Go back to bed, get some sleep, tomorrow you begin to see a whole new world." She left the room.

Demi smiled. "Yes, you will." Someone was smiling down on her. She went back to bed.

*****

Marna and Sasha entered a clearing. A small brook ran through it, rocks were scattered about, and patches of flowers bloomed to welcome spring. Marna sat down on a large boulder by the brook, wiping her brow and Sasha sat besider her. After looking around warily, Marna reached for the canteen hooked to her belt, took a drink, and offered it to Sasha.

"Thanks," Sasha tipped the canteen up and took a swallow, bringing it back to her lap and drawing in a cleansing breath.

"Have you gotten anything else?"

Sasha closed her eyes and tracked. "No, nothing. She must not be using her abilities."

"Anything in the area you tagged earlier?"

"No, nothing."

"Keep trying." Marna stood up, looking around the clearing, they had been walking for hours it seemed but the darkness still pressed down on them. However, that's not what worried her. She and Sasha still remained alone in this realm, no other human to speak of, no animal had so much as crossed their path, no Pierre, and no Demi. She found herself waiting for something to happen, something out of the ordinary, something that moved them forward, something – sinister. She heard a deep growl, it sounded close by. Gasping, she turned toward the noise. Nothing but inky blackness. "Sasha," she whispered, "we need to move on. That one sounded a little too close for comfort." She

glanced at the dark woodline nervously, then tapped Sasha's shoulder. "Come on," she started to walk away, but when she noticed Sasha didn't move, she looked down at her. The younger woman was still as stone, staring at the forested area they had just come from. Marna moved her eyes in that direction. Instantly two dark forms crossed the wooded line into clearing. They were cats, black as the night with green eyes and large heads. Marna froze. "Shit," she whispered, enter Pierre's dream-invader entertainment. "Sasha, don't make any sudden moves."

"You don't have to tell me twice." She hissed. She eased herself to a standing position. "How sweet of him to send one for each of us."

The surroundings changed. They were standing in the middle of a coliseum, enclosed in cement. The cats moved forward cautiously. Crowds were cheering. Marna and Sasha were dressed in white gowns, draping off the shoulder on one side, brass belts around their waists. Their hair was loose, on their heads was tiaras of rhinestones and sapphires, their feet were dressed with flat foot sandals, and in their hands appeared swords. "Now I know what a mouse feels like." Across the circular, dirt, arena a doorway appeared out of nowhere. "Great, he's giving us a fighting chance. The only problem is we have to make it through his pets to get there." The cats started to fan out around them as the crowd burst out in excited blood lust.

Sasha put her back against Marna's stayin in step with her as they spun slowly with their swords ready. "What do we do now."

Marna swallowed. "We've got one shot, Sasha, but you have to trust me, and once we connect, you can't let go."

"Marna, if you can get us out of here in once piece I'll hold on to whatever you say."

Marna chuckled. She glanced up at the crowd, she saw him standing there, but refused to look into his eyes. "All right, shields up." Sasha did as she said.

'You can't escape, came a whispered reply but come to me and I'll let your friend live.' Pierre intruded her thoughts

'Sorry, not in the mood for bargaining with the devil today,' she answered

'Ahh, Ma cher, you wound my heart'

'That ain't all I'm going to wound by the time I'm done with you, Sucker.'

I can give you a life like no other.

'Sorry, not into rape of the soul.' She blocked communication. Pierre waved his hand and the cats let out a yell and ran toward them.

"Take my hand !" She yelled to Sasha, who immediately replied, and simultaneously Marna threw up her cloak, spun on her feet, grabbed Sasha and jumped, landing them both on the ground, rolling away as the panthers landed where they had stood moments before. The only thing there, was Sasha's sword, she had lost it on impact. Marna noticed she still had Sasha's hand. "You okay." Sasha nodded. She looked up. The mist was still swirling around them, which meant her cloak was still up. "Come on, we've got to keep moving." She stood up and turned toward the door as the cats circled the area, looking for their prey. Marna and Sasha, hand in hand, ran toward the large opening at the back of the arena. 50 feet, 25 feet; the crowd's displeasure thundered in her ears as they demanded their blood lust be satisfied. 10 feet, "Almost there !" Out of nowhere Marna felt Sasha ripped away from her and she was slammed, face first, into the packed ground as the cloak disipated around her.

She lifted her head up. Sasha kicked and screamed as a guard dragged her back toward the arena. "No !" Marna pushed herself up, but as she tried to make it toward Sasha, another guard got between them and slammed her down, her sword slipped from her hands and meaty hands went around her throat, She pulled at his hands to try to keep him from strangling her. She Kicked up but he was able to dodge her blows. She felt around for a rock, something, and she immediately felt her hand hit something hard and cold. A piece of Cement! She grabbed it and swung up, catching him at the temple. She sprung herself up from the ground, and before he had a chance to get his bearings, she had her *sword and advanced on him sinking it deep into his left quadrant, through his heart. He faded from the dream. She wiped the blood off her face, and looked toward the area she had last seen Sasha struggling with her assailant and was in time to see her captor drag her toward the cats. Sasha's screams echoed in her head as she struggled to get away. She started to run toward them, but a third cat jumped into her path. She stopped, facing off with the animal, her eyes locked with the cat, she frantically looked around for a weapon. The crowd cheered, Sasha screamed. The cat readied to pounce. 'What a way to go, as cat chow.' PJ appeared between her and the cat.*

"PJ, no, get out of there." She reached for him, but he shrugged her off. He and the cat seemed to be in a face off of some kind, the cat growled a couple of times, and then he calmed and laid down. Marna grabbed PJ by the shoulder and eased him back, she watched as the cat commenced cleaning himself.

"We need to go." PJ said, turning toward her. "He's coming for us."

"Sasha." Marna shoved PJ behind her and looked up in time to see the guard lift Sasha up and throw her into the arena and raise her hands up in defense as the cats pounced on her. Her screams filled the arena. Saaashaaaa! Nooooo! She brought her and to her mouth. PJ grabbed the other one and closed his eyes as Pierre made his way down the steps between seats.

~~~~~

Marna! Get out! Now! The security blanket engulfed her, and she woke up screaming and crying out for Sasha. She struck out as strong arms circled around her. "Marna! It's me. It's Tanner !" He gave her a hard shake to bring her around. She looked at him, blankly at first, then she focused. Tears streamed down her face, bile rose in her throat.

"Tell them to check on Sasha?" she ordered.

"What?"

"Just do it! " She cried. Tanner pulled out his GPC and punched in the one button intercom to reach Keys."PJ" She ran out of the bedroom and into the hallway toward PJ's room. Tanner followed as his GPC beeped.

Keys face swam to focus. "What is it, Tanner, what's happened."

"Keys, Marna said to check Sasha." He appeared in the hall, just at Marna came out of PJ's room.

She grabbed Tanner's link. "Key's just do it !" Tears streamed down her face, "Please."

Keys looked confused and alarmed at the same time. "Marna, what's happened?"

"Just do it Keys." She pleaded. He turned away from the GPC and motioned to somebody behind him. Seconds later, they heard Bryan's voice in the background.

"Oh my. . . Keys, you need to come, now." His voice had a heightened sound of fear. Keys got up, and walked into Sasha's room. The video caught arterial spray on her headboard.

Keys moved quickly out of the room and came back on the screen. "She's gone." Marna retched and ran toward the bathroom.

"Keys, what the hell just happened?" Tanner asked.

The older man looked stricken. "I suspect Pierre just made his next move. The dream realm just crossed into reality.." He signed off. Tanner swallowed as he closed the GPC and heard water running in Marna's bathroom.

"Dear God what do we do now?" he whispered. He let his head drop into his hands and then ran them through his hair.

Chapter Fourteen

Marna sat on the couch in Keys' Zurich apartment. Tanner had tried to get her to stay away, but she wouldn't, she couldn't. He had called Rose and Kurt to stay with the children and had accompanied her to Keys' suite. Bryan was supervising the loading of the van for the trip to the airfield, while the local CSU was combing Sasha's room for clues to an intruder, but they all knew they wouldn't find one. What had killed Sasha was not of this world. She sniffed as Tanner brought her some tea.

"Marna, this isn't your fault," he said softly. His heart ached to see her in such distress.

"I should have watched the parameters closer. I knew the power Pierre held in that realm."

"He would have used something to distract you. There was a reason he put you and Sasha together." Marna nodded. Sasha was younger, weaker than Marna and only possessed passive abilities. She could not fight off an attack as someone else could have. She also didn't have PJ."

"I can't get her screams out my head, Tanner. Oh God, they were so loud, so pathetic, she was so scared." Her hands trembled, causing her tea to slosh over the cup's brim. Tanner retrieved the teacup from her trembling grip, and placed it on the coffee table, and then he took her hands in his. She didn't pull them away. "I thought I had saved her. I thought we had escaped." She pulled her hands free and wiped at her face.

"He probably had an Observer nearby, they probably penetrated the cloak."

"I should have thought of that, Tanner, I should have considered that. Oh my God, Sasha, I'm so sorry." She dropped her head in her hands.

He pulled her into his arms as she cried. "Shhhh, it's okay." She leaned into him.

Kyle watched from a chair across the room in shocked silence. Sasha gone? She had been his partner for four years. "How are you, Son?" Keys said as he came and sat beside him and patted his knee.

"I'm not sure. Is this real, Keys? God . . ." he swallowed. "The marks on her body, the look in her eyes. How can he force the horrors of a nightmare to the reality of life?"

"Pierre is a powerful adversary. He wanted to make a statement." He sighed moving his gaze toward Marna. "I think he made it loud and clear. Marna's a wreck. It may be a long time before she can bury this."

"Have you been able to get anything coherent out of her?"

He shook his head. "uh, nuh. She's still in a state of shock. I'm hoping Tanner has better luck, with that. They're good friends as well as partners." He pulled his eyes back to Kyle. The boy continued to watch Tanner and Marna. "Kyle, you had a pretty rough experience and now this thing with Sasha. Why don't you go with Bryan to the plane to board early . . ." He gestured to Bryan.

"I'm fine." Kyle said, his words a little too stern.

"No, you're not. I've lost one agent tonight. I don't want to lose another. Please, Son, I'm begging you. We'll be along as soon as they get Sasha taken care of. We're taking her home for autopsy and burial." Kyle looked at Keys, his face showed signs of sorrow and concern.

"Okay." His voice was calmer. He carefully pushed himself up and walked, favoring his right side, toward the door with Bryan. Keys let his eyes follow him to the door then he let them drift back to Tanner and Marna.

"Marna's getting her own fan club," Ventura said as he walked up to Keys. He saw Kyle glance Marna's way once more before he followed Bryan out the door.

"Huh?" Keys looked Ventura's way, and then nodded. "These things have a way of working themselves out."

"Until then?"

"They're all professionals; they'll figure a way around it."

"I don't think they're all aware of the storm brewing." He glanced Tanner's way.

"He will be." He stepped back as they wheeled Sasha out in a body bag. He caught Marna's eye across the room.

Marna returned his gaze and then watched as they wheeled the gurney out the door. "What happens now?" She asked Tanner.

"They get her ready for the trip home and then they send her back to Maine. Her family claims the body, and we bury another agent with honors." Tanner answered quietly.

"She was so young, Tanner," Marna said, "Keys said she had only been with Guardian WIT five years. She was senior partner in her and Kyle's team, but still so very young."

"You can't go on blaming yourself."

"I just can't get the look on her face, when she saw those cats, out of my mind."

"Marna, look at me." He took her hands and she turned her eyes toward him. "What happened, everything in the dream realm, Lamontage owns. He's the one who has Sasha's blood on his hands, the only one." His eyes strayed to the angry red marks circling her neck, anger ripped through him. "And he almost had yours on them too." He drew in a breath to gain control of his emotions. "You are free of guilt. We've all been there. Sometimes, the simple truth is the bad guy gets a point on the scorecard."

"Well our scorecard isn't looking too good right now, Tanner, first Demi, now Sasha. When is it all going to stop? When are good people going to stop dying because of me?" She sniffed and rubbed at the fresh tears spilling onto her face.

Keys appeared before them with a box of tissues. Tanner looked up at him, his eyes pleading with his mentor, Marna's hand resting comfortably in his, he was at a loss for words. He had never seen her like this. "Unfortunately, Marna, it will probably never end." Keys sat down on the coffee table across from her. He believed being truthful was the only way to reach her. She had a very valuable gift and unfortunately there were people out there that wanted to possess it, possess her. He drew in a breath. It was time to take off the kid gloves with his newest agent. He loved her like a daughter, but coddling her was not going to keep her alive. "Oh I could lie to you and say that we take Pierre out, it will end or maybe after the next one, or the one after that and so on, but the truth is, Marna, there will always be someone else. Another greedy Bastard wanting what you have."

"I can't handle the agents that have fallen. Tate, Sherry, Sasha, J--" She choked back a sob. "Jeff. I don't think I can handle it anymore."

Keys' eyes flashed. He lowered his voice to a stern whisper. "Agent Farlow, do you think you are the only agent that has been the center of an investigation by which other agents have fallen." She looked him in the eye, saw something she had never before seen aimed at her. His eyes were hot with anger and his voice tight with emotion. It snapped her out of her stupor.

"Keys, I--"

"You what?" He demanded. "You want to show the enemy how weak you are? Make it easier for him to get to you?"

"Keys, now's not the – " Tanner interjected, anger seeping into his voice.

"Stand down, Williams." Keys ordered. "This does not concern you."

"Keys – " Tanner's voice became tight.

"No, Tanner, he's right – " She squeezed his hand, and glanced his way. "I'm making myself and all of you vulnerable." She drew in a breath and let it out. She thought about Key's wife. She had fallen because of him. Jeff had fallen to save Rose, and she knew he would do it again, even knowing the outcome. "This isn't just about me. This is about the entire Guardian family. We just lost a member of our family, and another one is still out there suffering God knows what at the hands of that monster, and I'm being selfish." She brought her eyes back to Keys. "I'm sorry. I guess I just needed to be reminded of that."

"We all have those moments." He drew in a breath. "Do you feel up to going back?"

"Keys?" Tanner interjected, but Keys silenced him with a glance.

"Going back – You mean?" He nodded. She remember the experience in the restaurant – It seemed so long ago – so much had happened, but in truth it had only been a couple of days. "Why?" Her hand trembled; Tanner pressed it more firmly to let her know he would not leave her side. He would stay with her as long as needed.

"Sometimes a second look, a more distant look, can fill in the blanks, possibly give us a clue."

"You're thinking you can tap into Sasha's tracking if you go back there," Tanner stated. Keys nodded.

Marna sniffed. "Is that even possible? I mean with Sasha gone?"

Keys chose his next words carefully. "She wasn't gone at that moment in time, Marna. It's just walking through your memory. Pierre can't hurt you. However, the exercise may give us a clue as to Demi's whereabouts. We can stop any time you want, simply by breaking contact. Are you willing to try?"

She sniffed, wiped at a stray tear, and looked Keys way, then at Tanner. "Will you go too?" Tanner looked Keys way for verification, Keys nodded. She returned her eyes to Keys. "You really think this will work?"

"It's worth a try."

"All right then." She drew in a breath, wiped her hands on her jeans, reached her hand out to him, and tightened her grip on Tanner's hand. Within moments their abilities interwove, became one.

They were encircled in a cloaking mist and crackling current of natural energy. Then they found themselves standing on the outskirts of the dream's beginnings. Marna took a breath. Tanner pressed her hand and concentrated on encircling her with his blocking, but instead he encircled them all. He looked Keys way, and Keys winked at him. Marna's magnifying ability. They all moved their eyes to the unfolding of the dream before them. Marna remembered every detail as it replayed.

~~~~~

"Why are you here?"

Marna saw herself pull her gun and pivot on the balls of her feet pointing it, ready to fire. Her apparition sighed heavily, when she saw who stood before her. *"Sasha." She brought her hand back to her side, looking around. "Guess I could ask you the same thing."* Marna remembered the recognition that had overcome her at that moment. *"Sasha, do you have dream weaving abilities?" Sasha shook her head. "Dream walking?" Again, the young woman shook her head. "Ahh, hell."* Marna watched herself pulled Sasha further into the brush.

"What?" Sasha queried.

"Lamontage." Marna found herself searching the horizon with her past apparition. "I think we're about to become the stars in his latest nightmare movie script."

"Double hell." Sasha echoed and looked around. "What do you think he's up to?"

Being outsiders looking in, they actually saw the fading of the scenes as Pierre had changed them. It was like watching a life size television when the screen faded to dark. *They were deep in the forest. The clearings and the paths were gone. Sunlight barely made it between the canopies of leaves. Monkeys sounded off and swung from tree limb to tree limb, a big cat cried from somewhere off to their right. A wolf cried from somewhere deeper in the foliage. A Coyote's triumphant bark sounded off to the left. Marna watched as her apparition brought the gun up, the barrel parallel to her nose, facing upward. A nod in Sasha's direction and Sasha mirrored the action. The look on Sasha's face exposed the fear she felt within.* Marna shivered as the memory brought back the emotion she felt at that moment then she felt Tanner take a step closer to her, she looked his way, he slipped an arm around her waist, held her close, she let her head fall onto his shoulder. She returned her attention to the apparitions. "You okay?" he whispered, and she nodded.

"Sasha, listen to me," the dream-Marna hissed, *"the only way we're going to survive this, is together. There has to be a reason he pulled us into this vortex, I'm not sure what his sick game is, but I'm not about to let him win. Do you understand?"* Sasha nodded. She thought about their combined abilities. The dream-Marna looked puzzled, and then seconds later her whole face changed. *"Sasha, can you get a lock on Demi."*

"I-I don't know, I don't have anything of hers to use as a guide."

More indecision, then "You, don't need it here, Sasha." Sasha looked at her. "I don't have time to explain now, just close your eyes and combine your locating and tracking ability."

"Okay." Sasha closed her eyes as she focused her energies on finding Demi. Dream-Marna nervously kept her eyes moving on the surrounding forestland. Finally, Sasha opened them and turned her head toward Marna. *"A house, north of here."*

"Did she know you were there?"

Sasha shook her head. "No. She was sleeping on some canopy bed."

"Drugged?"

"Couldn't tell."

"Lead the way, Sash."

~~~~~

Suddenly the scene froze, as if somebody had hit the pause button on a DVD. She quickly turned her eyes on Keys. He had his eyes closed, he was trying to plug into Sasha's tracking ability and Marna, with closed eyes, plugged in her budding locating ability. Pictures flashed before her eyes. She saw several cars driving up a highway. She tried to focus on a sign, a landscape, anything that might give her a hint. Then 89 north flittered across her mind, and then she saw mountains, a small town, a deserted country road, and then a Villa, circled with bursting spring flowers on a lush green lawn. A sign with Ambrosian Hill village burned into it, filled her mind's eye. She faltered, and Keys broke contact. They returned and she gasped for air.

"Slow deep breaths, Marna." He turned to Tanner. "Get her some water, Tanner, please." Tanner disappeared and returned a few seconds later with a tall glass of water. Marna took it and took a long, cool drink. She drew in a breath and let it out. Her heartbeat returned to normal, and her breathing steadied.

"Tell me what happened, Marna? What frightened you?"

"I-I don't know. It wasn't anything in the vision, it was almost like something took hold of me and stole the air from my lungs, and I couldn't breathe." She sighed. "The sign said Ambrosian Hill Village. Have you ever heard of such a place?'"

"No, however, there are many unclaimed villages in the mountains of America. Friends of Freedom rebels set up many small settlements during the conflicts, throughout New England, that to this day are unknown. Some hikers have come across some, but most are ghost towns by now. They chose the mountains, because it was a strategic war move. It allowed visual superiority and safety to their numbers. Most of the government troops couldn't get to them without FOF criers seeing them and sounding the alarm . . . It wouldn't take much to make a settlement up there and go undetected for years, especially if you have your own source for food and supplies. Which most of them did, they had their own Eco-Systems."

"Why would anybody want to hide so well?"

"Stay off the radar." He looked thoughtful. "My contacts said they believed Pierre joined up with some Gypsies." He brought his eyes to theirs. Maybe a certain tribe thought it a good place to claim as their own when the conflicts ended and life got back to normal. Most people yearned to be among civilization again, so a lot of those mountain villages were deserted by their members, making it primary real estate for those wanting to continue to go undetected.." He drew in a breath, remained thoughtful for a moment, then drew a breath. "You two go ahead to the jet; I'm going to make a few calls. Sew up things here, and then I'll be along." He glanced at his watch, "shouldn't have any trouble getting out of here by noon at the latest."

"Okay." Tanner assisted Marna off the couch and taking her hand, led her out of the apartment. Keys watched them go He suspected their fight with Lamontage was about to heat up and judging by the actions of Tanner and Kyle, so was Marna's personal life.

Sighing, he grabbed his GPC and hit a number on the keypad. The screen swam to life and Devon Ruletto came into focus, as did the FWPA icon behind him of the earth with a ring around it and FWPA piercing through both. "Keys, enjoying Switzerland are you?"

"Not really, no. We just lost an agent to one of Lamontage's dream attacks."

The man's face sobered. "I'm sorry to hear that." Government agencies rarely saw eye to eye, but when an agent fell, no matter the branch, every officer felt the pain. "How close are you to catching the Bastard?"

"He's in the States."

"What?" He searched through the neat piles on his desk and found a file, opening it. "Damn, how did I miss that?" His voice betrayed the level of self-annoyance he had at that point.

"My Intel says he's in New England."

Ruletto shuffled through a few pages within the folder, and pulled out a printed sheet of paper with a 4X6 photo attached. "Yeah, looks like he may have passed a traffic camera late last night." He brought his eyes back to the screen. "I'm sorry, Keys, it looks like I dropped the ball on this one. How can we help?"

"We're flying in tonight. He not only killed one of my agents, he abducted another. Her name is Demi Spencer. If you plug her name into the Guardian database you'll find her."

Devin turned toward his computer screen and hit a few keys. He let out a low whistle. "Lady Irish from Tarot, do you think she's still alive?" He turned to face the screen as he asked the question.

"Yes, she's only a means to an end. He's actually after Marna."

"Marna ---The Farlow woman?" he looked puzzled, "How's she tie in to this?"

"Pierre wants her; I think he plans on using Demi to get her. He made his first move during the Bradshaw investigation and he's been haunting her dreams ever since. He's tried more than once to take control of her as well as send out Liberatores foot soldiers to do the deed. My gut tells me he's going to offer up an exchange."

"Spencer for Farlow?" Keys nodded. "Makes sense from what we know about this sociopath. What else?"

"Intel has come to me that he's stashed her in a place called Ambrosian Hill Village. Have you ever heard of it?"

Ruletto was thoughtful for a moment then shook his head. "Doesn't sound familiar."

"I think it might be one of the old FOF villages."

Ruletto nodded, "hmm, that makes sense, if you're going to hide a captive, where better than an unregistered village or town? There were many exoduses on a massive scale going on during that time, and they weren't exactly government friendly. It could take a while to search the records thoroughly enough, not to mention the interviews that we need to do with former residents. It's like searching for a needle in a haystack, Keys. Does your girl have that kind of time? Have you got anything else to help narrow it down?"

"Ambrose is an old Gypsy surname, try focusing on the North American population first, and then move to the Rom population. They're lifestyles are the ones that created many hidden villages. I'll swing by your office next week to check on your progress."

"Okay, I'll put a couple of agents on this right away." He jotted down something on his pad, "I am sorry for your loss Keys," Keys nodded, swallowing back the lump in his throat. Ruletto shook his head and looked at the screen. "We'll help you with whatever resources we can spare. You have safe travels and I'll see you next week. Tell Farlow to hang in there we've got her back."

"I will." He signed off, grabbed his bag, and headed for the door.

*****

Marna's head rested on Tanner's lap, her body covered with a light blanket as she stretched out on seat section B3. She had dozed off shortly after take-off. They had been in the air for several hours, and they were finally in US airspace. Tanner hit the button on his ereader. Kyle watched from two stations down, his eyes burning with anger. "Better turn those lasers down, Brother, before you burn a hole in the side of the plane." Ventura sat down placing a can of ice tea in front of Kyle.

Kyle looked at Ventura. "How long?"

"Excuse me?"

"How long has something been going on between them?"

Ventura glanced toward Marna and Tanner. "There is no 'something' moron, their friends. He was there when her husband died. He's been there to get her through the aftermath."

"He sure doesn't look at her like they're just friends."

"Look, kid, this may be beyond your capability of understanding, but when you walk through hell together, you come out the other side depending on each other, watching each other's back and yes you become tight."

"I got that."

"Do you, Rigby? Do you really? Because if you did, you would know there is no room on this team for jealousy or behavior liken to that of the wronged football player in high school. You keep your eye on the ball and your focus on the investigation, because if you can't, you don't belong on the WIT." He passed a glance over his shoulders. "A day may come when you need them to get you out of a jam or they need you, and if your head isn't on straight, someone is going to die, and that, Brother, is going to be on your head, and yours alone. So reign it in and step off your high horse, focus on developing friendships on this team before you think about chasing skirts, we've lost too many people over the last couple of years to have others fall because of our own actions or mistakes. Do you understand what I'm saying, Rigby?"

Kyle looked down at his hands, Sasha's mangled body flashed before his eyes. He brought his eyes back up to Ventura. "Yeah. I do."

"I hope so, because you'll soon find out that when it really matters, it's the team as a whole that counts, not the he's and she's." He sighed, Kyle had the makings of a good agent, but easily sidetracked and when going up against an enemy like Lamontage, his actions could mean life or death for the person going through the door with him. "Get some rest. Keys is trying to find old FOF towns for us to investigate. He thinks Lamontage has stashed Demi in one of them." Nodding, Ventura pushed away from the table, and went to watch the chess game between Isaiah and Bryan. "Who's winning?"

"I think it's a draw," said Isaiah.

"Really?" Ventura glanced over the board and moved Isaiah's queen, taking out Bryan's rook and leaving a clear path open to his King. "Check." Isaiah's mouth dropped wide open, and then shaped into a wide grin.

"Now how is that fair? Really? You got help from the peanut Gallery."

"That's the Peter Gallery to you, Rush." He grinned and winked at the boy, tousled his hair, and moved away from the table, leaving Bryan to find a way to rescue his King. He slid into the seat next to Heidi, who was helping the twins make jewelry. "Very nice," he said as they strung the glass beads into beautifully crafted necklaces.

"Colorful," she smiled at the girls, "why don't you two go grab us a soda?" Peter offered her his. "No thank you cowboy, I don't want your slobber all over my lips."

"Don't know what you're missing," he said, winking at the girls, changing to the seat across from her, "some women find my slobber very welcome indeed." The girls giggled and ran off toward the kitchen after a chorus of ewwws.

"After they get their distemper shot," she grinned.

"Oh, Heidi, you just haven't known me long enough to see the Ventura magic." He waggled his fingers.

"Lord help me, I hope I never do." She shook her head then gestured toward Kyle with it. "What goes on with our problem child?"

"School-boy crush." He took a sip of his ice tea.

"Really?" She chuckled, "Does the object of his desire know about this?"

"Not sure," he glanced Marna's way, "she might."

"So I guess you had to give him some of that old Ventura wisdom."

He smiled, "Somethin' like that."

"Don't beat the kid down too hard. Marna is a captivating woman."

"And way out of his league," he said, glancing toward Tanner and Marna. Heidi followed his gaze.

"Wanna wager on who finds the glass slipper first?"

Ventura feigned wounded shock. "Why, Schaefer, you misread me. I will not wager on matters of the heart." He placed his hand over his heart.

"Fifty bucks says Kyle wins with his dangerous and risky attitude toward life."

Ventura scoffed. "Really, Schaefer, are you kidding me? Whoever wins the heart of our fair maiden will have to win the heart of her ten kids as well. I'm not sure the boy wonder can handle the challenges of being an insta-daddy, especially in those numbers. That would call him to put someone else first. My money is on Tanner," he leaned forward, raised his hand, and started ticking points off on his fingers, "he's responsible, established, has rapport with the kids, considerate, capable and their good friends. You gotta be friends before you can take a step into something more meaningful." He leaned back with a satisfied grin.

She leaned forward and lowered her voice. "A woman with that much responsibility all day needs a little walk on the wild side at night to feel alive." She grinned as Ventura raised his brow then she leaned back and played her lower lip with her teeth. She looked thoughtful as Ventura challenged her with his eyes. "You're on, Cowboy." She winked as the girls returned, and Ventura left them to head toward the kitchen.

Tanner eased himself away from Marna, replaced his lap with a cushion, put his ereader on the table, and pushed away from the seating section. He headed toward the kitchen and pulled two cups out of the cupboard, flipping them right side up, reaching for the freshly brewed pot, and pouring the liquid into them. He raised one to his lips and looked out over the plane. "How is she?" Ventura asked as he dumped his ice tea, tossed the can into the recycling bucket, and poured a cup of coffee instead.

"I don't know. She's slept the entire trip." He took another sip. "Seeing those cats pounce on Sasha, hearing her screams. I think it may haunt her for a while."

Ventura took a drink. "We all live with our nightmares. She'll pull out of it."

"You're probably right," he smiled at him, "excuse me." He took the second cup with him, returned to his seat, and gently woke Marna up. The PA system sparked to life with the announcement of their approach to Maine, and a promise of starting their descent in twenty minutes. The kids cheered, and Marna smiled, thanked Tanner for the coffee, took a sip, tossed the blanket aside, buckled herself in, and turned to look out the window. She and Tanner talked quietly as the plane grew closer to home.

*****

Monday morning, Marna putted around the kitchen. The kids were off to school, and Keys' meeting wasn't until ten. She had thrown on a light blue sweater, low-riding jeans, and a pair of her favorite sneakers, before taking Amanda sue and PJ to their first day of school. She had introduced them using their new names, and returned home to ready the house for the big strategic planning meeting. Keys had feelers out to try to find the possible hidden village Lamontage was keeping Demi. The temperature was supposed to warm up later, but she could smell spring in the air already this morning when she was out. The coffee maker beeped a signal to let her know it was finished brewing. She grabbed her cup and poured herself some, adding her favorite flavoring syrup and cream.

Taking her Investigative Science text from the bar, she went and sat down at the table and pulled out her computer tablet, signed on to her student account, found the folder holding the class paperwork, and pulled out the questionnaire and the crime scene photo they had handed out just before vacation. It was due tomorrow morning. She chuckled. Here she was constantly on the children's cases to get their work done in a timely fashion and she had put this one worksheet off until the day before it was due. "Not smart, Farlow." She shook her head. Her eyes bounced between the photo and the worksheet steadily for the next twenty minutes.

1) What is unusual about the body position?
2) There is one marker missing, where should it be?
3) Should the crime scene be larger than it is?
4) What does the blood pattern say?

When she finished looking over the twenty questions, she went down to the bottom of the page and wrote out the summary of her findings. The believed height of the individual who had shot the victim, the perceived guess that had caused the fatal injury, and if there was anything missing from the scene that may have been there at the time of the homicide. She then went down to the next section of the paper and read the next step of the work sheet.

Now that you have exercised your traditional investigative skills, how would you use your psychic abilities to enhance your skills in reading this crime scene? "Oh, you're a mean one, Mr. Finch." She said and brought the eraser of the pencil to her lower lip, bringing the crime scene photo into her field of vision yet again. She thought about her abilities and wrote them out on paper. Then she circled the ones that would be of use at this particular scene and wrote out her psychic evaluation of the scene. Combining the two skills, she wrote a probable evaluation of the murder of this woman. It took place by her car, in a parking lot. The body wasn't moved and there appeared to be nothing missing so it was not probable that this killing could be included with the local serial killings that the chapter discussed earlier. Someone she knew in a fit of rage most likely committed it. Conclusion? A crime of passion.

"There. Done." She sent the file off to the professor with an acknowledgement that she would see him in class tomorrow. She slid her tablet back into her bag, and picked up her coffee. Somewhere outside her house, in the neighborhood, she heard car doors shut, a dog barked, and a child's gleeful giggles drifted through the early morning air. She smiled at the safe sounds of home.

The sun started breaking up the early morning cloud cover and coming through her blind slats. She glanced at the clock. She still had time to go straighten up the upstairs rooms, so she jogged up the stairs and started toward the back of the upper hallway and into the first room. She straightened sheets and pulled up comforters. Amanda Sue and PJ were using cots, one set up in Isaiah's room and one set up in the girls' room, but she made a mental note to go on line to order new furniture. Some rearranging was going to have to happen to accommodate two more children. Maybe she'd hire a contractor to finish the second half of the basement, and turn it into a living space for Isaiah then they would have to move the laundry room.

Okay maybe that same contractor could add on to the entire house; put another room on the second floor, a laundry room on the first, and the finished room in the basement. That would be the better way to go. Isaiah would have his own room, Moses and PJ could share a room, and Mary and

Amanda Sue could share a room. That sounded about right. She looked at her watch. She had time. She'd go online for a little while, before the big meeting, and check Jaben's list; a list of home improvement specialists in the area and see if she could find one that wouldn't put her in the poor house while she accommodated her growing family.

She stepped into the hallway, that's when she heard it. Breaking glass, her head jerked up, and she tuned in her listening ability. I *want it clean . . . in and out with the prize.*

Yeah, I hear you.

Seriously, Martin, I don't want to die today. From what I hear, she's powerful.

That's why we have this. Now shut up!

She hadn't had a chance to fine-tune her Listening skills very much but Keys did give her a crash course. *'Background noises are just as important, Marna, listen for them too.'* She focused, standing very still, not letting anything else interfere. She heard what she was looking for. She heard a conversation going on in the background, very low, a radio, No it was a television, hers. Whoever the intruders were, they were downstairs! The glass she heard must have been someone breaking a pane in her French door. Her gun, then she remembered it was downstairs, locked in the desk drawer in the den. She had left it down there when they had arrived home Friday night. "Smart move, Farlow." She muttered to herself.

She looked at the span of empty space between herself and her bedroom where her backup was. Too much open space she thought. They would see her for sure. The click of a lock, barely audible, yet it thundered in her ears, the squeak of hinges. God help her, they were in her house! Glass crunching underfoot as they stepped over the threshold. She reached for her GPC. It wasn't in its case, hooked to her belt. She opened her psychic channels wide, *911! MF WIT-6150 intruders, possibly two in my house backup needed.* She sent out the distress signal, via the psychic hotline, it was her only choice then she shut it down.

Silence from the floor below. One of them must have been a tracker and caught the use of her abilities on their radar. Cloak? She thought that over as she sunk back into the shadow of the alcove between the girls' room and the linen closet. She held her breath. A stair squeaked. She recognized it as the fourth one up. However, it was only once. One was coming upstairs. The other must have been searching downstairs, but he would soon join his friend. Two possibilities with the cloak, if one was an Observer, they would see right through it, but it might buy her some time. The tracker could hone in, but his findings would be approximate. That far outweighed the dangers of not using it. She cloaked. A whirling mist encircled her.

The intruder chuckled. "Wise play, lass, but dat only delays de inevitable," Martin Freeman muttered, "She's up 'ere, Vince, she's got no way oyt." All talk stopped while Martin waited for his partner to join him. She inched her way around the alcove toward the girls' room. She charted her path carefully. If she could make it to Isaiah's room, there was a fire escape outside his window. She could make a run for it. She moved as slow as she dared.

"Where is she?"

"De alcove over dare, she's usin' a cloak, an' mind they want 'er alive if possible." They moved toward her. "Our employer doesn't care, but de wan retrievin' 'er for 'ill pay a 'andsum price for de lassy." She was almost across the hall. Martin was studying the hallway with intensity. She froze. "Dare !" He yelled as he pointed to the space between the girls' and the boys' room. Marna made a run for it and the next thing she knew, they blasted her with a cold current, and trapped her in the bluish force field she recognized from the restaurant. "Stick her !" Martin ordered. A gun went off and Martin's man fell to the floor with a cry of pain. The syringe fell from his grasp as he grabbed his knee and fell to the floor.

"Don't move a muscle or I'll blow your brains all over the wall," Kyle hissed. He held his gun steadily on Martin, while leaning on the casing.

"Oi flip dis up a notch an' Marna Farlow is naw more."

"Your finger even has a muscle spasm, near that button, and you will be no more. Go ahead give me a reason to put your miserable ass down !" Kyle's features darkened, his eyes flashed.

"Yer can't take us both oyt alone." The man on the floor pulled a gun, and readied it to fire, pointing it at Kyle.

"I'm willing to accept the challenge, if you are." Kyle raised a brow and in a lightening quick movement of his hand, he put a bullet in Vince's gun hand, causing him to lose the gun, and then another bullet hit the gun, sending it flying across the floor. Before Martin could blink, Kyle had trained the gun back on him.

"Hmm Impressive, Agent Rigby."

"Now it's down to me and you, scumbag."

"Is it now? Are ya sure?"

"Enough with the head games, I'm through playing. Take that damn taser off of her! That's the last time I'm asking nicely." Martin released the button, turning off the beam. Marna collapsed, and then rolled herself away from Martin. "Now put it on the floor, and kick it toward me." Martin bent down to put the taser on the floor but instead, he fell to the floor raised the taser flipped it on, and imprisoned Kyle with the beam. Kyle got off one shot, before he fell victim to its numbing beam; his gun fell from his hand and slid to the hardwood floor out of his reach. His body arched with the intensity of the beam.

"Kyle !" Marna cried, she pushed herself up, and slammed her body into Martin, upsetting his balance and causing the taser to fall, but the laser had done its damage, Kyle was paralyzed, he couldn't move, and had no control over his limbs. Beads of sweat formed as he tried to reach for his gun. Marna and Martin became a tangled heap of arms and legs. She slammed his head into the hardwood floor, and he countered with kicking up at her and flipping her over his head. She landed hard on her back, the wind knocked out of her. Martin then grabbed the Taser and aimed, but she rolled out of the beams reach. In an instant, she had bent her back and was springing back to her feet, diving when he aimed for another shot. She saw Vince's gun, and looked back, Martin aimed, she pushed up, dived for the gun, checked the chamber, rolled to her back, and fired, she caught him in the shoulder Martin's body jerked, the taser falling and rolling away, commotion could be heard out front. Martin glanced around, "We'll meet again, Lass." He turned, ran toward Isaiah's room, and then he was gone. She let her arms down. She took a breath, using the stair railing to stand up.

There was no warning. No time to react. Vince must have had a back up, she heard the explosion, felt the bullet rip into her side and burn a path through her chest. Using the wall for support, she aimed her gun and fired one final shot, hitting him between the eyes. Vince died instantly, just before she slid down to the floor, leaving a crimson trail on the stark white wall. Blood quickly stained her shirt. She was having trouble breathing, Kyle could see that. Tears formed at the corner of his eyes. Marna was dying and he was helpless to save her.

"Marna !" Tanner came around the corner of the landing and went to her aid. Bryan came up behind him, and moved to Kyle, checking his vitals.

"Stay with me?" Tanner said, grabbing towels from the linen closet, and using them to staunch the bleeding. Marna's eyes focused on him.

"I'm s-sorry." She whispered.

"Don't talk. We'll talk later, you stay with me."

"Kyle?"

"Bryan's checking him out now." He looked toward Bryan and Kyle. He looked gray around the edges. Ventura and Heidi appeared on scene next. "Pete call 911, we've got two down !"Ventura quickly pulled out his GPC. Keys came up the stairs behind them. The others dispersed around the house. Keys went to Kyle's side. To Kyle, Keys words sounded tinny when he spoke. "Can you hear me, Son?" He moved his eyes from side to side. Keys turned away. "What's their ETA?" He queried of Ventura.

"Three minutes." His eyes moved back to Kyle, then to Marna and Tanner. "Tanner?"

"She's bleeding badly, and her breathing's labored pulse slow but steady. She's conscious and aware." Tanner turned back to Marna. "Stay with me, Marna, Just stay with me." He took her hand, and held it close to his chest, while he staunched the bleeding with his other one over the towel on her wound. Kyle heard Ventura say something before Keys responded. "No, not GSW, I'm thinking taser, but an altered one." Kyle heard more conversation between Ventura and Williams. Their voices sounded tinny, and far away. He couldn't hear anything from Marna. He heard Ventura say Marna's name.

"GSW," Tanner verified, "One to the side, but it's done some damage on the inside. Won't know how much 'til we get her to the ER." Kyle's heart sank. He had failed to protect her. The Bastard had gotten her, and by the tension in everybody's voice, he knew it was bad.

"He's gone." Schaefer verified as she came back to the landing. They could hear sirens fast approaching the house. Kyle started fading, his breathing was becoming slow and raspy.

"Hang on, Son, just hang on." Keys knelt beside him and took his hand, "There here."

"What do we have?" On paramedic asked.

"Taser injury and GSW. The latter is pretty serious." Keys verified, and the first team stooped to help Marna.

The second team that came in took over with Kyle. "He's losing consciousness. Let's get that heart monitor on." Keys stepped back, watching intensely as the paramedics did their jobs. He felt so totally helpless.

"He's having palpitations. Shock him. Let's see if we can get a sinus rythm" They pulled out their defibulator, and shocked Kyle, his body jerked. Keys looked from one to the other. He ran a shaky hand over his mouth.

"We're losing her! Get that IV up now! She's losing too much blood, we need to transport!"

"Marna, stay with us !" Tanner cried as the paramedics hooked her up with a breathing bag. He followed them downstairs, ran beside her, and climbed into the ambulance with her. After regulating his heart, they followed in another ambulance with Kyle. Keys rode with him.

Ventura watched as the second ambulance departed. "Allright. let's tear this place apart and find the Bastard."

*****

The next few hours – days – weeks – Marna didn't know how long, passed in a whirl of activity, she would later describe as flashes of disjointed memories.

Paramedics . . Oxygen mask. . . concerned friends,. . . family. . . colleagues —. . . darkness

She heard Keys order, "lockdown all exits and entrances to the compound; nobody in or out," darkness again.

Operating room lights . . . Alarms, her body floating above her.. . . Her head filled with scattered dreams about intruders.

Through the veil of confusion and darkness, she saw Tanner hovering above her, looking down at her with so much love and tenderness in his eyes. More Alarms. Tanner's eyes filling with tears and fear. Tanner holding her hand, kissing the back, begging her to come back to them . . . More.darkness.

There were vague memories, shadows really, of people coming by her bed, talking to her. Tanner sitting beside her, reading. Kyle limped up to her bedside, talked to her and kissed her forehead then he was gone. Rose reading to her from a book. Keys sitting by her bedside, looking through a magazine. Colleagues blocking her channels because she was too weak to block her own. Keys standing over her talking to the clinic doctor.

It was well in to the afternoon on day number whatever, when she was finally able to open her eyes and focus enough to see her surroundings.

She was in the intensive care unit. Two security personnel stood guard outsider her room. Machines beat a steady rhythm around her. Keys stepped up to the bedside. "Welcome back, Marna." He said softly, reading her vitals off the screens.

"Kyle?" Her voice sounded hoarse, even to her.

Keys fed her some ice chips. "He's fine. He's already been released and sent home." There was no permanent damage done from the taser. He has to take it easy for a few days, as the jolt aggravated the injuries he already had, and then report for a few therapy sessions, before he can control his abilities and his limbs fully, but he's alive.

She tried to move, but a pain shot through her chest and shoulder. "Ahh." Keys brought the trapeze from the bar, over her bed, and assissted her as she pull herself forward while he adjusted the pillows behind her, and the he supported her back as she eased herself onto them. "How long have I been out?"

"five days."

"fi – " She drew in a breath and closed her eyes, wishing away the dizziness. "The kids must be worried sick."

"Heidi and Peter have been splitting shifts with Rose and Tanner to care for them. They've been in here a few times, but you've been out of it."

"What the heck did he hit me with?" She glanced at her arm, held close to her body with a body sling.

"The Thunder 227 bullet, it's fairly new on the market, made distinctly for military use. It enters the body then splits like a T. It entered your side and traveled upward. It broke a couple of ribs that in turn pierced a lung, and clipped your aortic artery before it lodged itself in your scapula. You were bleeding internally. It took six hours for them to repair the damage. They lost you once in the ambulance, and once in the ER and resuscitated you. If we hadn't gotten there when we did, we'd be burying you next to Jeff."

She closed her eyes as more dizziness engulfed her. He gave her a few more ice chips then he put them back on the table. "Feel up to answering some questions?" She nodded. "Did you recognize your attackers?"

"I knew one of them."

"How?"

"He approached me at the end of my last class, the day of the birthday party," she cleared her throat.

"He approached you how?"

"He wanted me to go to the college cafe with him, have coffee." She licked her lips, "said he had just transferred here from Dublin, Ireland."

"Did he give his name?"

Marna closed her eyes, even her established memories were disjointed, "Martin ah," she concentrated, "Martin Freeman." Keys wrote the information down.

"Did he say where he was staying?"

"Tanner asked him before we left the lecture hall. Something about the guy made him suspicious. He said he was staying in the Barns building."

"Okay we'll send a CS unit out there," he said picking up his GPC, and hitting a button, Ventura swam to focus on his screen.

"Yeah, Keys?"

"Pete, take a team out to the Barns building on campus. Our suspect was living there prior to spring break."

"How's Marna doing?"

"She's awake, but I think her memory may need a little jogging. The attack and pain meds may have scrambled a few things, I'm going to help her pick through it all.

"Okay, Boss, we're heading out to Barns now."

"Keep me posted, and no one is to approach this man alone, we're down three, let's not give them any more of an advantage."

"Got it," Ventura said then disconnected.

Keys turned off his GPC and returned to Marna's bedside. "Marna, I need to try and unscramble some of the details from the intrusion, can you help me do that?"

She drew in a breath and let it out slowly. "I'll try."

"Now you said there were only two assailants, this Martin Freeman and the one that was killed.," Marna nodded.

"Were they working for someone or were they working on their own?"

Marna closed her eyes and let the memories flood her mind. Echoes of the attack came back to her. *Our employer doesn't care, but de wan he's retrievin' 'er for 'ill pay a 'andsum price for de lassy.* "They were working for someone. Martin talked about an employer. How they were going – " She swallowed, Keys patiently waited, " – ah going to sell me to some client or something like that."

Keys became troubled. Lamontage hadn't sent them. He would not have been interested in selling her. He wanted to possess her. There was another batter at play here, "Did he say anything that would reveal his employer?

She shook her head. "No."

"Could you tell what abilities he had?"

"Martin was a tracker. I'm not sure if the other one was an Observer, or just very practiced at seeing movement where there shouldn't be any."

"What do you mean?"

"I cloaked, but they managed to get through it and zap me with the taser."

"Can you think of anything that may help us find Martin?" She was tiring.

She closed her eyes, and tried hard to focus. "I winged him."

"Are you sure?"

"Yes, I got him in the shoulder. It was just before the team got there." Keys nodded. He remembered the gunfire. "He used the fire escape, outside Isaiah's window, to escape."

"A team went through the fire escape. We found some fabric, and blood. The lab is working to find a DNA match now."

"Good." She leaned her head back, closed her eyes."

"You get some rest now." He pushed the button on the Morphine drip.

"Mhmm." She said and slipped back under.

He lifted his eyes toward the door as someone stepped over the threshold. "How are you feeling, Kyle?"

"Better. How is she?"

"She was awake for a few minutes. She gave me a lead. Could you sit with her, while I join the others? I just gave her some more Morphine. She should sleep for a while." He smiled, "she could use the extra blocking."

"Of course." Kyle went to the chair and grabbed a magazine.

"I'll call with an update later."

"Thanks." Keys walked by him, reached out, squeezed the boy's shoulder, and continued out the door.

*****

Ventura nodded to Sarah Justice and Barry McGellan as they took position outside the room Freeman occupied. They had canvassed the Barns building, questioned many Barns residents, flashing and flashed the composite around. Their efforts were rewarded when a couple of the female students remembered his accent. Now they readied their weapons. "Martin Freeman, this is Peter Ventura from Guardian WIT. We need to talk to you." No response. Ventura repeated his request, still no response. He nodded to the security team and one member used a door laser to cut through the door hinges and latch, while another used a wood plunger grips to keep the door from falling in. Within seconds, they had removed the door and Ventura, Schaefer, West and McGellan moved in, followed by the security team.

They fanned out around the small dorm apartment, and cleared it. Ventura turned toward the security team. "recanvas the others on this floor, I want a timeline done of this guy's movements from the moment he stepped foot on this compound. I want to know what he ate for breakfast, how often he ordered out, and how many times he used the latrine. After nodding agreements, the team left.

"Hey, Ventura, you're going to want to see this," Schaefer called.

Ventura followed her voice to a walk-in closet, Freeman had altered to become a small office. There was a bulletin board with an outline of Marna's life, complete with pictures and timeline of her daily activities. "He's been watching her."

"Her taking the kids to school, her going to the market, her on campus," He pointed out photos as he spoke, "there's the night of the party." He indicated a picture of Marna on her back porch talking with Keys."

"Who is this guy?"

"I don't know, but this house isn't from around here." She pulled a picture down. It was a snap shot of a Villa set in a mountain backdrop with Magnolia's blooming on trees in the front horseshoe drive. On the front steps were three children, two boys and one girl, and toward the lower left front field of the photo was a dark haired woman in a broomstick skirt.

"Gypsies?" Ventura queried.

"Yeah but are they who he works for or are they his family? Could the Irish thing be an act?" Schaefer questioned.

"Keep looking," Ventura said, "Take that picture to Sarah, see if she can get a read on it. Meanwhile, I'll have Barry do a reading on the desk top, we'll see how long it's actually been since he's been here." One of Barry's abilities was Impressionism. He was able to read impressions off inanimate objects that would give investigators the amount of time that had lapsed since the owner had used it. Though it wasn't an exact science, Ventura had found it very helpful, in the past, on missing person cases and Homicides."

"On it." Heidi moved out in search of Sarah. Ventura called Barry into the room and told him to see if he could get a read on the desktop PC. "Computers are used for everything; see if he's used it recently."

Barry holstered his gun, and approached the computer. Sitting down, he placed both hands on the key board, closed his eyes and emptied everything out of his mind but the pattern of usage on the object below his fingertips. He sensed the tapping of keys, the mindset of the individual using it. He was excited but anxious. He focused on the time set of usage. He could almost hear the thoughts of the individual. Keys said one day the breakthrough may happen, but not today. He pulled his hands away. "This computer has been used within the last two hours."

"Thanks, Barry. Wait here for CS, I want that taken and checked out for emails and IP addresses."

"Yes, Sir."

Ventura pegged Keys. "Yes, Peter?"

"Freeman has been in his place within the last two hours."

"He's still on the compound."

"At least he was two hours ago." Heidi appeared before him, with the picture. "Hang on a minute, Keys." He nodded to Heidi, who pulled out her GPC and joined the conference. "We found a picture of a Villa in his apartment. Older in style, but it wasn't abroad. Looks to be here in the states."

"What about it Schaefer?" Keys queried. "Could it be where he is hiding?"

"No, when Sarah took it, she didn't see Lamontage. She saw some woman."

"Odd."

"Maybe she's who hired him to retrieve her."

"Maybe. Wrap things up, and return to Marna's, I've got Rose watching over the children, but I don't want her on her own." Keys signed off, and turned toward the street. He had come back to look over the fire escape again and take some notes. He was on Marna's front porch now. He pushed his GPC back into its carrier on his belt. He looked up as Tanner's Camaro came to a stop by the side of the road and he stepped out, engaging the locks. He seemed distracted as he made his way up the slate walkway. He didn't know Keys was standing there until he was almost on top of him.

"Keys," he said, nodding his acknowledgement, "how's Marna?"

"She woke up long enough to answer some questions this afternoon." Tanner sighed heavily and Keys could see his eye moisten.

"Thank God." He leaned into the porch railing, bowed his head, pinched the bridge of his nose, and took a deep breath before returning his eyes to Keys'. "She remember anything?"

"Yes, she did. The second attacker, the one that got away, was named Martin Freeman."

"The one from the lecture hall? That Martin Freeman?"

"Yes, that one."

"Damn, I knew I should have run a check on him?"

"Why didn't you?" Keys looked steadily at him.

"Marna asked me not to. She said she didn't feel threatened by him."

Keys leaned into the railing opposite him. "If you had, you would have found out that there was no Martin Freeman registered on the compound, neither in Ireland nor in the transfer office here."

"What are you saying, Keys?" Tanner looked at him, his mouth had run dry, a lump the size of a gulf ball formed in his throat, and just as dense.

"I'm saying that had you followed your instincts, Agent Williams, you would have discovered that Martin Freeman simply does not exist in the Guardian circle."

"Oh my . . ." He lowered himself to the porch and sat, rubbing a hand over his mouth then let it fall listlessly between his knees. "I enabled him to walk a path to her front door. She could have died because of me."

"But she didn't."

"Damn, Keys, when I think of what could have happened." He pushed himself up and walked a few paces away.

"But it didn't, Tanner." Keys got up and went to his side. He didn't want to jump the boy, but he had to be aware of how dangerous an oversight he had made. "Son, you are a Feeler, when your instincts tell you there is something off, than you damn well better listen to them. Marna is going to be okay, we got to her in time, and you kept her with us. However, it is going to take a while for her to get back on her feet. As Guardians, we can't afford to make those kinds of mistakes. Especially when we deal with the type of enemies, we deal with. Your oversight put down not one but two agents that need recovery time now. That sets us back on this investigation. I need you on the top of your game. If you have suspicions, you do what you can to alleviate them."

Tanner nodded. "Yes, Sir." He accepted Keys' dressing down, had he been in Keys shoes he would have done the same thing. He was right. Two agents could have died because of his negligence to follow through on his suspicions. "How's, Kyle?"

"He's doing okay, His memory still has holes, and he still has pain in his legs, but he's a strong young man, he'll be fine. I left him with Marna for a while. He feels better, knowing he can still be actively involved in the investigation. The rest of the team is at Freeman's place, tearing it apart. I'm leaving you and Rose here with the children. I don't think Freeman has left the compound. He'll try again. You keep the children safe." Tanner nodded. Keys wished him goodbye and headed back down the walkway, while he turned to enter the house.

From an abandoned house, two blocks away Martin watched with binoculars trained on Marna's house. Keys was right, he wouldn't give up. He would lay low until Marna returned home, and then he would make another attempt. He pulled his cell out of his pocket when it vibrated and looked at the screen, and lifted it to his ear. "Yeah . . . first attempt failed . . . don't worry I'll get her . . . well you didn't tell me I was grabbing the fricken queen of England . . . Hospital is too risky. . . Guardian has this place locked down tighter then the Fed . . . I told you I'll get, her you just need to trust me." He cut the conversation off, and slipped the phone back in his pocket, ignoring it when it rang again. "You'll get your windfall, woman, just be patient." He returned the binoculars to his eyes, and resumed his watch of the Farlow house.

Chapter Fifteen

Marna was drifting, she couldn't open her eyes to see where she was going but she felt the familiar weightlessness. She knew the dream wasn't natural, she was going there by invitation and she wasn't alone. Finally, she felt some of her control return; she opened her eyes to darkness. The room was cold, she was alone but she wasn't, she could feel a presence. Her breath made clouds before her.

She was lying in her hospital bed. She looked around the room, nothing seemed strange or out of the ordinary. She could see people, in the hallway moving about, beyond the open door. A nurse came through the door, she walked over to the bedside, checked her IV, "Can I have another blanket?" She queried. The nurse didn't even acknowledge she had heard her and went about her business. "Please, I'm cold."

"They can't hear you," she recognized the voice. Icy fear gripped her heart, making it hard to breathe.

"No, no, no." She frantically searched for her call button.

"Looking for this?" He appeared at the foot of her bed, holding her call button. Only this time he was wearing a flannel shirt and a pair of jeans, no robe. He stood there, his salt and pepper hair pulled tight in a tail, reaching his mid-shoulders, and his body as large as a gorilla and just as rigid. He was wearing the cross around his neck. "Ma, Cher. Don't look so frightened. I wish not to hurt you, only to love you, treasure you." He approached her, she shrunk away.

"No, leave me alone. Somebody please help me! She cried and she tried to get up, but discovered she was strapped down; her hands and feet strapped to the bedrails."

"No !" She pulled at the restraints. The hospital bed melted away, she was on the cot in the tower. The bedrails became the headboard and footboard of that horrible little cot. "No !" He stood above her.

"Such strength, such power." His hands hovered over her chest. She felt shockwaves go through her body. She screamed, her body arching, then she was standing beside him. Demi was on the cot. She was the one screaming. He was hurting her. Her body arching as electrical current after electrical current surged through it.

"Marna! help me!" She gasped in between surges.

"Stop! Stop hurting her!" She pushed out at him but he held her off with his hand creating an invisible wall between them. Demi screamed again.

"Stop! Please !" Currents surged through her. Pain ripped through her chest. She grabbed at it. "Stop, make it stop." She gasped and collapsed. Sasha lay next to her. Her skin shredded by those horrible beasts, her eyes unfocused. "Oh God, make it stop!"

He was crouching beside her, "you alone can make it stop, Ma Cher, you can end the suffering for everyone, just come to me. Come to me, and I give her back her life, he looked toward Demi, who now was laying where Sasha had lain, staring into space, her breath coming in gasps. You for her. Stay away and she will die. It really is quite simple." He raised his hand, closed his fist Demi screamed, Marna covered her ears. Pain ripped through her chest again, she couldn't breathe . . .

~~~~~

Kyle awoke to the shrills of alarms. Marna was flat lining, medical staff was pouring in. The doctor came in, looked into her eyes, "pupils fixed and dilated." He and an orderly started CPR "Bring me the defibrillator, we're losing her !" Kyle stepped back in shock. More medical staff swarmed down on her, one pushed him toward the door.

"You need to leave, now !" The nurse ordered.

"I need a chest tube!" the doctor yelled.

The nurse again tried to push him out the door. He tried to fight. The orderly came over and held him back. "Go, now, we're doing everything we can." Kyle backpedaled out of the room. The door closed, curtains closed. He watched as medical staff ran in and out of the room. Everybody was in red alert mode. Phones rang. The PA system buzzed to life and he recognized the name of her surgeon as it echoed in the hallway. The phone rang the nurse answered it. "OR three, right." She hung up, and ran to Marna's door. "They're prepping OR three." He heard metal clattering, and then he saw them push her bed quickly out of the room, and down the hallway, one nurse was standing on the lowered rail doing compressions, another was using a bag to help her breath. He ran up to the one nurse left behind, the one that was meant to stay at the desk.

"What's going on? What happened?"

The nurse turned toward him. "Are you family?"

"No. A friend."

"Then I'm sorry, it's against policy to discuss a patient's medical condition with someone other than family." He let his gaze stray down the hallway as the elevator door closed, the physician barking out orders. The nurse touched his shoulder. "Does she have family?" He nodded. "Call them." He nodded again. "What about you, do you have someone who can wait with you?"

"Y-Yeah."

"Good." She went back to her desk as he headed toward the colorful vinyl chairs in the impersonal waiting room. He covered his face and collapsed into a chair. "God no, not Marna, please not Marna. You need to help her be strong, help her fight. Help her live." He sent up a fervent prayer. He didn't believe himself to be on the top of God's list of prayer buddies, but hoped he would listen to him anyway, and then he took out his GPC, hitting a button on the key pad to leave video format dormant, he hit phone, then he hit speed dial and pulled the GPC to his ear. "Something's happened . . . Her heart. . . They just rushed her off to surgery . . . she was just laying there, no movement on her monitors. . . They made me leave . . .She wasn't responding to CPR." His voice broke and he sniffed. "I'm scared, Dad, I think we're going to lose her. . . Okay." He hung up his phone and walked to Marna's room. Bandages and various other disposable medical items, covered in blood, littered the floor. A nurse walked into the room.

"You really shouldn't be in here right now. If you go sit in the waiting room, I can clean up this mess." She was a petite thing with blonde wavy hair, and sea-green eyes.

"How," He nailed her to the wall with his eyes, "How bad is she?"

"I can't tell you that. It's against policy."

"I don't give a damn about policy !" He fought to control his emotions. "All this . . ." he waved his hand around the room, "tells me a tale of its own. How bad is she?"

The young woman looked helpless. "I-I can't," Kyle could tell by the way her eyes averted his, that something was very, very wrong. He didn't press anymore; he waved his hand, and went to the window, opened it and took two or three deep cleansing breaths to still the nausea in his stomach, and then he just stared out over the parking lot.

He heard the disturbances as she moved around the room; the rattling of the mop bucket, the wheels of the biohazard material bucket, the squealing wheels of a new bed getting rolled in and then the whisper of material as it was made fresh. "Is there something I can get you? Coffee, a soda?" She offered him some time later, touching his bicep with gentle fingers. He shook his head and pressed the palm of his hand to the window casing. Tears stung his eyes as he heard her scurry away. In the hallway, he heard the elevators ding and footsteps as people moved about. The PA system was going off. Footsteps approached, the door hinges squeaked.

"Kyle?" Keys said as he entered the room and approached him.

He glanced his way. "She's – ah, she's still in surgery."

"I know I stopped at the desk."

"I hope you got more out of them than I did." He retorted.

"Son, come, let's sit." Kyle let Keys lead him to the chairs against the wall on their right. "Can you tell me what happened?" Get him talking Keys thought; get his mind moving away from what was happening in Marna's surgery right now "Start from the beginning."

He sniffed. "Ah, she was sleeping. I gave her the extra blocking you requested." Keys nodded, "then I grabbed a magazine from the basket by the chair. The last thing I remember was reading an article on sports cars; Mustangs," Keys smiled, Kyle had always loved Mustangs. "Then I – I must have fallen asleep, because the next thing I remember is the machines going crazy, the alarms going off, her flat-lining. The medical staff came in, started CPR and then they swept her away to surgery." He drew in a breath, looked out the window, and then returned his gaze to Keys. "Can't you find out what's going on? I mean what good is it to be the all mighty Dr. Keys if you can't pull rank and find out stuff like that?"

"Kyle, I'm going to forget you said that because of your state of mind." Keys said firmly, "there are protocols in place, and they're in place to protect agents from people who mean to cause them harm. Rose called me, right after I got off the phone with you, the hospital had called her and she was on her way here. We met in the lobby. She's checking her status right now. She is Marna's sister. She's the one with the rights to find out these things. She'll give us an update as soon as she finds out anything."

"Oh, yeah, I forgot about her." Kyle pushed out of the chair and moved away from him. Keys let out a frustrated sigh.

Rose came into the room. The tension was evident as she looked from one to the other. "Am I interrupting something?"

"No." Keys assured her with a smile. Kyle turned to look at her. "What were you able to find out?"

"Marna's heart suffered a tachycardia, meaning her heart started beating extremely fast and that threw her into cardiac arrest. It's always a possibility in injuries such as hers, but when they went to use the Defib on her, they noticed hematomas—brusing — on her chest – again – always a possibility, considering her recent surgery but their concern was the fresh bruising. They suspected she was bleeding into her chest cavity, most likely causing blood to pool around her heart and lungs. This in turn caused restrictions to movement of the organs. They had to do something to alleviate it, to restore breathing and regular heart function. Their suspicions were confirmed when they inserted a chest tube, blood poured into the catch all dish. They had to take her in to emergency surgery to find out where the bleeder was. They aren't sure where it's coming from though. They've stabilized her for now and they're trying to find and repair the leak. She'll be in surgery for a few more hours, why don't you two go down to the cafe and get some coffee, I'll give you a call as soon as she's back in her room."

"Come on, Kyle, she's in the best of hands," Keys encouraged. Kyle nodded and Keys waved him ahead and they went to the elevators.

*****

Tanner paced the floor. Dinner was done, the dishwasher purred in the kitchen, and the kids had long since gone to bed. Rose and he had sat down to watch some TV drama dealing with cops and procedure, when the call had come through about Marna, now he had a hard time sitting still awaiting word on her progress. Impressions of that last night in Switzerland kept flashing through his mind. He shouldn't have been so short with her. He should have just held her, told her he understood. He knew how hard it had been for her to let go of Jeff. He shouldn't have pushed so hard, shouldn't have revealed his feelings to her, put her under that kind of pressure. His GPC beeped. He pulled it out to look at the screen. It was Ventura. "Yeah, Pete."

"What's going on?" Ventura queried.

"Marna dipped. She had some kind of cardiac episode. Rose went to the hospital to check on her."

"You're covering the house by yourself?" Ventura queried in a tight voice.

"Yeah, why?" He queried, "It's not like I haven't done solo acts before?" His eyes narrowed, something was off, "The kids are asleep, and I just did a parameter check. Things are secure. What's going on, Pete? What aren't you telling me?"

"Stay inside, Tech found something on Freeman's computer that could be a game changer, at the very least, it's troubling. Martin wasn't working for Lamontage."

"What? Who then, and why come after Marna?"

"It's not Marna he and his cohort were after, well they were but not in the way we think. It's too complicated to get into over the phone," Ventura said, "Make sure the place is locked down, and keep your weapon handy. We have reason to believe he's coming for a repeat performance and soon. You shouldn't be stepping out on your own. You need someone to cover your back. We're on our way, but we're about 20 minutes out. I'll radio HQ for backup, have them send a unit up to secure the premises and, Williams, I'm serious, lock that place down tight." Ventura hung up. Tanner moved around the lower floor, checking and rechecking all the locks on windows and doors, and then he repeated the process on the second floor. When he came back downstairs, he was on high alert and his senses were so piqued he felt he would know if a mouse was watching him from a dark corner of the kitchen.

Headlights scraped across the front windows and Tanner heard the engine of a car turn off by the front curb. He went toward the door and moved the curtain aside to look. It was a Guardian security cruiser. He closed the curtain and let out a breath, leaning his forehead against the door casing. Phew! It was then that the sensation came over him. He was not alone and he knew it, felt it; another presence, a menacing shroud fell over the entire room. He slowly reached up, as if he was going to work the chain lock, and moved quickly to the light switch, flipping it to off, and plunging the room into darkness. He dived to the side, behind a small entry lip in the wall, just before the blue taser beam struck where he had been standing. A jagged rip appeared in the door. He took a breath as sweat beaded his forehead. Damn! The intruder must have slipped in while he was up reading a story to Mary and Amanda Sue or possibly, while he did his parameter check. He lowered himself to a sitting position on the floor but didn't speak a word, for fear of giving away his whereabouts. He had one thing on him, he knew the house, and Martin Freeman did not.

Tanner closed his eyes to try to picture the room with its furnishings in his head. He belly crawled to the couch, stayed low behind the back panel, undoing the safety strap that held his gun in the holster and pulled the Glock out, feeling the cool metal in his hand. He loaded a round into the chamber and raised himself just enough so he could glance toward the stairs. He had to protect the children. He didn't know what Freeman wanted, but for Marna, he had to protect the children if it was the last thing he did. He crawled to the end of the couch, heard the intruder hit his foot on the magazine rack. That was on his right, the opposite end of the couch. All movement stopped and he tried to get a fix on the man. A small rustle of material, Martin was almost around the back of the couch. He started counting in his head. . .one. . . two. . . th. . .and he made a dash for the overstuffed chair, a few feet away from the stairs, the taser beam fired after him . . . He returned fired in the general direction Martin was in. . .As he was about to dive, his foot caught on the corner of the couch. He felt the pain rip through his ankle before he felt himself fall . . .

*****

Kyle paced the waiting room floor. Keys' GPC vibrated; he took it out of his pocket and saw he had an email from Peter. He fired up his internet screen, and clicked on the email. It downloaded pictures. He frowned, confused. Kyle glanced his way. "What is it?"

"Ah, pictures Ventura just zapped me. They came from Freeman's computer."

"The guy who was after Marna?"

"Yes. Hmmm. Excuse me a moment, will you? I'm just going to call him to get some clarification." Kyle shrugged and went back to his pacing.

Keys looked his way, and then walked a pace or two away and hit his intercom call button. Ventura's face appeared on the screen. "Yeah, Keys?"

"I just got your pictures."

"Yeah, a little unsettling don't you think?"

It was then that he noticed Ventura's surroundings. "Are you in the car?"

"Yeah, Heidi and I are on our way to Marna's, we sent a security unit up there. Williams is there by himself. No backup."

"I'm afraid I dropped the ball on that one, I thought he would be okay, considering Lamontage's ultimate goal."

"An understandable oversight considering most of our time on this case has been chasing after Lamontage and he has been after Marna. None of us would have expected this development."

"Did the techs find anything else in the folder, on the computer?"

"No nothing, just the pictures and the emails, no signature, couldn't even trace the IP address; the signal was bouncing all over the world. Tech team said it was going to take a while to get even an approximation of where it came from. The account number is also going to be hard to pin down. Not sure what is going on or why Freeman's for hire job is related to our case." Heidi's muffled voice came from somewhere in the background. "Shit! Gotta Go, Keys, Tanner just sent out a 911."

"Keep me informed." He heard Ventura's quick verification and the acceleration of the motor, just before he signed off.

Keys closed down his communicator. He looked toward Kyle, who was sitting down now with his head in his hands. Rose was at the desk finishing a conversation on the phone. She verified some kind of order, noted it on a chart, and then hung up. She caught Keys' eyes, nodded and headed toward Kyle. Keys walked over.

"Kyle." Keys said, putting his hand on Kyle's shoulder. Kyle looked up and saw Rose approaching them. He stood quickly, looking at her with anxious eyes.

"She's out of surgery and on her way back up. We'll keep her under light sedation for a couple of days. Apparently, she had an embolism, near her aortic artery, which gave way, induced by the stress of the surgery and it bled into her chest cavity. They've repaired it. Her heart is again beating normally. The next twenty-four hours will be crucial. We'll keep her here for a few days to make sure she remains quiet and subdued, and she'll probably need assistance around the house when she does go home, but I don't foresee a problem in that regard." She smiled, one thing she had learned about Guardian, they took care of their own. "As of right now, things look good." Keys smiled, placing a hand on Kyle's back, while the boy bent at the waist and rested his hands on his knees, drawing in some deep breaths, and then Keys hugged Rose.

"Thank you, Rose."

"Can I stay with her?" Kyle swung his head toward her, looking up.

"For a while, Kyle, but you need to get your rest too. You're not too far out from traumatic injuries yourself. You may feel better, but let's not overdue it okay. I'll be here the rest of the night and she'll be okay."

Kyle straightened up and put his hands on his waist, taking a deep breath. He tilted his head in Keys direction. "Thanks for coming."

"You knew I would." He patted the boys arm. "But you heard what Rose said, only for a little while."

"Yeah." Kyle studied his face. "You're worried about something else or someone else," Keys locked eyes with the boy, Rose left the two to chat. "I recognize the furrowed brow. The distant gaze, you want to be here, but you need to be there," Kyle drew in a breath, "to help them."

Keys took a breath, "I have other agents that can handle it," he sighed, "I need to be here with you."

"No you don't." Kyle said, not bitterly. "You need to be where Guardian takes you, Dad, where your agents need you to be. I've always known that, may not have liked it, but I've known it."

Keys looked steadily at the boy, never wavering from his gaze. "Kyle, No matter where Guardian takes me, no matter who needs me, you know that all of that doesn't matter---none of that is more important to me than you are." He put his hand on the back of Kyle's head. "None of it."

"I know, Dad," he sighed then he did the unexpected and pulled his father into a hug. Surprised, Keys hesitated then he wrapped his arms tightly around Kyle. "Thank you for just being Dad tonight." Kyle said in a husky voice.

"You're welcome, Son," he hugged the boy tightly again then separated and brought his eyes to Kyle's face, studying it, "and it's Dad who's saying you need your rest. No matter who else I worry about, you are first on my mind, always."

"I will, I promise," he smiled, glanced at the floor, swallowed, and then brought his eyes back to Keys'. "Who is it? Who's in trouble?"

"Tanner just sent out a 911."

Concern passed over Kyle's features. "He's at Marna's, with the kids?" Keys verified with a nod. "Then you need to go."

"Ventura and Schaefer are on their way there. Security teams have already been dispersed."

Kyle looked steadily at him. He remembered a time, not so long ago, that he had to send out a 911 and he was grateful for the team's quick response. Tanner was alone, he needed help. The team needed to go, that included Keys. "Dad, get out of here. He's there with the kids. What happens if he's outnumbered or outgunned? Don't worry about Marna. I'll stick close to her." They looked toward Marna's room as a medical team rolled her gurney toward it. "Go." he said with more urgency.

"Call me if anything changes."

"I will." Kyle watched as Keys stepped onto the elevator, touched by the fact that he would have stayed with him if he had requested him to. Though he had often felt he had taken a back seat to Guardian while growing up, the thought always left him almost the instant it had invaded his mind, because the reasons they kept their relationship secret from many people was for Kyle's own safety and he knew that. He understood that. Keys had enemies, e.g. Lamontage, that would not hesitate to hurt Kyle to get to him. Kyle had seen plenty of those sorts of attacks in other agents' families in the four years he had been with Guardian WIT, so even though he didn't always agree with it, he knew it was for the right reasons.

Kyle had his own reasons for keeping his identity under wraps, he wanted to make it in Guardian on his own, and he didn't want to make it up the ranks on his father's name, nor did he want it to reflect badly on his father if he did something stupid and spontaneous, which he had done on occasion. They had agreed, and Kyle had taken his grandmother's maiden name and had climbed the ladder on his own. He was in WIT of his own accord, not because he cashed in on Frederick Keys name or reputation. They were both proud of that accomplishment. Only Guardian members that needed to know were aware of the blood ties between Kyle and Frederick Keys, Sherry Sylvester and Thomas Tate were among them. That's how it would remain until Kyle said otherwise.

He was proud of his father, and he loved him very much. He knew those feelings were returned, and yes they got frustrated with each other sometimes and Keys had reamed Kyle out a few times, rightfully so, but he had learned from it. Many agents that came into Guardian didn't have the kind of support from family that he did, because of that, he didn't mind sharing his father with them or with the organization, because he knew he would always rank first with Keys when push came to shove.

He turned on his feet, walked across the hall, stepped into Marna's room, and stood back while they hooked her up to all the medical machines. He waited patiently for them to finish then he pulled his chair closer to her bed, took her hand and kissed the back of it. "I'm here, Marna. I'll be here until you wake up."

*****

Tanner finished keying in his distress signal and pulled deeper into the shadow of the chair. He didn't dare use his abilities because Freeman could track. Marna found that out. He looked down at his swollen ankle. He had twisted it when he had dived for the chair. He bit his lower lip as spasms of pain traveled up his calf and burst into his kneecap. . What he didn't understand is why the house? Why tonight? Marna was still in the hospital. Just what did Ventura mean by his comments? His ankle throbbed. He flexed it and bit harder on his lip and closed his eyes as more pain shot up his leg.

"Uncle Tanner?" His head jerked up. Mary! No, now was not the time for distraction. "Uncle Tanner, why are the lights out?" A step creaked. She was coming down stairs! He caught a flash of moonlight reflect off something as it swung across his field of vision. The taser! He was going to shoot Mary. NO! He made his move. He jumped up, got off a couple of shots, which forced Martin to dive for cover. Then he ran toward the stairs, fired off more shots, before he ran up them, ignoring his ankle pain, two at a time. The blue beam barely missed him as he grabbed Mary around the waist and dragged her to safety, pulling her close to his chest as he dived around the corner at the top landing and leaned against the wall. She screamed and he hugged her tightly with one arm, while he held his gun up with the other.

"You okay?" She nodded, her dark ringlets bouncing about her head. He smiled and kissed the top of her head. Martin fired another beam, which hit a large framed picture of the children, glass shattered as the picture fell to the steps. Isaiah peaked out of his room. Tanner beckoned him over. He was wincing as he shifted weight off his bad ankle. Sweat beaded his brow. "Isaiah, you and your siblings take the fire escape. There is a Security cruiser out front. Get to it. Ventura and Schaefer are on their way." The boy looked fearfully at him. "I'll explain later. Go !" He shoved him away.

"What about you?" Beth asked, coming to his side.

"I'm keeping him busy until you're all safely out of here. Now go."

"Why don't you let us help, Uncle Tanner?" Hannah queried.

He took them all in with a glance. Remembered how much they had come to mean to him since they had crashed into his life a year ago. "Not this time, sweetheart, he's got a weapon that could hurt you all. Go." He whispered and urged them on their way. He raised his hand to stop further protest from them and waved them away. They all filed toward Isaiah's room. Tanner fired a couple more shots as the kids made it across the hallway, forcing Martin to stay down, giving the children a few precious moments to gather in Isaiah's room.

With his back to the wall for support, Tanner slid himself to a standing position, fired a few shots, and half ran, half-hopped across the open space to Marna's room. Martin fired on him. Tanner felt the heat of the beam singe his clothing just before he dived into Marna's room. He returned fire.

Isaiah and the older girls quickly helped the others out the window, and toward the fire escape steps. Isaiah and Elizabeth swung their heads toward the closed door when they heard gunfire, more glass breaking and Martin's voice ring out. "Yer can't 'ide forever, Williams. Me boss wants yer an' oi aim ter deliver!"

Elizabeth started to go back, but Isaiah grabbed her arm, shook his head and pushed her toward the window. "We have to help him !" She hissed.

"He told us no. He knows what we can do, and he told us no, Beth, he has to have his reasons."

Beth looked at the window and then at Isaiah's door. She looked uncertain, then a certain resolve came over her features and Isaiah shook his head vehemently when he recognized it. "Get the others to the front porch and wait for me to open the door," she ordered and in an instant, she had broken free of his hold and dashed for the door.

"Beth, no !" Isaiah hissed and watched helplessly as she threw back the lock, and swung open the door. Martin swung his head in her direction. He fired on Isaiah, who scrambled and barely escaped. Beth Screamed. Tanner rolled to his stomach, aiming his weapon, in time to see Martin grab Beth's arm.

"Beth!" Tanner cried.

Martin Grinned. "er for ya, Williams! put yer gun down an' git yer arse oyt 'ere!"

"Let her go, Freeman! She's just a child!"

"Maybe, but she means somethin' to ya. I kin see dat." He chuckled. Tanner weighed his options. He couldn't shoot, because Beth was in his line of fire. He didn't understand this guy. If he wasn't working for Lamontage, whom did he work for?. Martin stood in a stream of moonlight had Beth pressed against him with the taser nozzle next to her carotid artery. He looked at his gun. He had two shots left. The rest of the team should be there soon, could he get Beth out of the line of fire and away from the house?

"Time's a tickin', Williams! ya for de lassy." Beth struggled against his hold. She looked around the hall for something to focus on. He shifted the Taser and pressed the muzzle tighter against her neck, hitting the button on the top. "Oi'm not a patient man, Williams. Do ya nu waaat a taser volt can do ter a child whaen de beam is directly on 'er artery? Instant death, me frund, that's waaat. I'll gie yer ter de count av tree ter muk yer mind, an' den oi drop 'er, Williams. Jist loike dat, drop 'er loike a fly wi' a swatter."

He recognized the look of resolve in Martin's eyes. He would kill her. She was nothing to him, just a means to an end. He saw the look in Beth's eyes. She was terrified. "All right !" He yelled. Taking a deep breath, he let his gun swing loose on his thumb, and tossed it away from him.

"Nigh come oyt av dare, 'ands up, Williams! nice an' slow loike."

Tanner stood up and limped into the hall with his hands in the air. "You okay, Beth?" She nodded. Tanner raised his eyes to Martin's. "All right, you've got me, now let her go."

"In due time, me frund, in due time. ya 'walk toward me, an' whaen oi 'av ya secured, i'll let de lass go, oi mean 'er naw 'arm, 'tis ya oi'm gettin' paid for." He beckoned with his head. Tanner limped slowly toward him, wincing with every step. He didn't want to make any sudden moves for fear Martin would perceive it wrong and hurt Beth. When he stepped in front of them, Martin grinned. "Nigh a go raun, an' put yer 'ands behind yer back, Williams." Tanner brought both his arms down in a C-curve and placed them behind his back. Martin kept the taser on Beth, but pulled out a zip-tie and handed it to her. "Dare lass, put dat raun 'is wrists nice an tight loike."

She held the tie, and dared a glance at Tanner. "It's okay, Beth, do as he says." Beth's eyes filled with tears as she circled the zip-tie around his wrists and pulled it tight. Martin gave it an extra pull, causing Tanner to wince. "You've got me, Freeman, now let her go." Martin looked at Beth and nodded his head toward the stairs. Beth turned around and gave Tanner a hug. *Be ready, Uncle Tanner.*

Tanner kept himself from reacting to her psychic message. He looked down at her and smiled. He had gotten her message loud and clear, but it seems Martin was oblivious to what had just passed. He nodded at her to let her know, he understood. "Go find your brothers and sisters, Beth." Beth nodded. She headed toward the stairs, looked back once and started down them. As soon as she hit the lower level, she steered herself toward the front door, opened it, and then melted into the shadows.

Tanner spoke, hoping to buy the kids some time. "Mind telling me what this is all about?"

" Someone is pure interested in gettin' their 'ands on yer." Martin said. "An' they're willin' ter pay a 'efty price for yer too."

"Are they asking you to commit murder too? You nearly got Marna killed the other day. She's still fighting for her life."

" She shud 'av done as oi asked. It wouldn't 'av 'appened. Didn't matter wan way or de other. De buyer didn't care if she made it alive, but yer," he chuckled, "Yer, me friend they want yer alive."

"Who are they? Don't I have a right to know who's paying the bounty on my head?"

Martin stared at him for a while then nudged him. "Let's go, Williams, oi got a delivery ter make," he said. Martin pushed him forward, Tanner stumbled toward the stairs then he started descending, step after painful step, ahead of his captor, almost stumbling twice before Martin caught him and forced him forward again. Tanner looked around carefully. He had not heard the front door shut but when he got to the lower level, he felt the breeze from outside. That's when he caught the movement out of the corner of his eye. Beth had not failed him. Martin pushed him a little harder toward the French doors. The landing stepped up. Tanner's foot hit it, and he went down face first. "Yer clumsy Bloak." He reached down to grab Tanner and pull him roughly to his feet.

Tanner had given them the opening, they joined hands. No, Marna wasn't with them, but they had done this before without her, Isaiah knew what he had to do. Their abilities intertwined, PJ and Amanda Sue added more possibilities to their collective, strengthened what they already had. This was the first time they had actually felt the surge, knew the joining of the collective. They knew what to do, knew they had to help. They all opened their channels. They felt what each other felt, could strengthen each other's abilities. Isaiah took his command. *Amanda Sue, block*! Her blocks helped the others, strengthened their shields. *Moses now!* Moses bilocated and appeared before Martin, causing him to jump back and release his hold on Tanner's arm. Tanner rolled onto his back, raised his feet and kicked up, pushing out, catching Martin in the ribs and lifting him in the air, pitching him over a chair. "Ahh !" Martin cried, aiming his Taser at Tanner and firing, Tanner dived behind a nearby chair. *Mary, Amanda sue Now!* The two girls focused and joined their shielding power. The protective bubble formed around them and they advanced on Martin. Martin's face filled with panic and astonishment. He aimed his Taser. *Beth now!* Beth focused and the Taser went flying across the room. Tanner jumped up and ran at Martin shoulders first. Martin grabbed a nearby stool and swung out, catching Tanner's mid section and dropping him to the floor. Martin pulled a Glock from the waistband of his pants, aiming it at Isaiah, shots rang out, he jerked, and fell backwards over an overturned chair, the life leaving his eyes as a circle of crimson stained his shirt. Ventura and Schaefer moved toward him, and a security team followed.

Disengage! Isaiah ordered. The force field retreated, and the children let go of their hold on each other's hands.

Schaefer moved toward Martin and checked his carotid. "He's dead," Then she glanced at the kids, while Ventura cut Tanner loose and helped him to the couch. "Nice job, kids."

"Thank you." They all said together then went to Tanner's side and circled him protectively.

Keys moved into the room, took in the surroundings and moved to the children's side. "Is everyone okay?"

"Yeah, with the exception of Freeman," Schaefer said, "he didn't fair so well."

He looked at Tanner who had an arm across his mid-section "are you okay, Son?"

"Yeah, I'm fine." He smiled at the kids. "Thanks to my back up team, otherwise I would be on a ride to where ever the hell this guy was taking me."

Keys looked at the children. He smiled with pride. They had initiated and performed a collective defense on their own, without Marna's help or direction. They had taken a step toward independence and knowing when to use their gifts to help another. "You did well. You should all be proud of yourself." He glanced at Schaefer. "Why don't you get the children settled back in, for the night, while I examine Tanner?" Objections filled the room from the children. Tanner chuckled and held up one of his hands, while he still held the other across his midsection.

"Easy now, guys, school tomorrow. You want your mom to kick my butt?" Tanner teased, "Haven't I been beat up enough for one night?" He raised an eyebrow. They were thoughtful for a moment, causing the adults to grin, and then they all laughed and wished everyone good night before heading upstairs.

Keys had Tanner strip his shirt off so he could check his ribs then he looked over his ankle. "I think you may have a bruised a rib or two and sprained your ankle," He said as he wrapped the ribs to give them support while they healed and then he wrapped the ankle. When he finished, he rolled his sleeves down. "You got lucky this time." Heidi came down and handed Tanner his gun. Tanner checked out the magazine and placed it back in his holster then allowed Keys to help him put his shirt back on. "Tell me what happened?"

He told Keys his version of events. "What happened to my back up? I saw them pull up."

"They're dead." Keys said. "Martin either came in later then you figured or he had a partner. The first team we sent up was killed in their car. We believe by a taser."

"Dammit! Johnson just had a baby a month ago." Tanner said dropping his head on the couch back and pinched the bridge of his nose. He swallowed, and remained silent for a moment before he returned his gaze to Ventura. His tone was strained, angry. "I thought Marna was the target. Why have I suddenly become the lead role in some twisted Saturday Night Thriller?"

Ventura tossed a folder on the table. "Sit, Tanner, I'll make you some tea." Schaefer said.

Tanner moved to the table, and sat down carefully, and winced. He slid the folder over to him, and opened the cover. There were pictures of him doing his daily activities, pictures of him on patrol, on the campus, on Marna's porch, playing basketball with her kids, washing his car, and some of him in Switzerland. There were pictures of him and Marna walking in the park, that private moment when he almost kissed her and the look on both their faces. He felt violated, betrayed. Who was intruding on his life and why? "What is all of this?"

"We don't know." Ventura tossed him another folder. "We found these on Freeman's computer as well." Tanner opened the second folder. There were several emails discussing negotiations between Freeman and some unknown subject calling themselves Gypwitch45 about abducting Tanner and delivering him to an unknown designation, revealed only if Martin had completed his mission. "We were hoping you could shed some light on the situation for us?"

He looked up from the emails and the pictures. "I have no idea. If he was after me, why hurt Marna? He is the one who shot her, right?"

"No. His partner was. But that's where the cases intersect and we don't know why. He's been stalking you obviously, and when he saw you spending so much time with her, maybe he figured . . ."

"I would have been here that day, and instead he got Kyle." Tanner looked thoughtful. "Wait a minute; didn't he say something about selling her?" He thought for a moment. "He said the one they're retrieving her for will pay a handsome price. Isn't that what Kyle said?" He looked toward Keys for confirmation.

Keys nodded. "Yes, something like that, Marna verified it."

"And tonight Martin said something about the buyer not caring if she made it to them alive, but that I was to be delivered alive."

Keys nodded. "So maybe this guy is some kind of retriever, bounty hunter for higher?" He turned toward Ventura. "Did they find anything about Marna or a negotiation exchange, concerning her?"

Ventura shook his head. "Not yet, but he encrypted every email folder he had. They're still working on them."

"Maybe Lamontage hired someone to get Marna for him," suggested Schaefer.

Keys shook his head. "No, He wants Marna alive. He wants to possess her."

"So what is your take on this, Keys?" Ventura queried. "Freeman's partner put Marna in the hospital,and put Kyle out of commission.Freeman almost got away with Tanner tonight,Why is he after both Marna and Tanner? If he doesn't work for Lamontage, who does he work for?"

"I can't answer that until we find out who hired Martin and his partner."

"They had the same taser the Liberatores had," Schaefer interjected.

"Yes, distributed by an online weapons sales company, weaponsarray.com or something along those lines, but it didn't come from the factory that way. Someone altered it into some kind of psychic warfare weaponry and that is what concerns me. If we have two different people using this altered weaponry, where are they getting it, and how do we shut them down? I have Guardian techs tearing apart the one we confiscated in Switzerland, and hopefully we'll find the answers and the signature of the maker, but until then . . ."

"So what do we do about this?" Tanner waved his hands over the folder.

"I have feelers out with FWPA. I sent them a picture of our friend. They might be able to find out who he really is," Keys sighed, "tonight, we get some rest. Look at all of this with fresh eyes in the morning."

"How do you want to work security?" Ventura queried, "now that we've got two agents with a price on their head?"

"Rose is at the hospital with Marna. She came through surgery well.They expect her to make a full recovery. I'll send Bryan down to relieve Kyle because he needs to get himself back in shape, before he can start protecting others again. I'll send a couple of security people down there too." He looked toward Ventura. "You and Heidi stay here; I want to continue to have a bubble of protection over this house and the children." The two of them nodded. His eyes moved to Tanner. Those pain killers should be taking effect soon."Tanner, you'll stay here as well, I want you under a security bubble too. You go to the den and get some rest." Tanner nodded, and eased himself up, and then dumped his remaining tea down the sink drain, putting the cup on the counter, and moved into the den. Keys took the folder, pushing the photos back into it, stopping when he saw the one of Tanner and Marna in the park in Switzerland. The look they exchanged said it all. The attraction was there for all to see.

 He didn't know how that story would end, but after seeing Kyle at the hospital tonight, all torn up about Marna, it could mean someone was heading for heartache. The worse part, they were all good people. Either match would benefit them and Guardian. He just didn't understand how he could not have seen it happening. How could he have not seen his Son, his pride and joy falling so fast and so hard? And Marna? She was just starting to put her life back together after the devastating loss of Jeff. Could she handle such a decision? Would she be strong enough to make the choice? She would be as gentle as she could. He knew that much of her, but a broken heart was inevitable. In the game of love, there were always casualties. Sighing, he pushed the picture in with the rest, and pushed the folders to the center of the table. He needed to call the hospital, check in and let Kyle know Bryan would be relieving him.

*****

Marna's head moved on the pillow, she let out a soft sigh. She felt her hand held firmly in enveloping warmth. She rolled her head to the side to see who was with her. Kyle was sitting in a chair next to her bed, his head resting on the arm curled over the railing and his breathing was slow and steady. She gently pulled her hand from his grasp and touched his arm. He lifted his head up and glanced at her. His arm had left a red impression on his forehead.

"Hi," she whispered.

"Hi yourself," he said, "You had me scared for a while there," he rubbed her head, and looked into her eyes, "how are you feeling? Are you in pain? Do you need a nurse?"

"No," her voice was very soft, barely above a whisper. "What happened? Her eyes moved around the room.

He gently ran the back of his fingers over her cheek. "You had some bleeding in your chest, but they fixed you up. They said a few days in here, and you'll be on your way to a full recovery."

"The kids?"

"Don't worry, we've got them covered."

"Mmm." She sighed again, and closed her eyes. Kyle thought she was going to sleep, and he just watched her for a moment. An overwhelming tenderness came over him he couldn't explain.

"Sweet dreams." He whispered.

Her eyes sprung open, she became agitated, fear shadowed over her features. "Lamontage!"

"What?" He became alarmed and looked around the room. "He's not here, Marna, he can't hurt you."

"No, no." Her alarm went off her heartbeat was climbing.

Rose rushed in. "What happened?"

Kyle looked helplessly at her. "I don't know. She woke up, and we were talking then she yelled out Lamontage's name and freaked."

"Rose, he's got Demi, he'll kill her if. . ."

"Marna, calm down or I'm going to have to increase your meds and put you under again. Do you hear me?"

"He wants, he wants." Kyle ran his hands through his hair and walked to the wall he and Keys had sat near earlier. He felt helpless. What was happening? Was it something he had said? Something he had done.

"Haldol !" Rose ordered the orderly who came in behind her.

"No, Rose, no." Marna pleaded. "I have to see Keys !" She became more agitated when the nurse with the syringe came in. "No, I can't, I can't, we have to save Demi." Rose held him off with a hand.

"Marna if you don't stop, I'll have to medicate you or you could start your bleeding again. Please just calm down !" Rose ordered.

"Okay, okay, I'll stop. Just don't make me sleep, don't make me sleep." Marna started breathing deeply. The machine readings decreased. She sat back calmly doing as Rose ordered, but her eyes were alert. Rose shook her head at the other nurse who put the syringe on the tray. Kyle walked back to the bed, reached over the rail, and took her hand his eyes were moist.

"Deep breaths, that's it." Rose continued to talk to her in soothing tones. She took her vitals, checked her stitches, and listened to her heart. She pressed around the new incision, and listened some more. Marna laid her head back. A tear slipped out of her eye and rolled down her cheek. Kyle reached up and wiped it away, looking into her eyes. He let his gaze slip to Rose who caught it and nodded, he drew in a deep breath. Rose took her stethoscope off, and put it around her neck. "Okay, it looks like you didn't do any damage with your little outburst, now how about you calmly tell me what is going on in that head of yours? What freaked you out to the point of needing sedation?"

"I need to see Keys."

"Tonight?" Marna nodded. "Marna, it's nearly eleven o'clock." Marna looked at her, pleading with her eyes. "All right, I'll call him, but only if you promise to lay back and stay calm."

"Okay." Rose left the room and came back in a few minutes later. "He's on his way, he said he's going to pick up Bryan on the way to relieve you Kyle, he wants you to go home and get some rest." Kyle nodded.

When Rose had left, Kyle sat back down beside her. "You okay?" His voice was low, caring.

She nodded. "Yeah, I'm sorry."

"No need to apologize, Marna, you just need to promise me you'll follow doctors orders or I'll put that syringe in your butt myself."

She grinned, "I'd like to see you try."

He chuckled, raising a brow. "Temptress." He brought her hand to his lips and kissed it. She winced and sank deeper into her pillow, pulling her hand away and crossing it over her side as a pain ripped through her. "You know, they have you hooked up to pain meds for a reason," he leaned closer, conspiratorially, "All you gotta do is push the little blue button on that there control panel," he pointed to the white box midway down the IV pole, "and it goes away," he whispered.

"Not until I talk to Keys, I need my head clear, just help me shift my position a little." He reached behind her, using the positioning pad underneath her, while she used the trapeze above her head, and repositioned herself. "Ahh,"

"You, okay." He stopped moving her pillows and brought his head back so he could see her face.

"Yeah, I'm fine, just help me sat back."

"Okay." He supported her behind her shoulders as she eased herself back on the pillows. "Better?"

"Yeah." He heard them shuffle in, before he turned to see them. He barely noticed the pause as Keys stopped a moment and watched him assist Marna. Again, he hoped his boy wasn't headed for heartache.

"Hello, Marna." Keys said coming over and kissing her forehead, then he caught Kyle's eyes and smiled. Kyle finished getting her positioned and backed off. "How are you feeling?"

"I've been better." She smiled at the newcomer. "Bryan, Hi."

"Hey, Marna, I hear you've had a rough day."

"That's what they tell me." She bit her lip, winced, drew in a painful breath, and started speaking again, "I slept through most of it." They all chuckled.

"I see your sense of humor is still intact," Keys said, "that's a plus to go through what you've gone through and still come out of it with a smile. Says a lot about you."

"It just hurts too much to laugh." She smiled, and turned to Keys, "how are the children?"

"They're fine. Everyone is taking a turn watching over them, and keeping your house from chaos, so you needn't worry. Just rest knowing we've all got you covered."

She gave a slight nod, drawing in a breath. "Have you caught him yet? Martin?"

Keys hesitated. "He's dead, Marna."

"How? When?"

"We'll get to all of that unpleasantness later, Rose said you needed to talk to me, and you were rather insistent, what was so important you couldn't get yourself a good night's sleep first?" He leaned on the bedrail and looked at her.

"Lamontage," she said with effort.

Keys frowned, curious, "What about him?"

"He invaded my dreams today." Kyle tensed, no wonder she was so upset, that was the reason she had gone into cardiac arrest. The Bastard had terrorized her to the point of kicking her heart into a tachycardia, before he let her come back. He would bet money on it. He mumbled an expletive, and walked across the room, staring out the window across the brightly lit parking lot.

Keys watched him go, and then returned his eyes to Marna. "Tell me about it," he encouraged.

"It was really ah--a bunch of flashes going through my head," she waved her hand before her eyes. Pictures of Sasha, she swallowed, —after — ah – after the attack, then I was tied down to this bed, then the bed at the tower, then Demi was tied down, then she was laying beside—" She drew in a breath as a tear slid down her face.

Keys urged her on, "what else?" He took her hand, rubbing the back and she gripped tightly to it, as if holding onto it would keep her anchored in this realm. "Take your time."

"—He – ah – he told me that I could make it all stop, all the pain, all the sorrow, and Demi — would – um – could get her life back if."

"If what, Marna," he spoke softly, knowing how important it was to keep her calm, yet needing the information she had to give.

"—If – ah – if I would go to him, become his, then he would leave everyone I love alone, and Demi would be returned to those that loved her."

Bryan put his hands on his waist, turned away, walked to the wall, leaning against it. Keys tried to reassure him with a glance. It had to be hard for him to hear this, because he knew that they could not give in to Pierre's demands, yet his heart wanted to do anything he could to stop Demi's suffering. "Is that all he said, Marna?"

She nodded. "Maybe I should."

Keys blew out a breath. He saw the horror spring into Kyle's eyes as he swung his head around. Keys shook his head slightly, assuring him that it wasn't happening. "No, Marna, we are not going to hand you over to him."

"You didn't see what he was doing to her. The horrible things he made her do."

"Which, Marna, he will do to you, probably much worse things he will do to you, if we give him the chance. No, Marna, we'll find another way to get to Lamontage."

She reached out and grabbed his arm with her other hand, "What if there is no other way? What if the only way to stop him from hurting Demi, Rose, the children, anyone I care for is for me to just go to him. Isn't sacrificing one to save the many worth it"

"Not in this sense it isn't, Marna. Lamontage has taken too many good people to allow him rights to you. You are not a sacrificial lamb to give to him to make him go away, because the truth is, he'll be back and he'll take more. That's what he does is take. Now I'm going to close this conversation and we aren't going to bring it up again, am I clear on that?" She nodded. Kyle drew in a breath and let it out as he lowered his head. "I've got people following the leads on the hidden villages in the area. Let's see where that leads before we lose hope in the path we're taking now." He smiled, took her hand and kissed her forehead. "You get some rest. Bryan will be here to keep Lamontage from breeching you again and I'll swing by tomorrow.Okay." She nodded, "good," he turned toward Kyle, who had moved up beside him again. "Kyle, are you ready?" He nodded and bent down to kiss Marna on the cheek, and squeezed her hand.

"I'll stop by tomorrow. You get some rest." She nodded, fighting back tears. Her mind returning to Lamontage's intrusion but she would do what Keys said and wait for the irons he had in the fire to pan out first. Bryan wished them both a good night and took up his vigil by the bed, thumbing through a magazine.

"I'm sorry, Bryan."

"For what." He answered softly, lifting his eyes to hers.

"I can't help her." Her voice broke. "I want to but I can't." Tears slipped down her cheeks.

Bryan sat up, leaning forward "Hey, I am grateful that you're willing to sacrifice yourself, but Keys is right, Marna, we can't do that. That would be playing into his hands, and then there is no guarantee he won't just kill her anyway. We'll do battle with Lamontage, Marna, but not that way. When we do meet Lamontage, it will be to bring him down. I don't want you to even think along those lines again, and I know Demi wouldn't even consider it for a minute." He took her hand, "you get some sleep and let someone take care of you for a change," she nodded.

Rose came in, checked her vitals, changed her dressings, and then dosed her with her pain medication and a mild sedative, the last thing Marna remembered was drifting off to a peaceful sleep, and the warmth of Bryan's protection encircling her and reinforcing her shields.

Chapter Sixteen

Kyle parted ways with Keys in the hospital parking lot. He started his car and sat back, letting it rumble. He had gotten the Camaro when he graduated high school. Keys had picked it up at a local auction for him. It was a classic Shelby Super Snake 2016 model, black and gold, in mint condition, and nothing but pure power. He had thought his father could walk on water that day and the car had been a prized possession of his ever since. He closed his eyes and let out a sigh, pinching the bridge of his nose. God he was so tired and heart weary. Sasha's death, Marna's near death. Evil forces were at work, trying to destroy all the good in his life.

He blew out a breath and pushed himself up in his seat. Then he fastened his seatbelt, shifted his car into reverse, backed out of his parking spot, and steered his way to the hospital bypass road. He planned on going home and getting some rest. His father was right about that much. His body needed to rest, but his mind wasn't as willing to shut down. He turned left onto Harris Avenue, and headed toward the business district. He slowed his car as he came to a red light and waited for it to turn green. His body went into autopilot but his mind went into hyper-warp; the look in Marna's eyes came back to haunt him; the fear, the pain, and then the resignation that the only way to keep everyone safe was to sacrifice herself. He could possibly chase the rest from his memory banks but he couldn't shake the steadiness in her voice when she made her offer Could she really be considering sacrificing herself to this prick because he made her a false promise? It had to be the meds messing with her head. She had to know the dangers of taking such a risk. He remembered his grandmother talking about false profits, he wondered if she meant men like Lamontage. The man was as deceitful as they get.

Then there was Sasha, he hadn't even taken the time to mourn his partner, his best friend. She had been a caring and forgiving woman, one of the few solid and stable people in his life. She had stuck with him through his reckless and chaotic behavior when most other agents would have run or at the very least, requested a new partner, and yes, she was one of the few that had known of his connection to Keys.

She understood his heart more than any romantic lover ever could, and yes, they had shared his bed a few times, but she also understood, as he had, there was really nothing there to grow. Had it affected their lives on the streets? Yes, in a good way, it made them stronger, made their psychic connection stronger, made their team stronger. He wondered if that was why Guardian had an unspoken don't ask, don't tell policy when it came to partners being sexually or romantically involved. Isn't that how his parents had started? They were partners and friends and they relied on each other to get out of tight spots, covered each other's back when they went through a door, but as far as he and Sasha had gone, a long-term romantic relationship never developed.

Because of all of these thoughts trolling through his mind, he knew there was no way he was going to sleep tonight, at least not right away, he was beginning to question his decision to turn his father's offer of a sedative down. A large, neon sign blinked red letters, announcing Jenna's Tavern, one of the compounds two bars. His peripheral vision reacted and he smiled, glancing toward it. Ah — the memories – before Bradshaw, before Switzerland, and definitely before Marna – he sobered, but then again, he thought, maybe one of his old haunts is just what he needed.

He sat for a moment pondering the thought, It was Wednesday; Ladies' night, live band night. He could think of several reasons why he shouldn't go, but one good reason why he should. His conscience and free spirit argued between themselves for a few more seconds before he flipped on his blinker and turned into the parking lot. He'd have a couple of drinks, listen to the band, and maybe take a few spins on the floor. No harm, no foul, right? It may be enough to relax him so he could do as Doctor Dad ordered and go home to get some real sleep, where Sasha's bloodied corpse, and Marna's wounded body didn't haunt his dreams.

He parked his Shelby, locked it up, slipped the keys into his pocket, and then he made steps toward the front door. He could hear – no – feel the bass already; it was coming in a slow steady vibration through his feet, via the parking lot. He passed the visiting band's bus and looked it over **Sweethearts 21** was painted in calligraphic letters on the side, and the four faces of the women in question, were computer painted above it. He smiled nostalgically. He knew the band well, He and Sasha used to come to hear them whenever they were in Maine. They were local, and had spent several years doing the tavern, and lounge circuit, but recently the right people had heard them and they had just released their first international single; 'A Rose of Many Colors'. He and Sasha used to listen to it in Switzerland, when they got together for a drink after work. His heart felt a little heavy. "I'll have one for you, Sash," he whispered then proceeded to the door, pushing inward and entering the tavern.

He smiled. The place hadn't changed much, but then he hadn't expected it to, secretly hoped it hadn't. The atmosphere brought him back to his earlier years; back when the biggest case he worked on was some teenager using his telekinesis for vandalism or the highlight of the night was stopping someone who believed the hover lever in the car turned it into a jet and the road was a runway. He shook his head and grinned at the memories.

The lighting was low and **Sweethearts 21** was batting out a new ballad on the slow spinning stage, centered on the ballroom sized dance floor. The stage's trim lights were wired into the sound system and tapped out the music rhythm with blinking, neon splendor. He grinned. Oh how he had missed American culture. "Hey, Kyle." A petite redhead said, pulling him out of his moment of reverie. She was delivering drinks to a table near the door. "Where ya been, Handsome? We thought you'd forgotten all about us."

"Never, Tiff, Never." He grinned and gave her a kiss on the cheek before she went to pick up another order. Tiffany Worgon, if he recalled correctly, she was a five star in his little black book. He watched her go then made his way to the bar. He had fond memories of Saturday nights, hook ups, and Jenna's Tavern. Sasha had accompanied him on many and watched his game in play. His only interest was whom he was going to go home with. On many of those occasions, he left Sasha with the keys to the Shelby, while he left with some new face in a short skirt, two sheets to the wind. She had overlooked a lot. He drew in a breath, swallowing the lump in his throat. He was going to miss her terribly.

"Regular, Kyle?" The bartender's voice interrupted his private thoughts. Her name was Sandy. Their relationship had lasted six months. His only monogamous relationship, during his first year on the compound, but she had wanted something more serious and he wasn't ready to settle down, they parted friends, and she later married a nice young man on the PS&S team.

"Thanks, Sandy."

"You got it, Gorgeous." She returned with a Sam Adams special and some chips. "Burger will be ready in a few." She wiped the counter down. "Where ya been, good lookin'? We were beginning to think you had vanished without a trace, though we saw no news reports on a missing Romeo." She winked, he chuckled, and she put her palms on the counter, leaning forward.

"I've actually been abroad on a missing person case for a year." He took a sip of his drink, let out a sigh and brought his eyes to her face. She was actually still a very good-looking woman and if circumstances had been different, in both their worlds, he might have tried another go around with her, "just got back last week."

"Did you find them?"

"Yeah, I did, and they're doing fine." His eyes drifted to the band.

"Romeo to the rescue," she grinned, "how come no ticker tape parade or hero's welcome? Doesn't seem fair."

He chuckled, glancing at her and returning his eyes to the band. "I don't need one. I'm just happy I was able to help."

"Hmm." She studied his features as a couple of girls passed by. A slow smile spread across her face, "Who is she?"

"What?"

"You're studying the band instead of making eyes at every girl as they pass by, and you haven't looked down my blouse once. Some woman has her hooks in you." He grinned and lowered his head, "She's gotta be somethin' special to lasso you, Romeo." He glanced her way and she saw it all reflected in his eyes. "Well I'll be damned, Romeo, someone who makes your eyes shine like that has got to be some kind of Juliette. Does she look at you the same way?" She smiled as he lowered his eyes to stare into the amber liquid in his mug, "If she doesn't, she will, or she deserves to lose you," he didn't answer.

"Order up !" She smiled, gave his hand a little squeeze, went off to get his order, and returned to hand him his burger.

"Want a refill?" He nodded and she left him to go down to the other end, returning moments later to replace his empty mug with a full one. Somebody yelled from the other end. "I'm coming wart face, hold your pants on. She winked at him and went to tend to the other customers. Kyle turned his attention to the band and ate his burger while he enjoyed his beer. When he finished, he signaled Sandy for another refill. He'd finish this drink and go home. He was right, being among old friends, had helped him relax.

"I thought that was you." A petite blonde scooted herself onto the stool beside him. "I didn't know you came here. I've been coming for months and haven't seen you before." Kyle studied the woman, trying to place the wavy hair and symmetrical features, enhanced with pastel colors, highlighting her striking, sea green eyes. He narrowed his eyes digging into his memory banks. He knew their paths had crossed somewhere; he just couldn't place the where. His eyes traveled the length of her body. She was wearing a short, Kelly green skirt, fishnet stockings, three-inch heels, the same shade of green as her skirt, and a white pull over sweater, embellished with rhinestones. "How's your friend?"

Kyle frowned, then it dawned on him, she was the nurse from the hospital, the one he had been so short with earlier "She's – ah – she's holding her own." He lowered his eyes a moment, and then brought them back to hers. "Look, I'm sorry about the way I jumped you earlier."

"Already forgotten." She brought up a perfectly manicured hand and waved his concern aside. "I wouldn't be doing my job if a friend or family member didn't yell at least once a week." She smiled, showing perfectly even, perfectly white teeth. Kyle chuckled. She caught Sandy's eyes as the woman headed toward them. "Coffee Brandy, Sandy."

"Sure thing, Giselle."

"Giselle," Kyle said, "and who, dare I ask, is holding you hostage?"

Giselle turned her face toward him. "Beg your pardon?"

"The meaning of Giselle is hostage. Originating in the tragic ballet about a fair maiden who is in love with a secretly engaged prince and when she finds it out, she goes mad and dies."

"Oh but don't forget the part about her going back to save the loser at great risk to herself."

"Ah, a noble woman," he said puckering his lips and narrowing his eyes in thought, "you're right, a much better stigma to be attached to. He tilted his head and raised his mug to her.

She accepted her drink, circled the glass a couple of times with the stirring stick, and then took a drink before she tilted her head toward him, her long blonde mane hanging loosely in waves to her lap. "That's the part that kept me from changing the name as I grew older."

"All of that aside, it is a very beautiful name." He smiled. "It suits you." Her face grew pink, he grinned. "Kyle Rigby." He offered her his name.

"Hello, Kyle Rigby." She shook his hand. "Do you want to get a table?" He looked uncertain. "I just saw one open up closer to the band. I just positively love this band and it is Ladies' night. I hate sitting at a table by myself, all the losers think you're fair game, and they never give you any peace all night, not to mention the ones that leave you room numbers." She puffed out a breath and raised her hand, palm out, "I promise, I'll keep your virtue intact, Mr. Kyle Rigby, I just don't want to be fighting off the wolves all night while I'm trying to listen to my favorite band."

Kyle smiled slowly. "Well when you put it that way, how can I say no to being a personal body guard to such a virtuous young woman and to, how did you say it, help keep the wolves at bay?"

"Great! Come on." She took his hand and led him through the narrow alley of the bar, and claimed a table for two a young woman was just clearing off. Positioned by an aisle in the first row, circling the ballroom floor, the table was perfect. Whistles and catcalls went across the room as **Sweethearts 21** finished a number and then went immediately into the interlude to their current hit single 'A Rose of Many Colors.' Giselle cheered and clapped as the lead vocalist started singing the first stanza.

You left me with a promise you'd return
All I have now is emptiness to burn
I come to give roses to this stone
and in the cold, I stand alone

Red is for the love we shared
Pink is for passion undenied
White is for how we cared
Blue is for the tears I cried
You have become my Rose of many colors . . .

A young woman came by and replaced their drinks. Kyle looked at it, was going to pass, but then he figured one more wouldn't hurt and then smiled up at her, caught for a moment by her dark eyes. He slipped a five-dollar tip into her apron pocket and winked at her. She winked back and moved to another table. He was beginning to relax and true to her word, Giselle had not asked for anything but stimulating conversation. He took a swig of his beer and listened to the rendition of the song. Considering it his tribute to Sasha, he pulled out his GPC, switched it to the nightlight app, and lifted it high swaying it to the tones of the ballad. Applause broke out and soon the 100 plus patrons, in the coliseum like circle, did the same thing. It was a sight to beholden. The lead singer caught his gaze and smiled. A message that she felt his pain, a gentle prodding and an alliance formed. She was a Feeler. He smiled as tears sprang to his eyes. With his free hand, he picked up his glass, lifted it in honor of their lost ones, and then he guzzled the remainder of his drink. It earned him a wink and a sad smile from the lead vocalist as the turntable stage slowly moved her on. It was an interlude that happens rarely in one's lifetime. The Server came by with another round. He looked at his watch then up at the girl, frowned for a moment, pealed another five from his wallet, handing it to her then nodded and continued to listen to the soothing voices of the up and coming band.

Two songs later, he felt the effects of his gusto. The room started spinning. He felt warm, and his thoughts were a jumbled mess. "I think it's time to call it a night," he said, grabbing the table edge as the dizziness moved in.

Giselle looked at him strangely, "What's wrong?" Her voice sounded muffled, as if they were under water.

"Guess I shouldn't have had that last one," he shook his head, "I can usually hold out better than this, I only had a few." He raised his hand to his head.

"You've been under a lot of stress," She reassured him. "Alcohol has a funny effect on us when that happens. Is there someone you want me to call?"

He reached for his GPC, opened it, and tried to focus on the screen, but it swam before his eyes. He closed it up and slipped it back into his jacket pocket. Warmth spread through his body, as if his blood was starting to heat up. "Perhaps I should get some air," he said, getting up and starting to stumble across the dance floor toward the exit door. Dancing couples pushed him away, making him stumble backwards into the wall that separated the bar from the ballroom. It kept him from falling. The more he tried to move, the more distorted things became. Conversations became nightmarishly distorted, people's faces elongated and his body started feeling strangely disconnected. He leaned his forehead against the wall, closed his eyes, swallowed, and took a deep breath. His uncertainty of what induced his state of being was becoming a rising fear. This wasn't affects from the alcohol. Opening his eyes, he dared another look around the room, still leaning on the wall for support. Everything was going in and out of focus, he felt like he was looking through a fish lens one moment and the next; down a narrow, distorted hall of mirrors. He felt the darkness curling in on his consciousness.

Had he been drugged? By who and why? For what? There wasn't anybody on the staff he didn't already know. Wait a minute, the girl who delivered his last drink. Something about her, he hadn't paid it much attention then because he was enjoying the band. Her eyes, they were familiar, she was familiar. He looked around the room trying to remember her features, but he was so into the band, so into the moment, remembering Sasha.

"Kyle?" He turned his head, Giselle stood beside him. Her features etched with concern.

"Gis – Giselle, I – I've been drug – drugged ."

"What?" She looked alarmed and glanced around the room.

"No. Don't look. I-I need to get out of here. N-need to c-call my father."

Her features shadowed in alarm, but to her credit, she didn't panic. "Okay, here, Lean on me, and I'll get you out of here and home. Then we can call whomever you want. What's your address?" He heard himself respond, and then he leaned into her as she carefully walked him toward the door.

"Whoa there, Kyle, a little too much?" Tiffany asked as Giselle struggled to keep them both upright.

"I'm sorry," Giselle said softly, "excuse us." Tiffany spun away, drink tray in her hand and cleared their path to the door. Giselle kicked it open with her foot, using their bodies to stabilize it then she half walked, half dragged him through it and over to a stone bench to their right. She helped him sit and crouched before him as he rested his elbows on his knees and forehead on his hands. "Deep breaths, Kyle, stay awake, don't lose consciousness." he gave her a nod, "I should call an ambulance."

"No!" he hissed, grabbing her wrist, "just get me home so I can call my dad, please, Giselle, he's a doctor. They may have an ambulance waiting."

"What?" He was scaring her; he needed her to stay calm. "Please Giselle. I-I'm a WIT agent, K-Keys is my father, just get me home – call him."

She pushed him back as he pitched forward some. "Okay – Okay, just hang on. . ." her footsteps echoed distortedly as she hurried away. The darkness pressed in on him. He wasn't going to make it. He pulled his phone from his pocket and focused hard on keyboard then punched Keys speed dial button, but the GPC slipped from his grasp as he lost grip control before he had a chance to talk to him. It fell to the ground, sliding under the car, in the parking spot, before him. He pitched forward; fell hard on the pavement, rolled over onto his back, and his head lolled to the side. He saw his father's face for a split second, tried to reach for the GPC, but a car pulled up, and he was lifted up and thrown into the trunk. He thought he heard his father urgently call his name but it blended in with the other jumble of voices he didn't recognize. He tried to move, tried to fight the people who were bonding his hands and feet with zip ties but his body would not respond to his brain's desperate pleas. His hooded captors took his gun and his wallet. Where was Giselle? What had happened to her? He started slipping into darkness as the trunk closed. As he drifted off, an icy fear gripped his heart, he somehow knew where his destination was and why. . .

*****

Dawn was just creeping over the almost deserted parking lot when Keys pulled his car into it. Flashing lights from the Security vehicles, and the paramedic vehicle were bringing in the new day as time marched on, but to him it stopped the minute he saw Kyle's face on his screen as his captors dragged him away. He hadn't felt that helpless since Lizzy's death. He pulled to the right and parked next to Kyle's Mustang. Ventura saw him roll in, and left the paramedics to work on Giselle. "How is she?" Keys asked as Ventura approached him.

"Aside from a bit of a headache, she says she's fine"

"Can she identify them?"

"Vaguely," he sighed, "she said one came up to her asking for directions while she was absently fishing for her keys, she told him she had an emergency with a friend, and that she redirected him inside to the bartender. The guy nodded and acted as if he was going to leave that's when they sucker punched her from behind. They slammed her head into the rooftop of her car two or three times and she lost consciousness. By the time she came to, he was gone and she was bloodied and disoriented. She made her way inside to get help. I'll question her further when the medics are done."

"Set her up with a reconstruction sketch artist, maybe he can pull more details from her." Keys sighed. "Did you find it?"

Ventura held up an evidence bag with Kyle's GPC inside. "Did he leave anything on your incoming?"

Keys shook his head, "nothing of significance." Keys remembered the heart wrenching moment when he answered Kyle's call , seen his son's eyes full of fear, confusion and desperation, seconds before he was taken by hooded thugs. Keys had to contact a tech team, activate the GPS on Kyle's phone, and disperse the SP&S team and a team of WIT Agents. When all was said and done, precious time had passed. Heidi came out of the building and walked over to them. "Anything?" He queried.

"The bartender remembers him coming in around midnight and having a couple of drinks to wind down before our damsel in distress over there approached him, and invited him to share a table in the band area with her. He had a couple more drinks and then she said he started stumbling around like he was having some kind of attack, pissing off a few dancers by bumping in to them on his way across the floor. Then he leaned on a wall before Blondie came over and helped him out of the building. The next thing she remembers is the girl running in with blood running down her face, saying someone had attacked her and Kyle in the parking lot, and he was gone. Their call came in moments after yours, Keys. The Staff and some patrons backed her up."

"What was he doing here?" Keys pressed, "I told him to go home."

"Bartender said he used to be a regular about a year ago. Guess Jenna's was the stomping grounds of our boy before he and Sasha went overseas. Sandy, the bartender, chatted with him a few minutes. She thought Blondie was the special lady he had hinted at that had calmed the wild streak in our prodigal son. When the girl arrived, she said they talked like they knew each other, but it was funny that before last night Giselle hadn't even mentioned him considering she had been a regular for a while now."

"Anything else?"

She drew in a breath. "Before he left to go abroad, she said they used to affectionately call him Romeo and that judging by their talk, he had finally found his Juliette." She and Ventura shared a glance.

"Giselle wasn't she." Keys said knowingly. He studied the young woman."She was the nurse on duty, at the hospital yesterday, when Marna had her trouble."

"You don't think she had anything to do with the snatch and grab do you?"

"She doesn't look like any body types I saw momentarily on the monitor," he glanced toward Ventura, "Pete what's your assessment?"

"No, I think it's just as she said. She came to hear the band, ran into Kyle, remembered him from the hospital, and when he got into trouble she tried to help. Wrong place wrong time maybe, but I don't think she was in on it."

"Okay, send a security officer with her, and have him stay with her. Then have a sketch artist sit with her, a Reconstructer may be the best route. People remember more than they think when they have chance encounters. The Reconstructer may hit pay dirt, make sure they're one of our best, I think Serena Blackwater just got off a case."

"Got it," Ventura nodded and Keys moved toward Kyle's car, pulling out the set of keys. He reached the Shelby and unlocked the door. Ventura and Schaefer stood and watched, "Hmm, why do you suppose he has the keys to that Baby?" Schaefer asked.

"If you look in Kyle's phone, Keys is also listed as his emergency contact too." Ventura said.

"A lot of agents do that, it's because their families are so far away and they're traveling abroad on cases. If they need medical attention fast, it's better to have a Guardian CEO/Team Leader watching their backs."

"I suppose, but most have others listed too," he jotted down a few things in his notebook. The paramedics let them know Giselle was available for questioning, and that they were getting ready to transport her. "Thanks," they walked over to the young woman on the gurney.

"Giselle Riley?" Schaefer queried.

"Yes?" She looked up at them. There was a six-inch gash in her forehead, held together by mediglue and steristrips, her left eye was swollen shut, and already starting to bruise, her top lip was split and swollen, her stockings were torn at the knees, and her shoes were scuffed. Techs had bandaged her left hand to the wrist. The poor kid took a heck of a beating. Schaefer caught her gaze with her own. She looked nervous and confused.

"Giselle, I'm Heidi Schaefer, this is my partner Peter Ventura, and we're from Guardian WIT. We're friends of Kyle's."

Tears sprang to her eyes. "I never should have left him. I should have had someone sit with him while I went to get the car. I should have insisted he let me call an ambulance."

"Kyle asked you not to, you were only trying to do what he wanted. Besides he was concerned about people impersonating medical personnel, right?" she nodded.

"There you go then," Shaefer said, taking her hand, "you are not at fault for anything that happened last night." The girl worried her lower lip with her teeth, "what we would like from you is once the doctors okay it, is for you to spend some time with one of our Reconstruction artists and see if you can help produce a sketch of the man that approached you."

"Sure." She nodded and let her head settle back against the pillows.

"Great," Ventura signaled to a nearby security officer, "Giselle, this is Officer Reynolds, he's going to accompany you to the hospital and stay with you until we're sure your okay. She nodded, and Ventura stepped back while they boarded the ambulance. He glanced Keys way, caught his eyes through the windshield of the Shelby, nodded and Keys watched as the emergency vehicle drove by with their lights flashing. He gave the young woman inside a sympathetic thought then continued his search. He opened the glove compartment, found Kyle's extra gun and badge, along with his apartment key card, his registration, and inspection. He found nothing that would explain the abduction. He closed it up.

He tried to remember the cases Kyle had worked over the last four years, trying to think if any of them might be seeking revenge. He couldn't think of any. He flipped the visors down; the passenger side first.Nothing there but a few bills, stamped and ready to mail out, he replaced them, and then flipped down the driver's side. Nothing accept for a sliding door in the center of the visor, he reached up, sliding it upwards, his heart stopped and an invisible hand twisted it until he felt a physical pain. Kyle had sewn a laminated picture into the material behind that door. It was a picture of him and Kyle standing in front of the car on Kyle's graduation day, their arms wrapped around each other. Kyle proudly displaying his diploma.

Keys had experienced a mixture of emotions that day. He felt pride, because of the man his son was becoming, sadness that his mother was not there to see it happening, cheated because work had made it a necessity to keep his boy in the shadow and hidden from many of his friends and colleagues. However, what he felt most was loss for the boy he had barely known and alienated from the man Kyle was trying to become. Kyle said he understood, but Keys' guilt always overshadowed the reassurance in his son's words. He swallowed and lifted shaky fingers to trace Kyle's image outline. "Promise me you'll hang on, Son, I will find you, because I can't, no, I won't lose you too. Please, God, keep him safe." Drawing a breath and letting it out between pursed lips, he pulled the door back into place and flipped the visor up, continuing his search for another twenty minutes. He was about to climb out and hand it over to the techs when his GPC beeped. He opened it up – Ventura's number — and answered the call. "Pete?"

"Keys you need to get to HQ ASAP." Several emotions etched Ventura's face, none of them pleasant or reassuring.

Keys was alarmed, "Kyle?"

"Kidnapper made contact."

"Who?"

"Lamontage."

For a moment, Keys couldn't breathe, seconds ticked by though they seemed like hours to him. No, no this wasn't happening. His number one enemy did not, could not, have his son but when he looked back at Ventura's face, he knew it to be so. "I'm on my way." He climbed out of the car, handed the keys to the closest tech, and ran to his own car, laying rubber down as he tore out of the parking lot."

As he turned onto the main road, his onboard GPC started beeping. He drew in a breath to steady his nerves and voice then he hit the answer button. Devin Ruletto swam into focus. "Keys."

"Not a good time, Devin."

"I heard the bulletin go out about Kyle. Any leads."

"Lamontage."

"God, Keys, I'm sorry." Devin's face filled with genuine sympathy. "You okay?"

"I will be once we bury the Bastard." He stopped at a light, and ran a hand over his face. He didn't want to talk about Kyle's situation right now. Even with his closest friend. He was too close to losing it. "Please tell me you've got some good news."

"I think so. I caught your data request on a Martin Freeman."

"What about him?" Keys pushed his car into gear.

"I ran his prints through our known alias' data base, his real name is Ambrose Stallman, he was a rising star on the FBI and FWPA most wanted lists during the 2030's."

"Really?" Keys flipped his blinker on, and turned onto Hollis Ave. "For what?"

"Demolition, political kidnapping, murder, you name it, he dropped out of sight round about 2037 after he made an assassination attempt on the president and his family. There was a rumor he had picked up the underground, bounty hunting profession."

"Not a rumor, he actually did. Any chatter on who hired him?"

"I was hoping you could tell me?"

"Techs are working on his computer. We're hoping we can find the ones who did. All we have is a screen name Gypwitch45. Any listing of his favorite haunts."

"No but I can give you the last lead they had on him before he dropped off the radar."

"Let's have it."

"Ambrosian Hill Village.." Keys eyes swung to the screen, the name that had come up during Marna's dream.

"Tell me you have coordinates."

"Just sent them out to your email."

Keys smiled, "Ruletto, I owe you a drink big time."

"And I will collect." He winked. "Go get your girl, Keys, and if there is anything we can do to help with Kyle's recovery and extraction mission, please call."

"Thank you." Keys sighed, swallowed back his emotion and signed off. He quickly punched in Ventura's number. Ventura picked up.

"Yeah Keys?"

"Devin Ruletto just found the location where Demi is being held. Get onto my computer, get the coordinates from my email, tell Bryan to commission a Guardian chopper, pull together a team, and go get her."

"Will do." He signed off, and Keys turned onto the private road that led to HQ, now if only they could help Kyle, but he somehow knew that Kyle's extraction wasn't going to be that easy. For some reason Demi was put on ice, and Freeman was a connection there, but his gut told him that Lamontage was done with her. Lamontage had a more powerful bargaining chip now and he knew it.

When he walked in to the meeting room, it took only one look at his Lieutenant's expression to verify that he was right. Somewhere outside the building, the chopper took off from the airfield. Outside the room, pedestrian traffic passed by just as it did any other day. Somebody coughed. Someone cleared his or her throat. Other agents in the room spoke together in low tones. Still others tapped keyboards, but nothing seemed to exist beyond the nightmare that began when he followed Ventura's gaze to one of the wall screens, on the curved wall, at the front of the room . . .

*****

Demi woke up to dead silence. She heard nothing, not a sound from the house beyond her room. She swung her legs around and pushed up off the bed. The sun was shining through the slats in the window. She walked over and peaked through them. Nobody puttered on the grounds below. What was going on?

She moved to her door and tried the knob, still locked. She heard movement beyond the door, snippets of a conversation. She pressed her ear to the interior surface. "What are you doing?"

"Jezebel said to get rid of her."

"Just like that

"They killed Stallman."

"What? Who?"

"The fool underestimated Guardian,"

"Is that why they left?"

"Yep, she's going back home."

"The old man died that's why. She's got designs on that daughter of hers marrying the prince."

"May be, but we need to do this and get out of here. Get the car."

"All right." She heard someone cross the hall and go down the stairs then she heard the key inserted into the lock and looked around the room frantically for a weapon . . .

*****

Keys took slow steady steps toward the command center as Ventura started the previously sent video. He watched Keys closely. The older man was terrified. The time stamp on the screen showed Lamontage had recorded the video an hour earlier, two hours after Kyle's initial abduction.

Kyle spit and sputtered as a servant threw a bucket of cold water at him. He coughed and opened his eyes, lifting his head to look around as he gasped for air. He was seated on a tall back,chair, bolted to the floor by its frame, his arms uncomfortably stretched around the high back, secured at the wrists with zip ties, his ankles secured to the front legs, by the same method. He raised his eyes to the man before him, immediately recognizing him. Before his thinking was clear enough to look away, Lamontage had taken hold of his senses. He intruded into his mind, took control of his connections, and he had done so too quickly for Kyle to fend off the attack in his weakened state. Kyle could feel him probing, connecting. His head throbbed with from the merciless intrusion. He winced, but couldn't look away. Beads of sweat formed on his forehead with his fighting effort. "Oh, don't fight it, boy. You're nowhere near strong enough." He walked up and grabbed Kyle's hair pulling his head back, exposing his throat, teasing it with the flat blade of a knife. "Pity your father would not accept that himself."

"Lamontage," Kyle breathed, clenching his teeth, as he tried to break free of the man's control, mindful of the pressure of the blade.

"Hmm, you do your homework," Lamontage said, "then you know what I am capable of, and what I can and will do to your brain." His breath was hot on Kyle's face, "Without hesitation." to prove it, he probed hard, Kyle grunted from the invasion, but couldn't look away. Lamontage chuckled a cold, hollow sound then pulled the knife away, but not before nicking Kyle's neck. He felt the warmth of his blood leak down his neck. "I have taken residence in your brain, boy, now you are mine to toy with, but don't worry, I left enough awareness, so you can feel everything I do, and Fred can see it all." He let the boy's head fall forward and gave the side of it a shove. Kyle felt the muscles in his neck pull taut, then release.

He didn't lift his head as he tried to gain control of his breathing. "What do you want with me? Keys isn't going to hand Marna Farlow over to you."

"He will if he wants to save his son . . ." Lamontage spat as he stopped his circular path around Kyle's chair, took another handful of his hair and yanked his head. This time Kyle winced. He tried to hide his surprise from Lamontage but the latter got down in his face. "You have her eyes." When he released Kyle's hair this time, Kyle pulled away from him. He looked away, hiding the dismay that had crossed his features. "Does he tell you about her? Your mother?" Kyle didn't answer.

Keys ran a shaking hand over his face. The room around him had gone completely silent. Somewhere behind him, he heard someone close and lock the door to the room, and close the shades over the observation windows. He raised his eyes back to the screen.

"She was stronger than I thought. You were both supposed to die that night, but he must have found a way to save you at the sacrifice of sweet Lizzy." Kyle lowered his head to keep Pierre from seeing the tears that sprang to his eyes or how he drew his lower lip into his mouth and bit it with his teeth. Keys had told him the story of Lizzy's death, the horrible way Lamontage had killed her. His father's heroic rescue attempt. How he had lost Lizzy, and how it was touch and go for a few weeks with Kyle too, but Keys believed God had brought them through it to leave him the gift of he and Lizzy's precious boy. "Are you deaf, boy?" Lamontage queried, "Answer me!"

Sarah jumped in the conference room when Pierre's voice boomed through the loudspeakers. Heidi reached out and placed a hand on her shoulder. They both returned their eyes to the screen.

Kyle swung his head around and caught Lamontage's eyes with his own, angry and rebellious. "You Bastard! You dare to speak my mother's name with your vile tongue! Now you think you're going to ruin another good woman to feed your ungodly desires. Kill me now, because Marna Farlow will never fall into your hands! I'll send myself to hell before I let that happen!"

"Kyle, no," Keys whispered as he watched for Pierre's reaction to his son's daring outburst, hoping for the best, but knowing the worst.

Pierre's eyes flashed, he lifted his hand and closed his fist. Kyle couldn't breathe and crushing pain ripped through his entire body. His body tensed. His head fell forward as pain he had never before experienced encased his brain and made it feel like it was in a crushing vice. The groan started deep in his stomach and then he swung his head back and it escaped his mouth in a blood-curdling scream.

The agents turned away, Keys let his head fall forward, and his eyes filled with tears, as Kyle's scream seemed to go on forever. When merciful silence filled the room, and all they heard was Kyle gasping for air, they returned their eyes to the macabre scene unfolding on the screen before them.

Pierre grabbed his hair, yanked his head back, and lowered his lips to his ear,, "there are worse things than death, boy. You'd be smart to remember that." He shoved his head roughly, and he turned to one of the guards nearby. "Send this first video to Guardian headquarters with the link. Get the timer ready, and set up the feed then call me. I want Keys to know I'm serious when he gets the access.

"Yes, Master." A servant moved forward and injected Kyle in his Carotid artery, the boy was instanty unconscious.,For a while, anyway, Kyle would not suffer the pain Pierre had induced.

Keys turned away, walked to the nearest desk and in one huge sweep of his arms the files, lamp, laptop, everything on it became victim to his anger, nothing was immune and it all went flying to the floor. His anger spent, he started to collapse, and Ventura rushed forward, grabbed him and assisted him into the chair Shaefer provided. Then Keys let it all out, he sobbed with his elbows on his knees and his forehead resting on his hands. "Sarah, get some water," Ventura instructed. Sarah Justice moved out of the room. Ventura kicked the pulverized laptop aside, and pulled a chair up, sitting so he faced Keys. Sarah handed Keys the water. He took it with shaking hands and swallowed some of it before he set it aside. Ventura leaned forward, elbows on knees, eyes searching the older man's face. He kept his voice low, steady. "Dammit, Keys, why the hell didn't you tell us?" The words weren't angry or unkind, just curious.

Keys opened his hand, and worked at a piece of loose skin with the finger from the opposite one. He sniffed, drew in a shaky breath and let it out in a sigh. "We thought it best to keep it low profile, I didn't want my enemies to know his identity and Kyle was fiercely independent and—"

"He wanted to make it on his own," Heidi finished. Keys nodded.

"Tell me everything, Keys, and I mean it, we aren't going to know how to get him back if we ride in blind and don't know the history between you and Lamontage," Ventura stated.

Keys took a breath and repeated the entire story of the night he had lost Lizzy the same way he had told it to Marna earlier – god was it only a few weeks ago – with the small exception that Lizzy was in the late stages of her pregnancy for Kyle. That was why she could not be his backup on that fateful night, why he had to leave her alone. Ventura could sense the deep pain and guilt that Keys still carried and now the same enemy that took his wife had his son, "How did Kyle survive?" Ventura pressed.

"Af – ah – after I carried Lizzy to the sidewalk, I knew she wasn't going to make it but the baby was still moving, I could see him moving, he was still alive. I couldn't bear to lose him too, so I started CPR. The medics were there already, and —they – ah – saw what I saw so they worked fast and furious with me until they could hook her up to life support for transport, by then ambulances had started carrying the portable machines on board. They loaded her up, and rushed her to the nearest hospital with a neonatal and maternity ward. They kept her on life support for two more days before they delivered him emergency c-section."

"How far along was she?"

"Seven and a half months." He gazed off into space. "He was put into one of the, then experimental Gestation Chambers, and watched closely for the next six weeks. They weren't sure he was going to make it, but they fought and they fought hard to help him survive. I never knew how much a man could pray in a day until those six weeks. Every day I was with him," he chuckled, "even then Kyle was bent on doing his own thing, beating all odds. He grew stronger every day, and on his original due date, six weeks later, I took him home. It was one of happiest days of my life." Keys drew in a breath. "It eased some of the pain of the loss of my Lizzy."

"How did you keep him under wraps for so long?'

"His grandmother, Lizzy's mother, moved in to our home in Washington and she stayed with him, helped me raise him until she passed away while he was at college. It was then that he told me he wanted to move here to the compound and finish his education here. We had discovered his abilities during his teens, and he never did like having to keep them under wraps." He smiled at some long ago memory.

"What are his abilities, Keys? What does he have that we can possibly use to help him?"

"Ah, verified Blocker, Kyther, and recently he has shown signs of having the branch of a remote viewing collective ability known as Space Continuum."

"Like you do when you connect to another psychic and bring them through a recent memory?"

"Yes, similar to what our Reconstructors do with witnesses when their giving descriptions of perpetrators only more 3D."

"Kyle has that ability too?"

"He's showing signs of it, but it hasn't fully developed yet."

Ventura nodded. "So what happened after he decided to come to Guardian?"

"Except for a few select people, who were part of our everyday life e.g. my partner at the time, Thomas Fielding, Thomas Tate, Sherry Sylvester, Sasha and Devin Ruletto from FWPA, we decided it best no one knew his connection to me. He had already been using his grandmother's maiden name his whole life so we kept our relationship quiet. I had so many enemies out there, and then when Lamontage showed up on the radar again, I buried all the paper work that could lead to me. Had a judge friend of mine seal them as if they were adoption papers, and listed his grandmother as his adoptive parent."

"But he still got to them somehow."

"Had to," Keys sighed, "I thought we had taken every precaution."

Ventura sighed. "Keys, did it ever occur to you or that headstrong kid of yours that we could have provided a little extra protection, especially after he lost Sasha," he ran a hand over his mouth,"I'm guessing that's why he targeted her. Without her, Kyle had no protection. Tate and Sylvester were killed last year. After he discovered Demi, she may have been a ruse too."

Keys looked stricken. "I never even gave that a thought." Keys stood up and turned his back to Ventura, walked a few paces away and ran a hand over his balding head. "I thought we were safe, I didn't connect Sasha or Demi to Kyle's identity.."

"I'm guessing Kyle didn't either. Lamontage pulled Marna into the dream to lead us in the direction we took." Ventura sat back with a frustrated sigh. He understood Keys position, but it didn't make the job ahead of them any easier. "You played right into his hands, Keys, Your decision to keep us out of the loop gave him an open field to your son."

"Peter, not now," Schaefer said.

"No, Heidi, he's right," Keys agreed, "I should have at least shared it with the core team, especially after Demi's cover was blown. Kyle may have been protected and he wouldn't be in Lamontage's hell on earth right now." Keys walked to the command center and tapped the link on the touch screen menu provided with the video. A bunch of codes rolled up the screen. Keys watched them scroll by. People behind him started using expletives, and pushing computer keys.

"Sir, we're getting a live two-way feed from an unauthorized link. How do you want us to proceed?" Ventura, Heidi and Sarah circled Keys.

"Block sensitive material from Guardian records, but open two-way communication to this command center."

"Yes, Sir," more tapping of keys. The screen turned red then blue then Lamontage's face swam to focus on screen. He was standing foreground and Kyle was in the background straining against his guard's hold.

"Hello, Frederick," Lamontage's black eyes bore down on Keys. Keys kept his shields in place, and returned his steady gaze. He felt the probing, but he had learned long ago how to fight the intrusions of this enemy.

"Pierre, Kyle has nothing to do with our fight, let him go."

"You give me what I want and I give you your boy back."

"Dad! no! I don't care what he does to me, you keep this prick away from Marna !" Kyle cried, pushing forward against his guard's hands. Pierre turned, looked Kyle in the eyes, raised his hand, closed his fist, and Kyle's body tensed, and he fought to keep it in, but he eventually let the scream loose. Sarah and Heidi raised their hands to their mouths. Ventura clenched his fists at his side. Pierre released him and the guard let him go. His body slumped forward, and his head dropped as he gasped for air.

"Not much for manners, is he, Fred." He raised his hand and closed his fist again. They stood helpless while Kyle's blood-curdling screams bounced back at them from the walls around them.

"Stop it Pierre! Leave him alone !" Pierre made a face, and released Kyle,causing him to lurch forward again and continue to gasp for air.

Keys watched as his son tried to get air into his lungs, and how the boy's body shook with sobs. After a lengthy silence, he spoke, his voice tightly controlled. "I will kill you next time our paths cross, Pierre, count on it." Keys face was tense, when he brought his eyes back to Pierre's, his lips set in a straight line. "I promise you that."

"Farlow for the boy, Brother," Pierre stared at the screen, "I'll give you until Wednesday, Fred, and that's being generous." Pierre chuckled. "I'll even leave the live feed going so you can be reminded of what's at stake." He raised his hand and clenched his fist one more time, inducing more agonizing screams from Kyle, before he released him, "Wednesday, Keys, or is that woman more important to you than your own flesh and blood? More important than Lizzy's son?" he started to turn. Oh and don't get any ideas, the room will be monitored and your son will be punished severely if I sense any Guardian tricks. He waved his head and left the room, followed by the two guards. Before they heard the unmistakable sound of a heavy-duty metal door closing. Someone set the camera on a close up shot of Kyle's form, from the waist up.

Kyle's chest was rising and falling rapidly, while he tried to regain control of his breathing. "What's Wednesday, Keys?" Ventura asked. "The date is obviously important to him and I saw the look on your face when he said it. What is it?"

"The thirty-third anniversary of Lizzy's murder." He leaned his hands on the glass worktable before him, palms down. Ventura put a hand on Keys' shoulder, giving it a gentle squeeze.

"Dad," Kyle gasped for air as he spoke. All eyes lifted to the screen. Keys separated from the group and moved a step or two forward. His head was still bent forward, but Keys heard the strain in his voice.

"Son, I'm so sorry." Keys' voice was shaky, he drew air in between his teeth.

"Dad *cough*I *gasp* not your fault*gasp*" he lifted his head slowly, tears were in his eyes, and tracking down his face, "I'm as.*gasp*wheeze* as good as dead. You know – that *swallow* *cough*wheeze* he isn't going to let me . . ."*gasp*wheeze* me walk out – here *swallow* protect Marna, please *wheeze* P – promise me*swallow*you'll protect her. *cough*wheeze*I love you*cough*wheeze*gasp*" He laid his head back and took some deep breaths, then brought his head forward again, still breathing erratically. Talking was an effort for him. Keys hung his head, his shoulder lifted and dropped in his own silent anguish. Ventura moved up beside Keys.

"Kyle, this is Ventura."

*cough*wheeze*forced chuckle*"Ven – bet you want *gasp* kick my – ass *wheez*"

Ventura shook his head and let out a soft chuckle, "no, kid, there will be plenty of time for that later," he said softly, swallowing "right now, you concentrate on hanging in there. We're going to find you."

Kyle brought his head up, looking straight at the screen, meeting Ventura's eyes. "*cough*if I *gasp* don't make it *wheeze*cough* you take care of – Dad *wheeze* don't le *breath* let him give up."

"Oh God, Kyle," Keys said softly, lifting his eyes to meet his son's, seeing all the pain Lamontage had just induced reflected in them. Sarah went up to Keys.

"You got it, kid, but you needn't worry about that, you'll be here to do it yourself," Kyle nodded, "reserve your strength. I'm sure you'd like to join us when we bring him down." Kyle gave him a jerking nod, though his expression showed his doubt in Ventura's words, he let his head drop and Ventura muted communication from their side, keeping the video feed going.

"Pete, there has got to be something we can do," Heidi said, "I've never seen Keys so distraught."

"It would help if we knew where to start looking." His eyes strayed toward Keys. Sarah was sitting beside him, talking to him, reassuring him. "I hope Bryan is having better luck than we are." He glanced at the screen as Kyle drew in some more deep breaths. His breathing was uneven, but it was clear to him that it wasn't all because of what Pierre had just done. The kid was scared. He was crying. He hit a touch screen button and Kyle's a digital read of Kyles vitals popped up in the lower right hand corner. They were stabilizing. At least that was good news. "Dammit, Kyle, where the hell are you?" He moved closer to the screen and studied the surrounding room, looking for something that would give them a clue .

*****

Demi grabbed the lamp from her bedside stand and stepped in to the space behind the door, as it swung open, she would only have one chance at this. She raised her hands above her head as her would be killer stepped into the room. She swung the lamp swift and hard down on his head, his body tensed in surprise then he pitched forward onto the rug. "Nothing personal, Creep," she whispered, and pulled the Glock from his hand, and an extra clip from his belt, pushing the magazine into her jeans pocket. The cold metal butt of the Glock felt good in the palm of her hand. "Been a long time, Mate," She whispered to the gun, and searched his pockets, smiling when she pulled out his communication device. "A GPC 2000? Nice. Man after my own heart." She opened her door and looked up and down the hallway. Her gun held in standby position, as she slipped into the hallway. She dialed Bryan's number. She smiled when his face swam into focus on the LCD, and her heart gave a little leap. There were times in the last few weeks, she wondered if she would ever see him again. She grinned as his face went from confused suspicion, to relieved excitement, and then guarded joy.

"Demi." He said in a breathless whisper. She heard disturbance in the background.

"Hey, can you ask Daddy if I can come in from the cold now? I'm done with these people, they don't play fair." She kept her eyes moving up and down the hallway, and her voice low.

Tears filled his eyes, and he swallowed hard to regain control, she smiled. "Baby, we're in the air on our way to your suspected location. Are you okay? You're not hurt?"

"Aside from wanting a really long bubble bath, a night on the town, and a month's worth of R&R, I'm fine thanks to you and Marna. I have one down, and closing in on a second. Unfortunately, I think the rest split."

"How rude. Get invited to a party and then the hosts leave before we arrive, I'm hurt."

"You don't know the half of it. I'll fill you in on the one person that can strike fear into Lamontage."

"You mean besides Guardian."

"Yeah." She smiled. I'm going to leave this on, so you can get a lock on my exact location, while I finish checking things out."

She saw him mutter something to someone else on the chopper. "You be careful Demi, we're on the homestretch now."

"Careful is my middle name, Leannán." His eyes softened as he recognized the Irish word for Lover. She smiled, dropped the GPC by her former prison doorway and closed and locked the door behind her. Holding the gun with two hands as it led the way, she made a large swing in the upstairs hall and across the upper landing to the top of the stairs. Then she started descending cautiously down the stairs, her back to the wall, giving herself a wider field of vision. Her anxiety level rose with each step on magnificent stone staircase.

A car pulled up in front of the house as she stepped onto the bottom floor entryway. She stepped behind an imported tree plant and moved the curtain aside. The driver emerged from a running car and headed toward the door. Demi quickly moved to the opposite side of the doorway and moved into the shadows. The door opened and a stocky man of 5'6" came into the house, he went to the bottom of the steps. "Stu, come on. I just heard the locals offer assistance to Guardian over the scanner.

"Stu sends his regards." Demi said coming up behind him. She sensed his next move. "I've got an expert marksman score in speed, distance, and close proximity shooting. If you think you can get a shot off before I deliver one to the back of your skull, be my guest because I've been locked away and abused for a few weeks and I'm pretty pissed right now so just give me a reason," Her voice was tight and fierce, "Now take that gun and toss it down, then slide it back to me. The man considered his options for a few seconds then did as she asked. "Party pooper." She again raised an eyebrow. "Did I mention I'm a black belt too?" She grinned when he seemed to deflate. "Your scorecard is just not doing so well today is it, Cowboy?" She quickly kicked the gun behind her, and glanced around the room. Her eye caught what she was looking for. There was a hall closet under the stairs, "Over to the closet, go on." He moved over to the closet. "Open it." He did. "Go on, get on in there." He sighed and stepped into it.

"Hands on your head and down on your knees." The guy hesitated. "Oh come on, Rover, don't quit now, you're doing so well. You might even get best in show." She started to back out but she said. "Oh by the way, Sweetie, you got a cell phone?" He started to lower his hand. "Ah, ah, two fingers, nice and slow." He pulled out his communicator. "Ah, a GPC 2000, top of the line, your boss is a very generous person, maybe there's a call back number in here and I can ask her about a position – Oh yeah that's right – she wants me dead." She took the phone and slipped it into her jacket pocket. "Still I might just give her a call and thank her for her generous hospitality, but I won't be calling her for my next vacation." She inched out of the closet.

"Thank you so much for your cooperation, now you just sit tight until the big boys get here, which from what you just said, won't be long now and boy do we have nice accommodations for you." She closed the door, locked it, and slid a heavy bench in front of it. Her captive let out a string of expletives. "Language, Sir, Does your Teanga know you talk like that." She retrieved his gun, and put it in the waistband of her jeans and moved away, with her gun leading the way, to check the rest of the bottom floor and clear the residence for the crime scene team.

*****

Bryan closed his GPC and then moved over to where the techs were on board working the coordinate's location. Seconds later they gave him the thumbs up, and delivered the new coordinate's to the pilot. Brian drew in a breath and let it out slowly, then opened his GPC, and dialed Keys phone.

Ventura's face swam to view, making Bryan recheck the number dialed, "You dialed right, Bryan, I made him go into the dorm to try and get a couple of hours down time."

"What's happened?"

"Pierre sent him an anniversary present." An icy fear grabbed his gut, "Kyle's not . . ."

"No, but he's got us hooked up to a live feed of his torture chamber with the kid in the starring position, complete with timer. I'm trying to get demographics now."

"The Bastard knows how to twist the knife. Still the same demands?"

Ventura rubbed the back of his neck. "Yeah, he wants Marna. How's your progress? You reach the village yet?"

"Better. Demi, turned the tables on her captors, and got her hands on a GPC, and a weapon. She just hooked us up to her actual location, we're closing in now."

"She okay?"

"Says she is, she's got one down, and closing in on another then she's going to start clearing the residence. We'll fill you in more after we do the extraction."

"Thanks, Bryan." He disconnected the call.

"Good news?" Schaefer queried.

He smiled. "Yeah, for once it is." He glanced at the screen. Kyle's breathing had returned to normal, and he had laid his head back on the chair. He appeared to be sleeping. "It would be nice to get two for two."

"Find anything in the room that might help us."

He shook his head. "No they knew what they were doing when they did Kyle's close up. The rest of the room is out of our field of vision."

"Maybe when they return for another pep talk, Lamontage likes a wider view for his theatrics."

Ventura's head sprung up. "Yes he does." He quickly moved to the command post, "Todd put the first video up on screen three." His tech man did as ordered. "Pan slowly." The tech panned the video, "mute audio," the walls passed slowly on the screen, "move up . . . There stop," the tech stopped, "zoom in,"

Schaefer saw what he was getting at. There was a square glare at the far, upper right frame of the video around a sectioned wall. "Damn, Ventura, that's a window!"

He nodded and turned toward Todd. "Can you isolate that area and clean it up a bit, tone down the back lighting?"

"I'll give it a shot, Sir."

"Good Man." Ventura came back to the command post. "Hang on, kid, we just took a step closer." For the first time since they had received the first video, Ventura felt a bit of hope.

*****

Demi swung back around the family parlor to backtrack to the front entryway when she heard the front door open. She shrunk back to the wall and slid toward her destination. So many thoughts fled through her mind as she slowly approached the bend that would make her vulnerable to whoever came in the front. "Bring it on," she breathed. She would be nobody's victim this time. Either she would subdue her assailant or she would die trying. She reached the bend, her heart pounded in her chest, fight or flight screamed through her central nervous system, she chose the former, drew in a breath, put her gun in standby position. Movement on the stairs told her there was more of them. Another team? Her senses went into overdrive, she heard, no, she felt someone moving toward her. Taking one last deep breath, she moved quickly twisted on the ball of her left foot, brought her right foot around in a controlled arc, planted it on the floor, beyond the bend, in a two-foot foundation and aimed her gun. Her opponent took the mirror position to her, and seconds later lifted his gun, and relaxed his stance.

"Dammit, Demi! I could have killed you !" He drew in a deep breath, brought his free hand to his waist, and brought his eyes to hers where tears were pooling, making them liquid emeralds.

"Bryan," she breathed, she took in the sandy blonde hair, the hazel eyes, and relief just washed in waves through her body like the baptism of a new lease on life. The fight went out of her, her gun hand fell to her side, the gun falling to the floor, her knees felt like jello, and she started to go down. "Whoa !" In one liquid motion, Bryan slipped his gun into his holster, moved forward, caught her around the waist and wrapped his arms tightly around her going down with her to his knees. He then cradled her in his arms and pulled her closer to his body. He kissed her forehead. "It's okay. You're safe now." He held her as she buried her face in his shoulder and cried. She just let loose and sobbed. His men came in to tell him the building was secure, and he found out from Demi, between sobs, where the two men were that she had taken down. He told his men to secure them then he lifted her into his arms and stood up. He turned toward Misty Scofield. "Finish it up for me? I'm taking her out to the medics."

"You bet, Bryan." She nodded and watched him carry Demi out of the house, murmuring to her as he did.

She turned toward the other men. "Let's get these guys under wraps."

"You bet." They moved the bench out of the way, covered the door, and extracted the man from the closet, cuffed him and handed him off to be booked for attempted murder, accessory to kidnapping, human trafficking and whatever else they could stick on his growing list of offenses. The agent returned from upstairs.

"He's gone." He handed her the GPC 2000 with a gloved hand, still open and still dialed in to Bryan's number. She took it with a gloved hand, closed it and slipped it into an evidence bag, handing it off to the first crime scene attendant that passed.

"One less scumbag to nurture," she looked out the window toward the ambulance. "Let the coroner know he can take out the trash any time."

"Think she'll be okay?" He asked, following her gaze.

She glanced out the door where Bryan was holding Demi in his lap while the ambulance attendant checked her out. "I think with him in her corner, she couldn't be anything else but." She turned back toward him and smiled, "come on, let's finish up here so we can go home." The agent nodded. "Maybe we can find something that could help put Lucifer out of his misery."

"Yes, Ma'am." The team dispersed about the house to start collecting evidence.

*****

Ventura held the phone to his ear and sighed in relief. "No, Bryan, you stay with her until they release her, send your team ahead with the evidence and we'll send a return chopper back for you. . . no we'll call you if we need you . . . give her our best, and tell her to behave, we'll see her when they feel they can release her to the clinic. . . Okay. . ." Ventura closed his GPC and drew in a breath, allowing himself a moment to smile.

"Demi?" Schaefer queried.

He glanced her way. "Yeah, they've secured the house she was held in and Bryan has her at the local hospital. They're going to do a medical and psych eval on her before they send her home." He sighed, "she – ah – had a bit of a breakdown when Bryan got there. The doctors think it's because she was terrorized for so long."

"PTSD?" "

"Yeah, and now he's got another one of ours," he glanced toward the screen, "

"We'll get him back, Pete."

"Yeah, we will." He returned his gaze to her, and drew in a breath. "Demi was able to collect two GPC 2000s that belonged to her captors"

"Good girl," she said, looking toward the monitor, "think it will help?"

"It can't hurt, whoever he left her with, must have had some kind of contact with him. Maybe we can get a lock on Pierre's phone."

"We could only hope."

"Yeah," she said, then saw an unidentified female in a long robe and face veil come into the room with Kyle, "get the audio, Pete." He looked up, and quickly turned on input audio.

"I've brought you some water." She put a bowl of water and a washcloth on some kind of stand by his chair. She started wiping down his face, his neck, and then she undid his shirt and started wiping down his torso. Large purple bruises had started to form in his rib area.

Ventura sighed. "Looks like he may have some rib damage,"

"This guy has got to have a heart as cold as ice." Schaefer said as she watched the woman cut away his shirt.

"He has no heart, Heidi, just a cold black hole where one should be."

"God, Ventura, we have got to find him."

"I know."

The woman took his shredded shirt and tossed it aside. She pulled a rib vest from the pile of linen she had brought in with her and threaded it behind Kyle's back, bringing it under his arms and wrapping it around the front, fastening it with Velcro straps. Kyle leaned back in the chair and looked up at her veiled face. She went about her business doing her own thing. He said nothing, but brought his eyes to the camera, that's when Ventura saw it, it was subtle, but it was there.

Ventura's eyes narrowed, he turned toward Todd. "Todd Tape this segment."

"Yes, Sir."

"What are you thinking, Ventura?" Heidi queried

"The kid's eyes, he recognized her."

"The woman."

"How? I mean she's completely covered, but her – eyes." Her own eyes went back to the screen.

"Right. A man always notices a woman's eyes. A lot of the times they leave a lasting impression, he's seen them before."

"You're thinking last night at the bar."

"Yeah, I am. If we can get an impression off this video capture, we might be able to run the irises."

"Which are as good, if not better then fingerprints." Schaefer shook her head. "Damn, your good, Ventura."

"No, the kid is." The woman finished her nursing of Kyle's damaged ribs, and put some kind of poncho type shirt on him. He winced as he leaned backward.

"Do you want some water?" Kyle nodded. *She lifted a bottle of spring water to his lips and held it for him while he drank.*

"Thank you." *He said when she pulled it away. She looked at him oddly, and put the bottle back on the stand by his chair.*

"You shouldn't anger him." *Kyle lifted his eyes to hers.* *"You'd do better not to disagree with him."*

"I'll keep that in mind." *Kyle said and looked around the room. His breathing was back to normal, though his voice was hoarse.* *"What is this place? Some kind of prison?" He lifted his eyes briefly to the camera.*

"Good boy, Kyle," Ventura whispered. He opened up another wall monitor and pulled up a national map on the screen. He typed in the keyword prisons in North America: The map showed 20,000 as of 2020 then he typed in "deserted" and "private" the numbers dropped to 15000, he then added "secluded", knowing full well Lamontage would not have taken their boy to a populated area. The numbers dropped to 1500. He looked back at the screen "Come on, kid, I need more."

"I need to go," the woman said, "Do you want more water?" Kyle nodded. She brought the bottle to his lips again, and he drank some more. When he was done, she brought the bottle down, capped it and set it aside. "I'll bring you in something to eat later." She got up, dumped her basin of water down a sink, somewhere off camera, and then they heard the same sound as earlier, the clanging of steel on steel. Kyle laid his head back, drew in a breath pulled his head forward, muttered a curse, shook his head and then his head pitched forward and his breathing became slow and steady.

"They must have drugged him," Schaefer said.

Ventura nodded, "The water, but why? It's not as if he's going to attempt an escape. They've got him pretty well under control." He turned toward Todd. "Spool your capture and put it up, Monitor four." Todd nodded.

"Maybe a play to show us who's in charge," Schaefer shrugged, "At least we're a step closer than we were."

"How," Keys said as he made his way to the coffee maker, and poured himself a cup.

"You get any rest, Keys?" Ventura queried.

"Some. Thank you." He took a drink of coffee, and looked at the second panel. "Tell me what you've discovered.

"Kyle managed to send us a couple of subtle hints; he's being held in prison, and we should run a check on her." He sent a capture of the woman's face to monitor four. "He recognized her eyes. Todd is running a reverse Iris check on her now." Ventura drew in a breath as he saw a certain relief spread across the older man's face. "You trained him well, Dad."

"Yeah," Keys voice was hoarse, "he always was a smart kid." He took another sip of coffee. "What have you found on the prison hint?"

"I narrowed it down to 1500 by feeding in the key words we know, private, secluded, and deserted."

"Try New England."

Ventura fed in the new information, more red dots dropped off the map. "Two-hundred," Ventura said.

"Still a small needle in a huge haystack," Keys said, "And not a lot of time to find it," he sighed, and looked at screen four. "If we can get an ID on her, we might have a chance to get her to flip on Lamontage."

"If she's in the system for any reason, we'll get her," Ventura caught Keys' eyes. "We'll find him, Keys."

"I know," he nodded, taking another drink of coffee and stealing a glance at his son, frowned.

"They drugged him via water and our mystery woman doctored him up. Looks like Pierre's attack may have done some damage to his ribs."

Keys' eyes dropped to his coffee, "At least someone took mercy on him." He turned away. "What's the report on Demi? Ventura relayed Bryan's report.

"That's our girl," Keys smiled, "Bryan staying with her?"

"Yes."

"Good," he was nodding then his head swung back toward the monitor, "how long has Kyle been sleeping?"

"A few minutes, why?"

"Dammit! Pierre is going after Marna in the dream realm! He'll use Kyle as leverage." He turned to Ventura. "Call Tanner and tell him to meet me at the hospital. Call the clinic and warn Rose so she can block her. Sarah connect with Peter and try like hell to use the live feed to connect to Kyle's Kything ability, see if you can use your influencing abilities to stall Pierre's entrance."

"Okay !" She said, and grabbed Peter's hand. They closed their eyes, tried to match the frequency of the live feed to steer Kyle away from the REM sleep stage, while Keys jumped the next elevator, and urgently pushed the button to his parking garage level.

Chapter Seventeen

Giselle opened her eyes, and looked around the hospital room. She was terrified. Another nightmare, but she couldn't remember it. She pushed her head back into her pillow. Something about a home invasion, impressions of fear and horrible sadness. She closed her eyes, trying to remember it.

Rose came in. "Giselle, you need something?" Giselle looked at her puzzled. Rose indicated the call button mechanism. She was holding it in her hand, firmly pressing it with her thumb.

" I'm sorry. I must have had a muscle spasm while I was sleeping. She let it go and it fell back to the bedrail, where its wire was loosely clipped.

Rose smiled. "It happens. The Guardian Reconstruction artist is here to see you. Are you up for it?"

"Yes." She smiled, shifting herself up in bed. It might get rid of this unsettling feeling, the nightmare had left behind.

Rose stepped back, and nodded her head toward the door. Giselle heard the clipping of approaching heals, seconds before a striking woman of about thirty- five, peered around the curtain. Her dark, silky hair, pulled back from sharp features exposed evenly spaced, dark eyes set above high cheekbones on either side of a fleshy nose accentuating straight lips curved in a warm smile. She had adorned her 5'8", lean, 140-pound frame in a cerulean blue skirt suit, accenting her bronze skin. She held her body in a proud manner that had been a trademark of her Native American culture for decades. She offered Giselle a hand. "Hi, my name is Serena Blackwater," she said, her voice strong and direct.

"Giselle Riley," Giselle said, taking her hand.

"Good to meet you, Giselle," she sat on a chair next to the bed and placed her blue spring Jacket over the arm.

"Is there anything either of you would like before you get started?" Rose offered. Giselle shook her head, but Serena asked for coffee.

Serena returned her attention to Giselle as she pulled out her PC tablet, opened the cover, selected her desired stylist head, and smiled. "Let me explain how we're going to do this, Giselle. I am a Reconstruction artist, which is essentially the same as any artist, but with a little extra zing. What I'm going to do is help you reconstruct that night, frame by frame, by taking you back, rebuilding and extracting anything of importance. I'm going to help your senses remember the sounds, the smells, the tastes, and the feel of everything around you up to the moment the men approached, and attacked you, then abducted Kyle, "Do you understand?"

"I-I think so, but If I saw him at all, it was just for a second or two. My mind was on Kyle, on getting him help, and I was trying to get my keys out of my purse so I could unlock the car."

Serena smiled and looked the girl directly in the eye. "As humans, we all have automatic responses to what goes on around us. We see a movement or unexpected object in our peripheral vision, we turn to look at it and in that second, or that moment, our eyes pull in a lot of information and our mind computes the data to give us the outline, color, shading, contrast lines, and detail to say, oh it's a person, a car, or a spider. Are they talking, stopping, carrying groceries, or passing by? Then we react to it. We turn away, go about our business, answer a question, jump back, or assist if they are in need of help."

"What I can do, is help you reconstruct a second or a moment in that sequence of events. Zoom in. Freeze a frame, and give you a second glance. From there, we work together to extract the details. I ask you questions, you answer, and I put it down on paper in a sketch, and some side notes, but you have to trust me. Can do that?" Giselle nodded.

"Good . . ." She thanked Rose as she brought her the coffee, took a drink, set it on the bedside table, and then started. "Okay, Giselle, I want you to take a deep cleansing breath, get comfortable, and close your eyes." Giselle did as Serena asked. "Great, relax." Serena reached out and touched Giselle's hand. "Listen to my voice, I'm going to guide you through the night you met Kyle okay." Giselle nodded.

Giselle settled back on her pillow as the playback started in her mind. It was like walking through a black and white movie in which she had a starring role. She recounted how she had heard, from a patient, that her favorite band was appearing at Jenna's, and how she had wanted to hear them, Serena spoke softly, her voice even, soothing. "Fast forward, you're entering the bar."

Giselle described her meeting with Kyle, their conversation, and her impulsive request for him to join her at a table – the music, the crowd, the cell phone tribute, the last drink. "Freeze frame," Serena said softly. "Rewind. Slow motion," Her memory banks slowed the action in her mind as she watched the events play out like a black and white television program. "What is going on?"

"The crowd is hyped up. There is an interlude to 'Rose of Many Colors.' Our Server is bringing us another drink, but we hadn't ordered it, or maybe Kyle had. I look at him, he hesitates, he smiles at me. He looks at her – I do too. He seems confused. He's about to wave it away, but she says something I can't hear her. It is so loud. The cheering. The music."

"Cut out the background music. Focus on her. On her words. What is she saying?"

Giselle hesitated, frowned in concentration, *My treat.* She says it's her treat, he changes his mind, nods and waves her to put it down. He looks up at her, and frowns, like he's trying to figure something out. Maybe she's an old girlfriend. I looked up at her."

"Freeze Frame. What do you see?" Serena readied her stylus. She recalled a notice going out earlier about the possibility of someone drugging Kyle's last drink. In hindsight, a complimentary drink looked suspicious, especially if he didn't know woman. "Is she Caucasian, African American, Native American, Mexican,

"Asian American."

"Good. What shape is her face? Oval, round, Pixie?"

"Pixie."

"What color are her eyes? Are they far apart or close together? Round, slanted or oval? Deeply set or average or bulging?"

"Dark, close together, oval, Average."

Serena continued to make speedy strokes on her tablet. "Nose; large or small? Sharp, button, upturned or hawk?"

"Small, upturned."

"Lips? Full, thin, puckered or butterfly? Mouth? wide or small? What color lipstick is she wearing?" Giselle hesitated. Serena looked up and reached for her hand. "You're doing great, take your time. What is troubling you?"

"She's very beautiful, her features are perfect

Serena made some adjustments on her sketch. Giselle had just told her that they were looking for a woman with symmetrical features. "What about her mouth, Giselle, look at her mouth." Giselle drew in a breath.

"Full lips, pink lipstick."

"Hair color? side part or middle? up or down? length?"

"Black, straight, side part, It falls in her face, it's down, long. Why is it down? She's a server, shouldn't it be pulled up?" Serena made a note.

"When she spoke, do you remember if she had an accent?"

"No her English was very good, considering."

Serena's head shot up. "Considering what, Giselle?"

"She was wearing a foreign exchange pin from the college, she was a student." Serena finished her sketching and looked it over. She wrote some notes on the sketch.

"Did she have any marks on her face? A mole? Tatoos?"

"She had a mole in front of her ear, on her right cheek, it lined up with the corner of her eye, and a small tattoo of a capitalized L with a rifle through it on her neck, over her carotid artery. It swelled with every pulse beat. Creepy. She pulled a few more details to make the sketch unique, and then she decided it was time to move on, and then opened up a new page on her tablet.

"Forward. What's happening now?"

"She walks away, he watches her go and shrugs, then he looks back at the band, lifts his drink . . ." She recounted his strange behavior shortly thereafter. His fear that he'd been drugged. How he begged her to help him get home so he could call his father. Then she talked about her uneasiness about leaving him on the bench, while she went to the car.

"Slow motion; what's going on around you. Are there other cars in the parking lot? People standing around, employees taking a cigarette break."

"Cars in the lot, I don't see anyone standing around, but it feels creepy, like someone is watching me."

"Do any of the cars have anyone in them?"

"Yes, two sections over, a Taurus 2000, late model."

"Is it under a lot light?"

"Yes."

"Freeze Frame. What color is it? Can you see the license plate?"

"It's Blue, Caribbean Blue I think. No too far away, I can't read it."

"What are its colors?"

"Light blue background, with Light house foreground on the right---Maine, it's a Maine plate."

"Nice job, Giselle, Can you see how many are in it?"

"Two in the front, wait a minute, there's movement in the backseat. There are three of them."

"Good. Forward, then what happens?" Serena brought her through the process of describing the man that approached her as she had the girl, and sketched out a Dark haired man, thinning on the top with Gray eyes, deeply set, a jutting brow bone, sharply hooked nose, and a mustache over thin lips, when he spoke it was with a French accent. She moved her forward to the point when the man was moving on and she was pulling her keys out of her purse. "Slow motion . . . What's going on around you? What do you hear? What do you see?

"Scuffing, behind me, somebody clears their throat."

"Are the sounds close up or far away? Do you feel threatened?"

"Close, real close, I start to turn, but someone grabs my neck, I can't turn anymore. He braces himself with his other hand on the roof of my car and tells me not to scream or he'll kill me."

"Freeze Frame; what do you see on that arm, what's his voice like?"

"His arm has a scar, like someone cut him with a knife, he has an accent, German, I think."

"Is the arm bulky or thin, muscular or lean? Is the scar Vertical or horizontal, describe it?"

"Dark skinned, muscular. Vertical. It's the same shape as the tatoo on the girl's neck."

Serena made some strokes on her tablet. "Do you see anything in your peripheral vision, hair color? Smell anything"

"He had a hood on. I smelled Pipe tobacco, Apple. I smell it just before, no, no." Serena noticed her breathing was becoming fast, rapid; her pulse was increasing. Time to pull her back. She grabbed her hand.

"Okay, come on back, Giselle, you're safe, he can't hurt you anymore. It's only a memory." Giselle opened her eyes, gasped and looked around the room. She drew in some deep breaths. "That's it, you're fine." Serena felt her pulse slow with each cleansing breath. "You did well Giselle, you have an amazing sight for detail."

"Why couldn't I remember all that without doing this?"

"Our brain tends to discard things that, at a certain moment in time, seem unimportant, insignificant, or fearful, especially following a traumatic experience. It's a defense mechanism built in to our Psyche, but like a computer database, the information is stored there, you just have to know the right buttons to push to retrieve it. People like me just have the ability to bring you back to the moment, make you pause, and take a second look to bring out more details."

"Will it help?"

She smiled at the girl. "I think you just brought us several steps closer to finding out where we can find him, so yeah, it will help. You rest now. I'm going to send this information to WIT HQ and they'll put it into our data base as well as a few others and see what pops up." She stood and collected her jacket, threw her coffee cup in the trashcan, and smiled once more at the girl then stepped out of the room, hit touch buttons on her screen and pulled out her GPC.

Ventura picked up, "Serena, my sweet, where have they been hiding you?" His dark face filled her screen and split into a smile as he stepped away from the command center, where she saw commotion going on around him.

"Hey, Stud, you look busy so I won't keep you long. I just got through with your witness. I'm sending you sketches now."

"Sketches as in the plural form?" He raised a brow.

"I'm that good," she winked, "call me." She disconnected, closed her tablet and headed out of the hospital.

*****

Ventura went to the command center, opened Serena's email, and stared at the sketches. Keys was right, she was one of the best. He separated the notes from the sketches. "Todd split screen four." Todd let the frequencies continue to run, and split the screen. An empty space went up beside the woman from the video. On a hunch, Venura sent the sketch up beside the captured frame. "Run match probabilities on the eyes." Todd did. Almost instantly, it came back as a 90 percent positive. "Merge." The picture and the sketch merged. They fit right down to the mole on the face. "Got you." He hissed. "Run facial recognition. Split screen on five." Screen five on the wall to their right lit up, he sent up Serena's other two sketches. "Facial recognition on Five-B, Art signature five-A." Todd hit a few more buttons, and the computer started searching. "Broaden searches to Europe and Switzerland." The search scope broadened to databases worldwide.

"The net's tightening." Shaefer said.

"Yes it is."

"Pete," Sarah said, "Kyle's showing signs of distress, ready for more frequency connections."

"I got the search, you go," Schaefer said, before he spoke the words."

*****

Tanner stood from his position by Marna's bed when Keys walked in. Tanner nodded. Keys breathed out a sigh in relief. "Thank you for rushing over."

"What's happening Keys?

Keys drew in a breath. "There was an assassination attempt on Demi," alarm crossed his features but Keys held his hand up, "she managed to escape, Bryan will be escorting her here later after evaluation and treatment. She'll continue her treatments here if recommended." Tanner studied his features; Keys looked years older than he had just twenty-four hours before.

"Finally some points in our column." He glanced at Keys, knew there was more. "What's the rest?"

"Lamontage has Kyle."

"What? Why?" Tanner narrowed his eyes, studied Keys. There was more

"Kyle's my son," Keys eyes drifted to Tanner.

The air went out of Tanner's lungs. He opened his mouth to speak then closed it and lifted his eyes to the ceiling, brought his hands to his waist, drew in a breath, and let it out in a hard sigh. After a few seconds, he brought his eyes back to Keys, "Your – " he was furious and sympathetic at the same time. He went to the window, looked out and ran his fingers through his hair, drew in another breath and let it out. When he trusted his voice, he turned to face his mentor again, "that's a hell of a revelation to let loose now, Keys, especially with an adversary such as Pierre." He looked toward Marna, sleeping in her bed.

"That's not even in the cards, Tanner. Ventura is at HQ following up some leads to try and pin point where Pierre is keeping him."

"What kind of leads?" Tanner narrowed his eyes.

"He's threaded a live, untraceable, two-way video feed to HQ, complete with audio and Timer. He's giving us until Wednesday to make the trade." Keys words drifted off.

Tanner understood, his tone softened. "He's hurting him, and giving you a ringside seat." Keys, nodded with a softly voiced reply. Tanner turned away, ran a hand over his mouth, and then turned back toward him, "I'm sorry, Keys." He noticed Keys was trying hard to control his emotions, "how's he holding up?"

"As well as can be expected, looks like he's got rib damage. Lord knows if he has any brain cell damage from the vicious attacks. He's done several in a short time span. God knows what that's done to his emotional state."

Tanner let out a long breath. "Where'd he grab him?"

"Jenna's" Keys summarized the account of the night's events, as outlined by Giselle.

"And you don't think the girl had anything to do with it?"

"No, she's with Serena right now, reconstructing the night," Keys walked over to the window, "Kyle's trying to help with subtle hints that he picks up. We've got a female servant that we're running a reverse iris check on, and we know he's being kept in a secluded, deserted prison somewhere in New England."

"It's a start."

"Lamontage has the feed monitored so caution has to be taken with any communication we have with Kyle or he launches another attack." He turned and leaned his hips on the windowsill. "His screams are the worst to deal with. The kind of pain that induces that kind of screaming in a man . . .or the tears that follow . . ." He sniffed, "It's hard to sit by and watch that when you have an agent in that kind of trouble, but when that agent is also your son." Keys shook his head. Tanner drew in a breath, he could not even imagine the kind of pain and uncertainty that Keys was experiencing right now. What could one say? Were there any words that could ease the older man's burden? He just stayed silent and let Keys talk. "He – ah – he said that he was dead anyway, so Marna was to be protected at all costs," he sighed, "His reward for his noble words was another attack . More screams.He told me that he loved me," he chuckled, "he hasn't said that since he was ten." Tanner swallowed and patted Keys on the shoulder.

"What makes you think Lamontage will launch a dream weaving, attack tonight?"

"Lamontage had him drugged, earlier this evening, probably *Compliance*. He was out cold when I left." Keys cleared his throat and stood up.

"And you think he's going to use Kyle as a vehicle to get to Marna, break down her defenses."

"I don't think it, Son, I know it. It's just a matter of when he'll make his first attempt." As if on cue, Marna started murmuring in her sleep, Tanner brought his hand to his temple, wincing with pain. Keys became alarmed, "What is it, Son?"

"Attempted breech !" Beads of sweat started forming on his forehead. A harsh, severe pounding was starting behind his eyes. His knees threatened to buckle. His face crunched in his effort to fight the breach. Keys assisted Tanner to a chair, crouched before him then pulled out his GPC and pegged Shaefer. He glanced at Tanner, who had doubled over at the waist, elbows on his knees, hands putting pressure on his head to offset the pain.

"Schaefer."

"Heidi, Lamontage is making his move now !" Keys said.

"Yeah, I know, Kyle is showing signs of distress too." She glanced at the screen, Kyle's body was jerking and he was murmuring. "We've got two more frequencies to try."

"Hurry up and get them in!"

"Okay, Boss." She turned toward Todd and relayed Keys' ordered. Todd nodded. Ventura and Justice fought to connect. Keys signed off.

Keys shoved his GPC into his pocket then placed his hands on Tanner's forearms. "You think you can go in?" He queried of Tanner. Tanner nodded. "Good because it may be the only way we can fight him off this time. Come on." Keys helped him stand, and Tanner stumbled over to Marna grabbing her hand, Keys pushed the call button. Rose came in, took one look around and knew instantly a desperate situation was upon them. "Rose we need you, now !" She nodded, called for another nurse to cover the desk, closed and locked Marna's door then came forward and grabbed Tanner's hand. Keys completed the circle. Immediately they could feel their minds and souls interlacing, their power strengthening. Eyes closed, their minds focused on connecting and blocking. Immediately they entered Marna's subconscious. There was a fog circling around Marna. A barrier produced by pain and sedation medication.

Marna, open and connect, Keys ordered

Keys, what's going on? Marna responded, her voice sounding distant and out of sorts.

You're under attack. We need you to connect actively.

Marna struggled to gain control of her senses. It seemed like an eternity before she could finally fight the fog and become actively involved in the joining.

~~~~~

The connection made, the mist engulfed the team, and eventually brought them into the dream realm where they landed solidly on what appeared to be a city park. Justice and Ventura appeared to their right, and joined their circle, seconds later. Keys nodded at them, and they nodded back. Keys looked around and he saw Kyle sitting on a park bench bathed in the eerie glow of a single street lamp. Marna looked around puzzled, her gaze followed Keys'. "Keys, why is Kyle over there and not with us?" She hissed. Keys did not answer. She drew in a breath as tears stung her eyes. Her awareness piqued. The tethers that held her to the bed were not in this realm, her injuries not physically present. However, a dull throbbing in her chest reminded her she did have them. "I think it's time to fill me in." she whispered.

"Later, Marna." His eyes had locked on the approaching threat that had appeared out of the shadow by Kyle's bench, "right now stay focused on the task at hand, for our sakes and his."

"Lamontage. . ." she whispered.

"Yes," Ventura hissed, "and you and Kyle have become his King and queen in the latest game of chess against Keys."

"Oh, God," her hand went to her mouth, and she swallowed back the bile in her throat. Not another one. Not Kyle!

"Check," Pierre said. The team circled Marna protectively as Pierre moved forward.

"Rose, block !" Rose activated her blocking ability. She felt a surge of power as the strength of the collective created a multicolored wall of pure electricity between them and Pierre.

"Really, Brother, you think your collective theatrics will stop me? Here? In my realm?" His words got louder as he spoke until his voice became a bellowing storm that seemed to shake the world around them then he raised his hands, palm out and the electrical charge between them started losing power, and the wall started fading."

"Telekinesis!" Keys ordered. Rose and Sarah activated their ability as one, spreading it throughout the entire team, and they all concentrated on pushing Pierre back. He faltered and they forced him backward. Pierre started pushing back. One by one, they faltered the weakest falling first being pulled up and supported by the others. Strength renewed, they reinstated the offensive. The tug of war went on just a few moments but to those involved it seemed like hours, both sides getting weary. Keys was beginning to wonder if they were strong enough to fight Pierre, even to win just this battle, his knees buckled, he was going down.

Kyle watched in horror from his perch on the bench, he could not move. Pierre's power had him tethered where he was. He focused on the collective trying to help them, wanting to, but Pierre had severely reduced his ability to do so with his control. When he saw his father falter, an icy fear gripped his soul. He would not let his father die at the hands of the monster that took his mother. Nooooo !" he cried out and, as a last ditch effort, used all his strength to call up his blocking ability and transport it to the team's wall, it regained strength, Keys was able to regain his balance, and suddenly from somewhere on the right, flames shot out, and combined with the electric wall. The collision of flames and electricity sent Lamontage stumbling backwards, weakened, his hold on the team let loose, and he went down to his knees. Shaken, he pushed himself up and turned to Kyle raising his hand and closing his fist. Kyle's form stiffened, and his screams filled the dream realm.

"Kyle !" Marna cried, trying to break free from the team.

Keys pushed her back "You can't help him here," he hissed and he nodded to Tanner to take her. Tanner wrapped protective arms around her.

Marna fought Tanner's hold. "Marna, if you step away from us, you give Lamontage what he wants. We can't help Kyle, if we lose more to the man who has him." Marna put her hands over her ears, and buried her face in Tanner's chest. Keys watched in amazement as Pierre sank to the ground, his power leaving him. He quickly looked to the right, but all he caught was a figure running away in a hooded sweatshirt and pants. The realm started dissolving around them, and Kyle's screams followed them out of the realm as they're abilities sent them away from the destruction . . .

~~~~~

Ventura and Sarah broke contact first, Ventura waving at Todd to cut the frequency. The video showed Kyle in his chair screaming, head thrown back like a wolf howling for a lost pack member as Lamontage prolonged his pain. Ventura looked at Sarah, who nodded then turned his angry eyes on Lamontage, his hands clenched at his sides.

However, Pierre had to cut his control short in his weakened state and lean on a nearby chair for support. Kyle's screams suddenly stopped. He moaned pitifully as his head slammed forward and he gasped for air, sobbing. Pierre was breathing heavily, but his voice was strong and ferocious.

"A Pyrokinetic? You will be sorry. The son will pay for the sins of father." He breathed raising his hand again.

Ventura tried to stop him, "Lamontage no !"

Lamontage released another vicious attack on Kyle. Peter felt helpless, he didn't know how much more the kid could take, Sarah's eyes filled with tears and she looked away. Mercifully, Pierre couldn't hold the attack. Almost immediately, he released him, silence thundered around the prison and the command center. Pierre pushed himself to his feet, eyes flashing. "I can induce so much pain; Fred's son will wish himself dead and then stop it at the threshold of actual death. You tell Keys and Farlow they know my demands !" He was breathing heavy and turned to his men, nodding. They helped him to his feet, and then assisted him out.

Ventura kicked a chair across the room, causing Sarah to jump. He brought his hands to his waist, dropped his head, let loose a string of expletives, and then glanced at the video, noticed Kyle was alone, no guards. Pierre must have thought he had left the kid in such bad shape that he could do no damage or that after his display of power over Kyle, Guardian wouldn't do anything to overstep and risk causing Kyle more pain.

He was right to a point, and Peter had to be very careful but it was a window of opportunity he couldn't let slip away. He put his hands palms down on the command center, and leaned forward. "Kyle?" he hissed. No response, the kid had probably lost consciousness, his body probably induced unconsciousness, as a body will do, when it reaches a certain threshold of pain. He tried again, "Kyle?"

Kyle started coughing, wheezing and gasping, trying to get air into his lungs. Ventura looked up at the ceiling, let out a hard sigh; Sarah wiped tears from her face. "Kid, you are made from some kind of stock to take that punishment and still be here."

"*Cough*wheeze*Can't – take – much – more *gasp*why don't*gasp* he just*cough* *wheeze* kill – me gasp*just— want – stop – gasp* *wheez*"

"I know, Kid, I know." He could hear the strain in Kyle's voice, knew the sound of defeat. Ventura sought out Schaefer's eyes, and then returned his own to the monitor. "We've caught some leads, Kid, good ones. Do you understand what I'm saying?" Kyle lifted his head and looked through the strands of his unkempt, shoulder length hair, a flicker of knowing brought them to life. "All you have to do is hang on long enough for them to pan out." He held Kyle's gaze for a few seconds, before another coughing fit took hold of him. The message had gotten through. He understood that they were following up on what he had given them. He watched Kyle struggle to get comfortable. The strain and uncertainty in his movements made it clear how much pain this last attack had caused him.

"*cough*gasp*breath* – Dad ?"

"Don't you worry about him,leave that to us.." Kyle nodded painfully. He watched as they talked how Kyle's breathing became calmer. He wasn't fighting as hard to breathe. The wheezing and coughing subsided. "Breathe deep, Kid."

Kyle took Ventura's advice, but groaned with the effort, he brought his head forward, regaining control of his breathing, but his movements were stiff, guarded. He slowly sat up. "Marna?" He looked at the camera.

"She's fine, thanks to our uninvited guest." He frowned.

Nervously, Kyle scanned the room, waiting for the next attack; bracing himself for it.

Ventura was quick to reassure him. "He was in as rough a shape as the rest of us, had to be assisted out. I think your okay for tonight. Take advantage of it and get some rest. Know we've got your back." Ventura watched as Kyle gave a jerky nod, his features became tight, and then Kyle's eyes filled with tears. He bit his lower lip, lowered his head, and sniffed. Ventura killed all audio to give him some dignity, and then walked away from the command center, waving Sarah away too. He took a breath, swallowing the lump in his own throat, pulled out his GPC and dialed Keys. . .

*****

A collective gasp went around the room as they disconnected. Marna pulled her hands out and tried to regain control of her breathing as hyperventilation threatened to move in. She kept hearing Kyle's screams bouncing around inside her head. Rose went to her, took her vitals, and looked at her chart. Then she went to grab a shot from the stand by her bed. "No! no more medication. I need to think."

"Marna, you are not three days out of emergency surgery."

Marna reached up and squeezed Rose's hand as it gripped the railing. "Please, Rose, I'll be fine. I just need to catch my breath." Rose looked her in the eyes then nodded, Tanner and Keys stood at the foot of the bed, Tanner nervously watching the monitors. Marna closed her eyes, took some deep breaths, and when she stopped shaking enough to confront Keys, she opened her eyes and sought his out. "You better start explaining a few things, Keys, and I don't want to hear anything about postponement. You either tell me now why Pierre has Kyle or I find out myself." She looked steadily at him, eyes flashing. Tanner narrowed his eyes. Marna was sending out vibes a bit hard to understand

274

over this thing with Kyle. Did she care about him or was she just feeling an over powering guilt that he had become yet another pawn in Pierre's deadly game to claim her? He didn't know, but right now wasn't the time to analyze. Kyle was an agent in trouble and he needed everyone backing him up.

Keys sat down and Tanner put a hand on his shoulder, squeezing it once to offer him moral support. Keys started at the beginning and explained it all; his and Kyle's blood ties, Kyle's kidnapping, and Lamontage's demands. "Check," she repeated Pierre's ominous message, "that's what he meant." She sat back horrified.

"I'm sorry, Marna, I probably should have told the core team but we honestly assumed his identity was safe."

Her mind went back to that night in the hotel in Switzerland, would Kyle have told her, confided in her if they had taken that step? "Well you know what they say about assuming." She brought her thumbnail to her teeth. "You need to get me out of here." She looked from one to the other.

Tanner's head shot up. "Marna you can't be considering giving in to Lamontage's demands?" He was angry, fearful. "Even Kyle said not to let you consider that, you're nowhere near strong enough to fight him off."

"Easy, Tanner." Keys held his hand up. "Is that what you have in mind, Marna?"

She shook her head, "Not exactly."

"Marna, we can't even think about using you as bait in your condition. You saw what he did to Kyle," Tanner said, "If he uses even half of that power on you, he'll rip your insides to pieces again and you may not make it. It's too dangerous." He looked at Keys, "Keys tell her."

"Are you sure, Marna?"

"I can't be out of commission or in a weakened state going up against this monster, Keys, you said it yourself, I have to take a leap of faith some time. I think that time has come." She tamped down the swelling fear in her gut.

He nodded, "Yes, yes I think it has." He held her gaze, saw she was serious.

Tanner looked from one to the other, wondering what was transpiring between them then he remember that night so long ago, and again as recently as a few weeks. "Mary"

"They'll need to release me in to your care, Keys."

"If you're sure? I don't think there is any risk to her, she's become very strong." Marna nodded, "I'll get the paper work started, but you can sleep on it tonight, we can do this in the morning."

"Kyle may not have a lot of time, Keys. We need to counter attack as soon as possible . Go." He nodded and left the room.

Tanner went to sit on the bedside, taking her hands with his own, wrapping them in warmth. "Are you sure about this, Marna?" He whispered.

She looked him steadily in the eye, "If there is one thing I've learned since joining this agency. Guardian is a family. We watch each-others back. I couldn't help Sasha, or Demi in their hour of need, Pierre made sure of that. I have to do everything I can to help Kyle. Do you understand that, am I making any sense?"

"He moved his eyes over her features. A nagging fear began in his gut. He tamped it down. "Yeah, I guess I do," he captured her chin gently with his thumb and forefinger. She enclosed her fingers around his hand. "Putting others before you is what makes you who you are."

"I'm no saint, Tanner. I'm just doing what they would do for me."

"Funny, I can sure see a halo from where I sit." he whispered, brushing her features with his eyes and lifting a hand to brush a stray piece of hair behind her ear with his fingers. With the back of his finger, he traced her ear, her jaw line and then her lips. His head tilted slightly, lowering his lips toward hers . . .

"Took a few minutes, but I fina . . ." Keys looked up at the two of them and stopped. Tanner smiled, dropped his head, and cleared his throat. He pushed up off the bed, and turned toward Keys. Marna worried her lower lip with her teeth to keep from grinning.

"Did they agree?" Tanner asked

"Yeah. The paper work is done, and Rose is getting a wheel chair," He sighed. "While they weren't happy about it, they agreed if I promised to be your attending physician at home. I said I would."

"All right then," Marna said, let's get operation destroy Lamontage underway. Keys' GPC buzzed.

He pulled it out, looked at the LCD, switched it to privacy mode and pulled it to his ear. "Yeah, Ventura."

"Keys, How is everyone there?"

"Fine, we're taking Marna out of the hospital tonight."

"What?"

"She's ready to let Mary give her healing ability a shot." He glanced back at Marna, and then lowered his voice. "How's Kyle?"

"Lamontage had a temper tantrum and took it out on our boy, but he's a strong Kid, Keys, he's hanging in there, he was more concerned about you and Marna."

"You told him we were fine?"

"Yes, I did. I told him to get some rest. Lamontage was in pretty bad shape, so I doubt he has the strength to launch another attack tonight, our uninvited friend bought us a little time." He glanced back at the screen. Kyle had quieted and was sleeping. Down in the lower right corner, his vitals beat a steady reading of normalcy. "Who was our good Samaritan anyway?"

"I don't know, Pyrokinetics are a rare breed. Most come from a heritage almost extinct. They don't usually play for our side. I don't think Guardian has ever had one. Imagine my surprise when one showed up in the ring for us."

"Maybe a rogue on Pierre's side?" Ventura queried. "possibly one that escaped the massacre."

"I'll see what I can find out. They aren't sharing, whoever they are. He/She did, however, how us how to destroy him."

"Yeah he wasn't happy about it either. Fear is a weakness, Pierre doesn't like to feel."

"Neither is defeat, and he's smelling it," Keys voice held hope. Ventura's eyes strayed to the monitor. He would not let Keys know the kid was on the verge of giving up or at this point would welcome death.

"What about the ID on our mystery servant."

"Serena pulled three good sketches from our witness. The Server was a match for our servant, we're running facial on her now," Keys closed his eyes, of course. She would have been able to drug Kyle's drink with no one noticing. By going to Jenna's alone, Kyle made himself a target of opportunity that night. Easy pickings for Pierre, he drew in a breath.

"You said sketches?" He pulled himself away from the thoughts of mistakes made. "What else did she send you?"

"She gave us a sketch of the man that approached Giselle as well as the forearm of the one that attacked her. She was also able to uncover a tattoo worn by all three involved. The server and the guy who approached her, it was on their neck, and the one who beat her, it was on the inside forearm. We're running an art signature search and a facial on the suspects. There was commotion in the background. "Hang on, Keys, We've got a hit on the woman."

Keys closed his eyes and let out a sigh. "Who is she?" Dare he hope that the floodgates on this case were finally opening?

" Sanoya Faung aka; Sarah Fender She's been employed at Jenna's for a year. Has an apartment in the same building Kyle lived in."

"Vicinity to Kyle's?"

"Two doors down, same floor."

"Perfect approximation to keep tabs on him and watch his every move. Tail his car. She was stalking him."

"Witnesses we interviewed said that before Kyle and Sasha were transferred to Switzerland, he frequented Jenna's," Ventura verified.

"She was guaranteed a successful snatch. All she had to do was get a job there and wait for the moment of opportunity," Keys said, starting to see a troubling situation unfold, "Pierre has known for a while who Kyle is."

"Seems so," Ventura looked over the print out. "Well here's our link. She's on the FWPA watch list. Suspected ties to the Liberatores."

Keys tapped down his anger. How had she acquired employment on the Guardian Compound with a tie like that? "Bring her in, Peter. Once I get Marna settled, I'm bringing Tanner for interrogation. If they've cleared Demi, I'll see if she wants to tag team."

More commotion. "Just got a hit on the man that approached Giselle; Paul Sanyo, He's got an address in Portland. He's also on the watch list for suspected Liberatores ties," Ventura read more information. "There's more. He's Faung's Uncle."

"How did these people get on Compound grounds and through screening to get in our university?" He drew in a breath and let it out. "Have security call FWPA and the locals for a joint mission to his house, and bring him in. Then I want to know who was on duty at the security gate that night. Relieve them of duty. Start an investigation. I want to know how these people were able to get through screening, and put a net around my son!"

"You got it, Keys."

"Call me with updates."

"He returned to Marna's bedside. Tanner was just helping her to the wheelchair, Rose had brought in for her."

"Good news?"

"Let's hope." He nodded at Rose who pushed Marna out of the room. "Tanner, agents are attempting to bring in some suspects. I want you to run point on the interrogation. I'm going to check on Demi now. If her Psych eval is okay, I'll ask her to tag team with you, but let's get Marna settled first." Tanner nodded and they headed out of the room.

*****

Ventura jumped out of the van, Misty stayed behind to watch the monitors. The landlord verified the sketch was that of his tenant Sarah Fender. There was one heat signature in the apartment. Ventura told him to go in to his office and stay there. He ordered McGellan and Justice around back, and then he took two WIT people with him and six other security officers to help secure the other apartments. The woman was a terrorist and that is how they approached her. When he reached the front door, he nodded to Schaefer, who took her place on the opposite side, and each one had three security officers flanking them. He knocked on the door. "Sanoya Faung, Guardian WIT we need to talk to you!" Not a sound. He knocked again. "Sanoya Faung, Guardian WIT. Open this door, now !" They heard footsteps retreating in the opposite direction.

"She's running !" He spun on the balls of his feet, lifted his right leg, and kicked at the door. With a resounding crack, it caved. They moved in, guns ready, "McGellan, Justice, she's headed your way !" Sarah and Barry move in toward the fire escape and Sarah mounted it, while Barry covered her then scrambled up behind her, while she covered him. In the apartment, Ventura and Heidi moved from above to block off escape or retreat.

Sanoya ran down two flights of iron steps, hair flowing behind her, before she met Sarah and Barry, "Gun!" Sarah Justice called out as Sanoya turned to run back up the stairs, but she was met with the barrels of Ventura's and Shaefer's Glocks. "Your options are limited, Sanoya," Sanoya looked at her gun. Sarah could see her mind working. "Suicide by cop isn't the way to go, Sanoya, drop the gun."

"You don't understand!" She started to cry. " He'll kill me !"

"Who will, Sanoya? Paul? Pierre?" Justice continued. Sanoya looked over the rail of the fire escape. "No, that's not the answer. Let us help you." Justice slowly holstered her gun.

Sarah! Ventura opened a psychic line with her, holding his gun steadily on Sanoya.

She's terrified

She's Liberatores

I've got it covered. She sent him a knowing look. Ventura cautiously moved down two steps, Barry fixed his weapon steadily on Sanoya. Sanoya Kept a steady aim on Sarah.

"Sanoya look at me," the girl looked at her. I'm unarmed, but my friends, they're not, and they will shoot you, if you so much as twitch. I just want to talk. "Did they threaten to kill you if you didn't Drug Kyle?"

"He was always so nice to me."

"Kyle was always nice to you?" Justice pointedly put Kyle's name in her comments to humanize him, "his name is Kyle,"

"Yes, Kyle, he was always smiling and friendly. He asked about my classes, helped me with groceries, but he didn't seem to recognize me that night." Her tone changed a bit, she was angry, defiant.

Uh-oh, Justice had to get her to refocus; otherwise, she couldn't get control of her, or the situation. "He'd been gone a long time, Sanoya, Pierre had just killed his partner, a friend of his was in the hospital, he had recently been injured in a fight, he was overtired, and he'd had a couple of drinks. I'm sure if he had a chance to talk to you further, he would have recognized you but it was real busy at the tavern, wasn't it? A popular band was playing, right?"

"Maybe." She looked at the gun and then at Sarah. "But he remembered the others."

Peter followed Justice's lead. "He recognized you the night you helped him," he said. She stepped back, moved her eyes between the two of them as Ventura moved to her right. "When you tended his wounds, you gave him water. You took care of him." Her eyes seemed to pull something out of her memory. Fear flashed in her eyes. It dawned on Ventura that maybe Pierre had punished her for her kindness. That's why she hadn't been back since then. Her eyes suggested instability; Pierre's treatment had possibly pushed her to the edge, ready to tip. "He sent us to get you," so it was a little white lie, but maybe she would consider Kyle's friends alternate allies to Pierre.

"He did?"

Ventura nodded. "He wants you to help us find him." Her eyes narrowed again, she studied his face, looked back at Sarah.

"Let me have the gun, Sanoya," Sarah said reaching out her hand, "Kyle was good to you, you said so yourself. Now it's your turn to return the favor. Help us help him." Tears welled in the girl's eyes, her resolve left her, and she deflated, handing the gun to Justice.

"Hands behind your back, Sanoya," Ventura ordered. She complied without a fight. He cuffed her and handed her off to security for transport. He turned to Sarah. "Good call." he drew in a breath and let it out, "But if you ever retreat your weapon when you are facing an armed suspect, that unstable again, with no cover, I will kick your butt back to Safety and Security myself.."

"I knew you had my back, Lu. Besides I had her covered." She handed him the weapon with a knowing grin.

He narrowed his eyes, and then a flash of Justice's abilities passed before him. "Remote Influencer." He nodded. No wonder the woman was so compliant.

"I just had to find her soft spot and it happened to be Rigby."

He shook his head, grinning. "You and Rigby are going to be an interesting partnership to watch develop."

"If we ever get him back," she sighed.

"We will. Just next time give me a little warning before you give me grays."

She held her hand up. "Promise." He clamped her shoulder and gave it a gentle squeeze.

"You talked her down, took the lead, your collar."

"I won't argue." She smiled, while he chuckled.

"Let's go check the apartment out then we might make it to HQ in time to have popcorn and watch the fireworks, because our guys should be moving in on Paul Sanyo as we speak."

"Who's doing the interview?"

"Williams."

"I hear he's good."

"One of our best, let's go." They headed up the fire escape toward the apartment. If they got both the suspects, maybe one of them knew where Pierre was keeping Rigby.

*****

Marna smiled as Tanner helped her onto her couch. She drew in a sharp breath, "you okay?" He asked, concerned he had hurt her. He sat on the arm of the couch and helped her ease back, and then left his arm loosely on the back of the couch.

She nodded. "I'm fine, just stiff from not moving around for so long."

"Two open heart surgeries in as many weeks can make anyone a little sore," Keys said as he checked her vitals, "Things look good, Marna. How do you feel?" He sat on the coffee table in front of the couch, taking her pulse.

"I'd be lying if I said I wasn't anxious."

He patted her knee. "I'll be right here. If I see any threat, to either of you, I will call this whole thing off." Keys said and glanced at Tanner who had an arm draped around Marna's shoulders and his other arm across his lap, with his hand resting on the shoulder closest to him. He gave her an affectionate squeeze of support and she lifted her hand to his.

"Okay," she said, and he nodded to Rose who went upstairs and returned moments later, holding Mary's hand. The other children were trailing behind and they all claimed a spot on the steps. "Hey." She said to Mary, who gave her a hug, and the child's face expressed sympathy for Marna. Mary was feeling her pain.

"You're hurting," Mary said.

"Yes, but I'll be okay." She looked the child over, her curls twisted down the center of her back now and a bright pink headband held them away from her face. Her big blue eyes shined with her desire to help.

"You want me to help?"

"Do you want to?"

"Now that's a silly question." She frowned. "Of course I want to help." Tanner chuckled then grinned and Keys sat back with a smile on his face. Children saw the world in black and white, without all the shades of gray messing up the paths between problems and solutions.

"But you need to lie down." She turned to Keys. "Could you help her lay down, Dr. Keys, please?"

"Why yes, ma'am I think I can," he glanced at Tanner, "Tanner can you give me a hand." Tanner nodded and he supported the upper half of her body, while Keys swung her legs up to the couch cushions. They put cushions under her head, then they stepped aside as Mary moved her hands to where Marna's thin nightgown showed the outline of bandages.

"Close your eyes, Aunt Marna and think about getting better." Mary said with a matter of fact tone.

"Okay." She did, and within seconds, she felt Mary's hands gently touch her chest and shoulder then the familiar feeling of their connection. Marna could feel heat surge through the wounded areas of her body. Pleasant warmth engulfed her body, circled her heart and lungs, and then exited out in a soft sigh. For the watchers the sight surprised and amazed them. A golden halo of light encircled the two of them, and then a display of multicolored light. Rose brought her hand to her mouth as she saw a healthy color return to Marna's features.

When the lights and the halo subsided, Marna opened her eyes, and looked up into Mary's proud little face. Keys moved in and checked Mary's vitals first. She showed no signs of distress. Other than being fatigued, she seemed fine, and then he turned his attention to Marna. "How are you feeling Marna?"

"Tired, but better," Tanner helped her sit, she moved slowly, her shoulder still stiff from the injuries, but that would get better with use. Keys had her step into the Den, while the family waited anxiously, so he could check her wounds and incisions. Mission accomplished, Mary had healed the wounds from the inside out. Scars had formed, as they would have if she had healed naturally. He took the bandages off, and helped her pull her gown back in place. "Mary?"

"We'll keep a close eye on her tonight. I've asked Rose to stay, to watch over the both of you, but her vitals are fine. She may suffer some fatigue due to the energy drain, the use of the ability causes her.. You may suffer some fatigue as well, simply from the whole ordeal. Other than that, it looks like the healing was a success. I want you two to take it easy tonight and tomorrow, get your strength back." He assisted her up, and opened the door for them to exit the room, told the family what he had told her, and then his GPC beeped. He stepped away as the kids all made of Mary and Marna, and then Rose, in her most fearsome nurse voice, told Marna to lay on the couch, and the rest of them to finish their homework and get ready for bed.

Tanner sat on the coffee table. "How do you feel?" He asked softly, taking her hand.

"Tired," she sighed, adjusting her head on the pillow. "Keys said I would."

He held her hand loosely and with his free hand, he pushed strands of hair away from her face. "Medical degree's got to account for something. So I guess you should listen to him." He smiled, "you get some rest. We need you strong." Their eyes held for a long moment.

"Tanner," Keys said, "They've got the suspects and they're bringing them in."

"Right behind you," Tanner said and watched as Keys went out the front door. He bent down and kissed her forehead. "I'll be back later to relieve Rose from blocking. You try to get some sleep."

"Okay," she sighed, but held his hand for a moment longer. "Find out where they're keeping him, so we can bring him home please, Tanner," tears stung her eyes, "I don't want anybody else to die because of me."

"We'll do our best," He brought her hand to his lips, kissed it, gave it a slight squeeze, and followed Keys out the door.

Chapter Eighteen

At HQ, Tanner stood in the monitor room for the five digitized interrogation rooms on level 5. He studied the image of Sanoya Faung on the wall screen for room two. She sat in a metal chair with both her wrists cuffed to a bar welded to the matching table before her. She had her hands clasped and bounced her knees nervously as she looked around the sparsely furnished room. He glanced down at the folder and sifted through the notes on her capture, the photos of Kyle, Sanoya, and Sanoya's questionable connections.

When combined with other collected evidence, the most incriminating photos were the ones the investigators had retrieved from security cameras stationed around Jenna's parking lot, the one captured from a video camera attached to the revolving stage in the tavern, and those taken in Kyle's building. Her hair partially hid her face in the one from the stage, but the tattoo on her neck was visible and Giselle had filled in the blanks during her session with Serena. Advanced facial recognition was able to give them a ninety-five percent match that they were all the same woman, good enough when thrown into the mix with the rest.

Sarah Justice came through the door, handing him a coffee. He thanked her then sized her up with a glance. Her honey-colored hair hung loose to her shoulders and off set her round, ocean-colored eyes that, in the low lighting of the room, looked the shade of the sea at its deepest. She barely topped 5'2" but it was a compact wall of 132 lbs of pure muscle. Guardian had just recently promoted her to the WIT division, from safety and security; this would be her first major case. "Congratulations," he said. "Good bust to start your career at WIT with."

"Thanks." She took a sip of her coffee and approached the monitor. Sanoya kept looking up at the camera. "How are you going to approach her?"

He took a sip and glanced at the monitor. "I'm waiting to find out how Demi wants to do it. They cleared her for interrogation responsibilities, but not quite ready to give her the green light on fieldwork yet. I'm thinking if Pierre did attack Sanoya, as you suggested, because of her act of kindness to Kyle, it might be a good idea to have a soft touch in interrogation."

"You're probably right. Who's got the other one?"

"Keys is running point, with FWPA flanking him. He lives off compound, so we had to include FWPA and locals. They're doing the interrogation at Portland PD"

"You think they'll let us keep the collar?"

"I'll let Keys and Ruletto duke it out over that one. What's the update on Kyle?"

"Pierre has been down for eight hours, so Ventura has been encouraging him to rest and conserve strength. However, I suspect our interlude is about to end and soon. Men like Pierre don't stay off the stage for long. Let's hope whatever these two give us, will lead us to him. Pierre was not happy with the appearance the pyrokinetic. Kyle paid for it." She shook her head and suppressed a shudder. "Never knew humans could scream like that."

"He's in Hades, Justice; the only thing missing is the fire and gnashing of teeth." Tanner took a breath, "Keys have any leads on our unexpected ally?"

She shook her head. "No. He said the breed is very rare, and hardly ever on the good guys' side." She took another drink of coffee."They're running down leads through FWPA to see if any of their past cases have similar patterns that mark pyrokinetics."

"Well whoever it was has shown us how to take Pierre down."

"Or at least weaken him."

"All we need to do is overdose him, and watch him fall."

"Sounds cold when you say it like that, Williams,"

He lifted his cold, hard eyes to hers over the brim of his cup. "There is only one way to deal with a monster like Lamontage, Justice, you put him down." She opened her mouth to respond, but the entrance doors slid open and Demi and Bryan joined them.

"Hey, Spencer," Tanner walked over and gave her a hug, "Welcome home." He stepped away and gave Bryan a hearty handshake, but his eyes returned to Demi.

"Thanks, Tanner, How's Marna?" Demi asked as she passed him and walked over to look at the screen.

"Home, resting."

"Good, she's going to need all her strength for the battle ahead." Suppressing a shudder, he exchanged a look with Bryan and then with Sarah. Demi's voice was hollow, matter of fact, and held the tone of firsthand experience. "What do we know about our guest?"

"She was assigned to spy on Kyle's activities for at least eighteen months that we can verify. Moved into his building six months before he was sent to Switzerland, and I guess in that time they had a few encounters. He actually charmed the young lady to the point of her second guessing her assignment."

Demi chuckled. "That fits from what I know about him."

Tanner nodded, "She secured a job at his favorite haunt, waited for the opportunity, drugged him and made him vulnerable to her Uncle and two others; errand boys for Pierre Lamontage." Demi closed her eyes and suppressed a shudder. "He and the two associates grabbed Kyle and took him to Pierre."

"Has she ever been a victim of Pierre?"

Tanner looked at Bryan, he nodded. "We believe she has. Before Pierre's last attack on Guardian. Pierre sent her into Kyle with a bottle of drugged water, Compliance, I'm assuming. She took to time to clean him up and tend to his wound, including a rib wrap. She was never sent back to him. We're assuming Pierre found out about it, and disciplined her for her kindness." Demi nodded. That's exactly what Pierre would have done.

"During that same encounter, Kyle recognized her eyes, and gave us a subtle hint. Giselle Riley, our witness, had a session with Serena Blackwater, and gave us a sketch of the woman serving Kyle the suspected drink the night of the abduction. We took the image from the video capture of her assisting Kyle, merged the two images,ran facial recognition, and found her on the FWPA's terrorist watch list

She took a breath and turned to face Tanner. Her expression was determined. "Well then, I guess we need to see if she's more afraid of him than she is of us."

"Let's do it then," He waved her ahead, and the exited observation, heading down the hall to interrogation room two.

She reached for the folder, Tanner offered, opened it, saw pictures of Kyle before the kidnapping and after. She looked away for a second, bit her lower lip then returned her eyes to the photos. She saw more photos of Sanoya with other Liberatores suspects. "Has she ever been in any trouble before?" "Nothing but a few speeding tickets, she's stayed off the radar."

Outside the room, Tanner reached for the doorknob and studied her face. He narrowed his eyes. She looked at him quizzically. "What's your spidy sense telling you, Mr. Williams?"

"You don't have to do this, Spencer, I can call Justice in."

"Justice hasn't been on the receiving end of Lamontage's twisted control."

"Precisely why I'm wondering if this might be too close for you."

"Tanner, I'm fine really. I admit, the pictures of Kyle got to me, I know the level of pain he's enduring, the fear, the shame, and the desperation; it's like being on a deserted island with your worst nightmare, only the night never ends. You know morning is coming, but you don't know when, so you live in the dark until it does. There are moments you wish he would just end it all, but he won't and others that make you angry enough to fight him off but that only brings more pain, more punishment and that's his power over you. That's what gives Lamontage his twisted pleasure and that's what gives him the control." She drew in a breath before she continued.

"I know the urgency in finding Kyle, and putting an end to Lamontage. I also have several years of interrogation experience and I know better than anyone else what that young girl went through, so I'm the perfect person to ride second chair on this little soirée." Her features grew tense, as she raised her eyes to his. "So let me do my job," her green eyes flashed.

His jaw bunched then relaxed. "Allright Spencer, but just so you know,Kyle's life isn't the only one hanging in the balance here and if I sense a falter no matter how minor, I take over." He countered, his gaze never faltering from hers.

"Agreed," she said, "he won't have a chance at her, Tanner, we'll get him." She looked at the doorknob still held tightly in his hand. He sighed heavily and opened the door, allowing her to enter first. As soon as she crossed the threshold, she was all business. She had pulled her long red curls back in a single tail, her green eyes hard as stone. Her lips formed a straight line. She knew she could afford the young woman a certain bit of sympathy, but she had handed one of their own over to Pierre. Tanner took up a place by an exterior window, standing with arms across his chest, and feet crossed at the ankles, his face tight and tense. Bryan watched it on the hub screen. Demi slipped into the role of interrogator as easily as she always had. He smiled proudly as she tossed the heavy folder on the table, causing the girl to jump and look nervously from one to the other.

"That's my girl," he breathed, leaning his hand, palm down, on the wall beside the monitor.

"Let the show begin." Justice said as she stood beside Bryan watching the screen.

"Good afternoon, Sanoya." Demi said as she sat across from her, then opened up the folder and started sifting through the contents. Sanoya didn't answer, just looked to the side. "You've been a busy girl." She glanced through the file. "Takes a determined person to lure a WIT agent into a trap especially since we are generally not very trusting people to begin with."

Tanner carefully untangled his limbs and walked over to the table placing his hands, palms down, on the table beside Demi. "He trusted you. He felt safe in that tavern and you just took advantage," he narrowed his eyes, and Sanoya averted hers. "If it were up to me, I'd send you to death row myself."

"Easy Tanner." Demi said in a tone that said take it easy. Tanner pushed away from the table, and walked toward the wall behind Demi, sparing a glance at the camera mounted in the corner. They had established the good cop, bad cop roles. Demi was taking lead. He turned around hoping it wasn't a mistake. He leaned against the wall, his body tense, ready to move if Demi faltered. "You gotta forgive my friend; he gets a little testy when someone makes a reality show of a family member being blatantly tortured. It doesn't make for good viewing, and it pisses him off." Demi brought her hand up, resting her chin on curled fingers. With her free hand, she slid a picture of Paul Sanyo in front of Sanoya.

"Know him?" Demi drew in a breath, "looks like you do in this picture." She slid another one of the two suspects talking in front of a restaurant, not very good for your case." Sanoya looked away. Demi looked at Tanner who nodded subtly. They both had felt it. Fear. She pulled out another, "what about him," Demi slid a black and white print of Kyle across the table, and then narrowed her eyes. "You should, you live in the same apartment building, on the same floor; two doors down in fact. You've actually talked to him on occasion," she threw a picture down of the apartment house, of Sanoya's apartment, and then a security shot outside Kyle's apartment; they were both smiling and appeared to be talking, Kyle's keycard in his hand. "You also wrote him a few emails, thanking him for his assistance on a number of occasions," she slipped a couple of emails over to her, "and you served him a drink last Wednesday night at Jenna's," she tossed the video capture from the concert on top of the pile, Sanoya licked her lips nervously. "Let me tell you a little bit about him, help you fill in the blanks. He's handsome, charming, never hesitates when a friend needs help and he has a hero complex the size of Texas, with a heart to support it. It's because he cares, maybe to a fault, which makes him an easy target to a pretty face in trouble." Sanoya sniffed and wiped her finger under her nose. "He's got a father who loves him, and friends who are worried about him." Sanoya said nothing. Tanner watched in silence. He saw, first hand, how Demi Spencer had received her reputation as the best interrogator in the WIT. Sanoya's armor was chipping away a little at a time.

Demi pulled out the traffic cam shot of Jenna's parking lot. Sanoya was walking in the front door, her uniform on. She placed it on top of the others. "That was taken at the beginning of your shift that night. Bartender says you were on duty. Eye witness swears it was you who gave him his last drink of the evening," Sanoya looked away and Demi brought her hand down, entwining her fingers. "Funny thing about Compliance, it leaves trace evidence on the clothing the person was wearing at the time they were using it, or in your case, the time you were lacing Kyle's drink with it." Demi tapped Kyle's picture. Sanoya stayed silent.

Demi reached into the bin beside her chair and pulled out a uniform in a large evidence bag. "This is yours. Security forces found it in your apartment in your hamper. There was a receipt in it from that night, and traces of Compliance from the vile you had in your pocket," she said, "and this," she pulled out a little plastic tubular container secured in another bag, "is the vile in question. Tests match its contents to the trace in your uniform pocket." Her eyes watched the girl's face, oh yeah there it was, the vibes of feeling trapped. Her eyes slid toward Tanner, he had felt them too. "They found that in your vanity in the bathroom. You were there, you served his drink, and you have traces of the drug on your uniform. Looks like the evidence is stacking up against you, and if your Uncle," she tapped the picture of Paul Sanyo, "stays as tight lipped as you, you're the one with all the damming evidence. You know what that tells us?"

Tanner took his cue and approached, placed his hands on the table, beside Demi, and leaned forward. "It tells us that you and you alone, conspired to kidnap a federal agent! If he dies while in the hands of Lamontage, then it turns in to Conspiracy to commit murder !" He pushed away from the table, and moved to the other side of her, took the same pose and said, "I say we just lock her up! Put her in with the general population, no Guardian protection at all, she'll be dead within 72 hours." He leaned forward, until he was in Sanoya's face, his voice tight and fierce, "because as soon as you close your eyes, he'll come, you know he will." He let the ominous words hang in the room for a few seconds before he spoke again. "I know from what I've seen so far, no matter how loyal you've been, how much he professes to love you; it doesn't stop him from killing you and kicking you to the curb, like yesterday's trash, if you disappoint him." The girl winced and he drew away. Demi put a hand on his bicep, dismissing his attack. Normally he would have taken his exit at this point, but he did not want to leave Demi in the room without backup. Instead, he walked around the table, taking a spot by the door, ready to move in if needed.

Demi turned back to the girl and leaned in closer. "Sanoya we want to help you, but you have to help yourself," Demi said. "We can't protect you if you don't."

"I know what he did to you." Sanoya whispered. Demi felt like she couldn't breathe. She pulled her hands to her lap so Sanoya wouldn't see them tremor. For a moment, the walls felt like they were closing in. Bryan leaned into his hand as he watched from the hub. Tanner pushed away from the wall, but Demi shook her head, drawing in a breath. She knew to falter now would mean losing the ground they had gained. Tanner stopped his forward move but did not retreat. "I was there, getting my assignment, when – ah – ah – when they brought you in." She cleared her throat. "He was going to kill you – planned on killing you – you were lucky to get away."

"I know, but I have good friends who helped." Demi said, her voice steady, this is what they had hoped for. She had established rapport with Sanoya, a comradeship among souls who had suffered the same abuse. "They didn't give up and now he has Kyle," she said, taking out the three pictures they had captured of Kyle, from the live feed. She placed them in front of Sanoya. She looked down at them and covered her mouth with her hand. Demi spoke softly, her temporary falter passing, "the same friends want to help him and if you let them, you, but first you have to help us."

"I didn't want to do it." Sanoya whispered, running her fingers the image of Kyle, his head bowed after one of Pierre's attacks.

"Then help us find him, Sanoya," Demi refolded her hands before her, "help us stop Pierre from hurting him anymore."

Sanoya raised her eyes to Demi's and held her gaze. "Will you tell him I'm sorry, tell him they made me do it?"

Demi reached across the table, placing her hand over Sanoya's, giving it a friendly squeeze. "I'll do better than that. I'll tell him it was you who told us where to find him." She held the girl's eyes for a moment, before she spoke again,"where are they keeping him?"

Sanoya sniffed, wiping the tears from her face. "A year ago, Pierre bought the remains of Beals Island from the state of Maine. It was falling to ruins, and nobody wanted to go back there, considering what went on there; the horrible things the government did to people. The prison that was erected there during the conflicts, for government prisoners, mostly FOF members; it has been abandoned since the end of the conflicts in 2035, he has him in one of the EIT rooms." Demi glanced at Tanner, who made his way across the room, swung open the door, stepped into the corridor, jogged up it, and then entered the hub.He pulled his GPC from his pocket, and looked Bryan's way. "Your partner's good, Rush."

"Yes she is." He hugged Sarah and returned his eyes to the screen. Demi was patting the girl's hand. He excused himself and went into the corridor, appearing in room two seconds later. He smiled and nodded at Demi, who responded in kind. They caught each other's eyes in a glance that said volumes more ,in the few seconds they held it, than words could have said in a lifetime. They would finish taking her statement before she would go upstairs to meet with the Safety team and be placed into Guardian protection until they took Pierre down, Then she would face the charges brought against her.

Tanner opened his GPC and pressed Keys call button. The older man's face came into focus after a few rings. He was passing through a door. "Tell me you've got something, Tanner. Paul Sanyo is refusing to talk even though he knows he'll probably be dead by morning."

"Tell FWPA they can have him. Sanoya came through. Pierre is keeping Kyle at the old Winters FOF Prison on Beals Island." Tanner watched Keys eyes grow misty, before he closed them and the tension just seemed to slip away from his face and form. Tanner gave him a few seconds to pull it together, before they spoke again.

Keys cleared his throat. "Call Ventura and update him. I'll call in the rest. Grab Sarah and meet me at the command center in two hours for a briefing. It's time we show Pierre who is in control."

"Yes, Sir, it is." Tanner nodded, closed out communication and turned toward Sarah, "Justice," Sarah swung her head his way, "Keys wants us at the command center for a briefing in two hours. Let's bury this Viper for good." Justice nodded and followed Tanner into the elevator, while he called Ventura.

*****

Ventura watched the live feed. Still no sign of Pierre, he glanced at his watch, it had been almost eleven hours. The door to the command center opened, and Marna walked in, followed by Schaefer. "There she is." He walked over and gave her a hug. "How are you?"

"I'm better," Marna said.

"Good to hear." He followed her gaze to the wall screen. "Pierre hasn't hurt him since our Rendezvous', as a matter of fact, I haven't seen him." As if on cue, the heavy door opened and they heard approaching footfalls. He propelled Marna toward Heidi. "Get her out of sight. We don't need to tip our hand yet."

"Keys !" Pierre's voice boomed, causing Kyle's head to snap up, and his eyes to open in startled wakefulness. Automatic reflex had him tipping his body away from Pierre.

Ventura faced Pierre down. "Keys isn't here, Pierre, you'll have to deal with me." Just then, the door opened, and Keys walked in, followed by Tanner and Justice. Keys had thought it wise to leave Bryan and Demi out of this take down. New evidence had shown itself in another case Guardian had simmering on a back burner; one Bryan and Demi were already familiar with. He had sent them to join the FWPA Task Force.

"Hello, Fred." Keys waved Tanner and Sarah toward the table just out of view of the wall screen and went to join Ventura by the command center. They had to be careful not to let on that they knew where Pierre was or what they were planning.

His eyes sought out Kyle first. "How are you holding up, Son?"

"I'm okay, Dad." Kyle swallowed painfully. Keys gave him a nod, and returned his eyes to Pierre. "What do you want, Pierre?"

"I've raised my price."

"What?" Keys demanded. "What more could we possibly have that you want?"

"I want Marna Farlow and the Pyrokinetic."

Keys drew in a breath and expelled, he had known that was coming. "Pierre, I don't know who that was. Their arrival was as surprising to us as it was to you."

In answer, Pierre raised his fist and twisted it to attack Kyle. Other Agents turned away. Marna's eyes filled with tears and she broke away from the rest, moving to the command center. Keys put his hands on her shoulders but she shook them off. "Lamontage, stop it! If you want me, just tell me when and where and I'll be there !" Her voice caught. "Just leave him alone, please." Keys head shook.

"Marna, No!"

"Keys, there is no other way!" She said waving him away.

Pierre released his hold. Kyle lifted desperate eyes to the camera. "*gasp*Marna *cough* no! *cough*wheeze*. . ."

"No, Kyle, I won't – no I can't – let you or anyone else die because of me." Kyle yanked at his restraints, and then dropped his head defeated, trying get control of his breathing. Tanner stood off to the side watching the exchange, eyes narrowed.

"Why would I take your offer now?" Pierre challenged her.

"Because I'm all you're going to get, Lamontage, that's part of the bargain. You take me and it ends there. You leave everyone else that I care about alone. Her eyes strayed to Kyle and he gets to come back home, otherwise there is no deal." Her eyes narrowed and she faced him off. She never blinked, never wavered. She felt his probing, felt him trying to intrude, but he would only see what she allowed him to see. Tanner and Misty were joining forces to help her shields block his intrusion.

"Oh and one more thing. Keys comes with me and gets his son. The deal goes down in 48 hours; Wednesday is too long to wait. Kyle needs medical attention and he is not going to be denied it any longer, nor are you going to be allowed to cause him and his family anymore pain." She looked him in the eye, but he could not get control of her.

He let out a wry chuckle. "Pretty demanding Bitch, aren't you." He looked at Kyle then brought his eyes back to hers. "Why would I settle for you when I could have both you and the Pyrokinetic?"

"Because, like Keys told you, he isn't part of Guardian. We don't know who he is or where he is." Her eyes strayed to Kyle, trying to tell him not to say anything offensive to Pierre or anger him in any way. She brought them back to Pierre. "Come on, Lamontage, you trying to tell me with your resources you can't find one psychic fire starter?" She crossed her arms and raised her eyebrow in a challenge. "Maybe you're not all that powerful after all."

Pierre's eyes narrowed, his features bunched then released. "You will not be so smug when I have you."

Marna hid the creeping fear in her heart, and kept a steady gaze on his face. "Does that mean we have a deal?"

"Hmmm – I suppose it does – I will call you an hour before the exchange with the where and when." He raised his hand and closed his fist. Kyle groaned, fighting the pain from the attack, but eventually his head fell back, his torso tightened and the horrific screams came. They assauled the ears of everyone present, until, mercifully, his body shut down and he passed out. Pierre released him. "Just a reminder of what will happen if you try any Guardian tricks." Pierre left the room.

"Ventura !" Keys ordered. Marna's hand shot to her mouth, tears stinging her eyes. The rest of the team came to the command center. Tanner came up behind Marna and put his hands on her shoulders. Ventura called Kyle's vitals up on the screen. "Breathing is irregular, heartbeat a little rapid, but they're stabilizing. Many more attacks like that, however, he could go into cardiac arrest. He's suffering from dehydration, malnutrition, possibly has a couple of fractured ribs that could totally break and pierce a lung." He ran a hand over his face, letting out a hard sigh. "In his weakened condition, it won't take much to send him over the edge." He killed the audio, and turned toward Marna, impressed with her performance. "Nicely done."

She drew in a deep breath to try to calm the shaking of her body. "Think he bought it?"

"I don't think he would have agreed to the exchange if not."

"What about Kyle? How will we let him know?"

"We'll connect with him later," Keys said, glancing at the screen. "Right now let's go over to the conference table and go over the plan." Marna crossed her arms before her and took the two steps down to the conference area. Tanner followed her to the table, pulled a chair out for her, and then sat in the one next to it. Keys took his spot by the west wall and hit a couple of buttons. Doors slid open, revealing a wall screen and allowing a touch screen table to slide out of a hidey-hole beside him. He hit the touch screen and a map of Maine appeared on the monitor then he grabbed a wireless remote. Beals Island was shaded in red. He took a quiet breath before he began. "Beals Island, in the early part of the century, was a small village of 500 plus residents. During the conflicts – " he hit a button on his remote, the screen filled with the ruins of several homes." In 2020, in accordance with the updated Martial Law order, the government had the right to take over any property, private or otherwise if they felt it was necessary for national security," another click on the remote, another slide appeared, this one was a man of Iranian-American heritage. "This is Fatih Arjmand Winters, the incumbent president, at the time. He wanted an Island off the East Coast to build a prison for captured FOF fighters so they could use ETI (Enhanced Interrogation Techniques) on them and get information about the FOF network in the nation; the kind he had adopted, came from the new radical allies Iran and Syria. It soon earned the same reputation as Gitmo had during the war on terror, only now these techniques were being used against American citizens. Friends of Freedom members who dared to stand against Winters and the new socialist/communist leadership he was establishing here in America."

"FOF joined forces with the residents of Beals and fought the government forces off for two weeks. It was long enough to allow for a mass exodus to other FOF holdings here in the states before the government sent in Air support, via air drones with surgical precision, just as they had in Iraq and Afghanistan in the nineties and the early part of this century. Most of the residents had been evacuated by that time but when it was all said and done there were 200 dead, several wounded, and the island was leveled " he flipped to another picture of a large concrete structure, surrounded by a chain link, electrified fence. Winters hired a government contractor to erect the prison and some government force offices in the early 2020s. By late 2024, it earned a reputation as Winters' Island of death. Those that weren't executed for treason, found a way to exit this world of their own accord." He ran a hand over his mouth and put up another slide, "When the conflicts ended in 2035, and FOF stood with thousands of Americans to remove Winters and hold the first democratic election in 15 years, anthropologists were brought in to find the remains of the prisoners identify them and send them home to be properly buried."

He changed to another screen to pictures of people carefully digging up remains. "When the government had taken over the Island, they destroyed the bridge between it and Jonesport, so the only way to get to it now is by boat, helicopter or if you want to get creative, mini submarine." He left the last picture up. The listeners were solemn. "I am not surprised Pierre has taken this Island over, it is highly convenient, and easily secured. Now Marna has given him the 48-hour deadline. We need to reach him in less than that to keep the element of surprise on our side."

"How are we doing our approach?" Tanner asked.

"There is no moon tomorrow night. We're taking advantage of that." He changed the screen to a satellite image of Beals Island and her surrounding waterways. Then pulled out a stylus and started mapping out their approach. He put an X off the coast of the Island. "We will be sailing the Guardian Elizabeth, from the compound, and anchor her outside of Alley Bay. She is a new vessel, and we are still in the experimental stages, but she is a cloaked boat and radar blind. This will be her maiden voyage. However, we need every advantage we can get." He circled the prison, dead center of the Island, surrounded on three sides by forestry. He drew arrows, from the Elizabeth position, to a rocky area where a lighthouse stood. "This is our Rendezvous point. From there, we are on foot, through the forestry, heading east, until we reach the exterior prison wall." He finished his arrows. "A Jammer control will be sent out from the ship, disabling cameras, electricity and radio controls." He drew in a breath before he continued. "We will go in to full psychic contact only, so make sure your shields are in place. He's going to check."

"The jam will give us forty minutes to breech, seek, find, and extract Kyle from the EIT rooms. He will have guards. Most likely Liberatores foot soldiers, not possessing abilities. Be aware and prepared for some hand to hand. Do not use your weapons unless there is positively no other alternative. It could alert them to our presence, and endanger the mission, yourselves and Kyle." A tall, slender man came in, followed by two others, each carrying a mid-sized bin. Keys attention drifted toward them, "thanks Bill, hand them out please," he said and returned his attention back to the team. "Each of you is receiving the Guardian P2041. This your new standard weapon. It has 12 levels of electrical streams, and one recently added flame throwing level. It has been in development for six years. I will explain the use of this unique weapon in a moment." He nodded to the men as the team looked over the weapon. Its shape mimicked that of their service Glock, it was lightweight and black. It was trigger controlled, and on the side, within reach of their thumb, was two controls. The first had three color-coded sections and three laser levels within that, beside that was a Pyro flame button with three levels, simply expressed as plastic, wood, and steel. Next item set before them was a charging chamber, with an outlet plug on the back of it, and a formed housing on the inside for the gun with two prongs protruding from the bottom. The housing had a lift top door that closed and locked over the piece. "Set it aside, and we will get back to that in a moment." They all finished looking over the weapon then set it aside, returning their attention to the screen.

"The Elizabeth will be loaded with Blaze charges; these charges are unique in that they are a two part missile. The Missile Tactical Team will place electrically charged housing targets on the exterior prison walls, and a honing device set within them. Agents from the munitions team will be tending these while we go in and work the extraction. Once we have Kyle and are free from the prison grounds, we will lock Pierre within. Elizabeth will release her blaze missiles which will be guided to the electrical charge boxes and the building will be engulfed in a circle of electrical fire."

"Pierre will become powerless," Ventura said.

Keys nodded solemnly. "A final missile will then be sent to destroy the prison and anyone left within."

"Wait a minute," Sarah said, "We aren't taking them in to custody?"

Keys shook his head. "Pierre is too powerful an enemy to take into custody, Sarah, He and the Liberatores have left a trail of death spanning two decades, men women, children, he has no discrimination of who he eliminates. Agents from Guardian WIT, FBI, CIA, FWPA, HLS, SS, FEDPOL, Interpol, and US Marshals have fallen at his hands. He has assassinated many world leaders and their families before, during, and after the conflicts. He is marked for elimination. We are the only ones with the capability of doing it. Agencies across the globe are in agreement with this." He aimed his eyes right at hers. "If you don't think you can handle this type of take down, then Guardian WIT isn't the place for you, because that is what we do. They call us in when all other methods are exhausted; we go after the worst of the worst of psychic enemies. Our targets are rarely the kind you can bring home alive. It does happen on occasion but this is not one of them."

The rest of the team looked her way. She licked her lips nervously. "Yes, Sir."

"Good." He looked at his watch. "Okay, now for the Guardian P2041," everyone picked up the weapon and looked it over. "WIT members will be the only ones in possession of this weapon for the time being. As I said this weapon has been in development for six years. However, recent events have forced me to ask the weapons development team to enhance it. They've been designed as an alternate weapon to the traditional firearm.

As you saw in Switzerland Tasers are quickly replacing the traditional law enforcement weapons. These weapons are similar to those with a couple of twists." He showed them the adjustment buttons on the side. "First off, these weapons throw off streams or lasers of electricity, not wires and connecting probes. It is much lighter than the traditional weapon. He lifted it a couple of times to prove his point then he pointed out controls on the side. There are twelve levels of electrical charges. The first four are stun levels. Each level increases the stun power a notch or two to stun different individuals of different weights. The stream level is enough to make them feel uncomfortable and temporarily weaken muscle control so you can gain control of your subject, but not enough to kill or incapacitate. The next six levels are to incapacitate, same format. Station four is what is different and uniquely designed for the psychic criminals we deal with. The three levels will weaken or interrupt the use of a target's abilities, by confusing signals to their brain. These are the ones you will be using most, as they are the ones used for psychic control. Tomorrow, you will have yours set at station three, level three. He demonstrated by setting it up to the highest level. When aimed at a major artery or the heart, from up to six feet away, the stream produced will send an electrical charge through the body that will kill a target of mild to normal class. In Pierre's sense, however, you'll need four streams on him to encase him completely in an electrical field and a fifth person to activate the flame throwing stream." He moved his finger to the flame activation button. This will create the same effect we saw in the dream realm. Held for a length of time, he will weaken, he will not be able to escape the Elizabeth attack, giving us the chance to extract Kyle and evacuate the prison,"

"The other part of this weapon is the charging housing. If you look it over, it is pretty self-explanatory. The battery is a special battery that will shut down when fully charged, so there is no danger in burning cells so I recommend you charge your weapon after every shift unless it is not used during your shift, then you are good to go for several days. Any questions?" They all looked around the table but nobody spoke. Though the task before them was unpleasant, they knew there was no other option. He sighed, looked at his watch again, and said, "Go home, spend time with your families, get at least eight hours down time. I want you all back here by four tomorrow afternoon to prep for the mission."

Keys dismissed them, wandered over to the command center, and looked at the screen. Kyle looked still as death, his head still lay back and his face had taken on a very pale color. His eyes strayed to the ticking vitals reading. They had returned to normal. That at least was a small comfort. Behind him, chairs scraped against the floor as the team got up and left. The door opened and voices drifted in as agents left the room and others passed by. There were hushed words behind him then he heard more shuffled movement and someone stepped up behind him. "You okay?" Marna asked, placing a hand on his shoulder.

He smiled, placing his hand over hers. "He looks so frail."

Her eyes strayed to the screen. "Pierre hasn't been easy on him."

"No, he's been very cruel, even for Pierre. Sins of the father." he sighed, "this was exactly what we were trying to avoid by hiding his identity." He stared at his son then sighed, "I missed so much, Marna. Made him grow up in a different state than I, saw him a couple of times a month, missed ball games, wrestling matches, didn't dare bring him to agency Christmas parties, functions. Outings such as zoos and carnivals always had a protection detail attached from a select few that knew the truth. God." He looked at the ceiling, blinking his eyes. "To think of everything I deprived myself of, deprived him of, now I may lose him anyway to the forces I was trying to protect him from."

"No," She sniffed, "You – we are not going to lose him, Keys," She looked him in the eye, "you've got to believe that," her eyes grew misty, her voice strained, "We are going in there tomorrow night and we are going to get him out. You will have lots of time to make up for what you lost," she drew in a breath, "okay, maybe the zoo and carnivals are out," Keys chuckled, "but you will make new and lasting memories with your son and no more hiding because the secret's out." She swallowed and looked him in the eye. "You have to believe in yourself, Keys, believe in the team that you have trusted to watch his back." He looked into her eyes and was suddenly aware that somewhere the tables had turned and she was the one offering him the comfort he needed, and she was doing it because she cared for him, for Kyle, for her team. His face crumbled and his resolve gave, Marna wrapped her arms around him and let him cry. Tanner came in, she shook her head, so he let himself back out then closed and locked the door. They had made plans for dinner, but he would wait for her downstairs.

After a few seconds, out of the corner of her eye, Marna caught movement on the screen. She turned to look. One of the guards came in and dumped water on Kyle's face, he shook his head, and brought it forward. She reached down and hit audio. Keys stepped away to rein in his emotions.

"Master said to let you have some water." Kyle looked at it warily, he needed it, but he didn't trust it to be clean. "What, you think we poisoned it or something?" the guard shrugged, "not my problem if you don' drink it, you're the one suff'erin'." Kyle licked his cracking lips, and decided to drink some of it. He nodded his head carefully. The guard brought the bottle to his lips and tipped it up, allowing Kyle to drink a few swallows. He coughed. "Easy now, you don' wanna drown afore you go home to daddy." Kyle's eyes shot to the prison monitor and held Marna's gaze. Something passed through them. Fear? Anger? Desperation? The man offered him more water. He took more and then drew in a breath. Keys rejoined Marna at the console, Kyle's eyes moved to him, he frowned, and then his eyes returned to the guard. "There that should hold you for a while." The guard left the room. Kyle watched him go then returned his eyes to the monitor.

"Are you alone, Son?" Keys asked softly, Kyle's eyes slid toward the door then back, and he nodded. "Are they monitoring this conversation?" Kyle looked toward another space in the room then shook his head once. "If you can find the strength, secure your shields and close your eyes. Focus on Marna and me. Can you do that, Son?" Kyle looked confused, but did it anyway. Keys turned, spoke a few quiet words to Todd, barely audible to anyone but the two of them, returned his gaze to Kyle, and then reached out to take Marna's hand. The drifted through space, and landed in the yard, outside the prison. Kyle looked around, but he couldn't move, Pierre's tethers held him fast. Marna and Keys appeared before him, walls of protection went around them as she combined her cloak and Locating ability with Keys' Space Continuum ability.

"Where is this place?" Kyle asked looking around.

"Somewhere near where he's holding you, but we can only keep you here for a short time."
"How did I get here?"

"It's a collective ability known as space continuum. I have it and you are showing signs of the early stages of it. Marna's Magnifying, and Locating ability directed us and her cloaking will protect us from detection for a short time.. I wasn't sure it would work, but I had to try it "

He tried to move. *"Why can't I move?"*

"Pierre is too powerful to break the bindings of his control. It was iffy that we could get you this far, but worth the risk."

Kyle looked Marna's way. *"Marna, you can't trade yourself for me."* he moved his eyes to his father's, *"Dad, you can't let her."*

"That was to divert Pierre's attention, make him think he's getting his way. We have a plan in motion. We know where you are, Son," Kyle's eyes closed in relief, *"We're coming for you tomorrow night. I just need you to hang on that long, do you think you can?"*

Kyle nodded jerkily and opened his eyes. When he raised them to Keys, Marna could see the raw emotion in them. *"I'm scared, Dad."* His voice sounded strained.

"I know but it will be over tomorrow night, I promise."

"Don't promise something like that, Dad. He's so powerful. I don't think I've seen anyone more so."

"We're pretty powerful too, and we've got love on our side," tears glistened in Kyle's eyes and he formed a straight line with his lips, holding his emotions in check. Keys wanted to grab his son and tell him it was okay but that desire would have to wait. Touching him could alert Pierre to the intrusion. *"We need to go. We don't want Pierre to know we have pierced his shroud around you, but I need you to hang on, Son, the Calvary's coming."*

"Charging on their mighty white steeds." Kyle said in a tight voice. Keys looked at his son; he was speechless for a second as he remembered a little boy saying that at night, when Daddy promised he had scared away the monsters under his bed.

"To take care of those monsters and their dirty deeds." Keys whispered and nodded as he faded out, and then they were back at the command center.

Kyle opened his eyes, looked at the screen, and nodded once. The hint of a smile played across his dried, cracked lips, and then he looked away from the screen. Keys killed the audio, turning to Marna. "Go home, Marna get some rest, help the kids with their homework, be a parent and leave this all behind for a few hours."

"What about you?"

"I'm staying here," He looked at the screen. "I can't touch him, but I'm going to stay with him, just so he knows he's not alone." She nodded and left the room, taking the elevator to the ground floor where Tanner waited for her.

"How is he?"

"Scared," She started walking toward the exit door and he picked up pace beside her, "blames himself. He took all the precautions to protect his child and evil forces got to him anyway."

Tanner shook his head as he went to the passenger side of the Camaro to open the door for her, "tough spot to be in," he sighed, "where would you like to stop for dinner?"

She stood with her hands on the door casing, "Could we just," she shrugged, "you know, get a couple of party Pizza's and take them home to share with the kids instead?"

He smiled as he ran his thumbs over the back of her hands. He got it, he understood. "I think that's a great idea. Do we want Hawaiian or Pepperoni and sausage?"

"Can we get one of each?"

"You bet." he said softly. He brought his hand up to push her hair back, then he put his hand on her shoulder. "Maybe we can find a great family flick while we're at it."

"I think I'd like that and so would the kids."

"Then it's a date." He grinned, brought his hand up to her cheek, ran his thumb over her cheekbone and returned it to the door, holding it while she slid in, and then he closed it. Seconds later, he slid behind the steering wheel, reached over, squeezed her hand, and drove out of the HQ parking garage, pointing the car to the highway. Family night sure beat being alone in his apartment this evening, he looked her way, caught her eye, smiled and drove on.

*****

Marna used the remote to flick off the television and the blue ray player as the credits rolled up the screen. She sat on the couch, legs folded under her, Tanner's arm loosely on the back of the couch behind her. "Okay, troops, off to bed."

"But there is no school tomorrow." Mary quipped.

"But it is about three hours past your bed time, come on." She passed a glance at Tanner, before she headed up the stairs to get the children settled. He started moving about downstairs picking up paper plates, cups, and plastic utensils then he pulled out a storage container and put the leftover pizza into it, placing it in the refrigerator. While he heard the stories commence, he grabbed her teapot, filled it, and placed it on the stove, turning on the burner. He took a couple of cups down from the cupboard to the counter and placed tea bags in them. He raised his eyes to the window, over the sink, looking out over the road beyond it, his mind wandered back to the command center. Marna's conversation with Kyle, the vibes were there. He had tried to ignore them, tried to set them aside, but they were there.

There was something between them, something that went a bit deeper than the superficial friendship developed while they were partners in that trek across Switzerland. He just wasn't sure what, and he was too cowardly to ask. It was easier to deny what he had felt. The teapot whistled, he poured the water into the cups. He felt her before he saw her. He turned around and leaned his hips against her counter, taking a sip of the hot liquid his eyes raised to hers over the rim of the cup, through the steam. He brought his cup down. "I made you tea."

"And cleaned up, I see." She looked around the lower floor.

He shrugged, "You were busy with the kids, figured I was down here, might as well."

She pushed away from the casing and approached the counter, accepting the cup as he handed it to her. "You are a domesticated man, Tanner Williams."

He winced. "Don't let that get out around the office please," his lips curved into a smile, "I'm still getting razzed about the Nanny gig."

She threw her head back and laughed; it was spontaneous and felt good.

He feigned offence, "I'm glad you find my soul scarring so amusing."

She drew in a breath, chuckled and brought her eyes to his, "I somehow doubt that you will have any lasting psychological effects from that, Tanner Williams." She brought her tea to the dining room, set the cup down on the table and started looking through the pile of mail that had been building up during her stay in the hospital. She separated the bills from the school notices and junk mail. She filed the junk in the recycling bin, school papers to one side, and the bills she brought the den. When she returned she saw the folders marked with Freeman's name, uncovered now, in the middle of the table. "Tanner, what are these?" She lifted the top folder.

He almost choked on his tea, he had forgotten about those. "Just some things they found on Freeman's computer." He moved toward the table, but Marna had placed the folders in front of her and started looking through the contents. He stopped when she looked up from the photos. "Tanner, what's this mean?" She stopped after a few photos and caught his eyes with hers, "and don't tell me it's nothing to worry about."

"I wouldn't insult your intelligence that way, Marna." He looked down at the photos then brought his eyes to hers; he hadn't wanted to worry her. "Martin was a bounty hunter. Keys thinks I was his target."

"Bounty hunter?" Her eyes moved back and forth, as she tried to make sense of it all. She opened up the other folder, and saw the emails. "Who?"

"We don't know?" He took her shoulders and turned her toward him. "The emails never give a name, and the IP address was bounced all over the globe."

"The night he was killed?" She looked up at him.

He let go of her shoulders and brought his hands to his waist. "He almost had me out the door. If it hadn't been for the kids, he would have. They formed their collective and saved my butt, and then Peter and Heidi came in and finished the job."

"When he attacked the first time?"

"We're not sure why. We think the same person who hired him to get me, hired him to get you. They're still decoding his encrypted files. We do know is it wasn't Lamontage. There was a third person involved that may or may not have had something to do with the current case."

"And you people didn't think I had a right to know about this !" She shuffled through the photos some more. These are surveillance photos of my house, Tanner! My family !" She looked at some more, "of my kids – of us !" She brought her eyes to the last one of them in Switzerland. Memories of that day, of those feelings, crashed to the surface, she brought her hand to her mouth, "and the person that hired him is still out there," she stared at the photo, touched it.

"Marna – " He reached out to her, she moved away. He felt her disappointment in the agency but most of all, her disappointment in him. He didn't know what to say. How to assure her that it wasn't a deliberate deceit. "Perhaps I should go." he said. She nodded.

He stepped away, set his cup on the counter, stepped into the living room, grabbed his jacket from the back of the chair, and stood for a moment looking at her. He sighed and walked to the front door, but before he left, he turned it back. "For what it's worth, Marna, I wasn't trying to hide anything from you, I just simply forgot. With everything going on with Kyle, it seemed pointless to me to worry about a few pictures on a dead man's computer. It fell to the bottom of my list of priorities." Marna heard the door click shut after he walked out. She moved to the window and looked out in time to see him pull away from the curb. She walked back over to the table and in one angry sweep, she swept the folders off the table, the contents spewed all over the floor and then she sat in a chair, lowering her head to her arms and cried.

~~~~~

"Feel better?"

Marna lifted her eyes to the apparition before her, wiping her eyes. "Manda." Amanda looked around the floor, "not that I'm disappointed to see you have a little rebellion in you after all these years. Guardian is good for you; it's making you more aggressive I like it."

Marna chuckled. "You here to tell me what an idiot I am for letting him walk out tonight?"

"No, mmm, well yeah maybe just a little bit." She lifted her thumb and forefinger up in a pinch pose and grinned.

"Save it," Marna got up and moved to a chair placing her hands on the back of it, "he lied to me."

"No he didn't."

"What do you call this?" She said waving her hands at the photos and emails on the floor."

"Saving you the worry of the dreary details," Marna's mouth dropped.

"Come on, Marny! He's human, and he did tell you he forgot."

"He put the kids in danger."

"No he didn't. That was Beth's call." She waved her hand and showed Marna a few scenes from the night in question. "He told them to get out." Amanda let the images fade away. "Beth's the one who came back, and spurred the rest of them." She shrugged, "what can I say, she's like her mother and a handful for you I'm afraid," she sighed, raising her brow, "anyway, he was willing to go to whatever horrible fate that awful man was taking him to as long as the kids were safe. Beth is the one who rallied the troops. She did me proud." She smiled and looked at her sister. "He's a good man, Marny, and the children love him." She studied her sister. "You're disappointed, maybe even a little angry and I understand that, but that's not all there is to it, is it?" Marna shrugged. "He scares you, what you feel for him, scares you."

"I don't know what I feel for him, Manda."

"Bull cocky. You care for him, but you're holding off taking it to the next level." She eyed her sister as she put it all together. "The question is why?"

"I'm just not ready, Manda."

"Oh yeah you are, but he represents something real, something lasting. Then there's the other one."

"I care for them both, Manda, now Kyle's life hangs in the balance and Tanner has a price on his head." She raised her eyes to her sister "They could both die. I don't want to feel that pain again, Manda, I can't. It will kill me."

"I suppose you could grow old, gray and crotchety like the old maid across the street from Grandma's house."

"At least her heart was in one piece."

"And all shriveled up. Marny, feeling love, holding it, having it hold you. That is what makes us feel alive, that is what makes our world go round. Never having that again to nourish and grow, you might as well be a Rose in a heat wave. Think about it. You take that leap of faith. I'll bet there will be a pair of strong arms ready to catch you. Whose they are, well now, that is up to you isn't it?" She winked. "Call him." Amanda faded out.

~~~~~

Marna lifted her head, the clock on the wall chimed in the midnight hour. "Manda, you sure have a way about you, even in death," she breathed. A feather of a draft went across her cheek. She smiled and picked up the photos and emails, slipping them back into the folder jackets, then she picked up her GPC, called up the text app, typed in *I understand*, and sent it out to Tanner.

Looking around the lower floor to make sure all was in order, she started shutting out the lights, locking the doors, and checking the windows. She had just started up the stairs, when her doorbell chimed. She glanced at her watch and went to the window, peaking around the curtain. Frowning she opened the door. "Tanner?"

He was looking toward the cruiser by the front curb, but when she spoke, he turned toward her, his brown eyes uncertain, his demeanor apologetic. "I'm sorry, Marna, your right, I should have told you."

She stepped aside and let him in. "I've been driving around since I left here, trying to justify why I kept it from you, but the only thing I could come up with is that I care too much." He caught her eyes. "You're more to me than just a partner and maybe, after tonight, that will remain one sided. Maybe I deserve that. You were in the hospital recovering from what that Bastard had done to you and You were so unstable." His voice caught. "Then Lamontage attacked, and that made you even less stable." He reached up and brushed loose strands of hair from her face, "I didn't want to risk losing you." His fingers lightly brushed her cheek. She closed her eyes as his feathery touch sent shockwaves through her body. He pulled his hand away, resting it on her shoulder.

"It may have been selfish of me, and I hope you can forgive me." he brought his other hand up to her other shoulder, then his voice lowered as he brought his forehead to hers, looking into her eyes.

"I can't promise it won't ever happen again, Marna, I wish I could but I'm human and damn girl, I have feelings for you, strong feelings. Feelings I can't ignore. Sure, I can immerse myself in work for distraction but at the end of the day, well, there you are," he smiled, "I will try to curb my protective ways, but if this thing is going anywhere, you'll just have to be patient with me. I'll probably be explaining myself again for some other infraction or line I've crossed. For now, maybe having you understand where I'm coming from is enough." He lifted his head away and scanned her face with his eyes. She looked away. He sighed, let his hands slide down her arms and took her hands in his then kissed her forehead. "I'll see you tomorrow," he said softly then turned to leave.

She gripped his hands tighter to stop him. "Don't go, Tanner," she said softly, her eyes moving over his face until they found his. "Stay," slivers of moonlight speared his features as it came through the slatted blinds, his eyes reflecting it back to her. She reached up and touched his face with her fingertips.

He closed his eyes, let out a slow sigh, took her hand, and kissed the palm then moved his lips to the tips themselves. Then he opened his eyes and lifted them to her face. He brought his hand up to palm her cheek, tracing her lips with his thumb. He slowly lowered his lips to hers and captured them with the gentleness of a summer breeze. He moved his hands to her back, caressing it, then to her sides, the kiss deepening. When he came up for air, he slipped out of his jacket and tossed it onto a nearby chair then he kissed her again. This time it was deeper, more demanding. Doors opened, connections made, their hearts thudded in their chests. He ran his hands up her outline, over her shoulders, caressed the curve of her neck with his forefingers. He pulled away, breathless, and rested his forehead on hers, gazing into her eyes. "Are you sure?" He whispered. In answer, she raised her lips to his and kissed him with as much need as she felt him holding back.

He crushed her to him, his lips finding her neck, and then with a groan, he cradled her in his arms and carried her up the stairs to her room, kicking the door closed behind him. He laid her gently on the bed, pulled off his gun holster and placed it on the bed stand closest to him. Then he brought his lips to hers again, their kisses became deeper, more urgent. They rolled and there breath became quick and fast. Their clothes fell to the floor as he trailed kisses across her jawline, down the curve of her neck, across her collarbone, over the mounds of her breasts and back to her lips. She let herself get lost in his eyes, in his kisses, in his touch, in his arms. He explored, enticed, and pleased and so did she. They held nothing back. Their connection cemented their hearts, bodies, minds and souls; they became one, both physically and psychically. The bond forming was sweet and satisfying. They knew what each other desired and they delivered. They traveled to euphoria, and went over the edge together, in perfect harmony. "Singura mea iubire," he whispered in her ear as they lay together and their hearts settled to a normal beat. When he lifted his head to look into her eyes, every feeling, every raw end of his emotion was there in his eyes.

She reached up and caressed his face with her fingers. "I'm so sorry, I've – "

"Shh," he said and kissed her lips in sweet surrender.

*****

Tanner's head moved restlessly on the pillow.

Floating faces, fire, screams, children running for their lives. He saw a teenager, a girl, running into the woods, people chasing her, her blonde trailing behind her. Woods, boulders, she tripped, she fell. Somebody came up behind her. She turned around, and screamed. Tanner rolled over murmuring. A home, A woman fighting someone off, a young boy watching from his bedroom. A man tears something from the womans arms, she screams, the man slaps her, she falls.

"NO!" Tanner yelled bolting up in bed. He looked around the room and untangled his legs from the sheet, swinging them off the bed, and sitting up. He tried to regain control of his breathing, and slow down his heart rate. The nightmares were coming more frequently now, at least a couple times a week. Each one was more vivid than the last. He scrubbed his face with his hands then pushed them through his hair.

He started when he felt hands touch his back and jerked away. "Tanner?" Marna queried, "You okay?" She reached out for his back again, rubbing his shoulders. "You're trembling." She moved closer to him, molded herself to his back, her chin on his shoulder, and her arms wrapped around his midriff.

He covered her hands with his, and pressed his temple into hers, "just a nightmare, I'm sorry I woke you."

"Do you want to talk about it?"

"No, I don't really remember it; just a bunch of unexplainable images that make no sense." He twisted around, and pushed her back onto the bed. She laughed, "besides, I can think of something else, I'd rather be doing," he nuzzled her neck..

"Really?" she queried, "what would that be?" She grinned up at him, her hair haloed her head in soft waves. Her beauty astounded him. Her inner strength made him greatly admire her. His lips curved into a lazy smile as his finger traced across her color bone, and over the swells of her breasts peaking above the sheet line.

"Really, Marna Farlow? Now you're going to be coy?" He grinned, and ran his hand across her stomach, up her side and around her shoulder, palming her cheek. He lowered his lips to hers, and she melted into his arms .

Two hours later, he held her in his arms while she slept. She was curved into him with her head on his chest, breathing steady and deep. Making love to her was everything he had imagined and more. They fit. If it was possible to fall fast and hard, he had. He could not imagine his life without her in it now. She shifted in her sleep, murmuring. "Shh," he crooned, not sure if she had heard him, but he did it anyway. He ran his fingertips through her silky hair, kissed her forehead and glanced at the clock, on her bedside stand, 4:00 AM. There was eleven hours before they were to report to HQ for the preparations. He figured he better try and shut down for a few hours or he'd be no good to anyone.

He kissed Marna's forehead again, rested his cheek on the top of her head, and then he closed his eyes. *Tanner, let me in*. His eyes flew open. He looked at Marna, thinking she may have said something but she slept on. He looked around the room; the wind gently blew the curtains about, night crickets sang their tune, while the ocean played in the background. Man, he really was tired if he was hearing voices on the wind, or the effects of his earlier dream had made him more jumpy than he thought.

He closed his eyes again and felt himself drifting off to the sound of distant ocean waves. *She's not for you*. His eyes flew open and he looked around the room, still nothing. The wind had picked up, but nothing more. Pulling up his shields, and including Marna in his blocking, he wrapped a protective arm around her, and drifted into a restless sleep. He did not see the shimmering apparition at the foot of the bed or feel the hate she openly held for Marna as she slept on in the protective circle of his arms.

Enjoy it while you can, Marna Farlow, because in the end he will be mine. The image faded and Marna's head moved about on the pillow. Tanner rolled to his side and instinctively tightened his hold on her.

Chapter nineteen

An array of smells penetrated Marna's senses. Coffee. Bacon. Blueberry Muffins? She glanced at her clock. Bold red letters told her it was 9:00 AM. What the? She tried to remember if someone was here for protection duty, and then the memories washed over her. The Pizza, the movie, she and Tanner's argument, his return, their night together, she drew in a satisfied breath, and rolled over. He was up already. So were the kids. She bolted up. The kids! Did they know? "Good going, Farlow," she scolded herself. She hurriedly got up, threw her robe on and pattered into the bathroom to shower and dress.

Twenty minutes later, she opened her door and heard excited voices from the kitchen. She made her way to the top of the stairs, her footfalls muffled by her favorite slippers, just in time to hear Tanner say, "Go long !" Then she saw Isaiah run backwards as a can of frozen orange juice sailed through the air into the living room. He caught it just before his legs hit the arm of the couch, and he collapsed into the overstuffed cushions. She let out a startle yelp, before she covered her mouth with her hand. The rooms below went silent.

"Uh-oh,"" Mary said, turning back to her job of buttering toast with Amanda Sue, Jacob and PJ.

"Busted," Joseph said, and went back to setting the table with David, and Moses.

Isaiah scrambled up to go mix the juice, averting his eyes. Hannah dumped scrambled eggs into a bowl and Elizabeth dumped another batch of muffins into a basket.

Tanner looked at her and grinned, "Coffee?" The look he gave her was so boyish and so endearing she couldn't help but grin back, shaking her head. "If you promise not to throw it across my living room, I'd love some."

"Scout's honor," he said, making the scout's symbol with his fingers. The kids broke out laughing. Tanner pulled a cup down, filled it, and handed it to her as she walked into the kitchen. Then he went back to flipping pancakes and turning sausages. She wandered around the kitchen to see what was on the menu, and happened to catch sight of the den. It didn't escape her notice that the day bed was unmade, Tanner's shoes were on the floor, and his jacket hung over the back of the chair by the roll top. She glanced at him and he winked. He had risen early, despite his restless night, to set things up so the kids wouldn't know about their night together. His actions touched her so deeply that tears sprang to her eyes, and a warm glow engulfed her from the depths of her soul outward. "Let's eat," Tanner said, giving Marna's side a discreet caress. She took a breath as the kids all took trays and bowls to the table so they could all eat together.

During the meal, they talked about the day's upcoming activities. Isaiah had football practice; he was catching a ride with Tammy's mom as was Hannah and Elizabeth for cheerleading practice. Rose would be picking up Mary, Amanda Sue, PJ and Jacob for the first backyard session of the camping season. The triplets were going to little league practice with their friend Bobby. To Marna, it all seemed so normal. After breakfast clean up, they were all out the door by noon. Keys called to tell Marna that Patty McGellan and two S&S agents would be watching over the children during the mission. Tanner straightened up the den, made sure there was a team out front and decided he would go home, change his clothes, and swing by to pick her up at 3:30.

He grabbed his jacket and took her hand while they walked to the door together. "Thanks for your discretion," she said.

"You'll tell them when you're ready." He brought her hand to his lips, "until then, discretion is my middle name." He brought his hand to her face, and lowered his head to capture her lips in a sweet, gentle kiss. When he had his full, he rested his forehead on hers. "You intoxicate me, Marna Farlow, and no matter what happens out there tonight – last night, this morning, what you gave me and what we shared – I will treasure it, all of it, forever." Her hand went up to his face and he lowered his lips to hers again, pulled her tightly against him, and deepened the kiss, she felt dizzy and a little intoxicated herself. Then he pulled away, took a breath, pressed her hand with gentle pressure, and smiled. "I'll see you at 3:30." She nodded and stepped back while he left the house. She watched him until his Camaro pulled away from the curb then she closed the door, leaned against it, and drew in some deep breaths to calm the fear and tremors that had decided to take over her body.

The possibilities of what could happen tonight, during the extraction, poured over her like a tidal wave. She felt claustrophobic, making her unable to catch her breath. She slid her back down the door, until she was sitting on the floor. She drew up her knees, put her forehead on them, and arms over her head. She tried to regain control of her breathing. No, life wouldn't be that cruel. It wouldn't take another chance at happiness from her grasp. They were all going to be fine, the team, Tanner, Kyle, Keys, everyone would be fine. She brought her head back against door and wiped at the tears on her face. She had to believe that. Taking a deep breath, she pushed herself off the floor and went toward the stairs. She would clean the bedrooms and ignore the sense of foreboding coming over her, dismissing it as fear induced. Last night was making her jittery she was open to worrying about him, about them, more so than before. That's all this sense of foreboding was – had to be.

*****

Tanner picked her up promptly at 3:30. She climbed in his Camaro, shut the door but said nothing and put her head on the back of the seat, closing her eyes. She fought the nausea that was threatening to beat her brunch back up as it crawled up her esophagus. Her face revealed the strain she was feeling. He shifted in to gear and headed out, reaching down to grasp her hand. It was cold and clammy. Concern etched his features. Had last night been too much, too soon? Was she struggling to find a way to tell him it was a mistake? "You okay?"

Her tone was edged with anger, "You mean aside from the fact that we're about to go face one of the deadliest men on the planet, that Kyle could die if we screw up, that the same team that walks in there may not walk out." She opened her eyes, turned her head and searched out his, her voice softening, "that we may not walk out."

He moved his eyes back to the road, his face muscles bunched then released. He signaled right onto Hollis Avenue. "You think like that, Marna, we'll be defeated before we start."

"I can't help but think like that, Tanner." she said softly, "the odds are so stacked against us here," her eyes returned to the road.

"Don't you have faith in the team, in me, in yourself?" He pressed, the words sounded crueler than he intended, but he had to shock her out of this stupor.

"That's not fair."

"Marna if even one agent goes in there with an attitude of defeat, we're all dead. Pierre will sense that and use it. We have to be strong, we have to be capable, and most of all we have to be united."

"The collective wins it all. Is that it?" She asked bitterly.

"Yes, Marna, that's the heart of Guardian. That is what makes us strong where others have failed." He didn't bother stating the obvious; that if she were on her own, she would not be safe nor would her family because there were people out there wanting to control her magnifying ability, wanting to control her.

"What if I don't want that, what if all I want is a life where my kids go to school, I go to work, ball games, competitions, recitals. No homicidal maniacs knocking at my door, or tearing up my house. No more strangers watching my house or no more worrying about protection for me and my family," she spat, "Why can't I just have that?"

"If that's what you wanted, Marna, you wouldn't be where you are right now."

She sniffed, closed her eyes and let her head fall back on the seat again. "I'm scared, Tanner," the words were barely audible, her bottom lip quivered

He could lie, give her a little bravado, but exactly what would that accomplish? "Me too," he said, bringing her hand to his lips. They sat in silence as he turned onto Harris Drive, and a few minutes later into the underground parking structure of HQ. Marna reached for her door handle. "Marna," he stopped her, she looked over at him. His hand reached up for her face, and his lips found hers in a deep, soul-reaching kiss that opened their doors and their connections.

Marna melted into the kiss, into the feelings they were sharing. When they pulled apart, they were both breathless. "Remember that," he whispered, "all of it," he outlined her face with a feathery touch of his fingers, "remember last night and remember these words. . ." She searched his face with her eyes. "We have unfinished business, you and I, and I intend to see it through. Remember I'm waiting at the end of this mission to pick up where we left off." She felt encompassing warmth fill her and felt a peace overcome her.

"You too," she said, reaching for his face, "Don't make me walk out of there alone."

"No way, Numai iubirea mea, we're in this together," he smiled and caught her chin between his thumb and forefinger, giving her another quick kiss before they pulled apart as another car pulled in to the parking garage. By the time they were climbing out of their car, Ventura and Schaefer were waiting for them by theirs. They waved. The four of them turned and headed toward the elevator.

*****

When they reached the conference room, Keys had a table laden with bakery breads, deli meats, cheese, and salads. Paper plates, utensils, napkins, cups and various soft drinks also claimed space on the table by a pot of fresh coffee, hot water and pouches of hot cocoa and tealeaves. "Going to be a long one," Ventura said.

"A lot to go over," piped Schaefer.

"Only thing missing is the priest of last rites," said a man Marna didn't recognize. He was a compact 5'4" with a wrestler's build and a boxer's face.

"With an attitude like that, Cardoza, you'll be the first to fall," Ventura stated, giving him a raised eyebrow. The chastised agent finished collecting his food and scuttled off to find his seat.

While the others were dishing their plates, Marna walked over to the command center. She looked at the wall screen. Keys had switched off the audio. Kyle's vitals registered within a safe range, considering what he had been going through. However, she could see that every attempt at movement caused him much pain, he rolled his head to try to loosen the muscles across the top of his shoulders, and again he winced. He lifted his eyes to the monitor and caught hers, his cracked lips curved slightly, but the smile did not reach his eyes. He was tired, in pain, and worn thin. His spirit almost broken.

He had lost weight during his captivity and he was dangerously close to losing his will to fight. She swallowed, and reached for the audio button. Fear flashed in his eyes and he shook his head once then turned it to the left. They were monitoring him. Contacting him now could blow the whole mission. She curled her fingers and her hand retreated. He lowered his head and Tanner came up behind her. "How's he doing?"

"Not good," she said before she headed toward the conference room. Tanner raised his eyes and happened to catch Kyle watching her retreat. The expression on his face was hard to read. Tanner blew out a sigh and followed her into the conference room.

When the last of the agents had filled their plates and sat at the table. Keys came over to the wall screen, hit a couple of buttons on the control panel, and lifted his eyes to the team. They were the best of the best Guardian had to offer, and it tore at him to know that the possibility existed some may not return with them. Two departements were represented at this table, on one end was WIT; Peter, Heidi, Marna, Tanner, Barry, Sarah, Cardoza, Misty and Chris and the tech team from the ship sat at the other end with the bomb layers.

"Good evening," he started the meeting. A chorus of the mixed voices responded. "Tonight's mission could possibly be one of the most important ones you have ever been sent on. Pierre

Lamontage is not only smart, he is dangerous and deadly so. He will not hesitate to wipe all of you out in a single sweep and is not responsive to reason. There is no other solution to this mission than the safe extraction of Agent Rigby at the demise of Pierre Lamontage. The orders to this mission are to protect your back, protect your partner's back, find and extract Agent Rigby with as little confrontational action as possible, do not engage with Lamontage until you are all together, unless absolutely necessary, and then shoot to kill. Any questions?" He looked around the table. Not a single agent raised a hand. They knew he spoke the truth. He moved on.

"Could I have your attention on the screen please?" All eyes went to the screen. After our meeting yesterday, I made a few calls and had this delivered to me. This is the last blue print and floor plan ever filed of Winters Prison in 2030." He nodded to an agent who flipped out the lights, and then he pulled out a laser pointer. "The prison itself was state of the art, with three floors. The section we are most interested in is this." He pointed out the basement level. On this level are the EIT rooms. There are ten of them. We are not sure which one he is keeping Kyle in, though we suspect it to be this one," he drew a circle around a block on the left side last in the row, "Ventura was able to clean up a video capture on a window behind Kyle," Keys changed screen and showed the blown up version. The frame of the window is on the back wall and it shows the fencing and trees, no other part of the building is visible." He brought their attention back to the blueprints and circled the area believed to be what Ventura had seen in the window frame. It was the back fencing. The building was rectangular shape, and the front facing pointed to an area that had once been a school, now it was the remains of a personnel dorm and cafeteria. He droned on as Marna studied the blueprint.

The room around her disappeared. She was in a corridor of cement. She was frantically searching for someone. She was opening the doors, looking beyond them into the rooms. Every door yielded emptiness. Suddenly she pulled a door open, and there was Kyle lying on the floor. Behind him stood Pierre, he was laughing, saying something to her, but there was no audio. She looked around. Tanner was not with her. Pierre kicked Kyle toward her, she saw his body tense, and then his mouth opened in silent screams. Then she felt the compression in her head, the icy grip on her heart, she couldn't breathe . . . she was clawing at her neck, trying to get air. Her nails dug gouges in her soft flesh. "Marna !" She felt herself being shaken. Hard. She was gasping for breath, trying to get air into her deprived lungs. Her eyes refocused on Tanner's, his full of concern, he was holding her biceps. The other agents in the room had turned her way, Keys was looking at her, fear etched in his features.

"He knows we're coming." She whispered, but in the room, among the other agents, it sounded like thunder rattling the walls. I don't know how, but he knows." She brought her eyes to Keys, who left his spot by the wall screen, and went around the corner wall to look at the screen. The chair was empty. Kyle was gone! In his place was a large sign that said **game on**. Keys had to grip the command center to catch his breath. The rest of the team moved to the command center. They all exchanged glances among themselves.

Keys pushed himself to an erect position and stared at the ominous message. "Grab your gear, suit up and be at the boat in ten minutes. He wants to play, we'll play."

*****

"You okay?" Tanner asked as he handed Marna a coffee.

"Yeah," she whispered, her hand automatically going to her neck, "I'm sorry I scared you."

He sat down beside her. "Scared. No," He whispered and tilted his head, "Terrified. Yes." He took a sip of his own coffee and screwed up his nose, "definitely not the Corner Cafe."

She grinned, taking a sip, screwed up her features, "no, definitely not," she tilted her head in his direction, "is this where they get the expression 'puts hair on your chest?'"

He grinned, raised his cup to his mouth, and looked through a veil of steam, scanning the other agents, checking for unwanted listeners. "Let's hope not, I think yours is just fine without it."

Her face turned ten shades of red and she almost choked on a mouth full of coffee, "Tanner!" she hissed, covering her mouth with her fingers.

"Well it is," he said, his tone matter of fact. He grinned and brought his cup to his lips again. "I'll have to inspect it later to make sure though." This time, she couldn't stop her reaction, coffee spewed from her mouth. All heads turned their way. Tanner took the cup and patted her back, "easy now, gotta watch that stuff, it can get pretty rugged. You okay?" She coughed and then shot daggers at him from her eyes. She took her coffee back, and swallowed another mouthful, but didn't ease up the death stare coming at him through the veil of steam.

Ventura let his hands dropped between his knees, and he turned his head from the momentary entertainment to look at Schaefer and did a hand me the dough gesture with his fingers. "She could have just choked on coffee, just as it appears." Schaefer hissed.

"Yeah, and I've got some waterfront property in the everglades you really ought to consider buying, comes complete with your choice of Guard 'Gators',." he whispered. "Come on, pay up," his mouth twitched.

"That is so cold, Ventura, and while we're on our way to a rescue mission."

"Hey if I'm gonna die tonight, I wanna make sure my family can pay for the services." Schaefer opened her mouth to speak, but decided against it and closed it, shook her head, and pulled out a bill handing it to him. "Nice doing business with you."

"You are a very strange man, Ventura."

"Hey there is only one Peter Ventura, no cloning of this bad boy, and one of these days you'll realize how lucky you are to know him," He winked, put the money in his shirt pocket, and spared a look back at Tanner and Marna. "Besides they fit."

Schaefer shook her head, but was spared from giving a retort, because Keys came to the front of the passenger section, moved his eyes around the hull taking in all his agents, and said, "Meet me at the lifeboats, we're about to anchor.."

Forty minutes later, they were all pulling their rafts onto shore and burying them under loose brush. The Elizabeth had cloaked herself, and jammed all radio communications between ship and teams. The electricity was down within seconds of them hitting shoreline. They dispersed into the forested area around the prison, heading toward their destination.

Keys, Tanner, Marna,Peter and Heidi made up the first WIT team; McGellan, Justice, Cardoza, Schofield and Smith made up the second WIT team "Psychic connections only. Make sure your shields stay up, and stay together. You know the drill if you come upon Pierre. Make sure Kyle is out of danger and attack." They all nodded, checked their P2041 weapons, and then parted ways.

Keys decided on a frontal attack with his team, and the second team would approach from the East. The tech team would set up the charges as soon as WIT entered the building. He only hoped they could find Kyle and leave in the reasoned amount of time. If Pierre did indeed know they were coming, like they suspected, he would want easy access off the island as soon he had Marna. "Move out," Keys ordered. The teams pulled on their night goggles and moved cautiously forward.

They had worn dark clothing to decrease their chances of detection, Lamontage was sure to have men stationed throughout the island. The first encounter was almost immediate. All Marna heard was a grunt from behind her as a soldier came down hard on Tanner, from an obscured tree branch. The soldier had his hands around Tanner's throat, and he was trying to break the attacker's grip. Ventura pounced and grabbed the man from behind, yanking him off. The man pulled a knife, and while Ventura was dodging the knife,Tanner jumped to his feet, and shouldered the man off balance. The soldier thrust the knife forward; Tanner dodged, grabbed his wrist, and slammed it into a nearby boulder, heard the wrist bone break, which caused him to drop the knife. Then Tanner doubled his fist and slammed it hard into the man's jaw. The man was down. Keys tossed them a couple of zip ties, and Ventura dragged him to a tree, brought his arms around the trunk, and attached his wrists behind it.

Then Tanner pulled the second zip, and tightly bound his ankls. Marna covered his mouth with some duct tape. "You two okay?" Keys asked. They nodded and the team moved on, keeping their eyes alert, scanning the trees as much as they did the forestry around them.

Two more Liberatores attacked from trees and they brought them down in the same manner. The fourth, however, was prepared. Marna was walking along and she stumbled, falling face first into the path. The soldier had rigged up a trip wire across her path. Tanner went back to help her, but before he reached her, a Liberatores was on top of her. Tanner stopped.Terrified. The man dragged her to her feet, pulled her back against him, his arm across her chest, and a knife tightly against her throat. "Easy . . ." Tanner said.

"Drop it or I drop her," he hissed, his words heavy with a French accent. The other team members quickly took cover. Keys gave Ventura a signal wave, and he disappeared into the darkness. Tanner set his weapon on the ground before him.

"Now back away from it." Tanner took three steps back. He looked at Marna. *You okay*? He connected to her psychically.

yes

Keep your eyes on me.

Okay. She looked into his eyes. The soldier started dragging her back with him. Panic seized her.

Marna, focus! Tanner ordered. *Remember our promise.* Marna searched his eyes. He kept his focus on her, but spoke to the soldier, "Let her go, and you can walk away. Take her and I'll hunt you down and plant you in the ground you stand on." his voice was low, fierce.

"You think I fear you?" His chuckle dripped with evil. "The Master will be pleased with my trophy." He brought his lips to Marna's ear, "He has plans for you, Madame." Marna made a noise as he tightened his grip on her chest and he dragged her backward a couple more steps. Tanner glanced at his weapon, seconds before he caught movement out of the corner of his eye, Ventura was perched and ready to strike at a tree, two steps back from the soldier. Tanner started counting down to himself. Three – Two – One, Ventura sprung. Marna fell forward and quickly rolled out of the way. The soldier rolled over, pushed himself up, and slashed the air with his knife.Ventura jumped back, the blade narrowly missing his midsection. Tanner dived for his Taser, rolled to his back, aimed, and blasted, catching the man in his chest. The soldier yelled and fell backward, his body jerked with the electrical charges coursing through it. When it stopped, his head lolled to the side and the last thing his eyes saw, before his life slipped away, was a tree on the wood line. Tanner pushed himself up and ran forward, helping Marna to her feet. Instinctively, he wrapped his arms around her, and held her tightly for a few seconds, and then he set her away from him.

"You okay?" She nodded, drawing in some deep breaths, while Ventura used his foot to roll the soldier into the darkness of the forest. He walked up to the two of them and put a hand on her bicep, raising his eyebrows in question. She nodded. He nodded back and moved beyond them and the team once again moved forward. This time Tanner took up the back.

Their team brought down four more soldiers; team two brought down three. Keys believed they had come to the end of the guards in the woods, didn't believe they would run into any. They pushed on. He looked at his watch. They were already 20 minutes out from their start time, when they finally started seeing the cement structure through the wood-line. Keys held up his hand to halt their approach. He sent out a verification request to the others and discovered both teams were ready to move in. He called them all together, and pulled out the map, laying it on a nearby boulder. "There are only three areas he would have taken Kyle," Keys instructed as he smoothed the map. "He could have possibly moved him to another EIT room." Keys splayed his fingers and waved over the area, or he could have moved him up a floor to cellblock one. "Having him in this area," Keys waved his hand over another section, "would allow him to have access to his own quarters as well, and the final area would be here." He pointed to the service area; the kitchen, storage rooms and bunker areas. These areas would give him the advantage. They are deeper into the bowels of the building, and leave little space for escape. If he sees no way out."

"He'll take us all with him," Schaefer said.

"How do you want us to proceed, Keys?" Ventura queried.

He sighed, "Marna?"

She looked up at him. "Yeah, Keys."

"There are two ways we can approach this. One way is I can order everyone to start topside and go down, the other is for you take this, "he pulled out a tassel of white and gold with gold plated numbers 2029 hanging from it, "and exercise your Locating ability."

She looked up at him, "Keys, I haven't spent a lot of time working with that." The rest of the team circled around her.

"Marna, please, it could not only give us the element of surprise, it could cut our time of finding the target in half."

She looked at Tanner. He nodded. She reached out for the tassel and gripped it in her hands. Taking a deep breath, she focused on nothing but Kyle. The sounds of the forest drifted away, the nervous shifting of her colleagues drifted away. Flashes started going through her mind. Kyle graduating, Kyle standing with his father, Kyle in the chair, tied down, Kyle hanging from a ceiling beam by his wrists. She stopped herself and looked around, he was in a commercial style kitchen, and Pierre was with him. In his hand, Pierre held a small black box. She focused hard on the object and gasped. She returned her attention to Kyle. His head hung, suspended between arms, his breathing erratic. Her eyes moved to his waist where Velcro attached a wide belt snugly – " Oh my"

"Marna, what is it?" Keys queried."

"He's in the service block, Keys, the kitchen, but there's more." She chewed on her lower lip, Keys waited patiently. He could tell by the look in her eyes, it wasn't good news.

"What is it, Marna?"

"Pierre has him wired with explosives." Agents around her let loose expletives. Keys took a breath and let his head fall. "He's holding the detonator, Keys. I saw two entrances. Frontal attack and bulk head." She took a breath. "Either way he's going to see us coming."

"Well then let's not disappoint him. Team two take the bulk head," he sighed, "We'll go in the front, stay close and stay safe." They readied their weapons and moved in. . . .

*****

Kyle hung by his wrists from a rustic beam, that stretched across the length of the kitchen. His shoulders screamed out in protest, his joints felt like they were on fire, and he was barely able to extend his toes on the floor below him. His mouth was taped shut, but the thing that terrified him the most was the belt of explosives Pierre had placed around his waist.

Pierre had chloroformed him and moved him to the service area block. When he came out of the Chloroform stupor, he was hanging as an animal up for slaughter. He tried to release the strain in his shoulders by sharing the weight on his feet. His body swung sideways with every movement causing even more pain. Nothing he did would alleviate it. He groaned as his body swayed and white, hot pain shot through his shoulders."Save your strength, Boy, there really isn't any way to adjust your comfort." Kyle closed his eyes swallowing down the nausea that was induced by drugs and pain. He just wanted it all to stop. At this point, he would even welcome death. The lights flickered, went off, and emergency lights came on. It was then that he heard a thud from the floor above.

He stopped his fidgeting and swung his head toward the main entrance to the block. "Here comes Daddy, Boy, to your rescue with his loyal posse bringing up the rear." Kyle watched the door and he could hardly breathe, "Are you ready to watch him die?" Tears stung Kyle's eyes, he looked up at his hands, down at his feet, and then at the belt of explosives. He wasn't even going to be able to save his father without blowing them all up. Guilt washed over him. He couldn't let his father die at the hands of this mad man. That option wasn't even on the table. . .

*****

Keys raised two, then four then three fingers (2-4-3). Two —guards – four – o;clock – three seconds to stage scene before take down. Ventura and Tanner held their weapons up as they saw the gate locked on the inside. They crouched behind the vegetation growing against the outer wall, but kept from contacting it, Ventura nodded toward the rock on the ground next to Keys feet. He grabbed it, and threw it at the gate. Sparks flew everywhere, lighting the night. Marna fell to the ground, rolled into the path leading to the entrance of the prison, four feet from the front of the gate. She lay in a prone position. Ventura and Tanner waited, Keys and Schaefer shrunk further into the shadows. They heard guards running to the gate.

The guards were rattled on in German, one guard told the other to check her vitals, and he would cover him. They unlocked the gate, and stepped out from behind the safety of the walls. They never knew what hit them when the streams struck their backs. They were dead in seconds. Keys and Heidi pulled them out of view and the four of them stepped into the yard . . .

With Barry leading, Team Two moved toward the back of the building, while team one headed for the warden's office. They all stayed to the shadows, so as not to be seen. Keys signaled Ventura and Tanner forward, he, Schaefer and Marna brought in the rear. Keys nodded and Ventura moved around the corner and peaked into a window. He signaled two and four with his fingers then formed a right angle with his thumb and forefinger; two guards – four feet to the right, and then he slithered back to the door's edge. Keys nodded and lifted thumb and forefinger in the shape of a gun, and then sliced the air with his hand, palm down (shoot to kill).

Ventura nodded, looked at the team and reached for the doorknob, turned it slowly, and then opened it quickly. Tanner dropped down and somersaulted to the desk, aiming and firing; one guard went down, his body twitching. Marna rolled in on his heels and took out the second one, while he was still trying to connect what had just happened to his partner. He tilted to the left and rolled down the stairs. She stayed low, held her weapon on the doorway, while the others moved in, and moved forward, she and Tanner took up the rear . . .

*****

Barry gave the signal that they had two guards watching the bulkhead. Hedges had formed an alcove area between a dead garden and the bulkhead. However, between their positions, by the corner of a shed and the hedge there was a wide span of open space. The guards would surely see them before they could get close enough for a surprise attack. He pulled back and thought about the best way to take these men down. Then it dawned on him, a vaulting assault would be the best way to go. He motioned Cardoza, Smith and Justice forward, and looked around the area. He found what he wanted tucked behind a supply of wall coverings to his right; a small piece of plywood 2'X2'. He, picked it up, and handed it to the two men, and then he gave the team instructions.

Cardoza gave Justice his weapon, and he and Smith crouched making a step vault by placing the wood between them and holding the edges in their hands. Misty kept her eyes and gun trained on where they had just come from. Barry took position by Cardoza, and looked Sarah's way; she nodded in response, and backed up a few paces to enable a running start. He started countdown – three – the vault had to be done right or Sarah could be hurt. The two men kept focused on each other two – Sarah . took the position of a racer ready to take off – one – Sarah took off. The men launched her simultaneously with her vault. They were in perfect sync. She sailed into the air in a perfect arc, aimed her weapons, and took out both the guards with streams to their hearts, and then as she started on the downward slope. She tucked her body close, and in perfect harmony with gravity, hit the ground in a perfect roll, coming to a safe stop, six feet from the bulkhead, simultaneously tossing Cardoza his weapon as he and the others moved forward to remove the bodies. Then carefully, very carefully, two men at each door, they opened the bulkhead as noiselessly as possible before moving down the stairs to the door below. Cardoza and Justice went down the steps backwards ready should the enemy approach from behind.

Using the fire stream setting on steel, Barry melted the padlock off the entrance door then pushed it open and entered the wine cellar. Wine bottles lined the shelves against each wall and many stand alone wooden shelves, placed in rows, on the concrete floor. Four doors leading to other parts of the prison were spaced on the interior walls., "Misty?" Barry whispered.

Misty nodded and tilted her head. Various sounds assaulted her ears until she caught Pierre's words. *Are you ready to watch him die? Kyle groaned softly.* She pointed her taser to a door on the end of the third row of wines, "There," she whispered, "they're in there."

Keys we have a lock on their position Barry sent a Psychic message to Keys.

Hold steady, Barry, we have just breeched the Warden's office, we are on our way down.

Got it, Boss. Barry held up his hand and put a halt to their approach, they would hold position until Keys said otherwise. . .

*****

Keys team moved down the circular stairs painfully slow as cellblock, by cellblock, they searched the surroundings for a hostile presence, before they moved down to the next level.

Charges set, Keys, fifteen minutes to launch a voice drifted into his head, and he quickly twisted his watch. He sent out a multiple warning to all involved. The rescuers picked up the pace as fast as they dared. Keys team closed in on the EIT level. Here they didn't get as easy a pass as they had before.

Keys heard voices, angry and German. He halted his team. *Marna, how many?* She tilted her head and focused. She counted and held up four fingers.

What's your flavor of choice, Keys? Ventura queried, looking at his watch T-13 and counting. Keys held his hand up, pushed outward at the wall, and then flattened his hand and pushed it downward back to the wall, (approach slowly, use caution). The team backed into the shadows and lined up, backs to the wall, two members guns aimed up, two with guns aimed down. Keys was running point, they eased themselves down one-step at a time their approach as quiet as a church mouse.

Moments later, Keys waved Marna and Tanner forward, head motioning toward the EIT door. *Cloak, enter quick and hard then be ready.* He communicated. They nodded. That action would draw the attention of the guards and they would take out the first wave. Next he turned toward Ventura and Schaefer, pointed to Peter, the stairs and raised two fingers. Peter understood. He was to move down two steps to the landing and hold. He moved into position, his back pressed against the wall, tilting his weapon toward the stairs. Then Keys moved his eyes to Heidi's, *Over the banister, landing hard on the steps below and lure them out. Then you and Pete take them out.* She nodded, and moved closer to the railing. Keys would then move in and take care of any remaining combatants.

They needed to synchronize the assault perfectly for the safety of the entire team. Keys ordered Heidi and Marna to cloak those closest to them and raised a finger. He crouched low and move across the landing, moving into the corner, and blending in with the shadows. The jamming had caused the electricity to fail throughout the building and forced the generator to click on, so they used the resulting shadows to their advantage. The deeper they went into the building, the heavier they got. He would not fire unless necessary, because that could cause the soldiers to move in the opposite direction they needed them to go. Eventually he wanted it down to just them and Pierre. It was a showdown long in coming, and if it was the last thing he did on this earth, Pierre would die today.

He raised three fingers and ticked them off, counting backwards. As soon as the last went down. The plan went into motion. The girls cloaked. Marna and Tanner moved to the EIT door, pushing it open, and passing through it, separating inside. An ominous red light spilled over the stairs, before it closed behind them. Conversation stopped below before there was a quick, German exchange, followed by approaching footfalls. Two! Keys sent out a message that two soldiers were approaching. Cloaks stayed in place, Keys sunk as far back as he could.

The first one went into the EIT block.

"You're just in time for our Water Boarding special," Marna said, the soldier turned toward her, and raised his weapon, "or are you more into cattle prodding?" Before he could fire, Tanner took him down with a stream to his back. He moved forward to catch him before he fell and dragged him into one of the interior rooms, placing him on the floor.

Tanner looked at her. "Cattle Prodding? Really Farlow?"

"What else was I going to say?" She challenged, lifting a hand to their surroundings. The door to the EIT room opened, and they swung their weapons toward it . . .

While they were taking down their man, the second man was turning toward Heidi with weapon raised as she vaulted over the railing; Ventura took him out with a kill stream to his back, and rushed forward to catch him. As soon as Heidi's feet hit her targeted step, she brought down one of the two below, and as the second advanced on her, Keys scrambled from his corner and took him down. Ventura dragged his man into the EIT room and caught Tanner's last remark as he hoisted his man into a nearby chair.

"Sounds Kinky to me," he winked and waved them forward, "Keys and Heidi took the last two out, let's move. We're almost home." Tanner and Marna closed in behind Ventura and left the EIT room, heading down the stairs toward the room in question, taking up position outside of it.

Keys looked at his watch and back at his team, "T- 7 before missile launch. From there thirty seconds to get out. We exit through bulkhead. Clear?" he whispered. They all nodded. Keys contacted Barry. *Barry, team one in position. Be ready to attack.* Barry's team got ready. *BREECH!* . . .

*****

Kyle winced as he again tried to relieve the pressure on his shoulder joints. He drew in a breath, closed his eyes. He had heard nothing else since that first thud. Perhaps it was just wishful thinking; even Pierre's stature had relaxed some. Kyle started thinking of different things to ignore the pain in his shoulders, memories from his childhood.

The ones that came to mind were the few cherished ones he had of his father, those rare moments when he had him to himself. His father sitting with him on the floor of his room, playing war with his toy soldiers. His father dressing up as Frankenstein on Halloween and taking him trick or treating. Those nights when his father would scare away the monsters under the bed, before he read him that bedtime story. The memories continued to flow through his head. Memories of his father standing beside him after his high school graduation, and every year when his father would take him to his mother's grave, on her birthday, to leave her favorite flowers and tell him stories about her. Those he cherished the most. He could swear he felt her presence surround them.

He had so many good memories of his father, could they really be at an end? He hadn't always been gracious to him, and sometimes he had even been downright resentful, but as he got older and especially after he joined the ranks of Guardian, he understood it all. Would he never be able to say goodbye? Would he die in this horrific prison? At the hands of the man that took his mother? He dropped his head, and bit his lower lip, as he felt another sheering pain rip through his arm and across his shoulders. When the spasm passed, he lifted his head and caught sight of something familiar, caught sight of something hopeful. Keys looked at him through the small porthole window in the kitchen door and nodded. Kyle felt tears sting the back of his eyes, tried to shake his head, warn his father off, but the effort was too painful, he swallowed back a groan. Three seconds later, both teams burst into the room all weapons trained on Pierre. He laughed, raised the detonator in his hand. "One move, Keys, and we all have an explosive ending to our little drama." Kyle closed his eyes, waiting for the bomb to go off.

Keys stared at Pierre and spoke in a voice cold as steel, "I told you, Pierre, if we ever crossed paths again, I'd kill you. Sarah !" Sarah's eyes narrowed, the remote flew out of his hand and skittered across the floor. "Now !" Keys bellowed. Justice and Smith fired streams from Barry's team and Schaefer and Ventura fired from Keys team. They caught Pierre in the electronic wall.

"Keys, your toys and games have no effect on me. He raised his hands and started to absorb the energy, it sparked with the intrusion.

"Yeah, so you've said, but this time your games will be your undoing?" Keys said taking aim and fired the jet stream of flames, which caught the wall and a ring of electronic fire encircled him. The effect was immediate, Pierre faltered. "Not so smug now, are you, Pierre?" he hissed.

Keys kept his eyes on Pierre. *T-minus three, Keys,* a voice crashed into his head. *Get out of there!* "Marna, Tanner, get Kyle out of here !" Marna and Tanner moved forward and carefully removed the the bomb belt from Kyle's waist, and setting it on a nearby counter. Tanner took a knife from his pocket and cut the ropes, while Marna took the tape from his mouth and they looped his arms around their shoulders and headed toward the root cellar. "Misty, Barry, Cardoza, go !" They took up the rear, covering them if there should be any soldiers left standing. Pierre crumbled to the floor. *T-minus one, Keys!* "Keep fire and begin retreat!" He ordered as he and the remaining four agents began to back out of the room, while keeping Pierre imprisoned in the electronically charged fire field. Pierre started taking labored breaths. His strength was leaving him. "Smith, Justice go!" They dropped their streams and took off.

"Ventura, Schafer, move!"

"What about you?" Ventura demanded.

"I'm right behind you !" They lifted fire and the other two ran through the door. Keys crouched, lett his eyes capture Pierre's, carefully holding his gaze. "How's it feel, Brother, to know mine is the last face you'll ever see?" His voice was fierce, his eyes cold as steel.

"I'll take you to Hell with me," Pierre gasped and he pulled another detonator from his jacket, lifting his finger. *Missles launched – t-minus 30 seconds, until impact – Keys'* eyes' widened. He jumped up and ran for the wine cellar door . . .

*****

Barry and Smith came up behind Marna and Tanner and lifted Kyle's legs. They ran through the wine cellar, through the root cellar, up the stairs and across the prison grounds to the gate. Then they brought him to the edge of the wood line. Tanner pulled off his jacket and rolled it up to put it under Kyle's head as they laid him down. "Give me some water and the first aid pack !" He ordered, and gently lifted Kyle's head to give him a drink. Kyle coughed, turned his head away, and automatically brought his arm across his midsection. "Easy, Buddy, you're pretty banged up." Kyle tried to draw in some air, but was only able to draw in shallow breaths. Tanner lifted the water bottle, Kyle nodded, and he gave him some more. Kyle drank slower, and pulled away. Barry and Smith came to their aide. Tanner lifted his head toward Smith. "You've got combat medical experience right?"

"Yeah seven years with the freedom conflicts here in the states.." The agent's blonde head was graying around the temples, and his skin scarred from a burn received during combat. His eyes were a fading blue in a face etched with lines of seeing way too many horrors in a lifetime.

"Start a drip, he needs fluids. We won't know about kidney damage until we get him to a hospital, but for now we can get him hydrated." Smith nodded and holstered his weapon, reaching in the medical pack for the IV already set up, and unwound the tubing, handing the bag to Marna.

"Hold it up, so gravity can work it." Marna nodded as she held up the bag and watched him search hurriedly for a vein. He finally teased one to the skin surface by slapping Kyle's hand and pushed the IV needle into it. Kyle winced and Marna rubbed his hair back from his face. He reached his hand up to grab hers, curving his lips into a tight smile. Tanner slowly removed the wrap from his midsection, and gingerly felt around the ribs. He looked at Smith, who responded with a nod. Kyle let out a muted groan, biting down on his peeling lower lip. Smith searched out Kyle's eyes. "Looks like you have a few cracked ribs here, Kid, maybe a couple of broken ones too, won't know until we're able to do X-rays. How's your breathing?" Kyle nodded slowly, "I need you to stay as still as possible, because all it takes is the displacement of one of those broken ones, and you could pierced a lung, then you're in a hell of a lot of trouble, understand what I'm saying?" Kyle nodded, "I'm going to give you something for the pain, after I finish my exam. It'll make you a bit more comfortable.." Next, he checked his shoulders by lifting up his arms, one at a time, and moving them about. Kyle groaned as his joints protested, and pain shot through his arms. "How tied on the rafter?"

"Three maybe four hours."

Chris nodded. "Right or left."

"Both bad, right's worse." He breathed. "Okay I'm going to sling it and then strap the whole set up to your chest. I'm betting you have some muscle, tissue, tendons and ligament damage, but we'll know better after X-rays. He nodded to Tanner, who handed him a sling with a body strap attached. He applied that. Ventura and Heidi ran to their meeting place. "Where's Keys?" Cardoza asked.

Ventura looked around. "He said he'd be right behind us."

"Cardoza, assist Smith," Tanner said, and Cardoza switched places with him. Tanner started running back toward the prison,

"Tanner, no !" Marna cried, standing up. Ventura took off after him.

The Elizabeth launched the first missile with a loud pop. All heads turned toward the water. "Dear God, they're launching the missiles," Schaefer said, letting her eyes stray to the prison gate in time to see the left section explode in a burst of flames. Seconds later, the first Missile made its mark and exploded the administration area of the building.

Kyle bolted up, ignoring the pain in his midsection. "DAD!!! !" Shaefer's hand went to her mouth.

Tears sprang to Marna's eyes and she swallowed back the bile in her throat, "Tanner," she whispered, "Please no, Tanner." The tears had spilled over onto her face, tracking down her cheeks. Two more missiles hit their targets.

The party near the wood line held their breath. Smith and Cardoza made Kyle lay back down. He was too weak to fight them. Smith patted his shoulder as tears slipped down Kyle's cheek, "Daddy," he whispered. All eyes were on the prison as the rest of the missiles hit their marks and the prison became an electronically charged fireball. Marna's eyes fastened on the front gates. She didn't even notice when Smith had taken the bag from her grasp and hooked it on to an extended tree branch. The surroundings were silent, but for the crackling flames of the burning prison.

No, he wasn't gone. She wouldn't believe it. Wouldn't she have felt a great loss if . . . A sound drifted through her reverie . . . someone was clapping, then cheering, and then whistling. Soon others joined the first. She shook herself out of her stupor and refocused on the prison gate. A form was taking shape in the smoky veil from the fire, no three forms blended together. Ventura and Tanner were assisting Keys, who was limping. Three other agents ran forward and took charge of Keys, while Ventura and Tanner leaned on their knees and took deep breaths. They looked at each other, shook hands and then pulled each other into a congratulatory man hug. The cheering got louder, and then they turned to look at their cheering colleagues. Peter headed further up the hill as colleagues gave him back slaps and congratulations. Shaefer gave him a hug and smiled. "You scared the hell out of us, Partner."

"I scared myself, but he would have done the same for any of us." He winked and wrapped an arm around her as he accepted the water another colleague was holding out for him.

Tanner scanned the wood line and his eyes stopped when he saw her. Tears were freely pouring down her face. She started walking, then picked up the pace and before long, her pace quickened to a dead run, until he caught her up in his arms, hugged her close and kissed her temple, oblivious to who was watching. Let them, he didn't care. He wanted the world to know how much he loved this woman..

Agents assisted Keys to Kyle's side, and he sat on the ground beside him, pulling him into his arms in a carful hug. The older man wept and held him tight as Kyle closed his eyes and returned his father's embrace. The crowd around them dispersed to allow them a little privacy. Kyle's eyes opened for a moment and he saw Tanner and Marna walking back toward the others hand in hand, but surprisingly enough he did not feel angry or cheated. Tanner was a good man. He didn't think twice about going in after Keys, and if Kyle had to step aside, he would do so for Tanner. Marna deserved the best and the most happiness life had to give. If Tanner could give that to her than they belonged together. The way she looked at him said it all. He closed his eyes and held onto his father. After a moment longer, Keys carefully laid him back down and took his hand, brushing his hair aside and slapping the side of his face gently. "Welcome back, Son," he said softly

"Dr. Keys," Smith said, "We need to wrap that ankle.

The ear buds flared to life. "Status check, Keys?"

"Target eliminated, two injured. We need airlift. Extraction was a Success." He heard cheering in the background on the boat and smiled.

"We're sending out a, med team now, Sir, ETA ten minutes." There was chatter in the background. "Air lift will meet you at the old school grounds north from prison, Elizabeth will wait for your team's return."

"We'll be there." Keys turned to the rest of the team. "Let's make a stretcher for Kyle and go home." While a team dispersed to get the materials needed, Keys returned to Kyle's side and Smith wrapped his ankle and made him a crutch out of a tree branch.

After the stretcher was assembled, with an emergency blanket and some tree branches held together by twine, Tanner, Ventura, Cardoza, and McGellan gently lifted Kyle onto it, the IV pole, made of a stripped down branch, was attatched to a corner, and six agents took the frame. The fluids had helped some. His features looked less drawn than before. Smith stood beside him with a syringe.

"Kyle, I'm going to give you that pain meds now. It'll make the trek a little more comfortable, okay?" Kyle nodded and watched as Smith injected the meds into his IV. Then he turned his head, saw Marna smiling down at him, felt her take his hand, and then everything swam around him as the meds took effect and darkness mercifully took him in. For the first time in days, he didn't fear it, he welcomed it.

Epilogue

The next thing Kyle remembered was waking up in a hospital bed, feeling disoriented and foggy. He fought to keep his eyes open and his mind focused. They had wrapped his ribs comfortably, placed his right arm in a chest sling that kept it stationary. Someone had raised the head of this bed to a 45-degree angle, so he could breathe easier, and a thousand jackhammers were tattering away inside his head.

A bedside table was across his bed with a glass of apple juice and a glass of water placed upon it. IV tubing ran to the veins in his hand and wrist. His mouth felt like stuffed cotton. He tried to reach for the table but his left shoulder felt stiff and sore. "Ahh." He let out a groan.

"Here, let me help." Giselle appeared from somewhere to his left. There was bruising on the left side of her face, yellowing at the edges, from her cheek to forehead, and a three inch scar marred the brow above her left eye. She was wearing lavender scrubs and her long, blonde hair was pulled back in a French braid. She pulled the table out of the way, and moved in beside the bed then smiled, "Apple or water?" she asked.

"Water, please." He rasped. She held the cup out for him then supported his elbow as he shakily took hold of the cup and guided the straw to his mouth. He took two long sips then let go of the water and she put it back on the table. She reached behind her, brought forth a pillow, and stuffed it under his arm offering a little more support.

"There that should make it a little easier." He bent his elbow up, and ran the back of his hand shakily over her bruised face. "Did they do that to you?" She nodded; reflex had her reaching up toward her face. Kyle gently took her hand. "I'm sorry."

"Wasn't your fault, Kyle. I'm sorry I left you there alone. I should have . . ."

"No . . . you have nothing to be sorry for." He smiled, wincing when it pulled on his dried, chapped lips.

"Oh." She pulled her hand away, and reached for the bedside stand, pulling out a tube of balm. Putting some on her finger, she gently applied it to his lips. He watched her eyes as she did it.

"Thank you." He said as she put it back in the drawer.

"My job," she replied with a smile.

He took her hand. "No, I mean thank you for everything." His eyes were heavy, and felt sleep coming again.

She smiled down at him. "You're welcome," she said still holding his hand as he faded out. Next time he opened his eyes, there was a pair of crutches resting against the wall, and Keys was sitting in the chair, next to them dozing, head on his hand, elbow on the chair arm.

"Dad?" Keys opened his eyes.

"Hey, Son," Keys pushed himself up from the chair and hobbled over to the bed, using the rail to assist his weight bearing, "How do you feel?"

"I've been better." He cleared his throat, brought his eyes to the crutches, then back to his father's. "What happened in there?"

"Pierre had another trick up his sleeve. He had a second detonator; He figured if he was going, he was taking me with him." Kyle closed his eyes and pressed his head into the pillow, swallowing. Then he returned his gaze to Keys. He brought his hand up to cover the one his father had on the bedrail. It felt leathery and aged.

"How'd you get away?" He asked softly.

"I ran for the wine cellar, closed the door, and dived behind some old cement blocks, butted up against a wall. Unfortunately, when I dived, I knocked one loose and it fell on my ankle, fracturing it. Tanner and Ventura came in and dragged me into the yard just before the first missile strike. We took cover behind an old barricade. After the missiles had hit the other sections of the prison, we made our way out and you know the rest."

"Is he dead?" Keys looked confused by Kyle's words. "Lamontage. Is he dead? Can we say, beyond a reasonable doubt, that the Bastard is dead?"

"Yes." Again, Kyle closed his eyes and turned his face toward the ceiling, this time in relief. "GCSU went over the prison with a fine tooth comb, they found his burned skull and other bones belonging to him. He's gone, Kyle. He won't ever come back to haunt us again. I only wish we had gotten to him before he got to you. Before he put you through the hell he put you through." His voice broke. He drew in a breath before he spoke again. "I spent so many years trying to protect you, but when it mattered most I failed you."

When Kyle brought his eyes back to Keys, they were moist, "Don't, Dad, please, don't let him have the victory here. I'm going to be okay," he sighed, "We're going to be okay and Mom can finally rest in peace." He closed his eyes as a wave of dizziness and drowziness overcame him. He took a deep breath, and then half opened his eyes to look at Keys face, he could feel himself drifting off again.

Keys took his son's hand, and then rubbed his forehead. "Yes she can, Son," a smile played at his lips. "Yes she can."

"I love you, D . . ." his voice drifted as he faded out again.

"I love you too, Son," Keys kissed him on the forehead, ran his fingers through his hair, and then returned to his seat. . .

The next face that came into focus was Ventura. He was talking to the doctor at the foot of the bed. He glanced toward Kyle, curved his lips in a smile, and then shook the doctor's hand. Kyle watched him as he moved toward him. The afternoon sun slanted across Ventura's dark skin. "Hey, Kid, how are you feeling?"

"Can't seem to stay awake," Kyle said, shifting his head some, his eyelids still felt heavy.

"Yeah they've got you on a steady flow of some pretty heavy narcotics, Lamontage did some damage to your insides with his attacks. They had to do some repair work. Luckily, the time without nourishment or water didn't affect your Kidneys. That was our greatest concern. The last of the tests came back this morning; you passed with flying colors. You've been fading in and out for six days now, but it was either that or put you in a medically induced coma, so you could heal. Your Dad thought the former the better idea and we're all taking shifts by your bed to make sure you behave." Ventura grinned, Kyle chuckled then winced, and then he turned his head toward the chair and brought his eyes back to Peter. "I sent him home, he needed rest. I don't think he's had a good solid eight since nightmare-A-Lamontage began."

Kyle repositioned his head as the wave of drowsiness swept over him again. "Good, thank you, Vent . . ." He closed his eyes and his breathing became even and deep.

"You're welcome, Kid." He adjusted the blankets and then sat in the chair earlier vacated by Keys, taking up a magazine and reading.

When Kyle came up for air the next time, the morning sun was streaming through the windows. He shifted his head and Tanner was walking in with two cups of coffee. He handed one to Marna, who was sitting in the chair. "Hey, you." She said getting up and going to the bedside, smiling. "How are you feeling?"

"Better," he said, trying to shift up.

"Tanner, could you?" Marna asked, he nodded and put the coffees on the bedside table, going to the other side and together they used the positioning sheet to pull him up a little bit. "Better?" He nodded. They straightened the blankets, and gently positioned his arms on top of them. "Do you want some water?" He nodded, so she took it from the bedside table and handed it to him. He took it and sipped, handing it back to her. His hands were still shaky, but not as bad. His lips were healing well, and he was receiving fewer spasms from his ribs.

"How's Dad?"

"I haven't seen him for a couple of days," she said, "he debriefed us all that first day and then he was a permanent fixture by your bedside, until Ventura sent him home. I think he'll be back this afternoon."

He nodded and brought his eyes back to Tanner. "Thank you for going back for him."

"Not doing anything anybody else wouldn't have done."

"Nobody else made that first move, Williams, you did – you and Ventura. Thank you."

"Keys would have done the same for us," Tanner stated.

Kyle nodded, knowing he spoke the truth. Keys would have risked it all for one of his agents in a heartbeat, Kyle knew this. Tanner's phone rang. Marna glanced up and saw a frown appear on his brow. "Problem?"

He brought his eyes to hers. "Not sure. I've got to take this. Will you two excuse me?"

"Go ahead." She followed him out the door with her eyes.

"Means a lot to you, doesn't he?"

She brought her eyes back to Kyle's and sighed. "We don't need to talk about this right now, Kyle."

"He's a good man, Marna," He reached up, to take her hand and rubbed her fingers with his thumb. You have a connection, a bond. If my spidy sense isn't too far off, it's pretty strong."

"That obvious?" She queried, he nodded. Color rushed to her cheeks, "I'm sorry."

He shook his head, "Don't apologize for making the right choices in your life, Marna," he glanced her way and smiled," these last couple weeks have taught me that." He put his head back on the pillow, swallowing. "My chances with you were slim to start with. I think I always knew that. Your connection with Williams was already there, I saw that during that first briefing, I just chose to ignore it." He winked and she smiled. "Besides, to get my head on straight, I've got weeks of mandatory therapy to deal with and some lost time to make up for with Dad." He gave her hand a gentle squeeze. "I'm going to need a friend to keep me on the right track." He returned his eyes to hers. "Don't happen to know anyone who might be up for the job do you?"

"I think I might, yeah," she grinned. She covered his hand with her other one. They turned their heads as Keys made his way in with the crutches. "How are you, feeling, Keys?"

"Better," he looked at Kyle. "How are you doing today, Son?"

"I think I might actually speak a full sentence before I pass out," he smiled.

"Small blessings," Keys said with a grin and hobbled over to pat his son's hand. "The doctors say your new X-rays look good." He nodded, and then frowned when Tanner walked in. His expression looked stricken, shocked.

"Tanner, what's wrong?" Marna asked.

"Marna, can I see you for a moment, in the hall."

"Of course," she excused herself and Keys watched the couple leave the room.

"Dad, do you know what's going on?" Kyle asked.

Keys drew a breath, "I'm afraid Tanner's past is about to come knocking on his door."

"Is that bad or good?"

"Depends on how he handles it I suppose," he smiled, "we all have journeys to make, pasts to come to grip with." Kyle nodded and looked toward the door, hoping if Tanner's past was about to disrupt his life, that Marna wasn't in the line of fire.

*****

Two days later, Marna lay in Tanner's arms, watching the sunrise over the horizon. Rose and Kurt had taken the kids on a camping trip to the White Mountains, for Memorial Day Weekend, so she and Tanner could have the weekend together. She lifted herself up on her elbow and traced her fingers through the fine hairs on his chest. "How long will you be gone?" she asked softly.

He smiled, and pushed her hair behind her shoulder. "The lawyer said it could take three to six months to settle the estate."

The phone call at the hospital had been from Andrew McNamara, a lawyer in charge of his grandfather's estate.

Andreas Raleigh had died suddenly, earlier in the month, and Andrew McNamara esquire had said that Tanner had been named sole heir to his property, but there was much to deal with before it could be finalized and he could take the reins on the various business interests...

"Why so long?" She shifted around and put her chest on his, her arm beside him.

"I guess my grandfather had a lot of property holdings that need to be dealt with." His hand slipped up her side and around her back caressing it, "sure you don't want to come?"

She grinned, "What about the kids?"

"Bring them."

"There still in school, Tanner."

"We could hire a Nanny." He wiggled his eyebrows. She chuckled.

"Hard to find one that can fill the shoes of the last," she said with a sigh for emphasis.

He looked thoughtful, "Guess I have to agree with you there," he smiled bringing his hand up her side around her shoulder, and tracing her face with his finger, "Okay, then as soon as school lets out."

"If we're not on a case."

"You have vacation time, Mea numai Iubirii," he whispered. She felt chills go down her back as he caressed it.

"What does that mean?" She queried softly, giving him a lazy smile

"My only love." He wrapped his legs around hers and rolled her over, pinning her wrists to the bed. She giggled and then he lowered his lips to hers reaching into her soul with his kiss, she responded in kind. His hands slid down her arms, and down the outline of her body, across her stomach and gently brushing over her breasts before they returned to her hands and he intertwined his fingers with hers. His kisses trailed across her jaw and down her neck and across her collarbone. "Mea numai lubirii," He whispered into her ear and proceeded to go another round of sweet, gentle love making. She had become the only thing he lived for. Being away from her for three weeks would be hard, but three to six months was going to drive him crazy. Their connection had become so strong, he doubted nothing short of death would separate them.

Three hours later they had showered, dressed and shared a small, solemn breakfast. The clock chimed in 9:00 a.m. and they were saying goodbye at her door. His grandfather's village was in the western portion of the Ossipcc Mountains. It was a gypsy town built on 6300 acres of estate property dubbed Castle in the Clouds before the Freedom Conflicts. The village sprouted up in 2028-2030, and had remained intact until now. It was a small village, barely 500 residents, but Andreas had been the leader of the clan. A beloved King from what the lawyer had said, and his loss was deeply felt. Keys had a jet flying out to a private airfield, near the village, to pick up some documents on a case, and he had offered Tanner the use of the jet as well. McNamara would pick him up there and drive him to the village. The jet was to be airborne in forty minutes. He brought his hand to her face and kissed her. When he came up for air, he brought his forehead down on hers. "I already miss you, Marna Farlow."

She swallowed, "Me too." Then she kissed him again.

He groaned when he pulled away. "You keep that up, I'm going to miss my plane," He breathed. She pulled her lower lip between her teeth, and stepped away. "I'll call you tonight."

"I'll be waiting.." She nodded, but her lip quivered. He caught her chin with his forefinger and thumb, giving her one more kiss, and then he hurried out the door, bags in hand. She watched him throw his luggage in the car, and then he turned to wave to her, before he ran around to the driver's side and climbed in. He looked up, waving one more time. As he drove away Marna felt it come on, couldn't stop it from happening.

She couldn't breathe, but there was no fog, no interlude, it just happened, the vision took hold and showed his car explode as it drove away. She grabbed the casing for support, and lowered her head to catch her breath and when she raised her head to look, there had been no explosion, she just saw his taillights turning down Camel toward the airfield. Her whole body trembled. She closed her door, and slid, her back against the door, to the floor. Tears sprang to her eyes and overflowed onto her face. She took deep breaths to get control of her breathing. What had just happened? What did it mean? She picked up her phone to call Keys.

Excerpt for
Gems of Jealousy
Book 3 of the Guardian WIT Series
Fall/winter 2013

Gems of Jealousy

The service had been nice. He had a freezer full of food that he would probably never eat on his own. He thought of Marna and the kids. They were his family too and he missed them terribly. He chuckled when he thought of how quick that food would be gone with that brood. He remembered the look in Marna's eyes when he had left her, felt the despair of the separation they would have to endure while he settled his grandfather's estate. He missed her the moment he drove away, his heart hurt and his arms ached to hold her. He'd called her every night, and though they'd joke about phone sex, they would never do it, but just to see her face on his screen was enough. He would call her tonight and tell her about the service; how heartwarming it had been to see the whole town turn out, and hear the people speak of the love they had held for Andreas Raleigh; their King, their leader, their friend.

His grandfather had been a caring man and many had wanted to show their respects. Many gave Tanner love and support and welcomed him into the village family. They had asked him if he planned to stay, and he had politely said, though he appreciated their gracious outpouring of love and acceptance, he had built a life elsewhere and had a family of his own. Many had smiled and given him an attaboy slap though some had just nodded and moved on. He felt their disapproval of his choice to live outside the fold, but his heart belonged to Marna, the children, and Guardian. That was his life, that's where he belonged. He loved his grandfather, but his mother's people were not his people. Their village was not his. One particular woman still kept sweeping through his mind. She had introduced herself as a dear friend of his mother's, "best friends," really she had said. Jezzy or was it Jizzy? He couldn't remember. She had dark hair, and alluring dark eyes, but when she smiled, it did not reach her eyes. He had felt vibes from her that weren't unpleasant, yet not fully pleasant either. However, it had passed as she had flittered away and the next person in line drew him into a hearty hug calling him the long lost Son.

The last guests had left hours ago and now he wandered around this big empty house, a Villa was the real estate label for it alone. The gypsies loved their heritage. All the homes in this little Mountain Village were styled after the ones in Romania, his mother's homeland. He tapped the corner of the envelope on his palm. The clock on the wall hauntingly chimed in the 6:00 PM hour. Marna would not be home until later that evening, the twins had a cheerleading competition tonight, so he decided now was as good a time as any. He ran up the Marble, stone staircase, took a direct left at the top of them, and then went to the white door at the end of the hall with the cauliflower shaped doorknob. He stopped outside it and drew in a breath.

McNamara told him he would find his connection to his mother's family, his heritage, their history, all of it, behind this door. He tipped the envelope, and the key slid into his hand. He inserted it into the door, and unlocked it in one liquid motion and then he flipped on the light switch to his right, jogging up the stairs.

It all flooded back to him as soon as he stepped onto the floor at the top of the stairs. The Christmases, the Thanksgivings, the birthday cards. It wasn't until after he had lost his sister, during the first few years of the Freedom Conflicts, did Andreas Raleigh realize how much his daughter had meant to him so, against the wishes of the tribe, he made steps to bring her and her family back into his life. However, they were not allowed to step foot into the village.

Tanner's mother had done the unthinkable and left her pending marriage to a wealthy elder in favor of marrying an outsider, the DA of Harrisville New Hampshire; David Harris Williams. It didn't matter that the love they had would top mountains only that Darla Kathryn Raleigh had rebelled against tradition, against acceptance with her people. She broke the rules.

Tanner drew in a breath and looked around. It was all here, packed in boxes and trunks. He felt another stabbing need for Marna, he wanted her to be a part of this, be a part of him finding out who he was. The baby grand piano, in the far corner of the room, was the first item to catch his eye. It was cherry oak in coloring and cobwebs stretched between its sturdy legs,but he didn't notice any of that, only what was displayed on top; pictures of his mother and her family framed by many different sizes and colors. He approached it, reached out his hand and grabbed the first one, blowing the dust off, and wiping it clean with his hand.

It was a Christmas shot. He recognized his mother right away with her sleek dark hair and symmetrical features. She had been a beautiful child, had grown into a beautiful woman. In this picture, she looked up at her father with open adoration in front of a Christmas tree, decorated with cookies, candy canes, and chains made of glittered paper. He replaced the picture and picked up another. In this one, her father was getting ready to push her on a bike, while her older sister, Dominique, the aunt he never met, cheered her on. They had tied balloons to the handlebars. The balloons said Happy Birthday. He smiled. One by one, he picked them up, looked them over, and saw his mother grow from a child with eyes full of wonder to a woman with eyes full of disillusionment. He'd like to know what cause that pain in her eyes.

"I'm sorry it was so hard for you, Mom." He replaced her graduation picture and noticed one tucked in the back. Behind all the others. He frowned, reaching for it. His mother wasn't in this one. His grandfather was standing beside another man, they were young, twenties or thirties he presumed, and they were holding a large, green stone between them.

"His name was Melbourne," Andrew McNamara said from the doorway. Tanner turned toward him. "He and your grandfather were good friends. He was the founder of the Friends of Freedom. That picture was taken in front of one of the three Emerald mines that now belong to you." He handed him a folder. "Melbourne was killed in the very beginning of the Freedom Conflicts, leaving your grandfather the sole owner of the mines. His share would have gone to his daughters, but with them gone, they transfer to you.

"Didn't Melbourne have family?"

"Yes, but he also owned six other Emerald mines. He was your grandfather's silent partner. He fronted the money to get your grandfather started. Andreas is the one who made them a success. He sold his ownership shares to Andreas a year before he died, making Andreas sole owner and now you are along with several other money funds, this house, this village. All of it goes to you, Son,"

"That's why you called me." Tanner said, sinking onto the piano bench.

"Yes, Son, We just have to settle any outstanding financial issues, and he bequeathed a few things to some charities, but the bulk of it is yours, Mr. Williams, you are about to become a very Wealthy man." He pulled out another folder. "These are the financial records, read them through and digest it. The Will reading is Next Friday morning 9:00 AM in my office. Then the fun really begins. Records transfers and such.." He looked around the room. "Andreas was a good man, Mr. Williams, and he loved you and your mother very much, but there are others who think you don't deserve anything so expect a fight,"

"What do you mean?"

He pulled out another folder. "Here's the autopsy report. Find out for yourself."

"What are you suggesting, Mr. McNamara?"

"That before you accept anything at face value in this village, you know all the facts," he looked around the room again. "There's a lot of history in here, not all of it pretty." He caught Tanner's gaze, "Equip yourself before you go up against anyone within the boundaries of this village and watch your back." He sighed, "Other than that, take some time to get to know your family, Mr. Williams, and know them well."

"I will, thank you." He shook hands with the lawyer and watched him go with wary eyes. He heard the door below close and opened the autopsy folder, looking it over. He frowned and pulled out his GPC, Keys swam into focus.

"Tanner, how are you?"

"Not quite sure."

"Of course." Keys stated with a nod of understanding. "What can I do?"

"Andrew McNamara, my grandfather's lawyer, paid me a very strange visit tonight. I'm a bit distressed."

"Tell me about it?" Keys encouraged. Tanner gave him the cliff notes version.

Keys frowned. "Fax me the autopsy, Tanner. I'll have our lab people look it over. Meanwhile you watch yourself out there and if you have a safe place to keep the other papers, keep them there. Do not share this information with anyone."

"What about Marna?"

"We'll bring her in if we have to, but right now let's just keep it low profile."

"All right." He signed off and left the attic, heading for his grandfather's bedroom, where he was staying, opened up the wall safe, and placed the legal documents inside. Then he took the autopsy report over to the fax machine and sent it out, returning that to the safe as well. When he was done, he locked it up and slid the wall panel back in place. Before he had turned around, glass shattered behind him, he dived for the floor, pulled his gun out of his bedside stand, flipped out the light, and did a Somersault to the window, peaking through the now broken pane. In the distance, he could see two riders on horses, heading away from the Villa. He pointed his gun out the window and did a sweep but there was no one else around. He flipped on his light and looked at the floor. A huge, gray rock lay in the middle, two feet from the bed, and on it, a message – *Outsider!* He picked it up to look it over then let it slip back to the floor. "Guess you weren't kidding, were you McNamara? His eyes went to the window and he sighed. It had already started. He put in a call to his grandfather's caretaker, then to the villages' equivalent to a constable and the local police. They both reported they would be there in thirty minutes.

His laptop started beeping, there was a video call coming through on his *Homespot* page. He moved to his desk, and hit the enter button to answer. Marna's face appeared before him. "Hey, I was going to call you a little later," he said, "How was the competition?"

"The girls' team won second place," she smiled, but after her eyes searched his face, her expression changed. "Hey, you okay?"

"I am now," he said smiling. The broken window, the lawyers foreboding message, and the unanswered mystery of the autopsy all but forgotten as he looked into those beautiful blue eyes. It could almost make him forgot they were so far apart. Almost. "I miss you like crazy."

"You just miss practicing football in my living room."

His eyes took on a teasing glint, "and other places." He grinned. His tone caused her face to color slightly. They chatted on, and when the doorbell rang, he said goodbye with a promise he would call her later that night .